EVELYN WAUGH

The Complete Short Stories
and Selected Drawings

Edited and introduced by
Ann Pasternak Slater

EVERYMAN'S LIBRARY

Alfred A. Knopf New York Toronto

190

THIS IS A BORZOI BOOK

PUBLISHED BY ALFRED A. KNOPF, INC.

First included in Everyman's Library, 1998 (UK), 2000 (US)
Copyright © 1998 by The Estate of Evelyn Waugh
This edition published by arrangement with Little, Brown and
Company, (Inc.). All rights reserved.
Introduction, Bibliography and Chronology Copyright © 1998 by
David Campbell Publishers Ltd.
Typography by Peter B. Willberg

ISBN 0-375-40430-9

Book Design by Barbara de Wilde and Carol Devine Carson

Printed and bound in Germany
by Graphischer Grossbetrieb Pössneck GmbH

EVELYN WAUGH

CONTENTS

THE COMPLETE SHORT STORIES OF EVELYN WAUGH
(with dates of composition)

INTRODUCTION

At the age of seven, Waugh began his diary: 'My History. My name is Evelyn Waugh I go to Heath Mount school ...' A year later he tried again, with more panache:

> My HISTORY
> BY E. WAUGH
> AT SCHOOL & HOME
> ILASTRATED BY THE AUTHER
> WRITEN AT THE AGE OF EIGHT

Throughout his life, Waugh turned his own experiences into fiction; throughout much of his life, too, he was preoccupied with the graphic arts. Until well after he left Oxford his ambitions were to be an artist rather than a writer. Among his Juvenilia are two short stories composed entirely of succinctly titled pictures (see p. 524). At Lancing School he earned a guinea a time designing book jackets for his father's firm, Chapman and Hall; these supplemented the normal one pound a term the boys could expect to spend on tuck. At Oxford Waugh was, on his own admission, pre-eminent not as a writer but as a provider of decorative drawings for undergraduate magazines. When he began, reluctantly, to write, his first novels were published with his own illustrations – six and a title page for *Decline and Fall, An Illustrated Novelette*, another nine for *Black Mischief*, a cover and frontispiece for *Vile Bodies*. This collection of short stories is interspersed with hitherto unreproduced drawings from Waugh's undergraduate years, whose originals are now exceedingly rare, difficult to locate and vulnerable to loss. One of the many ways in which this volume comes full circle is that its penultimate story, 'Love Among the Ruins', is also ilastrated by the auther – or, in his later, more elegantly ironic mode, supplied 'with decorations by various eminent hands including the author's'. Waugh's fine economy of line is hardly changed from his undergraduate *chef d'oeuvre*, 'The Tragical Death of Mr. Will. Huskisson', to this late story's pastiche Canovas with their tongue-in-cheek inscriptions, '*Canova fec. Moses delin. Waugh perfec.*' (Canova made it; Moses drew it; Waugh completed it).

There is certainly a self-conscious unity to Waugh's canon. This collection opens with his first published work (excluding his undergraduate ephemera). 'The Balance' is extraordinarily ambitious and accomplished, both for a young man of twenty-three, and absolutely. In it, we are instantly peppered by that fusillade of unattributed dialogue which was later to become one of Waugh's trademarks. There are four speakers here – Basil, Imogen, and two others. The attentive reader will have no difficulty in identifying who says what:

'Do you know, I don't think I *can* read mine. It's rather unkind.'
'Oh, Basil, you must.'
'Please, Basil.'
This always happened when Basil played paper games.
'No, I can't, look it's all scrumbled up.'
'Oh, Basil, dearest, do.'
'Oh, Basil, *please.*'
'Darling Basil, you must.'
'No, I won't. Imogen will be in a rage with me.'
'No, she won't, will you, Imogen?'
'Imogen, tell him you won't be in a rage with him.'
'Basil, *do* read it please.'
'Well, then, if you promise you won't hate me' – and he smoothed out the piece of paper.

The last story Waugh wrote begins in exactly the same mode, with the now aged Basil Seal and Peter Pastmaster, throwbacks from his earliest fiction, as two old buffers trying to make themselves heard above the din of a literary banquet:

'Yes.'
'What d'you mean: "Yes"?'
'I didn't hear what you said.'
'I said he made off with all my shirts.'
'It's not that I'm the least deaf. It's simply that I can't concentrate when a lot of fellows are making a row.'
'There's a row now.'
'Some sort of speech.'
'And a lot of fellows saying: "Shush".'
'Exactly. I can't concentrate. What did you say?'

Waugh always relished circular form. *Decline and Fall* and *Scoop* both come full circle, leaving their heroes where they began. In his last work, the autobiographical *A Little Learning* (1964), his seven-year-old diary entry, 'My History', is reproduced with the teasing title, 'First Draft of This Work, September 1911'.

It is curious that Waugh never chose to reprint 'The Balance'. In this collection all his short stories have been gathered together for the first time. Three he refrained from reprinting for obvious reasons. In each case they were pot-boiling contributions to a series commissioned by the popular press: 'The Manager of "The Kremlin"' for *John Bull*'s 'Real-Life Stories – by Famous Authors'; 'Too Much Tolerance' for the same paper's 'The Seven Deadly Sins of Today'; 'The Sympathetic Passenger' for the 'Tight Corner' series in the *Daily Mail*. None are worth reprinting on literary merit alone. All three are further disfigured by the papers' routine mincing of Waugh's prose into hiccupping paragraphs of two or three sentences at a gulp. Of the Juvenilia Waugh deemed only 'The Curse of the Horse Race' to show any merit, contributing this tale of gambling and mayhem to an anthology inappropriately titled *Little Innocents*. 'A House of Gentlefolks' was another early contribution to a collection of short stories, *The New Decameron*. Waugh also extracted a chapter from *Vile Bodies* to pose as another short story for *The New Decameron*, a serendipitous practice he continued for a lifetime. Since this and other prepublished segments from novels in progress are available in their proper form elsewhere, and only temporarily masqueraded as short stories for the sake of Waugh's wallet, they have been omitted from this collection. 'Compassion' is an interesting antithetical example. It was originally written, as a short story, for the Catholic literary magazine *The Month*, which Waugh was eager to support. Twelve years later it was incorporated with alterations in *Unconditional Surrender*, the final volume of the *Sword of Honour* trilogy. It has never been reprinted and appears here for the first time since 1949. 'The Man Who Liked Dickens' is a similar case; this is the short story Waugh wrote while travelling in British Guiana, which provided the germ for *A Handful of Dust* and was assimilated into the ending of that novel a year later. It, too, was never included in Waugh's collections of short stories and has not been reprinted since the thirties. 'Work Suspended' was begun in 1939 as a novel which Waugh rated *of Youth* in its accurately disenchanted portrayal of school life. Alec, however, is an unsullied presence; he is the hero's soldier brother Ralph, admiringly presented at the end of the fragment, and quoted with naive adulation: 'One of the awfully clever things Ralph had said was that life should be divided into water-tight compartments ...' (a platitude of Alec's also reverently recorded in Waugh's diary). The real interest of this material is what Waugh was to make of it in his late fragment, 'Charles Ryder's Schooldays', when he returned to the Lancing diaries with appalled, acid detachment. Meanwhile, 'Fragment of a Novel' shows a reputable if uncritically self-absorbed stage in Waugh's early development. The manuscript also bears witness to the positive influence Waugh's father had on his early writing, firmly annotating a sentence in which Waugh offered his hero two alternative motivations with the reproof: 'This sentence means nothing. *You* know whether he liked. The author is *omni-scient.*' Two years later, Pound was to score the margin of *The Waste Land* in similar terms: 'make up yr mind you Tiresias if you know know damn well or else you dont'.

Waugh was serious at Lancing. He was serious about the Dilettanti, the political, literary and arts club of which he was joint founder, and whose progressive misspellings he wryly chronicles in his autobiography. He was serious about decorative script, which he was being taught by Francis Crease; he was serious about getting into Oxford. 'At Oxford I was reborn in full youth', his autobiography records. Following the activities of Waugh and his friends through the pages of *Isis* and *Cherwell*, one is enviously struck by the amount of fun they had. The masthead Waugh designed for *The Cherwell* shows a stage on which dangle the university puppets: the Union debater, betailed, bespectacled; the don; the tankard-toting plus-foured hearty; the aesthete; the drunkard, supine. In the drawings further types spin past on the merry-go-round of university life – the seven sleepers in the Union Library, the garrulous scouts, the men of the different clubs, the drinkers of angostura and soda, of beer and of brandy. Waugh devotes a painstaking series over six weeks to The Seven Deadly Sins, his irreverent New Heptalogue. At the same time his caricatures memorably por-tray friends and contemporaries – Richard Pares, his first love;

INTRODUCTION

the admired Harold Acton. He reports the Union debates, writes film reviews, book reviews, on rare occasions a leader, and contributes profiles of Acton and Cruttwell, his unfortunate history tutor, to the series of Isis Idols. With John Sutro, one of many eccentric friends, he founds the Oxford Railway Club and writes learnedly tongue-in-cheek letters about slip-carriages and the complexities of the railway timetable. He devotes a two-page spread to The Great Bulldog Insurance Scheme, a spoof *Insurance against Proctorial Depredations* whose premiums are tailored to the flamboyance or drabness of the various colleges (from Keble, 1od, to Christ Church, £450, and Magdalen, no insurance undertaken), and whose questionnaire blandly enquires: Are you leading a Double or Single Life? Do you suffer from a University Chest? Have you during the last $21\frac{1}{4}$ days been to any Lecture or exposed to any other infectious Disease? Have you ever stood for Parliament? If so, did it stand for you?

In the summer term of his second year Waugh ran a Children's Corner with the incontrovertible credo, 'we are all of us young at Oxford – (who are wise?) – and do not need a psychology textbook to cause us to yearn once more for the nursery floor'. It figured three pets, Ann the Ant, Ludovic the Snail, and Bertram the Bumble Bee, and was conducted in the avuncular letters of Uncle Alfred and the equally avuncular letters of Auntie Ermyntrude. One of Waugh's drawings (p. 200) shows the pets' visit to the Editor of *Isis*, whom they find in bed at 12.30 pm. Uncle Alfred's letters are full of wise saws and winsome witticisms. At the end of term his last letter is suffused by an inextricable mix of genuine nostalgia and tongue-in-cheek nursery morality that throws a playful, half-ironic, half-direct light on Waugh's own beliefs.

Above all in life, Uncle Alfred urges you to laugh and preserve what is called 'a sense of humour'. You must, of course, never ridicule anything which is good, but it is better to smile good-humouredly at a wicked action than to be resentful. Laughter is the jam in life's sandwich. Uncle Alfred has gained much amusement in regarding men far away like ants ...

With all this activity, no wonder there was little time for study, or even for serious fiction. Of the seven Oxford items only two are outstanding. 'Edward of Unique Achievement' must be the work described in *A Little Learning* as 'a quite funny short story in which an earnest student might find hints of my first novel'. The wittily convoluted narrative describes how Edward, an exceptionally ordinary undergraduate, murders his history tutor, how the crime is blamed on the drunken Lord Poxe, and the corrupt college authorities circumvent the law by hushing up the crime and imposing a derisory fifteen shilling fine. The initial sequence of events in *Decline and Fall* inverts this template: Paul Pennyfeather, a nonentity like Edward, is unjustly accused of exhibitionism when the drunken members of the Bollinger Club debag him and pursue him across the college quad. The drunken lords are milched for sumptuous fines but escape all other blame; Paul, the blameless nobody, is summarily expelled for flagrant indecency. The amused, worldly portrayal of immorality, injustice, corrupt authority and abrupt, unmerited reversals of fortune is very similar in both works.

'Edward of Unique Achievement', like 'The Curse of the Horse Race', is an exercise in fantasy doubtless born of Waugh's deep loathing of his own history tutor, the unfortunate Mr. Cruttwell. It also draws on a memorable morning in Waugh's first term, when his melancholy scout woke him with the words, 'Half-past seven and the Principal's dead' – marginally heightened in the narrator's first hearing of the crime: 'It reached me through my scout who called me with: "Half-past seven, sir, and Lord Poxe has murdered Mr. Curtis."' The story thus bears a straightforward relationship to Waugh's own undergraduate life, and to his subsequent fiction, the threads leading clearly from one to the other. 'Antony, Who Sought Things That Were Lost', the other significant Oxford story, is inherently weaker, but betrays a fundamental duality that was to haunt Waugh's later work.

It was written for Harold Acton's *The Oxford Broom*, and in *A Little Learning* is noted only for betraying the influence of James Branch Cabell's *Jurgen*, 'that preposterously spurious artefact, which quite captivated me at the age of nineteen'. *Jurgen* is a long, elaborately illustrated Beardsleyesque romance in appallingly ornate prose. In Waugh's more restrained derivative Count Antony, a gentle idealist, is imprisoned as a revolutionary sympathizer in the ducal castle dungeons, where his beloved, the Lady Elizabeth, insists on sharing his imprisonment. Their marriage is consummated among the toads and dripping walls, and daily Count Antony serves her on his knees. But with time the love of the Lady Elizabeth fades to great weariness; they sleep apart in the cell they share, and at last she turns to the lame and pock-marked turnkey.

And she put her hands in his hair and she leaned her breast against his and so the Lady Elizabeth, who had known the white arms of Antony, loved this turnkey who was ugly and low born. And Antony made no sound but lay in his corner burdened with his ague and the great chain which he could barely move; but in his eyes there was pain as is seldom seen in men.

This is *A Handful of Dust* in embryo. The hero is called by his friends ' "Antony, who sought things that were lost" because he seemed always to be seeking in the future for what had gone before'. He is the clearly assonating progenitor of Tony Last, whose anachronistic Arthurian values of courtly love and honour are tragically out of place in the modern world of short-lived adulteries in Mrs. Beaver's service flats. The Lady Elizabeth, weary of her devotion and imprisonment, is Tony's wife Brenda, frequently described by her friends as the captive princess of a fairy-tale. Beaver, her vulgar lover, is the turnkey. The similarities are not merely coincidental. Both works draw on a contradictory impulse in Waugh. On the one hand is his nostalgia for an ideal past, expressed in the painstaking penmanship of his illuminated lettering; in his first published works after leaving Oxford, the essay on the Pre-Raphaelite Brotherhood and the *Life of Rossetti*; in the Arcadian image of Oxford in *Brideshead*; most clearly of all in his Lancing prize poem, *The Return of Launcelot*. On the other is the cynicism of the disappointed idealist. Of the prize poem, Waugh comments in his autobiography, 'It was characteristic of me at that period that I chose, not a story of heroism or romance, but the nostalgic, disillusioned musing of Sir Bedivere after the death of Arthur.' Those musings hit a recognizable note:

> Then cried Sir Launcelot, 'Are things thus changed
> Since Galahad from Camelot rode out

White armoured; and in green Sir Tristram ranged
The country round with tournament and bout,
That tradesmen rise and from their ramparts shout
Thus at their lords? . . .'

The people reply:

'The age of knights is over. He who buys
Now rules. For in the west King Arthur fell
And with him all his knightly army lies.
This is the age of shops and merchandise!'

The same horror at an ideal world fallen to Hetton Abbey's
commercially viable silver fox farm and the huckster ascend-
ancy of Hooper and Trimmer overcasts the ends of *A Handful of
Dust*, *Brideshead Revisited* and the *Sword of Honour* trilogy. When
Waugh's own first wife, Evelyn, cuckolded him with John Heygate, 'the basement boy', as Waugh scathingly called him, the
worst episode of his own life fell into a pattern of associations
which he had already begun to explore in his late adolescence.
In just the same way, numerous Hardy poems explored the ironies of past passion and present chill, before life, obedient to
the Wildean imperative, copied art and provided him with the
unexpected death of his own once adored, now disregarded
wife. Hardy's best poems are driven by the ultimate Satire of
Circumstance, that an author's fictional predilections sensitize
him to their subsequent chance approximation in reality. The
fantasy becomes painfully true. Furthermore, because the
experience touches on a central nerve, the writer often makes
his greatest work out of it, as Waugh did with *A Handful of Dust*
and Hardy did with the poems of 1912–13.

'The Balance' is the last of Waugh's juvenilia and his first
mature work; the last story to be written before he began life as a
novelist, and yet formally outstanding as his most experimental
piece of short fiction. Its three layers are typographically distinguished – the main narrative (roman) presented as a silent film
whose captions (bold) are commented on by a cinema audience
including two housemaids and a Cambridge undergraduate
(italics). The cinematic mode further allows Waugh to juxtapose
actual narrative with the fantastical suicide scenarios morbidly
projected by Adam, the hero. Numerous techniques Waugh was

to make his own appear here for the first time. The recurrent use of sustained, unattributed dialogue, handled with mastery from its very inception. The one-sided telephone conversation, from whose disjointed replies the entire exchange can be inferred. The swift, sure establishment of character by setting, as Adam visits the Oxford rooms of one student friend after another. The speed and narrative economy of cross-cut scenes. The conscious exploitation of conflicting generic modes, light-heartedly identified in the film's initial caption ('The "Art title" shows a still life of a champagne bottle, glasses, and a comic mask – or is it yawning?'), and expanded in the responses of Gladys and Ada:

Closeup of Adam. He is a young man of about twenty-two, clean-shaven, with thick, very dark hair. He looks so infinitely sad that even Ada is shaken.
Can it be funny?
'Buster Keaton looks sad like that sometimes – don't 'e?'
Ada is reassured.
Buster Keaton looks sad; Buster Keaton is funny. Adam looks sad; Adam is funny. What could be clearer?

Behind all these techniques the influence of the cinema is paramount. On going down from Oxford Waugh had spent an enjoyable summer making a film, *The Scarlet Woman*, with a number of his university friends. It is a fantastic farrago concerning a Catholic plot to convert the Prince of Wales which is foiled by a lady of loose habits (played by Elsa Lanchester, later wife of Charles Laughton). Waugh played the homosexual Dean of Balliol (with a blond wig and much fondling of the Prince of Wales), and a dissolute lord (with a mean burnt-cork moustache). The film, inevitably for the time, is silent; its witty captions are written by Waugh; its level of technical competence is unsteady. The wild vacillations of speed in Colonel Blount's film in *Vile Bodies* come direct from Waugh's own film-making experiences, which are first parodied in 'The Balance':

The film becomes obscure – after the manner of the more modern Continental studies: the saxophonist has become the vortex of movement; faces flash out and disappear again; fragmentary captions will not wait until they are read.

'Well, I do call this soft.'
A voice with a Cambridge accent from the more expensive seats says,
'Expressionismus.'
Gladys nudges Ada and says, 'Foreigner.'

Yet what failed in *The Scarlet Woman* – which was, after all, only a light-hearted game – was transformed in Waugh's fiction. In 'The Balance' he uses cinematic techniques because the story is recounted as a film: in his later work cinematic techniques are appropriated, without apology, as his chosen medium for prose narrative. Waugh has found his voice.

*

Waugh had left Oxford with a Third. His letters rob this of surprise. 'I have schools at the end of next term,' he writes to one friend. 'Between whiles I read *Alice in Wonderland*. It is an excellent book I think.' And to another, 'Do let me most seriously advise you to take to drink. There is nothing like the aesthetic pleasure of being drunk ... That is the greatest thing Oxford has to teach.' There were, however, a few other life lessons still to be learned. On his return to London, Waugh tried in vain to get a variety of jobs, even selling toothbrushes; he attended art school; he finally found employment in a Welsh boarding-school. He began writing *The Temple at Thatch*, a novel in which the black magic explored in the undergraduate short story, 'Unacademic Exercise', was to be continued. But when he sent the first chapters to Harold Acton the response was discouraging. 'Too English for my exotic taste,' Acton wrote. 'Too much nid-nodding over port.' Waugh consigned the manuscript to the school furnace. A series of further disappointments drove him to attempt suicide. He left his clothes with a quotation from Euripides on a moonlit Welsh beach, and swam out to sea. Jellyfish turned him back. 'As earnest of my intent,' he writes in the last lines of his autobiography, 'I had brought no towel. With some difficulty I dressed and tore into small pieces my pretentious classical tag ... Then I climbed the sharp hill that led to all the years ahead.'

'The Balance' draws on several of these experiences: art school, depression, attempted suicide, even the pretentious classical tag, which is further ridiculed in the story by a grammatical howler ('MORITURUS TE SALUTANT'). But 'The Balance' initiated Waugh's gradual ascent from the depths. While teaching, he wrote his essay on the P.R.B. and then *Rossetti, His Life and Works*; while writing, he met and fell in love with Evelyn Gardner; proposed; began *Decline and Fall*; married – and with the publication of his first novel that first sharp hill was crested and the ground fell away beneath his feet once more. Waugh had started *Vile Bodies* in the light-hearted mode of *Decline and Fall*, spending his weeks out of London composing and returning to his wife at weekends. Her affair with John Heygate came as a complete surprise. 'Evelyn's defection was preceded by no sort of quarrel or estrangement,' he wrote to Harold Acton. 'I did not know it was possible to be so miserable & live but I am told that this is a common experience.' Fourteen months after his marriage Waugh was divorced; in the autumn of 1930 he was received into the Catholic Church. The couple had agreed not to have children when they married; later, this was to facilitate the annulment of the marriage. At the time, it came to symbolize the meaninglessness of their contract.

*

'Reticence' is a term recurring with a strong positive charge in Waugh's work. Only the first two stories following the breakdown of his marriage reflect this profoundly painful experience, and do so coolly and obliquely. 'Love in the Slump' pointedly introduces the marriage of Tom Watch and Angela Trench-Troubridge as 'completely typical of all that was most unremarkable in social conditions', and recounts, with remorseless flatness, the unremitting sequence of trivial events in which newly-wed husband and wife fail to meet until after the honeymoon, when an alternative relationship is already in place. Marriage entails neither love nor children. Both partners are equally, selfishly feckless. The narrative is studiously deadpan; authorial disapprobation is implicit and even-handed. 'Too Much Toleration' is the cautionary tale of an amiable naif in revolt against his firm Victorian upbringing. His indiscriminate liberalism exposes him to the greed and rapacity of his business partner, wife, son, and a whole continent of dishonest commercial clients. Two leitmotifs dominate the tale – the central figure's insistence on seeing everyone as 'a jolly good fellow', and his refusal to accept or even recognize his own responsibility for his unfortunate experiences:

'My wife left me,' he said simply. 'It was a great surprise. I can't to this day think why. I always encouraged her to do what she wanted.'

The nursery morality once playfully espoused by Uncle Alfred in *The Isis* Children's Corner is sorely wanting in this world. Indeed, its shocking absence will underlie Waugh's profoundly moral ironies in most of the fiction after his wife's desertion.

Waugh collected the majority of the short stories written between 1930 and 1936 in *Mr. Loveday's Little Outing and Other Sad Stories*. Easily the best is the shortest and most frivolous. 'Cruise' is *Clarissa* shrunk in the wash – a delightful degradation of the epistolary novel's grand passions and profound moral dilemmas to a flutter of feather-headed postcards. These 'Letters from a Young Lady of Leisure' breathlessly recount an ever-accelerating round of shipboard romances, quarrels, engagements and estrangements in a delectably apt evocation of the girl's delivery. When Waugh first started writing *Scoop* he confided to his diary, 'it is light and excellent'. 'Cruise', too, is light and excellent – and, uniquely, displays Waugh's novelistic techniques, elsewhere imperceptibly deployed across the extended fabric of the novels, in sharp miniature. This method consists of a number of recurring motifs, repeated with variation at increasing speed – the narrator's serial amours with a corking young man met at breakfast, the purser, a pansy (not a pansy? a pansy), the corker; her brother Bertie's no less heady round from booze to baroque art to the unspeakable Miss P. with her yachting cap to Algerian tarts back to booze again. Rotating more slowly are Papa on a walkout with Lady M., and Bill the sad divorcé, unreticent about his ex-wife to each of the passengers in turn. Motionless at the heart of the merry-go-round is Mum, stolidly buying a shawl at every port. Repeated phrases, 'goodness how decent', 'goodness how sad', deliriously abbreviated to 'G how S', spin the narrative ever faster, till the S.S. *Glory of Greece* returns to dock at Monte Carlo and the characters roll to rest in their proper beds. The circular motifs of *Decline and Fall* and *Vile Bodies*, the great wheel of Luna Park, the motor-racing track, the car skidding faster and faster in Agatha Runcible's fevered imagination, here find diminutive perfection.

Many of the other stories are formally less original, resorting to the traditional narrative twist – the sting in the tail of the unposted invitations in 'Bella Fleace Gave a Party', the bitten nose in 'On Guard', the benevolent lunatic's little treat of murder in 'Mr. Loveday's Little Outing'. The last tale of the collection, 'Winner Takes All', reverses this somewhat predictable form by having the ultimate twist of no twist. Every decent-minded reader will hope, from page to page, for the unfortunate younger brother's luck to turn, the title wickedly encouraging the false expectation that it can't possibly give the whole story away. No such thing. The story is what its title says, and the caddish elder brother prospers to the bitter end. The unremitting narrative progression, already noted in 'Love in the Slump', recurs here and in a number of these stories. The social world Waugh portrays is amoral, remorseless. The tone of the collection is correspondingly chilly and detached. Paradox and irony abound. 'Period Piece', like 'Cruise', figures a finely individualized female narrator, a spinster whose tale of aristocratic impotence, adultery and illegitimacy is delivered in the silkiest, genteelest of tones. This story, too, is all about reticence, Lady Amelia paradoxically remarking, 'I invariably find modern novels painfully reticent', an enigma she later clarifies: 'You couldn't write about the things which actually happen. People are so used to novels that they would not believe them.'

However, Waugh's novels and short stories, for all their apparent improbabilities, are pre-eminently about things which actually happen, and we do believe in them. This is partly because of his authoritative evocation of setting and the half-glimpsed reappearances of a wide cast of characters established in *Decline and Fall* and *Vile Bodies* – Lady Metroland, Viola Chasm, the Anchorages – which create a sense of solidity, a familiar world. 'Incident in Azania', one of the finest short stories of this period, unabashedly confesses its roots in *Black Mischief*, and flourishes from plantation in that dark soil. Bretherton, Reppington, Major Lepperidge, and the atrocious Mr. Youkoumian are all old friends, Matodi and the Union Club familiar territory. And yet this apparently improbable tale is also firmly rooted in reality. In September 1932 two British subjects were kidnapped by Chinese bandits in Manchuria and held to ransom for seven weeks. The newspaper reports on the captivity of Mrs. 'Tinko' Pawley and Mr. Corkran have long been forgotten. Yet they make supremely funny reading, and Waugh clearly followed the story with relish. The bandits' demands were preposterous: 1,100,000 dollars in ransom, 240 rifles and 38,000 rounds of cartridges, 6 machine rifles, 4 carbines, 200 ounces of opium, several rolls of silk, 100 gold rings and 60 gold watches. The demands were accompanied by ferocious threats: the captives' flesh and ears were to be chopped off and sent to Mrs. Pawley's father, husband, and the Asiatic Petroleum Company. From day to day the papers detailed the dispatch of parcels (a pipe and tobacco hidden in an old shoe for Mr. Corkran; cigarettes, a novel, toffee, a Christmas pudding). Waugh registered everything: the journalists' affectation of concern ('the safe receipt of a woollen sweater by the captives has given a grain of comfort here'); their titillatory evocation of cruelty ('they were bound by thin ropes which went round the tops of their necks and their arms ...'); above all, the curiously jaunty letters of the captives themselves:

'It is pretty well hell here. We are beastly bored. We received the parcels and everything OK. Next time the messengers come they must bring $30,000 and 200 ounces of opium, or else goodbye ears.'

At the foot of Mrs. Pawley's letter, Mr. Corkran has added the following note: 'Above confirmed. Bung-ho! for now. Many thanks for whisky. Tinko has drunk most of it, but I have had my share. See you soon. – Charles.'

The captives' final liberation by the Japanese was also strangely anticlimactic: 'They were free, but could not realize it, and showed no excitement when told they were to be released ...' All these details were seized on and rationalized in Waugh's masterly version of the story, where it is only very gradually intimated, from Prunella's letters, that her ordeal is not exactly life-threatening ('Dearest Dad, Not those records. The dance ones...'); that, far from being kidnapped, she went into hiding with the shadowy remittance man from Kenya in order to raise a ransom for them to return to England and marry.

to Chapter VI of *A Handful of Dust*, 'Du Côté de Chez Todd',
reveals the decisive economy with which the short story is transformed and absorbed into the novel's black denouement.
Waugh begins by making a small number of routine adjustments: Mr. McMaster becomes Mr. Todd (a memento mori);
the Shiriana Indians are the Pie-Wies; Paul Henty is Tony Last.
Henty's delirious approach to McMaster's house is expanded,
Tony's hallucinations picking up a number of details from earlier in the novel. The flashback giving Henty's pre-history is cut.
Thereafter the novel and story are substantially identical. It is
astonishing how little has been altered to effect the seamless
transformation of Henty to Tony; how well the story stood as
an independent entity; how inevitably, aesthetically predeter-
mined it appears as the penultimate chapter of the novel.

Some contemporary response to the black ending of *A Handful of Dust* was, however, critical. In self-defence Waugh wrote to
his friend Henry Yorke (the novelist Henry Green), 'I think I
agree that the Todd episode is fantastic. It is a "conceit" in the
Webster manner – wishing to bring Tony to a sad end I made it
an elaborate & improbable one . . . But the Amazon stuff had to
be there. The scheme was a Gothic man in the hands of savages
– first Mrs. Beaver etc., then the real ones . . .' Yet when the
novel was first published in serial form in England and America,
its fifth and last chapter provided an alternative, 'happy' ending,
disdainfully titled 'By Special Request'. The implication of the
title seems clear. You want a happy ending? I'll show you a
happy ending. In it, we are given the resolution the captive
Henty dreamed of with such longing – the leisurely river journey
to Belem, the big liner to Europe, the shy meeting with his
wife . . . '*Darling*, you've been much longer than you said. I quite
thought you were lost . . .' But in 'By Special Request' Tony's
untroubled return to Hetton is, in its own way, even bleaker
than the novel's Amazonian denouement. As Waugh once pointed out, the novel was 'about humanism', that is, about man
without God. Throughout the novel Tony is presented as an
innocent, a Gothic man of outdated ideals, an Antony who
sought things that were lost. And yet Waugh also shows a distressing spiritual lack, even in his hero. The point is first made in
the germinal 'The Man Who Liked Dickens', and then deployed

with significant emphasis throughout the novel. 'Do you believe in God?' Mr. McMaster asks. 'I've never really thought about it much,' Henty replies. In 'By Special Request', when Tony travels wearily back to Hetton with Brenda, that moral lack is made painfully evident as he fails to confront his wife with her adultery, or question their reunion:

He woke . . . to find that the question which neither he nor Brenda had asked, was answered. This should have been a crisis; his destinies had been at his control; there had been things to say, a decision to make, affecting every hour of his future life. *And he had fallen asleep.*

Through an act of spiritual sloth, the sin of accidie, Tony drifts back into a false marriage. Thoughtlessly, he eases himself into the immoral mores of his time. Secretly, he takes over Brenda's London flat for affairs of his own. In *A Handful of Dust* Tony as Todd's victim is a tragic hero of some moral worth. In Tony the smug survivor of 'By Special Request', Waugh dispassionately delineates another fall of man, familiar, unfrightening, and none the less appalling.

*

For many years Waugh had believed that, as a Catholic, he would not be able to marry again. In 1936 the annulment of his marriage to Evelyn Gardner was agreed by Rome. The publication of *Mr. Loveday's Little Outing and Other Sad Stories* helped raise funds for his marriage to Laura Herbert. With marriage and a fine home, the gift of his wife's grandmother, seven years of rootlessness came to an end. *Scoop*'s long gestation straddled the three years of his engagement, marriage, and the birth of his first child. It is written in the familiar, cinematic-satiric style of the earlier novels. But Waugh was becoming restive with the skills he knew too well. He was much occupied with restoring and furnishing his home, collecting Victoriana, and acquiring the ways of a country gentleman. A number of his journalistic essays in this period show his discriminating sociological observation of his surroundings, the villages with their still surviving Georgian mansions, the architecture of unspoiled rural England and the nature of its inhabitants. His evocation of the gentleman's house, half a mile from the village, could well describe Piers Court, his own home,

'standing', as the house agents say, 'in twenty acres of park-like grounds; three acres of well matured gardens; entrance lodge, carriage drive, stabling for twelve and other outbuildings ... four recep., ten bed, usual offices, water by gravitation. Electric light available in near future. A feature of the property is the wealth of period decoration.' A lovely house where an aged colonel plays wireless music to an obese retriever.

At the same time as Waugh was turning to the art of the nineteenth century and the architecture of the eighteenth, his style was also yearning towards a greater Augustan amplitude, a dignified orotundity of diction distinctly perceptible in these journalistic essays and the first short story he wrote after his marriage, 'An Englishman's Home'. Even while composing *A Handful of Dust* Waugh had confessed to his friend Katharine Asquith that it was 'very difficult to write because for the first time I am trying to deal with normal people instead of eccentrics. Comic English character parts [are] too easy when one gets to be thirty.' 'An Englishman's Home' is peopled with the recognizable figures of a quiet English village – Lady Peabury at Much Malcock House, Colonel Hodge at the Manor, the artistic, childless Hornbeams at the Old Mill – and Mr. Beverley Metcalfe, Waugh's semi-parodic alter ego, the new owner of Much Malcock Hall. Like Waugh, Mr. Metcalfe 'had made a study and noted the points of true countrymen. Had he been of literary habit and of an earlier generation, his observations might have formed a little book of aphorisms ...' The true countrymen of this story, with their finely judged and jealously guarded social differences, are lovingly, sardonically observed. In the unhurried narrative of their reluctantly joined ranks in the face of a common enemy, the suburban developer, we come to recognize a new note in Waugh's work.

'An Englishman's Home' marks Waugh's climacteric, a moment of change as decisive as his debut in 'The Balance'. The significance of both, as minor works, has gone unnoticed. Yet Waugh was well aware of what he was up to, and in 'Work Suspended' his hero, the successful detective-story writer John

Plant, is another unflattering alter ego who speaks for his author. 'I have been writing for over eight years,' Plant tells his publisher, 'and am nearing a climacteric.'

'I don't quite follow,' said Mr. Benwell anxiously.

'I mean a turning point in my career.'

'Oh, dear, I hope you're not thinking of making a contract elsewhere?'

'No, no, I mean that I feel in danger of turning into a stock bestseller ... It seems to me I am in danger of becoming mechanical, turning out year after year the kind of book I know I can write well. I feel I have got as good as I can be at this particular sort of writing. I need new worlds to conquer.' ...

'You've not been writing *poetry* in Morocco?'

'No, no ... it won't be anything like that. Just some new technical experiments. I don't suppose the average reader will notice them at all.'

For the average reader, the change may only become obvious with *Brideshead Revisited*, the post-war novel in which Waugh's Catholic themes are first paramount, and in which the style of his earlier novels gives place to a more traditional, nineteenth-century mode of narrative – first-person, nostalgic, richly descriptive. Yet 'Work Suspended' is the progenitor of *Brideshead*, and, had its composition not been broken off by the war, all the signs are that it would have been the better novel.

It seems probable that 'Work Suspended' was projected as a *Bildungsroman*, depicting the spiritual growth of the pointedly named John Plant, from a life of successful authorship and emotional sterility, to personal engagement and finally, we may infer, religious commitment. This trajectory is suggested by the allusive title of the novel's first chapter, 'My Father's House'. Ostensibly, it describes the narrator's return to England after the death of his father, to oversee the sale of his paternal home, and introduces a theme of house-hunting continued in the second chapter, when Plant's patrimony enables him to search for a country mansion after years of bachelor rootlessness. The first chapter's title, however, significantly echoes St. John's Gospel, 'In my Father's house are many mansions'. Had the novel been completed, we might guess that it would take the path followed by its successor, *The Sacred and Profane Memories of Captain Charles Ryder, or Brideshead Revisited* – whose first projected title was *The Household of the Faith*. There is a telling exchange towards the end of *Brideshead* which throws further light on the enigmatic 'Work Suspended':

'It's frightening,' Julia once said, 'to think how completely you have forgotten Sebastian.'

'He was the forerunner.'

'That's what you said in the storm. I've thought since, perhaps I am only a forerunner too.'

'Perhaps,' I thought, while her words hung in the air between us . . . 'perhaps all our loves are merely hints and symbols . . .'

'Work Suspended' begins with Plant wintering in Fez to complete his latest detective story. He is an unappealing hero – prim, conceited, godless, emotionally barren, satisfied by weekly congress with a Berber prostitute. His long-repressed emotions are first released on his return to England as he stands in his father's deserted studio. The dam is breached, and the novel's second chapter traces Plant's emotional growth as he falls in love with the pregnant wife of a literary friend. Lucy's pregnancy and his quickening love follow a parallel course till her baby is born and his love dies. What is most interesting about this second chapter, however, is that it contains a second love in embryo between Plant and Lucy's teenage cousin Julia, an engaging, bright, outspoken schoolgirl who has long admired Plant's books and now falls, unabashedly, for the man. Plant the narrator is preoccupied by his sexless calf-love for Lucy; in Waugh's supremely delicate handling the reader can trace, unbeknownst to the narrator, the beginning of a more genuine relationship between Plant, paternal, amused, benevolent, and the spontaneous, emotionally generous Julia. Perhaps all these loves were also intended to be merely hints and symbols of an ultimately discovered divine love – but the novel was aborted, and we will never know.

'Work Suspended' was begun and abandoned in 1939. It was published in its original form, as 'Two Chapters of an Unfinished Novel', in 1942. In the dedicatory epistle Waugh stated dispassionately, 'So far as it went, this was my best writing.' To finish it, however, 'would be vain, for the world in which and for which it was designed, has ceased to exist'. Consequently it was reissued in 1949, together with a cut selection of the short stories,* in a radically truncated form which transformed it from a fragment to a self-enclosed artistic whole. Among its many cuts are a series of passages in which Waugh describes his own aesthetic in the ironically downgraded version of an author of detective stories – his dislike of unnecessary effects, and his predilection for what he later termed elegance and variety of contrivance. In both versions Plant disdains serialization, which destroys 'the delicate fibres of a story'. 'Work Suspended' is rich with such delicate fibres, plot-lines skilfully laid for later detonation, which Waugh ruthlessly cut from the second version. It seems clear, for instance, that the domestic couple employed by Plant's father, the Jellabys, will later blackmail the son for his Academician father's secondary income as a forger of old masters. F. J. Stopp, the author of the first critical study of Waugh, suggests that Atwater, the sponger who accidentally killed Plant's father and then attaches himself to the son, will, at a later point in the novel, be murdered by him. Since we hear Plant, in a drunken moment, rashly inviting the unspeakable Atwater ('I've got a house in the country, plenty of room. Stay as long as you like. Die there.'), the suggestion seems both probable and rich with delicious possibilities, not least that of the master of crime fiction having to hide his own act of murder. Stopp was entertained as a house-guest by Waugh while preparing his book, and it seems probable that the hint is authorially sanctioned.

Waugh's other alterations show his care in updating the text – modifying the casual anti-Semitism of Plant's father, a redoubtable reactionary eccentric, for instance, and changing the subjects of his paintings to reflect the imminent war. The unfinished novel's two chapters become Part One and Part Two, neatly balanced by the twin titles, 'A Death' and 'A Birth', so eradicating the most significant thread laid by the original first chapter's title. Finally, the work is closed by a bleak 'Postscript', firmly shutting down all the beginnings lovingly initiated in the novel's original form:

*'Love in the Slump', 'Out of Depth', 'Incident in Azania' and 'By Special Request' were dropped.

EVELYN WAUGH

The date of this child's birth was 25 August, 1939, and while Lucy was still in bed the air-raid sirens sounded the first false alarm of the second World War. And so an epoch, my epoch, came to an end ... My father's death, the abandonment of my home, my literary innovations, my house in the country – all these had seemed to presage a new life. The new life came, not by my contrivance.

In 1939 Waugh had only been married two years. As Europe edged towards war, the new life he had begun to contrive for himself – his family, his house in the country, his literary innovations – was increasingly difficult to sustain. His first response was to turn his back. In May he ironized his own anathema to the wireless in 'The Sympathetic Passenger'. But when Lady Diana Cooper visited him in late June, she still had to listen to radio news bulletins outside the house, sitting in her car. His attitude changed when war was declared. He was eager and impatient to enlist; he served with the Marines and later the Commandos and saw active service in Dakar, Bardia and the last days of the Battle of Crete. On the long sea-voyage home from that defeat he cast his eyes back to the first months of the phoney war, and wrote *Put Out More Flags* in his old, inimitable satiric mode. But the literary innovations initiated in 'Work Suspended' were not forgotten. In 1944 he was given leave from service, to write *Brideshead Revisited*. Six months later he was sent on the British Military Mission to the Partisans in Yugoslavia, which was later to provide the material for 'Compassion'. He was demobbed in 1945; *Brideshead* was published, and he returned home.

*

Waugh's comments on 'Work Suspended' dwelt on its lost world. 'An epoch, my epoch, came to an end.' 'The world in which and for which it was designed, has ceased to exist.' His response to the war was to write the novel that lamented what it had lost. After *Brideshead* he turned his gaze even further back and began *Helena*, a Catholic historical novel in the tradition of Newman's *Callista*, celebrating the life of the saint credited with finding the remains of the True Cross. In the same year, 1945, he turned his retrospective gaze over his own life and, on rereading his Lancing diaries, began 'Charles Ryder's Schooldays', whose first and only chapter was discovered in the files of his literary agent in 1982.

Waugh's references to this work in the Diaries betray his uncertainty about its form. 'Yesterday I read through my Lancing diaries with unmixed shame,' he writes in late September. A week later, with satisfaction: 'I have begun a novel of school life in 1919 – as untopical a theme as could be found.' And within another month: 'I have written more of the school story.' It stands perfectly well as a short story, but the surviving typescript is headed 'Chapter One. Ryder by Gaslight' and, like 'Work Suspended', reveals a number of discrete threads apparently laid for later development. The work is chiefly fascinating for its scrupulously objective re-creation of the adolescent hero, whose experiences derive directly from Waugh's own memories and the record of the Lancing diaries. The 'Fragment of a Novel' of Waugh's Lancing days had been defiantly dedicated to 'myself, Evelyn Arthur St. John Waugh, to whose sympathy and appreciation alone it owes its being'. Now the dedicatee is scrutinized with distinctly diminished sympathy. 'If what I wrote was a true account of myself,' Waugh observed of the schoolboy diaries in *A Little Learning*, 'I was conceited, heartless, and cautiously malevolent.'

I should like to believe that even in this private journal I was dissembling a more generous nature; that I absurdly thought cynicism and malice the marks of maturity. I pray it may be so. But the damning evidence is there, in sentence after sentence on page after page, of consistent caddishness.

As in an appalled confessional, Waugh's autobiography returns repeatedly to his 'covert self-seeking', to the bullying in which he was 'not high-spirited or courageous but full of malice and calculation', driven by 'the fear that I myself might at any moment fall from favour'. The resulting story, 'Charles Ryder's Schooldays', is a conscious riposte to *Tom Brown's Schooldays* (to which it once refers) and bears the same critical relationship to its original as Golding's *Lord of the Flies* to *Coral Island*. It is, too, as merciless a re-creation of adolescence as Joyce's *Stephen Hero* – and fails for much the same reason, that the author's comprehensive, scrupulous realism plunges us into a world whose petty absorptions are ultimately tedious. There is too wide an imbalance between the minutiae of school life so important to the hero, and the reader's sympathy. And yet the reader's growing dislike of the hero is precisely the story's point.

Waugh's re-creation of his shameful past is ruthless. In the Lancing diaries the bright, heartless voice of the sixteen-year-old is unmistakably audible:

Last night we had a rather good rag with O'Connor in the dormitory by saying our dibs before he came up and then refusing to when he told us. He is really awfully officious.

Poor O'Connor recurs all too often in the diary, the butt of rag after rag. In the story he is O'Malley. His persecution is preceded by a single episode of the senior boys' psychological bullying of a miserable new boy. The reader's sympathies are thus clearly engaged with the victim. Thereafter, the sustained pack-hunting of O'Malley is built up over the entire chapter. As in 'Work Suspended', Waugh employs a skewed narrative perspective: the reader observes events through the cold eyes of Charles Ryder, feeling, as Charles does not, the misery of O'Malley, and hearing, as Charles will not, the warnings of Mr. Graves, the master whose overtures he rebuffs.

Waugh's Lancing diaries are painfully pretentious ('A tale told by a madman full of wind and fury, signifying nothing'; 'I am weary of an old passion and thoroughly depressed' – neither Shakespeare nor Dowson's 'Cynara' escape misquotation). Life is crude, art is not. Ryder's diary is a refined mockery of such pretensions: '*The day before yesterday this time I was in my dinner-jacket just setting out for dinner at the d'Italie with Aunt Philippa* ... Quantum mutatus ab illo Hectore. *We live in watertight compartments.*' That quip about watertight compartments was Alec's aphorism, transferred without irony to Ralph in 'Fragment of a Novel', where it was pronounced 'awfully clever'. Waugh's self-indulgence diminished with age. In his Lancing diaries a coarse prank had won the inappropriate accolade, 'It really is most subtly funny.' On a single page of Ryder's diary three deeply unfunny schoolboy jokes are pronounced 'very witty', their sequence skilfully descending from a cod Latin mispronunciation to a crass act of vandalism. And yet Waugh sympathetically details Ryder's absorption in his practice of ornamental lettering, copying – absurdly, but engagingly – an inappropriate Georgian poem in a crabbed thirteenth-century script with florid fifteenth-century capitals. In the Diaries the uptight young Waugh records briefly, 'Fremlin and I returned early from our walk and helped Gordon to mend his printing press. It would be priceless to have one but they are rather costly.' Gordon is the model for the novel's tactful and intelligent Mr. Graves. Ryder's pretence of haughty reluctance when Graves invites him in to his study to unpack his Victorian hand-press is finely conveyed, as are his unacknowledged excitement as they work together, and the repellent hypocrisy with which the whole episode is misrepresented in his diary. In this unfinished novel Waugh successfully conveys not only Ryder's public persona – priggish, pretentious, cynical, self-seeking, a real bastard – and his equally unpleasant self-projection in his diary, but also the more complex, intelligent, artistically absorbed personality the young Waugh had partially hidden from his own Lancing diaries. 'I would like to believe that even in this private journal I was dissembling a more generous nature,' Waugh had said. In *Charles Ryder's Schooldays* he re-creates with admirable even-handedness all the schoolboy's moral deficiencies – to which every bosom will return an uneasy echo – without obscuring the finer qualities that herd membership demands to be kept hidden.

*

Waugh's post-war shorter fiction follows no clear pattern, except that it is suffused by disillusion with the present and a yearning for a more civilized past. 'Scott-King's Modern Europe' (1947) is an accomplished novella drawing on a recent jaunt to a Spanish centenary celebration of 'a Thomist philosopher whose name escapes me', and his former familiarity with the Balkans during the Military Mission to Yugoslavia. It is a comic account of the kind of academic jamboree later thoroughly anatomized in Lodge's *Small World*, simultaneously playing lightly with the perils and confusions of a newly created totalitarian state, the Republic of Neutralia. Scott-King is yet another ironic, partial self-portrait – a dim Classics master characterized by a recurrent refrain as 'an adult, an intellectual, a classical scholar, almost a poet'. Scott-King, unlike Waugh, is the only professor attending the centenary celebration who is familiar with its subject, a little-known Renaissance poet named Bellorius, whose magnum opus Scott-King has translated into Spenserian stanzas. That unpublished translation is a sly side-swipe at Waugh's adolescent literary endeavour, the Lancing prize poem, *The Return of Launcelot*, also painfully composed in Spenserian stanzas ('and most of them are complete balls', Waugh confided to his diary at the time).

'Tactical Exercise' is a callous tale in the manner of the pre-war collection, driven by the traditional final narrative twist. When first published in the *Strand* in 1947 it was preceded by an Osbert Lancaster cartoon of Waugh, and a two-page introduction by John Betjeman that sounds distinctly ghost-written. Betjeman begins by making claims for Waugh as a scholar – a claim already half-ironized in Scott-King, and later repeated in the overt self-portrait of Gilbert Pinfold, 'who was neither a scholar nor a regular soldier' and yet 'the part for which he cast himself was a combination of eccentric don and testy colonel'. Nevertheless, Waugh's skills are indeed also scholarly. As Betjeman points out, his fiction is remarkable for its 'precise and selective observation of details of furniture, architecture, clothes, food, landscape'. His discrimination and impartiality are qualities proper to good scholarship. But he is above all a Catholic, since *A Handful of Dust* electing to show people ' "in the round", as he calls it, that is to say in their relation to their Creator and an eternal scheme of things'. Within such a perspective Betjeman rightly asserts that 'Tactical Exercise' is 'a morality': 'Notice the utter destruction in which the scene is set. How the characters are chaotic inhabitants of chaos. No wonder the sin of hatred breeds another sin, that of murder. Evil breeds evil.'

It is easy to misread 'Tactical Exercise' merely as a murder story, without crediting its savage moral dimension. Betjeman's guidance is salutary. Waugh abhorred the post-war world portrayed here – London in ruins, the men war-wounded, the women at work, deprivation and ugliness everywhere. The unamiable hero, John Verney, is welcomed back to his wife's paternal home with a pointed half-quotation of Milton: 'Welcome to Chaos and Old Night'. The story's very first sentence betrays its inverted values by the most diminutive of linguistic adjustments:

John Verney married Elizabeth in 1938, but it was not until the winter of 1945 that he came to hate her steadily and fiercely.

Merely by the addition of 'but' Waugh conveys an implicit expectation on the part of the reader that, had it not been for the war's interruption, Verney would have hated his wife sooner.

'Love Among the Ruins' takes Waugh's disenchantment with the contemporary world even further. It is, as the subtitle ominously warns, 'A Romance of the Near Future', an imminent, Orwellian, futuristic dystopia in which all the gifts Betjeman rightly identified, of precise social observation and economic evocation of setting, are necessarily forfeit. Waugh had read *Animal Farm* with delight; *Nineteen Eighty-Four*, he wrote to Orwell in the year of its publication, 'failed to make my flesh creep as presumably you intended', because it denied the existence of the soul, and furthermore Winston's rebellion was false because it took the form of 'fucking in the style of Lady Chatterley – finding reality through a sort of mystical union with the Proles in the sexual act'. 'Love Among the Ruins' can be read as a counter-fiction to *Nineteen Eighty-Four*, where the dystopic element lies precisely in futurity's denial of all spiritual and private personal values, Christmas is a meaningless Santa-Claus-Tide and the love-affair of Miles Plastic and the bearded Clara is sacrificed to abortion, sterility, and her dancing career. It was begun in 1950, the year of Orwell's death, abandoned, 'and resumed with the realization that the characters lacked substance for more than a short story'. Its publication coincided inopportunely with the coronation of Queen Elizabeth II. In 1953 Waugh analysed its mixed reception in an article for the *Spectator* in which he pronounced his own estimation with equanimity: 'It is a brief, very prettily produced fantasy about life in the near future with certain obvious defects.' Presumably among these he would himself have numbered its similarity in some details (such as state-supplied euthanasia) to *Brave New World*, as well as the rudimentary nature of its characters and its uncharacteristic lack of solidity of specification. 'Basil Seal Rides Again' (1963), Waugh's last work of fiction, is by contrast wickedly engaging in his original satiric manner, a delightful and wholly frivolous portrait of himself as Basil Seal, thwarting the ill-judged marriage of a favourite daughter.

None of these late short stories have the seriousness of 'Compassion', which derives from Waugh's experiences in wartime Yugoslavia, and describes Major Gordon's attempts to assist a group of Jewish displaced persons in the face of hostility and resistance from Tito's partisans. The story was written in 1949 and filleted into the third part of his war trilogy, *Unconditional Surrender*, in 1962. It is seriously weakened in this adaptation, partly because it is broken up to make way for other strands of plot, partly because the reticence characterizing all Waugh's work prompted him to cut from the story revealing passages analysing Major Gordon's gradual involvement with the Jews:

Major Gordon was not an imaginative man. He saw the complex historical situation in which he had participated, quite simply in terms of friends and enemies and the paramount importance of the war-effort. He had nothing against Jews and nothing against communists. He wanted to defeat the Germans and go home. Here it seemed were a lot of tiresome civilians getting in the way of this object ...

... But another part of his mind was all the time slowly being set in motion. He had seen something entirely new, which needed new eyes to see clearly: humanity in the depths, misery of quite another order from anything he had guessed before. He was not as yet conscious of terror or pity. His steady Scottish mind would take some time to assimilate the experience.

The suffering of the Jews, Waugh is telling us, is a tragedy – one that Major Gordon has not yet recognized, but which Waugh's narrative identifies in its reference to Aristotle's description of tragedy arousing pity and terror. In the small area of his competence, however, Major Gordon fails to avert tragedy, and although the majority of the local refugees reach Palestine, the Kanyi couple are executed. The final passage of 'Compassion' (pp. 439–440), in which the chaplain offers his interpretation of Major Gordon's failure, is also cut from *Unconditional Surrender*. It provides the germ for the central moral aphorism fuelling the *Sword of Honour* trilogy, the pronouncement of Guy Crouchback's father, that 'quantitative judgements don't apply'.

*

Waugh's sympathetic, profoundly human handling of the Jewish victims in 'Compassion' raises the vexed question of his prejudices. In the earlier part of this collection sensitive readers may find themselves shocked by casual mockery of vulnerable minority groups – the working class, women, blacks, Jews, foreigners, homosexuals, lunatics. There are several answers to this. Frequently, the remarks are made by Waugh's characters rather than in his own authorial voice. Plant's father, for instance, is characterized by his robust indulgence in a variety of prejudices, from unabashed anti-Semitism to rabid anti-Post-Impressionism. When the young lady of 'Cruise' is intrigued by a fellow passenger of ambiguous sexual orientation it is natural for her to speculate on whether he is 'a pansy'. This delineation of social prejudices and the language in which they are expressed is part of Waugh's meticulous observation of his contemporary world. Yet it has to be admitted that Waugh's own tones can be distinctly heard in the unacceptable pronouncements of Plant's father, whose derision of Cézanne is closely allied to Waugh's mockery of Joyce and Picasso. Plant's father doggedly maintained Dreyfus's guilt until the popular tide turned, the early thirties brought rising anti-Semitism, and he took up the Jewish cause in a number of unpublished letters to *The Times*. Waugh, like Plant senior, is incorrigibly contrary, and any social, moral, or aesthetic piety is liable to prompt an ostentatious counter-reaction.

There is a telling moment in 'Charles Ryder's Schooldays' when Charles identifies a new note in his inner counsels,

a voice, as it were, from a more civilized age, as from the chimney corner in mid-Victorian times there used to break sometimes the sardonic laughter of grandmama, relic of Regency, a clear, outrageous, entirely self-assured disturber among the high and muddled thoughts of her whiskered descendants.

EVELYN WAUGH

Comedy, and even more so satire, is by its very nature transgressive, challenging and ridiculing society's respectable norms. Waugh's infringement of social taboos problematic for the present-day demands of political correctness is mostly to be found in the earlier work of the thirties. There, in his lighter comedy, we hear the sardonic laughter of an outrageous disturber of the high-minded proprieties of our present age. This, however, is an element of Waugh's comedy, not his satire. Waugh himself habitually denied his status as a satirist, claiming that contemporary society lacked its prerequisite, a stable system of values. Yet Waugh's Catholicism provided the structure society lacked. From *Vile Bodies* onwards the main objects of Waugh's comedy are serious. The nursery morality natural to him was continually outraged by society's casual transgressions. The majority of the short stories prior to his second marriage are fuelled by disapprobation of the casual morality of his contemporary world. With the overt Catholic perspective subsequent to *A Handful of Dust* the objects of his satire are preeminently identifiable by their spiritual deficiencies, and the social prejudices lightly exploited in the early work become signs of moral inadequacy. The corrupt John Verney in 'Tactical Exercise', for instance, is anti-Semitic, and in 'Compassion' the self-seeking Bakic lacks all charity in his handling of the Jewish refugees.

*

Evelyn Waugh's short stories do not exhibit the uniform proficiency demonstrated by Kipling and Chekhov, the masters of the genre. Conversely, their very heterogeneity is their strength. This collection, spanning an entire creative lifetime and embraced by Waugh's first and last works of fiction, is remarkable for its unpredictable variety of matter, manner and form. In its restless flux Waugh's kaleidoscopic development is reflected. Many of the best are aborted novels, yearn towards novel status, or incubate materials later to be found fully-fledged in the novels. The Irish landscape blurred by moss so vividly evoked at the beginning of 'Bella Fleace Gave a Party' recurs, much expanded, in Ambrose Silk's flight to Ireland at the end of *Put Out More Flags*, where it becomes a moral emblem of his culpably ill-defined spiritual landscape. Waugh probably refrained from republishing 'Incident in Azania' after its appearance in *Mr. Loveday's Little Outing and Other Sad Stories*, not because it was potentially libellous (which would have inhibited its original publication), but because he pillaged it for a number of ideas re-employed in *Scoop*'s satire of journalists. The ruse employed by the spoof property developers in 'An Englishman's Home' is vastly expanded and improved in Basil Seal's exploitation of the Connolly children as a threatened billet in *Put Out More Flags*. Lord Cornphillip's willing legitimation of his wife's bastard for base motives of revenge in 'Period Piece' is radically reversed in *Unconditional Surrender*, where Guy Crouchback remarries his ex-wife Virginia, pregnant by Trimmer, not merely as an act of chivalry to her, but to protect the soul of the unborn child, an act of grace. In an unusually self-revealing essay entitled 'People Who Want to Sue Me', Waugh once exclaimed:

> If only the amateurs would get it in their heads that novel writing is a highly skilled and laborious trade. One does not just sit behind a screen jotting down other people's conversation. One has for one's raw material every single thing one has ever seen or heard or felt, and one has to go over that vast, smouldering rubbish-heap of experience, half-stifled by the fumes and dust, scraping and delving until one finds a few discarded valuables.
>
> Then one has to assemble these tarnished and dented fragments, polish them, set them in order, and try to make a coherent and significant arrangement of them.

Waugh's oeuvre is uniquely derivative from his own experiences. From fact to fiction, his life is passed through the multiple filters provided by the diaries, letters, travel books, journalism, the short stories and the novels. In this collection we are privileged to enter the studio of this scavenger and supreme craftsman, to watch him at work, and admire his array of polished, completed artefacts.

Ann Pasternak Slater

MAJOR PRIMARY TEXTS

1. FICTION

Decline and Fall, An Illustrated Novelette, Chapman & Hall, 1928; Doubleday, Doran, New York, 1929.

Vile Bodies, Chapman & Hall, 1930; Cape, Smith, New York, 1930.

Black Mischief, Chapman & Hall, 1932; Farrar & Rinehart, New York, 1932.

A Handful of Dust, Chapman & Hall, 1934; Farrar & Rinehart, New York, 1934.

Mr. Loveday's Little Outing and Other Sad Stories, Chapman & Hall, 1936; Little, Brown, Boston, 1936.

Scoop: A Novel About Journalists, Chapman & Hall, 1938; Little, Brown, Boston, 1938.

Put Out More Flags, Chapman & Hall, 1942; Little, Brown, Boston, 1942.

Work Suspended, Chapman & Hall, 1942.

Brideshead Revisited: The Sacred and Profane Memories of Captain Charles Ryder, Chapman & Hall, 1945; Little, Brown, Boston, 1945.

Scott-King's Modern Europe, Chapman & Hall, 1947; Little, Brown, Boston, 1949.

The Loved One, Chapman & Hall, 1948; Little, Brown, Boston, 1948.

Work Suspended and Other Stories Written Before the Second World War, Chapman & Hall, 1949.

Helena, Chapman & Hall, 1950; Little, Brown, Boston, 1950.

Men At Arms, Chapman & Hall, 1952; Little, Brown, 1952.

Love Among the Ruins: A Romance of the Near Future, Chapman & Hall, 1953.

Tactical Exercise (US edition of short stories), Little, Brown, Boston, 1954.

Officers and Gentlemen, Chapman & Hall, 1955; Little, Brown, Boston, 1955.

The Ordeal of Gilbert Pinfold, Chapman & Hall, 1957; Little, Brown, Boston, 1957.

Unconditional Surrender, Chapman & Hall, 1961; US edition: *The End of the Battle*, Little, Brown, Boston, 1961.

Basil Seal Rides Again or The Rake's Regress, Chapman & Hall, 1963; Little, Brown, Boston, 1963.

Sword of Honour. A Final Version of the Novels: *Men at Arms* (1952),

Officers and Gentlemen (1955), and *Unconditional Surrender* (1961), Chapman & Hall, 1965; Little, Brown, Boston, 1966.

DAVIS, ROBERT MURRAY, ed., *Evelyn Waugh, Apprentice: The Early Writings, 1910-1927*, Pilgrim Books, Oklahoma, 1985.

2. TRAVEL

Labels, A Mediterranean Journal, Duckworth, 1930; US edition: *A Bachelor Abroad, A Mediterranean Journal*, Cape, Smith, New York, 1930.

Remote People, Duckworth, 1931; US edition: *They Were Still Dancing*, Farrar & Rinehart, New York, 1932.

Ninety-Two Days, The Account of a Tropical Journey Through British Guiana and Part of Brazil, Duckworth, 1934; Farrar & Rinehart, New York, 1934.

Waugh in Abyssinia, Longman, Green & Co., 1936; Longman, Green & Co., New York, 1936.

Robbery Under Law: The Mexican Object-Lesson, Chapman & Hall, 1939; US edition: *Mexico: An Object Lesson* Little, Brown, Boston, 1939.

The Holy Places, The Queen Anne Press, 1952; Queen Anne Press and British Book Center, New York, 1953.

A Tourist in Africa, Chapman & Hall, 1960; Little, Brown, Boston, 1960.

3. BIOGRAPHY, AUTOBIOGRAPHY, AND OTHER

Rossetti, His Life and Works, Duckworth, 1928; Dodd, Mead & Co., New York, 1928.

Edmund Campion: Jesuit and Martyr, Longman's, 1935; Sheed & Ward, New York, 1935.

The Life of the Right Reverend Ronald Knox, Chapman & Hall, 1959; US edition: *Monsignor Ronald Knox*, Little, Brown, Boston, 1959.

A Little Learning. The First Volume of an Autobiography, Chapman & Hall, 1964; Little, Brown, Boston, 1964.

AMORY, MARK, ed., *The Letters of Evelyn Waugh*, Weidenfeld & Nicolson, 1980.

DAVIE, MICHAEL, ed., *The Diaries of Evelyn Waugh*, Weidenfeld & Nicolson, 1976.

GALLAGHER, DONAT, ed., *The Essays, Articles and Reviews of Evelyn Waugh*, Methuen, 1983.

COOPER, ARTEMIS, ed., *Mr. Wu and Mrs. Stitch: The Letters of Evelyn Waugh and Diana Cooper*, Hodder & Stoughton, 1991.

MOSLEY, CHARLOTTE, ed., *The Letters of Nancy Mitford and Evelyn Waugh*, Hodder & Stoughton, 1996.

Waugh is one of the great letter-writers.

EVELYN WAUGH

SECONDARY TEXTS

1. BIOGRAPHY AND PERSONAL REMINISCENCE

DONALDSON, FRANCES, *Evelyn Waugh. Portrait of a Country Neighbour*, Weidenfeld & Nicolson, 1967. A well-written, warm and honest portrait of Waugh from the late forties.

HASTINGS, SELINA, *Evelyn Waugh: A Biography*, Sinclair-Stevenson, 1994. Lively and sympathetic.

PATEY, DOUGLAS LANE, *The Life of Evelyn Waugh: A Critical Biography*, Blackwell, 1998. An intelligent intellectual biography.

PRYCE-JONES, DAVID, ed., *Evelyn Waugh and His World*, Weidenfeld & Nicolson, 1973. Essays and photographs by friends on different aspects of Waugh.

ST JOHN, JOHN, *To the War With Waugh*, Leo Cooper, 1973. Written by a fellow-member of the Royal Marines.

STANNARD, MARTIN, *Evelyn Waugh: The Early Years 1903–1939*, Dent, 1986, and *Evelyn Waugh: No Abiding City 1939–1966* Dent, 1992. Admirably industrious and full documentation, marred by a lack of sympathy.

SYKES, CHRISTOPHER, *Evelyn Waugh: A Biography*, Collins, 1975. Factually inaccurate, but with the vitality and insight of critical friendship.

2. BIBLIOGRAPHY

Necessary tools for the Waugh scholar:

DAVIS, ROBERT MURRAY, *A Catalogue of the Evelyn Waugh Collection at the Humanities Research Center, The University of Texas at Austin*, Whitston Publishing Co., New York, 1981.

DAVIS, ROBERT MURRAY, Paul A. Doyle, Heinz Kosok, Charles E. Linck Jr., *Evelyn Waugh: A Checklist of Primary and Secondary Material*, Whitston Publishing Co., New York, 1972.

3. CRITICISM

DAVIS, ROBERT MURRAY, *Evelyn Waugh, Writer*, Pilgrim Books, Oklahoma, 1981. Full-length study using fascinating unpublished manuscript variants.

HOLLIS, CHRISTOPHER, 'Evelyn Waugh', British Council 'Writers and their Work' series, Longman's, 1966. Brief and pithy.

LODGE, DAVID, 'Evelyn Waugh', Columbia University Press, 1971. Broad, fast-moving and suggestive essay by a fellow-Catholic novelist.

PASTERNAK SLATER, ANN, 'Waugh's Handful of Dust: Right Things in Wrong Places', *Essays in Criticism*, January 1982, pp. 48- 68. Establishes some essential Waugh techniques.

SELECT BIBLIOGRAPHY

STANNARD, MARTIN, ed., *Evelyn Waugh: The Critical Heritage*, Routledge & Kegan Paul, 1984. All the contemporary reviews.

STOPP, FREDERICK J., *Evelyn Waugh, Portrait of an Artist*, Chapman & Hall, 1958. The first and best critical study of Waugh.

WILSON, EDMUND, ' "Never Apologise, Never Explain": The Art of Evelyn Waugh', *Classics and Commercials. A Literary Chronicle of the Forties*, W. H. Allen, 1951, pp. 140–6. A judicious eulogy, followed by post-*Brideshead* disillusion in 'Splendors and Miseries of Evelyn Waugh', ibid., pp. 298–305.

CHRONOLOGY

DATE	AUTHOR'S LIFE	LITERARY CONTEXT
1898	Birth of Alec Waugh, Evelyn's brother.	
1903	28 October: birth of Evelyn Waugh to Arthur and Catherine Waugh in Hampstead.	James: *The Ambassadors.* Shaw: *Man and Superman.*
1904		Conrad: *Nostromo.*
1905		James: *The Golden Bowl.* Forster: *Where Angels Fear to Tread.*
1908		Forster: *A Room with a View.* Bennett: *The Old Wives' Tale.* Grahame: *The Wind in the Willows.*
1910	Attends Heath Mount Preparatory School.	Forster: *Howards End.*
1911	Begins keeping a diary.	Lawrence: *The White Peacock.* Beerbohm: *Zuleika Dobson.*
1912		Beerbohm: *A Christmas Garland.* Brooke: *Collected Poems.* Shaw: *Pygmalion.*
1913		Lawrence: *Sons and Lovers.* Proust: *A la Recherche du temps perdu* (to 1927). Conrad: *Chance.*
1914		Joyce: *Dubliners.*
1915		Ford: *The Good Soldier.* Conrad: *Victory.* Buchan: *The Thirty-nine Steps.* Woolf: *The Voyage Out.*
1916		Joyce: *A Portrait of the Artist as a Young Man.*
1917	Alec Waugh's *Loom of Youth* published. Evelyn attends Lancing College, Sussex.	Yeats: *The Wild Swans at Coole.* Eliot: *Prufrock and Other Observations.*
1918		Brooke: *Collected Poems.*
1919		Shaw: *Heartbreak House.* Beerbohm: *Seven Men.* Firbank: *Valmouth.*
1920		Pound: *Hugh Selwyn Mauberley.*

Emmeline Pankhurst founds the Women's Social and Political Union.

Russo-Japanese war. Franco-British *entente cordiale*.
Liberal government in Britain: Campbell-Bannerman Prime Minister. First Russian revolution.

Asquith becomes Prime Minister.

Death of Edward VII.

Coronation of George V. Agadir crisis. Industrial unrest in Britain.

Outbreak of World War I.
Asquith forms coalition government with Balfour.

Easter Rising in Dublin. Lloyd George becomes Prime Minister.

Bolshevik revolution in Russia. US joins war.

Armistice. Women over 30 gain vote.
Versailles peace conference.

League of Nations formed. Prohibition in the US.

DATE	AUTHOR'S LIFE	LITERARY CONTEXT
1921		Huxley: *Crome Yellow*. Pirandello: *Six Characters in Search of an Author*.
1922	January: attends Hertford College, Oxford, as a Scholar reading History. Begins contributing graphics, and later pieces to undergraduate magazines.	Joyce: *Ulysses*. Eliot: *The Waste Land*. Housman: *Last Poems*. Fitzgerald: *The Beautiful and the Damned*.
1923		Cummings: *The Enormous Room*. Firbank: *The Flower Beneath the Foot*. Huxley: *Antic Hay*.
1924	Leaves Oxford with a third-class degree. Begins novel, *The Temple at Thatch*. Makes film, *The Scarlet Woman*. Attends Heatherley's Art School, London.	Forster: *A Passage to India*. Shaw: *Saint Joan*. Ford: *Parade's End* (to 1928).
1925	Schoolmaster at Arnold House, Llanddulas, Denbighshire (January–July). Destroys *The Temple at Thatch* on Harold Acton's criticism. Attempts suicide. Writes 'The Balance'. Begins as schoolmaster in Aston Clinton, Berkshire (September).	Fitzgerald: *The Great Gatsby*. Kafka: *The Trial*.
1926	*P.R.B.: An Essay on the Pre-Raphaelite Brotherhood 1847–1854* privately printed. 'The Balance' published.	Faulkner: *Soldier's Pay*. Nabokov: *Mary*. Henry Green: *Blindness*. Firbank: *Concerning the Eccentricities of Cardinal Pirelli*.
1927	Sacked from Aston Clinton (February). Story for *The New Decameron* commissioned; writes 'The Tutor's Tale: A House of Gentlefolks'. Temporary schoolmaster in London, also contributing to *The Daily Express*. Meets Evelyn Gardner (April). Writes *Rossetti, His Life and Works*. Takes carpentry lessons. proposes to Evelyn Gardner (December).	Woolf: *To the Lighthouse*. Hemingway: *Men Without Women*. Dunne: *An Experiment with Time*.
1928	Begins writing *Decline and Fall*. *Rossetti* published (April). Marries Evelyn Gardner (June). *Decline and Fall* published (September).	Lawrence: *Lady Chatterley's Lover*. Woolf: *Orlando*. Yeats: *The Tower*. Lewis: *The Childermass*. Nabokov: *King, Queen, Knave*.

CHRONOLOGY

HISTORICAL EVENTS

Establishment of USSR. Stalin becomes General Secretary of the Communist party Central Committee. Mussolini marches on Rome. Coalition falls and Bonar Law forms Conservative ministry.

Baldwin becomes Prime Minister. Women gain legal equality in divorce suits. Hitler's coup in Munich fails. German hyper-inflation.

First Labour government formed by Ramsay MacDonald. Hitler in prison. Death of Lenin. Baldwin becomes Prime Minister again after a Conservative election victory.

Locarno conference.

British general strike. First television demonstrated.

Lindbergh makes first solo flight over Atlantic.

Hoover becomes US President. Stalin de facto dictator in USSR: first Five Year Plan. Women's suffrage in Britain reduced from age 30 to age 21.

DATE	AUTHOR'S LIFE	LITERARY CONTEXT
1929	Mediterranean cruise with his wife (February–March). *Vile Bodies* begun. Marriage breaks down (July). Divorce (September).	Faulkner: *The Sound and the Fury*. Cocteau: *Les Enfants terribles*. Hemingway: *A Farewell to Arms*. Henry Green: *Living*. Priestley: *The Good Companions*. Remarque: *All Quiet on the Western Front*.
1930	*Vile Bodies* published (January). Received into the Catholic Church; *Labels, A Mediterranean Journal* published (September). Travels to Abyssinia to report coronation of Haile Selassie for *The Times* (October–November); travels in East and Central Africa.	Eliot: *Ash Wednesday*. Faulkner: *As I Lay Dying*. Nabokov: *The Defence*.
1931	Returns to England (March). *Remote People* completed (August) and published (November). *Black Mischief* begun (September).	Faulkner: *Sanctuary*. Woolf: *The Waves*.
1932	Working on film scenario for Ealing Studios (January–February). Writes 'Excursion in Reality' (March). *Black Mischief* completed (June) and published (October). Sails for British Guiana (December).	Huxley: *Brave New World*. Faulkner: *Light in August*. Betjeman: *Mount Zion*. Nabokov: *Glory*.
1933	Travels in British Guiana and Brazil (January–May). Writes 'The Man Who Liked Dickens' (February). Meets 'white mouse named Laura' Herbert at Herbert family home in Italy (September). 'Out of Depth' and *Ninety-Two Days* written (October–November).	Malraux: *La Condition humaine*. Stein: *The Autobiography of Alice B. Toklas*.
1934	In Fez, Morocco, begins *A Handful of Dust* (January–February). *Ninety-Two Days* published (March) and *A Handful of Dust* completed (April). Expedition to Spitzbergen in the Arctic (July–August). *A Handful of Dust* published (September). Begins *Edmund Campion: Jesuit and Martyr* (September); writes 'Mr Crutwell's Little Outing' and 'On Guard'.	

CHRONOLOGY

HISTORICAL EVENTS

Wall Street crash. First year of the Depression.

Gandhi begins civil disobedience campaign in India. Nazis win seats from the moderates in German election.

Britain abandons Gold Standard.

Unemployment in Britain reaches 2.8 million. F. D. Roosevelt's landslide victory in US presidential election.

Hitler becomes Chancellor of Germany. Roosevelt's 'New Deal' in US.

Riots in Paris; Doumergue forms National Union ministry to avert civil war. Dollfuss murdered in attempted Nazi coup in Austria.

DATE	AUTHOR'S LIFE	LITERARY CONTEXT
1935	Completes *Campion* (May); writes 'Winner Takes All' (July). Travels to Abyssinia to report on imminent Italian invasion for *The Daily Mail* (August–December).	Isherwood: *Mr. Norris Changes Trains*. Eliot: *Murder in the Cathedral*. Odets: *Waiting for Lefty*. Graham Greene: *England Made Me*.
1936	Writes *Waugh in Abyssinia* (April–October). Annulment to first marriage agreed by Rome (July); engagement to Laura Herbert. Returns to Abyssinia to report on Italian occupation (July–September). *Waugh in Abyssinia* published. *Scoop* begun (October).	Faulkner: *Absalom, Absalom!* Nabokov: *Despair*.
1937	Marriage to Laura Herbert (17 April); honeymoon in Italy. Decides to rewrite *Scoop* (July). Moves into Piers Court, Stinchcombe, Gloucestershire (August).	Hemingway: *To Have and Have Not*. Orwell: *The Road to Wigan Pier*. Sartre: *La Nausée*. Betjeman: *Continual Dew*. Steinbeck: *Of Mice and Men*.
1938	Birth of daughter, Teresa Waugh (March). *Scoop* published (May). Two trips, both with Laura: to Hungary (May) and Mexico (August–October). Writes 'An Englishman's Home' and begins *Robbery Under Law: The Mexican Object-Lesson*.	Graham Greene: *Brighton Rock*. Beckett: *Murphy*. Orwell: *Homage to Catalonia*.
1939	Completes *Robbery Under Law*; writes 'The Sympathetic Passenger' (May). Begins *Work Suspended*. *Robbery Under Law* published (June). Birth of son, Auberon Waugh (November). Joins Royal Marines (December) and abandons *Work Suspended*.	Joyce: *Finnegans Wake*. Eliot: *The Family Reunion*. Steinbeck: *The Grapes of Wrath*. Henry Green: *Party Going*. Auden: *Journey to a War*. Isherwood: *Goodbye to Berlin*.
1940	Expedition to Dakar, West Africa (August–September). Transfers to Commandos in Scotland (November). Birth and death of daughter, Mary Waugh (December).	Hemingway: *For Whom the Bell Tolls*. Graham Greene: *The Power and the Glory*. Dylan Thomas: *Portrait of the Artist as a Young Dog*. Faulkner: *The Hamlet*. Henry Green: *Pack my Bag: A Self-Portrait*. Betjeman: *Old Lights for New Chancels*.

CHRONOLOGY

HISTORICAL EVENTS

Italy invades Abyssinia. Anti-Jewish Nuremberg laws passed in Germany.

Spanish civil war begins. Abdication crisis in Britain. Hitler and Mussolini form Rome–Berlin Axis. Moscow 'Show Trials' begin. Blum forms Popular Front ministry in France.

Japanese invade China. Baldwin retires and Neville Chamberlain becomes Prime Minister.

Germany annexes Austria. Munich crisis.

Nazi-Soviet pact. Germany invades Czechoslovakia and Poland; Britain and France declare war (September 3).

Germany invades Norway and Denmark. Churchill becomes Prime Minister. Dunkirk. Italy declares war on Britain and France. Fall of France. Battle of Britain. The Blitz.

DATE	AUTHOR'S LIFE	LITERARY CONTEXT
1941	Sails for service in Egypt (February); raid on Bardia (April). At Battle of Crete (May). Disillusioned with war. July–August, on circuitous route home, writes *Put Out More Flags*. Rejoins Royal Marines (September).	Acton: *Peonies and Ponies*. Fitzgerald: *The Last Tycoon*.
1942	*Put Out More Flags* published. Transfers to Blues, Special Service Brigade; birth of daughter, Margaret Waugh (June). *Work Suspended* published (December).	Anouilh: *Eurydice*. Sartre: *Les Mouches*. Camus: *L'Etranger*, *Le Mythe de Sisyphe*.
1943	Transferred to London (March). Father dies (June).	Davies: *Collected Poems*. Henry Green: *Caught*.
1944	Given leave to write (January); begins *Brideshead Revisited* (January–June). Birth of daughter, Harriet Waugh (May). On British Military Mission to the Partisans in Yugoslavia (from July).	Eliot: *Four Quartets*. Anouilh: *Antigone*. Camus: *Caligula*. Sartre: *Huis Clos*.
1945	Returns to London (March). *Brideshead Revisited* published and *Helena* begun (May). Demobbed; returns to Piers Court.	Broch: *The Death of Virgil*. Betjeman: *New Bats in Old Belfries*. Orwell: *Animal Farm*. Henry Green: *Loving*. Mitford: *The Pursuit of Love*.
1946	*When the Going was Good* published (selection from previous travel books). Travels to Nuremberg (March) and Spain (June). Writes 'Scott-King's Modern Europe' and *Wine in Peace and War*.	Rattigan: *The Winslow Boy*. Cocteau: *L'Aigle à deux têtes*. Henry Green: *Back*. Dylan Thomas: *Deaths and Entrances*.
1947	Visits New York and Los Angeles for projected film of *Brideshead Revisited* (January–March). Writes 'Tactical Exercise'. Writes first draft of *The Loved One* (May–July). Birth of son, James Waugh (June). Visits Scandinavia (August–September).	Mann: *Doctor Faustus*. Camus: *La Peste*. Diary of Anne Frank is published. Henry Green: *Concluding*.

CHRONOLOGY

DATE	AUTHOR'S LIFE	LITERARY CONTEXT
1948	*The Loved One* published (February). Begins lecture tour in USA (October).	Eliot: *Notes Towards the Definition of Culture.* Graham Greene: *The Heart of the Matter.* Faulkner: *Intruder in the Dust.* Henry Green: *Nothing.* Acton: *Memoirs of an Aesthete.*
1949	Returns from America (March). 'Compassion' published.	Orwell: *Nineteen Eighty-Four.* De Beauvoir: *The Second Sex.* Graham Greene: *The Third Man.* Mitford: *Love in a Cold Climate.* Miller: *Death of a Salesman.*
1950	Birth of son, Septimus Waugh (July). *Helena* published. Last visit to America.	Hemingway: *Across the River and into the Trees.* Eliot: *The Cocktail Party.* Henry Green: *Doting.*
1951	Middle East tour for *Life Magazine* (January–March). Writes *Men at Arms* (June–December).	Salinger: *The Catcher in the Rye.* Powell: *A Question of Upbringing* (the first of the 12 novels comprising *A Dance to the Music of Time* (1952–75). Mitford: *The Blessing.*
1952	Writes *The Holy Places* and 'Love Among the Ruins'. *Men at Arms* published (September). Christmas in Goa.	Beckett: *Waiting for Godot.* Miller: *The Crucible.*
1953	Begins *Officers and Gentlemen* (March).	Hartley: *The Go-Between.*
1954	Voyage to Ceylon and mental breakdown (February). Contributes to "U" and "non U" debate. Death of his mother (December).	
1955	*Officers and Gentlemen* published (May). Trip to Jamaica, writing *The Ordeal of Gilbert Pinfold* (from December).	Nabokov: *Lolita.* Miller: *A View from the Bridge.* Graham Greene: *Loser Takes All, The Quiet American.* Murdoch: *Under the Net.*
1956	Moves to Combe Florey, Taunton, Somerset.	Beckett: *Molloy.* Camus: *La Chute.* Faulkner: *Requiem for a Nun.* Mitford, Waugh, Betjeman et al: *Noblesse Oblige.*

CHRONOLOGY

HISTORICAL EVENTS

Marshall Aid: US contributes $5.3 billion for European recovery. Soviet blockade of West Berlin: Allied airlifts begin (to 1949). State of Israel founded. Apartheid introduced in South Africa. Yugoslavia under Tito expelled from Comintern. National Health Service inaugurated in Britain.

Federal and Democratic Republics established in Germany. People's Republic of China proclaimed. Korean war begins (to 1953). NATO founded.

McCarthy witch hunts – persecution of Communists throughout US.

Conservatives return to power in Britain. Burgess and Maclean defect to USSR.

Death of George VI: accession of Elizabeth II.

Stalin dies and is succeeded by Khrushchev.

Vietnam war begins. Nasser gains power in Egypt.

West Germany joins NATO.

Suez crisis. Invasion of Hungary by USSR.

DATE	AUTHOR'S LIFE	LITERARY CONTEXT
1957	*Pinfold* completed (January) and published (July). First plans for *Unconditional Surrender* (July).	Camus: *L'Exil et le Royaume*. Pasternak: *Doctor Zhivago*. Pinter: *The Birthday Party*. Nabokov: *Pnin*. Spark: *The Comforters*.
1958	Travels to Rhodesia (February–March), collecting material for—	Betjeman: *Collected Poems*.
1959	*The Life of the Right Reverend Ronald Knox* published (October).	Spark: *Memento Mori*. Eliot: *The Elder Statesman*. Graham Greene: *The Complaisant Lover*. Beckett: *Endgame*.
1960	*A Tourist in Africa* published.	Spark: *The Ballad of Peckham Rye*. Updike: *Rabbit, Run*. Pinter: *The Caretaker*. Betjeman: *Summoned by Bells*.
1961	*Unconditional Surrender* published (September). Trip to West Indies with his daughter Margaret (November–February).	Graham Greene: *A Burnt-Out Case*. Albee: *The American Dream*. Huxley: *Religion without Revelation*. Mitford: *Don't Tell Alfred*. Spark: *The Prime of Miss Jean Brodie*.
1962	Working on *A Little Learning*. Begins 'Basil Seal Rides Again' (August).	Albee: *Who's Afraid of Virginia Woolf?* Isherwood: *Down There on a Visit*.
1963	Publication of 'Basil Seal Rides Again'.	Stoppard: *A Walk on Water*. Pinter: *The Lover*. Spark: *The Girls of Slender Means*.
1964	Serial publication of *A Little Learning* (June–July).	Sartre: *Les Mots*. Ayme: *The Minotaur*. Isherwood: *A Single Man*.
1965	War trilogy revised and published as *Sword of Honour* (September).	Pinter: *The Homecoming*. Albee: *Tiny Alice*.
1966	Evelyn Waugh dies on Easter Sunday, 10 April, at Combe Florey.	Albee: *A Delicate Balance*.

CHRONOLOGY

TEXTUAL NOTE

The stories reprinted here have been drawn from a variety of sources, not necessarily those of first publication. Magazine editors felt free to meddle: Waugh complained that both the American and English magazine versions of 'The Man Who Liked Dickens' were cut and rewritten by others in an excess of enthusiasm, while *Harper's Bazaar* ill-advisedly regularized the narrator's breathless lack of punctuation in its version of 'Cruise'. Preference has therefore been shown, where possible, to texts most likely to have been overseen by Waugh himself. Consequently 'Love in the Slump', 'Excursion in Reality', 'Incident in Azania', 'Bella Fleace Gave a Party', 'Cruise', 'Out of Depth', 'By Special Request', 'Period Piece', 'On Guard', 'Mr. Loveday's Little Outing' and 'Winner Takes All' have been taken from Waugh's first collection of short stories, *Mr. Loveday's Little Outing and Other Sad Stories* (1936), and 'An Englishman's Home' from *Work Suspended and Other Stories Written Before the Second World War* (1949). The rest are taken from the place of first publication, as detailed on pp. 593–5, with two exceptions. 'The Man Who Liked Dickens' comes from *A Century of Horror Stories*, edited by Dennis Wheatley (1935), collated with the earlier English and American magazine versions. 'Compassion' was first published in America under a different title, but appeared in an enlarged form in England shortly afterwards – the version reproduced here (for details, see p. 594). Footnotes and headnotes to the stories are Waugh's own, except in the case of *Work Suspended*, where the footnotes record variants between the copy-text of 1942, and its revised version of 1949.

The pictures have been drawn from the collections held by the Bodleian Library, Oxford, and the Harry Ransom Humanities Research Center, The University of Texas at Austin. They represent nearly everything that survives of Waugh's graphic work in the Oxford undergraduate magazines, *The Isis*, *The Cherwell* and *The Oxford Broom*; a selection from the book-plates and dust jackets designed by him, and the best of his contributions to *The Golden Hind* and *The London Mercury*, where he appeared in the company of such artists as Jack B. Yeats, Gwen Raverat, and Eric Gill. With one exception, 'The Tragical Death of Mr. Will. Huskisson', preference has been shown for works that have not been published elsewhere. 'Scaramel' was Waugh's undergraduate *nom de plume* for both graphic and literary works.

ACKNOWLEDGEMENTS

———

I would like to express my gratitude to the Harry Ransom Research Center, The University of Texas at Austin, for permission to reproduce the pictures facing pages 134, 162, 182, 404, 524, 558 and 592, and the Bodleian Library, Oxford, for permission to reproduce the pictures facing pages 38, 50, 56, 66, 72, 86, 102, 112, 118, 146, 154, 174, 200, 220, 224, 320, 350, 418, 440, 518, 530, 534, 548, 552, 564, 570, 578, 580, 584 and 588.

I am particularly grateful to Rachel Howarth, Leslie Wearb and Tara Wenger of the Harry Ransom Research Center, and Jackie Merralls, Susan Harris, Vivien Bradley and Nick Cistone at the Bodleian Library, for their painstaking assistance, and above all to Jenny Harrington, Jane Holloway and Helen Oldfield for inestimable help.

EVELYN WAUGH

THE COMPLETE SHORT STORIES

AND

SELECTED DRAWINGS

THE BALANCE

*A Yarn of the Good Old Days of Broad Trousers
and High Necked Jumpers*

INTRODUCTION

"DO YOU know, I don't think" I *can* read mine. It's rather unkind."

"Oh, Basil, you must."

"Please, Basil."

This always happened when Basil played paper games.

"No, I can't, look it's all scrumbled up."

"Oh, Basil, dearest, do."

"Oh, Basil, *please.*"

"Darling Basil, you must."

"No, I won't. Imogen will be in a rage with me."

"No, she won't, will you, Imogen?"

"Imogen, tell him you won't be in a rage with him."

"Basil, *do* read it please."

"Well, then, if you promise you won't hate me" – and he smoothed out the piece of paper.

"Flower – Cactus.

"Drink – Rum.

"Stuff – Baize.

"Furniture – Rocking-Horse.

"Food – Venison.

"Address – Dublin.

"And Animal – Boa constrictor."

"Oh, Basil, how marvellous."

"Poor Adam, I never thought of him as Dublin, of course it's perfect."

"Why Cactus?"

"So phallic, my dear, and prickly."

"And such vulgar flowers."

"Boa constrictor is brilliant."

3

"Yes, his digestion you know."

"And can't sting, only crush."

"And fascinates rabbits."

"I must draw a picture of Adam fascinating a rabbit," and then, "Imogen, you're not going?"

"I must. I'm terribly sleepy. Don't get drunk and wake me up, will you?"

"Imogen, you *are* in a rage with me."

"My dear, I'm far too tired to be in a rage with anybody. Good night."

The door shut.

"My dear, she's furious."

"I knew she would be, you shouldn't have made me read it."

"She's been very odd all the evening, I consider."

"She told me she lunched with Adam before she came down."

"I expect she ate too much. One does with Adam, don't you find?"

"Just libido."

"But you know, I'm rather proud of that character all the same. I wonder why none of us ever thought of Dublin before."

"Basil, do you think Imogen *can* have been having an *affaire* with Adam, really?"

CIRCUMSTANCES

NOTE. – No attempt, beyond the omission of some of the aspirates, has been made at a phonetic rendering of the speech of Gladys and Ada; they are the cook and house-parlourmaid from a small house in Earls Court, and it is to be supposed that they speak as such.

The conversations in the film are deduced by the experienced picture-goer from the gestures of the actors; only those parts which appear in capitals are actual "captions".

THE COCKATRICE CLUB 2.30 A.M.
A CENTRE OF LONDON NIGHT LIFE.

The "Art title" shows a still life of a champagne bottle, glasses, and a comic mask – or is it yawning?

"Oh, Gladys, it's begun; I knew we'd be late."

"Never mind, dear, I can see the way. Oh, I say — I am sorry. Thought the seat was empty — really I did."

Erotic giggling and a slight struggle.

"Give over, can't you, and let me get by — saucy kid."

"'Ere you are, Gladys, there's two seats 'ere."

"Well I never — tried to make me sit on 'is knee."

"Go on. I say, Gladys, what sort of picture is this — is it comic?"

The screen is almost completely dark as though the film has been greatly over-exposed. Fitful but brilliant illumination reveals a large crowd dancing, talking and eating.

"No, Ada — that's lightning. I dare say it's a desert storm. I see a picture like that the other day with Fred."

EVERYBODY LOVES MY BABY.

Close up: the head of a girl.

"That's 'is baby. See if she ain't."

It is rather a lovely head, shingled and superbly poised on its neck. One is just beginning to appreciate its exquisite modelling — the film is too poor to give any clear impression of texture — when it is flashed away and its place taken by a stout and elderly man playing a saxophone. The film becomes obscure — after the manner of the more modern Continental studios: the saxophonist has become the vortex of movement; faces flash out and disappear again; fragmentary captions will not wait until they are read.

"Well, I do call this soft."

A voice with a Cambridge accent from the more expensive seats says, "Expressionismus."

Gladys nudges Ada and says, "Foreigner."

After several shiftings of perspective, the focus becomes suddenly and stereoscopically clear. The girl is seated at a table leaning towards a young man who is lighting her cigarette for her. Three or four others join them at the table and sit down. They are all in evening dress.

"No, it isn't comic, Ada — it's Society."

"Society's sometimes comic. You see."

6 EVELYN WAUGH

The girl is protesting that she must go.

"Adam, I must. Mother thinks I went out to a theatre with you and your mother. I don't know what will happen if she finds I'm not in."

There is a general leave-taking and paying of bills.

"*I say, Gladys, 'e's 'ad a drop too much, ain't 'e?*"

The hero and heroine drive away in a taxi.

Half-way down Pont Street, the heroine stops the taxi.

"Don't let him come any farther, Adam. Lady R. will hear."

"Good night, Imogen dear."

"Good night, Adam."

She hesitates for a moment and then kisses him.

Adam and the taxi drive away.

Close up of Adam. He is a young man of about twenty-two, clean-shaven, with thick, very dark hair. He looks so infinitely sad that even Ada is shaken.

Can it be funny?

"*Buster Keaton looks sad like that sometimes – don't 'e?*"

Ada is reassured.

Buster Keaton looks sad; Buster Keaton is funny. Adam looks sad; Adam is funny. What could be clearer?

The cab stops and Adam gives it all his money. It wishes him "Good night" and disappears into the darkness. Adam unlocks the front door.

On his way upstairs he takes his letters from the hall table; they are two bills and an invitation to a dance.

He reaches his room, undresses and sits for some time wretchedly staring at himself in the glass. Then he gets into bed. He dare not turn out the light because he knows that if he does the room will start spinning round him; he must be there thinking of Imogen until he becomes sober.

The film becomes darker. The room begins to swim and then steadies itself. It is getting quite dark. The orchestra plays very softly the first bars of "Everybody loves my baby". It is quite dark.

Close up: the heroine.

Close up: the hero asleep.

Fade out.

NEXT MORNING 8.30 A.M.

The hero still asleep. The electric light is still burning.

A disagreeable-looking maid enters, turns out the light and raises the blind.

Adam wakes up.

"Good morning, Parsons."

"Good morning, sir."

"Is the bathroom empty?"

"I think Miss Jane's just this minute gone along there."

She picks up Adam's evening clothes from the floor.

Adam lies back and ponders the question of whether he shall miss his bath or miss getting a place at the studio.

Miss Jane in her bath.

Adam deciding to get up.

Tired out but with no inclination to sleep, Adam dresses. He goes down to breakfast.

"*It can't be Society, Gladys, they aren't eating grape fruit.*"

"*It's such a small 'ouse too.*"

"*And no butler.*"

"*Look, there's 'is little old mother. She'll lead 'im straight in the end. See if she don't.*"

"*Well, that dress isn't at all what I call fashionable, if you ask me.*"

"*Well, if it isn't funny and it isn't murder and it isn't Society, what is it?*"

"*P'r'aps there'll be a murder yet.*"

"*Well, I calls it soft, that's what I calls it.*"

"*Look now, 'e's got a invitation to a dance from a Countess.*"

"*I don't understand this picture.*"

The Countess's invitation.

"*Why, there isn't even a coronet on it, Ada.*"

The little old mother pours out tea for him and tells him about the death of a friend in the *Times* that morning; when he has drunk some tea and eaten some fish, she bustles him out of the house.

Adam walks to the corner of the road, where he gets on to a bus. The neighbourhood is revealed as being Regent's Park.

THE CENTRE OF LONDON'S QUARTIER LATIN
THE MALTBY SCHOOL OF ART.

No trouble has been spared by the producers to obtain the right atmosphere. The top studio at Maltby's is already half full of young students when Adam enters. Work has not yet started, but the room is alive with busy preparation. A young woman in an overall – looking rather more like a chorus girl than a painter – is making herself very dirty cleaning her palette; another near by is setting up an easel; a third is sharpening a pencil; a fourth is smoking a cigarette in a long holder. A young man, also in an overall, is holding a drawing and appraising it at arm's length, his head slightly on one side; a young man with untidy hair is disagreeing with him. Old Mr. Maltby, an inspiring figure in a shabby silk dressing-gown, is telling a tearful student that if she misses another composition class, she will be asked to leave the school. Miss Philbrick, the secretary, interrupts the argument between the two young men to remind them that neither of them has paid his fee for the month. The girl who was setting up the easel is trying to borrow some "fixative"; the girl with the cigarette-holder lends her some. Mr. Maltby is complaining of the grittiness of the charcoal they make nowadays. Surely this is the Quartier Latin itself?

The "set", too, has been conscientiously planned. The walls are hung with pots, pans and paintings – these last mainly a series of rather fleshly nudes which young Mr. Maltby has been unable to sell. A very brown skeleton hangs over the dais at the far end.

"*I say, Gladys, do you think we shall see 'is models?*"

"*Coo, Ada, you are a one.*"

Adam comes in and goes towards the board on which hangs a plan of the easel places; the girl who was lending the "fixative" comes over to him, still smoking.

"THERE'S A PLACE EMPTY NEXT TO ME, DOURE, DO COME THERE."

Close up of the girl.

"*She's in love with 'im.*"

Close up of Adam.

"*'E's not in love with 'er, though, is 'e, Ada?*"

The place the girl points out is an excellent one in the second row; the only other one besides the very front and the very back is round at the side, next to the stove. Adam signs his initials opposite this place.

"I'M SORRY – I'M AFRAID THAT I FIND THE LIGHT WORRIES ME FROM WHERE YOU ARE – ONE GETS SO FEW SHADOWS – DON'T YOU FIND?"

The girl is not to be discouraged; she lights another cigarette.

"I SAW YOU LAST NIGHT AT THE COCKATRICE – YOU DIDN'T SEE ME THOUGH."

"THE COCKATRICE – LAST NIGHT – OH YES – WHAT A PITY!"

"WHO WERE ALL THOSE PEOPLE YOU WERE WITH?"

"OH, I DON'T KNOW, JUST SOME PEOPLE, YOU KNOW."

He makes a movement as if to go away.

"WHO WAS THAT GIRL YOU WERE DANCING WITH SO MUCH – THE PRETTY ONE WITH FAIR HAIR – IN BLACK?"

"OH, DON'T YOU KNOW HER? YOU MUST MEET HER ONE DAY – I SAY, I'M AWFULLY SORRY, BUT I MUST GO DOWN AND GET SOME PAPER FROM MISS PHILBRICK."

"I CAN LEND YOU SOME."

But he is gone.

Ada says, "Too much talk in this picture, eh, Gladys?" and the voice with the Cambridge accent is heard saying something about the "elimination of the caption".

ONE OF LIFE'S UNFORTUNATES.

Enter a young woman huddled in a dressing-gown, preceded by young Mr. Maltby.

"*The model – coo – I say.*"

She has a slight cold and sniffles into a tiny ball of handkerchief; she mounts the dais and sits down ungracefully. Young

Mr. Maltby nods good morning to those of the pupils who catch his eye; the girl who was talking to Adam catches his eye; he smiles.

"'*E's in love with 'er.*"

She returns his smile with warmth.

Young Mr. Maltby rattles the stove, opens the skylight a little and then turns to the model, who slips off her dressing-gown and puts it over the back of the chair.

"Coo – I say. Ada – my!"

"Well I never."

The young man from Cambridge goes on talking about Matisse unfalteringly as though he were well accustomed to this sort of thing. Actually he is much intrigued.

She has disclosed a dull pink body with rather short legs and red elbows; like most professional models her toes are covered with bunions and malformed. Young Mr. Maltby sets her on the chair in an established Art School pose. The class settles to work.

Adam returns with some sheets of paper and proceeds to arrange them on his board. Then he stands for some time glaring at the model without drawing a line.

"'*E's in love with 'er.*" But *for once Ada's explanation is wrong* – and then begins sketching in the main lines of the pose.

He works on for five or six minutes, during which time the heat of the stove becomes increasingly uncomfortable. Old Mr. Maltby, breathing smoke, comes up behind him.

"Now have you placed it? What is your centre? Where is the foot going to come? Where is the top of the head coming?"

Adam has not placed it; he rubs it out angrily and starts again.

Meanwhile a vivid flirtation is in progress between young Mr. Maltby and the girl who was in love with Adam. He is leaning over and pointing out mistakes to her; his hand rests on her shoulder; she is wearing a low-necked jumper; his thumb strays over the skin of her neck; she wriggles appreciatively. He takes the charcoal from her and begins drawing in the corner of her paper; her hair touches his cheek; neither of them heed the least what he is drawing.

"*These Bo'emians don't 'alf carry on, eh, Gladys?*"

In half an hour Adam has rubbed out his drawing three times. Whenever he is beginning to interest himself in some particular combination of shapes, the model raises her ball of handkerchief to her nose, and after each sniff relapses into a slightly different position. The anthracite stove glows with heat; he works on for another half-hour.

THE ELEVEN O'CLOCK REST.

Most of the girls light cigarettes; the men, who have increased in number with many late arrivals, begin to congregate away from them in the corner. One of them is reading *The Studio*. Adam lights a pipe, and standing back, surveys his drawing with detestation.

Close up; Adam's drawing. It is not really at all bad. In fact it is by far the best in the room; there is one which will be better at the end of the week, but at present there is nothing of it except some measurements and geometrical figures. Its author is unaware that the model is resting; he is engaged in calculating the medial section of her height in the corner of the paper.

Adam goes out on to the stairs, which are lined with women from the lower studio eating buns out of bags. He returns to the studio.

The girl who has been instructed by young Mr. Maltby comes up to him and looks at his drawing.

"Rather Monday morningish."

That was exactly what young Mr. Maltby had said about hers.

The model resumes her pose with slight differences; the paper bags are put away, pipes are knocked out; the promising pupil is calculating the area of a rectangle.

The scene changes to

158 PONT STREET. THE LONDON HOUSE OF MR. CHARLES AND LADY ROSEMARY QUEST.

An interior is revealed in which the producers have at last made some attempt to satisfy the social expectations of Gladys and Ada. It is true that there is very little marble and no footmen in powder and breeches, but there is nevertheless an undoubted air of grandeur about the high rooms and Louis Seize furniture, and there *is* a footman. The young man from Cambridge estimates the household at six thousand a year, and though somewhat overgenerous, it is a reasonable guess. Lady Rosemary's collection of Limoges can be seen in the background.

Upstairs in her bedroom Imogen Quest is telephoning.

"*What a lovely Kimony, Ada.*"

Miss Philbrick comes into the upper studio at Maltby's, where Adam is at last beginning to take some interest in his drawing.

"MISS QUEST WANTS TO SPEAK TO YOU ON THE TELEPHONE, MR. DOURE. I told her that it was against the rules for students to use the telephone except in the luncheon hour" (there is always a pathetic game of make-believe at Maltby's played endlessly by Miss Philbrick and old Mr. Maltby, in which they pretend that somewhere there is a code of rules which all must observe), "but she says that it is most important. I do wish you would ask your friends not to ring you up in the mornings."

Adam puts down his charcoal and follows her to the office.

There over the telephone is poor Miss Philbrick's notice written in the script writing she learned at night classes in Southampton Row.

"Students are forbidden to use the telephone during working hours."

"Good morning, Imogen."

"Yes, quite safely – very tired though."

"I can't, Imogen – for one thing I haven't the money."

"No, you can't afford it either. Anyway, I'm dining with Lady R. to-night. You can tell me then, surely?"

"Why not?"

"Who lives there?"

"Not that awful Basil Hay?"

"Well, perhaps he is."

"I used to meet him at Oxford sometimes."

"WELL, IF YOU'RE SURE YOU CAN PAY I'LL COME TO LUNCHEON WITH YOU."

"WHY THERE? IT'S FRIGHTFULLY EXPENSIVE."

"STEAK-TARTARE – WHAT'S THAT?"

The Cambridge voice explains, "Quite raw, you know, with olives and capers and vinegar and things."

"My dear, you'll turn into a werewolf."

"I should love it if you did."

"Yes, I'm afraid I *am* getting a little morbid."

"One-ish. Please don't be too late – I've only three-quarters of an hour."

"Good-bye, Imogen."

So much of the forbidden conversation is audible to Miss Philbrick.

Adam returns to the studio and draws a few heavy and insensitive lines.

He rubs at them but they still show up grubbily in the pores of the paper. He tears up his drawing; old Mr. Maltby remonstrates; young Mr. Maltby is explaining the construction of the foot and does not look up.

Adam attempts another drawing.

Close up of Adam's drawing.

"*'E's thinking of 'er.*" Unerring Ada!

"*These films would be so much more convincing if they would only employ decent draughtsmen to do the hero's drawings for him – don't you think?*" Bravo, the cultured bourgeoisie!

TWELVE O'CLOCK.

There is a repetition of all the excursions of eleven o'clock.

The promising pupil is working out the ratio of two cubes. The girl who has been learning the construction of the foot comes over to him and looks over his shoulder; he starts violently and loses count.

Adam takes his hat and stick and goes out.

Adam on a 'bus.

Adam studying Poussin at the National Gallery.

Close up of Adam studying Poussin.

"*'E's thinking of 'er.*"

The clock of St. Martin-in-the-Fields strikes one. Adam leaves the National Gallery.

TEN MINUTES PAST ONE. THE DINING-ROOM
OF THE RESTAURANT DE LA TOUR DE FORCE.

Enter Adam; he looks round but as he had expected, Imogen
has not yet arrived. He sits down at a table laid for two and waits.

Though not actually in Soho, the Tour de Force gives unmistakably an impression half cosmopolitan, half theatrical, which
Ada would sum up in the word "Bo'emian". The tables are well
spaced and the wines are excellent though extremely costly.

Adam orders some sherry and waits, dividing his attention
between the door through which Imogen will enter and the
contemplation of a middle-aged political lawyer of repute who
at the next table is trying to keep amused a bored and exquisitely
beautiful youth of eighteen.

QUARTER TO TWO.

Enter Imogen.

The people at the other tables say, "Look, there's Imogen
Quest. I can't see what people find in her, can you?" or else,
"I wonder who that is. Isn't she attractive?"

"My dear, I'm terribly late. I am sorry. I've had the *most* awful
morning shopping with Lady R."

She sits down at the table.

"You haven't got to rush back to your school, have you?
Because I'm never going to see you again. The most awful
thing has happened – you order lunch, Adam. I'm very
hungry. I want to eat a *steak-tartare* and I don't want to drink
anything."

Adam orders lunch.

"LADY R. SAYS I'M SEEING TOO MUCH OF YOU.
ISN'T IT TOO AWFUL?"

*Gladys at last is quite at home. The film has been classified. Young love is
being thwarted by purse-proud parents.*

Imogen waves aside a wagon of *hors d'œuvre.*

"We had quite a scene. She came into my room before I was
up and wanted to know all about last night. Apparently she heard
me come in. And, oh Adam, I can't tell you what dreadful things

she's been saying about you. My dear, *what* an odd luncheon – you've ordered everything I most detest."

Adam drinks soup.

"THAT'S WHY I'M BEING SENT OFF TO THATCH THIS AFTERNOON. And Lady R. is going to talk to you seriously to-night. She's put Mary and Andrew off so that she can *get you alone*. Adam, how can you expect me to eat all this? and you haven't ordered yourself anything to drink."

Adam eats an omelette alone. Imogen crumbles bread and talks to him.

"But, my dear, you mustn't say anything against Basil because I simply adore him, and he's got the loveliest, vulgarest mother – you'd simply love her."

The *steak-tartare* is wheeled up and made before them.

Close up; a dish of pulverized and bleeding meat: hands pouring in immoderate condiments.

"Do you know, Adam, I don't think I do want this after all. It reminds me so of Henry."

HALF-PAST TWO.

Adam has finished luncheon.

"SO YOU SEE, DEAR, WE SHALL NEVER, NEVER MEET AGAIN – PROPERLY I MEAN. Isn't it just too like Lady R. for words."

Imogen stretches out her hand across the table and touches Adam's.

Close up; Adam's hand, a signet ring on the little finger and a smudge of paint on the inside of the thumb. Imogen's hand – very white and manicured – moves across the screen and touches it.

Gladys gives a slight sob.

"YOU DON'T MIND TOO DREADFULLY – DO YOU, ADAM?"

Adam does mind – very much indeed. He has eaten enough to be thoroughly sentimental.

The Restaurant de la Tour de Force is nearly empty. The political barrister has gone his unregenerate way; the waiters stand about restlessly.

Imogen pays the bill and they rise to go.

"Adam, you must come to Euston and see me off. We can't part just like this – for always, can we? Hodges is meeting me there with the luggage."

They get into a taxi.

Imogen puts her hand in his and they sit like this for a few minutes without speaking.

Then Adam leans towards her and they kiss.

Close up: Adam and Imogen kissing. There is a tear (which finds a ready response in Ada and Gladys, who sob uncontrollably) in Adam's eye; Imogen's lips luxuriously disposed by the pressure.

"*Like the Bronzino Venus.*"

"IMOGEN, YOU NEVER REALLY CARED, DID YOU? IF YOU HAD YOU WOULDN'T GO AWAY LIKE THIS. IMOGEN, DID YOU EVER CARE – REALLY?"

"HAVEN'T I GIVEN PROOF THAT I DID. Adam dear, why will you always ask such tiresome questions. Don't you see how impossible it all is? We've only about five minutes before we reach Euston."

They kiss again.

Adam says, "Damn Lady R."

They reach Euston.

Hodges is waiting for them. She has seen about the luggage; she has seen about tickets; she has even bought magazines; there is nothing to be done.

Adam stands beside Imogen waiting for the train to start; she looks at a weekly paper.

"Do look at this picture of Sybil. Isn't it odd? I wonder when she had it taken."

The train is about to start. She gets into the carriage and holds out her hand.

"Good-bye, darling. You will come to mother's dance in June, won't you? I shall be miserable if you don't. Perhaps we shall meet before then. Good-bye."

The train moves out of the station.

Close up. Imogen in the carriage studying the odd photograph of Sybil.

Adam on the platform watching the train disappear.
Fade out.

"*Well, Ada, what d'you think of it?*"

"*Fine.*"

"*It is curious the way that they can never make their heroes and heroines talk like ladies and gentlemen – particularly in moments of emotion.*"

A QUARTER OF AN HOUR LATER.

Adam is still at Euston, gazing aimlessly at a bookstall. The various prospects before him appear on the screen.

Maltby's. The anthracite stove, the model, the amorous student – ("*the Vamp*"), the mathematical student, his own drawing.

Dinner at home. His father, his mother, Parsons, his sister with her stupid, pimply face and her dull jealousy of all Imogen said and did and wore.

Dinner at Pont Street, head to head with Lady Rosemary.

Dinner by himself at some very cheap restaurant in Soho. And always at the end of it, Solitude and the thought of Imogen.

Close up: Adam registering despair gradually turning to resolution.

Adam on a 'bus going to Hanover Gate.

He walks to his home.

Parsons. Parsons opens the door. Mrs. Doure is out; Miss Jane is out; no, Adam does not want any tea.

Adam's room. It is a rather charming one, high at the top of the house, looking over the trees. At full moon the animals in the Zoological Gardens can be heard from there. Adam comes in and locks the door.

Gladys is there already.

"*Suicide, Ada.*"

"*Yes, but she'll come in time to stop 'im. See if she don't.*"

"*Don't you be too sure. This is a queer picture, this is.*"

He goes to his desk and takes a small blue bottle from one of the pigeon holes.

"*What did I tell yer? Poison.*"

"*The ease with which persons in films contrive to provide themselves with the instruments of death . . .*"

He puts it down, and taking out a sheet of paper writes.
"*Last message to 'er. Gives 'er time to come and save 'im. You see.*"

"AVE IMPERATRIX IMMORTALIS, MORITURUS TE SALUTANT."

Exquisitely written.
He folds it, puts it in an envelope and addresses it.
Then he pauses, uncertain.
A vision appears:
The door of Adam's room. Mrs. Doure, changed for dinner, comes up to it and knocks; she knocks repeatedly, and in dismay calls for her husband. Professor Doure tries the door and shakes it. Parsons arrives and Jane. After some time the door is forced open; all the time Professor Doure is struggling with it, Mrs. Doure's agitation increases. Jane makes futile attempts to calm her. At last they all burst into the room. Adam is revealed lying dead on the floor. Scene of unspeakable vulgarity involving tears, hysteria, the telephone, the police. Fade out.
Close up. Adam registering disgust.
Another vision:
A native village in Africa on the edge of the jungle; from one of the low thatch huts creeps a man naked and sick to death, his wives lamenting behind him. He drags himself into the jungle to die alone.
"*Lor, Gladys. Instruction.*"
Another vision:
Rome in the time of Petronius. A young patrician reclines in the centre of his guests. The producers have spared no effort in creating an atmosphere of superb luxury. The hall, as if in some fevered imagining of Alma Tadema, is built of marble, richly illumined by burning Christians. From right and left barbarian slave boys bring in a course of roasted peacocks. In the centre of the room a slave girl dances to a puma. Exit several of the guests to the vomitorium. Unborn pigs stewed in honey and stuffed with truffles and nightingales' tongues succeed the peacocks. The puma, inflamed to sudden passion, springs at the girl and bears her to the ground; he stands over her, one paw planted upon her

breast from which ooze tiny drops of blood. She lies there on the Alma Tadema marble, her eyes fixed upon the host in terrified appeal. But he is toying with one of the serving boys and does not notice her. More guests depart to the vomitorium. The puma devours the girl. At length, when the feast is at its height, a basin of green marble is borne in. Water, steaming and scented, is poured into it. The host immerses his hand, and a negro woman who, throughout the banquet has crouched like some angel of death beside his couch, draws a knife from her loin cloth and buries it deep in his wrist. The water becomes red in the green marble. The guests rise to go, and with grave courtesy, though without lifting himself from the couch, he bids them each farewell. Soon he is left alone. The slave boys huddle together in the corners, their bare shoulders pressed against each other. Moved by savage desire, the negress begins suddenly to kiss and gnaw the deadening arm. He motions her listlessly aside. The martyrs burn lower until there is only a faint glimmer of light in the great hall. The smell of cooking drifts out into the terrace and is lost on the night air. The puma can just be discerned licking its paws in the gloom.

Adam lights a pipe and taps restlessly with the corner of the envelope on the writing-table. Then he puts the bottle in his pocket and unlocks the door.

He turns and walks over to his book-shelves and looks through them. Adam's book-shelves; it is rather a remarkable library for a man of his age and means. Most of the books have a certain rarity and many are elaborately bound; there are also old books of considerable value given him from time to time by his father.

He makes a heap on the floor of the best of them.

MR. MACASSOR'S BOOKSHOP.

There is about Mr. Macassor's bookshop the appearance of the private library of an ancient and unmethodical scholar. Books are everywhere, on walls, floor and furniture, as though laid down at some interruption and straightway forgotten. First editions and early illustrated books lie hidden among Sermons and

Blue Books for the earnest adventurer to find. Mr. Macassor hides his treasures with care.

An elderly man is at the moment engaged in investigating a heap of dusty volumes while Mr. Macassor bends longingly over the table engrossed in a treatise on Alchemy. Suddenly the adventurer's back straightens; his search has been rewarded and he emerges into the light, bearing a tattered but unquestionably genuine copy of the first edition of "Hydrotaphia". He asks Mr. Macassor the price. Mr. Macassor adjusts his spectacles and brushes some snuff from his waistcoat and, bearing the book to the door, examines it as if for the first time.

"Ah, yes, a delightful work. Yes, yes, marvellous style," and he turns the pages fondly, "The large stations of the dead," what a noble phrase. He looks at the cover and wipes it with his sleeve. "Why, I had forgotten I had this copy. It used to belong to Horace Walpole, only someone has stolen the bookplate – the rascal. Still, it was only the Oxford one – the armorial one, you know. Well, well, sir, since you have found it I suppose you have the right to claim it. Five guineas, shall I say. But I hate to part with it."

The purchaser is a discerning man. Had he seen this same book baldly described in a catalogue he would not have paid half this price for it in its present condition, but the excitement of pursuit and the pride of discovery more even than the legends of Strawberry Hill have distorted his sense of values. One cannot haggle with Mr. Macassor as with some mere tradesman in Charing Cross Road. The purchaser pays and goes away triumphant. It is thus that Mr. Macassor's son at Magdalen is able to keep his rooms full of flowers and, during the season, to hunt two days a week.

Enter Adam from a taxi laden with books. Mr. Macassor offers him snuff from an old tortoiseshell box.

"IT'S A SAD THING TO HAVE TO SELL BOOKS, MR. DOURE. Very sad. I remember as if it was yesterday, Mr. Stevenson coming in to me to sell his books, and will you believe it, Mr. Doure, when it came to the point, after we had arranged everything, his heart failed him and he took them all away again. A great book-lover, Mr. Stevenson."

Mr. Macassor adjusts his spectacles and examines, caressingly, but like some morbid lover fastening ghoulishly upon every imperfection.

"Well, and how much were you expecting for these?"

Adam hazards, "Seventeen pounds," but Mr. Macassor shakes his head sadly.

Five minutes later he leaves the shop with ten pounds and gets into his taxi.

PADDINGTON STATION.

Adam in the train to Oxford; smoking, his hands deep in his overcoat pockets.

"*'E's thinking of 'er.*"

OXFORD.

KNOW YOU HER SECRET NONE CAN UTTER; HERS OF THE BOOK, THE TRIPLE CROWN? Art title showing Book and Triple Crown; also Ox in ford.

General prospect of Oxford from the train showing reservoir, gas works and part of the prison. It is raining.

The station; two Indian students have lost their luggage. Resisting the romantic appeal of several hansom cab-drivers – even of one in a grey billycock hat, Adam gets into a Ford taxi. Queen Street, Carfax, the High Street, Radcliffe Camera in the distance.

"*Look, Ada, St. Paul's Cathedral.*"

King Edward Street. The cab stops and Adam gets out.

LORD BASINGSTOKE'S ROOMS. KING EDWARD STREET.

Interior of Lord Basingstoke's rooms. On the chimney-piece are photographs of Lord Basingstoke's mother and two of Lord Basingstoke's friends, wearing that peculiarly inane and serene smile only found during the last year at Eton and then only in photographs. Some massive glass paper weights and cards of invitation.

On the walls are large coloured caricatures of Basil Hay drawn by himself at Eton, an early nineteenth-century engraving of Lord Basingstoke's home; two unfinished drawings by Ernest Vaughan of the Rape of the Sabines and a wool picture of two dogs and a cat.

Lord Basingstoke, contrary to all expectation, is neither drinking, gaming, nor struggling with his riding boots; he is engaged on writing a Collections Paper for his tutor.

Lord Basingstoke's paper in a pleasant, childish handwriting. "BRADLAUGH v. GOSSETT. THIS FAMOUS TEST CASE FINALLY ESTABLISHED THE DECISION THAT MARSHAL LAW IS UNKNOWN IN ENGLAND."

He crosses out "marshal" and puts "martial"; then sits biting his pen sadly.

"Adam, how lovely; I had no idea you were in Oxford."

They talk for a little while.

"RICHARD, CAN YOU DINE WITH ME TO-NIGHT. YOU MUST. I'M HAVING A FAREWELL BLIND." Richard looks sadly at his Collections Paper and shakes his head.

"My dear, I simply can't. I've got to get this finished by to-night. I'm probably going to be sent down as it is."

Adam returns to his taxi.

MR. SAYLE'S ROOMS IN MERTON.

Flowers, Medici prints and Nonesuch Press editions. Mr. Sayle is playing "L'Après midi d'un Faun" on the gramophone to an American aunt. He cannot dine with Adam.

MR. HENRY QUEST'S ROOMS IN THE UGLIER PART OF MAGDALEN.

The furniture provided by the College has been little changed except for the addition of some rather repulsive cushions. There are photographs of Imogen, Lady Rosemary and Mr. Macassor's son winning the Magdalen Grind. Mr. Henry Quest has just given tea to two freshmen; he is secretary of the J.C.R. His face, through the disability of the camera, looks nearly black, actually it forms a patriotic combination with his Bullingdon tie; he has a fair moustache.

Adam enters and invites him to dinner. Henry Quest does not approve of his sister's friends; Adam cannot stand Imogen's brother; they are always scrupulously polite to each other.

"I'M SORRY, ADAM, THERE'S A MEETING OF THE CHATHAM HERE TO-NIGHT. I SHOULD HAVE LOVED TO, OTHERWISE. Stay and have a cigarette, won't you? Do you know Mr. Trehearne and Mr. Bickerton-Gibbs?"

Adam cannot stop, he has a taxi waiting.

Henry Quest excuses his intrusion to Messrs. Trehearne and Bickerton-Gibbs.

MR. EGERTON-VERSCHOYLE'S ROOMS IN PECKWATER.

Mr. Egerton-Verschoyle has been entertaining to luncheon. Adam stirs him with his foot; he turns over and says:

"There's another in the cupboard – corkscrew's behind the thing, you know..." and trails off into incoherence.

MR. FURNESS'S ROOMS IN THE NEXT STAIRCASE.

They are empty and dark. Mr. Furness has been sent down.

MR. SWITHIN LANG'S ROOMS IN BEAUMONT STREET.

Furnished in white and green. Water colours by Mr. Lang of Wembley, Mentone and Thatch. Some valuable china and a large number of magazines. A coloured and ornamented decanter of Cointreau on the chimney-piece and some gold-beaded glasses. The remains of a tea-party are scattered about the room, and the air is heavy with cigarette smoke.

Swithin, all in grey, is reading the *Tatler*.

Enter Adam; effusive greetings.

"Adam, do look at this photograph of Sybil Anderson. Isn't it too funny?"

Adam has seen it.

They sit and talk for some time.

"Swithin, you must come and dine with me to-night – please."

"Adam, I can't. Gabriel's giving a party in Balliol. Won't you be there? Oh no, of course, you don't know him, do you? He came up last term – such a dear, and *so* rich. I'm giving some people dinner first at the Crown. I'd ask you to join us, only I don't honestly think you'd like them. It is a pity. What about to-morrow? Come over to dinner at Thame to-morrow."

Adam shakes his head. "I'm afraid I shan't be here," and goes out.

AN HOUR LATER.

Still alone, Adam is walking down the High Street. It has stopped raining and the lights shine on the wet road. His hand in his pocket fingers the bottle of poison.

There appears again the vision of the African village and the lamenting wives.

ST. MARY'S CLOCK STRIKES SEVEN.

Suddenly Adam's step quickens as he is struck by an idea.

MR. ERNEST VAUGHAN'S ROOMS.

They stand in the front quadrangle of one of the uglier and less renowned colleges midway between the lavatories and the chapel. The window blind has become stuck half-way up the window so that by day they are shrouded in a twilight as though of the Nether world, and by night Ernest's light blazes across the quad, revealing interiors of unsurpassed debauchery. Swithin once said that, like Ernest, Ernest's rooms were a pillar of cloud by day and a pillar of fire by night. The walls are devoid of pictures except for a half-finished drawing of Sir Beelzebub calling for his rum, which, pinned there a term ago, has begun to droop at the corners, and, spattered with drink and leant against by innumerable shoulders, has begun to take on much the same *patina* as the walls. Inscriptions and drawings, ranging from almost inspired caricature to meaningless or obscene scrawlings, attest Ernest's various stages of drunkenness.

"Who is this Bach? I have not so much as heard of the man.

E. V." runs across the bedroom door in an unsteady band of red chalk, "UT EXULTAT IN COITU ELEPHAS, SIC RICARDUS," surmounting an able drawing of the benign Basingstoke.

A large composition of the Birth of Queen Victoria can be traced over the fireplace. There are broken bottles and dirty glasses and uncorrected galley proofs on the table; on the corner of the chimney-piece a beautiful decanter, the broken stopper of which has been replaced by a cork. Ernest is sitting in the broken wicker chair mending the feathers of some darts with unexpected dexterity. He is a short, sturdy young man, with fierce little eyes and a well-formed forehead. His tweeds, stained with drink and paint, have once been well-made, and still preserve a certain distinction. Women undergraduates, on the rare occasions of his appearance at lectures, not infrequently fall in love with him.

"*Bolshevist.*" It is a reasonable mistake, but a mistake. Until his expulsion for overdue subscriptions, Ernest was a prominent member of the Canning.

Adam goes through the gateway into Ernest's College where two or three youths are standing about staring vacantly at the notice-boards. As Adam goes by, they turn round and scowl at him.

"Another of Vaughan's friends."

Their eyes follow him across the quad, to Ernest's rooms.

Ernest is somewhat surprised at Adam's visit, who, indeed, has never shown any very warm affection for him. However, he pours out whisky.

HALF AN HOUR LATER.

It has begun to rain again. Dinner is about to be served in Ernest's College and the porch is crowded by a shabby array of gowned young men vacantly staring at the notice-boards. Here and there a glaring suit of "plus fours" proclaims the generosity of the Rhodes Trust. Adam and Ernest make their way through the cluster of men who mutter their disapproval like peasants at the passage of some black magician.

"IT'S NO GOOD TAKING ME TO ANY CLUB, DOURE, I'VE BEEN BLACK-BALLED FOR THE LOT."

"*I should imagine that would have happened – even in Oxford.*"

AN HOUR LATER. AT THE CROWN.

Adam and Ernest are just finishing dinner; both show marked signs of intoxication.

The dining-room at the Crown bears little resemblance to Adam's epicurean dream. The walls, pathetically frescoed with views of Oxford, resound with the clattering of dirty plates. Swithin's dinner-party has just left, leaving the room immeasurably more quiet. The three women who up till now have been playing selections from Gilbert and Sullivan in the corner have finished work and begun eating their dinner. An undergraduate who has very grandly signed the bill is engaged in an argument with the manager. At a table near Adam's three young men with gowns wound round their throats have settled themselves and ordered coffee and cream cakes; while they are waiting they discuss the Union elections.

Adam orders more double whiskies.

Ernest insists on sending a bottle of gin over to the party at the next table. It is rejected with some resentment, and soon they rise and go away.

Adam orders more double whiskies.

Ernest begins drawing a portrait of Adam on the table-cloth.

He entitles it "*Le vin triste*", and, indeed, throughout dinner, Adam has been growing sadder and sadder as his guest has grown more happy. He drinks and orders more with a mechanical weariness.

At length, very unsteadily, they rise to go.

From now onwards the film becomes a series of fragmentary scenes interspersed among hundreds of feet of confusion.

"*It's going queer again, Ada. D'you think it's meant to be like this?*"

A public-house in the slums. Adam leans against the settee and pays for innumerable pints of beer for armies of ragged men. Ernest is engrossed in a heated altercation about birth control with a beggar whom he has just defeated at "darts".

Another public-house: Ernest, beset by two panders, is loudly maintaining the abnormality of his tastes. Adam finds a bottle of gin in his pocket and attempts to give it to a man; his wife interposes; eventually the bottle falls to the floor and is broken.

Adam and Ernest in a taxi; they drive from college to college, being refused admission. Fade out.

GABRIEL'S PARTY in Balliol is being an enormous success. It is a decorous assembly mostly sober. There are bottles of champagne and decanters of whisky and brandy, but most of Gabriel's guests prefer dancing. Others sit about and talk. They are large, well-furnished rooms, and the effect is picturesque and agreeable. There are a few people in fancy dress – a Queen Victoria, a Sapphist and two Generals Gordon. A musical comedy actor, who is staying the week-end with Gabriel, stands by the gramophone looking through the records; as becomes a guest of honour he is terribly bored.

Henry Quest has escaped from the Chatham and is talking about diplomatic appointments, drinking whisky and regarding everyone with disapproval. Lord Basingstoke stands talking to him, with his mind still worrying about the Constitution of the Commonwealth of Australia. Swithin is making himself quite delightful to the guest of honour. Mr. Egerton-Verschoyle sits very white, complaining of the cold.

Enter Mr. Sayle of Merton.

"GABRIEL, DO LOOK WHO I'VE FOUND IN THE QUAD. MAY I BRING HIM IN?" He pulls in Adam, who stands with a broken gin bottle in one hand staring stupidly about the room.

Someone pours him out a glass of champagne.

The party goes on.

A voice is heard roaring "ADAM" outside the window, and suddenly there bursts in Ernest, looking incredibly drunk. His hair is disordered, his eyes glazed, his neck and face crimson and greasy. He sits down in a chair immobile; someone gives him a drink; he takes it mechanically and then pours it into the carpet and continues to stare before him.

"ADAM, IS THIS IMPOSSIBLE PERSON A FRIEND OF YOURS? DO FOR GOODNESS' SAKE TAKE HIM AWAY. GABRIEL WILL BE FURIOUS."

"HE'S THE MOST MARVELLOUS MAN, HENRY. YOU JUST DON'T KNOW HIM. COME AND TALK TO HIM."

And to his intense disgust Henry is led across the room and introduced to Ernest. Ernest at first does not seem to hear, and then slowly raises his eyes until they are gazing at Henry; by a further effort he continues to focus them.

"QUEST? ANY RELATION TO ADAM'S WOMAN?"

There is about to be a scene. The musical comedy actor feels that only this was needed to complete the melancholy of the evening. Henry is all indignation and contempt. "IMOGEN QUEST IS MY SISTER IF THAT'S WHAT YOU MEAN. WHO THE DEVIL ARE YOU AND WHAT DO YOU MEAN BY SPEAKING ABOUT HER LIKE THAT?"

Gabriel flutters ineffectually in the background. Richard Basingstoke interposes with a genial, "Come on, Henry, can't you see the frightful man's blind drunk?" Swithin begs Adam to take Ernest away. Everybody is thrown into the utmost agitation.

But Ernest, in his own way, saves everyone from further anxiety.

"DO YOU KNOW, I THINK I'M GOING TO BE SICK?"

And makes his way unmolested and with perfect dignity to the quad. The gramophone starts playing "Everybody loves my baby". Fade out.

THE OXFORD CITY LIBERAL ASSOCIATION DANCE AT THE TOWN HALL.

Tickets are being sold at the door for 1s. 6d.

Upstairs there is a table with jugs of lemonade and plates of plum cake. In the main hall a band is playing and the younger liberals are dancing. One of the waitresses from the Crown sits by the door fanning her face with a handkerchief.

Ernest, with a radiant smile, is slowly walking round the room offering plum cake to the couples sitting about. Some giggle and take it; some giggle and refuse; some refuse and look exceedingly haughty.

Adam leans against the side of the door watching him.

Close up; Adam bears on his face the same expression of blind misery that he wore in the taxi the night before.

LE VIN TRISTE.

Ernest has asked the waitress from the Crown to dance with him. It is an ungainly performance; still sublimely contented he collides with several couples, misses his footing and, but for his partner, would have fallen. An M.C. in evening dress asks Adam to take him away.

Broad stone steps.

Several motors are drawn up outside the Town Hall. Ernest climbs into the first of them – a decrepit Ford – and starts the engine. Adam attempts to stop him. A policeman hurries up. There is a wrenching of gears and the car starts.

The policeman blows his whistle.

Half-way down St. Aldates the car runs into the kerb, mounts the pavement and runs into a shop window. The inhabitants of St. Aldates converge from all sides; heads appear at every window; policemen assemble. There is a movement in the crowd to make way for something being carried out.

Adam turns and wanders aimlessly towards Carfax.

St. Mary's clock strikes twelve.

It is raining again.

Adam is alone.

HALF AN HOUR LATER. AN HOTEL BEDROOM.

Adam is lying on his face across the bed, fully clothed. He turns over and sits up. Again the vision of the native village; the savage has dragged himself very near to the edge of the jungle. His back glistens in the evening sun with his last exertion. He raises himself to his feet, and with quick unsteady steps reaches the first bushes; soon he is lost to view.

Adam steadies himself at the foot of the bed and walks to the dressing-table; he leans for a long time looking at himself in the glass.

He walks to the window and looks out into the rain.

Finally he takes the blue bottle from his pocket, uncorks it, smells it, and then without more ado drinks its contents. He makes a wry face at its bitterness and stands for a minute uncertain. Then moved by some odd instinct he turns out the light and curls himself up under the coverlet.

At the foot of a low banyan tree the savage lies very still. A large fly settles on his shoulder; two birds of prey perch on the branch above him, waiting. The tropical sun begins to set, and in the brief twilight animals begin to prowl upon their obscene questings. Soon it is quite dark.

A photograph of H.M. the King in naval uniform flashes out into the night.

GOD SAVE THE KING.

The cinema quickly empties.

The young man from Cambridge goes his way to drink a glass of Pilsen at Odenino's.

Ada and Gladys pass out through ranks of liveried attendants.

For perhaps the fiftieth time in the course of the evening Gladys says, "Well, I do call it a soft film."

"Fancy 'er not coming in again."

There is quite a crowd outside, all waiting to go to Earls Court. Ada and Gladys fight manfully and secure places on the top of the 'bus.

"'Ere, 'oo are yer pushing? Mind out, can't yer?"

When they arrive home they will no doubt have some cocoa before going to bed, and perhaps some bread and bloater paste. It has been rather a disappointing evening on the whole. Still, as Ada says, with the pictures you has to take the bad with the good.

Next week there may be something really funny.

Larry Semon or Buster Keaton – who knows?

CONCLUSION

I

The tea grew cold upon the chamber cupboard and Adam Doure stared out into the void.

The rain of yesterday had cleared away and the sun streamed into the small bedroom, lighting it up with amiable and unwelcome radiance. The distressing sound of a self-starter grappling in vain with a cold engine rang up from the yard below the window. Otherwise everything was quiet.

He cogitated: therefore he was.

From the dismal array of ills that confronted him and the confused memories that lay behind, this one proposition obtruded itself with devastating insistence. Each of his clearing perceptions advanced fresh evidence of his existence; he stretched out his limbs fully clothed under the counterpane and gazed at the ceiling with uncomprehending despair, while memories of the preceding evening, of Ernest Vaughan with swollen neck and staring eye, of the slum bar and the eager faces of the two pimps, of Henry, crimson and self-righteous, of shop girls in silk blouses eating plum cake, of the Ford wrecked in the broken window, fought for precedence in his awakening consciousness until they were established in some fairly coherent chronological order; but always at the end there remained the blue bottle and the sense of finality rudely frustrated. It stood upon the dressing-table now, emptied of all its power of reprieve, while the tea grew cold upon the chamber cupboard.

After all the chaotic impressions which he had thus painfully and imperfectly set in order, the last minutes before he had turned out the light stood out perfectly clearly. He could see the white, inconsolable face that had stared out at him from the looking-glass; he could feel at the back of his tongue the salt and bitter taste of the poison. And then as the image of the taste began to bulk larger in his field of consciousness, as though with the sudden breaking down of some intervening barrier another memory swept in on him blotting out all else with its intensity. He remembered as in a nightmare, remote, yet infinitely clear, his awakening in the darkness with the coldness of death about his heart; he had raised himself from the bed and stumbled to the window and leant there, he did not know how long, with the cold air in his face and the steady monotone of the rain fighting with the drumming of blood in his head. Gradually, as he stood there motionless, nausea had come upon him; he had fought it back, his whole will struggling in the effort; it had come again; his drunken senses relaxed their resistance, and with complete abandonment of purpose and restraint, he vomited into the yard below.

Slowly and imperceptibly the tea grew cold on the chamber cupboard.

II

Centuries ago, in his dateless childhood, Ozymandias had sprung to the top of the toy cupboard tired of Adam's game. It was a game peculiar to himself and Ozymandias which Adam had evolved, and which was only played on the rare occasions of his being left alone. First, Ozymandias had to be sought from room to room, and when at last he was found, borne up to the nursery and shut in. He would watch him for some minutes as he paced the floor and surveyed the room with just the extreme tip of his tail expressing his unfathomable contempt for European civilization. Then armed with a sword, gun, battledore, or an armful of bricks to throw, and uttering sadistic cries, Adam would pursue him round and round the room, driving him from refuge to refuge, until almost beside himself with rage and terror, he crouched jungle-like with ears flattened back and porpentine hair. Here Adam would rest, and after some slight pause the real business of the game began. Ozymandias had to be won back to complacency and affection. Adam would sit down on the floor some little way from him and begin calling to him softly and endearingly. He would lie on his stomach with his face as near Ozymandias as he would allow and whisper extravagant eulogies of his beauty and grace; mother-like he would comfort him, evoking some fictitious tormentor to be reproached, assuring him that he was powerless to hurt him any more; Adam would protect him; Adam would see that the horrible little boy did not come near him again. Slowly Ozymandias' ears would begin to come forward and his eyes begin to close, and the delectable exercise invariably ended with caresses of passionate reconciliation.

On this particular afternoon, however, Ozymandias had refused to play, and the moment Adam brought him into the nursery, had established himself in unassailable sanctuary at the top of the toy cupboard. He sat there among the dust and broken toys, and Adam, foiled in his purpose, sat gloomily beneath calling to him. But Adam – at the age of seven – was not easily discouraged, and soon he began pushing up the nursery table towards the cupboard. This done he lifted the soldier box into it, and above this planted a chair. There was not room, turn it how he might, for all four legs to rest on the box, but content with an unstable equilibrium, Adam poised it upon three and mounted. When his hands were within a few inches of Ozymandias' soft fur an unwary step on to the unsupported part of the chair precipitated him and it, first on to the table and then with a clatter and cry on to the floor.

Adam had been too well brought up to remember very much of his life in the days before he went to his private school, but this incident survived in his memory with a clearness, which increased as he became farther removed from it, as the first occasion on which he became conscious of ill as a subjective entity. His life up till this time had been so much bounded with warnings of danger that it seemed for a moment inconceivable that he could so easily have broken through into the realm of positive bodily harm. Indeed, so incompatible did it seem with all previous experience that it was some appreciable time before he could convince himself of the continuity of his existence; but for the wealth of Hebraic and mediaeval imagery with which the idea of life outside the body had become symbolized, he could in that moment easily have believed in his own bodily extinction and the unreality of all the sensible objects about him. Later he learned to regard these periods between his fall and the dismayed advent of help from below, as the first promptings towards that struggle for detachment in which he had, not without almost frantic endeavour, finally acknowledged defeat in the bedroom of the Oxford hotel.

The first phase of detachment had passed and had been succeeded by one of methodical investigation. Almost simultaneously with his acceptance of his continued existence had come the conception of pain – vaguely at first as of a melody played by another to which his senses were only fitfully attentive, but gradually taking shape as the tangible objects about him gained in reality, until at length it appeared as a concrete thing, external but intimately attached to himself. Like the pursuit of quicksilver with a spoon, Adam was able to chase it about the walls of his consciousness until at length he drove it into a corner in which he could examine it at his leisure. Still lying perfectly still, just as he had fallen, with his limbs half embracing the wooden legs of the chair, Adam was able, by concentrating his attention upon each part of his body in turn, to exclude the disordered sensations to which his fall had given rise and trace the several constituents of the bulk of pain down their vibrating channels to their sources in his various physical injuries. The process was nearly complete when the arrival of his nurse dissolved him into tears and scattered his bewildered ratiocinations.

It was in some such mood as this that, an hour or so after his awakening, Adam strode along the towing path away from Oxford. He still wore the clothes in which he had slept, but in his intellectual dishevelment he had little concern for his appearance. All about him the shadows were beginning to dissipate and give place to clearer images. He had breakfasted in a world of phantoms, in a great room full of uncomprehending eyes, protruding grotesquely from monstrous heads that lolled over steaming porridge; marionette waiters had pirouetted about him with uncouth gestures. All round him a macabre dance of shadows had reeled and flickered, and in and out of it Adam had picked his way, conscious only of one insistent need, percolating through to him from the world outside, of immediate escape from the scene upon which the bodiless harlequinade was played, into a third dimension beyond it.

And at length, as he walked by the river, the shapes of the design began to advance and recede, and the pattern about him and the shadows of the night before became planes and masses and arranged themselves into a perspective, and like the child in the nursery Adam began feeling his bruises.

Somewhere among the red roofs across the water bells were ringing discordantly.

Two men were fishing on the bank. They looked curiously at him and returned their attention to their barren sport.

A small child passed him sucking her thumb in Freudian ecstasy.

And after a time Adam left the footpath and lay down under a bank and by the Grace of God fell asleep.

III

It was not a long or an unbroken sleep, but Adam rose from it refreshed and after a little while resumed his journey.

On a white footbridge he paused, and lighting his pipe, gazed down into his ruffled image. A great swan swept beneath him with Spenserian grace, and as the scattered particles of his reflection began to reassemble, looking more than ever grotesque in contrast with the impeccable excellence of the bird, he began half-consciously to speak aloud:

"So, you see, you are after all come to the beginning of another day." And as he spoke, he took from his pocket the envelope addressed to Imogen and tore it into small pieces. Like wounded birds they tumbled and fluttered, until reaching the water they became caught up in its movement and were swept out of sight round the bend of the river towards the city, which Adam had just left.

The reflection answered: "Yes, I think that that was well done. After all, 'imperatrix' is not a particularly happy epithet to apply to Imogen, is it? – and, by the way, are you certain that she can understand Latin? Suppose that she had had to ask Henry to translate it to her!

"But, tell me, does this rather picturesque gesture mean that you have decided to go on living? You seemed so immovably resolved on instant death yesterday, that I find it hard to believe you can have changed your mind."

ADAM: I find it hard to believe that it was I who yesterday was so immovably resolved. I cannot explain but it seems to me as though the being who survives, I must admit, with very great clearness in my memory, was born of a dream, drank and died in a dream.

THE REFLECTION: And loved in a dream, too?

ADAM: There you confound me, for it seems to me that that love of his alone does partake of reality. But perhaps I am merely yielding to the intensity of the memory. Indeed I think that I am. For the rest that being had no more substance than you yourself, whom the passage of a bird can dissolve.

REFLECTION: That is a sorry conclusion, for I am afraid that you are trying to dismiss as a shadow a being in every way as real as yourself. But in your present mood it would be useless to persuade you. Tell me instead, what was the secret which you learned, asleep there in the grass?

ADAM: I found no secret – only a little bodily strength.

REFLECTION: Is the balance of life and death so easily swayed?

ADAM: It is the balance of appetite and reason. The reason remains constant – the appetite varies.

REFLECTION: And is there no appetite for death?

ADAM: None which cannot be appeased by sleep or change or the mere passing of time.

REFLECTION: And in the other scale no reason?

ADAM: None. None.

REFLECTION: No honour to be observed to friends? No interpenetration, so that you cannot depart without bearing away with you something that is part of another?

ADAM: None.

REFLECTION: Your art?

ADAM: Again the appetite to live – to preserve in the shapes of things the personality whose dissolution you foresee inevitably.

REFLECTION: That is the balance then – and in the end circumstance decides.

ADAM: Yes, in the end circumstance.

CONTINUATION

They have all come over to Thatch for the day; nine of them, three in Henry Quest's Morris and the others in a huge and shabby car belonging to Richard Basingstoke. Mrs. Hay had only expected Henry Quest and Swithin, but she waves a plump hand benignly and the servants busy themselves in finding more food. It is so nice living near Oxford, and Basil's friends always *look* so charming about the place even if they are rather odd in their manners sometimes. They all talk so quickly that she can never hear what they are saying and they never finish their sentences either – but it doesn't matter, because they always talk about people she doesn't know. Dear boys, of course they don't mean to be rude really – they are so well bred, and it *is* nice to see them making themselves really at home. Who are they talking about now?

"No, Imogen, *really*, he's getting rather impossible."

"I can't tell you what he was like the other night."

"The night you came down here."

"Gabriel was giving a party."

"And he didn't know Gabriel and he hadn't been asked."

"And Gabriel didn't want him – did you, Gabriel?"

"Because you never know what he is going to do next."

"And he brought in the *most dreadful* person."

"Quite, quite drunk."

"Called Ernest Vaughan, you wouldn't have met him. Just the *most awful* person in the world. Gabriel was perfectly sweet to him."

Dear boys, so young, so intolerant.

Still, if they must smoke between courses, they might be a little more careful with the ash. The dark boy at the end – Basil always forgot to introduce his friends to her – was quite ruining the table.

"Edwards, give the gentleman next to Lord Basingstoke another ash-tray."

What were they saying?

"D'you know, Henry, I think that that was rather silly of you? Why should I mind what some poor drunk says about me?"

What a sweet girl Imogen Quest was. So much *easier* than her father. Mrs. Hay was always rather afraid of Imogen's father. She was afraid Henry was going to be like him. How charming she looks now. She cannot understand why all the boys aren't in love with her. When Mrs. Hay was young, they would have been. None of Basil's friends seemed quite the "marrying sort" somehow. Now if only Basil would marry someone like Imogen Quest. . . .

"But do you know, I think I've met Ernest Vaughan? Or at least someone pointed him out to me once. Didn't you, Swithin?"

"Yes. You said you thought he was rather attractive."

"*Imogen!*"

"*My dear.*"

"I think he is. Isn't he short and dirty with masses of hair?"

"Always drunk."

"Yes, I remember. I think he looked very charming. I want to meet him properly."

"Imogen, you can't, *really*. He is *too* awful."

"Didn't he do those pictures in Richard's room? Richard, will you invite me to meet him one day?"

"No, Imogen, really I couldn't."

"Then someone must – Gabriel, you will, *please*. I insist on meeting him."

Dear children, so young, so *chic*.

"Well, I think it's perfectly beastly of you all. But I will meet him all the same. I'll get Adam to arrange it."

The table was ruined.

"Edwards, I think it's almost fine enough to have coffee outside."

The Seven Deadly Sins. No. I

The intolerable wickedness of him who drinks alone.

'The Seven Deadly Sins. No. 1. The intolerable wickedness of him who drinks alone', *The Cherwell*, 17 October 1923, p. 238.

A HOUSE OF GENTLEFOLKS

I ARRIVED at Vanburgh at five to one. It was raining hard by now and the dreary little station yard was empty except for a deserted and draughty-looking taxi. They might have sent a car for me.

How far was it to Stayle? About three miles, the ticket collector told me. Which part of Stayle might I be wanting? The Duke's? That was a good mile the other side of the village.

They really might have sent a car.

With a little difficulty I found the driver of the taxi, a sulky and scorbutic young man who may well have been the bully of some long-forgotten school story. It was some consolation to feel that he must be getting wetter than I. It was a beastly drive.

After the cross-roads at Stayle we reached what were obviously the walls of the park, interminable and dilapidated walls that stretched on past corners and curves with leafless trees dripping on to their dingy masonry. At last they were broken by lodges and gates, four gates and three lodges, and through the ironwork I could see a great sweep of ill-kept drive.

But the gates were shut and padlocked and most of the windows in the lodges were broken.

"There are some more gates further on," said the school bully, "and beyond them, and beyond them again. I suppose they must get in and out somehow, sometimes."

At last we found a white wooden gate and a track which led through some farm buildings into the main drive. The park land on either side was railed off and no doubt let out to pasture. One very dirty sheep had strayed on to the drive and stumbled off in alarm at our approach, continually looking over its shoulder and then starting away again until we overtook it. Last of all the house came in sight, spreading out prodigiously in all directions.

The man demanded eight shillings for the fare. I gave it to him and rang the bell.

After some delay an old man opened the door to me.

"Mr. Vaughan," I said. "I think his Grace is expecting me to luncheon."

"Yes; will you come in, please?" and I was just handing him my hat when he added: "I am the Duke of Vanburgh. I hope you will forgive my opening the door myself. The butler is in bed to-day – he suffers terribly in his back during the winter, and both my footmen have been killed in the war." *Have been killed* – the words haunted me incessantly throughout the next few hours and for days to come. That desolating perfect tense, after ten years at least, probably more ... Miss Stein and the continuous present; the Duke of Vanburgh and the continuous perfect passive. ...

I was unprepared for the room to which he led me. Only once before, at the age of twelve, had I been to a ducal house, and besides the fruit garden, my chief memory of that visit was one of intense cold and of running upstairs through endless passages to get my mother a fur to wear round her shoulders after dinner. It is true that that was in Scotland, but still I was quite unprepared for the overpowering heat that met us as the Duke opened the door. The double windows were tight shut and a large coal fire burned brightly in the round Victorian grate. The air was heavy with the smell of chrysanthemums, there was a gilt clock under a glass case on the chimney-piece and everywhere in the room stiff little assemblages of china and bric-à-brac. One might expect to find such a room in Lancaster Gate or Elm Park Gardens where the widow of some provincial knight knits away her days among trusted servants. In front of the fire sat an old lady, eating an apple.

"My dear, this is Mr. Vaughan, who is going to take Stayle abroad – my sister, Lady Emily. Mr. Vaughan has just driven down from London in his motor."

"No," I said, "I came by train – the 12.55."

"Wasn't that very expensive?" said Lady Emily.

Perhaps I ought here to explain the reason for my visit. As I have said, I am not at all in the habit of moving in these exalted circles, but I have a rather grand godmother who shows a sporadic interest in my affairs. I had just come down from Oxford, and was very much at a loose end when she learned unexpectedly that the Duke of Vanburgh was in need of a tutor to take his grandson and heir abroad – a youth called the Marquess of Stayle, eighteen years old. It had seemed a tolerable way in which to spend the next six months, and accordingly the thing had been arranged. I was here to fetch away my charge and start for the Continent with him next day.

"Did you say you came by train?" said the Duke.

"By the 12.55."

"But you said you were coming by motor."

"No, really, I can't have said that. For one thing I haven't got a motor."

"But if you hadn't said that, I should have sent Byng to meet you. Byng didn't meet you, did he?"

"No," I said, "he did not."

"Well, there you see."

Lady Emily put down the core of her apple and said very suddenly:

"Your father used to live over at Oakshott. I knew him quite well. Shocking bad on a horse."

"No, that was my uncle Hugh. My father was in India almost all his life. He died there."

"Oh, I don't think he can have done that," said Lady Emily; "I don't believe he even went there – did he, Charles?"

"Who? what?"

"Hugh Vaughan never went to India, did he?"

"No, no, of course not. He sold Oakshott and went to live in Hampshire somewhere. He never went to India in his life."

At this moment another old lady, almost indistinguishable from Lady Emily, came into the room.

"This is Mr. Vaughan, my dear. You remember his father at Oakshott, don't you? He's going to take Stayle abroad – my sister, Lady Gertrude."

Lady Gertrude smiled brightly and took my hand.

"Now I knew there was someone coming to luncheon, and then I saw Byng carrying in the vegetables a quarter of an hour ago. I thought, now he ought to be at Vanburgh meeting the train."

"No, no, dear," said Lady Emily. "Mr. Vaughan came down by motor."

"Oh, that's a good thing. I thought he said he was coming by train."

II

The Marquess of Stayle did not come in to luncheon.

"I am afraid you may find him rather shy at first," explained the Duke. "We did not tell him about your coming until this morning. We were afraid it might unsettle him. As it is he is a little upset about it. Have you seen him since breakfast, my dear?"

"Don't you think," said Lady Gertrude, "that Mr. Vaughan had better know the truth about Stayle? He is bound to discover it soon."

The Duke sighed: "The truth is, Mr. Vaughan, that my grandson is not quite right in his head. Not mad, you understand, but noticeably under-developed."

I nodded. "I gathered from my godmother that he was a little backward."

"That is largely why he never went to school. He went to a private school once for two terms, but he was very unhappy and the fees were very high; so I took him away. Since then he has had no regular education."

"No education of any sort, dear," said Lady Gertrude gently.

"Well, it practically amounts to that. And it is a sad state of affairs, as you will readily understand. You see, the boy will succeed me and – well, it is very unfortunate. Now there is quite a large sum of money which his mother left for the boy's education. Nothing has been done with it – to tell you the truth, I had forgotten all about it until my lawyer reminded me of it the other day. It is about thirteen hundred pounds by now, I think. I have talked the matter over with Lady Emily and Lady Gertrude, and we came to the conclusion that the best thing to do would be to send him abroad for a year with a tutor. It might make a difference. Anyway, we shall feel that we have done our duty by the boy." (It seemed to me odd that they should feel that about it, but I said nothing.) "You will probably have to get him some clothes too. You see he has never been about much, and we have let him run wild a little, I am afraid."

When luncheon was over they brought out a large box of peppermint creams. Lady Emily ate five.

III

Well, I had been sent down from Oxford with every circumstance of discredit, and it did not become me to be over nice; still, to spend a year conducting a lunatic nobleman about Europe was rather more than I had bargained for. I had practically made up my mind to risk my godmother's displeasure and throw up the post while there was still time, when the young man made his appearance.

He stood at the door of the dining-room surveying the four of us, acutely ill at ease but with a certain insolence.

"Hullo, have you finished lunch? May I have some peppermints, Aunt Emily?"

He was not a bad-looking youth at all, slightly over middle height, and he spoke with that rather agreeable intonation that gentlepeople acquire who live among servants and farm hands. His clothes, with which he had obviously been at some pains, were unbelievable – a shiny blue suit with four buttons, much too small for him, showing several inches of wrinkled woollen sock and white flannel shirt. Above this he had put on a stiff evening collar and a very narrow tie, tied in a sailor-knot. His hair was far too long, and he had been putting water on it. But for all this he did not look mad.

"Come and say, 'How do you do?' to your new tutor," said Lady Gertrude, as though to a child of six. "Give him your right hand – that's it."

He came awkwardly towards me, holding out his hand, then put it behind him and then shot it out again suddenly, leaning his body forward as he did so. I felt a sudden shame for this poor ungraceful creature.

"How-d'you-do?" he said. "I expect they forgot to send the

car for you, didn't they? The last tutor walked out and didn't get here until half-past two. Then they said I was mad, so he went away again. Have they told you I'm mad yet?"

"No," I said decidedly, "of course not."

"Well, they will then. But perhaps they have already, and you didn't like to tell me. You're a gentleman, aren't you? That's what grandfather said: 'He's a bad hat, but at least he's a gentleman.' But you needn't worry about me. They all say I'm mad."

Anywhere else this might have caused some uneasiness, but the placid voice of Lady Gertrude broke in:

"Now, you mustn't talk like that to Mr. Vaughan. Come and have a peppermint, dear." And she looked at me as though to say, "What did I tell you?"

Quite suddenly I decided to take on the job after all.

An hour later we were in the train. I had the Duke's cheque for £150 preliminary expenses in my pocket; the boy's preposterous little wicker box was in the rack over his head.

"I say," he said, "what am I to call you?"

"Well, most of my friends call me Ernest."

"May I really do that?"

"Yes, of course. What shall I call you?"

He looked doubtful. "Grandfather and the aunts call me Stayle; everyone else calls me 'my Lord' when they are about and 'Bats' when we are alone. It's short for 'Bats in the Belfry', you know."

"But haven't you got a Christian name?"

He had to think before he answered. "Yes – George Theodore Verney."

"Well, I'm going to call you George."

"Will you really? I say, have you been to London a lot?"

"Yes, I live there usually."

"I say. D'you know I've never been to London? I've never been away from home at all – except to that school."

"Was that beastly?"

"It was —" He used a ploughboy's oath. "I say, oughtn't I to say that? Aunt Emily says I shouldn't."

"She's quite right."

"Well, she's got some mighty queer ideas, I can tell you," and for the rest of the journey he chatted freely. That evening he evinced a desire to go to a theatre, but remembering his clothes, I sent him to bed early and went out in search of friends. I felt that with £150 in my pocket I could afford champagne. Besides, I had a good story to tell.

We spent the next day ordering clothes. It was clear the moment I saw his luggage that we should have to stay on in London for four or five days; he had nothing that he could possibly wear. As soon as he was up I put him into one of my overcoats and took him to all the shops where I owed money. He ordered lavishly and with evident relish. By the evening the first parcels had begun to arrive and his room was a heap of cardboard and tissue-paper. Mr. Phillrick, who always gives me the impression that I am the first commoner who has dared to order a suit from him, so far relaxed from his customary austerity as to call upon us at the hotel, followed by an assistant with a large suitcase full of patterns. George showed a well-bred leaning towards checks. Mr. Phillrick could get two suits finished by Thursday, the other would follow us to the Crillon. Did he know anywhere where we could get a tolerable suit of evening clothes ready made? He gave us the name of the shop where his firm sold their misfits. He remembered his Lordship's father well. He would call upon his Lordship for a fitting to-morrow evening. Was I sure that I had all the clothes I needed at the moment? He had some patterns just in. As for that little matter of my bill – of course, any time that was convenient to me. (His last letter had made it unmistakably clear that he must have a cheque on account before undertaking any further orders.) I ordered two suits. All of this George enjoyed enormously.

After the first morning I gave up all attempt at a tutorial attitude. We had four days to spend in London before we could start and, as George had told me, it was his first visit. He had an unbounded zeal to see everything, and, above all, to meet people; but he had also a fresh and acute critical faculty and a natural fastidiousness which shone through the country bumpkin. The first time he went to a revue he was all agog with excitement; the theatre, the orchestra, the audience all enthralled him. He insisted on being there ten minutes before the time; he insisted on leaving ten minutes before the end of the first act. He thought it vulgar and dull and ugly, and there was so much else that he was eager to see. The dreary "might-as-well-stay-here-now-we've-paid" attitude was unintelligible to him.

In the same way with his food, he wished to try all the dishes. If he found he did not like anything, he ordered something else. On the first evening we dined out he decided that champagne was tasteless and disagreeable and refused to drink it again. He had no patience for acquiring tastes, but most good things pleased him immediately. At the National Gallery he would look at nothing after Bellini's "Death of Peter Martyr".

He was an immediate success with everyone I introduced him to. He had no "manner" of any kind. He said all he thought with very little reticence and listened with the utmost interest to all he heard said. At first he would sometimes break in with rather disturbing sincerity upon the ready-made conversations with which we are mostly content, but almost at once he learned to discern what was purely mechanical and to disregard it. He would pick up tags and phrases and use them with the oddest twists, revitalizing them by his interest in their pictur-esqueness.

And all this happened in four days; if it had been in four months the change would have been remarkable. I could see him developing from one hour to the next.

On our last evening in London I brought out an atlas and tried to explain where we were going. The world for him was divided roughly into three hemispheres – Europe, where there had been a war; it was full of towns like Paris and Buda-Pest, all equally remote and peopled with prostitutes; the East, a place full of camels and elephants, deserts and dervishes and nodding man-darins; and America, which besides its own two continents included Australia, New Zealand, and most of the British Empire not obviously "Eastern"; somewhere, too, there were some "savages".

"We shall have to stop the night at Brindisi," I was saying.

"Then we can get the Lloyd Trestino in the morning. What a lot you're smoking!"

We had just returned from a tea and cocktail party. George was standing at the looking-glass gazing at himself in his new clothes.

"You know, he has made this suit rather well, Ernest. It's about the only thing I learned at home – smoking, I mean. I used to go up to the saddle-room with Byng."

"You haven't told me what you thought of the party."

"Ernest, why are all your friends being so sweet to me? Is it just because I'm going to be a duke?"

"I expect that makes a difference with some of them – Julia for instance. She said you looked so fugitive."

"I'm afraid I didn't like Julia much. No, I mean Peter and that funny Mr. Oliphant."

"I think they like you."

"How odd!" He looked at himself in the glass again. "D'you know, I'll tell you something I've been thinking all these last few days. I don't believe I really am mad at all. It's only at home I feel so different from everyone else. Of course I don't know much...I've been thinking, d'you think it can be grandfather and the aunts who are mad, all the time?"

"They're certainly getting old."

"No, mad. I can remember some awfully dotty things they've done at one time or another. Last summer Aunt Gertrude swore there was a swarm of bees under her bed and had all the gardeners up with smoke and things. She refused to get out of bed until the bees were gone – and there weren't any there. And then there was the time grandfather made a wreath of strawberry-leaves and danced round the garden singing 'Cook's son, Dook's son, son of a belted earl'. It didn't strike me at the time, but that was an odd thing to do, wasn't it? Anyway, I shan't see them again for months and months. Oh, Ernest, it's too wonderful. You don't think the sleeves are too tight, do you? Are people black in Athens?"

"Not coal black – mostly Jews and undergraduates."

"What's that?"

"Well, Peter's an undergraduate. I was one until a few weeks ago."

"I say, do you think people will take me for an under-graduate?"

IV

It seems to me sometimes that Nature, like a lazy author, will round off abruptly into a short story what she obviously intended to be the opening of a novel.

Two letters arrived for me by the post next morning. One was from my bank returning the Duke's cheque for £150 marked "Payment Stopped"; the other from a firm of solicitors enjoining me that they, or rather one of them, would call upon me that morning in connection with the Duke of Vanburgh's business. I took them in to George.

All he said was: "I had a sort of feeling that this was all too good to last."

The lawyer duly arrived. He seemed displeased that neither of us was dressed. He intimated that he wished to speak to me alone.

His Grace, he said, had altered his plans for his grandson. He no longer wished him to go abroad. Of course, between ourselves we had to admit that the boy was not quite sane ... very sad ... these old families ... putting me in such a difficult position in case anything happened.... His Grace had talked it over with Lady Emily and Lady Gertrude.... It really was too dangerous an experiment ... besides, they had especially kept the boy shut away because they did not want the world to know ... discredit on a great name ... and, of course, if he went about, people were bound to talk. It was not strictly his business to discuss the wisdom of his client's decision, but, again between ourselves, he had been very much surprised that his Grace had ever considered letting the boy leave home.... Later perhaps, but not yet ... he would always need watching. And of course there was a good deal of money coming to him. Strictly between ourselves, his Grace was a great deal better off than people supposed ... town property ... death duties ... keeping up Stayle ... and so on.

He was instructed to pay the expenses incurred up to date and to give me three months' salary . . . most generous of his Grace, no legal obligation. . . . As to the clothes . . . we really seemed rather to have exceeded his Grace's instructions. Still, no doubt all the things that had not been specially made could be returned to the shops. He would give instructions about that . . . he was himself to take Lord Stayle back to his grandfather.

And an hour later they left.

"It's been a marvellous four days," said George; and then: "Anyway, I shall be twenty-one in three years and I shall have my mother's money then. I think it's rather a shame sending back those ties though. Don't you think I could keep one or two?"

Five minutes later Julia rang up to ask us to luncheon.

The horrid sacrilege of those that illtreat books

'The Seven Deadly Sins. No. 2. The horrid sacrilege of those that illtreat books', *The Cherwell*, 27 October 1923, p. 14.

THE MANAGER OF
"THE KREMLIN"

THIS STORY was told me in Paris very early in the morning by the manager of a famous night club, and I am fairly certain that it is true.

I shall not tell you the real name of the manager or of his club, because it is not the sort of advertisement he would like, but I will call them, instead, Boris and "The Kremlin".

"The Kremlin" occupies a position of its own.

Your hat and coat are taken at the door by a perfectly genuine Cossack of ferocious appearance; he wears riding-boots and spurs, and the parts of his face that are not hidden by beard are cut and scarred like that of a pre-war German student.

The interior is hung with rugs and red, woven stuff to represent a tent. There is a very good *tsigain* band playing gipsy music, and a very good jazz-band which plays when people want to dance.

The waiters are chosen for their height. They wear magnificent Russian liveries, and carry round flaming skewers on which are spitted onions between rounds of meat. Most of them are ex-officers of the Imperial Guard.

Boris, the manager, is quite a young man; he is 6 ft. 5$\frac{1}{2}$ in. in height. He wears a Russian silk blouse, loose trousers and top boots, and goes from table to table seeing that everything is all right.

From two in the morning until dawn "The Kremlin" is invariably full, and the American visitors, looking wistfully at their bills, often remark that Boris must be "making a good thing out of it". So he is.

Fashions change very quickly in Montmartre, but if his present popularity lasts for another season, he talks of retiring to a villa on the Riviera.

One Saturday night, or rather a Sunday morning, Boris did

me the honour of coming to sit at my table and take a glass of
wine with me. It was then that Boris told his story.

His father was a general, and when the war broke out Boris
was a cadet at the military academy.

He was too young to fight, and was forced to watch, from
behind the lines, the collapse of the Imperial Government.

Then came the confused period when the Great War was
over, and various scattered remnants of the royalist army, with
half-hearted support from their former allies, were engaged in a
losing fight against the Bolshevists.

Boris was eighteen years old. His father had been killed and
his mother had already escaped to America.

The military academy was being closed down, and with
several of his fellow cadets Boris decided to join the last royalist
army which, under Kolchak, was holding the Bolshevists at bay
in Siberia.

It was a very odd kind of army. There were dismounted
cavalry and sailors who had left their ships, officers whose
regiments had mutinied, frontier garrisons and aides-de-camp,
veterans of the Russo-Japanese war, and boys like Boris who were
seeing action for the first time.

Besides these, there were units from the Allied Powers, who
seemed to have been sent there by their capricious Governments
and forgotten; there was a corps of British engineers and some
French artillery; there were also liaison officers and military
attachés to the General Headquarters Staff.

Among the latter was a French cavalry officer a few years
older than Boris. To most educated Russians before the war
French was as familiar as their own language.

Boris and the French attaché became close friends. They
used to smoke together and talk of Moscow and Paris before
the war.

As the weeks passed it became clear that Kolchak's campaign
could end in nothing but disaster.

Eventually a council of officers decided that the only course open was to break through to the east coast and attempt to escape to Europe.

A force had to be left behind to cover the retreat, and Boris and his French friend found themselves detailed to remain with this rearguard. In the action which followed, the small covering force was completely routed.

Alone among the officers Boris and his friend escaped with their lives, but their condition was almost desperate.

Their baggage was lost and they found themselves isolated in a waste land, patrolled by enemy troops and inhabited by savage Asiatic tribesmen.

Left to himself, the Frenchman's chances of escape were negligible, but a certain prestige still attached to the uniform of a Russian officer in the outlying villages.

Boris lent him his military overcoat to cover his uniform, and together they struggled through the snow, begging their way to the frontier.

Eventually they arrived in Japanese territory. Here all Russians were suspect, and it devolved on the Frenchman to get them safe conduct to the nearest French Consulate.

Boris' chief aim now was to join his mother in America. His friend had to return to report himself in Paris, so here they parted.

They took an affectionate farewell, promising to see each other again when their various affairs were settled. But each in his heart doubted whether chance would ever bring them together again.

Two years elapsed, and then one day in spring a poorly-dressed young Russian found himself in Paris, with three hundred francs in his pocket and all his worldly possessions in a kitbag.

He was very different from the debonair Boris who had left the military academy for Kolchak's army. America had proved to be something very different from the Land of Opportunity he had imagined.

His mother sold the jewels and a few personal possessions she had been able to bring away with her, and had started a small dressmaking business.

There seemed no chance of permanent employment for Boris, so after two or three months of casual jobs he worked his passage to England.

During the months that followed, Boris obtained temporary employment as a waiter, a chauffeur, a professional dancing-partner, a dock-labourer, and he came very near to starvation.

Finally, he came across an old friend of his father's, a former first secretary in the diplomatic corps, who was now working as a hairdresser.

This friend advised him to try Paris, where a large Russian colony had already formed, and gave him his fare.

It was thus that one morning, as the buds were just beginning to break in the Champs Elysées and the *couturiers* were exhibiting their Spring fashions, Boris found himself, ill-dressed and friend-less, in another strange city.

His total capital was the equivalent of about thirty shillings; and so, being uncertain of what was to become of him, he decided to have luncheon.

An Englishman finding himself in this predicament would no doubt have made careful calculations.

He would have decided what was the longest time that his money would last him, and would have methodically kept within his budget while he started again "looking for a job".

But as Boris stood working out this depressing sum, something seemed suddenly to snap in his head.

With the utmost privation he could hardly hope to subsist for more than two or three weeks.

At the end of that time he would be in exactly the same position, a fortnight older, with all his money spent and no nearer a job.

Why not now as well as in a fortnight's time? He was in Paris, about which he had read and heard so much. He made up his mind to have one good meal and leave the rest to chance.

He had often heard his father speak of a restaurant called Larue. He had no idea where it was, so he took a taxi.

He entered the restaurant and sat down in one of the red-plush seats, while the waiters eyed his clothes with suspicion.

He looked about him in an unembarrassed way. It was quieter and less showy in appearance than the big restaurants he had passed in New York and London, but a glance at the menu told him that it was not a place where poor people often went.

Then he began ordering his luncheon, and the waiter's manner quickly changed as he realized that this eccentrically dressed customer did not need any advice about choosing his food and wine.

He ate fresh caviare and *ortolansan porto* and *crepes suzettes*; he drank a bottle of vintage claret and a glass of very old *fine champagne*, and he examined several boxes of cigars before he found one in perfect condition.

When he had finished, he asked for his bill. It was 260 francs. He gave the waiter a tip of 26 francs and 4 francs to the man at the door who had taken his hat and kitbag. His taxi had cost 7 francs.

Half a minute later he stood on the kerb with exactly 3 francs in the world. But it had been a magnificent lunch, and he did not regret it.

As he stood there, meditating what he could do, his arm was suddenly taken from behind, and turning he saw a smartly dressed Frenchman, who had evidently just left the restaurant. It was his friend the military attaché.

"I was sitting at the table behind you," he said. "You never noticed me, you were so intent on your food."

"It is probably my last meal for some time," Boris explained, and his friend laughed at what he took to be a joke.

They walked up the street together, talking rapidly. The Frenchman described how he had left the army when his time of service was up, and was now a director of a prosperous motor business.

"And you, too," he said. "I am delighted to see that you also have been doing well."

"Doing well? At the moment I have exactly 3 francs in the world."

"My dear fellow, people with 3 francs in the world do not eat caviare at Larne."

Then for the first time he noticed Boris' frayed clothes. He had only known him in a war-worn uniform and it had seemed natural at first to find him dressed as he was.

Now he realized that these were not the clothes which prosperous young men usually wear.

"My dear friend," he said, "forgive me for laughing. I didn't realize.... Come and dine with me this evening at my flat, and we will talk about what is to be done."

"And so," concluded Boris, "I became the manager of 'The Kremlin'. *If I had not gone to Larne that day it is about certain we should never have met!*

"My friend said that I might have a part in his motor business, but that he thought anyone who could spend his last 300 francs on one meal was ordained by God to keep a restaurant.

"So it has been. He financed me. I collected some of my old friends to work with us. Now, you see, I am comparatively a rich man."

The last visitors had paid their bill and risen, rather unsteadily, to go. Boris rose, too, to bow them out. The daylight shone into the room as they lifted the curtain to go out.

Suddenly, in the new light, all the decorations looked bogus and tawdry; the waiters hurried away to change their sham liveries. Boris understood what I was feeling.

"I know," he said. "It is not Russian. It is not anything even to own a popular night club when one has lost one's country."

That grim act parricide

'The Seven Deadly Sins. No. 5. That grim act parricide', *The Cherwell*,
17 November 1923, p. 77.

LOVE IN THE SLUMP

I

THE MARRIAGE of Tom Watch and Angela Trench-Troubridge was, perhaps, as unimportant an event as has occurred within living memory. No feature was lacking in the previous histories of the two young people, in their engagement, or their wedding, that could make them completely typical of all that was most unremarkable in modern social conditions. The evening paper recorded:

"This has been a busy week at St. Margaret's. The third fashionable wedding of the week took place there this afternoon, between Mr. Tom Watch and Miss Angela Trench-Troubridge. Mr. Watch, who, like so many young men nowadays, works in the city, is the second son of the late Hon. Wilfrid Watch of Holyborne House, Shaftesbury; the bride's father, Colonel Trench-Troubridge, is well known as a sportsman, and has stood several times for Parliament in the Conservative interest. Mr. Watch's brother, Captain Peter Watch of the Coldstream Guards, acted as best man. The bride wore a veil of old Brussels lace lent by her grandmother. In accordance with the new fashion for taking holidays in Britain, the bride and bridegroom are spending a patriotic honeymoon in the West of England."

And when that has been said there is really very little that need be added.

Angela was twenty-five, pretty, good-natured, lively, intelligent and popular – just the sort of girl, in fact, who, for some mysterious cause deep-rooted in Anglo-Saxon psychology, finds it most difficult to get satisfactorily married. During the last seven years she had done everything which it is customary for girls of her sort to do. In London she had danced on an average four evenings a week, for the first three years at private houses, for the last four at restaurants and night clubs; in the country she had been slightly patronizing to the neighbours and had taken parties to the hunt ball which she hoped would shock them; she had worked in a slum and a hat shop, had published a novel, been bridesmaid eleven times and godmother once; been in love, unsuitably, twice; had sold her photograph for fifty guineas to the advertising department of a firm of beauty specialists; had got into trouble when her name was mentioned in gossip columns; had acted in five or six charity matinées and two pageants, had canvassed for the Conservative candidate at two General Elections, and, like every girl in the British Isles, was unhappy at home.

In the Crisis years things became unendurable. For some time her father had shown an increasing reluctance to open the London house; now he began to talk in a sinister way about "economies", by which he meant retiring permanently to the country, reducing the number of indoor servants, stopping bedroom fires, cutting down Angela's allowance and purchasing a mile and a half of fishing in the neighbourhood, on which he had had his eye for several years.

Faced with the grim prospect of an indefinitely prolonged residence in the home of her ancestors, Angela, like many a sensible English girl before her, decided that after her two unhappy affairs she was unlikely to fall in love again. There was for her no romantic parting of the ways between love and fortune. Elder sons were scarcer than ever that year and there was hot competition from America and the Dominions. The choice was between discomfort with her parents in a Stately Home or discomfort with a husband in a London mews.

Poor Tom Watch had been mildly attentive to Angela since her first season. He was her male counterpart in about every particular. Normally educated, he had, after taking a Third in History at the University, gone into the office of a reliable firm of chartered accountants, with whom he had worked ever since. And throughout those sunless city afternoons he looked back wistfully to his undergraduate days, when he had happily followed the normal routine of University success by riding second on a borrowed hunter in the Christ Church "grind", breaking furniture with the Bullingdon, returning at dawn through the window after dances in London, and sharing dingy but expensive lodgings in the High with young men richer than himself.

Angela, as one of the popular girls of her year, used to be a frequent visitor to Oxford and to the houses where Tom stayed during the vacation, and as the bleak succession of years in his accountant's office sobered and depressed him, Tom began to look upon her as one of the few bright fragments remaining from his glamorous past. He still went out a little, for an unattached young man is never quite valueless in London, but the late dinner parties to which he went sulkily, tired by his day's work and out of touch with the topics in which the débutantes attempted to interest him, served only to show him the gulf that was widening between himself and his former friends.

Angela, because (as cannot be made too clear) she was a thoroughly nice girl, was always charming to him, and he returned her interest gratefully. She was, however, a part of his past, not of his future. His regard was sentimental but quite unaspiring. She was a piece of his irrecapturable youth; nothing could have been more remote from his attitude than to think of her as a possible companion for old age. Accordingly her proposal of marriage came to him as a surprise that was by no means welcome.

They had left a particularly crowded and dull dance, and were eating kippers at a night club. They were in the intimate and slightly tender mood which always developed between them when Angela had said in a gentle voice:

"You're always so much nicer to me than anyone else, Tom; I wonder why?" and before he could deflect her – he had had an unusually exacting day's business and the dance had been stupefying – she had popped the question.

"Well, of course," he had stammered, "I mean to say there's nothing I'd like more, old girl. I mean, you know, of course I've always been crazy about you . . . But the difficulty is I simply can't afford to marry. Absolutely out of the question for years, you know."

"But I don't think I should mind being poor with you, Tom; we know each other so well. Everything would be easy."

And before Tom knew whether he was pleased or not, the engagement had been announced.

He was making eight hundred a year; Angela had two hundred. There was "more coming" to both of them eventually. Things were not too bad if they were sensible about not having children. He would have to give up his occasional days of hunting; she was to give up her maid. On this basis of mutual sacrifice they arranged for their future.

It rained heavily on the day of the wedding, and only the last-ditchers among the St. Margaret's crowd turned out to watch the melancholy succession of guests popping out of their dripping cars and plunging up the covered way into the church. There was a party afterwards at Angela's home in Egerton Gardens. At half-past four, the young couple caught a train at Paddington for the West of England. The blue carpet and the striped awning were rolled away and locked among candle-ends and hassocks in the church store-room. The lights in the aisles were turned out and the doors locked and bolted. The flowers and shrubs were stacked up to await distribution in the wards of a hospital for incurables in which Mrs. Watch had an interest. Mrs. Trench-Troubridge's secretary set to work dispatching silver-and-white cardboard packets of wedding cake to servants and tenants in the country. One of the ushers hurried to Covent Garden to return his morning coat to the firm of gentlemen's outfitters from whom it was hired. A doctor was summoned to attend the bridegroom's small nephew, who, after attracting considerable attention as page at the ceremony by his outspoken comments, developed a high temperature and numerous disquieting symptoms of food-poisoning. Sarah Trumpery's maid discreetly returned the travelling clock which the old lady had inadvertently pouched from among the wedding presents. (This foible of hers was well known and the detectives had standing orders to avoid a scene at the reception. It was not often that she was asked to weddings nowadays. When she was, the stolen presents were invariably returned that evening or on the following day.) The bridesmaids got together over dinner and fell into eager conjecture about the intimacies of the honeymoon, the odds in this case being three to two that the ceremony had not been anticipated. The Great Western express rattled through the sodden English counties. Tom and Angela sat glumly in a first-class smoking carriage, discussing the day.

"It was so wonderful neither of us being late."

"Mother fussed so . . ."

"I didn't see John, did you?"

"He was there. He said good-bye to us in the hall."

"Oh, yes . . . I hope they've packed everything."

"What books did you bring?"

A thoroughly normal, uneventful wedding.

Presently Tom said: "I suppose in a way it's rather unenterprising of us, just going off to Aunt Martha's house in Devon. Remember how the Lockwoods went to Morocco and got captured by brigands?"

"And the Randalls got snowed up for ten days in Norway."

"We shan't get much adventure in Devon, I'm afraid."

"Well, Tom, we haven't really married for adventure, have we?"

And, as things happened, it was from that moment onwards that the honeymoon took an odd turn.

II

"D'you know if we change?"

"I rather think we do. I forgot to ask. Peter got the tickets. I'll get out at Exeter and find out."

The train drew into the station.

"Shan't be a minute," said Tom, shutting the door behind him to keep out the cold. He walked up the platform, purchased a West country evening paper, learned that they need not change and was returning to his carriage when his arm was seized and a voice said:

"Hello, Watch, old man! Remember me?" And with a little difficulty he recognized the smiling face of an old school acquaintance. "See you've just got married. Congratulations. Meant to write. Great luck running into you like this. Come and have a drink."

"Wish I could. Got to get back to the train."

"Heaps of time, old man. Waits twelve minutes here. Must have a drink."

Still searching his memory for the name of his old friend, Tom went with him to the station buffet.

"I live fifteen miles out, you know. Just come in to meet the train. Expecting some cow-cake down from London. No sign of it ... Well, all the best." .

They drank two glasses of whisky – very comforting after the cold train journey. Then Tom said:

"Well, it's been jolly seeing you. I must get back to the train now. Come with me and meet my wife."

But when they reached the platform, the train was gone.

"I say, old man, that's darned funny, you know. What are you going to do? There's not another train to-night. Tell you what, you'd better come and spend the night with me and go on in the morning. We can wire and tell your wife where you are."

"I suppose Angela will be all right?"

"Heavens, yes! Nothing can happen in England. Besides, there's nothing you can do. Give me her address and I'll send a wire now, telling her where you are. Jump into the car and wait."

Next morning Tom woke up with a feeling of slight apprehension. He turned over in bed, examining with sleepy eyes the unaccustomed furniture of the room. Then he remembered. Of course he was married. And Angela had gone off in the train, and he had driven for miles in the dark to the house of an old friend whose name he could not remember. It had been dinner-time when they arrived. They had drunk Burgundy and port and brandy. Frankly, they had drunk rather a lot. They had recalled numerous house scandals, all kinds of jolly insults to chemistry masters, escapades after dark when they had gone up to London to the "43". What was the fellow's name? It was clearly too late to ask him now. And anyway he would have to get on to Angela. He supposed that she had reached Aunt Martha's house safely and had got his telegram. Awkward beginning to the honeymoon – but then he and Angela knew each other so well . . . It was not as though this were some sudden romance.

Presently he was called. "Hounds are meeting near here this morning, sir. The Captain wondered if you'd care to go hunting."

"No, no! I have to leave immediately after breakfast."

"The Captain said he could mount you, sir, and lend you clothes."

"No, no! Quite impossible."

But when he came down to breakfast and found his host filling a saddle flask with cherry-brandy, secret threads began to pull at Tom's heart.

"Of course we're a comic sort of pack. Everyone turns out, parson, farmers, all kinds of animals. But we generally get a decent run along the edge of the moor. Pity you can't come out. I'd like you to try my new mare, she's a lovely ride . . . a bit fine for this type of country, perhaps . . ."

Well, why not? . . . after all, he and Angela knew each other so well . . . it was not as though . . .

And two hours later Tom found himself in a high wind galloping madly across the worst hunting country in the British Isles – alternations of heather and bog, broken by pot-holes, boulders, mountain streams and disused gravel pits – hounds streaming up the valley opposite, the mare going perfectly, farmers' boys on shaggy little ponies, solicitors' wives on cobs, retired old sea-captains bouncing about eighteen hands high, vets and vicars plunging on all sides of him, and not a care in his heart.

Two hours later still he was in less happy circumstances, seated alone in the heather, surrounded on all sides by an unbroken horizon of empty moor. He had dismounted to tighten a girth, and galloping across a hillside to catch up with the field, his mount had put her foot in a rabbit hole, tumbled over, rolled perilously near him, and then regaining her feet, had made off at a brisk canter towards her stable, leaving him on his back, panting for breath. Now he was quite alone in a totally strange country. He did not know the name of his host or of his host's house. He pictured himself tramping from village to village saying: "Can you tell me the address of a young man who was hunting this morning? He was in Butcher's house at Eton!" Moreover, Tom suddenly remembered he was married. Of course he and Angela knew each other so well . . . but there were limits.

At eight o'clock that evening a weary figure trudged into the gas-lit parlour of the Royal George Hotel, Chagford. He wore sodden riding boots and torn and muddy clothes. He had wandered for five hours over the moor, and was hungry. They provided him with Canadian cheese, margarine, tinned salmon, and bottled stout, and sent him to sleep in a large brass bedstead which creaked as he moved. But he slept until half-past ten next morning.

The third day of the honeymoon started more propitiously. A bleak sun was shining a little. Stiff and sore in every muscle, Tom dressed in the still damp riding clothes of his unknown host and made inquiries about reaching the remote village where his Aunt Martha's house stood, and where Angela must be anxiously awaiting him. He wired to her: "*Arriving this evening. Will explain. All love,*" and then inquired about trains. There was one train in the day which left early in the afternoon and, after three changes, brought him to a neighbouring station late that evening. Here he suffered another check. There was no car to be hired in the village. His aunt's house was eight miles away. The telephone did not function after seven o'clock. The day's journey in damp clothes had set him shivering and sneezing. He was clearly in for a bad cold. The prospect of eight miles' walk in the dark was unthinkable. He spent the night at the inn.

The fourth day dawned to find Tom speechless and nearly deaf. In this condition the car came to conduct him to the house so kindly lent for his week's honeymoon. Here he was greeted with the news that Angela had left early that morning.

"Mrs. Watch received a telegram, sir, saying that you had met with an accident hunting. She was very put out as she had asked several friends to luncheon."

"But where has she gone?"

"The address was on the telegram, sir. It was the same address as your first telegram . . . No, sir, the telegram has not been preserved."

So Angela had gone to his host near Exeter; well, she could jolly well look after herself. Tom felt far too ill to worry. He went straight to bed.

The fifth day passed in a stupor of misery. Tom lay in bed listlessly turning the pages of such books as his aunt had collected in her fifty years of vigorous out-of-door life. On the sixth day conscience began to disturb him. Perhaps he ought to do something about Angela. It was then the butler suggested that the name in the inside pocket of the hunting coat would probably be that of Tom's late, Angela's present host. Some work with a local directory settled the matter. He sent a telegram.

"*Are you all right? Awaiting you here. Tom,*" and received the answer:

"*Quite all right. Your friend divine. Why not join us here. Angela.*"

"*In bed severe cold. Tom.*"

"*So sorry darling. Will see you in London or shall I join you. Hardly worth it is it. Angela.*"

"*Will see you London. Tom.*"

Of course Angela and he knew each other very well . . .

Two days later they met in the little flat which Mrs. Watch had been decorating for them.

"I hope you've brought all the luggage."

"Yes, darling. What fun to be home!"

"Office to-morrow."

"Yes, and I've got hundreds of people to ring up. I haven't thanked them for the last batch of presents yet."

"Have a good time?"

"Not bad. How's your cold?"

"Better. What are we doing to-night?"

"I promised to go and see mama. Then I said I would dine with your Devon friend. He came up with me to see about some cow-cake. It seemed only decent to take him out after staying with him."

"Quite right. But I think I won't come."

"No, I shouldn't. I shall have heaps to tell her that would bore you."

That evening Mrs. Trench-Troubridge said: "I thought Angela was looking sweet to-night. The honeymoon's done her good. So sensible of Tom not to take her on some exhausting trip on the Continent. You can see she's come back quite rested. And the honeymoon is so often such a difficult time particularly after all the rush of the wedding."

"What's this about their taking a cottage in Devon?" asked her husband.

"Not *taking* dear, it's being given them. Near the house of a bachelor friend of Tom's apparently. Angela said it would be such a good place for her to go sometimes when she wanted a change. They can never get a proper holiday because of Tom's work."

"Very sensible, very sensible indeed," said Mr. Trench-Troubridge, lapsing into a light doze, as was usual with him at nine in the evening.

'The Seven Deadly Sins. No. 6. That dull, old sin Adultery', *The Cherwell*, 24 November 1923, p. 110.

TOO MUCH TOLERANCE

A ROUND, amiable face, reddened rather than browned by the tropical sun; round, rather puzzled grey eyes; close-cut sandy hair; a large, smiling mouth; a small sandy moustache; clean white duck suit and sun helmet – a typical English commercial agent stopping between ships at a stifling little port on the Red Sea.

We were the only Europeans in the hotel. The boat for which we were both waiting was two days late. We spent all our time together.

We went round the native bazaar and played interminable games of poker dice at the café tables. In these circumstances a casual acquaintance easily assumes a confidential tone.

At first naturally enough we talked of general subjects – local conditions and race problems.

"Can't understand what all the trouble's about. They're all jolly chaps when you get to know them." British officials, traders, Arabs, natives, Indian settlers – they were all to my new friend jolly good chaps.

Such an odd thing they couldn't get on better. Of course, different races had different ideas – some didn't wash, some had queer ideas about honesty, some got out of hand at times when they'd had too much to drink.

"Still," he said, "that's nobody's business but their own. If only they'd all let each other alone to go their own ways there wouldn't be any problems. As for religions, well, there was a lot of good in them all – Hindu, Mahommedan, Pagan: the missionaries did a lot of good, too – Wesleyan, Catholic, Church of England, all jolly good fellows."

People in remote parts of the world tend to have unshakable views on every topic. After a few months spent among them it was a relief to come across so tolerant and broad a mind.

On the first evening I left my companion with a feeling of warm respect. Here at last, in a continent peopled almost

exclusively by fanatics of one kind or another, I thought I had
found a nice man.

*   *   *

Next day we got on to more intimate subjects and I began to learn
something of his life. He was now nearer fifty than forty years of
age, though I should have thought him younger.

He had been an only son, brought up in an English provincial
town in a household where rigid principles of Victorian decorum
dominated its members.

He had been born late in his parents' life, and all his memories
dated from after his father's retirement from a responsible Government post in India.

It was alien to his nature to admit the existence of discomfort
or disagreement, but it was clear from his every reference to it
that his home had not been a congenial one.

Exact rules of morals and etiquette, ruthless criticism of
neighbours, an insurmountable class-barrier raised against all
who were considered socially inferior, hostile disapproval of
superiors – these were clearly the code of my friend's parents,
and he had grown up with a deep-rooted resolution to model his
own life on opposite principles.

I had been surprised on the evening of our first meeting to
discover the nature of his work. He was engaged in selling sewing-machines on commission to Indian store-keepers up and
down the East African coast.

It was clearly not the job for which his age and education
should have fitted him. Later I learned the explanation.

He had gone into business on leaving his public school, had
done quite well, and eventually, just before the war, had set up on
his own with the capital left him at his father's death.

"I had bad luck there," he said. "I never feel quite to blame
over what happened. You see, I'd taken a chap into partnership
with me. He'd been a clerk with me in the office, and I'd always
liked him, though he didn't get on very well with the other
fellows.

"He got sacked just about the time I came in for some money.
I never quite made out what the trouble was about, and anyway it

was none of my business. The arrangement seemed rather lucky at first, because my partner wasn't fit for military service, so all the time I was in the army he was able to look after things at home.

"The business seemed to be going very well, too. We moved to new offices and took on a larger staff, and all through the war we were drawing very decent dividends. But apparently it was only temporary prosperity.

"When I got back after the Armistice I didn't pay a great deal of attention to my affairs, I'm afraid. I was glad to be home and wanted to make the most of peace. I left my partner to manage everything, and I suppose I more or less let things slide for two years.

"Anyway, I didn't know how bad things were until he suddenly told me that we should have to go into liquidation.

"Since then I've been lucky in getting jobs, but it isn't quite the same as being one's own master."

He gazed out across the quay, turning his glass idly in his hand. Then, as an after-thought, he made an illuminating addition to his story.

"One thing I'm very glad of," he said, "my partner didn't come down with me. Almost immediately after we closed down he opened on his own in the same way of business on quite a large scale. He's a rich man now."

Later in the day he surprised me by casually mentioning his son.

"Son?"

"Yes. I've a boy of twenty-seven at home. Awfully nice fellow. I wish I could get back more often to see him. But he's got his own friends now and I dare say he's happy by himself. He's interested in the theatre.

"It's not a thing I know much about myself. All his friends are theatrical, you know, jolly interesting.

"I'm glad the boy has struck out for himself. I always made a point of never trying to force his interest in anything that didn't attract him.

"The only pity is that there's very little money in it. He's always hoping to get a job either on the stage or the kinema, but it's difficult if you don't know the right people, he says, and that's expensive.

"I send him as much as I can, but he has to be well dressed, you know, and go about a good deal and entertain, and all that takes money. Still, I expect it'll lead to something in the end. He's a jolly good fellow."

But it was not until some days later, on board ship, when we were already berthed at the port where he was due to disembark next day, that he mentioned his wife.

We had had many drinks to wish each other good luck on our respective journeys. The prospect of immediate separation made mutual confidence easier than it would be between constant companions.

"My wife left me," he said simply. "It was a great surprise. I can't to this day think why. I always encouraged her to do just what she wanted.

"You see, I'd seen a lot of the Victorian idea of marriage, where a wife was supposed to have no interests outside her housekeeping, and the father of the family dined at home every evening. I don't approve of that.

"I always liked my wife to have her own friends and have them in the house when she wanted and to go out when she wanted and I did the same. I thought we were ideally happy.

"She liked dancing and I didn't, so when a chap turned up who she seemed to like going about with, I was delighted. I'd met him once or twice and heard that he ran after women a good bit, but that wasn't my business.

"My father used to keep a strict division among his friends, between those he saw at home and those he met in the club. He wouldn't bring anyone to his house whose moral character he didn't wholly approve of. I think that's all old-fashioned rot.

"Anyway, to cut a long story short, after she'd been going out with this fellow for some time she suddenly fell in love and went off with him. I'd always liked him, too. Jolly good sort of fellow.

I suppose she had a perfect right to do what she preferred. All the same, I was surprised. And I've been lonely since."

At this moment two fellow-passengers whose acquaintance I had been scrupulously avoiding came past our table. He called them to our table, so I wished him "Good-night" and went below.

I did not see him to speak to next day, but I caught a brief glimpse of him on the pier, supervising the loading of his crate of sample sewing-machines.

As I watched, he finished his business and strode off towards the town – a jaunty, tragic little figure, cheated out of his patrimony by his partner, battened on by an obviously worthless son, deserted by his wife, an irrepressible, bewildered figure striding off under his bobbing topee, cheerfully butting his way into a whole continent of rapacious and ruthless jolly good fellows.

'The Seven Deadly Sins. No. 7. The grave discourtesy of such a man as will beat his host's servant', *The Cherwell*, 24 November 1923, p. 116.

EXCURSION IN REALITY

I

THE COMMISSIONAIRE at Espinoza's restaurant seems to maintain under his particular authority all the most decrepit taxicabs in London. He is a commanding man; across his great chest the student of military medals may construe a tale of heroism and experience; Boer farms sink to ashes, fanatical Fuzzi-wuzzies hurl themselves to paradise, supercilious mandarins survey the smashing of their porcelain and rending of fine silk, in that triple row of decorations. He has only to run from the steps of Espinoza's to call to your service a vehicle as crazy as all the enemies of the King-Emperor.

Half-a-crown into the white cotton glove, because Simon Lent was too tired to ask for change. He and Sylvia huddled into the darkness on broken springs, between draughty windows. It had been an unsatisfactory evening. They had sat over their table until two because it was an extension night. Sylvia would not drink anything because Simon had said he was broke. So they sat for five or six hours, sometimes silent, sometimes bickering, sometimes exchanging listless greetings with the passing couples. Simon dropped Sylvia at her door; a kiss, clumsily offered, coldly accepted; then back to the attic flat, over a sleepless garage, for which Simon paid six guineas a week.

Outside his door they were sluicing a limousine. He squeezed round it and climbed the narrow stairs, that had once echoed to the whistling of ostlers, stamping down to stables before dawn. (Woe to young men in Mewses! Oh woe, to bachelors half in love, living on £800 a year!) There was a small heap of letters on his dressing-table, which had arrived that evening while he was dressing. He lit his gas fire and began to open them. Tailor's bill £56, hosier £43; a reminder that his club subscription for that year had not yet been paid; his account from Espinoza's with a note informing him that the terms were strict, net cash monthly,

73

and that no further credit would be extended to him; it "appeared from the books" of his bank that his last cheque overdrew his account £10 16s. beyond the limit of his guaranteed overdraft; a demand from the income-tax collector for particulars of his employees and their wages (Mrs. Shaw, who came in to make his bed and orange juice for 4s. 6d. a day); small bills for books, spectacles, cigars, hair lotion and Sylvia's last four birthday presents. (Woe to shops that serve young men in Mewses!)

The other part of his mail was in marked contrast to this. There was a box of preserved figs from an admirer in Fresno, California; two letters from young ladies who said they were composing papers about his work for their college literary societies, and would he send a photograph; press cuttings describing him as a "popular", "brilliant", "meteorically successful", and "enviable" young novelist; a request for the loan of two hundred pounds from a paralysed journalist; an invitation to luncheon from Lady Metroland; six pages of closely reasoned abuse from a lunatic asylum in the North of England. For the truth, which no one who saw into Simon Lent's heart could possibly have suspected, was that he was in his way and within his limits quite a famous young man.

There was a last letter with a typewritten address which Simon opened with little expectation of pleasure. The paper was headed with the name of a Film Studio in one of the suburbs of London. The letter was brief and business-like.

Dear Simon Lent (a form of address, he had noted before, largely favoured by the theatrical profession),

I wonder whether you have ever considered writing for the Films. We should value your angle on a picture we are now making. Perhaps you would meet me for luncheon to-morrow at the Garrick Club and let me know your reactions to this. Will you leave a message with my night-secretary some time before 8 a.m. to-morrow morning or with my day-secretary after that hour.

                                 Cordially yours,

Below this were two words written in pen and ink which seemed to be *Jewee Mecceee* with below them the explanatory typescript (*Sir James Macrae*).

Simon read this through twice. Then he rang up Sir James Macrae and informed his night-secretary that he would keep the luncheon appointment next day. He had barely put down the telephone before the bell rang.

"This is Sir James Macrae's night-secretary speaking. Sir James would be very pleased if Mr. Lent would come round and see him this evening at his house in Hampstead."

Simon looked at his watch. It was nearly three. "Well ... it's rather late to go so far to-night ..."

"Sir James is sending a car for you."

Simon was no longer tired. As he waited for the car the telephone rang again. "Simon," said Sylvia's voice; "are you asleep?"

"No, in fact I'm just going out."

"*Simon* . . . I say, was I beastly to-night?"

"Lousy."

"Well, I thought you were lousy too."

"Never mind. See you sometime."

"Aren't you going to go on talking?"

"Can't, I'm afraid. I've got to do some work."

"*Simon*, what *can* you mean?"

"Can't explain now. There's a car waiting."

"When am I seeing you – to-morrow?"

"Well, I don't really know. Ring me up in the morning. Good night."

A quarter of a mile away, Sylvia put down the telephone, rose from the hearthrug, where she had settled herself in the expectation of twenty minutes' intimate explanation and crept disconsolately into bed.

Simon bowled off to Hampstead through deserted streets. He sat back in the car in a state of pleasant excitement. Presently they began to climb the steep little hill and emerged into an open space with a pond and the tops of trees, black and deep as a jungle in the darkness. The night-butler admitted him to the low Georgian house and led him to the library, where Sir James Macrae was standing before the fire, dressed in ginger-coloured plus fours. A table was laid with supper.

"Evening, Lent. Nice of you to come. Have to fit in business when I can. Cocoa or whisky? Have some rabbit pie, it's rather good. First chance of a meal I've had since breakfast. Ring for some more cocoa, there's a good chap. Now what was it you wanted to see me about?"

"Well, I thought *you* wanted to see *me*."

"Did I? Very likely. Miss Bentham'll know. She arranged the appointment. You might ring the bell on the desk, will you?"

Simon rang and there instantly appeared the neat night-secretary.

"Miss Bentham, what did I want to see Mr. Lent about?"

"I'm afraid I couldn't say, Sir James. Miss Harper is responsible for Mr. Lent. When I came on duty this evening I merely found a note from her asking me to fix an appointment as soon as possible."

"Pity," said Sir James. "We'll have to wait until Miss Harper comes on to-morrow."

"I think it was something about writing for films."

"Very likely," said Sir James. "Sure to be something of the kind. I'll let you know without delay. Thanks for dropping in." He put down his cup of cocoa and held out his hand with unaffected cordiality. "Good night, my dear boy." He rang the bell for the night-butler. "Sanders, I want Benson to run Mr. Lent back."

"I'm sorry, sir. Benson has just gone down to the studio to fetch Miss Grits."

"Pity," said Sir James. "Still, I expect you'll be able to pick up a taxi or something."

II

Simon got to bed at half-past four. At ten minutes past eight the telephone by his bed was ringing.

"Mr. Lent? This is Sir James Macrae's secretary speaking. Sir James's car will call for you at half-past eight to take you to the studio."

"I shan't be ready as soon as that, I'm afraid."

There was a shocked pause; then, the day-secretary said: "Very well, Mr. Lent. I will see if some alternative arrangement is possible and ring you in a few minutes."

In the intervening time Simon fell asleep again. Then the bell woke him once more and the same impersonal voice addressed him.

"Mr. Lent? I have spoken to Sir James. His car will call for you at eight forty-five."

Simon dressed hastily. Mrs. Shaw had not yet arrived, so there was no breakfast for him. He found some stale cake in the kitchen cupboard and was eating it when Sir James's car arrived. He took a slice down with him, still munching.

"You needn't have brought that," said a severe voice from inside the car. "Sir James has sent you some breakfast. Get in quickly; we're late."

In the corner, huddled in rugs, sat a young woman in a jaunty red hat; she had bright eyes and a very firm mouth.

"I expect that you are Miss Harper."

"No. I'm Elfreda Grits. We're working together on this film, I believe. I've been up all night with Sir James. If you don't mind I'll go to sleep for twenty minutes. You'll find a thermos of cocoa and some rabbit pie in the basket on the floor."

"Does Sir James live on cocoa and rabbit pie?"

"No; those are the remains of his supper. Please don't talk. I want to sleep."

Simon disregarded the pie, but poured some steaming cocoa into the metal cap of the thermos flask. In the corner, Miss Grits composed herself for sleep. She took off the jaunty red hat and laid it between them on the seat, veiled her eyes with two blue-pigmented lids and allowed the firm lips to relax and gape a little. Her platinum-blonde wind-swept head bobbed and swayed with the motion of the car as they swept out of London through converging and diverging tram lines. Stucco gave place to brick and the façades of the tube stations changed from tile to concrete; unoccupied building plots appeared and newly planted trees along unnamed avenues. Five minutes exactly before their arrival at the studio, Miss Grits opened her eyes, powdered her nose, touched her lips with red, and pulling her hat on to the side of her scalp, sat bolt upright, ready for another day.

Sir James was at work on the lot when they arrived. In a white-hot incandescent hell two young people were carrying on an infinitely tedious conversation at what was presumably the table of a restaurant. A dozen emaciated couples in evening dress danced listlessly behind them. At the other end of the huge shed some carpenters were at work building the façade of a Tudor manor house. Men in eye-shades scuttled in and out. Notices stood everywhere. *Do not Smoke. Do not Speak. Keep away from the high-power cable.*

Miss Grits, in defiance of these regulations, lit a cigarette, kicked some electric apparatus out of her path, said, "He's busy. I expect he'll see us when he's through with this scene," and disappeared through a door marked *No admittance.*

Shortly after eleven o'clock Sir James caught sight of Simon. "Nice of you to come. Shan't be long now," he called out to him. "Mr. Briggs, get a chair for Mr. Lent."

At two o'clock he noticed him again. "Had any lunch?"

"No," said Simon.

"No more have I. Just coming."

At half-past three Miss Grits joined him and said: "Well, it's been an easy day so far. You mustn't think we're always as slack as this. There's a canteen across the yard. Come and have something to eat."

An enormous buffet was full of people in a variety of costume and make-up. Disappointed actresses in languorous attitudes served cups of tea and hard-boiled eggs. Simon and Miss Grits ordered sandwiches and were about to eat them when a loud-speaker above their heads suddenly announced with alarming distinctness, "Sir James Macrae calling Mr. Lent and Miss Grits in the Conference Room."

"Come on, quick," said Miss Grits. She bustled him through

the swing doors, across the yard, into the office buildings and up a flight of stairs to a solid oak door marked *Conference. Keep out.*

Too late.

"Sir James has been called away," said the secretary. "Will you meet him at the West End office at five-thirty."

Back to London, this time by tube. At five-thirty they were at the Piccadilly office ready for the next clue in their treasure hunt. This took them to Hampstead. Finally at eight they were back at the studio. Miss Grits showed no sign of exhaustion.

"Decent of the old boy to give us a day off," she remarked. "He's easy to work with in that way – after Hollywood. Let's get some supper."

But as they opened the canteen doors and felt the warm breath of light refreshments, the loud-speaker again announced: "Sir James Macrae calling Mr. Lent and Miss Grits in the Conference Room."

This time they were not too late. Sir James was there at the head of an oval table; round him were grouped the chiefs of his staff. He sat in a greatcoat with his head hung forward, elbows on the table and his hands clasped behind his neck. The staff sat in respectful sympathy. Presently he looked up, shook himself and smiled pleasantly.

"Nice of you to come," he said. "Sorry I couldn't see you before. Lots of small things to see to on a job like this. Had dinner?"

"Not yet."

"Pity. Have to eat, you know. Can't work at full pressure unless you eat plenty."

Then Simon and Miss Grits sat down and Sir James explained his plan. "I want, ladies and gentlemen, to introduce Mr. Lent to you. I'm sure you all know his name already and I daresay some of you know his work. Well, I've called him in to help us and I hope that when he's heard the plan he'll consent to join us. I want to produce a film of *Hamlet*. I daresay you don't think that's a very original idea – but it's Angle that counts in the film world. I'm going to do it from an entirely new angle. That's why I've called in Mr. Lent. I want him to write dialogue for us."

"But, surely," said Simon, "there's quite a lot of dialogue there already?"

"Ah, you don't see my angle. There have been plenty of productions of Shakespeare in modern dress. We are going to produce him in modern speech. How can you expect the public to enjoy Shakespeare when they can't make head or tail of the dialogue. D'you know I began reading a copy the other day and blessed if *I* could understand it. At once I said, 'What the public wants is Shakespeare with all his beauty of thought and character translated into the language of everyday life.' Now Mr. Lent here was the man whose name naturally suggested itself. Many of the most high-class critics have commended Mr. Lent's dialogue. Now my idea is that Miss Grits here shall act in an advisory capacity, helping with the continuity and the technical side, and that Mr. Lent shall be given a free hand with the scenario . . ."

The discourse lasted for a quarter of an hour; then the chiefs of staff nodded sagely; Simon was taken into another room and given a contract to sign by which he received £50 a week retaining fee and £250 advance.

"You had better fix up with Miss Grits the times of work most suitable to you. I shall expect your first treatment by the end of the week. I should go and get some dinner if I were you. Must eat."

Slightly dizzy, Simon hurried to the canteen where two languorous blondes were packing up for the night.

"We've been on since four o'clock this morning," they said, "and the supers have eaten everything except the nougat. Sorry."

Sucking a bar of nougat Simon emerged into the now deserted studio. On three sides of him, to the height of twelve feet, rose in appalling completeness the marble walls of the scene-restaurant; at his elbow a bottle of imitation champagne still stood in its pail of melted ice; above and beyond extended the vast gloom of rafters and ceiling.

"*Fact*," said Simon to himself, "the world of action . . . the pulse of life . . . Money, hunger . . . *Reality*."

Next morning he was called with the words, "Two young ladies waiting to see you."

"Two?"

Simon put on his dressing-gown and, orange juice in hand, entered his sitting-room. Miss Grits nodded pleasantly.

"We arranged to start at ten," she said. "But it doesn't really matter. I shall not require you very much in the early stages. This is Miss Dawkins. She is one of the staff stenographers. Sir James thought you would need one. Miss Dawkins will be attached to you until further notice. He also sent two copies of *Hamlet*. When you've had your bath, I'll read you my notes for our first treatment."

But this was not to be; before Simon was dressed Miss Grits had been recalled to the studio on urgent business.

"I'll ring up and tell you when I am free," she said.

Simon spent the morning dictating letters to everyone he could think of; they began – "*Please forgive me for dictating this, but I am so busy just now that I have little time for personal correspondence . . .*" Miss Dawkins sat deferentially over her pad. He gave her Sylvia's number.

"Will you get on to this number and present my compliments to Miss Lennox and ask her to luncheon at Espinoza's . . . And book a table for two there at one forty-five."

"Darling," said Sylvia, when they met, "why were you out all yesterday and *who* was that voice this morning?"

"Oh, that was Miss Dawkins, my stenographer."

"Simon, what *can* you mean?"

"You see, I've joined the film industry."

"*Darling*. Do give me a job."

"Well, I'm not paying much attention to casting at the moment – but I'll bear you in mind."

"Goodness. How you've changed in two days!"

"Yes!" said Simon, with great complacency. "Yes, I think I have. You see, for the first time in my life I have come into contact with Real Life. I'm going to give up writing novels. It was a mug's game anyway. The written word is dead – first the papyrus, then the printed book, now the film. The artist must no longer work alone. He is part of the age in which he lives; he must share (only of course, my dear Sylvia, in very different proportions) the weekly wage envelope of the proletarian. Vital art implies a corresponding set of social relationships. Co-operation ... co-ordination ... the hive endeavour of the community directed to a single end ..."

Simon continued in this strain at some length, eating meantime a luncheon of Dickensian dimensions, until, in a small, miserable voice, Sylvia said: "It seems to me that you've fallen for some ghastly film star."

"O God," said Simon, "only a virgin could be as vulgar as that."

They were about to start one of their old, interminable quarrels when the telephone boy brought a message that Miss Grits wished to resume work instantly.

"So that's her name," said Sylvia.

"If you only knew how funny that was," said Simon, scribbling his initials on the bill and leaving the table while Sylvia was still groping with gloves and bag.

As things turned out, however, he became Miss Grits' lover before the week was out. The idea was hers. She suggested it to him one evening at his flat as they corrected the typescript of the final version of their first treatment.

"No, really," Simon said aghast. "No, really. It would be quite impossible. I'm sorry, but ..."

"Why? Don't you like women?"

"Yes, but ..."

"Oh, come along," Miss Grits said briskly. "We don't get much time for amusement ..." And later, as she packed their manuscripts into her attaché case she said, "We must do it again if we have time. Besides I find it's so much easier to work with a man if you're having an *affaire* with him."

III

For three weeks Simon and Miss Grits (he always thought of her by this name in spite of all subsequent intimacies) worked together in complete harmony. His life was re-directed and transfigured. No longer did he lie in bed, glumly preparing himself for the coming day; no longer did he say every morning 'I *must* get down to the country and finish that book' and every evening find himself slinking back to the same urban flat; no longer did he sit over supper tables with Sylvia, idly bickering; no more listless explanations over the telephone. Instead he pursued a routine of incalculable variety, summoned by telephone at all hours to conferences which rarely assembled; sometimes to Hampstead, sometimes to the studios, once to Brighton. He spent long periods of work pacing up and down his sitting-room, with Miss Grits pacing backwards and forwards along the other wall and Miss Dawkins obediently perched between them, as the two dictated, corrected and redrafted their scenario. There were meals at improbable times and vivid, unsentimental passages of love with Miss Grits. He ate irregular and improbable meals, bowling through the suburbs in Sir James's car, pacing the carpet dictating to Miss Dawkins, perched in deserted lots upon scenery which seemed made to survive the collapse of civilization. He lapsed, like Miss Grits, into brief spells of death-like unconsciousness, often awakening, startled, to find that a street or desert or factory had come into being about him while he slept.

The film meanwhile grew rapidly, daily putting out new shoots and changing under their eyes in a hundred unexpected ways. Each conference produced some radical change in the story. Miss Grits in her precise, unvariable voice would read out the fruits of their work. Sir James would sit with his head in his hand, rocking slightly from side to side and giving vent to occasional low moans and whimpers; round him sat the experts – production, direction, casting, continuity, cutting and costing managers, bright eyes, eager to attract the great man's attention with some apt intrusion.

"Well," Sir James would say, "I think we can O.K. that. Any suggestions, gentlemen?"

There would be a pause, until one by one the experts began to deliver their contributions... "I've been thinking, sir, that it won't do to have the scene laid in Denmark. The public won't stand for travel stuff. How about setting it in Scotland – then we could have some kilts and clan gathering scenes?"

"Yes, that's a very sensible suggestion. Make a note of that, Lent..."

"I was thinking we'd better drop this character of the Queen. She'd much better be dead before the action starts. She hangs up the action. The public won't stand for him abusing his mother."

"Yes, make a note of that, Lent."

"How would it be, sir, to make the ghost the Queen instead of the King..."

"Yes, make a note of that Lent..."

"Don't you think, sir, it would be better if Ophelia were Horatio's sister. More poignant, if you see what I mean."

"Yes, make a note of that..."

"I think we are losing sight of the essence of the story in the last sequence. After all, it is first and foremost a Ghost Story, isn't it?..."

And so from simple beginnings the story spread majestically. It was in the second week that Sir James, after, it must be admitted, considerable debate, adopted the idea of incorporating with it the story of *Macbeth*. Simon was opposed to the proposition at first, but the appeal of the three witches proved too strong. The title was then changed to *The White Lady of Dunsinane*, and he and Miss Grits settled down to a prodigious week's work in rewriting their entire scenarios.

IV

The end came as suddenly as everything else in this remarkable episode. The third conference was being held at an hotel in the New Forest where Sir James happened to be staying; the experts had assembled by train, car and motor-bicycle at a moment's notice and were tired and unresponsive. Miss Grits read the latest scenario; it took some time, for it had now reached the stage when it could be taken as "white script" ready for shooting. Sir James sat sunk in reflection longer than usual. When he raised his head, it was to utter the single word:

"No."

"No?"

"No, it won't do. We must scrap the whole thing. We've got much too far from the original story. I can't think why you need introduce Julius Cæsar and King Arthur at all."

"But, sir, they were your own suggestions at the last conference."

"Were they? Well, I can't help it. I must have been tired and not paying full attention . . . Besides, I don't like the dialogue. It misses all the poetry of the original. What the public wants is Shakespeare, the whole of Shakespeare and nothing but Shakespeare. Now this scenario you've written is all very well in its way – but it's not Shakespeare. I'll tell you what we'll do. We'll use the play exactly as he wrote it and record from that. Make a note of it, Miss Grits."

"Then you'll hardly require my services any more?" said Simon.

"No, I don't think I shall. Still, nice of you to have come."

Next morning Simon woke bright and cheerful as usual and was about to leap from his bed when he suddenly remembered the events of last night. There was nothing for him to do. An empty day lay before him. No Miss Grits, no Miss Dawkins, no scampering off to conferences or dictating of dialogue. He rang up Miss Grits and asked her to lunch with him.

"No, quite impossible, I'm afraid. I have to do the continuity for a scenario of St. John's Gospel before the end of the week. Pretty tough job. We're setting it in Algeria so as to get the atmosphere. Off to Hollywood next month. Don't suppose I shall see you again. Good-bye."

Simon lay in bed with all his energy slowly slipping away. Nothing to do. Well, he supposed, now was the time to go away to the country and get on with his novel. Or should he go abroad?

Some quiet café-restaurant in the sun where he could work out those intractable last chapters. That was what he would do...sometime...the end of the week perhaps.

Meanwhile he leaned over on his elbow, lifted the telephone and, asking for Sylvia's number, prepared himself for twenty-five minutes' acrimonious reconciliation.

' R.U.R. '

'Theatre' (column head cartoon), *The Isis*, 28 November 1923, p. 21 and thereafter.

INCIDENT IN AZANIA

Azania is a large, imaginary island off the East Coast of Africa; in character and history a combination of Zanzibar and Abyssinia. At the end of Black Mischief *the native administration was overthrown and a joint protectorate established by the British and French. Several of the characters in this story appeared in* Black Mischief.

I

THE UNION club at Matodi was in marked contrast to the hillside, bungalow dwellings of the majority of its members. It stood in the centre of the town, on the water front; a seventeenth-century Arab mansion built of massive whitewashed walls round a small court; latticed windows overhung the street from which, in former times, the women-folk of a great merchant had watched the passing traffic; a heavy door, studded with brass bosses gave entrance to the dark shade of the court, where a little fountain sprayed from the roots of an enormous mango; and an open staircase of inlaid cedar-wood led to the cool interior.

An Arab porter, clothed in a white gown scoured and starched like a Bishop's surplice, crimson sash and tarboosh, sat drowsily at the gate. He rose in reverence as Mr. Reppington, the magistrate, and Mr. Bretherton, the sanitary-inspector, proceeded splendidly to the bar.

In token of the cordiality of the Condominium, French officials were honorary members of the Club, and a photograph of a former French President ("We can't keep changing it," said Major Lepperidge, "every time the frogs care to have a shimozzle") hung in the smoking room opposite the portrait of the Prince of Wales; except on Gala nights, however, they rarely availed themselves of their privilege. The single French journal to which the Club subscribed was *La Vie Parisienne*, which, on this particular evening, was in the hands of a small man of plebeian appearance, sitting alone in a basket chair.

Reppington and Bretherton nodded their way forward. "Evening, Granger." "Evening, Barker." "Evening, Jagger," and then in an audible undertone Bretherton inquired, "Who's the chap in the corner with *La Vie?*"

"Name of Brooks. Petrol or something."

"Ah."

"Pink gin?"

"Ah."

"What sort of day?"

"Bad show, rather. Trouble about draining the cricket field. No subsoil."

"Ah. Bad show."

The Goan barman put their drinks before them. Bretherton signed the chit.

"Well, cheerioh."

"Cheerioh."

Mr. Brooks remained riveted upon *La Vie Parisienne.*

Presently Major Lepperidge came in, and the atmosphere stiffened a little. (He was O.C. of the native levy, seconded from India.)

"Evening, Major," from civilians. "Good evening, sir," from the military.

"Evening. Evening. Evening. Phew. Just had a very fast set of lawner with young Kentish. Hot service. Gin and lime. By the way, Bretherton, the cricket field is looking pretty seedy."

"I know. No subsoil."

"I say, that's a bad show. *No subsoil.* Well, do what you can, there's a good fellow. It looks terrible. Quite bare and a great lake in the middle."

The Major took his gin and lime and moved towards a chair; suddenly he saw Mr. Brooks, and his authoritative air softened to unaccustomed amiability. "Why, hallo, Brooks," he said. "How are you? Fine to see you back. Just had the pleasure of seeing your daughter at the tennis club. My missus wondered if you and she would care to come up and dine one evening. How about Thursday? Grand. She'll be delighted. Good-night you fellows. Got to get a shower."

The occurrence was sensational. Bretherton and Reppington looked at one another in shocked surprise.

Major Lepperidge, both in rank and personality, was the leading man in Matodi – in the whole of Azania indeed, with the single exception of the Chief Commissioner at Debra Dowa. It was inconceivable that Brooks should dine with Lepperidge. Bretherton himself had only dined there once and *he* was Government.

"Hullo, Brooks," said Reppington "Didn't see you there behind your paper. Come and have one."

"Yes, Brooks," said Bretherton. "Didn't know you were back. Have a jolly leave? See any shows?"

"It's very kind of you, but I must be going. We arrived on Tuesday in the *Ngoma*. No, I didn't see any shows. You see, I was down at Bournemouth most of the time."

"One before you go."

"No really, thanks, I must get back. My daughter will be waiting. Thanks all the same. See you both later."

Daughter...?

II

There were eight Englishwomen in Matodi, counting Mrs. Bretherton's two-year-old daughter; nine if you included Mrs. Macdonald (but no one *did* include Mrs. Macdonald who came from Bombay and betrayed symptoms of Asiatic blood. Besides, no one knew who Mr. Macdonald had been. Mrs. Macdonald kept an ill-frequented *pension* on the outskirts of the town named "The Bougainvillea"). All who were of marriageable age were married; they led lives under a mutual scrutiny too close and unremitting for romance. There were, however, seven unmarried Englishmen, three in Government service, three in commerce and one unemployed, who had fled to Matodi from his creditors in Kenya. (He sometimes spoke vaguely of "planting" or "prospecting", but in the meantime drew a small remittance each month and hung amiably about the Club and the tennis courts.)

Most of these bachelors were understood to have some girl at home; they kept photographs in their rooms, wrote long letters regularly, and took their leave with hints that when they returned they might not be alone. But they invariably were. Perhaps in precipitous eagerness for sympathy they painted too dark a picture of Azanian life; perhaps the Tropics made them a little addle-pated....

Anyway, the arrival of Prunella Brooks sent a wave of excitement through English society. Normally, as the daughter of Mr. Brooks, oil company agent, her choice would have been properly confined to the three commercial men – Mr. James, of the Eastern Exchange Telegraph Company, and Messrs. Watson and Jagger, of the Bank – but Prunella was a girl of such evident personal superiority, that in her first afternoon at the tennis courts, as has been shown above, she transgressed the shadow line effortlessly and indeed unconsciously, and stepped straight into the inmost sanctuary, the Lepperidge bungalow.

She was small and unaffected, an iridescent blonde, with a fresh skin, doubly intoxicating in contrast with the tanned and desiccated tropical complexions around her; with rubbery, puppyish limbs and a face which lit up with amusement at the most barren pleasantries; an air of earnest interest in the opinions and experiences of all she met; a natural *confidante*, with no disposition to make herself the centre of a group, but rather to tackle her friends one by one, in their own time, when they needed her; deferential and charming to the married women; tender, friendly, and mildly flirtatious with the men; keen on games but not so good as to shake masculine superiority; a devoted daughter denying herself any pleasure that might impair the smooth working of Mr. Brooks's home – "No, I *must* go now. I couldn't let father come home from the Club and not find me there to greet him" – in fact, just such a girl as would be a light and blessing in any outpost of the Empire. It was very few days before all at Matodi were eloquent of their good fortune.

Of course, she had first of all to be examined and instructed by the matrons of the colony, but she submitted to her initiation with so pretty a grace that she might not have been aware of the dangers of the ordeal. Mrs. Lepperidge and Mrs. Reppington put her through it. Far away in the interior, in the sunless secret places, where a twisted stem across the jungle track, a rag fluttering to the bough of a tree, a fowl headless and full spread by an old stump marked the taboo where no man might cross, the Sakuya women chanted their primeval litany of initiation; here on the hillside the no less terrible ceremony was held over Mrs. Lepperidge's tea table. First the questions; disguised and delicate over the tea cake but quickening their pace as the tribal rhythm waxed high and the table was cleared of tray and kettle, falling faster and faster like ecstatic hands on the taut cow-hide, mounting and swelling with the first cigarette; a series of urgent, peremptory interrogations. To all this Prunella responded with docile simplicity. The whole of her life, upbringing and education were exposed, examined and found to be exemplary; her mother's death, the care of an aunt, a convent school in the suburbs which had left her with charming manners, a readiness to find the right man and to settle down with him whenever the Service should require it; her belief in a limited family and European education, the value of sport, kindness to animals, affectionate patronage of men.

Then, when she had proved herself worthy of it, came the instruction. Intimate details of health and hygiene, things every young girl should know, the general dangers of sex and its particular dangers in the Tropics; the proper treatment of the other inhabitants of Matodi, etiquette towards ladies of higher rank, the leaving of cards.... "*Never* shake hands with natives, however well educated they think themselves. Arabs are quite different, many of them very like gentlemen ... no worse than a great many Italians, really ... Indians, luckily, you won't have to meet ... never allow native servants to see you in your dressing-gown ... and be *very* careful about curtains in the bathroom – *natives peep* ... never walk in the side streets alone – in fact you have no business in them at all ... never ride outside the compound alone. There have been several cases of bandits ... an American missionary only last year, but he was some kind of non-Conformist ... *We owe it to our men folk* to take no unnecessary

risks ... a band of brigands commanded by a Sakuya called
Joab ... the Major will soon clean him up when he gets the levy
into better shape ... they find their boots very uncomfortable at
present[1] ... meanwhile it is a very safe rule to take a *man* with you
everywhere. ..."

III

And Prunella was never short of male escort. As the weeks
passed it became clear to the watching colony that her choice had
narrowed down to two – Mr. Kentish, assistant native commissioner, and Mr. Benson, second lieutenant in the native levy; not
that she was not consistently charming to everyone else – even to
the shady remittance man and the repulsive Mr. Jagger – but by
various little acts of preference she made it known that Kentish
and Benson were her favourites. And the study of their innocent
romances gave a sudden new interest to the social life of the town.
Until now there had been plenty of entertaining certainly –
gymkhanas and tennis tournaments, dances and dinner parties,
calling and gossiping, amateur opera and church bazaars – but it
had been a joyless and dutiful affair. They knew what was
expected of Englishmen abroad; they had to keep up appear-
ances before the natives and their co-protectionists; they had to
have something to write home about; so they sturdily went
through the recurring recreations due to their station. But with
Prunella's coming a new lightness was in the air; there were more
parties and more dances and a point to everything. Mr. Brooks,
who had never dined out before, found himself suddenly popular,
and as his former exclusion had not worried him, he took his
present vogue as a natural result of his daughter's charm, was
pleased by it and mildly embarrassed. He realized that she would
soon want to get married and faced with equanimity the prospect
of his inevitable return to solitude.

Meanwhile Benson and Kentish ran neck and neck through
the crowded Azanian spring and no one could say with

1 See *Black Mischief*.

confidence which was leading – betting was slightly in favour of Benson, who had supper dances with her at the Caledonian and the Polo Club Balls – when there occurred the incident which shocked Azanian feeling to its core. Prunella Brooks was kidnapped.

The circumstances were obscure and a little shady. Prunella, who had never been known to infringe one jot or tittle of the local code, had been out riding alone in the hills. That was apparent from the first, and later, under cross-examination, her syce revealed that this had for some time been her practice, two or three times a week. The shock of her infidelity to rule was almost as great as the shock of her disappearance.

But worse was to follow. One evening at the Club, since Mr. Brooks was absent (his popularity had waned in the last few days and his presence made a painful restraint) the question of Prunella's secret rides was being freely debated, when a slightly fuddled voice broke into the conversation.

"It's bound to come out," said the remittance man from Kenya, "so I may as well tell you right away. Prunella used to ride with *me*. She didn't want us to get talked about, so we met on the Debra Dowa road by the Moslem Tombs. I shall miss those afternoons very much indeed," said the remittance man, a slight, alcoholic quaver in his voice, "and I blame myself to a great extent for all that has happened. You see, I must have had a little more to drink than was good for me that morning and it was very hot, so with one thing and another, when I went to change into riding breeches I fell asleep and did not wake up until after dinner time. And perhaps that is the last we shall ever see of her..." and two vast tears rolled down his cheeks.

This unmanly spectacle preserved the peace, for Benson and Kentish had already begun to advance upon the remittance man with a menacing air. But there is little satisfaction in castigating one who is already in the profound depths of self-pity and the stern tones of Major Lepperidge called them sharply to order. "Benson, Kentish, I don't say I don't sympathize with you boys and I know exactly what I'd do myself under the circumstances. The story we have just heard may or may not be the truth. In either case I think I know what we all feel about the teller. But that can wait. You'll have plenty of time to settle up when we've got Miss Brooks safe. That is our first duty."

Thus exhorted, public opinion again rallied to Prunella, and the urgency of her case was dramatically emphasized two days later by the arrival at the American Consulate of the Baptist missionary's right ear loosely done up in newspaper and string. The men of the colony – excluding, of course, the remittance man – got together in the Lepperidge bungalow and formed a committee of defence, first to protect the women who were still left to them and then to rescue Miss Brooks at whatever personal inconvenience or risk.

IV

The first demand for ransom came through the agency of Mr. Youkoumian. The little Armenian was already well known and, on the whole, well liked by the English community; it did them good to find a foreigner who so completely fulfilled their ideal of all that a foreigner should be. Two days after the foundation of the British Womanhood Protection Committee, he appeared at the Major's orderly room asking for a private audience, a cheerful, rotund, self-abasing figure, in a shiny alpaca suit, skull cap and yellow, elastic-sided boots.

"Major Lepperidge," he said, "you know me; all the gentlemen in Matodi know me. The English are my favourite gentlemen and the natural protectors of the under races all same as the League of Nations. Listen, Major Lepperidge, I ear things. Everyone trusts me. It is a no good thing for these black men to abduct English ladies. I fix it O.K."

To the Major's questions, with infinite evasions and circumlocutions, Youkoumian explained that by the agency of various cousins of his wife he had formed contact with an Arab, one of whose wives was the sister of a Sakuya in Joab's band; that Miss Brooks was at present safe and that Joab was disposed to talk business. "Joab make very stiff price," he said. "He want one undred thousand dollars, an armoured car, two machine guns, a undred rifles, five thousand rounds of ammunition, fifty orses, fifty gold wrist watches, a wireless set, fifty cases of whisky, free pardon and the rank of honorary colonel in the Azanian levy."

"That, of course, is out of the question."

The little Armenian shrugged his shoulders. "Oh, well, then he cut off Miss Brooks' ears all same as the American clergyman. Listen, Major, this is one damn awful no good country. I live ere forty years, I know. I been little man and I been big man in this country, all same rule for big and little. If native want anything you give it im quick, then work ell out of im and get it back later. Natives all damn fool men but very savage all same as animals. Listen, Major, I make best whisky in Matodi – Scotch, Irish, all brands I make im; I got very fine watches in my shop all same as gold, I got wireless set, – armoured car, orses, machine guns is for you to do. Then we clean up tidy bit fifty-fifty, no?"

V

Two days later Mr. Youkoumian appeared at Mr. Brooks's bungalow. "A letter from Miss Brooks," he said. "A Sakuya fellow brought it in. I give im a rupee."

It was an untidy scrawl on the back of an envelope.

> *Dearest Dad,*
> *I am safe at present and fairly well. On no account attempt to follow the messenger. Joab and the bandits would torture me to death. Please send gramophone and records. Do come to terms or I don't know what will happen.*
> *Prunella.*

It was the first of a series of notes which, from now on, arrived every two or three days through the agency of Mr. Youkoumian. They mostly contained requests for small personal possessions . . .

> *Dearest Dad,*
> *Not those records. The dance ones. . . . Please send face cream in pot in bathroom, also illustrated papers . . . the green silk pyjamas . . . Lucky Strike cigarettes . . . two light drill skirts and the sleeveless silk shirts . . .*

The letters were all brought to the Club and read aloud, and as the days passed the sense of tension became less acute, giving way to a general feeling that the drama had become prosaic.

"They are bound to reduce their price. Meanwhile the girl is safe enough," pronounced Major Lepperidge, voicing authoritatively what had long been unspoken in the minds of the community.

The life of the town began to resume its normal aspect – administration, athletics, gossip; the American missionary's second ear arrived and attracted little notice, except from Mr. Youkoumian, who produced an ear trumpet which he attempted to sell to the mission headquarters. The ladies of the colony abandoned the cloistered life which they had adopted during the first scare; the men became less protective and stayed out late at the Club as heretofore.

Then something happened to revive interest in the captive. Sam Stebbing discovered the cypher.

He was a delicate young man of high academic distinction, lately arrived from Cambridge to work with Grainger in the immigration office. From the first he had shown a keener interest than most of his colleagues in the situation. For a fortnight of oppressive heat he had sat up late studying the texts of Prunella's messages; then he emerged with the startling assertion that there was a cypher. The system by which he had solved it was far from simple. He was ready enough to explain it, but his hearers invariably lost hold of the argument and contented themselves with the solution.

" . . . you see you translate it into Latin, you make an anagram of the first and last words of the first message, the second and last but one of the third when you start counting from the centre onwards. I bet that puzzled the bandits . . ."

"Yes, old boy. Besides, none of them can read anyway . . ."

"Then in the fourth message you go back to the original system, taking the fourth word and the last but three . . ."

"Yes, yes, I see. Don't bother to explain any more. Just tell us what the message really says."

"It says, 'DAILY THREATENED WORSE THAN BREATH.'"

"Her system's at fault there, must mean 'death'; then there's a word I can't understand – PLZGF, no doubt the poor child was in great agitation when she wrote it, and after that TRUST IN MY KING."

This was generally voted a triumph. The husbands brought back the news to their wives.

" . . . Jolly ingenious the way old Stebbing worked it out. I won't bother to explain it to you. You wouldn't understand. Anyway, the result is clear enough. Miss Brooks is in terrible danger. We must all do something."

"But who would have thought of little Prunella being so clever . . ."

"Ah, I always said that girl had brains."

VI

News of the discovery was circulated by the Press agencies throughout the civilized world. At first the affair had received wide attention. It had been front page, with portrait, for two days, then middle page with portrait, then middle page half way down without portrait, and finally page three of the *Excess* as the story became daily less alarming. The cypher gave the story a new lease of life. Stebbing, with portrait, appeared on the front page. Ten thousand pounds was offered by the paper towards the ransom, and a star journalist appeared from the skies in an aeroplane to conduct and report the negotiations.

He was a tough young man of Australian origin and from the moment of his arrival everything went with a swing. The colony sunk its habitual hostility to the Press, elected him to the Club, and filled his leisure with cocktail parties and tennis tournaments. He even usurped Lepperidge's position as authority on world topics.

But his stay was brief. On the first day he interviewed Mr. Brooks and everyone of importance in the town, and cabled back a moving "human" story of Prunella's position in the heart of the colony. From now onwards to three millions or so of readers Miss Brooks became Prunella. (There was only one local celebrity whom he was unable to meet. Poor Mr. Stebbing had "gone under" with the heat and had been shipped back to England on sick leave in a highly deranged condition of nerves and mind.)

On the second day he interviewed Mr. Youkoumian. They sat down together with a bottle of mastika at a little round table behind Mr. Youkoumian's counter at ten in the morning. It was three in the afternoon before the reporter stepped out into the white-dust heat, but he had won his way. Mr. Youkoumian had promised to conduct him to the bandits' camp. Both of them were pledged to secrecy. By sundown the whole of Matodi was discussing the coming expedition, but the journalist was not embarrassed by any inquiries; he was alone that evening, typing out an account of what he expected would happen next day.

He described the start at dawn... "grey light breaking over the bereaved township of Matodi... the camels snorting and straining at their reins... the many sorrowing Englishmen to whom the sun meant only the termination of one more night of hopeless watching... silver dawn breaking in the little room where Prunella's bed stood, the coverlet turned down as she had left it on the fatal afternoon..." He described the ascent into the hills — "... luxuriant tropical vegetation giving place to barren scrub and bare rock..." He described how the bandits' messenger blindfolded him and how he rode, swaying on his camel through darkness, into the unknown. Then, after what seemed an eternity, the halt; the bandage removed from his eyes... the bandits' camp. "... twenty pairs of remorseless eastern eyes glinting behind ugly-looking rifles..." here he took the paper from his machine and made a correction; the bandits' lair was to be in a cave "... littered with bone and skins." ... Joab, the bandit chief, squatting in barbaric splendour, a jewelled sword across his knees. Then the climax of the story; Prunella bound. For some time he toyed with the idea of stripping her, and began to hammer out a vivid word-picture of her girlish frame shrinking in the shadows, Andromeda-like. But caution restrained him and he contented himself with "... her lovely, slim body marked by the hempen ropes that cut into her young limbs . . ." The con-cluding paragraphs related how despair suddenly melted to hope in her eyes as he stepped forward, handing over the ransom to the bandit chief and "in the name of the *Daily Excess* and the People of Great Britain restored her to her heritage of freedom".

It was late before he had finished, but he retired to bed with a sense of high accomplishment, and next morning deposited his manuscript with the Eastern Exchange Telegraph Company before setting out with Mr. Youkoumian for the hills.

The journey was in all respects totally unlike his narrative. They started, after a comfortable breakfast, surrounded by the well wishes of most of the British and many of the French colony, and instead of riding on camels they drove in Mr. Kentish's baby Austin. Nor did they even reach Joab's lair. They had not gone more than ten miles before a girl appeared walking alone on the track towards them. She was not very tidy, particularly about the hair, but, apart from this, showed every sign of robust well-being.

"Miss Brooks, I presume," said the journalist, unconsciously following a famous precedent. "But where are the bandits?"

Prunella looked inquiringly towards Mr. Youkoumian who, a few steps in the rear, was shaking his head with vigour. "This British newspaper writing gentleman," he explained, "e know all same Matodi gentlemen. E got the thousand pounds for Joab."

"Well, he'd better take care," said Miss Brooks, "the bandits are all round you. Oh you wouldn't see them, of course, but I don't mind betting that there are fifty rifles covering us at this moment from behind the boulders and bush and so on." She waved a bare, suntanned arm expansively towards the innocent-looking landscape. "I hope you've brought the money in gold."

"It's all here, in the back of the car, Miss Brooks."

"Splendid. Well, I'm afraid Joab won't allow you into his lair, so you and I will wait here, and Youkoumian shall drive into the hills and deliver it."

"But listen, Miss Brooks, my paper has put a lot of money into this story. I got to see that lair."

"I'll tell you all about it," said Prunella, and she did.

"There were three huts," she began, her eyes downcast, her hands folded, her voice precise and gentle as though she were repeating a lesson, "the smallest and the darkest was used as my dungeon."

The journalist shifted uncomfortably. "Huts," he said. "I had formed the impression that they were caves."

"So they were," said Prunella. "Hut is a local word for cave. Two lions were chained beside me night and day. Their eyes glared and I felt their foetid breath. The chains were of a length so that if I lay perfectly still I was out of their reach. If I had moved hand or foot . . ." She broke off with a little shudder . . .

By the time that Youkoumian returned, the journalist had material for another magnificent front-page splash.

"Joab has given orders to withdraw the snipers," Prunella announced, after a whispered consultation with the Armenian. "It is safe for us to go."

So they climbed into the little car and drove unadventurously back to Matodi.

VII

Little remains of the story to be told. There was keen enthusiasm in the town when Prunella returned, and an official welcome was organized for her on the subsequent Tuesday. The journalist took many photographs, wrote up a scene of homecoming that stirred the British public to the depths of its heart, and soon flew away in his aeroplane to receive congratulation and promotion at the *Excess* office.

It was expected that Prunella would now make her final choice between Kentish and Benson, but this excitement was denied to the colony. Instead, came the distressing intelligence that she was returning to England. A light seemed to have been extinguished in Azanian life, and in spite of avowed good wishes there was a certain restraint on the eve of her departure – almost of resentment, as though Prunella were guilty of disloyalty in leaving. The *Excess* inserted a paragraph announcing her arrival, headed ECHO OF KIDNAPPING CASE, but otherwise she seemed to have slipped unobtrusively from public attention. Stebbing, poor fellow, was obliged to retire from the service. His mind seemed permanently disordered and from now on he passed his time, harmlessly but unprofitably, in a private nursing home, working out hidden messages in Bradshaw's Railway Guide. Even in Matodi the kidnapping was seldom discussed.

One day six months later Lepperidge and Bretherton were sitting in the Club drinking their evening glass of pink gin. Banditry was in the air at the moment for that morning the now memberless trunk of the American missionary had been found at the gates of the Baptist compound.

"It's one of the problems we shall have to tackle," said Lepperidge. "A case for action. I am going to make a report of the entire matter."

Mr. Brooks passed them on his way out to his lonely dinner table; he was a rare visitor to the Club now; the petrol agency was uniformly prosperous and kept him late at his desk. He neither remembered nor regretted his brief popularity, but Lepperidge maintained a guilty cordiality towards him whenever they met.

"Evening, Brooks. Any news of Miss Prunella?"

"Yes, as a matter of fact I heard from her to-day. She's just been married."

"Well I'm blessed ... I hope you're glad. Anyone we know?"

"Yes, I am glad in a way, though of course I shall miss her. It's that fellow from Kenya who stayed here once; remember him?"

"Ah, yes, him? Well, well ... Give her my salaams when you write."

Mr. Brooks went downstairs into the still and odorous evening. Lepperidge and Bretherton were completely alone. The Major leant forward and spoke in husky, confidential tones.

"I say, Bretherton," he said. "Look here, there's something I've often wondered, strictly between ourselves, I mean. Did you ever think there was anything fishy about that kidnapping?"

"*Fishy*, sir?"

"Fishy."

"I think I know what you mean, sir. Well some of us *have* been thinking, lately . . ."

"Exactly."

"Not of course anything definite. Just what you said yourself, sir, *fishy.*"

"Exactly . . . Look here, Bretherton, I think you might pass the word round that it's not a thing to be spoken about, see what I mean? The missus is putting it round to the women too . . ."

"Quite, sir. It's not a thing one wants talked about . . . Arabs, I mean, and frogs."

"Exactly."

There was another long pause. At last Lepperidge rose to go. "I blame myself," he said. "We made a great mistake over that girl. I ought to have known better. After all, first and last when all's said and done, Brooks *is* a commercial wallah."

'Men Who Talk Too Much', *The Isis*, 14 June 1922, p. 18. [J.C.R. = Junior Common Room. The Union = the Oxford debating society. Scouts = college servants.]

BELLA FLEACE GAVE A PARTY

BALLINGAR IS four and a half hours from Dublin if you catch the early train from Broadstone Station and five and a quarter if you wait until the afternoon. It is the market town of a large and comparatively well-populated district. There is a pretty Protestant Church in 1820 Gothic on one side of the square and a vast, unfinished Catholic cathedral opposite it, conceived in that irresponsible medley of architectural orders that is so dear to the hearts of transmontane pietists. Celtic lettering of a sort is beginning to take the place of the Latin alphabet on the shop fronts that complete the square. These all deal in identical goods in varying degrees of dilapidation; Mulligan's Store, Flannigan's Store, Riley's Store, each sells thick black boots, hanging in bundles, soapy colonial cheese, hardware and haberdashery, oil and saddlery, and each is licensed to sell ale and porter for consumption on or off the premises. The shell of the barracks stands with empty window frames and blackened interior as a monument to emancipation. Someone has written *The Pope is a Traitor* in tar on the green pillar box. A typical Irish town.

Fleacetown is fifteen miles from Ballingar, on a direct uneven road through typical Irish country; vague purple hills in the far distance and towards them, on one side of the road, fitfully visible among drifting patches of white mist, unbroken miles of bog, dotted with occasional stacks of cut peat. On the other side the ground slopes up to the north, divided irregularly into spare fields by banks and stone walls over which the Ballingar hounds have some of their most eventful hunting. Moss lies on everything; in a rough green rug on the walls and banks, soft green velvet on the timber – blurring the transitions so that there is no knowing where the ground ends and trunk and masonry begin. All the way from Ballingar there is a succession of whitewashed cabins and a dozen or so fair-size farmhouses; but there is no gentleman's house, for all this was Fleace property in the days before the Land Commission. The demesne land is all that belongs to Fleacetown now, and this is let for pasture to neighbouring farmers. Only a few beds are cultivated in the walled kitchen garden; the rest has run to rot, thorned bushes barren of edible fruit spreading everywhere among weedy flowers reverting rankly to type. The hot-houses have been draughty skeletons for ten years. The great gates set in their Georgian arch are permanently padlocked, the lodges are derelict, and the line of the main drive is only just discernible through the meadows. Access to the house is half a mile further up through a farm gate, along a track befouled by cattle.

But the house itself, at the date with which we are dealing, was in a condition of comparatively good repair; compared, that is to say, with Ballingar House or Castle Boycott or Knode Hall. It did not, of course, set up to rival Gordontown, where the American Lady Gordon had installed electric light, central heating and a lift, or Mock House or Newhill, which were leased to sporting Englishmen, or Castle Mockstock, since Lord Mockstock married beneath him. These four houses with their neatly raked gravel, bathrooms and dynamos, were the wonder and ridicule of the country. But Fleacetown, in fair competition with the essentially Irish houses of the Free State, was unusually habitable.

Its roof was intact; and it is the roof which makes the difference between the second and third grade of Irish country houses. Once that goes you have moss in the bedrooms, ferns on the stairs and cows in the library, and in a very few years you have to move into the dairy or one of the lodges. But so long as he has, literally, a roof over his head, an Irishman's house is still his castle. There were weak bits in Fleacetown, but general opinion held that the leads were good for another twenty years and would certainly survive the present owner.

Miss Annabel Rochfort-Doyle-Fleace, to give her the full name under which she appeared in books of reference, though she was known to the entire countryside as Bella Fleace, was the last of her family. There had been Fleces and Fleysers living about Ballingar since the days of Strongbow, and farm buildings marked the spot where they had inhabited a stockaded fort two centuries before the immigration of the Boycotts or Gordons or Mockstocks. A family tree emblazed by a nineteenth-century genealogist, showing how the original stock had merged with the equally ancient Rochforts and the respectable though more recent Doyles, hung in the billiard-room. The present home had been built on extravagant lines in the middle of the eighteenth century, when the family, though enervated, was still wealthy and influential. It would be tedious to trace its gradual decline from fortune; enough to say that it was due to no heroic debauchery. The Fleaces just got unobtrusively poorer in the way that families do who make no effort to help themselves. In the last generations, too, there had been marked traces of eccentricity. Bella Fleace's mother – an O'Hara of Newhill – had from the day of her marriage until her death suffered from the delusion that she was a negress. Her brother, from whom she had inherited, devoted himself to oil painting; his mind ran on the simple subject of assassination and before his death he had executed pictures of practically every such incident in history from Julius Caesar to General Wilson. He was at work on a painting, his own murder, at the time of the troubles, when he was, in fact, ambushed and done to death with a shot-gun on his own drive.

It was under one of her brother's paintings – Abraham Lincoln in his box at the theatre – that Miss Fleace was sitting one colourless morning in November when the idea came to her to give a Christmas party. It would be unnecessary to describe her appearance closely, and somewhat confusing, because it seemed in contradiction to much of her character. She was over eighty, very untidy and very red; streaky grey hair was twisted behind her head into a horsy bun, wisps hung round her cheeks; her nose was prominent and blue veined; her eyes pale blue, blank and mad; she had a lively smile and spoke with a marked Irish intonation. She walked with the aid of a stick, having been lamed many years back when her horse rolled her among loose stones late in a long day with the Ballingar Hounds; a tipsy sporting doctor had completed the mischief, and she had not been able to ride again. She would appear on foot when hounds drew the Fleacetown coverts and loudly criticize the conduct of the huntsman, but every year fewer of her old friends turned out; strange faces appeared.

They knew Bella, though she did not know them. She had become a by-word in the neighbourhood, a much-valued joke.

"A rotten day," they would report. "We found our fox, but lost again almost at once. But we saw Bella. Wonder how long the old girl will last. She must be nearly ninety. My father remembers when she used to hunt – went like smoke, too."

Indeed, Bella herself was becoming increasingly occupied with the prospect of death. In the winter before the one we are talking of, she had been extremely ill. She emerged in April, rosy cheeked as ever, but slower in her movements and mind. She gave instructions that better attention must be paid to her father's and brother's graves, and in June took the unprecedented step of inviting her heir to visit her. She had always refused to see this young man up till now. He was an Englishman, a very distant cousin, named Banks. He lived in South Kensington and occupied himself in the Museum. He arrived in August and wrote long and very amusing letters to all his friends describing his visit, and later translated his experiences into a short story for the *Spectator*. Bella disliked him from the moment he arrived. He had horn-rimmed spectacles and a B.B.C. voice. He spent most of his time photographing the Fleacetown chimney-pieces and the moulding of the doors. One day he came to Bella bearing a pile of calf-bound volumes from the library.

"I say, did you know you had these?" he asked.

"I did," Bella lied.

"All first editions. They must be extremely valuable."

"You put them back where you found them."

Later, when he wrote to thank her for his visit – enclosing prints of some of his photographs – he mentioned the books again. This set Bella thinking. Why should that young puppy go poking round the house putting a price on everything? She wasn't dead yet, Bella thought. And the more she thought of it, the more repugnant it became to think of Archie Banks carrying off her books to South Kensington and removing the chimney-pieces and, as he threatened, writing an essay about the house for the *Architectural Review*. She had often heard that the books were valuable. Well, there were plenty of books in the library and she did not see why Archie Banks should profit by them. So she wrote a letter to a Dublin bookseller. He came to look through the library, and after a while he offered her twelve hundred pounds for the lot, or a thousand for the six books which had attracted Archie Banks's attention. Bella was not sure that she had the right to sell things out of the house; a wholesale clearance would be noticed. So she kept the sermons and military history which made up most of the collection, the Dublin bookseller went off with the first editions, which eventually fetched rather less than he had given, and Bella was left with winter coming on and a thousand pounds in hand.

It was then that it occurred to her to give a party. There were always several parties given round Ballingar at Christmas time, but of late years Bella had not been invited to any, partly because many of her neighbours had never spoken to her, partly because they did not think she would want to come, and partly because they would not have known what to do with her if she had. As a matter of fact she loved parties. She liked sitting down to supper in a noisy room, she liked dance music and gossip about which of the girls was pretty and who was in love with them, and she liked drink and having things brought to her by men in pink evening coats. And though she tried to console herself with contemptuous reflections about the ancestry of the hostesses, it annoyed her very much whenever she heard of a party being given in the neighbourhood to which she was not asked.

And so it came about that, sitting with the *Irish Times* under the picture of Abraham Lincoln and gazing across the bare trees of the park to the hills beyond, Bella took it into her head to give a party. She rose immediately and hobbled across the room to the bell-rope. Presently her butler came into the morning-room; he wore the green baize apron in which he cleaned the silver and in his hand he carried the plate brush to emphasize the irregularity of the summons.

"Was it yourself ringing?" he asked.

"It was, who else?"

"And I at the silver!"

"Riley," said Bella with some solemnity, "I propose to give a ball at Christmas."

"Indeed!" said her butler. "And for what would you want to be dancing at your age?" But as Bella adumbrated her idea, a sympathetic light began to glitter in Riley's eye.

"There's not been such a ball in the country for twenty-five years. It will cost a fortune."

"It will cost a thousand pounds," said Bella proudly.

The preparations were necessarily stupendous. Seven new servants were recruited in the village and set to work dusting and cleaning and polishing, clearing out furniture and pulling up carpets. Their industry served only to reveal fresh requirements; plaster mouldings, long rotten, crumbled under the feather brooms, worm-eaten mahogany floorboards came up with the tin tacks; bare brick was disclosed behind the cabinets in the great drawing-room. A second wave of the invasion brought painters, paperhangers and plumbers, and in a moment of enthusiasm Bella had the cornice and the capitals of the pillars in the hall regilded; windows were reglazed, banisters fitted into gaping sockets, and the stair carpet shifted so that the worn strips were less noticeable.

In all these works Bella was indefatigable. She trotted from drawing-room to hall, down the long gallery, up the staircase, admonishing the hireling servants, lending a hand with the lighter objects of furniture, sliding, when the time came, up and down the mahogany floor of the drawing-room to work in the French chalk. She unloaded chests of silver in the attics, found long-forgotten services of china, went down with Riley into the cellars to count the few remaining and now flat and acid bottles of champagne. And in the evenings when the manual labourers had retired exhausted to their gross recreations, Bella sat up far into the night turning the pages of cookery books, comparing the estimates of rival caterers, inditing long and detailed letters to the agents for dance bands and, most important of all, drawing up her list of guests and addressing the high double piles of engraved cards that stood in her escritoire.

Distance counts for little in Ireland. People will readily drive three hours to pay an afternoon call, and for a dance of such importance no journey was too great. Bella had her list painfully compiled from works of reference, Riley's more up-to-date social knowledge and her own suddenly animated memory. Cheerfully, in a steady childish handwriting, she transferred the names to the cards and addressed the envelopes. It was the work of several late sittings. Many of those whose names were transcribed were dead or bedridden; some whom she just remembered seeing as small children were reaching retiring age in remote corners of the globe; many of the houses she wrote down were blackened shells, burned during the troubles and never rebuilt; some had "no one living in them, only farmers". But at last, none too early, the last envelope was addressed. A final lap with the stamps and then later than usual she rose from the desk. Her limbs were stiff, her eyes dazzled, her tongue cloyed with the gum of the Free State post office; she felt a little dizzy, but she locked her desk that evening with the knowledge that the most serious part of the work of the party was over. There had been several notable and deliberate omissions from that list.

"What's all this I hear about Bella giving a party?" said Lady Gordon to Lady Mockstock. "I haven't had a card."

"Neither have I yet. I hope the old thing hasn't forgotten me. I certainly intend to go. I've never been inside the house. I believe she's got some lovely things."

With true English reserve the lady whose husband had leased Mock Hall never betrayed the knowledge that any party was in the air at all at Fleacetown.

As the last days approached Bella concentrated more upon her own appearance. She had bought few clothes of recent years, and the Dublin dressmaker with whom she used to deal had shut up shop. For a delirious instant she played with the idea of a journey to London and even Paris, and considerations of time

alone obliged her to abandon it. In the end she discovered a shop
to suit her, and purchased a very magnificent gown of crimson
satin; to this she added long white gloves and satin shoes. There
was no tiara, alas! among her jewels, but she unearthed large
numbers of bright, nondescript Victorian rings, some chains and
lockets, pearl brooches, turquoise earrings, and a collar of gar-
nets. She ordered a coiffeur down from Dublin to dress her hair.

On the day of the ball she woke early, slightly feverish with
nervous excitement, and wriggled in bed till she was called, restlessly rehearsing in her mind every detail of the arrangements.
Before noon she had been to supervise the setting of hundreds of
candles in the sconces round the ball-room and supper-room,
and in the three great chandeliers of cut Waterford glass; she had
seen the supper tables laid out with silver and glass and stood the
massive wine coolers by the buffet; she had helped bank the
staircase and hall with chrysanthemums. She had no luncheon
that day, though Riley urged her with samples of the delicacies
already arrived from the caterer's. She felt a little faint; lay down
for a short time, but soon rallied to sew with her own hands the
crested buttons on to the liveries of the hired servants.

The invitations were timed for eight o'clock. She wondered
whether that were too early – she had heard tales of parties that
began very late – but as the afternoon dragged on unendurably,
and rich twilight enveloped the house, Bella became glad that she
had set a short term on this exhausting wait.

At six she went up to dress. The hairdresser was there with a
bag full of tongs and combs. He brushed and coiled her hair and
whiffed it up and generally manipulated it until it became orderly
and formal and apparently far more copious. She put on all her
jewellery and, standing before the cheval glass in her room, could
not forbear a gasp of surprise. Then she limped downstairs.

The house looked magnificent in the candle-light. The band
was there, the twelve hired footmen, Riley in knee breeches and
black silk stockings.

It struck eight. Bella waited. Nobody came.

She sat down on a gilt chair at the head of the stairs, looked
steadily before her with her blank, blue eyes. In the hall, in the

cloakroom, in the supper-room, the hired footmen looked at one another with knowing winks. "What does the old girl expect? No one'll have finished dinner before ten."

The linkmen on the steps stamped and chafed their hands.

At half-past twelve Bella rose from her chair. Her face gave no indication of what she was thinking.

"Riley, I think I will have some supper. I am not feeling altogether well."

She hobbled slowly to the dining-room.

"Give me a stuffed quail and a glass of wine. Tell the band to start playing."

The *Blue Danube* waltz flooded the house. Bella smiled approval and swayed her head a little to the rhythm.

"Riley, I am really quite hungry. I've had nothing all day. Give me another quail and some more champagne."

Alone among the candles and the hired footmen, Riley served his mistress with an immense supper. She enjoyed every mouthful.

Presently she rose. "I am afraid there must be some mistake. No one seems to be coming to the ball. It is very disappointing after all our trouble. You may tell the band to go home."

But just as she was leaving the dining-room there was a stir in the hall. Guests were arriving. With wild resolution Bella swung herself up the stairs. She must get to the top before the guests were announced. One hand on the banister, one on her stick, pounding heart, two steps at a time. At last she reached the landing and turned to face the company. There was a mist before her eyes and a singing in her ears. She breathed with effort, but dimly she saw four figures advancing and saw Riley meet them and heard him announce:

"Lord and Lady Mockstock, Sir Samuel and Lady Gordon."

Suddenly the daze in which she had been moving cleared. Here on the stairs were the two women she had not invited – Lady Mockstock the draper's daughter, Lady Gordon the American.

She drew herself up and fixed them with her blank, blue eyes. "I had not expected this honour," she said. "Please forgive me if I am unable to entertain you."

The Mockstocks and the Gordons stood aghast; saw the mad blue eyes of their hostess, her crimson dress; the ball-room beyond, looking immense in its emptiness; heard the dance music echoing through the empty house. The air was charged with the scent of chrysanthemums. And then the drama and unreality of the scene were dispelled. Miss Fleace suddenly sat down, and holding out her hands to her butler, said, "I don't quite know what's happening."

He and two of the hired footmen carried the old lady to a sofa. She spoke only once more. Her mind was still on the same subject. "They came uninvited, those two . . . and nobody else."

A day later she died.

Mr. Banks arrived for the funeral and spent a week sorting out her effects. Among them he found in her escritoire, stamped, addressed, but unposted, the invitations to the ball.

'An Impression of the Union Library, A.D. 1922', *The Isis*, 18 October 1922, p. 20.

CRUISE

Letters from a Young Lady of Leisure

DARLING,
   Well I said I would write and so I would have only goodness
it was rough so didnt. Now everything is a bit more alright so I
will tell you. Well as you know the cruise started at Monte Carlo
and when papa and all of us went to Victoria we found that the
tickets didnt include the journey there so Goodness how furious
he was and said he wouldnt go but Mum said of course we must
go and we said that too only papa had changed all his money into
Liri or Franks on account of foreigners being so dishonest but he
kept a shilling for the porter at Dover being methodical so then he
had to change it back again and that set him wrong all the way to
Monte Carlo and he wouldnt get me and Bertie a sleeper and
wouldnt sleep himself in his through being so angry Goodness
how Sad.

   Then everything was much more alright the purser called him
Colonel and he likes his cabin so he took Bertie to the casino
and he lost and Bertie won and I think Bertie got a bit
plastered at least he made a noise going to bed he's in the next
cabin as if he were being sick and that was before we sailed. Bertie
has got some books on Baroque art on account of his being at
Oxford.

   Well the first day it was rough and I got up and felt odd in the
bath and the soap wouldnt work on account of salt water you see
and came into breakfast and there was a list of so many things
including steak and onions and there was a corking young man
who said we are the only ones down may I sit here and it was
going beautifully and he had steak and onions but it was no good
I had to go back to bed just when he was saying there was nothing
he admired so much about a girl as her being a good sailor
goodness how sad.

The thing is not to have a bath and to be very slow in all movements. So next day it was Naples and we saw some Bertie churches and then that bit that got blown up in an earthquake and a poor dog killed they have a plaster cast of him goodness how sad. Papa and Bertie saw some pictures we weren't allowed to see and Bill drew them for me afterwards and Miss P. tried to look too. I havent told you about Bill and Miss P. have I? Well Bill is rather old but clean looking and I dont suppose hes very old not really I mean and he's had a very disillusionary life on account of his wife who he says I wont say a word against but she gave him the raspberry with a foreigner and that makes him hate foreigners. Miss P. is called Miss Phillips and is lousy she wears a yachting cap and is a bitch. And the way she makes up to the second officer is no ones business and its clear to the meanest intelligence he hates her but its part of the rules that all the sailors have to pretend to fancy the passengers. Who else is there? Well a lot of old ones. Papa is having a walk out with one called Lady Muriel something or other who knew uncle Ned. And there is a honeymoon couple very embarrassing. And a clergyman and a lovely pansy with a camera and white suit and lots of families from the industrial north.

So Bertie sends his love too. XXXXXX etc.

Mum bought a shawl and an animal made of lava.

Post-card

This is a picture of Taormina. Mum bought a shawl here. V. funny because Miss P. got left as shed made chums only with second officer and he wasnt allowed ashore so when it came to getting into cars Miss P. had to pack in with a family from the industrial north.

S.S. *Glory of Greece*

Darling,

Hope you got P.C. from Sicily. The moral of that was not to make chums with sailors though who I've made a chum of is the purser who's different on account he leads a very cynical life with a gramophone in his cabin and as many cocktails as he likes and welsh rabbits sometimes and I said but do you pay for all these drinks but he said no so that's all right.

So we have three days at sea which the clergyman said is a good thing as it makes us all friendly but it hasn't made me friendly with Miss P. who won't leave poor Bill alone not taking any more chances of being left alone when she goes ashore. The purser says theres always someone like her on board in fact he says that about everyone except me who he says quite rightly is different goodness how decent.

So there are deck games they are hell. And the day before we reach Haifa there is to be a fancy dress dance. Papa is very good at the deck games expecially one called shuffle board and eats more than he does in London but I daresay its alright. You have to hire dresses for the ball from the barber I mean we do not you. Miss P. has brought her own. So I've thought of a v. clever thing at least the purser suggested it and that is to wear the clothes of one of the sailors I tried his on and looked a treat. Poor Miss P.

Bertie is madly unpop, he wont play any of the games and being plastered the other night too and tried to climb down a ventilator and the second officer pulled him out and the old ones at the captains table look *askance* at him. New word that. Literary yes? No?

So I think the pansy is writing a book he has a green fountain pen and green ink but I couldnt see what it was. XXXX Pretty good about writing you will say and so I am.

Post-card

This is a photograph of the Holyland and the famous sea of Gallillee. It is all v. Eastern with camels. I have a lot to tell you about the ball. *Such* goings on and will write very soon. Papa went off for the day with Lady M. and came back saying enchanting woman Knows the world.

S.S. *Glory of Greece*

Darling,

Well the Ball we had to come in to dinner in our clothes and everyone clapped as we came downstairs. So I was pretty late on account of not being able to make up my mind whether to wear the hat and in the end did and looked a corker. Well it was rather a faint clap for me considering so when I looked about there were about twenty girls and some women all dressed like me so how cynical the purser turns out to be. Bertie looked horribly dull as an apache. Mum and Papa were sweet. Miss P. had a ballet dress from the Russian ballet which couldnt have been more unsuitable so we had champagne for dinner and were jolly and they threw paper streamers and I threw mine before it was unrolled and hit Miss P. on the nose. Ha ha. So feeling matey I said to the steward isnt this fun and he said yes for them who hasnt got to clear it up goodness how Sad.

Well of course Bertie was plastered and went a bit far particularly in what he said to Lady M. then he sat in the cynical pursers cabin in the dark and cried so Bill and I found him and Bill gave him some drinks and what do you think he went off with Miss P. and we didnt see either of them again it only shows into what degradation the Demon Drink can drag you him I mean.

Then who should I meet but the young man who had steak and onions on the first morning and is called Robert and said I have been trying to meet you again all the voyage. Then I bitched him a bit goodness how Decent.

Poor Mum got taken up by Bill and he told her all about his wife and how she had disillusioned him with the foreigner so tomorrow we reach Port Said d.v. which is latin in case you didn't know meaning God Willing and all go up the nile and to Cairo for a week.

Will send P.C. of Sphinx.

XXXXXX

Post-card

This is the Sphinx. Goodness how Sad.

Post-card

This is temple of someone. Darling I cant wait to tell you I'm engaged to Arthur. Arthur is the one I thought was a pansy. Bertie thinks egyptian art is v. inartistic.

Post-card

This is Tutankhamens v. famous Tomb. Bertie says it is vulgar and is engaged to Miss P. so hes not one to speak and I call her Mabel now. G how S. Bill wont speak to Bertie Robert wont speak to me Papa and Lady M. seem to have had a row there was a man with a snake in a bag also a little boy who told my fortune which was v. prosperous Mum bought a shawl.

Post-card

Saw this Mosque today. Robert is engaged to a new girl called something or other who is lousy.

S.S. *Glory of Greece*

Darling,

Well so we all came back from Egypt pretty excited and the cynical purser said what news and I said *news* well Im engaged to Arthur and Bertie is engaged to Miss P. and she is called Mabel now which is hardest of all to bear I said and Robert to a lousy girl and Papa has had a row with Lady M. and Bill has had a row with Bertie and Roberts lousy girl was awful to me and Arthur was sweet but the cynical purser wasnt a bit surprised on account he said people always get engaged and have quarrels on the Egyptian trip every cruise so I said I wasnt in the habit of getting engaged lightly thank you and he said I wasnt apparently in the habit of going to Egypt so I wont speak to him again nor will Arthur.

All love.

S.S. *Glory of Greece*

Sweet,

This is Algiers *not* very eastern in fact full of frogs. So it is all off with Arthur I was right about him at the first but who I am engaged to is Robert which is *much* better for all concerned really particularly Arthur on account of what I said originally first impressions always right. Yes? No? Robert and I drove about all day in the Botanic gardens and Goodness he was Decent. Bertie got plastered and had a row with Mabel – Miss P. again – so thats all right too and Robert's lousy girl spent all day on board with second officer. Mum bought shawl. Bill told Lady M. about his disillusionment and she told Robert who said yes we all know so Lady M. said it was very unreticent of Bill and she had very little respect for him and didnt blame his wife or the foreigner.

Love.

Post-card

I forget what I said in my last letter but if I mentioned a lousy man called Robert you can take it as unsaid. This is still Algiers and Papa ate *dubious oysters* but is all right. Bertie went to a house full of tarts when he was plastered and is pretty unreticent about it as Lady M. would say.

Post-card

So now we are back and sang old lang syne is that how you spell it and I kissed Arthur but wont speak to Robert and he cried not Robert I mean Arthur so then Bertie apologized to most of the people hed insulted but Miss P. walked away pretending not to hear. Goodness what a bitch.

'The Great Club Problem', *The Isis*, 25 October 1922, p. 10. [O.U.D.S. = the Oxford University Dramatic Society.]

THE MAN WHO LIKED
DICKENS

ALTHOUGH Mr. McMaster had lived in Amazonas for nearly sixty years, no one except a few families of Shiriana Indians was aware of his existence. His house stood in a small savannah, one of those little patches of sand and grass that crop up occasionally in that neighbourhood, three miles or so across, bounded on all sides by forest.

The stream which watered it was not marked on any map; it ran through rapids, always dangerous and at most seasons of the year impassable, to join the upper waters of the River Urari-cuera, whose course, though boldly delineated in every school atlas, is still largely conjectural. None of the inhabitants of the district, except Mr. McMaster, had ever heard of the republic of Colombia, Venezuela, Brazil or Bolivia, each of whom had at one time or another claimed its possession.

Mr. McMaster's house was larger than those of his neighbours, but similar in character – a palm thatch roof, breast high walls of mud and wattle, and a mud floor. He owned the dozen or so head of puny cattle which grazed in the savannah, a plantation of cassava, some banana and mango trees, a dog, and, unique in the neighbourhood, a single-barrelled, breech-loading shotgun. The few commodities which he employed from the outside world came to him through a long succession of traders, passed from hand to hand, bartered for in a dozen languages at the extreme end of one of the longest threads in the web of commerce that spreads from Manáos into the remote fastness of the forest.

One day while Mr. McMaster was engaged in filling some cartridges, a Shiriana came to him with the news that a white man was approaching through the forest, alone and very sick. He closed the cartridge and loaded his gun with it, put those that were finished into his pocket and set out in the direction indicated.

The man was already clear of the bush when Mr. McMaster reached him, sitting on the ground, clearly in a very bad way. He was without hat or boots, and his clothes were so torn that it was only by the dampness of his body that they adhered to it; his feet were cut and grossly swollen, every exposed surface of skin was scarred by insect and bat bites; his eyes were wild with fever. He was talking to himself in delirium, but stopped when Mr. McMaster approached and addressed him in English.

"I'm tired," the man said; then: "Can't go any farther. My name is Henty and I'm tired. Anderson died. That was a long time ago. I expect you think I'm very odd."

"I think you are ill, my friend."

"Just tired. It must be several months since I had anything to eat."

Mr. McMaster hoisted him to his feet and, supporting him by the arm, led him across the hummocks of grass towards the farm.

"It is a very short way. When we get there I will give you something to make you better."

"Jolly kind of you." Presently he said: "I say, you speak English. I'm English, too. My name is Henty."

"Well, Mr. Henty, you aren't to bother about anything more. You're ill and you've had a rough journey. I'll take care of you."

They went very slowly, but at length reached the house.

"Lie there in the hammock. I will fetch something for you."

Mr. McMaster went into the back room of the house and dragged a tin canister from under a heap of skins. It was full of a mixture of dried leaf and bark. He took a handful and went outside to the fire. When he returned he put one hand behind Henty's head and held up the concoction of herbs in a calabash for him to drink. He sipped, shuddering slightly at the bitterness. At last he finished it. Mr. McMaster threw out the dregs on the floor. Henty lay back in the hammock sobbing quietly. Soon he fell into a deep sleep.

"Ill-fated" was the epithet applied by the press to the Anderson expedition to the Parima and upper Uraricuera region of

Brazil. Every stage of the enterprise from the preliminary arrangements in London to its tragic dissolution in Amazonas was attacked by misfortune. It was due to one of the early setbacks that Paul Henty became connected with it.

He was not by nature an explorer; an even-tempered, good-looking young man of fastidious tastes and enviable possessions, unintellectual, but appreciative of fine architecture and the ballet, well travelled in the more accessible parts of the world, a collector though not a connoisseur, popular among hostesses, revered by his aunts. He was married to a lady of exceptional charm and beauty, and it was she who upset the good order of his life by confessing her affection for another man for the second time in the eight years of their marriage. The first occasion had been a short-lived infatuation with a tennis professional, the second was a captain in the Coldstream Guards, and more serious.

Henty's first thought under the shock of this revelation was to go out and dine alone. He was a member of four clubs, but at three of them he was liable to meet his wife's lover. Accordingly he chose one which he rarely frequented, a semi-intellectual company composed of publishers, barristers, and men of scholarship awaiting election to the Athenaeum.

Here, after dinner, he fell into conversation with Professor Anderson and first heard of the proposed expedition to Brazil. The particular misfortune that was retarding arrangements at that moment was the defalcation of the secretary with two-thirds of the expedition's capital. The principals were ready – Professor Anderson, Dr. Simmons the anthropologist, Mr. Necher the biologist, Mr. Brough the surveyor, wireless operator and mechanic – the scientific and sporting apparatus was packed up in crates ready to be embarked, the necessary facilities had been stamped and signed by the proper authorities, but unless twelve hundred pounds was forthcoming the whole thing would have to be abandoned.

Henty, as has been suggested, was a man of comfortable means; the expedition would last from nine months to a year; he could shut his country house – his wife, he reflected, would want to remain in London near her young man – and cover more than the sum required. There was a glamour about the whole journey which might, he felt, move even his wife's sympathies. There and then, over the club fire, he decided to accompany Professor Anderson.

When he went home that evening he announced to his wife: "I have decided what I shall do."

"Yes, darling?"

"You are certain that you no longer love me?"

"*Darling*, you *know*, I *adore* you."

"But you are certain you love this guardsman, Tony what-ever-his-name-is, more?"

"Oh, yes, *ever* so much more. Quite a different thing altogether."

"Very well, then. I do not propose to do anything about a divorce for a year. You shall have time to think it over. I am leaving next week for the Uraricuera."

"Golly, where's that?"

"I am not perfectly sure. Somewhere in Brazil, I think. It is unexplored. I shall be away a year."

"But darling, how ordinary! Like people in books – big game, I mean, and all that."

"You have obviously already discovered that I am a very ordinary person."

"Now, Paul, don't be disagreeable – oh, there's the telephone. It's probably Tony. If it is, d'you mind terribly if I talk to him alone for a bit?"

But in the ten days of preparation that followed she showed greater tenderness, putting off her soldier twice in order to accompany Henty to the shops where he was choosing his equipment and insisting on his purchasing a worsted cummerbund. On his last evening she gave a supper party for him at the Embassy to which she allowed him to ask any of his friends he liked; he could think of no one except Professor Anderson, who looked oddly dressed, danced tirelessly and was something of a failure with everyone. Next day Mrs. Henty came with her husband to the boat train and presented him with a pale blue, extravagantly soft blanket, in a suède case of the same colour furnished with a zip fastener and monogram. She kissed him goodbye and said, "Take care of yourself in wherever it is."

Had she gone as far as Southampton she might have witnessed two dramatic passages. Mr. Brough got no farther than the gangway before he was arrested for debt – a matter of £32; the publicity given to the dangers of the expedition was responsible for the action. Henty settled the account.

The second difficulty was not to be overcome so easily. Mr. Necher's mother was on the ship before them; she carried a missionary journal in which she had just read an account of the Brazilian forests. Nothing would induce her to permit her son's departure; she would remain on board until he came ashore with her. If necessary, she would sail with him, but go into those forests alone he should not. All argument was unavailing with the resolute old lady, who eventually, five minutes before the time of embarkation, bore her son off in triumph, leaving the company without a biologist.

Nor was Mr. Brough's adherence long maintained. The ship in which they were travelling was a cruising liner taking passengers on a round voyage. Mr. Brough had not been on board a week and had scarcely accustomed himself to the motion of the ship before he was engaged to be married; he was still engaged, although to a different lady, when they reached Manáos and refused all inducements to proceed farther, borrowing his return fare from Henty and arriving back in Southampton engaged to the lady of his first choice, whom he immediately married.

In Brazil the officials to whom their credentials were addressed were all out of power. While Henty and Professor Anderson negotiated with the new administrators, Dr. Simmons proceeded up river to Boa Vista where he established a base camp with the greater part of the stores. These were instantly commandeered by the revolutionary garrison, and he himself imprisoned for some days and subjected to various humiliations which so enraged him that, when released, he made promptly for the coast, stopping at Manáos only long enough to inform his

colleagues that he insisted on leaving his case personally before
the central authorities at Rio.

Thus, while they were still a month's journey from the start of
their labours, Henty and Professor Anderson found themselves
alone and deprived of the greater part of their supplies. The
ignominy of immediate return was not to be borne. For a short
time they considered the advisability of going into hiding for six
months in Madeira or Tenerife, but even there detection seemed
probable; there had been too many photographs in the illustrated
papers before they left London. Accordingly, in low spirits, the
two explorers at last set out alone for the Uraricuera with little
hope of accomplishing anything of any value to anyone.

For seven weeks they paddled through green, humid tunnels
of forest. They took a few snapshots of naked, misanthropic
Indians; bottled some snakes and later lost them when their
canoe capsized in the rapids; they overtaxed their digestions,
imbibing nauseous intoxicants at native galas; they were robbed
of the last of their sugar by a Guianese prospector. Finally,
Professor Anderson fell ill with malignant malaria, chattered
feebly for some days in his hammock, lapsed into coma and
died, leaving Henty alone with a dozen Maku oarsmen, none
of whom spoke a word of any language known to him. They
reversed their course and drifted down stream with a minimum
of provisions and no mutual confidence.

One day, a week or so after Professor Anderson's death, Henty
awoke to find that his boys and his canoe had disappeared during
the night, leaving him with only his hammock and pyjamas some
two or three hundred miles from the nearest Brazilian habitation.
Nature forbade him to remain where he was although there
seemed little purpose in moving. He set himself to follow the
course of the stream, at first in the hope of meeting a canoe. But
presently the whole forest became peopled for him with frantic
apparitions, for no conscious reason at all. He plodded on, now
wading in the water, now scrambling through the bush.

Vaguely at the back of his mind he had always believed that
the jungle was a place full of food; that there was danger of snakes
and savages and wild beasts, but not of starvation. But now he

observed that this was far from being the case. The jungle consisted solely of immense tree trunks, embedded in a tangle of thorn and vine rope, all far from nutritious. On the first day he suffered hideously. Later he seemed anaesthetized and was chiefly embarrassed by the behaviour of the inhabitants who came out to meet him in footman's livery, carrying his dinner, and then irresponsibly disappeared or raised the covers of their dishes and revealed live tortoises. Many people who knew him in London appeared and ran round him with derisive cries, asking him questions to which he could not possibly know the answer. His wife came, too, and he was pleased to see her, assuming that she had got tired of her guardsman and was there to fetch him back; but she soon disappeared, like all the others.

It was then that he remembered that it was imperative for him to reach Manáos; he redoubled his energy, stumbling against boulders in the stream and getting caught up among the vines. "But I mustn't waste my strength," he reflected. Then he forgot that, too, and was conscious of nothing more until he found himself lying in a hammock in Mr. McMaster's house.

His recovery was slow. At first, days of lucidity alternated with delirium; then his temperature dropped and he was conscious even when most ill. The days of fever grew less frequent, finally occurring in the normal system of the tropics, between long periods of comparative health. Mr. McMaster dosed him regularly with herbal remedies.

"It's very nasty," said Henty, "but it does do good."

"There is medicine for everything in the forest," said Mr. McMaster; "to make you well and to make you ill. My mother was an Indian and she taught me many of them. I have learned others from time to time from my wives. There are plants to cure you and give you fever, to kill you and send you mad, to keep away snakes, to intoxicate fish so that you can pick them out of the water with your hands like fruit from a tree. There are medicines even I do not know. They say that it is possible to

bring dead people to life after they have begun to stink, but I have
not seen it done."

"But surely you are English?"

"My father was – at least a Barbadian. He came to British
Guiana as a missionary. He was married to a white woman but he
left her in Guiana to look for gold. Then he took my mother. The
Shiriana women are ugly but very devoted. I have had many.
Most of the men and women living in this savannah are my
children. That is why they obey – for that reason and because I
have the gun. My father lived to a great age. It is not twenty years
since he died. He was a man of education. Can you read?"

"Yes, of course."

"It is not everyone who is so fortunate. I cannot."

Henty laughed apologetically. "But I suppose you haven't
much opportunity here."

"Oh yes, that is just it. I have a great many books. I will show
you when you are better. Until five years ago there was an
Englishman – at least a black man, but he was well educated in
Georgetown. He died. He used to read to me every day until he
died. You shall read to me when you are better."

"I shall be delighted to."

"Yes, you shall read to me," Mr. McMaster repeated, nodding
over the calabash.

During the early days of his convalescence Henty had little
conversation with his host; he lay in the hammock staring up at
the thatched roof and thinking about his wife, rehearsing over
and over again different incidents in their life together, including
her affairs with the tennis professional and the soldier. The days,
exactly twelve hours each, passed without distinction. Mr.
McMaster retired to sleep at sundown, leaving a little lamp
burning – a hand-woven wick drooping from a pot of beef fat –
to keep away vampire bats.

The first time that Henty left the house Mr. McMaster took
him for a little stroll around the farm.

"I will show you the black man's grave," he said, leading him
to a mound between the mango trees. "He was very kind to me.
Every afternoon until he died, for two hours, he used to read to

me. I think I will put up a cross – to commemorate his death and your arrival – a pretty idea. Do you believe in God?"

"I've never really thought about it much."

"You are perfectly right. I have thought about it a *great* deal and I still do not know . . . Dickens did."

"I suppose so."

"Oh yes, it is apparent in all his books. You will see."

That afternoon Mr. McMaster began the construction of a headpiece for the negro's grave. He worked with a large spokeshave in a wood so hard that it grated and rang like metal.

At last when Henty had passed six or seven consecutive days without fever, Mr. McMaster said, "Now I think you are well enough to see the books."

At one end of the hut there was a kind of loft formed by a rough platform erected up in the eaves of the roof. Mr. McMaster propped a ladder against it and mounted. Henty followed, still unsteady after his illness. Mr. McMaster sat on the platform and Henty stood at the top of the ladder looking over. There was a heap of small bundles there, tied up with rag, palm leaf and raw hide.

"It has been hard to keep out the worms and ants. Two are practically destroyed. But there is an oil the Indians know how to make that is useful."

He unwrapped the nearest parcel and handed down a calf-bound book. It was an early American edition of *Bleak House*.

"It does not matter which we take first."

"You are fond of Dickens?"

"Why, yes, of course. More than fond, far more. You see, they are the only books I have ever heard. My father used to read them and then later the black man . . . and now you. I have heard them all several times by now but I never get tired; there is always more to be learned and noticed, so many characters, so many changes of scene, so many words . . . I have all Dickens's books except those that the ants devoured. It takes a long time to read them all – more than two years."

"Well," said Henty lightly, "they will well last out my visit."

"Oh, I hope not. It is delightful to start again. Each time I think I find more to enjoy and admire."

They took down the first volume of *Bleak House* and that afternoon Henty had his first reading.

He had always rather enjoyed reading aloud and in the first year of marriage had shared several books in this way with his wife, until one day, in one of her rare moments of confidence, she remarked that it was torture to her. Sometimes after that he had thought it might be agreeable to have children to read to. But Mr. McMaster was a unique audience.

The old man sat astride his hammock opposite Henty, fixing him throughout with his eyes, and following the words, soundlessly, with his lips. Often when a new character was introduced he would say, "Repeat the name, I have forgotten him," or, "Yes, yes, I remember her well. She dies, poor woman." He would frequently interrupt with questions; not as Henty would have imagined about the circumstances of the story – such things as the procedure of the Lord Chancellor's Court or the social conventions of the time, though they must have been unintelligible, did not concern him – but always about the characters. "Now, why does she say that? Does she really mean it? Did she feel faint because of the heat of the fire or of something in that paper?" He laughed loudly at all the jokes and at some passages which did not seem humorous to Henty, asking him to repeat them two or three times; and later at the description of the sufferings of the outcasts in "Tom-all-Alone's" tears ran down his cheeks into his beard. His comments on the story were usually simple. "I think that Dedlock is a very proud man," or, "Mrs. Jellyby does not take enough care of her children." Henty enjoyed the readings almost as much as he did.

At the end of the first day the old man said, "You read beautifully, with a far better accent than the black man. And you explain better. It is almost as though my father were here again." And always at the end of a session he thanked his guest courteously. "I enjoyed that very much. It was an extremely distressing chapter. But, if I remember rightly, it will all turn out well."

By the time that they were well into the second volume, however, the novelty of the old man's delight had begun to wane, and Henty was feeling strong enough to be restless. He touched more than once on the subject of his departure, asking about canoes and rains and the possibility of finding guides. But Mr. McMaster seemed obtuse and paid no attention to these hints.

One day, running his thumb through the pages of *Bleak House* that remained to be read, Henty said, "We still have a lot to get through. I hope I shall be able to finish it before I go."

"Oh yes," said Mr. McMaster. "Do not disturb yourself about that. You will have time to finish it, my friend."

For the first time Henty noticed something slightly menacing in his host's manner. That evening at supper, a brief meal of farine and dried beef eaten just before sundown, Henty renewed the subject.

"You know, Mr. McMaster, the time has come when I must be thinking about getting back to civilization. I have already imposed myself on your hospitality for too long."

Mr. McMaster bent over his plate, crunching mouthfuls of farine, but made no reply.

"How soon do you think I shall be able to get a boat? . . . I said how soon do you think I shall be able to get a boat? I appreciate all your kindness to me more than I can say, but . . ."

"My friend, any kindness I may have shown is amply repaid by your reading of Dickens. Do not let us mention the subject again."

"Well, I'm very glad you have enjoyed it. I have, too. But I really must be thinking of getting back . . ."

"Yes," said Mr. McMaster. "The black man was like that. He thought of it all the time. But he died here . . ."

Twice during the next day Henty opened the subject but his host was evasive. Finally he said, "Forgive me, Mr. McMaster, but I really must press the point. When can I get a boat?"

"There is no boat."

"Well, the Indians can build one."

"You must wait for the rains. There is not enough water in the river now."

"How long will that be?"

"A month . . . two months . . ."

They had finished *Bleak House* and were nearing the end of *Dombey and Son* when the rain came.

"Now it is time to make preparations to go."

"Oh, that is impossible. The Indians will not make a boat during the rainy season – it is one of their superstitions."

"You might have told me."

"Did I not mention it? I forgot."

Next morning Henty went out alone while his host was busy, and, looking as aimless as he could, strolled across the savannah to the group of Indian houses. There were four or five Shirianas sitting in one of the doorways. They did not look up as he approached them. He addressed them in the few words of Maku he had acquired during the journey but they made no sign whether they understood him or not. Then he drew a sketch of a canoe in the sand, he went through some vague motions of carpentry, pointed from them to him, then made motions of giving something to them and scratched out the outlines of a gun and a hat and a few other recognizable articles of trade. One of the women giggled, but no one gave any sign of comprehension, and he went away unsatisfied.

At their midday meal Mr. McMaster said, "Mr. Henty, the Indians tell me that you have been trying to speak with them. It is easier that you say anything you wish through me. You realize, do you not, that they would do nothing without my authority. They regard themselves, quite rightly in most cases, as my children."

"Well, as a matter of fact, I was asking them about a canoe."

"So they gave me to understand . . . and now if you have finished your meal perhaps we might have another chapter. I am quite absorbed in the book."

They finished *Dombey and Son*; nearly a year had passed since Henty had left England, and his gloomy foreboding of permanent exile became suddenly acute when, between the pages of *Martin Chuzzlewit*, he found a document written in pencil in irregular characters.

Year 1919

I James McMaster of Brazil do swear to Barnabas Washington of Georgetown that if he finish this book in fact Martin Chuzzlewit I will let him go away back as soon as finished.

There followed a heavy pencil *X*, and after it: *Mr. McMaster made this mark signed Barnabas Washington.*

"Mr. McMaster," said Henty. "I must speak frankly. You saved my life, and when I get back to civilization I will reward you to the best of my ability. I will give you anything within reason. But at present you are keeping me here against my will. I demand to be released."

"But, my friend, what is keeping you? You are under no restraint. Go when you like."

"You know very well that I can't get away without your help."

"In that case you must humour an old man. Read me another chapter."

"Mr. McMaster, I swear by anything you like that when I get to Manáos I will find someone to take my place. I will pay a man to read to you all day."

"But I have no need of another man. You read so well."

"I have read for the last time."

"I hope not," said Mr. McMaster politely.

That evening at supper only one plate of dried meat and farine was brought in and Mr. McMaster ate alone. Henty lay without speaking, staring at the thatch.

Next day at noon a single plate was put before Mr. McMaster, but with it lay his gun, cocked, on his knee, as he ate. Henty resumed the reading of *Martin Chuzzlewit* where it had been interrupted.

Weeks passed hopelessly. They read *Nicholas Nickleby* and *Little Dorrit* and *Oliver Twist*. Then a stranger arrived in the savannah, a half-caste prospector, one of that lonely order of men who wander for a lifetime through the forests, tracing the little streams, sifting the gravel and, ounce by ounce, filling the little leather sack of gold dust, more often than not dying of exposure and starvation with five hundred dollars' worth of gold hung around their necks. Mr. McMaster was vexed at his arrival, gave him

farine and *passo* and sent him on his journey within an hour of his
arrival, but in that hour Henty had time to scribble his name on a
slip of paper and put it into the man's hand.

From now on there was hope. The days followed their unvary-
ing routine; coffee at sunrise, a morning of inaction while Mr.
McMaster pottered about on the business of the farm, farine and
passo at noon, Dickens in the afternoon, farine and *passo* and
sometimes some fruit for supper, silence from sunset to dawn
with the small wick glowing in the beef fat and the palm thatch
overhead dimly discernible; but Henty lived in quiet confidence
and expectation.

Some time, this year or the next, the prospector would arrive
at a Brazilian village with news of his discovery. The disasters to
the Anderson expedition would not have passed unnoticed.
Henty could imagine the headlines that must have appeared in
the popular press; even now probably there were search parties
working over the country he had crossed; any day English voices
might sound over the savannah and a dozen friendly adventurers
come crashing through the bush. Even as he was reading, while
his lips mechanically followed the printed pages, his mind wandered away from his eager, crazy host opposite, and he began to
narrate to himself incidents of his homecoming – the gradual re-
encounters with civilization; he shaved and bought new clothes at
Manáos, telegraphed for money, received wires of congratulation; he enjoyed the leisurely river journey to Belem, the big liner
to Europe; savoured good claret and fresh meat and spring
vegetables; he was shy at meeting his wife and uncertain how to
address ... "*Darling*, you've been much longer than you said.
I quite thought you were lost ..."

And then Mr. McMaster interrupted. "May I trouble you to
read that passage again? It is one I particularly enjoy."

The weeks passed; there was no sign of rescue, but Henty
endured the day for hope of what might happen on the morrow;
he even felt a slight stirring of cordiality towards his gaoler and was
therefore quite willing to join him when, one evening after a long
conference with an Indian neighbour, he proposed a celebration.

"It is one of the local feast days," he explained, "and they have been making *piwari*. You may not like it, but you should try some. We will go across to this man's home to-night."

Accordingly after supper they joined a party of Indians that were assembled round the fire in one of the huts at the other side of the savannah. They were singing in an apathetic, monotonous manner and passing a large calabash of liquid from mouth to mouth. Separate bowls were brought for Henty and Mr. McMaster, and they were given hammocks to sit in.

"You must drink it all without lowering the cup. That is the etiquette."

Henty gulped the dark liquid, trying not to taste it. But it was not unpleasant, hard and muddy on the palate like most of the beverages he had been offered in Brazil, but with a flavour of honey and brown bread. He leant back in the hammock feeling unusually contented. Perhaps at that very moment the search party was in camp a few hours' journey from them. Meanwhile he was warm and drowsy. The cadence of song rose and fell interminably, liturgically. Another calabash of *piwari* was offered him and he handed it back empty. He lay full length watching the play of shadows on the thatch as the Shirianas began to dance. Then he shut his eyes and thought of England and his wife and fell asleep.

He awoke, still in the Indian hut, with the impression that he had outslept his usual hour. By the position of the sun he knew it was late afternoon. No one else was about. He looked for his watch and found to his surprise that it was not on his wrist. He had left it in the house, he supposed, before coming to the party.

"I must have been tight last night," he reflected. "Treacherous drink, that." He had a headache and feared a recurrence of fever. He found when he set his feet to the ground that he stood with difficulty; his walk was unsteady and his mind confused as it had been during the first weeks of his convalescence. On the way across the savannah he was obliged to stop more than once, shutting his eyes and breathing deeply. When he reached the house he found Mr. McMaster sitting there.

"Ah, my friend, you are late for the reading this afternoon. There is scarcely another half hour of light. How do you feel?"

"Rotten. That drink doesn't seem to agree with me."

"I will give you something to make you better. The forest has remedies for everything; to make you awake and to make you sleep."

"You haven't seen my watch anywhere?"

"You have missed it?"

"Yes. I thought I was wearing it. I say, I've never slept so long."

"Not since you were a baby. Do you know how long? Two days."

"Nonsense. I can't have."

"Yes, indeed. It is a long time. It is a pity because you missed our guests."

"Guests?"

"Why, yes. I have been quite gay while you were asleep. Three men from outside. Englishmen. It is a pity you missed them. A pity for them, too, as they particularly wished to see you. But what could I do? You were so sound asleep. They had come all the way to find you, so – I thought you would not mind – as you could not greet them yourself I gave them a little souvenir, your watch. They wanted something to take home to your wife who is offering a great reward for news of you. They were very pleased with it. And they took some photographs of the little cross I put up to commemorate your coming. They were pleased with that, too. They were very easily pleased. But I do not suppose they will visit us again, our life here is so retired . . . no pleasures except reading . . . I do not suppose we shall ever have visitors again . . . well, well, I will get you some medicine to make you feel better. Your head aches, does it not . . . We will not have any Dickens to-day . . . but to-morrow, and the day after that, and the day after that. Let us read *Little Dorrit* again. There are passages in that book I can never hear without the temptation to weep."

Dust jacket for *Labels, A Mediterranean Journal,* September 1930.

OUT OF DEPTH

I

RIP HAD got to the decent age when he disliked meeting new people. He lived a contented life between New York and the more American parts of Europe and everywhere, by choosing his season, he found enough of his old acquaintances to keep him effortlessly amused. For fifteen years at least he had dined with Margot Metroland during the first week of his visit to London, and he had always been sure of finding six or eight familiar and welcoming faces. It is true that there were also strangers, but these had passed before him and disappeared from his memory, leaving no more impression than a change of servants at his hotel.

To-night, however, as he entered the drawing-room, before he had greeted his hostess or nodded to Alastair Trumptington, he was aware of something foreign and disturbing. A glance round the assembled party confirmed his alarm. All the men were standing save one; these were mostly old friends interspersed with a handful of new, gawky, wholly inconsiderable young men, but the seated figure instantly arrested his attention and froze his bland smile. This was an elderly, large man, quite bald, with a vast white face that spread down and out far beyond the normal limits. It was like Mother Hippo in *Tiger Tim*; it was like an evening shirt-front in a du Maurier drawing; down in the depths of the face was a little crimson smirking mouth; and, above it, eyes that had a shifty, deprecating look, like those of a temporary butler caught out stealing shirts.

Lady Metroland seldom affronted her guests' reticence by introducing them.

"Dear Rip," she said, "it's lovely to see you again. I've got all the gang together for you, you see," and then noticing that his eyes were fixed upon the stranger, added, "Doctor Kakophilos,

135

this is Mr. Van Winkle. Doctor Kakophilos," she added, "is a
great magician. Norah brought him, I can't think why."

"Musician?"

"Magician. Norah says there's nothing he can't do."

"How do you do?" said Rip.

"Do what thou wilt shall be the whole of the law," said
Dr. Kakophilos, in a thin Cockney voice.

"Eh?"

"There is no need to reply. If you wish to, it is correct to say
'Love is the law, Love under will.' "

"I see."

"You are unusually blessed. Most men are blind."

"I tell you what," said Lady Metroland. "Let's all have some
dinner."

It took an hour's substantial eating and drinking before Rip
began to feel at ease again. He was well placed between two
married women of his own generation, with both of whom, at one
time and another, he had had affairs; but even their genial gossip
could not entirely hold his attention and he found himself continually gazing down the table to where, ten places away, Dr.
Kakophilos was frightening a pop-eyed débutante out of all
semblance of intelligence. Later, however, wine and reminiscence began to glow within him. He remembered that he had
been brought up a Catholic and had therefore no need to fear
black magic. He reflected that he was wealthy and in good health;
that none of his women had ever borne him ill-will (and what
better sign of good character was there than that?); that it was his
first week in London and that everyone he most liked seemed to
be there too; that the wine was so copious he had ceased to notice
its excellence. He got going well and soon had six neighbours
listening as he told some successful stories in his soft, lazy voice; he
became aware with familiar, electric tremors that he had captured the attention of a lady opposite on whom he had had his eye
last summer in Venice and two years before in Paris; he drank a
good deal more and didn't care a damn for Dr. Kakophilos.

Presently, almost imperceptibly to Rip, the ladies left the dining-room. He found himself with a *ballon* of brandy and a cigar, leaning back in his chair and talking for about the first time in his life to Lord Metroland. He was telling him about big game when he was aware of a presence at his other side, like a cold draught. He turned and saw that Dr. Kakophilos had come sidling up to him.

"You will see me home to-night," said the magician. "You and Sir Alastair?"

"Like hell I will," said Rip.

"Like hell," repeated Dr. Kakophilos, deep meaning resounding through his horrible Cockney tones. "I have need of you."

"Perhaps we ought to be going up," said Lord Metroland, "or Margot will get restless."

For Rip the rest of the evening passed in a pleasant daze. He remembered Margot confiding in him that Norah and that silly little something girl had had a scene about Dr. Kakophilos and had both gone home in rages. Presently the party began to thin until he found himself alone with Alastair Trumptington drinking whiskeys in the small drawing-room. They said good-bye and descended the stairs arm-in-arm. "I'll drop you, old boy."

"No, old boy, *I'll* drop *you*."

"I like driving at night."

"So do I, old boy."

They were on the steps when a cold Cockney voice broke in on their friendly discussion.

"Will you please drop *me*?" A horrible figure in a black cloak had popped out on them.

"Where do you want to go?" asked Alastair in some distaste.

Dr. Kakophilos gave an obscure address in Bloomsbury.

"Sorry, old boy, bang out of my way."

"And mine."

"But you said you liked driving at night."

"Oh God! All right, jump in."

And the three went off together.

Rip never quite knew how it came about that he and Alastair
went up to Dr. Kakophilos's sitting-room. It was certainly not for
a drink, because there was none there; nor did he know how it
was that Dr. Kakophilos came to be wearing a crimson robe
embroidered with gold symbols and a conical crimson hat. It only
came to him quite suddenly that Dr. Kakophilos *was* wearing
these clothes; and when it came it set him giggling, so
uncontrollably that he had to sit on the bed. And Alastair
began to laugh too, and they both sat on the bed for a long
time laughing.

But quite suddenly Rip found that they had stopped laughing
and that Dr. Kakophilos, still looking supremely ridiculous in his
sacerdotal regalia, was talking to them ponderously about time
and matter and spirit and a number of things which Rip had got
through forty-three eventful years without considering.

"And so," Dr. Kakophilos was saying, "you must breathe
the fire and call upon Omraz the spirit of release and journey
back through the centuries and recover the garnered wisdom
which the ages of reason have wasted. I chose you because you
are the two most ignorant men I ever met. I have too much
knowledge to risk my safety. If you never come back nothing will
be lost."

"Oh, I say," said Alastair.

"And what's more, you're tipsy," said Dr. Kakophilos relaps-
ing suddenly into everyday speech. Then he became poetic again
and Rip yawned and Alastair yawned.

At last Rip said: "Jolly decent of you to tell us all this, old boy;
I'll come in another time to hear the rest. Must be going now, you
know."

"Yes," said Alastair. "A most interesting evening."

Dr. Kakophilos removed his crimson hat and mopped his
moist, hairless head. He surveyed his parting guests with undisguised disdain.

"Sots," he said. "You are partakers in a mystery beyond your
comprehension. In a few minutes your drunken steps will have
straddled the centuries. Tell me, Sir Alastair," he asked, his face
alight with ghastly, facetious courtesy, "have you any preference

with regard to your translation? You may choose any age you like."

"Oh, I say, jolly decent of you . . . Never was much of a dab at History you know."

"Say."

"Well, any time really. How about Ethelred the Unready? – always had a soft spot for him."

"And you, Mr. Van Winkle?"

"Well, if I've got to be moved about, being an American, I'd sooner go forwards – say five hundred years."

Dr. Kakophilos drew himself up. "Do what thou wilt shall be the whole of the law."

"I can answer that one. 'Love is the law, Love under will.' "

"God, we've been a long time in that house," said Alastair as at length they regained the Bentley. "Awful old humbug. Comes of getting tight."

"Hell, I could do with another," said Rip. "Know anywhere?"

"I do," said Alastair and, turning a corner sharply, ran, broadside on, into a mail van that was thundering down Shaftesbury Avenue at forty-five miles an hour.

When Rip stood up, dazed but, as far as he could judge, without specific injury, he was scarcely at all surprised to observe that both cars had disappeared.

There was so much else to surprise him; a light breeze, a clear, star-filled sky, a wide horizon unobscured by buildings. The moon, in her last quarter, hung low above a grove of trees, illumined a slope of hummocky turf and a herd of sheep, peacefully cropping the sedge near Piccadilly Circus and, beyond, was reflected in a still pool, pierced here and there with reed.

Instinctively, for his head and eyes were still aflame from the wine he had drunk and there was a dry, stale taste in his mouth, Rip approached the water. His evening shoes sank deeper with each step and he paused, uncertain. The entrance of the Underground Station was there, transformed into a Piranesi ruin; a black aperture tufted about with fern and some crumbling steps leading down to black water. Eros had gone, but the pedestal rose above the reeds, moss grown and dilapidated.

"Golly," said Mr. Van Winkle slowly, "the twenty-fifth century."

Then he crossed the threshold of the underground station and, kneeling on the slippery fifth step, immersed his head in the water.

Absolute stillness lay all around him except for rhythmic, barely audible nibbling of the pastured sheep. Clouds drifted across the moon and Rip stood awed by the darkness; they passed and Rip stepped out into the light, left the grotto and climbed to a grass mound at the corner of the Haymarket.

To the south, between the trees, he could pick out the silver line of the river. Warily, for the ground was full of pits and crevices, he crossed what had once been Leicester and Trafalgar Squares. Great flats of mud, submerged at high water, stretched to his feet over the Strand, and at the margin of mud and sedge was a cluster of huts, built on poles; inaccessible because their careful householders had drawn up the ladders at sunset. Two camp fires, almost extinct, glowed red upon platforms of beaten earth. A ragged guard slept with his head on his knees. Two or three dogs prowled below the huts, nosing for refuse, but the breeze was blowing from the river bank and, though Rip had made some noise in his approach, they gave no alarm. Limitless calm lay on all sides among the monstrous shapes of grass-grown masonry and concrete. Rip crouched in a damp hollow and waited for day.

It was still night, darker from the setting of the moon, when the cocks began to crow – twenty or thirty of them, Rip judged – from the roosts under the village. The sentry came to life and raked over the embers sending up a spatter of wood sparks.

Presently a thin line of light appeared downstream, broadening into delicate summer dawn. Birds sang all round him. Tousled households appeared on the little platforms before the huts; women scratching their heads, shaking out blankets, naked children. They let down ladders of hide and stick; two or three women padded down to the river with earthenware pots to draw water; they hitched up their clothes to the waist and waded thigh deep.

From where Rip lay he could see the full extent of the village. The huts extended for half a mile or so, in a single line along the bank. There were about fifty of them; all of the same size and character, built of wattle and mud with skin-lined roofs; they seemed sturdy and in good repair. A dozen or more canoes were beached along the mud flats; some of them dug-out trees, others of a kind of basketwork covered in skins. The people were fair-skinned and fair-haired, but shaggy, and they moved with the loping gait of savages. They spoke slowly in the sing-song tones of an unlettered race who depend on oral tradition for the preservation of their lore.

Their words seemed familiar yet unintelligible. For more than an hour Rip watched the village come to life and begin the routine of its day, saw the cooking-pots slung over the fires, the men going down and muttering sagely over their boats as longshoremen do; saw the children scrambling down the supports of the houses to the refuse below – and for perhaps the first time in his life felt uncertain of what he should do. Then with as much resolution as he could muster, he walked towards the village.

The effect was instantaneous. There was a general scramble of women for their children, a general stampede for the ladders. The men at the boats stopped fiddling with tackle and came lumbering up the banks. Rip smiled and walked on. The men got together and showed no inclination to budge. Rip raised his clasped hands and shook them amicably in the air as he had seen boxers do when entering the ring. The shaggy white men made no sign of recognition.

"Good morning," said Rip. "Is this London?"

The men looked at each other in surprise, and one very old white beard giggled slightly. After a painful delay the leader nodded and said, "Lunnon". Then they cautiously encircled him until, growing bolder, they came right up to him and began to finger his outlandish garments, tapping his crumpled shirt with their horny nails and plucking at his studs and buttons.

The women meanwhile were shrieking with excitement in the house-tops. When Rip looked up to them and smiled, they dodged into the doorways, peeping out at him from the smoky interiors. He felt remarkably foolish and very dizzy. The men were discussing him; they squatted on their hams and began to debate, without animation or conviction. Occasional phrases came to him, "white", "black boss", "trade", but for the most part the jargon was without meaning. Rip sat down too. The voices rose and fell liturgically. Rip closed his eyes and made a desperate effort to wake himself from this preposterous nightmare. "I am in London, in nineteen-thirty-three, staying at the Ritz Hotel. I drank too much last night at Margot's. Have to go carefully in future. Nothing really wrong. I am in the Ritz in nineteen-thirty-three." He said it over and over again, shutting his senses to all outward impression, forcing his will towards sanity. At last, fully convinced, he raised his head and opened his eyes . . . early morning on the river, a cluster of wattle huts, a circle of impassive barbarous faces . . .

II

It is not to be supposed that one who has lightly skipped five hundred years would take great notice of the passage of days and nights. Often in Rip's desultory reading, he had struck such phrases as, "From then time ceased to have any reality for her"; at last he knew what they meant. There was a time when he lived under guard among the Londoners; they fed him on fish and coarse bread and heady, viscous beer; often, in the late afternoon when the work for the day was over, the village women would collect round him in a little circle, watching all his movements with an intent scrutiny; sometimes impatiently (once a squat young matron came up to him and suddenly tweaked his hair) but more often shyly – ready to giggle or take flight at any unusual movement.

This captivity may have lasted many days. He was conscious of restraint and strangeness; nothing else.

Then there was another impression; the coming of the boss.

A day of excitement in the village; the arrival of a large mechanically propelled boat, with an awning and a flag; a crew of
smart negroes, all wearing uniforms of leather and fur although
it was high summer; a commander among the negroes issuing
orders in a quiet supercilious voice. The Londoners brought out
sacks from their huts and spread on the beach the things they had
recovered from the ruins by digging – pieces of machinery and
ornament, china and glass and carved stonework, jewellery and
purposeless bits of things they hoped might have value. The
blacks landed bales of thick cloth, cooking utensils, fish-hooks,
knife-blades and axe-heads; discussion and barter followed, after
which the finds from the diggings were bundled up into the
launch. Rip was led forward and presented, turned round and
inspected; then he too was put in the launch.

A phantasmagoric journey downstream; Rip seated on the
cargo; the commander puffing imperturbably at a cigar. Now
and then they stopped at other villages, smaller than London,
but built on the same plan. Here curious Englishmen
crowded the banks and paddled in to stare at him until per-
emptorily told to keep their distance. The nightmare journey
continued.

Arrival at the coast; a large military station; uniforms of
leather and fur; black faces; flags; saluting. A pier with a large
steamer alongside; barracks and a government house. A negro
anthropologist with vast spectacles. Impressions became more
vivid and more brief; momentary illumination like flickering
lightning. Someone earnestly trying to talk to Rip. Saying
English words very slowly; reading to him from a book, familiar
words with an extraordinary accent; a black man trying to read
Shakespeare to Rip. Someone measured his skull with calipers.
Growing blackness and despair; restraint and strangeness;
moments of illumination rarer and more fantastic.

At night when Rip woke up and lay alone with his thoughts
quite clear and desperate, he said: "This is not a dream. It
is simply that I have gone mad." Then more blackness and
wildness.

The officers and officials came and went. There was a talk of sending him "home". "Home," thought Rip and beyond the next official town, vague and more distant, he saw the orderly succession of characterless, steam-heated apartments, the cabin trunks and promenade decks, the casinos and bars and supper restaurants, that were his home.

And then later – how much later he could not tell – something that was new and yet ageless. The word "Mission" painted on a board; a black man dressed as a Dominican friar... and a growing clearness. Rip knew that out of strangeness, there had come into being something familiar; a shape in chaos. Something was being done. Something was being done that Rip knew; something that twenty-five centuries had not altered; of his own childhood which survived the age of the world. In a log-built church at the coast town he was squatting among a native congregation; some of them in cast-off uniforms; the women had shapeless, convent-sewn frocks; all round him dishevelled white men were staring ahead with vague, uncomprehending eyes, to the end of the room where two candles burned. The priest turned towards them his bland, black face.

"Ite, missa est."

III

It was some days after the accident before Rip was well enough to talk. Then he asked for the priest who had been by his head when he recovered consciousness.

"What I can't understand, Father, is how you came to be there."

"I was called in to see Sir Alastair. He wasn't badly hurt, but he had been knocked unconscious. You both had a lucky escape. It was odd Sir Alastair asking for me. He isn't a Catholic, but he seems to have had some sort of dream while he was unconscious that made him want to see a priest. Then they told me you were here too, so I came along."

Rip thought for a little. He felt very dizzy when he tried to think.

"Alastair had a dream too, did he?"

"Apparently something about the Middle Ages. It made him ask for me."

"Father," said Rip, "I want to make a confession . . . I have experimented in black art . . ."

IMPROBABILITIES.

I. A well-known Old Etonian coxes the New College Eight.

II. Someone tries to make a joke at the International Assembly.

III. The O.S.C.U. have a ' blind.'

'Improbabilities', *The Isis*, 21 June 1922, p. 9. [O.S.C.U. = the Oxford Students' Christian Union.]

BY SPECIAL REQUEST

An alternative ending to *A Handful of Dust*

This was used in the serialized version. It takes the place of Chapters V, VI and VII and would begin at page 241 of the book. The entire Brazilian incident is thus omitted. Tony Last leaves London on the breakdown of his wife's arrangements for divorce, and goes on a prolonged and leisurely cruise.

THE NEXT WINTER

I

THE LINER came into harbour at Southampton, late in the afternoon.

They had left the sun three days behind them; after the Azores there had been a high sea running; in the Channel a white mist. Tony had been awake all night, disturbed by the fog signals and the uncertainty of home-coming.

They berthed alongside the quay. Tony leant on the rail looking for his chauffeur. He had cabled to Hetton that he was to be met and would drive straight home. He wanted to see the new bathrooms. Half the summer workmen had been at Hetton. There would be several changes to greet him.

It had been an uneventful excursion. Not for Tony were the ardours of serious travel, desert or jungle, mountain or pampas; he had no inclination to kill big game or survey unmapped tributaries. He had left England because, in the circumstances, it seemed the correct procedure, a convention hallowed in fiction and history by generations of disillusioned husbands. He had put himself in the hands of a travel agency and for lazy months had pottered from island to island in the West Indies, lunching at Government Houses, drinking swizzles on club verandahs, achieving an easy popularity at Captains' tables; he had played deck quoits and ping-pong, had danced on deck and driven with new acquaintances, on well-laid roads amid tropical vegetation. Now he was home again. He had thought less and less of Brenda during the passing weeks.

Presently he identified his chauffeur among the sparse population of the quay. The man came on board and took charge of the luggage. The car was waiting on the other side of the customs sheds.

The chauffeur said, "Shall I have the big trunk sent on by train?"

"There's plenty of room for it behind the car, isn't there?"

"Well, hardly, sir. Her ladyship has a lot of luggage with her."

"Her ladyship?"

"Yes, sir. Her ladyship is waiting in the car. She telegraphed that I was to pick her up at the hotel."

"I see. And she has a lot of luggage?"

"Yes, sir, an uncommon lot."

"Well . . . perhaps you *had* better send the trunks by train."

"Very good, sir."

So Tony went out to the car alone, while his chauffeur was seeing to the trunks.

Brenda was in the back, shrunk into the corner. She had taken off her hat – a very small knitted hat, clipped with a brooch he had given her some years ago – and was holding it in her lap. There was deep twilight inside the car. She looked up without moving her head.

"Darling," she said, "your boat was *very* late."

"Yes, we had fog in the channel."

"I got here last night. The people in the office said you'd be in early this morning."

"Yes, we *are* late."

"You can never tell with ships, can you?" said Brenda.

There was a pause. Then she said, "Aren't you going to come in?"

"There's a fuss about the luggage."

"Blake will see to that."

"He's sending it by train."

"Yes, I thought he would have to. I'm sorry I brought so much . . . You see, I brought everything. I've turned against that flat . . . It never quite lost the smell. I thought it was just newness, but it got worse. You know – *radiator smell*. So what with one thing and another I thought, how about giving it up."

Then the chauffeur came back. He had settled everything about the luggage.

"Well, we'd better start right away."

"Very good, sir."

Tony got in beside Brenda, and the chauffeur shut the door on them. They ran through the streets of Southampton and out into the country. The lamps were already alight behind the windows they passed.

"How did you know I was coming this afternoon?"

"I *thought* you were coming this morning. Jock told me."

"I didn't expect to see you."

"Jock said you'd be surprised."

"How *is* Jock?"

"Something awful happened to him, but I can't remember what. I think it was to do with politics – or it may have been a girl. I can't remember."

They sat far apart, each in a corner. Tony was very tired after his sleepless night. His eyes were heavy and the lights hurt them when the car passed through a bright little town.

"Have you been having a lovely time?"

"Yes. Have you?"

"No, rather lousy really. But I don't expect you want to hear about that."

"What are your plans?"

"Vague. What are yours?"

"Vague."

And then in the close atmosphere and gentle motion of the car, Tony fell asleep. He slept for two and a half hours, with his face half hidden in the collar of his overcoat. Once, as they stopped at a level crossing, he half woke up and asked, deep down in the tweed, "Are we there?"

"No, darling. *Miles* more."

And then he fell asleep again and woke to find them hooting at the lodge gates. He woke, too, to find that the question which neither he nor Brenda had asked, was answered. This should have been a crisis; his destinies had been at his control; there had been things to say, a decision to make, affecting every hour of his future life. *And he had fallen asleep.*

Ambrose was on the drawbridge to greet them. "Good evening, my lady. Good evening, sir. I hope you have had an agreeable voyage, sir."

"Most agreeable, thank you, Ambrose. Everything quite all right here?"

"Everything *quite* all right, sir. There are one or two small things, but perhaps I had better mention them in the morning."

"Yes, in the morning."

"Your correspondence is all in the library, sir."

"Thank you. I'll see to all that to-morrow."

They went into the great hall and upstairs. A large log fire was burning in Guinevere.

"The men only left last week, sir. I think you will find their work quite satisfactory."

While his suitcase was being unpacked, Tony and Brenda examined the new bathrooms. Tony turned on the taps.

"I haven't had the furnace lighted, sir. But it was lit the other day and the result was quite satisfactory."

"Let's not change," said Brenda.

"No. We'll have dinner right away, Ambrose."

During dinner, Tony talked about his trip; of the people he had met, and the charm of the scenery, the improvidence of the negro population, the fine flavour of the tropical fruits, the varying hospitality of the different Governors.

"I wonder if we could grow Avocado pears, here, under glass," he said.

Brenda did not say very much. Once he asked her, "Have you been away at all?" and she replied "Me? No. London all the time."

"How is everybody?"

"I didn't see many people. Polly's in America."

And that set Tony talking about the excellent administration in Haiti. "They've made a new place of it," he said.

After dinner they sat in the library. Tony surveyed the substantial pile of letters that had accumulated for him in his absence. "I can't do anything about that to-night," he said. "I'm so tired."

"Yes, let's go to bed soon."

There was a pause, and it was then that Brenda said, "You aren't still in a rage with me, are you?... over that nonsense with Mr. Beaver, I mean?"

"I don't know that I was ever in a rage."

"Oh yes you were. Just at the end you were, before you went away."

Tony did not answer.

"You aren't in a rage, *are* you? I hoped you weren't, when you went to sleep in the car."

Instead of answering, Tony asked, "What's become of Beaver?"

"It's rather a sad story, do you really want to hear it?"

"Yes."

"Well, I come out of it in a very small way. You see, I just couldn't hold him down. He got away almost the same time as you.

"You see, you didn't leave me with very much money, did you? And that made everything difficult because poor Mr. Beaver hadn't any either. So everything was *most* uncomfortable.... And then there was a club he wanted to join – Brown's – and they wouldn't have him in, and for some reason he held *that* against me, because he thought I ought to have made Reggie help more instead of what actually happened, which was that Reggie was the chief one to keep him out. Gentlemen are so funny about their clubs, I should have thought it was heaven to have Mr. Beaver there, but they didn't.

"And then Mrs. Beaver turned against me – she was always an old trout anyway – and I tried to get a job with her shop, but no, she wouldn't have me on account she thought I was doing harm to Beaver. And then I had a job with Daisy trying to get people to go to her restaurant, but that wasn't any good, and those I got didn't pay their bills.

"So there was I living on bits from the delicatessen shop round the corner, and no friends much except Jenny, and I got to hate her.

"Tony, it was a lousy summer.

"And then, finally, there was an American vamp called Mrs. Rattery — *you know*, the Shameless Blonde. Well, my Mr. Beaver met her and from that moment I was nowhere. Of course she was just his ticket and he was bats about her, only she never seemed to notice him, and every time he met her she forgot she'd seen him before, and that was hard cheese on Beaver, but it didn't make him any more decent to me. And he wore himself to a shadow chasing after her and getting no fun, till finally Mrs. Beaver sent him away and he's got some job to do with her shop buying things in Berlin or Vienna.

"So that's that . . . *Tony*, I believe you're falling asleep again."

"Well, I didn't get any sleep at all last night."

"Come on, let's go up."

II

That winter, shortly before Christmas, Daisy opened another restaurant. Tony and Brenda were in London for the day, so they went there to lunch. It was very full (Daisy's restaurants were often full, but it never seemed to make any effect on the resulting deficit). They went to their table nodding gaily to right and left.

"All the old faces," said Brenda.

A few places away sat Polly Cockpurse and Sybil with two young men.

"Who was that?"

"Brenda and Tony Last. I wonder what's become of them. They never appear anywhere now."

"They never did much."

"I had an idea they'd split."

"It doesn't look like it."

"Come to think of it, I *do* remember some talk last spring," said Sybil.

"Yes, I remember. Brenda had a fancy for someone quite extraordinary. I can't remember who it was, but I know it was someone quite extraordinary."

"Wasn't that her sister Marjorie?"

"Oh no, *hers* was Robin Beasley."

"Yes, of course . . . Brenda's looking pretty."

"Such a waste. But I don't think she'd ever have the energy now to get away."

At Brenda and Tony's table they were saying, "I wish *you'd* see her."

"No, you *must* see her."

"All right, I'll see her."

Tony had to go and see Mrs. Beaver about the flat. Ever since his return they had been trying to sublet it. Now Mrs. Beaver had informed them that there was a tenant in sight.

So while Brenda was at the doctor's (she was expecting a baby) Tony went round to the shop.

Mrs. Beaver was surrounded with a new sort of lampshade made of cellophane and cork.

"*How* are you, Mr. Last?" she said, rather formally. "We haven't met since that *delightful* week-end at Hetton."

"I hear you've found a tenant for the flat."

"Yes, I think so. A young cousin of Viola Chasm's. Of course I'm afraid you'll have to make some slight sacrifice. You see the flats have proved *too* popular, if you see what I mean. The demand was so brisk that a great many other firms came into the market and, as a result, rents have fallen. *Everyone* is taking flats of the kind now, but the speculative builders are letting them at competitive rents. The new tenant will only pay two pounds fifteen a week and he insists on its being entirely repainted. *We* will undertake that, of course. I think we can make a very nice job of it for fifty pounds or so."

"You know," said Tony, "I've been thinking. It's rather a useful thing to have – a flat of that kind."

"It is *necessary*," said Mrs. Beaver.

"Exactly. Well I think I shall keep it on. The only trouble is that my wife is inclined to fret a little about the rent. My idea is to use it when I come to London instead of my club. It will be cheaper and a great deal more convenient. But my wife may not see it in that light . . . in fact . . ."

"I *quite* understand."

"I think it would be better if my name didn't appear on that board downstairs."

"Naturally. A number of my tenants are taking the same precaution."

"So that's all right."

"That's quite satisfactory. I daresay you will want some little piece of extra furniture – a writing-table, for instance."

"Yes, I suppose I had better."

"I'll send one round. I think I know just what will suit you."

The table was delivered a week later. It cost eighteen pounds; on the same day there was a new name painted on the board below.

And for the price of the table Mrs. Beaver observed absolute discretion.

Tony met Brenda at Marjorie's house and they caught the evening train together.

"Did you get rid of the flat?" she asked.

"Yes, that's all settled."

"Mrs. Beaver decent?"

"*Very* decent."

"So that's the end of that," said Brenda.

And the train sped through the darkness towards Hetton.

SIC TRANSIT GLORIA MUNDI.

'Sic Transit Gloria Mundi', *The Isis*, 7 February 1923, p. 10. [Part of the *Great Bulldog Insurance Scheme* (see Introduction, p. xvii). The silhouetted figures are a Proctor and two Bulldogs, the University police.]

PERIOD PIECE

L ADY AMELIA had been educated in the belief that it was the height of impropriety to read a novel in the morning. Now, in the twilight of her days, when she had singularly little to occupy the two hours between her appearance downstairs at quarter past eleven, hatted and fragrant with lavender water, and the announcement of luncheon, she adhered rigidly to this principle. As soon as luncheon was over, however, and coffee had been served in the drawing-room; before the hot milk in his saucer had sufficiently cooled for Manchu to drink it; while the sunlight, in summer, streamed through the Venetian blinds of the round-fronted Regency windows; while, in winter, the carefully stacked coal-fire glowed in its round-fronted grate; while Manchu sniffed and sipped at his saucer, and Lady Amelia spread out on her knees the various shades of coarse wool with which her failing eyesight now compelled her to work; while the elegant Regency clock ticked off the two and a half hours to tea time – it was Miss Myers' duty to read a novel aloud to her employer.

With the passing years Lady Amelia had grown increasingly fond of novels, and of novels of a particular type. They were what the assistant in the circulating library termed "strong meat" and kept in a hidden place under her desk. It was Miss Myers' duty to fetch and return them. "Have you anything of the kind Lady Amelia likes?" she would ask sombrely.

"Well, there's this just come in," the assistant would answer, fishing up a volume from somewhere near her feet.

At one time Lady Amelia had enjoyed love stories about the irresponsible rich; then she had had a psychological phase; at the moment her interests were American, in the school of brutal realism and gross slang. "Something else like *Sanctuary* or *Bessie Cotter*," Miss Myers was reluctantly obliged to demand. And as the still afternoon was disturbed by her delicately modulated tones enunciating page by page, in scarcely comprehensible idiom, the narratives of rape and betrayal, Lady Amelia would occasionally chuckle a little over her woolwork.

"Women of my age always devote themselves either to religion or novels," she said. "I have remarked among my few surviving friends that those who read novels enjoy far better health."

The story they were reading came to an end at half-past four.

"Thank you," said Lady Amelia. "That was *most* entertaining. Make a note of the author's name, please, Miss Myers. You will be able to go to the library after tea and see whether they have another. I hope you enjoyed it."

"Well, it was very sad, wasn't it?"

"Sad?"

"I mean the poor young man who wrote it must come from a terrible home."

"Why do you say that, Miss Myers?"

"Well, it was so far fetched."

"It is odd you should think so. I invariably find modern novels painfully reticent. Of course until lately I never read novels at all. I cannot say what they were like formerly. I was far too busy in the old days living my own life and sharing the lives of my friends – all people who came from anything but terrible homes," she added with a glance at her companion; a glance sharp and smart as a rap on the knuckles with an ivory ruler.

There was half-an-hour before tea; Manchu was asleep on the hearth rug, before the fireless grate; the sun streamed in through the blinds, casting long strips of light on the Aubusson carpet. Lady Amelia fixed her eyes on the embroidered, heraldic firescreen; and proceeded dreamily. "I suppose it would not do. You couldn't write about the things which actually happen. People are so used to novels that they would not believe them. The poor writers are constantly at pains to make the truth seem probable. Dear me, I often think, as you sit, *so kindly*, reading to me, 'If one was just to write down quite simply the events of a few years in *any* household one knows ... No one would believe it.' I can hear you yourself, dear Miss Myers, saying, 'Perhaps these things *do* happen, very occasionally, once in a century, in terrible homes'; instead of which they are constantly happening, every day, all round us – or at least, they were in my young days.

"Take for example the extremely ironic circumstances of the succession of the present Lord Cornphillip:

"I used to know the Cornphillips very well in the old days," said Lady Amelia – "Etty was a cousin of my mother's – and when we were first married my husband and I used to stay there every autumn for the pheasant shooting. Billy Cornphillip was a *very* dull man – very dull indeed. He was in my husband's regiment. I used to know a great many dull people at the time when I was first married, but Billy Cornphillip was notorious for dullness even among my husband's friends. Their place is in Wiltshire. I see the boy is trying to sell it now. I am not surprised. It was very ugly and very unhealthy. I used to dread our visits there.

"Etty was entirely different, a lively little thing with very nice eyes. People thought her fast. Of course it was a *very* good match for her; she was one of seven sisters and her father was a younger son, poor dear. Billy was twelve years older. She had been after him for years. I remember crying with pleasure when I received her letter telling me of the engagement . . . It was at the breakfast table . . . she used a very artistic kind of writing paper with pale blue edges and bows of blue ribbon at the corner . . .

"Poor Etty was always being artistic; she tried to do something with the house – put up peacocks' feathers and painted tambourines and some very modern stencil work – but the result was always depressing. She made a little garden for herself at some distance from the house, with a high wall and a padlocked door, where she used to retire to think – or so she said – for hours at a time. She called it the Garden of Her Thoughts. I went in with her once, as a great privilege, after one of her quarrels with Billy. Nothing grew very well there – because of the high walls, I suppose, and her doing it all herself. There was a mossy seat in the middle. I suppose she used to sit on it while she thought. The whole place had a nasty dank smell . . .

"Well we were all delighted at Etty's luck and I think she quite liked Billy at first and was prepared to behave well to him, in spite of his dullness. You see it came just when we had all despaired.

Billy had been the friend of Lady Instow for a long time and we were all afraid she would never let him marry but they had a quarrel at Cowes that year and Billy went up to Scotland in a bad temper and little Etty was staying in the house; so everything was arranged and I was one of her bridesmaids.

"The only person who was not pleased was Ralph Bland. You see he was Billy's nearest relative and would inherit if Billy died without children and he had got very hopeful as time went on.

"He came to a very sad end – in fact I don't know *what* became of him – but at the time of which I am speaking he was extremely popular, especially with women … Poor Viola Chasm was terribly in love with him. Wanted to run away. She and Lady Anchorage were very jealous of each other about him. It became quite disagreeable, particularly when Viola found that Lady Anchorage was paying her maid five pounds a week to send on all Ralph's letters to her – *before* Viola had read them, that was what she minded. He really had a most agreeable manner and said such ridiculous things … The marriage was a great disappointment to Ralph; he was married himself and had two children. She had a little money at one time, but Ralph ran through it. Billy did not get on with Ralph – they had very little in common, of course – but he treated him quite well and was always getting him out of difficulties. In fact he made him a regular allowance at one time, and what with that and what he got from Viola and Lady Anchorage he was really quite comfortable. But, as he said, he had his children's future to consider, so that Billy's marriage *was* a *great* disappointment to him. He even talked of emigrating and Billy advanced him a large sum of money to purchase a sheep farm in New Zealand, but nothing came of that because Ralph had a Jewish friend in the city who made away with the entire amount. It all happened in a very unfortunate manner because Billy had given him this lump sum on the understanding that he should not expect an allowance. And then Viola and Lady Anchorage were greatly upset at his talk of leaving and made other arrangements so that in one way and another Ralph found himself in very low water, poor thing.

"However he began to recover his spirits when, after two years, there was no sign of an heir. People had babies very much more regularly when I was young. Everybody expected that Etty would have a baby – she was a nice healthy little thing – and when she did not, there was a great deal of ill-natured gossip. Ralph himself behaved very wrongly in the matter. He used to make jokes about it, my husband told me, quite openly at his club in the worst possible taste.

"I well remember the last time that Ralph stayed with the Cornphillips; it was a Christmas party and he came with his wife and his two children. The eldest boy was about six at the time and there was a very painful scene. I was not there myself, but we were staying nearby with the Lockejaws and of course we heard all about it. Billy seems to have been in his most pompous mood and was showing off the house when Ralph's little boy said solemnly and very loudly, 'Daddy says that when I step into your shoes I can pull the whole place down. The only thing worth worrying about is the money.'

"It was towards the end of a large and rather old-fashioned Christmas party, so no one was feeling in a forgiving mood. There was a final breach between the two cousins. Until then, in spite of the New Zealand venture, Billy had been reluctantly supporting Ralph. Now the allowance ceased once for all and Ralph took it in very bad part.

"You know what it is – or perhaps, dear Miss Myers, you are so fortunate as not to know what it is – when near relatives begin to quarrel. There is no limit to the savagery to which they will resort. I should be ashamed to indicate the behaviour of these two men towards each other during the next two or three years. No one had any sympathy with either.

"For example, Billy, of course, was a Conservative. Ralph came down and stood as a Radical in the General Election in his own county and got in.

"This, you must understand, was in the days before the lower classes began going into politics. It was customary for the candidates on both sides to be men of means and, in the circumstances, there was considerable expenditure involved. Much more in fact

than Ralph could well afford, but in those days Members of
Parliament had many opportunities for improving their position,
so we all thought it a very wise course of Ralph's – the first really
sensible thing we had known him do. What followed was *very*
shocking.

"Billy of course had refused to lend his interest – that was only
to be expected – but when the election was over, and everybody
perfectly satisfied with the result, he did what I always consider a
Very Wrong Thing. He made an accusation against Ralph of
corrupt practices. It was a matter of three pounds which Ralph
had given to a gardener whom Billy had discharged for drunkenness. I daresay that all that kind of thing has ceased nowadays,
but at the time to which I refer, it was universally customary. No
one had any sympathy with Billy but he pressed the charge and
poor Ralph was unseated.

"Well, after this time, I really think that poor Ralph became a
little unsettled in his mind. It is a very sad thing, Miss Myers,
when a middle-aged man becomes obsessed by a grievance. You
remember how difficult it was when the Vicar thought that
Major Etheridge was persecuting him. He actually informed
me that Major Etheridge put water in the petrol tank of his
motor-cycle and gave sixpences to the choir boys to sing out of
tune – well it was like that with poor Ralph. He made up his
mind that Billy had deliberately ruined him. He took a cottage in
the village and used to embarrass Billy terribly by coming to
all the village fêtes and staring at Billy fixedly. Poor Billy was
always embarrassed when he had to make a speech. Ralph used
to laugh ironically at the wrong places but never so loudly that
Billy could have him turned out. And he used to go to public
houses and drink far too much. They found him asleep on the
terrace twice. And of course no one on the place liked to offend
him, because at any moment he might become Lord Cornphillip.

"It must have been a very trying time for Billy. He and Etty
were not getting on at all well together, poor things, and she spent
more and more time in the Garden of Her Thoughts and brought

out a very silly little book of sonnets, mostly about Venice and Florence, though she could never induce Billy to take her abroad. He used to think that foreign cooking upset him.

"Billy forbade her to speak to Ralph, which was very awkward as they were always meeting one another in the village and had been great friends in the old days. In fact Ralph used often to speak very contemptuously of his cousin's manliness and say it was time someone took Etty off his hands. But that was only one of Ralph's jokes, because Etty had been getting terribly thin and dressing in the *most* artistic way, and Ralph *always* liked people who were chic and plump – like poor Viola Chasm. Whatever her faults –" said Lady Amelia, "Viola was always chic and plump.

"It was at the time of the Diamond Jubilee that the crisis took place. There was a bonfire and a great deal of merry making of a rather foolish kind and Ralph got terribly drunk. He began threatening Billy in a very silly way and Billy had him up before the magistrates and they made an order against him to keep the peace and not to reside within ten miles of Cornphillip. 'All right,' Ralph said, in front of the whole Court, 'I'll go away, but I won't go alone.' And will you believe it, Miss Myers, he and Etty went off to Venice together that very afternoon.

"Poor Etty, she had always wanted to go to Venice and had written so many poems about it, but it was a great surprise to us all. Apparently she had been meeting Ralph for some time in the Garden of Her Thoughts.

"I don't think Ralph ever cared about her, because, as I say, she was not at all his type, but it seemed to him a very good revenge on Billy.

"Well, the elopement was far from successful. They took rooms in a very insanitary palace, and had a gondola and ran up a great many bills. Then Etty got a septic throat as a result of the sanitation and while she was laid up Ralph met an American woman who was *much* more his type. So in less than six weeks poor Etty was back in England. Of course she did not go back to

Billy at once. She wanted to stay with us, but, naturally, that wasn't possible. It was very awkward for everyone. There was never, I think, any talk of a divorce. It was long before that became fashionable. But we all felt it would be very inconsiderate to Billy if we had her to stay. And then, this is what will surprise you, Miss Myers, the next thing we heard was that Etty was back at Cornphillip and about to have a baby. It was a son. Billy was very pleased about it and I don't believe that the boy ever knew, until quite lately, at luncheon with Lady Metroland, when my nephew Simon told him, in a rather ill-natured way.

"As for poor Ralph's boy, I am afraid he has come to very little good. He must be middle-aged by now. No one ever seems to hear anything of him. Perhaps he was killed in war. I cannot remember.

"And here comes Ross with the tray; and I see that Mrs. Samson has made more of those little scones which you always seem to enjoy so much. I am sure, dear Miss Myers, you would suffer much less from your *migraine* if you avoided them. But you take so little care of yourself, dear Miss Myers ... Give one to Manchu."

Mr John Greenidge's Book

Book-plate for Mr. John Greenidge.

ON GUARD

I

MILLICENT BLADE had a notable head of naturally fair hair; she had a docile and affectionate disposition, and an expression of face which changed with lightning rapidity from amiability to laughter and from laughter to respectful interest. But the feature which, more than any other, endeared her to sentimental Anglo-Saxon manhood was her nose.

It was not everybody's nose; many prefer one with greater body; it was not a nose to appeal to painters, for it was far too small and quite without shape, a mere dab of putty without apparent bone structure; a nose which made it impossible for its wearer to be haughty or imposing or astute. It would not have done for a governess or a 'cellist or even for a post office clerk, but it suited Miss Blade's book perfectly, for it was a nose that pierced the thin surface crust of the English heart to its warm and pulpy core; a nose to take the thoughts of English manhood back to its schooldays, to the doughy-faced urchins on whom it had squandered its first affection, to memories of changing room and chapel and battered straw boaters. Three Englishmen in five, it is true, grow snobbish about these things in later life and prefer a nose that makes more show in public – but two in five is an average with which any girl of modest fortune may be reasonably content.

Hector kissed her reverently on the tip of this nose. As he did so, his senses reeled and in momentary delirium he saw the fading light of the November afternoon, the raw mist spreading over the playing fields; overheated youth in the scrum; frigid youth at the touchline, shuffling on the duckboards, chafing their fingers and, when their mouths were emptied of biscuit crumbs, cheering their house team to further exertion.

"You will wait for me, won't you?" he said.

"Yes, darling."

"And you will write?"

"Yes, darling," she replied more doubtfully, "sometimes . . . at least I'll try. Writing is not my best thing, you know."

"I shall think of you all the time Out There," said Hector. "It's going to be terrible – miles of impassable waggon track between me and the nearest white man, blinding sun, lions, mosquitoes, hostile natives, work from dawn until sunset singlehanded against the forces of nature, fever, cholera . . . But soon I shall be able to send for you to join me."

"Yes, darling."

"It's bound to be a success. I've discussed it all with Beck-thorpe – that's the chap who's selling me the farm. You see the crop has failed every year so far – first coffee, then seisal, then tobacco, that's all you can grow there, and the year Beckthorpe grew seisal, everyone else was making a packet in tobacco, but seisal was no good; then he grew tobacco, but by then it was coffee he ought to have grown, and so on. He stuck it nine years. Well if you work it out mathematically, Beckthorpe says, in three years one's bound to strike the right crop. I can't quite explain why but it is like roulette and all that sort of thing, you see."

"Yes, darling."

Hector gazed at her little, shapeless, mobile button of a nose and was lost again . . . "Play up, play up," and after the match the smell of crumpets being toasted over a gas-ring in his study . . .

II

Later that evening he dined with Beckthorpe, and, as he dined, he grew more despondent.

"Tomorrow this time I shall be at sea," he said, twiddling his empty port glass.

"Cheer up, old boy," said Beckthorpe.

Hector filled his glass and gazed with growing distaste round the reeking dining-room of Beckthorpe's club. The last awful member had left the room and they were alone with the cold buffet.

"I say, you know, I've been trying to work it out. It *was* in three years you said the crop was bound to be right, wasn't it?"

"That's right, old boy."

"Well, I've been through the sum and it seems to me that it may be eighty-one years before it comes right."

"No, no, old boy, three or nine or at the most twenty-seven."

"Are you sure?"

"Quite."

"Good . . . you know it's awful leaving Milly behind. Suppose it *is* eighty-one years before the crop succeeds. It's the devil of a time to expect a girl to wait. Some other blighter might turn up, if you see what I mean."

"In the Middle Ages they used to use girdles of chastity."

"Yes, I know. I've been thinking of them. But they sound damned uncomfortable. I doubt if Milly would wear one even if I knew where to find it."

"Tell you what, old boy. You ought to give her something."

"Hell, I'm always giving her things. She either breaks them or loses them or forgets where she got them."

"You must give her something she will always have by her, something that will last."

"Eighty-one years?"

"Well, say, twenty-seven. Something to remind her of you."

"I could give her a photograph – but I might change a bit in twenty-seven years."

"No, no, that would be most unsuitable. A photograph wouldn't do at all. I know what I'd give her. I'd give her a dog."

"Dog?"

"A healthy puppy that was over distemper and looked like living a long time. She might even call it Hector."

"Would that be a good thing, Beckthorpe?"

"Best possible, old boy."

So next morning, before catching the boat train, Hector hurried to one of the mammoth stores of London and was shown to the livestock department. "I want a puppy."

"Yes, sir, any particular sort?"

"One that will live a long time. Eighty-one years, or twenty-seven at the least."

The man looked doubtful. "We have some fine healthy puppies of course," he admitted, "but none of them carry a guarantee. Now if it was longevity you wanted, might I recommend a tortoise? They live to an extraordinary age and are very safe in traffic."

"No, it must be a pup."

"Or a parrot?"

"No, no, a pup. I would prefer one named Hector."

They walked together past monkeys and kittens and cockatoos to the dog department which, even at this early hour, had attracted a small congregation of rapt worshippers. There were puppies of all varieties in wire-fronted kennels, ears cocked, tails wagging, noisily soliciting attention. Rather wildly, Hector selected a poodle and, as the salesman disappeared to fetch him his change, he leant down for a moment's intense communion with the beast of his choice. He gazed deep into the sharp little face, avoided a sudden snap and said with profound solemnity:

"You are to look after Milly, Hector. See that she doesn't marry anyone until I get back."

And the pup Hector waved his plume of tail.

III

Millicent came to see him off, but, negligently, went to the wrong station; it could not have mattered, however, for she was twenty minutes late. Hector and the poodle hung about the barrier looking for her, and not until the train was already moving did he bundle the animal into Beckthorpe's arms with instructions to deliver him at Millicent's address. Luggage labelled for Mombasa, "Wanted on the voyage", lay in the rack above him. He felt very much neglected.

That evening as the ship pitched and rolled past the Channel lighthouses, he received a radiogram: *Miserable to miss you went Paddington like idiot thank you thank you for sweet dog I love him father minds dreadfully longing to hear about farm dont fall for ship siren all love Milly.*

In the Red Sea he received another. *Beware sirens puppy bit man called Mike.*

After that Hector heard nothing of Millicent except for a Christmas card which arrived in the last days of February.

IV

Generally speaking, Millicent's fancy for any particular young man was likely to last four months. It depended on how far he had got in that time whether the process of extinction was sudden or protracted. In the case of Hector, her affection had been due to diminish at about the time that she became engaged to him; it had been artificially prolonged during the succeeding three weeks, during which he made strenuous, infectiously earnest efforts to find employment in England; it came to an abrupt end with his departure for Kenya. Accordingly the duties of the puppy Hector began with his first days at home. He was young for the job and wholly inexperienced; it is impossible to blame him for his mistake in the matter of Mike Boswell.

This was a young man who had enjoyed a wholly unromantic friendship with Millicent since she first came out. He had seen her fair hair in all kinds of light, in and out of doors, crowned in hats in succeeding fashions, bound with ribbon, decorated with combs, jauntily stuck with flowers; he had seen her nose uplifted in all kinds of weather, had even, on occasions, playfully tweeked it with his finger and thumb, and had never for one moment felt remotely attracted by her.

But the puppy Hector could hardly be expected to know this. All he knew was that two days after receiving his commission, he observed a tall and personable man of marriageable age who treated his hostess with the sort of familiarity which, among the kennel maids with whom he had been brought up, meant only one thing.

The two young people were having tea together. Hector watched for some time from his place on the sofa, barely stifling his growls. A climax was reached when, in the course of some barely intelligible back-chat, Mike leant forward and patted Millicent on the knee.

It was not a serious bite, a mere snap, in fact; but Hector had small teeth as sharp as pins. It was the sudden, nervous speed with which Mike withdrew his hand which caused the damage; he swore, wrapped his hand in a handkerchief, and at Millicent's entreaty revealed three or four minute wounds. Millicent spoke harshly to Hector and tenderly to Mike, and hurried to her mother's medicine cupboard for a bottle of iodine.

Now no Englishman, however phlegmatic, can have his hand dabbed with iodine without, momentarily at any rate, falling in love.

Mike had seen the nose countless times before, but that afternoon, as it was bowed over his scratched thumb, and as Millicent said, "Am I hurting terribly?", as it was raised towards him, and as Millicent said, "There. Now it will be all right," Mike suddenly saw it transfigured as its devotees saw it and from that moment, until long after the three months of attention which she accorded him, he was Millicent's besotted suitor.

The pup Hector saw all this and realized his mistake. Never again, he decided, would he give Millicent the excuse to run for the iodine bottle.

V

He had on the whole an easy task, for Millicent's naturally capricious nature could, as a rule, be relied upon, unaided, to drive her lovers into extremes of irritation. Moreover she had come to love the dog. She received very regular letters from Hector, written weekly and arriving in batches of three or four according to the mails. She always opened them; often she read them to the end, but their contents made little impression upon her mind and gradually their writer drifted into oblivion so that when people said to her "How is darling Hector?" it came naturally to her to reply, "He doesn't like the hot weather much I'm afraid, and his coat is in a very poor state. I'm thinking of having him plucked," instead of, "He had a go of malaria and there is black worm in his tobacco crop."

Playing upon this affection which had grown up for him, Hector achieved a technique for dealing with Millicent's young men. He no longer growled at them or soiled their trousers; that merely resulted in his being turned from the room; instead, he found it increasingly easy to usurp the conversation.

Tea was the most dangerous time of day, for then Millicent was permitted to entertain friends in her sitting-room; accordingly, though he had a constitutional preference for pungent, meaty dishes, Hector heroically simulated a love of lump sugar. Having made this apparent, at whatever cost to his digestion, it was easy to lead Millicent on to an interest in tricks; he would beg and "trust", lie down as though dead, stand in the corner and raise a fore paw to his ear.

"What does S U G A R spell?" Millicent would ask and Hector would walk round the tea table to the sugar-bowl and lay his nose against it, gazing earnestly and clouding the silver with his moist breath.

"He understands everything," Millicent would say in triumph.

When tricks failed Hector would demand to be let out of the door. The young man would be obliged to interrupt himself to open it. Once on the other side Hector would scratch and whine for re-admission.

In moments of extreme anxiety Hector would affect to be sick – no difficult feat after the unwelcome diet of lump sugar; he would stretch out his neck, retching noisily, till Millicent snatched him up and carried him to the hall, where the floor, paved in marble, was less vulnerable – but by that time a tender atmosphere had been shattered and one wholly prejudicial to romance created to take its place.

This series of devices spaced out through the afternoon and tactfully obtruded whenever the guest showed signs of leading the conversation to a more intimate phase, distracted young man after young man and sent them finally away, baffled and despairing.

Every morning Hector lay on Millicent's bed while she took her breakfast and read the daily paper. This hour from ten to eleven was sacred to the telephone and it was then that the young men with whom she had danced overnight attempted to renew their friendship and make plans for the day. At first Hector sought, not unsuccessfully, to prevent these assignations by entangling himself in the wire, but soon a subtler and more insulting technique suggested itself. He pretended to telephone too. Thus, as soon as the bell rang, he would wag his tail and cock his head on one side in a way that he had learned was engaging. Millicent would begin her conversation and Hector would wriggle up under her arm and nuzzle against the receiver.

"Listen," she would say, "*someone* wants to talk to you. Isn't he an angel?" Then she would hold the receiver down to him and the young man at the other end would be dazed by a shattering series of yelps. This accomplishment appealed so much to Millicent that often she would not even bother to find out the name of the caller but, instead, would take off the receiver and hold it directly to the black snout, so that some wretched young man half a mile away, feeling, perhaps, none too well in the early morning, found himself barked to silence before he had spoken a word.

At other times young men, badly taken with the nose, would attempt to waylay Millicent in Hyde Park when she was taking Hector for exercise. Here, at first, Hector would get lost, fight other dogs and bite small children to keep himself constantly in her attention, but soon he adopted a gentler course. He insisted upon carrying Millicent's bag for her. He would trot in front of the couple and whenever he thought an interruption desirable he would drop the bag; the young man was obliged to pick it up and restore it first to Millicent and then, at her request, to the dog. Few young men were sufficiently servile to submit to more than one walk in these degrading conditions.

In this way two years passed. Letters arrived constantly from Kenya, full of devotion, full of minor disasters – blight in the seisal, locusts in the coffee, labour troubles, drought, flood, the local government, the world market. Occasionally Millicent read the letters aloud to the dog, usually she left them unread on her breakfast tray. She and Hector moved together through the leisurely routine of English social life. Wherever she carried her nose, two in five marriageable men fell temporarily in love; wherever Hector followed their ardour changed to irritation, shame and disgust. Mothers began to remark complacently that it was curious how that fascinating Blade girl never got married.

VI

At last in the third year of this régime a new problem presented itself in the person of Major Sir Alexander Dreadnought, Bart., M.P., and Hector immediately realized that he was up against something altogether more formidable than he had hitherto tackled.

Sir Alexander was not a young man; he was forty-five and a widower. He was wealthy, popular and preternaturally patient; he was also mildly distinguished, being joint-master of a Midland pack of hounds and a junior Minister; he bore a war record of conspicuous gallantry. Millie's father and mother were delighted when they saw that her nose was having its effect on him. Hector took against him from the first, exerted every art which his two and a half years' practice had perfected, and achieved nothing. Devices that had driven a dozen young men to frenzies of chagrin seemed only to accentuate Sir Alexander's tender solicitude. When he came to the house to fetch Millicent for the evening he was found to have filled the pockets of his evening clothes with lump sugar for Hector; when Hector was sick Sir Alexander was there first, on his knees with a page of *The Times*; Hector resorted to his early, violent manner and bit him frequently and hard, but Sir Alexander merely remarked, "I believe I am making the little fellow jealous. A delightful trait."

For the truth was that Sir Alexander had been persecuted long and bitterly from his earliest days – his parents, his sisters, his schoolfellows, his company-sergeant and his colonel, his colleagues in politics, his wife, his joint-master, huntsman and hunt secretary, his election agent, his constituents and even his

parliamentary private secretary had one and all pitched into
Sir Alexander, and he accepted this treatment as a matter of
course. For him it was the most natural thing in the world to
have his eardrums outraged by barks when he rang up the
young woman of his affections; it was a high privilege to retrieve
her handbag when Hector dropped it in the Park; the small
wounds that Hector was able to inflict on his ankles and wrists
were to him knightly scars. In his more ambitious moments he
referred to Hector in Millicent's hearing as "my little rival".
There could be no doubt whatever of his intentions and when
he asked Millicent and her mama to visit him in the country, he
added at the foot of the letter, "*Of course the invitation includes little
Hector.*"

The Saturday to Monday visit to Sir Alexander's was a nightmare to the poodle. He worked as he had never worked before;
every artifice by which he could render his presence odious was
attempted and attempted in vain. As far as his host was concerned, that is to say. The rest of the household responded well
enough, and he received a vicious kick when, through his own
bad management, he found himself alone with the second footman, whom he had succeeded in upsetting with a tray of cups at
tea time.

Conduct that had driven Millicent in shame from half the
stately homes of England was meekly accepted here. There were
other dogs in the house – elderly, sober, well-behaved animals at
whom Hector flew; they turned their heads sadly away from
his yaps of defiance, he snapped at their ears. They lolloped
sombrely out of reach and Sir Alexander had them shut away
for the rest of the visit.

There was an exciting Aubusson carpet in the dining-room to
which Hector was able to do irreparable damage; Sir Alexander
seemed not to notice.

Hector found a carrion in the park and conscientiously rolled
in it – although such a thing was obnoxious to his nature – and,
returning, fouled every chair in the drawing-room; Sir Alexander
himself helped Millicent wash him and brought some bath salts
from his own bathroom for the operation.

Hector howled all night; he hid and had half the household searching for him with lanterns; he killed some young pheasants and made a sporting attempt on a peacock. All to no purpose. He staved off an actual proposal, it is true – once in the Dutch garden, once on the way to the stables and once while he was being bathed – but when Monday morning arrived and he heard Sir Alexander say, "I hope Hector enjoyed his visit a little. I hope I shall see him here *very, very* often," he knew that he was defeated.

It was now only a matter of waiting. The evenings in London were a time when it was impossible for him to keep Millicent under observation. One of these days he would wake up to hear Millicent telephoning to her girl friends, breaking the good news of her engagement.

Thus it was that after a long conflict of loyalties he came to a desperate resolve. He had grown fond of his young mistress; often and often when her face had been pressed down to his he had felt sympathy with that long line of young men whom it was his duty to persecute. But Hector was no kitchen-haunting mongrel. By the code of all well-born dogs it is money that counts. It is the purchaser, not the mere feeder and fondler, to whom ultimate loyalty is due. The hand which had once fumbled with the fivers in the livestock department of the mammoth store, now tilled the unfertile soil of equatorial Africa, but the sacred words of commission still rang in Hector's memory. All through the Sunday night and the journey of Monday morning, Hector wrestled with his problem; then he came to the decision. *The nose must go.*

VII

It was an easy business; one firm snap as she bent over his basket and the work was accomplished. She went to a plastic surgeon and emerged some weeks later without scar or stitch. But it was a different nose; the surgeon in his way was an artist and, as

'The Rag Regatta', *The Isis*, 14 June 1922, p. 9. [The top two images are of 'the relentless and ubiquitous vendors of flags' and a presentation of St. George and the Dragon on a punt, both described in the accompanying report.]

MR. LOVEDAY'S LITTLE OUTING

"YOU WILL not find your father greatly changed," remarked Lady Moping, as the car turned into the gates of the County Asylum.

"Will he be wearing a uniform?" asked Angela.

"No, dear, of course not. He is receiving the very best attention."

It was Angela's first visit and it was being made at her own suggestion.

Ten years had passed since the showery day in late summer when Lord Moping had been taken away; a day of confused but bitter memories for her; the day of Lady Moping's annual garden party, always bitter, confused that day by the caprice of the weather which, remaining clear and brilliant with promise until the arrival of the first guests, had suddenly blackened into a squall. There had been a scuttle for cover; the marquee had capsized; a frantic carrying of cushions and chairs; a table-cloth lofted to the boughs of the monkey-puzzler, fluttering in the rain; a bright period and the cautious emergence of guests on to the soggy lawns; another squall; another twenty minutes of sunshine. It had been an abominable afternoon, culminating at about six o'clock in her father's attempted suicide.

Lord Moping habitually threatened suicide on the occasion of the garden party; that year he had been found black in the face, hanging by his braces in the orangery; some neighbours, who were sheltering there from the rain, set him on his feet again, and before dinner a van had called for him. Since then Lady Moping had paid seasonal calls at the asylum and returned in time for tea, rather reticent of her experience.

Many of her neighbours were inclined to be critical of Lord Moping's accommodation. He was not, of course, an ordinary inmate. He lived in a separate wing of the asylum, specially devoted to the segregation of wealthier lunatics. These were given every consideration which their foibles permitted. They might choose their own clothes (many indulged in the liveliest fancies), smoke the most expensive brands of cigars and, on the anniversaries of their certification, entertain any other inmates for whom they had an attachment to private dinner parties.

The fact remained, however, that it was far from being the most expensive kind of institution; the uncompromising address, "COUNTY HOME FOR MENTAL DEFECTIVES" stamped across the notepaper, worked on the uniforms of their attendants, painted, even, upon a prominent hoarding at the main entrance, suggested the lowest associations. From time to time, with less or more tact, her friends attempted to bring to Lady Moping's notice particulars of seaside nursing homes, of "qualified practitioners with large private grounds suitable for the charge of nervous or difficult cases", but she accepted them lightly; when her son came of age he might make any changes that he thought fit; meanwhile she felt no inclination to relax her economical régime; her husband had betrayed her basely on the one day in the year when she looked for loyal support, and was far better off than he deserved.

A few lonely figures in great-coats were shuffling and loping about the park.

"Those are the lower-class lunatics," observed Lady Moping. "There is a very nice little flower garden for people like your father. I sent them some cuttings last year."

They drove past the blank, yellow brick façade to the doctor's private entrance and were received by him in the "visitors room", set aside for interviews of this kind. The window was protected on the inside by bars and wire netting; there was no fireplace; when Angela nervously attempted to move her chair further from the radiator, she found that it was screwed to the floor.

"Lord Moping is quite ready to see you," said the doctor.

"How is he?"

"Oh, very well, very well indeed, I'm glad to say. He had rather a nasty cold some time ago, but apart from that his condition is excellent. He spends a lot of his time in writing."

They heard a shuffling, skipping sound approaching along the flagged passage. Outside the door a high peevish voice, which Angela recognized as her father's, said: "I haven't the time, I tell you. Let them come back later."

A gentler tone, with a slight rural burr, replied, "Now come along. It is a purely formal audience. You need stay no longer than you like."

Then the door was pushed open (it had no lock or fastening) and Lord Moping came into the room. He was attended by an elderly little man with full white hair and an expression of great kindness.

"That is Mr. Loveday who acts as Lord Moping's attendant."

"Secretary," said Lord Moping. He moved with a jogging gait and shook hands with his wife.

"This is Angela. You remember Angela, don't you?"

"No, I can't say that I do. What does she want?"

"We just came to see you."

"Well, you have come at an exceedingly inconvenient time. I am very busy. Have you typed out that letter to the Pope yet, Loveday?"

"No, my lord. If you remember, you asked me to look up the figures about the Newfoundland fisheries first?"

"So I did. Well, it is fortunate, as I think the whole letter will have to be redrafted. A great deal of new information has come to light since luncheon. A great deal . . . You see, my dear, I am fully occupied." He turned his restless, quizzical eyes upon Angela. "I suppose you have come about the Danube. Well, you must come again later. Tell them it will be all right, quite all right, but I have not had time to give my full attention to it. Tell them that."

"Very well, Papa."

"Anyway," said Lord Moping rather petulantly, "it is a matter of secondary importance. There is the Elbe and the Amazon and the Tigris to be dealt with first, eh, Loveday? . . . *Danube* indeed. Nasty little river. I'd only call it a stream myself. Well, can't stop, nice of you to come. I would do more for you if I could, but you see how I'm fixed. Write to me about it. That's it. *Put it in black and white.*"

And with that he left the room.

"You see," said the doctor, "he is in excellent condition. He is putting on weight, eating and sleeping excellently. In fact, the whole tone of his system is above reproach."

The door opened again and Loveday returned.

"Forgive my coming back, sir, but I was afraid that the young lady might be upset at his Lordship's not knowing her. You mustn't mind him, miss. Next time he'll be very pleased to see you. It's only to-day he's put out on account of being behindhand with his work. You see, sir, all this week I've been helping in the library and I haven't been able to get all his Lordship's reports typed out. And he's got muddled with his card index. That's all it is. He doesn't mean any harm."

"What a nice man," said Angela, when Loveday had gone back to his charge.

"Yes. I don't know what we should do without old Loveday. Everybody loves him, staff and patients alike."

"I remember him well. It's a great comfort to know that you are able to get such good warders," said Lady Moping; "people who don't know, say such foolish things about asylums."

"Oh, but Loveday isn't a warder," said the doctor.

"You don't mean he's cuckoo, too?" said Angela.

The doctor corrected her.

"He is an *inmate*. It is rather an interesting case. He has been here for thirty-five years."

"But I've never seen anyone saner," said Angela.

"He certainly has that air," said the doctor, "and in the last twenty years we have treated him as such. He is the life and soul of the place. Of course he is not one of the private patients, but we allow him to mix freely with them. He plays billiards excellently, does conjuring tricks at the concert, mends their gramophones, valets them, helps them in their crossword puzzles and various – er – hobbies. We allow them to give him small tips for services rendered, and he must by now have amassed quite a little fortune. He has a way with even the most troublesome of them. An invaluable man about the place."

"Yes, but why is he here?"

"Well, it is rather sad. When he was a very young man he killed somebody – a young woman quite unknown to him, whom he knocked off her bicycle and then throttled. He gave himself up immediately afterwards and has been here ever since."

"But surely he is perfectly safe now. Why is he not let out?"

"Well, I suppose if it was to anyone's interest, he would be. He has no relatives except a step-sister who lives in Plymouth. She used to visit him at one time, but she hasn't been for years now. He's perfectly happy here and I can assure you *we* aren't going to take the first steps in turning him out. He's far too useful to us."

"But it doesn't seem fair," said Angela.

"Look at your father," said the doctor. "He'd be quite lost without Loveday to act as his secretary."

"It doesn't seem fair."

II

Angela left the asylum, oppressed by a sense of injustice. Her mother was unsympathetic.

"Think of being locked up in a looney bin all one's life."

"He attempted to hang himself in the orangery," replied Lady Moping, "*in front of the Chester-Martins.*"

"I don't mean Papa. I mean Mr. Loveday."

"I don't think I know him."

"Yes, the looney they have put to look after Papa."

"Your father's secretary. A very decent sort of man, I thought, and eminently suited to his work."

Angela left the question for the time, but returned to it again at luncheon on the following day.

"Mums, what does one have to do to get people out of the bin?"

"The bin? Good gracious, child, I hope that you do not anticipate your father's return *here*."

"No, no. Mr. Loveday."

"Angela, you seem to me to be totally bemused. I see it was a mistake to take you with me on our little visit yesterday."

After luncheon Angela disappeared to the library and was soon immersed in the lunacy laws as represented in the encyclopaedia.

She did not re-open the subject with her mother, but a fortnight later, when there was a question of taking some pheasants over to her father for his eleventh Certification Party she showed an unusual willingness to run over with them. Her mother was occupied with other interests and noticed nothing suspicious.

Angela drove her small car to the asylum, and after delivering the game, asked for Mr. Loveday. He was busy at the time making a crown for one of his companions who expected hourly to be anointed Emperor of Brazil, but he left his work and enjoyed several minutes' conversation with her. They spoke about her father's health and spirits. After a time Angela remarked, "Don't you ever want to get away?"

Mr. Loveday looked at her with his gentle, blue-grey eyes. "I've got very well used to the life, miss. I'm fond of the poor people here, and I think that several of them are quite fond of me. At least, I think they would miss me if I were to go."

"But don't you ever think of being free again?"

"Oh yes, miss, I think of it – almost all the time I think of it."

"What would you do if you got out? There must be *something* you would sooner do than stay here."

The old man fidgeted uneasily. "Well, miss, it sounds ungrateful, but I can't deny I should welcome a little outing, once, before I get too old to enjoy it. I expect we all have our secret ambitions, and there *is* one thing I often wish I could do. You mustn't ask me what . . . It wouldn't take long. But I do feel that if I had done it, just for a day, an afternoon even, then I would die quiet. I could settle down again easier, and devote myself to the poor crazed people here with a better heart. Yes, I do feel that."

There were tears in Angela's eyes that afternoon as she drove away. "He *shall* have his little outing, bless him," she said.

III

From that day onwards for many weeks Angela had a new purpose in life. She moved about the ordinary routine of her home with an abstracted air and an unfamiliar, reserved courtesy which greatly disconcerted Lady Moping.

"I believe the child's in love. I only pray that it isn't that uncouth Egbertson boy."

She read a great deal in the library, she cross-examined any guests who had pretensions to legal or medical knowledge, she showed extreme goodwill to old Sir Roderick Lane-Foscote, their Member. The names "alienist", "barrister" or "government official" now had for her the glamour that formerly surrounded film actors and professional wrestlers. She was a woman with a cause, and before the end of the hunting season she had triumphed. Mr. Loveday achieved his liberty.

The doctor at the asylum showed reluctance but no real opposition. Sir Roderick wrote to the Home Office. The necessary papers were signed, and at last the day came when Mr. Loveday took leave of the home where he had spent such long and useful years.

His departure was marked by some ceremony. Angela and Sir Roderick Lane-Foscote sat with the doctors on the stage of the gymnasium. Below them were assembled everyone in the institution who was thought to be stable enough to endure the excitement.

Lord Moping, with a few suitable expressions of regret, presented Mr. Loveday on behalf of the wealthier lunatics with a gold cigarette case; those who supposed themselves to be emperors showered him with decorations and titles of honour. The warders gave him a silver watch and many of the non-paying inmates were in tears on the day of the presentation.

The doctor made the main speech of the afternoon. "Remember," he remarked, "that you leave behind you nothing but our warmest good wishes. You are bound to us by ties that none will forget. Time will only deepen our sense of debt to you. If at any time in the future you should grow tired of your life in the world, there will always be a welcome for you here. Your post will be open."

A dozen or so variously afflicted lunatics hopped and skipped after him down the drive until the iron gates opened and Mr. Loveday stepped into his freedom. His small trunk had already gone to the station; he elected to walk. He had been reticent about his plans, but he was well provided with money, and the general impression was that he would go to London and enjoy himself a little before visiting his step-sister in Plymouth.

It was to the surprise of all that he returned within two hours of his liberation. He was smiling whimsically, a gentle, self-regarding smile of reminiscence.

"I have come back," he informed the doctor. "I think that now I shall be here for good."

"But, Loveday, what a short holiday. I'm afraid that you have hardly enjoyed yourself at all."

"Oh yes, sir, thank you, sir, I've enjoyed myself *very much*. I'd been promising myself one little treat, all these years. It was short, sir, but *most* enjoyable. Now I shall be able to settle down again to my work here without any regrets."

Half a mile up the road from the asylum gates, they later discovered an abandoned bicycle. It was a lady's machine of some antiquity. Quite near it in the ditch lay the strangled body of a young woman, who, riding home to her tea, had chanced to overtake Mr. Loveday, as he strode along, musing on his opportunities.

Dust jacket for *Decline and Fall*, September 1928.

WINNER TAKES ALL

I

WHEN Mrs. Kent-Cumberland's eldest son was born (in an expensive London nursing home) there was a bonfire on Tomb Beacon; it consumed three barrels of tar, an immense catafalque of timber, and, as things turned out – for the flames spread briskly in the dry gorse and loyal tenantry were too tipsy to extinguish them – the entire vegetation of Tomb Hill.

As soon as mother and child could be moved, they travelled in state to the country, where flags were hung out in the village street and a trellis arch of evergreen boughs obscured the handsome Palladian entrance gates of their home. There were farmers' dinners both at Tomb and on the Kent-Cumberlands' Norfolk estate, and funds for a silver-plated tray were ungrudgingly subscribed.

The christening was celebrated by a garden-party. A princess stood Godmother by proxy, and the boy was called Gervase Peregrine Mountjoy St. Eustace – all of them names illustrious in the family's history.

Throughout the service and the subsequent presentations he maintained an attitude of phlegmatic dignity which confirmed everyone in the high estimate they had already formed of his capabilities.

After the garden-party there were fireworks and after the fireworks a very hard week for the gardeners, cleaning up the mess. The life of the Kent-Cumberlands then resumed its normal tranquillity until nearly two years later, when, much to her annoyance, Mrs. Kent-Cumberland discovered that she was to have another baby.

The second child was born in August in a shoddy modern house on the East Coast which had been taken for the summer so that Gervase might have the benefit of sea air. Mrs. Kent-Cumberland was attended by the local doctor, who antagonized her by his middle-class accent, and proved, when it came to the point, a great deal more deft than the London specialist.

Throughout the peevish months of waiting Mrs. Kent-Cumberland had fortified herself with the hope that she would have a daughter. It would be a softening influence for Gervase, who was growing up somewhat unresponsive, to have a pretty, gentle, sympathetic sister two years younger than himself. She would come out just when he was going up to Oxford and would save him from either of the dreadful extremes of evil company which threatened that stage of development – the bookworm and the hooligan. She would bring down delightful girls for Eights Week and Commem. Mrs. Kent-Cumberland had it all planned out. When she was delivered of another son she named him Thomas, and fretted through her convalescence with her mind on the coming hunting season.

II

The two brothers developed into sturdy, unremarkable little boys; there was little to choose between them except their two years' difference in age. They were both sandy-haired, courageous, and well-mannered on occasions. Neither was sensitive, artistic, highly strung, or conscious of being misunderstood. Both accepted the fact of Gervase's importance just as they accepted his superiority of knowledge and physique. Mrs. Kent-Cumberland was a fair-minded woman, and in the event of the two being involved in mischief, it was Gervase, as the elder, who was the more severely punished. Tom found that his obscurity was on the whole advantageous, for it excused him from the countless minor performances of ceremony which fell on Gervase.

III

At the age of seven Tom was consumed with desire for a model motor-car, an expensive toy of a size to sit in and pedal about the garden. He prayed for it steadfastly every evening and most mornings for several weeks. Christmas was approaching.

Gervase had a smart pony and was often taken hunting. Tom was alone most of the day and the motor-car occupied a great part of his thoughts. Finally he confided his ambition to an uncle. This uncle was not addicted to expensive present giving, least of all to children (for he was a man of limited means and self-indulgent habits) but something in his nephew's intensity of feeling impressed him.

"Poor little beggar," he reflected, "his brother seems to get all the fun," and when he returned to London he ordered the motor-car for Tom. It arrived some days before Christmas and was put away upstairs with other presents. On Christmas Eve Mrs. Kent-Cumberland came to inspect them. "How very kind," she said, looking at each label in turn, "how very kind."

The motor-car was by far the largest exhibit. It was pillar-box red, complete with electric lights, a hooter and a spare wheel.

"Really," she said. "How *very* kind of Ted."

Then she looked at the label more closely. "But how foolish of him. He's put *Tom's* name on it."

"There was this book for Master Gervase," said the nurse, producing a volume labelled "Gervase with best wishes from Uncle Ted".

"Of course the parcels have been confused at the shop," said Mrs. Kent-Cumberland. "This can't have been meant for Tom. Why, it must have cost six or seven pounds."

She changed the labels and went downstairs to supervise the decoration of the Christmas tree, glad to have rectified an obvious error of justice.

Next morning the presents were revealed.

"Oh, Ger. You *are* lucky," said Tom, inspecting the motor-car. "May I ride in it?"

"Yes, only be careful. Nanny says it was awfully expensive."

Tom rode it twice round the room. "May I take it in the garden sometimes?"

"Yes. You can have it when I'm hunting."

Later in the week they wrote to thank their uncle for his presents.

Gervase wrote: "*Dear Uncle Ted, Thank you for the lovely present. It's lovely. The pony is very well. I am going to hunt again before I go back to school. Love from Gervase.*"

"*Dear Uncle Ted,*" wrote Tom, "*Thank you ever so much for the lovely present. It is just what I wanted. Again thanking you very much. With love from Tom.*"

"So that's all the thanks I get. Ungrateful little beggar," said Uncle Ted, resolving to be more economical in future.

But when Gervase went back to school, he said, "You can have the motor-car, Tom, to keep."

"What, for *my own*?"

"Yes. It's a kid's toy, anyway."

And by this act of generosity he increased Tom's respect and love for him a hundredfold.

IV

The War came and profoundly changed the lives of the two boys. It engendered none of the neuroses threatened by pacifists. Air raids remained among Tom's happiest memories, when the school used to be awakened in the middle of the night and hustled downstairs to the basements where, wrapped in eiderdowns, they were regaled with cocoa and cake by the matron, who looked supremely ridiculous in a flannel nightgown. Once a Zeppelin was hit in sight of the school; they all crowded to the dormitory windows to see it sinking slowly in a globe of pink flame. A very young master whose health rendered him unfit for military service danced on the headmaster's tennis court crying, "There go the baby killers." Tom made a collection of "War Relics", including a captured German helmet, shell-splinters, *The Times* for August 4th, 1914, buttons, cartridge cases, and cap badges, that was voted the best in the school.

The event which radically changed the relationship of the brothers was the death, early in 1915, of their father. Neither knew him well nor particularly liked him. He had represented the division in the House of Commons and spent much of his time in London while the children were at Tomb. They only saw him on three occasions after he joined the army. Gervase and Tom were called out of the class-room and told of his death by the headmaster's wife. They cried, since it was expected of them, and for some days were treated with marked deference by the masters and the rest of the school.

It was in the subsequent holidays that the importance of the change became apparent. Mrs. Kent-Cumberland had suddenly become more emotional and more parsimonious. She was liable to unprecedented outbursts of tears, when she would crush Gervase to her and say, "My poor fatherless boy." At other times she spoke gloomily of death duties.

V

For some years in fact "Death Duties" became the refrain of the household.

When Mrs. Kent-Cumberland let the house in London and closed down a wing at Tomb, when she reduced the servants to four and the gardeners to two, when she "let the flower gardens go", when she stopped asking her brother Ted to stay, when she emptied the stables, and became almost fanatical in her reluctance to use the car, when the bath-water was cold and there were no new tennis-balls, when the chimneys were dirty and the lawns covered with sheep, when Gervase's cast-off clothes ceased to fit Tom, when she refused him the "extra" expense at school of carpentry lessons and mid-morning milk – "Death Duties" were responsible.

"It is all for Gervase," Mrs. Kent-Cumberland used to explain. "When he inherits, he must take over free of debt, as his father did."

VI

Gervase went to Eton in the year of his father's death. Tom would normally have followed him two years later, but in her new mood of economy, Mrs. Kent-Cumberland cancelled his entry and began canvassing her friends' opinions about the less famous, cheaper public schools. "The education is just as good," she said, "and far more suitable for a boy who has his own way to make in the world."

Tom was happy enough at the school to which he was sent. It was very bleak and very new, salubrious, progressive, prosperous in the boom that secondary education enjoyed in the years immediately following the war, and, when all was said and done, "thoroughly suitable for a boy with his own way to make in the world". He had several friends whom he was not allowed to invite to his home during the holidays. He got his House colours for swimming and fives, played once or twice in the second eleven for cricket, and was a platoon-commander in the O.T.C.; he was in the sixth form and passed the Higher Certificate in his last year, became a prefect and enjoyed the confidence of his house master, who spoke of him as "a very decent stamp of boy". He left school at the age of eighteen without the smallest desire to revisit it or see any of its members again.

Gervase was then at Christ Church. Tom went up to visit him, but the magnificent Etonians who romped in and out of his brother's rooms scared and depressed him. Gervase was in the Bullingdon, spending money freely and enjoying himself. He gave a dinner-party in his rooms, but Tom sat in silence, drinking heavily to hide his embarrassment, and was later sombrely sick in a corner of Peckwater quad. He returned to Tomb next day in the lowest spirits.

"It is not as though Tom were a scholarly boy," said Mrs. Kent-Cumberland to her friends. "I am glad he is not, of course. But if he had been, it might have been right to make the sacrifice and send him to the University. As it is, the sooner he Gets Started the better."

VII

Getting Tom started, however, proved a matter of some difficulty. During the Death Duty Period, Mrs. Kent-Cumberland had cut herself off from many of her friends. Now she cast round vainly to find someone who would "put Tom into something". Chartered Accountancy, Chinese Customs, estate agencies, "the City", were suggested and abandoned. "The trouble is, that he has no particular abilities," she explained. "He is the sort of boy who would be useful in anything – an all-round man – but, of course, he has no capital."

August, September, October passed; Gervase was back at Oxford, in fashionable lodgings in the High Street, but Tom remained at home without employment. Day by day he and his mother sat down together to luncheon and dinner, and his constant presence was a severe strain on Mrs. Kent-Cumberland's equability. She herself was always busy and, as she bustled about her duties, it shocked and distracted her to encounter the large figure of her younger son sprawling on the morning-room sofa or leaning against the stone parapet of the terrace and gazing out apathetically across the familiar landscape.

"Why can't you find something to *do*?" she would complain. "There are *always* things to do about a house. Heaven knows I never have a moment." And when, one afternoon, he was asked out by some neighbours and returned too late to dress for dinner, she said, "Really, Tom, I should have thought that *you* had time for that."

"It is a very serious thing," she remarked on another occasion, "for a young man of your age to get out of the habit of work. It saps his whole morale."

Accordingly she fell back upon the ancient country house expedient of Cataloguing the Library. This consisted of an extensive and dusty collection of books amassed by succeeding generations of a family at no time notable for their patronage of literature; it had been catalogued before, in the middle of the nineteenth century, in the spidery, spinsterish hand of a relative in reduced circumstances; since then the additions and disturbances had been negligible, but Mrs. Kent-Cumberland purchased a fumed oak cabinet and several boxes of cards and instructed Tom how she wanted the shelves renumbered and the books twice entered under Subject and Author.

It was a system that should keep a boy employed for some time, and it was with vexation, therefore, that, a few days after the task was commenced, she paid a surprise visit to the scene of his labour and found Tom sitting, almost lying, in an armchair, with his feet on a rung of the library steps, reading.

"I am glad you have found something interesting," she said in a voice that conveyed very little gladness.

"Well, to tell you the truth, I think I have," said Tom, and showed her the book.

It was the manuscript journal kept by a Colonel Jasper Cumberland during the Peninsular War. It had no startling literary merit, nor did its criticisms of the general staff throw any new light upon the strategy of the campaign, but it was a lively, direct, day-to-day narrative, redolent of its period; there was a sprinkling of droll anecdotes, some vigorous descriptions of fox-hunting behind the lines of Torres Vedras, of the Duke of Wellington dining in Mess, of a threatened mutiny that had not yet found its way into history, of the assault on Badajos; there were some bawdy references to Portuguese women and some pious reflections about patriotism.

"I was wondering if it might be worth publishing," said Tom.

"I should hardly think so," replied his mother. "But I will certainly show it to Gervase when he comes home."

For the moment the discovery gave a new interest to Tom's life. He read up the history of the period and of his own family. Jasper Cumberland he established as a younger son of the period, who had later emigrated to Canada. There were letters from him among the archives, including the announcement of his marriage to a Papist which had clearly severed the link with his elder brother. In a case of uncatalogued miniatures in the long drawing-room, he found the portrait of a handsome whiskered soldier, which by a study of contemporary uniforms he was able to identify as the diarist.

Presently, in his round, immature handwriting, Tom began working up his notes into an essay. His mother watched his efforts with unqualified approval. She was glad to see him busy, and glad to see him taking an interest in his family's history. She had begun to fear that by sending him to a school without "tradition" she might have made a socialist of the boy. When, shortly before the Christmas vacation, work was found for Tom she took charge of his notes. "I am sure Gervase will be extremely interested," she said. "He may even think it worth showing to a publisher."

VIII

The work that had been found for Tom was not immediately lucrative, but, as his mother said, it was a Beginning. It was to go to Wolverhampton and learn the motor business from the bottom. The first two years were to be spent at the works, from where, if he showed talent, he might graduate to the London show-rooms. His wages, at first, were thirty-five shillings a week. This was augmented by the allowance of another pound. Lodgings were found for him over a fruit shop in the outskirts of the town, and Gervase gave him his old two-seater car, in which he could travel to and from his work, and for occasional week-ends home.

It was during one of these visits that Gervase told him the good news that a London publisher had read the diary and seen possibilities in it. Six months later it appeared under the title *The Journal of an English Cavalry Officer during the Peninsular War. Edited with notes and a biographical introduction by Gervase Kent-Cumberland*. The miniature portrait was prettily reproduced as a frontispiece, there was a collotype copy of a page of the original manuscript, a contemporary print of Tomb Park, and a map of the campaign. It sold nearly two thousand copies at twelve-and-sixpence and received two or three respectful reviews in the Saturday and Sunday papers.

The appearance of the *Journal* coincided within a few days with Gervase's twenty-first birthday. The celebrations were extravagant and prolonged, culminating in a ball at which Tom's attendance was required.

He drove over, after the works had shut down, and arrived, just in time for dinner, to find a house-party of thirty and a house entirely transformed.

His own room had been taken for a guest ("as you will only be here for one night", his mother explained). He was sent down to the Cumberland Arms, where he dressed by candle-light in a breathless little bedroom over the bar, and arrived late and slightly dishevelled at dinner, where he sat between two lovely girls who neither knew who he was nor troubled to inquire. The dancing, afterwards, was in a marquee built on the terrace, which a London catering firm had converted into a fair replica of a Pont Street drawing-room. Tom danced once or twice with the daughters of neighbouring families whom he had known since childhood. They asked him about Wolverhampton and the works. He had to get up early next morning; at midnight he slipped away to his bed at the inn. The evening had bored him; because he was in love.

IX

It had occurred to him to ask his mother whether he might bring his fiancée to the ball, but on reflection, enchanted as he was, he had realized that it would not do. The girl was named Gladys Cruttwell. She was two years older than himself; she had fluffy, yellow hair which she washed at home once a week and dried before the gas-fire; on the day after the shampoo it was very light and silky; towards the end of the week, darker and slightly greasy. She was a virtuous, affectionate, self-reliant, even-tempered, unintelligent, high-spirited girl, but Tom could not disguise from himself the fact that she would not go down well at Tomb.

She worked for the firm on the clerical side. Tom had noticed her on his second day, as she tripped across the yard, exactly on time, bare-headed (the day after a shampoo) in a woollen coat and skirt which she had knitted herself. He had got into conversation with her in the canteen, by making way for her at the counter with a chivalry that was not much practised at the works.

His possession of a car gave him a clear advantage over the other young men about the place.

They discovered that they lived within a few streets of one another, and it presently became Tom's practice to call for her in the mornings and take her home in the evenings. He would sit in the two-seater outside her gate, sound the horn, and she would come running down the path to greet him. As summer approached they went for drives in the evening among leafy Warwickshire lanes. In June they were engaged. Tom was exhilarated, sometimes almost dizzy at the experience, but he hesitated to tell his mother. "After all," he reflected, "it is not as though I were Gervase," but in his own heart he knew that there would be trouble.

Gladys came of a class accustomed to long engagements; marriage seemed a remote prospect; an engagement to her sig-nified the formal recognition that she and Tom spent their spare time in one another's company. Her mother, with whom she lived, accepted him on these terms. In years to come, when Tom had got his place in the London show-rooms, it would be time enough to think about marrying. But Tom was born to a less patient tradi-tion. He began to speak about a wedding in the autumn.

"It would be lovely," said Gladys in the tones she would have employed about winning the Irish sweepstake.

He had spoken very little about his family. She understood, vaguely, that they lived in a big house, but it was a part of life that never had been real to her. She knew that there were Duchesses and Marchionesses in something called "Society"; they were encountered in the papers and the films. She knew there were directors with large salaries; but the fact that there were people like Gervase or Mrs. Kent-Cumberland, and that they could think of themselves as radically different from herself, had not entered her experience. When, eventually, they were brought together Mrs. Kent-Cumberland was extremely gracious and Gladys thought her a very nice old lady. But Tom knew that the meeting was proving disastrous.

"Of course," said Mrs. Kent-Cumberland, "the whole thing is quite impossible. Miss What-ever-her-name-was seemed a thoroughly nice girl, but you are not in a position to think of marriage. Besides," she added with absolute finality, "you must not forget that if anything were to happen to Gervase, you would be his heir."

So Tom was removed from the motor business and an opening found for him on a sheep farm in South Australia.

X

It would not be fair to say that in the ensuing two years Mrs. Kent-Cumberland forgot her younger son. She wrote to him every month and sent him bandana handkerchiefs for Christmas. In the first, lonely days he wrote to her frequently, but when, as he grew accustomed to the new life, his letters became less frequent she did not seriously miss them. When they did arrive they were lengthy; she put them aside from her correspondence to read at leisure and, more than once, mislaid them, unopened. But whenever her acquaintances asked after Tom, she loyally answered, "Doing splendidly. And enjoying himself *very* much."

She had many other things to occupy and, in some cases, distress her. Gervase was now in authority at Tomb, and the careful régime of his minority wholly reversed. There were six expensive hunters in the stable. The lawns were mown, bedrooms thrown open, additional bathrooms installed; there was even talk of constructing a swimming-pool. There was constant Saturday to Monday entertaining. There was the sale, at a poor price, of two Romneys and a Hoppner.

Mrs. Kent-Cumberland watched all this with mingled pride and anxiety. In particular she scrutinized the succession of girls who came to stay, in the irreconcilable, ever present fears that Gervase would or would not marry. Either conclusion seemed perilous; a wife for Gervase must be well-born, well-conducted, rich, of stainless reputation, and affectionately disposed to Mrs. Kent-Cumberland; such a mate seemed difficult to find. The estate was clear of the mortgages necessitated by death duties, but dividends were uncertain, and though, as she frequently pointed out, she "never interfered", simple arithmetic and her own close experience of domestic management convinced her that Gervase would not long be able to support the scale of living which he had introduced.

With so much on her mind, it was inevitable that Mrs. Kent-Cumberland should think a great deal about Tomb and very little about South Australia, and should be rudely shocked to read in one of Tom's letters that he was proposing to return to England on a visit, with a fiancée and a future father-in-law; that in fact he had already started, was now on the sea and due to arrive in London in a fortnight. Had she read his earlier letters with attention she might have found hints of such an attachment, but she had not done so, and the announcement came to her as a wholly unpleasant surprise.

"Your brother is coming back."

"Oh, good! When?"

"He is bringing a farmer's daughter to whom he is engaged – and the farmer. They want to come here."

"I say, that's rather a bore. Let's tell them we're having the boilers cleaned."

"You don't seem to realize that this is a serious matter, Gervase."

"Oh, well, you fix things up. I dare say it would be all right if they came next month. We've got to have the Anchorages some time. We might get both over together."

In the end it was decided that Gervase should meet the immigrants in London, vet them and report to his mother whether or no they were suitable fellow-guests for the Anchorages. A week later, on his return to Tomb, his mother greeted him anxiously.

"Well? You never wrote?"

"Wrote, why should I? I never do. I say, I haven't forgotten a birthday or anything, have I?"

"Don't be absurd, Gervase. I mean, about your brother Tom's unfortunate entanglement. Did you see the girl?"

"Oh, *that*. Yes, I went and had dinner with them. Tom's done himself quite well. Fair, rather fat, saucer-eyed, good-tempered I should say by her looks."

"Does she – does she speak with an Australian accent?"

"Didn't notice it."

"And the father?"

"Pompous old boy."

"Would he be all right with the Anchorages?"

"I should think he'd go down like a dinner. But they can't come. They are staying with the Chasms."

"Indeed! What an extraordinary thing. But, of course, Archie Chasm was Governor-General once. Still, it shows they must be fairly respectable. Where are they staying?"

"Claridges."

"Then they must be quite rich, too. How very interesting. I will write this evening."

XI

Three weeks later they arrived. Mr. MacDougal, the father, was a tall, lean man, with pince-nez and an interest in statistics. He was a territorial magnate to whom the Tomb estates appeared a cosy small-holding. He did not emphasize this in any boastful fashion, but in his statistical zeal gave Mrs. Kent-Cumberland some staggering figures. "Is Bessie your only child?" asked Mrs. Kent-Cumberland.

"My only child and heir," he replied, coming down to brass tacks at once. "I dare say you have been wondering what sort of settlement I shall be able to make on her. Now that, I regret to say, is a question I cannot answer accurately. We have good years, Mrs. Kent-Cumberland, and we have bad years. It all depends."

"But I dare say that even in bad years the income is quite considerable?"

"In a bad year," said Mr. MacDougal, "in a *very* bad year such as the present, the net profits, after all deductions have been made for running expenses, insurance, taxation, and deterioration, amount to something between" – Mrs. Kent-Cumberland listened breathlessly – "fifty and fifty-two thousand pounds. I know that is a very vague statement, but it is impossible to be more accurate until the last returns are in."

Bessie was bland and creamy. She admired everything. "It's so *antique*," she would remark with relish, whether the object of her attention was the Norman Church of Tomb, the Victorian panelling in the billiard-room, or the central-heating system which Gervase had recently installed. Mrs. Kent-Cumberland took a great liking to the girl.

"Thoroughly Teachable," she pronounced. "But I wonder whether she is *really* suited to Tom ... I *wonder* ..."

The MacDougals stayed for four days and, when they left, Mrs. Kent-Cumberland pressed them to return for a longer visit. Bessie had been enchanted with everything she saw.

"I wish we could live here," she had said to Tom on her first evening, "in this dear, quaint old house."

"Yes, darling, so do I. Of course it all belongs to Gervase, but I always look on it as my home."

"Just as we Australians look on England."

"Exactly."

She had insisted on seeing everything; the old gabled manor, once the home of the family, relegated now to the function of dower house since the present mansion was built in the eighteenth century – the house of mean proportions and inconvenient offices where Mrs. Kent-Cumberland, in her moments of depression, pictured her own, declining years; the mill and the quarries; the farm, which to the MacDougals seemed minute and formal as a Noah's Ark. On these expeditions it was Gervase who acted as guide. "He, of course, knows so much more about it than Tom," Mrs. Kent-Cumberland explained.

Tom, in fact, found himself very rarely alone with his fiancée. Once, when they were all together after dinner, the question of his marriage was mentioned. He asked Bessie whether, now that she had seen Tomb, she would sooner be married there, at the village church, than in London.

"Oh there is no need to decide anything hastily," Mrs. Kent-Cumberland had said. "Let Bessie look about a little first."

When the MacDougals left, it was to go to Scotland to see the castle of their ancestors. Mr. MacDougal had traced relationship with various branches of his family, had corresponded with them intermittently, and now wished to make their acquaintance.

Bessie wrote to them all at Tomb; she wrote daily to Tom, but in her thoughts, as she lay sleepless in the appalling bed provided for her by her distant kinsmen, she was conscious for the first time of a slight feeling of disappointment and uncertainty. In Australia Tom had seemed so different from everyone else, so gentle and dignified and cultured. Here in England he seemed to recede into obscurity. Everyone in England seemed to be like Tom.

And then there was the house. It was exactly the kind of house which she had always imagined English people to live in, with the dear little park – less than a thousand acres – and the soft grass and the old stone. Tom had fitted into the house. He had fitted too well; had disappeared entirely in it and become part of the background. The central place belonged to Gervase – so like Tom but more handsome; with all Tom's charm but with more personality. Beset with these thoughts, she rolled on the hard and irregular bed until dawn began to show through the lancet window of the Victorian-baronial turret. She loved that turret for all its discomfort. It was so antique.

XII

Mrs. Kent-Cumberland was an active woman. It was less than ten days after the MacDougals' visit that she returned triumphantly from a day in London. After dinner, when she sat alone with Tom in the small drawing-room, she said:

"You'll be very much surprised to hear who I saw to-day. *Gladys*."

"Gladys?"

"Gladys Cruttwell."

"Good heavens. Where on earth did you meet her?"

"It was quite by chance," said his mother vaguely. "She is working there now."

"How was she?"

"Very pretty. Prettier, if anything."

There was a pause. Mrs. Kent-Cumberland stitched away at a gros-point chair seat. "You know, dear boy, that *I never interfere*, but I have often wondered whether you treated Gladys very kindly. I know I was partly to blame, myself. But you were both very young and your prospects so uncertain. I thought a year or two of separation would be a good test of whether you really loved one another."

"Oh, I am sure she has forgotten about me long ago."

"Indeed, she has not, Tom. I thought she seemed a very unhappy girl."

"But how *can* you know, Mother, just seeing her casually like that?"

"We had luncheon together," said Mrs. Kent-Cumberland. "In an A.B.C. shop."

Another pause.

"But, look here, I've forgotten all about her. I only care about Bessie now."

"You know, dearest boy, I never interfere. I think Bessie is a delightful girl. But are you free? Are you free in your own conscience? You know, and I do not know, on what terms you parted from Gladys."

And there returned, after a long absence, the scene which for the first few months of his Australian venture had been constantly in Tom's memory, of a tearful parting and many intemperate promises. He said nothing. "I did not tell Gladys of your engagement. I thought you had the right to do that – as best you can, in your own way. But I did tell her you were back in England and that you wished to see her. She is coming here tomorrow for a night or two. She looked in need of a holiday, poor child."

When Tom went to meet Gladys at the station they stood for some minutes on the platform not certain of the other's identity. Then their tentative signs of recognition corresponded. Gladys had been engaged twice in the past two years, and was now walking out with a motor salesman. It had been a great surprise

when Mrs. Kent-Cumberland sought her out and explained that
Tom had returned to England. She had not forgotten him, for she
was a loyal and good-hearted girl, but she was embarrassed and
touched to learn that his devotion was unshaken.

They were married two weeks later and Mrs. Kent-
Cumberland undertook the delicate mission of "explaining
everything" to the MacDougals.

They went to Australia, where Mr. MacDougal very magnan-
imously gave them a post managing one of his more remote
estates. He was satisfied with Tom's work. Gladys has a large
sunny bungalow and a landscape of grazing-land and wire
fences. She does not see very much company nor does she
particularly like what she does see. The neighbouring ranchers
find her very English and aloof.

Bessie and Gervase were married after six weeks' engagement. They live at Tomb. Bessie has two children and Gervase
has six race-horses. Mrs. Kent-Cumberland lives in the house
with them. She and Bessie rarely disagree, and, when they do, it is
Mrs. Kent-Cumberland who gets her way.

The dower house is let on a long lease to a sporting manufac-
turer. Gervase has taken over the Hounds and spends money
profusely; everyone in the neighbourhood is content.

'Bertram, Ludovic, and Ann', *The Isis*, 24 May 1923, p. 23. [See Introduction, p. xvii.]

AN ENGLISHMAN'S HOME

I

MR. BEVERLEY METCALFE tapped the barometer in the back hall and noted with satisfaction that it had fallen several points during the night. He was by nature a sun-loving man, but he believed it was one of the marks of a true countryman to be eternally in need of rain. He had made a study and noted the points of true countrymen. Had he been of literary habit and of an earlier generation, his observations might have formed a little book of aphorisms. The true countryman wore a dark suit on Sundays unlike the flannelled tripper from the cities; he loved a bargain and would go to any expense to do his marketing by private treaty instead of through the normal channels of retail trade; while ostensibly sceptical and conservative he was readily fascinated by mechanical gadgets; he was genial but inhospitable, willing to gossip for hours across a fence with any passing stranger, but reluctant to allow his closest friends into his house.... These and a hundred other characteristics Mr. Metcalfe noted for emulation.

"That's what we need – rain," he said to himself, and opening the garden door stepped into the balmy morning air. There was no threat in the cloudless heavens. His gardener passed, pushing the water-barrow.

"Good morning, Boggett. The glass has dropped, I'm glad to say."

"Ur."

"Means rain."

"Noa."

"Down quite low."

"Ah."

"Pity to spend a lot of time watering."

"Them'll burn up else."

"Not if it rains."

"Am't agoin to rain. Don't never rain around heres except you can see clear down-over."

"See clear down-over?"

"Ur. Can always see Pilbury Steeple when rains a-coming."

Mr. Metcalfe accepted this statement gravely. "These old fellows know a thing or two that the scientists don't," he would often remark, simulating an air of patronage which was far from sincere. Boggett, the gardener, was not particularly old and he knew very little; the seeds he planted seldom grew; he wrought stark havoc whenever he was allowed to use the pruning-knife; his ambition in horticulture went no further than the fattening of the largest possible pumpkin; but Mr. Metcalfe regarded him with the simple reverence of peasant for priest. For Mr. Metcalfe was but lately initiated into the cult of the countryside, and any features of it still claimed his devotion – its agricultural processes, its social structure, its vocabulary, its recreations; the aspect of it, glittering now under the cool May sunshine, fruit trees in flower, chestnut in full leaf, the ash budding; the sound and smell of it – Mr. Westmacott calling his cows at dawn, the scent of wet earth and Boggett splashing clumsily among the wall-flowers; the heart of it – or what Mr. Metcalfe took to be its heart – pulsing all round him; his own heart beating time, for was he not part of it, a true countryman, a landowner?

He was, it is true, a landowner in rather a small way, but, as he stood on his terrace and surveyed the untroubled valley below him, he congratulated himself that he had not been led away by the house agents into the multitudinous cares of a wider territory. He owned seven acres, more or less, and it seemed to him exactly the right amount; they comprised the policies of the house and a paddock; sixty further acres of farmland had also been available, and for a day or two he had toyed with the rather inebriating idea of acquiring them. He could well have afforded it, of course, but to his habit of mind there was something perverse and downright wrong in an investment which showed a bare two per cent yield on his capital. He wanted a home, not a "seat", and he reflected on the irony of that word; he thought of Lord Brakehurst, with whose property he sometimes liked to say that his own "marched" – there was indeed a hundred yards of ha-ha between his paddock and one of Lord Brakehurst's pastures. What could be less sedentary than Lord Brakehurst's life, every day of which was agitated by the cares of his great possessions? No, seven acres, judiciously chosen, was the ideal property, and Mr. Metcalfe *had* chosen judiciously. The house-agent had spoken no more than the truth when he described Much Malcock as one of the most unspoilt Cotswold villages. It was exactly such a place as Mr. Metcalfe had dreamed of in the long years in the cotton trade in Alexandria. Mr. Metcalfe's own residence, known for generations by the singular name of Grumps, had been rechristened by a previous owner as Much Malcock Hall. It bore the new name pretty well. It was "a dignified Georgian house of mellowed Cotswold stone; four recep., six principal bed and dressing rooms, replete with period features". The villagers, Mr. Metcalfe observed with regret, could not be induced to speak of it as "the Hall". Boggett always said that he worked "up to Grumps", but the name was not of Mr. Metcalfe's choosing and it looked well on his notepaper. It suggested a primacy in the village that was not undisputed.

Lord Brakehurst, of course, was in a class apart; he was Lord Lieutenant of the County with property in fifty parishes. Lady Brakehurst had not in fact called on Mrs. Metcalfe, living as she did in a world where card-leaving had lost its importance, but, of the calling class, there were two other households in Much Malcock, and a border-line case – besides the vicar, who had a plebeian accent and an inclination to preach against bankers.

The rival gentry were Lady Peabury and Colonel Hodge, both, to the villagers, newcomers, but residents of some twenty years priority to Mr. Metcalfe.

Lady Peabury lived at Much Malcock House, whose chimneys, soon to be hidden in the full foliage of summer, could still be seen among its budding limes on the opposite slope of the valley. Four acres of meadowland lay between her property and Mr. Metcalfe's, where Westmacott's plump herd enriched the landscape and counter-balanced the slightly suburban splendour of her flower gardens. She was a widow and, like Mr. Metcalfe, had

come to Much Malcock from abroad. She was rich and kind and
rather greedy, a diligent reader of fiction, mistress of many Cairn
terriers and of five steady old maidservants who never broke the
Crown Derby.

Colonel Hodge lived at the Manor, a fine gabled house in the
village street, whose gardens, too, backed on to Westmacott's
meadow. He was impecunious but active in the affairs of the
British Legion and the Boy Scouts; he accepted Mr. Metcalfe's
invitation to dinner, but spoke of him, in his family circle, as "the
cotton wallah".

These neighbours were of unequivocal position; the Hornbeams at the Old Mill were a childless, middle-aged couple who
devoted themselves to craftsmanship. Mr. Hornbeam senior was
a genuine, commercial potter in Staffordshire; he supported
them reluctantly and rather exiguously, but this backing of
unearned quarterly cheques placed them definitely in the upper
strata of local society. Mrs. Hornbeam attended church and Mr.
Hornbeam was quite knowledgeable about vegetables. In fact,
had they preferred a tennis court to their herb garden, and had
Mr. Hornbeam possessed an evening-suit, they might easily have
mixed with their neighbours on terms of ostensible equality. At
the time of the Peace Ballot, Mrs. Hornbeam had canvassed
every cottage in bicycling distance, but she eschewed the
Women's Institute, and in Lady Peabury's opinion failed to pull
her weight in the village. Mr. Metcalfe thought Mr. Hornbeam
Bohemian, and Mr. Hornbeam thought Mr. Metcalfe Philistine.
Colonel Hodge had fallen out with them some time back, on a
question relating to his Airedale, and cut them year in, year out,
three or four times a day.

Under their stone-tiled roofs the villagers derived substantial
comfort from all these aliens. Foreign visitors impressed by the
charges of London restaurants and the splendour of the more
accessible ducal palaces often express wonder at the wealth of
England. A half has not been told them. It is in remote hamlets
like Much Malcock that the great reservoirs of national wealth
seep back to the soil. The villagers had their Memorial Hall and
their club. In the rafters of their church the death-watch beetle

had been expensively exterminated for them; their scouts had a bell tent and silver bugles; the district nurse drove her own car; at Christmas their children were surfeited with trees and parties and the cottagers loaded with hampers; if one of them was indisposed port and soup and grapes and tickets for the seaside arrived in profusion; at evening their menfolk returned from work laden with perquisites, and all the year round they feasted on forced vegetables. The vicar found it impossible to interest them in the Left Book Club.

"God gave all men all earth to love," Mr. Metcalfe quoted, dimly remembering the lines from a calendar which had hung in his office in Alexandria, "but since our hearts are small, Ordained for each one spot should prove, Beloved over all."

He pottered round to the engine-house where his chauffeur was brooding over batteries. He popped his head into another outbuilding and saw that no harm had befallen the lawnmower during the night. He paused in the kitchen garden to nip the blossom off some newly planted black-currant which must not be allowed to fruit that summer. Then, his round finished, he pottered in to breakfast.

His wife was already there.

"I've done my round," he said.

"Yes, dear."

"Everything coming along very nicely."

"Yes, dear."

"You can't see Pilbury Steeple, though."

"Good gracious, Beverley, why should you want to do that?"

"It's a sign of rain when you can."

"What a lot of nonsense. You've been listening to Boggett again."

She rose and left him with his papers. She had to see the cook. Servants seem to take up so much time in England; she thought wistfully of the white-gowned Berber boys who had pattered about the cool, tiled floors of her house in Alexandria.

Mr. Metcalfe finished his breakfast and retired to his study with pipe and papers. The *Gazette* came out that morning. A true countryman always reads his "local rag" first, so Mr. Metcalfe patiently toiled through the columns of Women's Institute doings and the reports of a Council meeting on the subject of sewage, before he allowed himself to open *The Times*.

Serene opening of a day of wrath!

II

Towards eleven o'clock Mr. Metcalfe put aside the crossword. In the lobby by the garden-door he kept a variety of garden implements specially designed for the use of the elderly. Selecting from among them one which had newly arrived, he sauntered out into the sunshine and addressed himself to the plantains on the lawn. The tool had a handsomely bound leather grip, a spliced cane handle and a head of stainless steel; it worked admirably, and with a minimum of effort Mr. Metcalfe had soon scarred a large area with neat little pits.

He paused and called towards the house, "Sophie, Sophie, come and see what I've done."

His wife's head emerged from an upper window. "Very pretty, dear," she said.

Encouraged, he set to work again. Boggett passed.

"Useful little tool this, Boggett."

"Ur."

"Think we ought to sow some seed in the bare patches?"

"Noa."

"You think the grass will grow over them?"

"Noa. Plantains'll come up again."

"You don't think I've killed the roots?"

"Noa. Makes the roots powerful strong topping 'em off same as you've done."

"Well, what ought I to do?"

"Bain't nothing you can do with plantains. They do always come up again."

Boggett passed. Mr. Metcalfe looked at his gadget with sudden distaste, propped it petulantly against the sundial, and with his hands in his pockets stared out across the valley. Even at this

distance Lady Peabury's aubretias struck a discordant note. His
eyes dropped and he noticed, casually at first, then with growing
curiosity, two unfamiliar figures among Westmacott's cows. They
were young men in dark, urban clothes, and they were very busy
about something. They had papers in their hands which they
constantly consulted; they paced up and down the field as though
measuring it; they squatted on their haunches as though roughly
taking a level; they pointed into the air, to the ground, and to the
horizon.

"Boggett," said Mr. Metcalfe sharply, "come here a minute."

"Urr."

"Do you see two men in Mr. Westmacott's field?"

"Noa."

"You don't?"

" 'Er bain't Mr. Westmacott's field. 'E've a sold of 'er."

"Sold it! Good heavens! Who to?"

"Couldn't rightly say who 'e've a sold 'er to. Gentleman from
London staying at the Brakehurst. Paid a tidy price for 'er too I've
a heard said."

"What on earth for?"

"Couldn't rightly say, but I reckon it be to build hisself
a house."

Build. It was a word so hideous that no one in Much Malcock
dared use it above a whisper. "Housing scheme", "Development", "Clearance", "Council houses", "Planning" – these
obscene words had been expunged from the polite vocabulary
of the district, only to be used now and then, with the licence
allowed to anthropologists, of the fierce tribes beyond the parish
boundary. And now the horror was in their midst, the mark of
Plague in the court of the Decameron.

After the first moment of shock, Mr. Metcalfe rallied for
action, hesitated for a moment whether or no to plunge down
the hill and challenge the enemy on his own ground, and decided
against it; this was the moment to act with circumspection. He
must consult Lady Peabury.

It was three-quarters of a mile to the house; the lane ran past the gate which gave access to Westmacott's field; a crazily-hung elm gate and deep cow-trodden mud, soon in Mr. Metcalfe's imagination, to give place to golden privet and red gravel. Mr. Metcalfe could see the heads of the intruders bobbing beyond the hedge; they bore urban, purposeful black hats. He drove on, miserably.

Lady Peabury was in the morning-room reading a novel; early training gave a guilty spice to this recreation, for she had been brought up to believe that to read a novel before luncheon was one of the gravest sins it was possible for a gentlewoman to commit. She slipped the book under a cushion and rose to greet Mr. Metcalfe.

"I was just getting ready to go out," she explained.

Mr. Metcalfe had no time for politenesses.

"Lady Peabury," he began at once, "I have very terrible news."

"Oh dear! Is poor Mr. Cruttwell having trouble with the Wolf Cub account again?"

"No; at least, he is; there's another fourpence gone astray; on the credit side this time, which makes it more worrying. But that isn't what I came about. It is something that threatens our whole lives. They are going to build in Westmacott's field." Briefly, but with emotion, he told Lady Peabury what he had seen.

She listened gravely. When he had finished there was silence in the morning-room; six little clocks ticked among the chintzes and the potted azaleas. At last Lady Peabury spoke:

"Westmacott has behaved very badly," she said.

"I suppose you can't blame him."

"I do blame him, Mr. Metcalfe, very severely. I can't understand it at all. He always seemed a very decent man. . . . I was thinking of making Mrs. Westmacott secretary of the Women's Institute. He had no right to do a thing like that without consulting us. Why, I look right on to that field from my bedroom windows. I could never understand why you didn't buy the field yourself."

It was let for £3 18s.; they had asked £170 for it; there was tithe and property tax on top of that. Lady Peabury knew this.

"Any of us could have bought it at the time of sale," said Mr. Metcalfe rather sharply.

"It always went with your house."

In another minute, Mr. Metcalfe felt, she would be telling him that *he* had behaved very badly; that *he* had always seemed a very decent man.

She was, in fact, thinking on just those lines at the moment. "I daresay it's not too late even now for you to make an offer," she said.

"We are all equally threatened," said Mr. Metcalfe. "I think we ought to act together. Hodge won't be any too pleased when he hears the news."

Colonel Hodge had heard, and he was none too pleased. He was waiting at the Hall when Mr. Metcalfe got back.

"Do you know what that scoundrel Westmacott has done?"

"Yes," said Mr. Metcalfe rather wearily, "I know." The interview with Lady Peabury had not gone off quite as he had hoped. She had shown no enthusiasm for common action.

"Sold his field to a lot of jerry builders."

"Yes, I know."

"Funny, I always thought it was *your* field."

"No," said Mr. Metcalfe, "never."

"It always used to go with this house."

"Yes, I know, but I didn't happen to want it."

"Well, it's put us all in a pretty nasty fix, I must say. D'you suppose they'd sell it back to you now?"

"I don't know that I want to buy it. Why, they'll probably want a building-land price – seventy or eighty pounds an acre."

"More, I daresay. But, good heavens man, you wouldn't let that stop you. Think how it would depreciate your property having a whole town of bungalows right under your windows."

"Come, come, Hodge. We've no reason to suppose that it will be bungalows."

"Well, villas then. You surely aren't sticking up for the fellows?"

"Certainly not. We shall all suffer very much from any development there. My belief is that it can be stopped by law; there's the Society for the Protection of Rural England. We could interest them in it. The County Council could be approached. We could write letters to the papers and petition the Office of Works. The great thing is that we must all stand together over this."

"Fat lot of change we shall get out of that. Think of the building that's gone on over at Metbury."

Mr. Metcalfe thought, and shuddered.

"I should say that this was one of the times when money talked loudest. Have you tried Lady Peabury?"

For the first time in their acquaintance Mr. Metcalfe detected a distinctly coarse strain in Colonel Hodge. "I have discussed it with her. She is naturally very much concerned."

"That field has always been known as Lower Grumps," said the Colonel, reverting to his former and doubly offensive line of thought. "It's not really her chicken."

"It is all our chickens," said Mr. Metcalfe, getting confused with the metaphor.

"Well, I don't know what you expect me to do about it," said Colonel Hodge. "You know how I'm placed. It all comes of that parson preaching Bolshevism Sunday after Sunday."

"We ought to get together and discuss it."

"Oh, we'll discuss it all right. I don't suppose we shall discuss anything else for the next three months."

No one in Much Malcock took the crisis harder than the Hornbeams. News of it reached them at midday by means of the village charwoman, who dropped in twice a week to despoil their larder. She told them with some pride, innocently assuming that all city gentlemen – as she continued to regard Mr. Hornbeam, in spite of his home-spuns and his beard – would welcome an addition to their numbers.

Nervous gloom descended on the Old Mill. There was no explosion of wrath as there had been at the Manor; no moral condemnation as at the House; no call to action as had come from the Hall. Hopeless sorrow reigned unrelieved. Mrs. Hornbeam's pottery went to pieces. Mr. Hornbeam sat listless at the loom. It was their working hour; they sat at opposite ends of the raftered granary. Often, on other afternoons, they sang to one another catches and refrains of folk music as their busy fingers muddled with the clay and the shuttles. To-day they sat in silence each, according to a Japanese mystical practice, attempting to drive the new peril into the World of Unbeing. It had worked well enough with Colonel Hodge and the Airedale, with the Abyssinian War, and with Mr. Hornbeam senior's yearly visit, but by sunset the new peril remained obstinately concrete.

Mrs. Hornbeam set their simple meal of milk, raisins, and raw turnip; Mr. Hornbeam turned away from his elm platter. "There is no place for the Artist in the Modern World," he said. "We ask nothing of their brutish civilization except to be left alone, to be given one little corner of land, an inch or two of sky where we can live at peace and occupy ourselves with making seemly and beautiful things. You wouldn't think it was too much to ask. We give them the entire globe for their machines. But it is not enough. They have to hunt us out and harry us. They know that as long as there is one spot of loveliness and decency left it is a standing reproach to them."

It was growing dark; Mrs. Hornbeam struck a flint and lit the rush lights. She wandered to the harp and plucked a few poignant notes. "Perhaps Mr. Metcalfe will stop it," she said.

"That we should be dependent for the essentials of life upon a vulgarian like that. . . ."

It was in this mood that he received an invitation from Mr. Metcalfe to confer with his neighbours at Much Malcock House on the following afternoon.

The choice of meeting place had been a delicate one, for Lady Peabury was loth to abdicate her position of general leadership or to appear as leader in this particular matter; on the other hand, it touched her too closely for her to be able to ignore it. Accordingly the invitations were issued by Mr. Metcalfe, who thereby accepted responsibility for the agenda, while the presence of the meeting in her morning-room gave something of the atmosphere of a Cabinet meeting at the Palace.

Opinion had hardened during the day and there was general agreement with Colonel Hodge's judgement: "Metcalfe has got us into this hole by not buying the field in the first place; it's up to him to get us out of it." Though nothing as uncompromising as this was said in front of Mr. Metcalfe, he could feel it in the air. He was the last to arrive. Lady Peabury's welcome to her guests had been lukewarm. "It is very kind of you to come. I really cannot think that it is necessary, but Mr. Metcalfe particularly wished it. I suppose he intends telling us what he is going to do." To Mr. Metcalfe she said, "We are full of curiosity."

"Sorry to be late. I've had a day of it, I can tell you. Been to all the local offices, got on to all the Societies, and I may as well tell you at once, there's nothing doing from that end. We are not even scheduled as a rural area."

"No," said Colonel Hodge, "I saw to that. Halves the potential value of one's property."

"*Schedules*," moaned Mr. Hornbeam, "that is what we have become. We must be *scheduled* to lead a free life."

". . . And so," persisted Mr. Metcalfe, in his board-room manner, "we are left to find the solution ourselves. Now this young man has no particular reason, I imagine, for preferring this district above any other in the country. The building has not yet begun; he has no commitments. I cannot help feeling that if he were tactfully approached and offered a reasonable profit on the transaction, he might be induced to re-sell."

"I am sure," said Lady Peabury, "we shall all owe a deep debt of gratitude to Mr. Metcalfe."

"Very public spirited of you," said Colonel Hodge.

"Profits, the cancer of the age . . ."

"I am perfectly willing," said Mr. Metcalfe, "to bear my share of the burden. . . ." At the word "share" his hearers stiffened perceptibly. "My suggestion is that we make a common fund proportionate to our present land holdings. By a rough calculation I work that out as being in the ratio of one to Mr. Hornbeam, two to Colonel Hodge, two to myself, and five to our hostess here. The figures could be adjusted," he added as he noted that his suggestion was falling a little flat.

"You can count me out," said Colonel Hodge. "Couldn't possibly run to it."

"And me," said Mr. Hornbeam.

Lady Peabury was left in, with a difficult hand to stake. Delicacy forbade recognition of the vital fact that Mr. Metcalfe was very much the richer – delicacy tempered with pride. The field must be saved, but there seemed no system of joint purchase by which she could honourably fail to bear the largest part. Duty called, clearly and unmistakably, to Mr. Metcalfe alone. She held her cards and passed the bidding. "Surely," she said, "as a business man you must see a great many objections to joint ownership. Do you propose to partition the field, or are we all to share the rent, the tithe and the tax? It would be highly inconvenient. I doubt if it is even legal."

"Certainly, certainly. I merely wished to assure you of my readiness to co-operate. The field, as such, is of no interest to me, I can assure you. I would willingly stand down."

There was a threat, almost a lack of politeness in his tone. Colonel Hodge scented danger.

"Wouldn't it be best," he said, "to find out first if this fellow is willing to re-sell? Then you can decide which of you keep it."

"I am sure we shall be very interested to hear the results of Mr. Metcalfe's negotiations," said Lady Peabury.

She should not have said that. She would gladly have recalled the words the moment after they were uttered. She had vaguely wanted to say something disagreeable, to punish Mr. Metcalfe for the discomfort in which she found herself. She had not meant to antagonize him, and this she had unmistakably done.

Mr. Metcalfe left the House abruptly, almost precipitately, and all that evening he chafed. For fifteen years Mr. Metcalfe had been president of the British Chamber of Commerce. He had been greatly respected by the whole business community. No one could put anything across him, and he would not touch anything that was not above-board. Egyptian and Levantine merchants who tried to interest Metcalfe in shady business went away with a flea in the ear. It was no good trying to squeeze Metcalfe. That was his reputation in the Union Club, and here, at home, in his own village, an old woman had tried to catch him napping. There was a sudden change. He was no longer the public-spirited countryman; he was cards-on-the-table-brass-tacks-and-twenty-shillings-in-the-pound-treat-him-fair-or-mind-your-step Metcalfe, Metcalfe with his back up, fighting Metcalfe once again, Metcalfe who would cut off his nose any day to spite his face, sink any ship for a ha'p'orth of tar that was not legally due, Metcalfe the lion of the Rotarians.

"She should not have said that," said Colonel Hodge, reporting the incident to his wife over their horrible dinner. "Metcalfe won't do anything now."

"Why don't *you* go and talk to the man who's bought the field?" said Mrs. Hodge.

"I might ... I think I will. ... Tell you what, I'll go now."

He went.

He found the man without difficulty, since there was no other visitor staying at the Brakehurst Arms. An enquiry from the landlord elicited his name – Mr. Hargood-Hood. He was sitting alone in the parlour, sipping whisky and soda and working at *The Times'* crossword.

The Colonel said, "Evening. My name is Hodge."

"Yes?"

"I daresay you know who I am."

"I'm very sorry, I'm afraid ..."

"I own the Manor. My garden backs on to Westmacott's field – the one you've bought."

"Oh," said Mr. Hargood-Hood, "was he called Westmacott? I didn't know. I leave all these things to my lawyer. I simply told him to find me a suitable, secluded site for my work. He told me last week he had found one here. It seems very suitable. But he didn't tell me anyone's name."

"You didn't pick this village for any particular reason?"

"No, no. But I think it perfectly charming," he added politely. There was a pause.

"I wanted to talk to you," said Colonel Hodge superfluously. "Have a drink."

"Thank you."

Another pause.

"I'm afraid you won't find it a very healthy site," said the Colonel. "Down in the hollow there."

"I never mind things like that. All I need is seclusion."

"Ah, a writer no doubt."

"No."

"A painter?"

"No, no. I suppose you would call me a scientist."

"I see. And you would be using your house for weekends?"

"No, no, quite the reverse. I and my staff will be working here all the week. And it's not exactly a house I'm building, although of course there will be living quarters attached. Perhaps, since we are going to be such close neighbours, you would like to see the plans. . . ."

". . . You never saw such a thing," said Colonel Hodge next morning to Mr. Metcalfe. "An experimental industrial laboratory he called it. Two great chimneys – have to have those, he said, by law, because of poison fumes, a water tower to get high pressures, six bungalows for his staff . . . ghastly. The odd thing was he seemed quite a decent sort of fellow. Said it hadn't occurred to him anyone would find it objectionable. Thought we should all be interested. When I brought up the subject of re-selling – tactful, you know – he just said he left all that to his lawyer. . . ."

III

Much Malcock Hall.

Dear Lady Peabury,

In pursuance of our conversation of three days ago, I beg to inform you that I have been in communication with Mr. Hargood-Hood, the purchaser of the field which separates our two properties, and his legal representative. As Col. Hodge has already informed you, Mr. Hargood-Hood proposes to erect an experimental industrial laboratory fatal to the amenities of the village. As you are doubtless aware, work has not yet been commenced, and Mr. Hargood-Hood is willing to re-sell the property if duly compensated. The price proposed is to include re-purchase of the field, legal fees and compensation for the architect's work. The young blackguard has us in a cleft stick. He wants £500. It is excessive, but I am prepared to pay half of this if you will pay the other half. Should you not accede to this generous offer I shall take steps to safeguard my own interests at whatever cost to the neighbourhood.

Yours sincerely,

Beverley Metcalfe.

P.S. – I mean I shall sell the Hall and develop the property as building lots.

Much Malcock House.

Lady Peabury begs to inform Mr. Metcalfe that she has received his note of this morning, the tone of which I am unable to account for. She further begs to inform you that she has no wish to increase my already extensive responsibilities in the district. She cannot accept the principle of equal obligation with Mr. Metcalfe as he has far less land to look after, and the field in question should rightly form part of your property. She does not think that the scheme for developing his garden as a housing estate is likely to be a success if Mr. Hargood-Hood's laboratory is as unsightly as is represented, which I rather doubt.

"All right," said Mr. Metcalfe. "That's that and be damned to her."

IV

It was ten days later. The lovely valley, so soon to be defiled, lay resplendent in the sunset. Another year, thought Mr. Metcalfe, and this fresh green foliage would be choked with soot, withered with fumes; these mellow roofs and chimneys which for two hundred years or more had enriched the landscape below the terrace, would be hidden by functional monstrosities in steel and glass and concrete. In the doomed field Mr. Westmacott, almost for the last time, was calling his cattle; next week building was to begin and they must seek other pastures. So, in a manner of speaking, must Mr. Metcalfe. Already his desk was littered with house-agents' notices. All for £500, he told himself. There would be redecorations; the cost and loss of moving. The speculative builders to whom he had viciously appealed showed no interest in the site. He was going to lose much more than £500 on the move. But so, he grimly assured himself, was Lady Peabury. She would learn that no one could put a fast one over on Beverley Metcalfe.

And she, on the opposing slope, surveyed the scene with corresponding melancholy. The great shadows of the cedars lay across the lawn; they had scarcely altered during her long tenancy, but the box hedge had been of her planting; it was she who had planned the lily pond and glorified it with lead flamingoes; she had reared the irregular heap of stones under the west wall and stocked it with Alpines; the flowering shrubs were hers; she could not take them with her where she was going. Where? She was too old now to begin another garden, to make other friends. She would move, like so many of her contemporaries, from hotel to hotel, at home and abroad, cruise a little, settle for prolonged rather unwelcome visits, on her relatives. All this for £250, for £12 10s. a year, for less than she gave to charity. It was not the money; it was Principle. She would not compromise with Wrong; with that ill-bred fellow on the hill opposite.

Despite the splendour of the evening an unhappy spirit obsessed Much Malcock. The Hornbeams moped and drooped; Colonel Hodge fretted. He paced the threadbare carpet of his smoking-room. "It's enough to make a fellow turn Bolshie, like that parson," he said. "What does Metcalfe care. He's rich. He can move anywhere. What does Lady Peabury care? It's the small man, trying to make ends meet, who suffers."

Even Mr. Hargood-Hood seemed affected by the general gloom. His lawyer was visiting him at the Brakehurst. All day they had been in intermittent, rather anxious consultation. "I think I might go and talk to that Colonel again," he said, and set off up the village street, under the deepening shadows, for the Manor House. And from this dramatic, last-minute move for conciliation sprang the great Hodge Plan for appeasement and peace-in-our-time.

V

"... the Scouts are badly in need of a new hut," said Colonel Hodge.

"No use coming to me," said Mr. Metcalfe. "I'm leaving the neighbourhood."

"I was thinking," said Colonel Hodge, "that Westmacott's field would be just the place for it. . . ."

And so it was arranged. Mr. Hornbeam gave a pound, Colonel Hodge a guinea, Lady Peabury £250. A jumble sale, a white-elephant-tea, a raffle, a pageant, and a house-to-house collection, produced a further 30s. Mr. Metcalfe found the rest. It cost him, all told, a little over £500. He gave with a good heart. There was no question now of jockeying him into a raw deal. In the rôle of public benefactor he gave with positive relish, and when Lady Peabury suggested that the field should be reserved for a camping site and the building of the hut postponed, it was Mr. Metcalfe who pressed on with the building and secured the old stone tiles from the roof of a dismantled barn. In the circumstances, Lady Peabury could not protest when the building was named the Metcalfe-Peabury Hall. Mr. Metcalfe found the title invigorating and was soon in negotiation with the brewery for a change of name at the Brakehurst Arms. It is true that Boggett still speaks of it as "the Brakehurst", but the new name is plainly lettered for all to read: The Metcalfe Arms.

And so Mr. Hargood-Hood passed out of the history of Much Malcock. He and his lawyer drove away to their home beyond the hills. The lawyer was Mr. Hargood-Hood's brother.

"We cut that pretty fine, Jock. I thought, for once, we were going to be left with the baby."

They drove to Mr. Hargood-Hood's home, a double quadrangle of mellow brick that was famous far beyond the county.

On the days when the gardens were open to the public, record crowds came to admire the topiary work, yews and boxes of prodigious size and fantastic shape which gave perpetual employment to three gardeners. Mr. Hargood-Hood's ancestors had built the house and planted the gardens in a happier time, before the days of property tax and imported grain. A sterner age demanded more strenuous efforts for their preservation.

"Well, that has settled Schedule A for another year and left something over for cleaning the fish-ponds. But it was an anxious month. I shouldn't care to go through it again. We must be more careful next time, Jock. How about moving east?"

Together the two brothers unfolded the inch ordnance map of Norfolk, spread it on the table of the Great Hall and began their preliminary, expert search for a likely, unspoilt, well-loved village.

'Cornish Landscape with White Cow in Thought', *The Cherwell*, 2 February 1924, p. 40.

THE SYMPATHETIC PASSENGER

As MR. JAMES shut the side door behind him, radio music burst from every window of his house. Agnes, in the kitchen, was tuned in to one station; his wife, washing her hair in the bathroom, to another.

The competing programmes followed him to the garage and into the lane.

He had twelve miles to drive to the station, and for the first five of them he remained in a black mood.

He was in most matters a mild-tempered person – in all matters, it might be said, except one; he abominated the wireless.

It was not merely that it gave him no pleasure; it gave active pain, and, in the course of years, he had come to regard the invention as being directed deliberately against himself, a conspiracy of his enemies to disturb and embitter what should have been the placid last years of his life.

He was far from being an old man; he was, in fact, in his middle fifties; he had retired young, almost precipitously, as soon as a small legacy had made it possible. He had been a lover of quiet all his life.

Mrs. James did not share this preference.

Now they were settled in a small country house, twelve miles from a suitable cinema.

The wireless, for Mrs. James, was a link with the clean pavements and bright shop windows, a communion with millions of fellow beings.

Mr. James saw it in just that light too. It was what he minded most – the violation of his privacy. He brooded with growing resentment on the vulgarity of womankind.

In this mood he observed a burly man of about his own age signalling to him for a lift from the side of the road. He stopped.

"I wonder if by any chance you are going to the railway station?" The man spoke politely with a low, rather melancholy voice.

"I am; I have to pick up a parcel. Jump in."

"That's very kind of you."

The man took his place beside Mr. James. His boots were dusty, and he sank back in his seat as though he had come from far and was weary.

He had very large, ugly hands, close-cut grey hair, a bony, rather sunken face.

For a mile or so he did not speak. Then he asked suddenly, "Has this car got a wireless?"

"Certainly not."

"What is that knob for?" He began examining the dashboard. "And that?"

"One is the self-starter. The other is supposed to light cigarettes. It does not work. If," he continued sharply, "you have stopped me in the hope of hearing the wireless, I can only suggest that I put you down and let you try your luck on someone else."

"Heaven forbid," said his passenger. "I detest the thing."

"So do I."

"Sir, you are one among millions. I regard myself as highly privileged in making your acquaintance."

"Thank you. It is a beastly invention."

The passenger's eyes glowed with passionate sympathy. "It is worse. It is diabolical."

"Very true."

"Literally diabolical. It is put here by the devil to destroy us. Did you know that it spread the most terrible diseases?"

"I didn't know. But I can well believe it."

"It causes cancer, tuberculosis, infantile paralysis, and the common cold. I have proved it."

"It certainly causes headaches," said Mr. James.

"No man," said his passenger, "has suffered more excruciating headaches than I.

"They have tried to kill me with headaches. But I was too clever for them. Did you know that the B.B.C. has its own secret police, its own prisons, its own torture chambers?"

"I have long suspected it."

"I *know*. I have experienced them. Now it is the time of revenge."

Mr. James glanced rather uneasily at his passenger and drove a little faster.

"I have a plan," continued the big man. "I am going to London to put it into execution. I am going to kill the Director-General. I shall kill them *all*."

They drove on in silence. They were nearing the outskirts of the town when a larger car driven by a girl drew abreast of them and passed. From inside it came the unmistakable sounds of a jazz band. The big man sat up in his seat, rigid as a pointer.

"Do you hear that?" he said. "*She's* got one. After her, quick."

"No good," said Mr. James. "We can never catch that car."

"We can try. We *shall* try, unless," he said with a new and more sinister note in his voice, "unless you don't want to."

Mr. James accelerated. But the large car was nearly out of sight.

"Once before," said his passenger, "I was tricked. The B.B.C. sent one of their spies. He was very like you. He pretended to be one of my followers; he said he was taking me to the Director-General's office. Instead he took me to a prison. Now I know what to do with spies. I kill them." He leaned towards Mr. James.

"I assure you, my dear sir, you have no more loyal supporter than myself. It is simply a question of cars. I cannot overtake her. But no doubt we shall find her at the station."

"We shall see. If we do not, I shall know whom to thank, and how to thank him."

They were in the town now and making for the station. Mr. James looked despairingly at the policeman on point duty, but was signalled on with a negligent flick of the hand. In the station yard the passenger looked round eagerly.

"I do not see that car," he said.

Mr. James fumbled for a second with the catch of the door and then tumbled out. "Help!" he cried. "Help! There's a madman here."

With a great shout of anger the man dodged round the front of the car and bore down on him.

At that moment three men in uniforms charged out of the station doorway. There was a brief scuffle; then, adroitly, they had their man strapped up.

"We thought he'd make for the railway," said their chief. "You must have had quite an exciting drive, sir."

Mr. James could scarcely speak. "Wireless," he muttered weakly.

"Ho, he's been talking to you about that, has he? Then you're very lucky to be here to tell us. It's his foible, as you might say. I hope you didn't disagree with him."

"No," said Mr. James. "At least, not at first."

"Well, you're luckier than some. He can't be crossed, not about wireless. Gets very wild. Why, he killed two people and half killed a third last time he got away. Well, many thanks for bringing him in so nicely, sir. We must be getting him home."

Home. Mr. James drove back along the familiar road.

"Why," said his wife when he entered the house. "How quick you've been. Where's the parcel?"

"I think I must have forgotten it."

"How very unlike you. Why, you're looking quite ill. I'll run in and tell Agnes to switch off the radio. She can't have heard you come in."

"No," said Mr. James, sitting down heavily. "Not switch off radio. Like it. Homely."

'The Union: Europe Listens where Oxford sleeps' (column head cartoon), *The Cherwell*, 10 November 1923, p. 51 and thereafter. [The standing figure is a student debater.]

WORK SUSPENDED

Two Chapters of an Unfinished Novel

To Alexander Woollcott

Dear Mr. Woollcott,

This is the book on which I was at work in September, 1939. It is now clear to me that even if I were again to have the leisure and will to finish it, the work would be vain, for the world in which and for which it was designed, has ceased to exist.

So far as it went, this was my best writing. Will you, who, in the past, have been so prodigal of encouragement, accept this fragment of what, complete, might have come within measurable distance of justifying your interest?

Yours sincerely,

Evelyn Waugh.

Summer, 1942.

This epistle was cut from the abbreviated version of *Work Suspended* published in 1949. In the pages that follow, divergencies from the 1942 text are recorded in the footnotes, and passages cut from the original text are enclosed in square brackets.

CHAPTER I
MY FATHER'S HOUSE[1]

At the time of my father's death I was in Morocco, at a small French hotel outside the fortifications of Fez. I had been there for six weeks, doing little else but write, and my book, *Murder at Mountrichard Castle*, was within twenty thousand words of its end. In three weeks I should pack it up for the typist; perhaps sooner, for I had nearly passed that heavy middle period where less conscientious writers introduce their second corpse. I was thirty-[three][2] years of age at the time, and a serious writer. I had always been a one-corpse man [and, as far as possible, a clean corpse man, eschewing the blood-transfusions to which most of my rivals resorted to revitalize their flagging stories; moreover, I eschewed anything that was even remotely sordid or salacious. My corpses, invariably, were male, solitary, of high position in the world and, as near as possible, bloodless. I abhorred blunt instruments and "features battered beyond recognition". Lord George Vanburgh, in *Death in the Dukeries*, was decapitated but only, it will be remembered, after he had been dead for some time through other causes. My poisons were painless; no character of mine ever writhed or vomited. Cardinal Vascari, in *Vengeance at the Vatican*, my first and in other ways my least successful story, met death in a model fashion, lapsing into coma while he sat at his window, one tranquil autumn evening, overlooking the Tiber; the fingers relaxed in the scarlet lap and the rosary with the missing decade – that ingenious clue – slipped unnoticed to the carpet. That was how John Plant's characters died.

On the other hand, while avoiding blood, I was tolerably free with the thunder. I despised a purely functional novel as I despised contemporary architecture; the girders and struts of

1 PART ONE
  A Death
2 four

the plot require adornment and concealment; I relish the masked buttresses, false domes, superfluous columns, all the subterfuges of literary architecture and the plaster and gilt of its decoration. A tenth of my writing or more – and some of the best of it – went on stage effects; sudden eddies of cold air would stir my curtains, candles guttered, horses lathered themselves to frenzy in their stalls; idiots gibbered; my policemen hunted their man in a landscape of crag, torrent, ruin, and fallen oak. And now and then, when the sequence of emotions I planned for my readers required a moment of revulsion and terror, I would kill an animal in atrocious circumstances – Lady Belinda's Blenheim spaniel, for example, in *The Frightened Footman*.

Murder at Mountrichard Castle bristled with Gothic enrichments and I was tolerably confident of its good reception. Success even at its first approach, failed to surprise me]. I took pains with my work and I [thought][1] it excellent. Each of my seven books sold better than its predecessor. Moreover, the sale was in their first three months, at seven and sixpence. I did not have to relabel the library edition for the bookstalls. People bought my books and kept them – not in the spare bedrooms but in the library, all seven of them together on a shelf. [My contract provided me with an advance on each book corresponding with the total earnings of the one before it.] In six weeks' time, when my manuscript had been typed, revised and delivered I should receive a cheque for something over nine hundred pounds. [This would pay off my overdraft and Income Tax and leave me with five hundred or so, on which, with another overdraft, I should live until my next book was ready. That was how I ordered my affairs.] Had I wished it, I could have earned considerably more. I never tried to sell my stories as serials; the delicate fibres of a story suffer when it is chopped up into weekly or monthly parts and never completely heal. Often, when I have been reading the work of a competitor, I have said, "She was writing with an eye on the magazines. She had to close this episode prematurely; she had to introduce that extraneous bit of melodrama, so as to make each

1 found

instalment a readable unit. Well," I would reflect, "she has a husband to support and two sons at school. She must not expect to do two jobs well, to be a good mother and a good novelist." I chose to live modestly on the royalties of my books.

I never found economy the least irksome; on the contrary I took pleasure in it. My friends, I know, considered me parsimonious; it was a joke among them, which I found quite inoffensive [, for there are two distinct kinds of meanness – those which come of loving money and of disliking it. Mine was the latter sort]. My ambition was to eradicate money as much as I could from my life [and to do so required planning]. I acquired as few possessions as possible. I preferred to pay interest to my bank rather than be bothered by tradesmen's bills. I decided what I wanted to do and then devised ways of doing it cheaply and tidily; money wasted meant more money to be earned. I disliked profusion[; it recalled stories in the *Daily Express* about prizefighters and comedians dying in penury...they had spent £200 a week, entertaining and lending; they had worn a new pair of black silk socks every evening; no old pal ever left them empty-handed...ten-shilling tips to commissionaires... Bohemians].

I chose my career deliberately at the age of twenty-one. I had a naturally ingenious and constructive mind and the taste for writing. I was youthfully zealous of good fame. There seemed few ways, of which a writer need not be ashamed, by which he could make a decent living. To produce something, saleable in large quantities to the public, which had absolutely nothing of myself in it; to sell something for which the kind of people I liked and respected, would have a use; that was what I sought, and detective stories fulfilled the purpose. They were an art which admitted of classical canons of technique and taste. [Their writing was painful – though much less painful than any other form would have been – because I have the unhappy combination of being both lazy and fastidious.] It was immune, anyway, from the obnoxious comment to which lighter work is exposed. "How you must revel in writing your delicious books, Mr. So-and-So." My friend Roger Simmonds, who was with me at the University and set up as a professional humorist at the same time as I wrote *Vengeance at the Vatican*, is constantly plagued by that kind of remark. Instead, women say to me, "How difficult it must be to think of all those complicated clues, Mr. Plant." I agree. "It *is*, intolerably difficult." "And do you do your writing here in London?" "No, I find I have to go away to work." "Away from telephones and parties and things?" "Exactly."

I had tried a dozen or more retreats in England and abroad – country inns, furnished cottages, seaside hotels out of the season – Fez was by far the best of them. It is a splendid, compact city and in early March, with flowers springing everywhere in the surrounding hills and in the untidy patios of the Arab houses, one of the most beautiful in the world. I liked the little hotel. It was cheap and rather chilly – an indispensable austerity. The food was digestible with, again, that element of sparseness which I find agreeable. It had an intermediate place between the semi-Egyptian splendours of the tourists' palace on the hill, and the bustling commercial hotels of the new town, half an hour's walk away. The clientele was exclusively French; the wives of civil servants and elderly couples of small means wintering in the sun. In the evening Spahi officers came to the bar to play bagatelle. I used to work on the verandah of my room, overlooking a ravine where Senegalese infantrymen were constantly washing their linen. My recreations were few and simple. Once a week after dinner I took the 'bus to the Moulay Abdullah; once a week I dined at the Consulate. The consul allowed me to come to him for a bath. I used to walk up, under the walls, swinging my sponge-bag, through the dusk. He, his wife and their governess were the only English people I met; the only people, indeed, with whom I did more than exchange bare civilities. Sometimes I visited the native cinema where old, silent films were shown in a babel of catcalls. On other evenings I took a dose of Dial and was asleep by half-past nine. In these circumstances the book progressed well. I have since, on occasions, looked back at them with envy.

As an odd survival of the age of capitulations there was at that time a British Post Office at the Consulate, used mainly, the French believed, for treasonable purposes by disaffected Arabs. When there was anything for me the postman used to come down the hill on his bicycle to my hotel. He had a badge in his cap and on his arm a brassard with the royal escutcheon; he invariably honoured me with a stiff, military salute which increased my importance in the hotel at the expense of my reputation as an innocent and unofficial man of letters. It was this postman who brought the news of my father's death in a letter from my Uncle Andrew, his brother.

My father, it appeared, had been knocked down by a motor car more than a week ago and had died without regaining consciousness. I was his only child and, with the exception of my uncle, his only near relative. "All arrangements" had been made. The funeral was taking place that day. "*In spite of your father's opinions, in the absence of any formal instructions to the contrary,*" my Uncle Andrew wrote, "*your Aunt and I thought it best to have a religious ceremony of an unostentatious kind.*"

"He might have telegraphed," I thought; and then, later, "Why should he have?" There was no question of my having been able to see my father before he died; participation in a "religious ceremony of an unostentatious kind" was neither in my line nor my father's; nor − to do him justice − in my Uncle Andrew's. It would satisfy the Jellabys.

With regard to the Jellabys my father always avowed a ruthlessness which he was far from practising; he would in fact put himself to considerable inconvenience to accommodate them, but in principle he abhorred any suggestion of discretion or solicitude. It was his belief that no one but himself dealt properly with servants. Two attitudes drove him to equal fury: what he called the "*pas-devant* tomfoolery" of his childhood − the precept that scandal and the mention of exact sums of money should be hushed in their presence − or the more recent idea that their quarters should be prettily decorated and themselves given opportunity for cultural development. "Jellaby has been with me twenty years," he would say, "and is fully cognisant of the facts of life. He and Mrs. Jellaby know my income to the nearest shilling and they know the full history of everyone who comes to this house. I pay them abominably and they supplement their wages by cooking the books. Servants prefer it that way. It

preserves their independence and self-respect. The Jellabys eat
continually, sleep with the windows shut, go to church every
Sunday morning and to chapel in the evening, and entertain
surreptitiously at my expense whenever I am out of the house.
Jellaby's a teetotaller; Mrs. Jellaby takes the port." He rang the
bell whenever he wanted anything fetched from upstairs and sat
as long as he wanted over his wine. "Poor old Armstrong," he
used to say of a fellow Academician, "lives like a Hottentot. He
keeps a lot of twittering women like waitresses in a railway-station
buffet. After the first glass of port they open the dining-room door
and stick their heads in. After the second glass they do it again.
Then instead of throwing something at them, Armstrong says,
'I think they want to clear' and we have to move out." But he had
a warm affection for the Jellabys, and I believe it was largely on
Mrs. Jellaby's account that he allowed himself to be put down for
the Academy. They, in their turn, served him faithfully. It would
have been a cruel betrayal to deny them a funeral service and
I am sure my father had them in mind when he omitted any
provision against it in his will. He was an exact man who would
not have forgotten a point of that kind. On the other hand, he
was a dogmatic atheist of the old-fashioned cast and would not
have set anything down which might be construed as apostasy.
He had left it to my Uncle Andrew's tact. No doubt, too, it was
part of my uncle's tact to save me the embarrassment of being
present.

II

I sat on my verandah for some time, smoking and considering
the situation in its various aspects. There seemed no good reason
for a change of plan. My Uncle Andrew would see to everything.
The Jellabys would be provided for. Apart from them my father
had no obligations. His affairs were always simple and in good
order. The counterfoils of his cheques and his own excellent
memory were his only account books; he had never owned any
investments except the freehold of the house in St. John's Wood
which he had bought with the small capital sum left him by my
mother. He lived up to his income and saved nothing. In him the

parsimony which I had inherited, took the form of a Gallic
repugnance to paying direct taxes or, as he preferred it, to
subscribing to "the support of the politicians". He had,
moreover, the conviction that anything he put by would be
filched by the radicals. Lloyd George's ascent to power was the
last contemporary event to impress him. Since then he believed,
or professed to believe, that public life had become an open
conspiracy for the destruction of himself and his class. This
class, of which he considered himself the sole survivor, and its
ways were for him the object of romantic loyalty; he spoke of it as
a Jacobite clan proscribed and dispersed after Culloden, in a way
which sometimes embarrassed those who did not know him well.
"We have been uprooted and harried," he would say. "There are
only three classes in England now, politicians, tradesmen and
slaves." Then he would particularize. "Seventy years ago the
politicians and the tradesmen were in alliance; they destroyed the
gentry by destroying the value of land; some of the gentry became
politicians themselves, others tradesmen; out of what was left
they created the new class into which I was born, the moneyless,
landless, educated gentry who managed the country for them.
My grandfather was a Canon of Christ Church, my father was in
the Bengal Civil Service. The capital they left their sons was their
education and their moral principles. Now the politicians are in
alliance with the slaves to destroy the tradesmen. They don't
need to bother about us. We are extinct already. I am a Dodo,"
he used to say, defiantly staring at his audience. "You, my poor
son, are a petrified egg." There is a caricature of him by Max
Beerbohm, in this posture, saying these words.

My choice of profession confirmed his view. "Marjorie
Steyle's boy works below the streets, in a basement, selling
haberdashery at four pounds a week. Dick Anderson has married
his daughter to a grocer. My son John took a second in Mods
and a first in Greats. He writes penny dreadfuls for a living," he
would say.

I always sent him my books and I think he read them. "At least
your grammar is all right," he once said. "Your books will
translate and that's more than can be said for most of these

fellows who set up to write Literature." He had a naturally
hierarchic mind and in his scheme of things, detective stories
stood slightly above the librettos of musical comedy and well
below political journalism. I once showed him a reference to
Death in the Dukeries by the Professor of Poetry, in which it was
described as "a work of art". "Anyone can buy a don," was his
only comment. But he was gratified by my prosperity. "Family
love and financial dependence don't go together," he said. "My
father made me an allowance of thirty shillings a week for the first
three years I was in London and he never forgave it me, *never*. He
hadn't cost his father a penny after he took his degree. Nor had *his*
father before him. You ran into debt at the University. That was a
thing I never did. It was two years before you were keeping
yourself and you went about as a dandy those two years, which
I never did while I was learning to draw. But you've done very
well. No nonsense about Literature. You've cut out quite a line
for yourself. I saw old Etheridge at the club the other evening. He
reads all your books, he told me, and likes 'em. Poor old Etheridge; he brought his boy up to be a barrister and he's still keeping
him at the age of thirty-seven."

My father seldom referred to his contemporaries without the
epithet "old" – usually as "poor old so-and-so", unless they had
prospered conspicuously when they were "that old humbug".
On the other hand, he spoke of men a few years his junior as
"whipper-snappers" and "young puppies". The truth was that he
could not bear to think of anyone as being the same age as
himself. It was all part of the aloofness that was his dominant
concern in life. It was enough for him to learn that an opinion of
his had popular support for him to question and abandon it. His
atheism was his response to the simple piety and confused agnosticism of his family circle. He never came to hear much about
Marxism; had he done so he would, I am sure, have discovered a
number of proofs of the existence of God. In his later years I
observed two reversions of opinion in reaction to contemporary
fashion. In my boyhood, in the time of their Edwardian popularity, he denounced the Jews roundly on all occasions, and later
attributed to them the vogue for post-impressionist painting –

"There was a poor booby called Cezanne, a kind of village idiot who was given a box of paints to keep him quiet. He very properly left his horrible canvases behind him in the hedges. The Jews discovered him and crept round behind him picking them up – just to get something for nothing. Then when he was safely dead and couldn't share in the profits they hired a lot of mercenary lunatics to write him up. They've made thousands out of it." To the last he maintained that Dreyfus had been guilty, but when, in the early thirties, anti-Semitism showed signs of becoming a popular force, he [justly pointed out in an unpublished letter to *The Times*, that the prime guilt in that matter lay with Gentile Prussians][1].

Similarly he was used to profess an esteem for Roman Catholics. "Their religious opinions are preposterous," he said. "But so were those of the ancient Greeks. Think of Socrates spending half his last evening babbling about the topography of the nether world. Grant them their first absurdities and you will find Roman Catholics a reasonable people – and they have civilized habits." Later, however, when he saw signs of this view gaining acceptance, he became convinced of the existence of a Jesuit conspiracy to embroil the world in war, and wrote several letters to *The Times* on the subject; they, too, were unpublished. But in neither of these periods did his opinions greatly affect his personal relations; Jews and Catholics were among his closest friends all his life.

My father dressed as he thought a painter should, in a distinct and recognizable garb which made him a familiar and, in his later years, a venerable figure as he took his exercise in the streets round his house. There was no element of ostentation in his poncho capes, check suits, sombrero hats and stock ties. It was rather that he thought it fitting for a man to proclaim unequivocally his station in life, and despised those of his colleagues who seemed to be passing themselves off as guardsmen and stockbrokers. In general he liked his fellow academicians, though I never heard him express anything but contempt for their work. He regarded the Academy as a club; he enjoyed the dinners and

1 supported the Jewish cause in many unpublished letters to *The Times*

frequently attended the schools, where he was able to state his
views on art in Johnsonian terms. He never doubted that the
function of painting was representational. He criticized his colleagues for such faults as incorrect anatomy, "triviality" and
"insincerity". For this he was loosely spoken of as a conservative,
but that he never was where his art was concerned. He
abominated the standards of his youth. He must have been an
intransigently old-fashioned young man, for he was brought up
in the hey-day of Whistlerian decorative painting and his first
exhibited work was of a balloon ascent in Manchester – a large
canvas crowded with human drama, in the manner of Frith. His
practice was chiefly in portraits – many of them posthumous – for
presentation to colleges and guildhalls. He seldom succeeded
with women whom he endowed with a statuesque absurdity
which was half deliberate, but given the robes of a Doctor of
Music or a Knight of Malta and he would do something fit to
hang with the best panelling in the country; given some whiskers
and he was a master. "As a young man I specialized in hair," he
would say, rather as a doctor might say he specialized in noses
and throats. "I paint it incomparably. Nowadays nobody has any
to paint," and it was this aptitude of his which led him to the long,
increasingly unsaleable series of historical and scriptural groups,
and the scenes of domestic melodrama by which he is known –
subjects which had already become slightly ludicrous when he
was in his cradle, but which he continued to produce year after
year while experimental painters came and went until, right at
the end of his life, he suddenly, without realizing it, found himself
in the fashion. The first sign of this was in [1929][1] when his "Agag
before Samuel" was bought at a provincial exhibition for 750
guineas. It was a large canvas at which he had been at work
intermittently since 1908. Even he spoke of it, with conscious
understatement, as "something of a white elephant". White
elephants indeed were almost the sole species of four-footed
animal that was not, somewhere, worked into this elaborate
composition. When asked why he had introduced such a variety

I   1935

of fauna, he replied, "I'm sick of Samuel. I've lived with him for twenty years. Every time it comes back from an exhibition I paint out [a Jew][1] and put in an animal. If I live long enough I'll have a Noah's ark in its background."

The purchaser of this work was Sir Lionel Sterne.

"Honest Sir Lionel," said my father, as he saw the great canvas packed off to Kensington Palace Gardens. "I should dearly have liked to shake his hairy paw. I can see him well – a fine, meaty fellow with a great gold watch-chain across his belly, who's been decently employed boiling soap or smelting copper all his life, with no time to read Clive Bell. In every age it has been men like him who kept painting alive."

I tried to explain that Lionel Sterne was the youthful and elegant millionaire who for ten years had been a leader of aesthetic fashion. "Nonsense!" said my father. "Fellows like that collect disjointed negresses by Gauguin. Only Philistines like my work and, by God, I only like Philistines."

There was also another, rather less reputable side to my father's business. He received a regular yearly retaining fee from Goodchild and Godley, the Duke Street dealers, for what was called "restoration". This sum was a very important part of his income; without it the comfortable little dinners, the trips abroad, the cabs to and fro between St. John's Wood and the Athenaeum, the faithful, predatory Jellabys, the orchid in his buttonhole – all the substantial comforts and refinements which endeared the world and provided him with his air of gentlemanly ease – would have been impossible to him. The truth was that, while excelling at Lely, my father could paint, very passably, in the manner of almost any of the masters of English portraiture and the private and public collections of the New World were richly representative of his versatility. Very few of his friends knew this traffic; to those who did, he defended it with complete candour. "Goodchild and Godley buy these pictures for what they are – my own work. They pay me no more than my dexterity merits. What they do with them afterwards is their own business. It would ill become

1 an Israelite

me to go officiously about the markets identifying my own handi-craft and upsetting a number of perfectly contented people. It is a great deal better for them to look at beautiful pictures and enjoy them under a misconception about the date, than to make them-selves dizzy by goggling at genuine Picassos."

It was largely on account of his work for Goodchild and Godley that his studio was strictly reserved as a workshop. It was a separate building approached through the garden and it was excluded from general use. Once a year, when he went abroad it was "done out"; once a year, on the Sunday before sending-in day at the Royal Academy it was open to his friends. He took a peculiar pleasure from the gloom of these annual tea-parties and was at the same pains to make them dismal as he was on all other occasions to enliven his entertainments. There was a species of dry, bright yellow, caraway cake which was known to my childhood as "Academy cake", which appeared then and only then, from a grocer in Praed Street; there was an enormous Worcester tea-service – a wedding present – which was known as "Academy cups"; there were "Academy sandwiches" – tiny, triangular and quite tasteless. All these things were part of my earliest memories. I do not know at what date these parties changed from being a rather tedious convention to what they certainly were to my father at the end of his life, a huge, grim and solitary jest. If I was in England I was required to attend and to bring a friend or two. It was difficult, until the last two years when, as I have said, my father became the object of fashionable interest, to collect guests. "When I was a young man," my father said, sardonically surveying the company, "there were twenty or more of these parties in St. John's Wood alone. People of culture drove round from three in the afternoon to six, from Campden Hill to Hampstead. To-day I believe our little gathering is the sole survivor of that deleterious tradition."

On these occasions his year's work – Goodchild and Godley's items excepted – would be ranged round the studio on mahogany easels; the most important work had a wall to itself against a background of scarlet rep. I had been present at the last of the parties the year before. The recollection was remarkable. Lionel

Sterne was there, Lady Metroland and a dozen fashionable connoisseurs. My father was at first rather suspicious of his new clients and suspected an impertinent intrusion into his own private joke, a calling of his bluff of seed-cake and cress sandwiches; but their commissions reassured him. People did not carry a joke to such extravagant lengths. Mrs. Algernon Stitch paid 500 guineas for his picture of the year – a tableau of contemporary life conceived and painted with elaborate mastery. My father attached great importance to suitable titles for his work, and after toying with "The People's Idol", "Feet of Clay", "Not on the First Night", "Their Night of Triumph", "Success and Failure", "Not Invited", "Also Present", he finally called this picture rather enigmatically "The Neglected Cue". It represented the dressing-room of a leading actress at the close of a triumphant first night. She sat at the dressing-table, her back turned on the company and her face visible in the mirror, momentarily relaxed in fatigue. Her protector with proprietary swagger was filling the glasses for a circle of admirers. In the background the dresser was in colloquy at the half-open door with an elderly couple of provincial appearance; it is evident from their costume that they have seen the piece from the cheaper seats, and a commissionaire stands behind them uncertain whether he did right in admitting them. He did not do right; they are her old parents arriving most inopportunely. There was no questioning Mrs. Stitch's rapturous enjoyment of her acquisition.

I was never to know how my father would react to his vogue. He could paint in any way he chose; perhaps he would have embarked on those vague assemblages of picnic litter which used to cover the walls of the Mansard Gallery in the early twenties; he might have retreated to the standards of the Grosvenor Gallery in the nineties. He might, perhaps, have found popularity less inacceptable than he supposed and allowed himself a luxurious and cosetted old age. He died with his [1932][1] picture still unfinished. I saw its early stage on my last visit to him; [it represented an old shipwright pondering on the idle dockyard where lay the great skeleton of the Cunarder that was later to be known as the *Queen Mary*. It was to have been called "Too Big?"][1] My father had given the man a grizzled beard and was revelling in it. That was the last time I saw him.

I had given up living in St. John's Wood for four or five years. There was never a definite moment when I "left home". For all official purposes the house remained my domicile. There was a bedroom that was known as mine; I kept several trunks full of clothes there and a shelf or two of books. I never set up for myself anywhere else, but during the last five years of my father's life I do not suppose I slept ten nights under his roof. This was not due to any estrangement. I enjoyed his company, and he seemed to enjoy mine[; had I settled there permanently, with a servant of my own and a separate telephone number, we might have lived together comfortably enough], but I was never in London for more than a week or two at a time, and I found that as an occasional visitor I strained and upset my father's household. He and they tried to do too much, and he liked to have his plans clear for some way ahead. "My dear boy," he would say on my first evening. "Please do not misunderstand me. I hope you will stay as long as you possibly can, but I do wish to know whether you will still be here on Thursday the fourteenth and if so, whether you will be in to dinner." So I took to staying at my club or with more casual hosts, and to visiting St. John's Wood as often as I could, but with formal prearrangements.

Nevertheless, I realized, the house had been an important part of my life. It had remained unaltered for as long as I could remember. It was a decent house, built in 1840 or thereabouts, in the contemporary Swiss mode of stucco and ornamental weather boards, one of a street of similar, detached houses when I first saw it. By the time of my father's death the transformation of the district, though not complete, was painfully evident. The skyline of the garden was broken on three sides by blocks of flats. The

---

1 it was to have been called "Again?" and represented a one-armed veteran of the First World War meditating over a German helmet.

first of them drove my father into a frenzy of indignation. He wrote to *The Times* about it, addressed a meeting of ratepayers and for six weeks sported a board advertising the house for sale. At the end of that time he received a liberal offer from the syndicate, who wished to extend their block over the site, and he immediately withdrew it from the market. ["I could tell they were Jews," he said, "by the smell of their notepaper."]

This was [in his anti-Semitic period; it was also] the period of his lowest professional fortunes, when his subject pictures remained unsold, the market for dubious old masters was dropping, and public bodies were beginning to look for something "modern" in their memorial portraits; the period, moreover, when I had finished with the University and was still dependent on my father for pocket money. It was a very unsatisfactory time in his life. I had not then learned to appreciate the massive defences of what people call the "border line of sanity", and I was at moments genuinely afraid that my father was going out of his mind; there had always seemed an element of persecution mania about his foibles which might, at a time of great strain, go beyond his control. He used to stand on the opposite pavement watching the new building rise, a conspicuous figure muttering objurgations. I used to imagine scenes in which a policeman would ask him to move on and be met with a wild outburst. I imagined these scenes vividly – my father in swirling cape being hustled off, waving his umbrella. Nothing of the kind occurred. My father, for all his oddity, was a man of indestructible sanity and in his later years he found a keen pleasure in contemplating the rapid deterioration of the hated buildings. "Very good news of Hill Crest Court," he announced one day. "Typhoid and rats." And on another occasion, "Jellaby reports the presence of [tarts][1] at St. Eustace's. They'll have a suicide there soon, you'll see." There was a suicide, and for two rapturous days my father watched the coming and going of police and journalists. After that fewer chintz curtains were visible in the windows, rents began to fall and the lift-man smoked on duty. My father observed and gleefully noted

[1] prostitutes

all these signs. Hill Crest Court changed hands; decorator's, plumber's and electrician's boards appeared all round it; a commissionaire with a new uniform stood at the doors. On the last evening I dined with my father he told me about a visit he had made there, posing as a potential tenant. "The place is a deserted slum," he said. "A miserable, down-at-heel kind of secretary took me round flat after flat – all empty. There were great cracks in the concrete stuffed up with putty. The hot pipes were cold. The doors jammed. He started asking three hundred pounds a year for the best of them and dropped to one hundred and seventy-five pounds before I saw the kitchen. Then he made it one hundred and fifty pounds. In the end he proposed what he called a 'special form of tenancy for people of good social position' – offered to let me live there for a pound a week on condition I turned out if he found someone who was willing to pay the real rent. 'Strictly between ourselves,' he said, 'I can promise you will not be disturbed.' Poor beast, I nearly took his flat, he was so paintable."

Now, I supposed, the house would be sold; another speculator would pull it to pieces; another great, uninhabitable barrack would appear, like a refugee ship in harbour; it would be filled sold, emptied, resold, refilled, re-emptied, while the concrete got discoloured and the green wood shrank, and the rats crept up in their thousands out of the metropolitan railway tunnel; and the trees and gardens all round it disappeared one by one until the place became a working-class district and at last took on a gaiety and life of some sort; until it was condemned by government inspectors and its inhabitants driven further into the country and the process began all over again. I thought of all this, sadly, as I looked out at the fine masonry of Fez, cut four hundred years back by Portuguese prisoners . . . I must go back to England soon to arrange for the destruction of my father's house. Meanwhile there seemed no reason for an immediate change of plan.

III

It was the evening when I usually visited the Moulay Abdullah – the walled *quartier toleré* between the old city and the ghetto. I had gone there first with a sense of adventure; now it had become part of my routine, a regular resort, like the cinema and the Consulate, one of the recreations which gave incident to my week and helped clear my mind of the elaborate villainies of Lady Mountrichard.

I dined at seven and soon afterwards caught my 'bus at the new gate. Before starting I removed my watch and emptied my pockets of all except the few francs which I proposed to spend – a superstitious precaution which still survived from the first evening, when memories of Marseilles and Naples had even moved me to carry a life preserver. The Moulay Abdullah was an orderly place, particularly in the early evening when I frequented it. I had formed an attachment [for it; it was the only]¹ place of its kind [I have ever found,] which endowed its trade with something approaching glamour. There really was a memory of "the East", as adolescents imagine it, in that silent courtyard with its single light, the negro sentries on either side of the lofty Moorish arch, the black lane beyond, between the walls and the water-wheel, full of the thump and stumble of French military boots and the soft pad and rustle of the natives, the second arch into the lighted bazaar, the bright open doors and the tiled patios, the little one-roomed huts where the women stood against the lamp-light – shadows without race or age – the larger houses with their bars and gramophones. I always visited the same house and the same girl – a chubby little Berber with the scarred cheeks of her people and tattooed ornaments – blue on brown – at her fore-head and throat. She spoke the peculiar French which she had picked up from the soldiers and she went by the unassuming, professional name of Fatima. Other girls of the place called themselves "Lola" and "Fifi"; there was even an arrogant, coal-black Sudanese named "Whiskey-soda". But Fatima had none of these airs; she was a cheerful, affectionate girl working hard to collect her marriage dot; she professed to like everyone in the house, even the proprietress, a forbidding [Jewess]² from Tetuan, and the proprietress's Algerian husband, who wore a

1 this sole
2 Levantine

European suit, carried round the mint tea, put records on the gramophone and collected the money. (The Moors are a strict people and take no share in the profits of the Moulay Abdullah.)

To regular and serious customers it was an inexpensive place – fifteen francs to the house, ten to Fatima, five for the mint tea, a few sous to the old fellow who tidied Fatima's alcove and blew up the brazier of sweet gum. Soldiers paid less, but they had to make way for more important customers; often they were penniless men from the Foreign Legion who dropped in merely to hear the gramophone and left nothing behind them but cigarette ends. Now and then tourists appeared with a guide from the big hotel, and the girls were made to line up and give a modest perform-ance of shuffling and hand clapping which was called a native dance. Women tourists particularly seemed to like these expedi-tions and paid heavily for them – a hundred francs or more. But they were unpopular with everyone, particularly with the girls, who regarded it as an unseemly proceeding. Once I came in when Fatima was taking part in one of these dances and saw her genuinely and deeply abashed.

On my first visit I told Fatima that I had a wife and six children in England; this greatly enhanced my importance in her eyes and she always asked after them.

"You have had a letter from England? The little ones are well?"

"They are very well."

"And your father and mother?"

"They, too."

We sat in a tiled hall, two steps below street level, drinking our mint tea – or, rather, Fatima drank hers while I let mine cool in the glass. It was a noisome beverage.

"Whiskey-soda lent me some cigarettes yesterday. Will you give her them?"

I ordered a packet from the bar.

"Yesterday I had a stomach-ache and stayed in my room. That is why Whiskey-soda gave me her cigarettes."

She asked about my business.

I had told her I exported dates.

The date market was steady, I assured her.

When I was in the Moulay Abdullah I almost believed in this aspect of myself as a philo-progenitive fruiterer; St. John's Wood and Mountrichard Castle seemed equally remote. That was the charm of the quarter for me – not its simple pleasures but its privacy and anonymity, the hide-and-seek with one's own personality which redeems vice of its tedium.

That night there was a rude interruption. The gramophone suddenly stopped playing; there was a scuttling among the alcoves; two seedy figures in raincoats strode across the room and began questioning the proprietress; a guard of military police stood at the street door. Raids of this kind, to round up bad characters, are common enough in French Protectorates. It was the first time I had been caught in one. The girls were made to stand along one wall while the detectives checked their medical certificates. Then two or three soldiers stood to attention and gave a satisfactory account of themselves. Then I was asked for my *carte d'identité*. By the capitulations the French police had little authority over British subjects, and since the criminal class of Morocco mostly possessed Maltese papers, this immunity was good ground for vexation. The detectives were surly fellows, African born. Even the sacred word "tourist" failed to soften them. Where was my guide? Tourists did not visit the Moulay Abdullah alone. Where was my passport? At my hotel. The Jamai Palace? No? Tourists did not stay at the hotel I mentioned. Was I registered at the police headquarters? Yes. Very well, I must come with them. In the morning I should have the opportunity to identify myself. A hundred francs, no doubt, would have established my respectability, but my money lay with my passport in the hotel. I did not relish a night in gaol in company with the paperless characters of the Moulay Abdullah. I told them I was a friend of the British Consul. He would vouch for me. They grumbled that they had no time for special enquiries of that kind. The Chief would see about it next morning. Then when I had despaired, they despaired too. There was clearly no money coming for them. They had been in the profession long enough to know that no lasting satisfaction results from vexing British subjects. There was a police post in the quarter and they consented to telephone from it. A few minutes later I was set at liberty with a curt reminder that it was advisable to keep my passport accessible if I wanted to wander about the town at night.

I did not return to Fatima. Instead I set off for the 'bus stop, but the annoyances of the night were not yet over. I was halted again at the gates and the interrogation was repeated. I explained that I had already satisfied their colleagues and been discharged. We re-enacted the scene, with the fading hope of a tip as the recurring motive. Finally they, too, telephoned to the Consulate and I was free to take my 'bus home.

They were still serving dinner at the hotel; the same game of billiards was in progress in the bar; it was less than an hour since I went out. But that hour had been decisive; I was finished with Fez; its privacy had been violated. My weekly visit to the Consulate could never be repeated on the same terms. Twice in twenty minutes the Consul had been called to the telephone to learn that I was in the hands of the police in the Moulay Abdullah; he would not, I thought, be censorious or resentful; the vexation had been mild and the situation slightly absurd – nothing more; but when we next met our relations would be changed. Till then they had been serenely remote; we had talked of the news from England and the Moorish antiquities. We had exposed the bare minimum of ourselves; now a sudden, mutually unwelcome confidence had been forced. The bitterness lay, not in the Consul knowing the fact of my private recreations, but in his knowing that I knew he knew. It was a salient in the defensive line between us that could only be made safe by a wide rectification of frontier or by a complete evacuation. I had no friendly territory into which to withdraw. I was deployed on the dunes between the sea and the foothills. The transports riding at anchor were my sole lines of support.

In the matter of Good Conscience, I was a man of few possessions and held them at a corresponding value. As a spinster in mean lodgings fusses over her fragments of gentility – a rosewood work-box, a Spode plate, a crested tea-kettle – which in a house of abundance would be risked in the rough and tumble of

general use, I set a price on Modesty which those of ampler
virtues might justly regard as fanciful.

Next day I set off for London with my book unfinished.

IV

I travelled from spring into winter; sunlit spray in the Straits of
Gibraltar changed to dark, heavy seas in the Bay of Biscay; fog off
Finisterre, fog in the Channel, clear, grey weather in the Thames
estuary and a horizon of factories and naked trees. We berthed in
London and I drove through cold and dirty streets to meet my
Uncle Andrew.

He told me the full circumstances of my father's death; the
commercial traveller, against whom a case was being brought for
reckless driving, had outraged my uncle by sending a wreath of
flowers to the funeral; apart from this everything had been
satisfactory. My uncle passed over to me the undertaker's
receipted account; he had questioned one or two of the items
and obtained an inconsiderable reduction. "I am convinced," my
uncle said, "that there is a great deal of sharp practice among
these people. They trade upon the popular conception of delicacy. In fact they are the only profession who literally rob the
widow and the orphan." I thanked my uncle for having saved me
£3 18s. It was a matter of principle, he said.

As I expected, I was my father's sole heir. Besides the house
and its contents I inherited £2,000 in an insurance policy which
my father had taken out at the time of his marriage and, without
my knowledge, kept up ever since. An injunction, in the brief will,
to "provide suitably" for the servants in my father's employment,
had already been obeyed. The Jellabys had been given £250. It
was clear from my father's words that he had no conception of
what a suitable provision should be. Neither had I, and I was
grateful to my uncle for taking responsibility in the matter. For
their part the Jellabys had expected nothing. My father, as long
ago as I could remember him, was accustomed to talk with relish
of his approaching death. I had heard him often admonish
Jellaby, "You have joined fortune with a poor man. Make what

you can while I still have my faculties. My death will be an occasion for unrelieved lamentation," and the Jellabys, in the manner of their kind, took his words literally, kept a keen watch on all sources of perquisite, and expected nothing. Jellaby took his cheque, my uncle said, without any demonstration of gratitude or disappointment, murmuring ungraciously that it would come in quite useful. No doubt he thought no thanks were due to my uncle, for it was not his money, nor to my father, for it was no intention of his to give it. It was a last, substantial perquisite.

The Jellabys had been much in my mind, off and on, during the journey from Fez. I had fretted, in a way I have, imagining our meeting and a scene of embarrassing condolence and reminiscence, questioning the propriety of removing them immediately, if ever, from the place where they had spent so much of their lives; I even saw myself, on the Jellabys' account, assuming my father's way of life, settling in St. John's Wood, entertaining small dinner parties, lunching regularly at my club and taking three weeks' holiday abroad in the early summer. As things turned out, however, I never saw the Jellabys again. They had done their packing before the funeral, and went straight to the railway station in their black clothes. Their plans had been laid years in advance. They had put away a fair sum and invested it in Portsmouth, not, as would have been conventional, in a lodging house, but in a small shop in a poor quarter of the town which enjoyed a brisk trade in second-hand wireless apparatus. Mrs. Jellaby's step-brother had been keeping the business warm for them and there they retired with an alacrity which was slightly shocking but highly convenient. I wrote to them some time later when I was going through my father's possessions, to ask if they would like to have some small personal memento of him; they might value one of his sketches, I suggested, for the walls of their new home. The answer took some time in coming. When it came it was on a sheet of trade paper with a printed heading "*T. JELLABY. Every Radio want promptly supplied for cash.*" Mrs. Jellaby wrote the letter. They had not much room for pictures, she said, but would greatly appreciate some blankets, as it was chilly at nights in Portsmouth; she specified a particular pair which my father had bought shortly before his death; they were lying, folded in the hot cupboard. . . .

Uncle Andrew gave me the keys of my father's house. I went straight there from lunching with him. The shutters were up and the curtains drawn; the water and electric light were already cut off; all this my uncle had accomplished in a few days. I stumbled among sheeted furniture to the windows and let in the daylight. I went from room to room in this way. The place still retained its own smell − an agreeable, rather stuffy atmosphere of cigar smoke and cantaloup; a masculine smell − women had always seemed a little out of place there, as in a London club on Coronation Day.

The house was sombre but never positively shabby so that, I suppose, various imperceptible renovations and replacements must have occurred from time to time. It looked what it was, the house of an unfashionable artist of the 1880s. The curtains and chair-covers were of indestructible Morris tapestry; there were Dutch tiles round the fireplaces; Levantine rugs on the floors; on the walls, Arundel prints, photographs from the old Masters, and majolica dishes. The furniture, now shrouded, had the inimitable air of having been in the same place for a generation; it was a harmonious, unobtrusive jumble of inherited rosewood and mahogany, and of inexpensive collected pieces of carved German oak, Spanish walnut, English chests and dressers, copper ewers and brass candlesticks. Every object was familiar and yet so much a part of its surroundings that later, when they came to be moved, I found a number of things which I barely recognized. Books, of an antiquated sort, were all over the house in a variety of hanging, standing and revolving shelves.

I opened the french windows in my father's study and stepped down into the garden. There was little of spring to be seen here. The two plane trees were bare; under the sooty laurels last year's leaves lay rotting. It was never a garden of any character. Once, before the flats came, we used to dine there sometimes, in extreme discomfort under the catalpa tree; for years now it had been a no-man's land isolating the studio at the further end; on one side, behind a trellis, were some neglected frames and beds

where my father had once tried to raise French vegetables. The
mottled concrete of the flats, with its soil pipes and fire escapes
and its rash of iron-framed casement windows, shut out half the
sky. The tenants of these flats were forbidden, in their leases, to
do their laundry, but the owners had long since despaired of a
genteel appearance, and you could tell which of the rooms
were occupied by the stockings hanging to dry along the win-
dow-sills.

In his death my father's privacy was still respected and no one
had laid dust-sheets in the studio. ["*Too Big?*"][1] stood as he had
left it on the easel. More than half was finished. My father made
copious and elaborate studies for his pictures and worked quickly
when he came to their final stage, painting over a monochrome
sketch, methodically, in fine detail, left to right across the canvas
as though he were lifting the backing of a child's "transfer". "Do
your thinking *first*," he used to tell the Academy students. "Don't
muddle it out on the canvas. Have the whole composition clear in
your head before you start," and if anyone objected that this was
seldom the method of the greatest masters, he would say, "You're
here to become Royal Academicians, not great masters. [This
was the way Ford Madox Brown worked, and it will be a great
day for English art when one of you is half as good as he was.] If
you want to write books on Art, trot round Europe studying the
Rubenses. If you want to learn to paint, watch me." The four or
five square feet of finished painting were a monument of my
father's art. There had been a time when I had scant respect for
it. Lately I had come to see that it was more than a mere matter of
dexterity and resolution. He had a historic position for he completed a period of English painting that through other circumstances had never, until him, come to maturity. Phrases, as
though for an obituary article, came to my mind – ". . . fulfilling
the broken promise of the young Millais . . . Winterhalter suffused
with the spirit of Dickens . . . English painting as it might have
been, had there not been any Aesthetic Movement . . . [the age of
the Prince Consort in contrast to the age of Victoria . . .]" and

1 "*Again?*"

with the phrases my esteem for my father took form and my sense of loss became tangible and permanent.

No good comes of this dependence on verbal forms. It saves nothing in the end. Suffering is none the less acute and much more lasting when it is put into words. In the house my memories had been all of myself – of the countless homecomings and departures of thirty-three years, of adolescence like a stained table-cloth – but in the studio my thoughts were of my father and grief, nearly a week delayed, overtook and overwhelmed me. It had been delayed somewhat by the strangeness of my surroundings and the business of travel, but most by this literary habit; it had lacked words. Now the words came; I began, in my mind, to lament my father [with prose cadences and classical allusions,] addressing, as it were, a funeral oration to my own literary memories, and sorrow, dammed and canalized, flowed fast.

For the civilized man there are none of those swift transitions of joy and pain which possess the savage; words form slowly like pus about his hurts; there are no clean wounds for him; first a numbness, then a long festering, then a scar ever ready to reopen. Not until they have assumed the livery of the defence can his emotions pass through the lines; sometimes they come massed in a wooden horse, sometimes as single spies, but there is always a Fifth Column among the garrison ready to receive them. Sabotage behind the lines, a blind raised and lowered at a lighted window, a wire cut, a bolt loosened, a file disordered – that is how the civilized man is undone.

I returned to the house and darkened the rooms once more, relaid the dust-sheets I had lifted and left everything as it had been.

V

The manuscript of *Murder at Mountrichard Castle* lay on the chest of drawers in my club bedroom, reproaching me morning, evening and night. It was promised for publication in June, and I had never before disappointed my publishers. This year, however, I should have to ask grace for a postponement. I made two attempts on it, bearing the pile of foolscap to an upper room of the club which was known as the library and used by the elder members for sleeping between luncheon and tea. But I found it impossible to take up the story with any interest[; I grew peevish about the time sequence, and half inclined to scrap all I had written and start anew; the murderess had had too much luck on the morning of the crime and the police were being unnaturally obtuse; they had reached a stage in the investigation when they must either tumble to the truth within six pages or miss it for ever; I could not go on piling up clue and counterplot; why should not the wrong man get hanged for a change or the murderess walk in her sleep and proclaim the whole story? I had gone stale on it]. So I went to my publisher and tried to explain.

"I have been writing for over eight years," I said, "and am nearing a climacteric."

"I don't quite follow," said Mr. Benwell anxiously.

"I mean a turning point in my career."

"Oh, dear, I hope you're not thinking of making a contract elsewhere?"

"No, no, I mean that I feel in danger of turning into a stock best-seller."

"If I may say so in very imminent danger," said Benwell, and he made me a kind of little bow from the seat of his swivel chair and smirked in the wry fashion people sometimes assume when they feel they have said something elaborately polite; a smile normally kept for his women writers; the word "climacteric" had clearly upset him.

"I mean, I am in danger of becoming purely a technical expert. Take my father – " Mr. Benwell gave a deferential grunt and quickly changed his expression to one of gravity suitable to the mention of someone recently dead. "He spent his whole life perfecting his technique. It seems to me I am in danger of becoming mechanical, turning out year after year the kind of book I know I can write well. I feel I have got as good as I ever can be at this particular sort of writing. I need new worlds to conquer." I added this last remark in compassion for

Mr. Benwell, whose gravity had deepened to genuine concern. I believed he would feel the easier for a little facetiousness – erroneously, for Mr. Benwell had suffered similar, too serious conversations with other writers than me.

"You've not been writing *poetry* in Morocco?"

"No, no."

"Sooner or later almost all my novelists come to me and say they have written poetry. I can't think why. It does them infinite harm. Only last week Roger Simmonds was here with a kind of a play. You never saw such a thing. All the characters were parts of a motor-car – not in the least funny."

"Oh, it won't be anything like that," I said. "Just some new technical experiments. I don't suppose the average reader will notice them at all."

"I hope not," said Mr. Benwell. "I mean, now you've found your public ... well, look at Simmonds [– magneto and sparking plugs and camshaft all talking in verse about communism. I don't know what to do about it at all. ... But I can count on your new novel for the autumn?"

"Yes."

"And we can list it as 'crime'?"

"Certainly."

Mr. Benwell saw me to the top of the stairs. "Interesting place, Morocco," he said. "The French are doing it very well]."

I knew what he was thinking: "The trouble about Plant is, he's come in for money."

In a way he was right. The money my father had left me and the proceeds which I expected from the sale of the house, relieved me of the need to work for two or three years[; once the necessity was removed there was little motive for writing]. It was a matter of pure athletics to go on doing something merely because one did it well. [This tedium was the price I must pay for my privacy, for the choice, which until lately had been a matter of special pride with me, of a trade which had nothing of myself in it.] The heap of foolscap began to disgust me. Twice I hid it under my shirts, twice the club valet unearthed it and laid it in the open.

I had nowhere to keep things, except in this little hired room above the traffic.

[As I returned from seeing Mr. Benwell, the club secretary waylaid me. Under Rule XLV, he reminded me, members might not occupy bedrooms for more than five consecutive nights. He did not mind stretching a point, he said, but if a member from out of town applied for a room and found them all engaged and wrote to the committee about it, where would he, the secretary, be? I promised to move out as soon as I could; I had a lot to attend to at the moment; perhaps he had seen that my father had just died. We both knew that it was unfair to bring this up, but it won me my point. For the time being I had lodging – a bed, a washbasin, a window in St. James's, a telephone, space enough for a fortnight's wardrobe. But I must start looking about for something more secure.]

This sense of homelessness was new to me. Before I had moved constantly from one place to another; every few weeks I would descend upon St. John's Wood with a trunk, leave some books, collect others, put away summer clothes for the winter; seldom as I slept there, the house in St. John's Wood had been my headquarters and my home; that earth had now been stopped and I thought, not far away, I could hear the hounds.

My worries at this period became symbolized in a single problem; what to do with my hats. I owned what now seemed a multitude of them, of one sort and another; two of them of silk – the tall hat I took to weddings and a second I had bought some years earlier when I thought for a time that I was going to take to fox-hunting; there were a bowler, a panama, a black, a brown and a grey soft hat, a green hat from Salzburg, a sombrero, some tweed caps for use on board ship and in trains – all these had accumulated from time to time and all, with the possible exception of the sombrero, were more or less indispensable. Was I doomed for the rest of my life to travel everywhere with this preposterous collection? At the moment they were, most of them, in St. John's Wood, but, any day now, the negotiations for the sale might be finished and the furniture removed, sold or sent to store.

Somewhere to hang up my hat, that was what I needed.

I consulted Roger Simmonds who was lunching with me. I felt as though I had known Roger all my life; actually I had first met him in our second year at Oxford; we edited an undergraduate weekly together and had been close associates ever since. He was one of the very few people I corresponded with when I was away; we met constantly when I was in London. Sometimes I even stayed with him, for he and half a dozen others constituted a kind of set. We had all known each other intimately over a number of years, had from time to time passed on girls from one to the other, borrowed and lent freely. When we were together we drank more and talked more boastfully than we normally did. We had grown rather to dislike one another; certainly when any two or three of us were alone, we blackguarded the rest, and if asked about them on neutral ground I denied their friendship. ["Blades?" I would say. "Yes, I used to see a lot of him, but we never seem to meet now he's in Parliament" or "Jimmie Rendall? Yes, I knew him well. Then he got taken up by Lord Monomark and that is the end of all friendship."] About Roger I used to say, "I don't think he's interested in anything except politics now."

This was more or less true. In the late twenties he set up as a writer and published some genuinely funny novels on the strength of which he filled a succession of [rather dazzling] jobs with newspapers and film companies, but lately he had married an unknown heiress, joined the [Communist][1] Party and become generally [respectable][2].

"I never wear a hat now I am married," said Roger virtuously. "Lucy says they're *kulak*. Besides I was beginning to lose my hair."

"My dear Roger, you've been bald as a coot for ten years. But it isn't only a question of hats. There are overcoats."

"Only in front. It's as thick as anything at the back. How many overcoats have you got?"

"Four, I think."

"Too many."

[1] Socialist
[2] conventional

We discussed it at length and decided it was possible to manage with three.

"Workers pawn their overcoats in June and take them out again in October," Roger said. He wanted to talk about his play, *Internal Combustion*. "The usual trouble with ideological drama," he said, "is that they're too mechanical. I mean the characters are economic types, not individuals, and as long as they look and speak like individuals it's bad art. D'you see what I mean?"

"I do, indeed."

"Human beings without human interest."

"Very true. I . . ."

"Well, I've cut human beings out altogether."

"Sounds rather like an old-fashioned ballet."

"*Exactly*," Roger said with great pleasure. "It *is* an old-fashioned ballet. I knew you'd understand. Poor old Benwell couldn't. The Finsbury International Theatre are sitting on it now, and if it's orthodox – and I *think* it is – they may put it on this summer if Lucy finds the money."

"Is she keen too?"

"Well, not very, as a matter of fact. You see, she's having a baby and that seems to keep her interested at the moment."

"But to return to the question of my hats . . ."

"I tell you what. Why don't you buy a nice quiet house in the country. I shall want somewhere to stay while this baby is born."

There was the rub. It was precisely this fear that had been working in my mind for days, the fear of making myself a sitting shot to the world. It lay at the root of the problem of privacy; the choice which torments to the verge of mania, between perpetual flight and perpetual siege; and the unresolved universal paradox of losing things in order to find them.

"Surely that is odd advice from a [communist][1]?"

Roger became suddenly wary; he had been caught and challenged in loose talk. "Ideally, of course, it would be," he said. "But I daresay that in practice, for the first generation, we shall allow a certain amount of private property where its value is

[1] Socialist

purely sentimental. Anyway, any investment you make now is bound to be temporary. That's why I feel no repugnance about living on Lucy's money..." Marxist ethics kept him talking until we had finished luncheon. Over the coffee he referred to Ingres as a "bourgeois" painter. When he left me I sat for some time in the leather armchair finishing my cigar. The club was emptying as the younger members went back to their work and their elders padded off to the library for the afternoon nap. I belonged to neither world. I had nothing whatever to do. At three in the afternoon my friends would all be busy and, in any case, I did not want to see them. I was ready for a new deal. I climbed to my room, began re-reading the early chapters of *Murder at Mount-richard Castle*, put it from me and faced the boredom of an afternoon in London. Then the telephone rang and the porter said, "Mr. Thurston is downstairs to see you."

"Who?"

"Mr. Thurston. He says he has an appointment."

"I don't know anything about him. Will you ask what he wants?"

A pause: "Mr. Thurston says will you see him very particular."

"Very well, I'll come down."

A tall young man in a raincoat was standing in the hall. He had reddish hair and an unusually low, concave forehead. He looked as though he had come to sell some hopelessly unsuitable commodity and had already despaired of success.

"Mr. Thurston?" He took my hand in a savage grip. "You say you have an appointment with me. I am afraid I don't remember it."

"No, well, you see I thought we ought to have a yarn, and you know how suspicious these porter-fellows are at clubs. I knew you wouldn't mind my stretching a point." He spoke with a kind of fierce jauntiness. "I had to give up my club. Couldn't run to it."

"Perhaps you will tell me what I can do for you."

"I used to belong to the Wimpole. I expect you know it?"

"I'm not sure that I do."

"No? You would have liked it. I could have taken you there and introduced you to some of the chaps."

"That, I gather, is now impossible."

"Yes. It's a pity. There are some good scouts there. I daresay you know the Batchelors?"

"Yes. Were you a member there, too?"

"Yes, at least not exactly, but a great pal of mine was – Jimmie Grainger. I expect you've often run across Jimmie?"

"No, I don't think I have."

"Funny. Jimmie knows almost everyone. You'd like him. I must bring you together." Having failed to establish contact, Thurston seemed now to think that responsibility for the conversation devolved on me.

"Mr. Thurston," I said, "is there anything particular you wished to say to me? Because otherwise . . ."

"I was coming to that," said Thurston. "Isn't there somewhere more private where we could go and talk?"

It was a reasonable suggestion. Two page boys sat on a bench beside us, the hall porter watched us curiously from behind his glass screen, two or three members passing through paused by the tape machine to take a closer look at my peculiar visitor. I was tolerably certain that he was not one of the enthusiasts for my work who occasionally beset me, but was either a beggar or a madman or both; at another time I should have sent him away, but that afternoon, with no prospect of other interest, I hesitated. "Be a good scout," he urged.

There is at my club a nondescript little room of depressing aspect where members give interviews to the press, go through figures with their accountants, and in general transact business which they think would be conspicuous in the more public rooms. I took Thurston there.

"Snug little place," he said[, surveying this dismal place]. "O.K. if I smoke?"

"Perfectly."

"Have one?"

"No thank you."

He lit a cigarette, drew a deep breath of smoke, gazed at the ceiling and, as though coming to the point, said, "Quite like the old Wimpole."

My heart sank. "Mr. Thurston," I said, "you have surely not troubled to come here simply in order to talk to me about [your club.][1]"

"No. But you see it's rather awkward. Don't exactly know how to begin. I thought I might lead up to it naturally. But I realize that your time's valuable, Mr. Plant, so I may as well admit right out that I owe you an apology."

"Yes?"

"Yes. I'm here under false pretences. My name isn't Thurston."

"No?"

"No. I'd better tell you who I am, hadn't I?"

"If you wish to."

"Well, here goes. I'm Arthur Atwater." The name was spoken with such an air of bravado, with such confidence of it making a stir, that I felt bewildered. It meant absolutely nothing to me. Where and how should I have heard it? Was this a fellow-writer, a distant cousin, a popular athlete? Atwater? Atwater? I repeated it to myself. No association was suggested. My visitor meanwhile seemed unconscious of how flat his revelation had fallen, and was talking away vehemently:

"Now you see why I couldn't give my name. It's awfully decent of you to take it like this. I might have known you were a good scout. I've been through Hell I can tell you ever since it happened. I haven't slept a wink. It's been terrible. You know how it is when one's nerve's gone. I shouldn't be fit for work now even if they'd kept me on in the job. Not that I care about that. Let them keep their lousy job. I told the manager that to his face. I wasn't brought up and educated to sell stockings. I ought to have gone abroad long ago. There's no opportunity in England now, unless you've got influence or are willing to suck up to a lot of snobs. You get a fair chance out there in the colonies where one man's as good as another and no questions asked."

I can seldom bear to let a mis-statement pass uncorrected. "Believe me, Mr. Atwater," I said. "You have a totally mistaken

1 the Wimpole Club?

view of colonial life. You will find people just as discriminating and inquisitive there as they are here."

"Not where I'm going," he said. "I'm clearing right out. I'm fed up. This case hanging over me and nothing to do all day except think about the accident. It *was* an accident too. No one can try and hang the blame on me and get away with it. I was on my proper side of the road and I hooted twice. It wasn't a Belisha crossing. It was my road. The old man just wouldn't budge. He saw me coming, looked straight at me, as if he was daring me to drive into him. Well, I thought I'd give him a fright. You know how it is when you're driving all day. You get fed to the teeth with people making one get out of their way all the time. I like to wake them up now and then when there's no copper near, and make them jump for it. It seems like an hour now, but it all happened in two seconds. I kept on, waiting for him to skip, and he kept on, strolling across the road as if he'd bought it. It wasn't till I was right on top of him I realized he didn't intend to move. Then it was too late to stop. I put on my brakes and tried to swerve. Even then I might have missed him if he'd stopped, but he just kept on walking right into me and the mudguard got him. That's how it was. No one can blame it on me."

It was just as my Uncle Andrew had described it.

"Mr. Atwater," I said, "do I understand that you are the man who killed my father?"

"Don't put it that way, Mr. Plant. I feel sore enough about it. He was a great artist. I read about him in the papers. It makes it worse, his having been a great artist. There's too little beauty in the world as it is. I should have liked to be an artist myself, only the family went broke. Father took me away from school young, just when I might have got into the eleven. Since then I've had nothing but odd jobs. I've never had a real chance. I want to start again, somewhere else."

I interrupted him, frigidly I thought. "And why, precisely, have you come to me?"

But nothing could disabuse him of the idea that I was well-disposed. "I knew I could rely on you," he said. "And I'll never forget it, not as long as I live. I've thought everything out. I've got a pal who went out to Rhodesia; I think it was Rhodesia. Somewhere in Africa, anyway. He'll give me a shakedown till I get on my feet. He's a great fellow. Won't he be surprised when I walk in on him! All I need is my passage money – third class, I don't care. I'm used to roughing it these days – and something to make a start with. I could do it on fifty pounds."

"Mr. Atwater," I said, "have I misunderstood you, or are you asking me to break the law by helping you to evade your trial and also give you a large sum of money?"

"You'll get it back, every penny of it."

"And our sole connection is the fact that, through pure insolence, you killed my father."

"Oh, well, if you feel like that about it . . ."

"I am afraid you greatly overrate my good nature."

"Tell you what. I'll make you a sporting offer. You give me fifty pounds now and I'll pay it back in a year plus another fifty pounds to any charity you care to name. How's that?"

"[I'm afraid there is no point in our discussing the matter.] Will you please go?"

"Certainly I'll go. If that's how you take it, I'm sorry I ever came. It's typical of the world," he said, rising huffily. "Everyone's all over you till you get into a spot of trouble. It's 'good old Arthur' while you're in funds. Then, when you need a pal it's 'you overrate my good nature, Mr. Atwater'. "

I followed him across the room, but before we reached the door his mood had changed. "You don't understand," he said. "They may send me to prison for this. That's what happens in this country to a man earning his living. If I'd been driving my own Rolls Royce they'd all be touching their caps. 'Very regrettable accident,' they'd be saying. 'Hope your nerves have not been shocked, Mr. Atwater,' – but to a poor man driving a two seater . . . Mr. Plant, your father wouldn't have wanted me sent to prison."

"He often expressed his belief that all motorists of all classes should be [treated as criminals][1]."

1 kept permanently in prison

Atwater received this with disconcerting enthusiasm. "And he was quite right," he cried in louder tones than can ever have been used in that room except [perhaps] during spring-cleaning. "I'm fed to the teeth with motor-cars. I'm fed to the teeth with civilization. I want to farm. That's a man's life."

"Mr. Atwater, will nothing I say persuade you that your aspirations are no concern of mine?"

"There's no call to be sarcastic. If I'm not wanted, you've only to say so straight."

"You are not wanted."

"Thank you," he said. "That's all I wanted to know."

I got him through the door, but half-way across the front hall he paused again. "I spent my last ten bob on a wreath."

"I'm sorry you did that. I'll refund it."

He turned on me with a look of scorn. "Plant," he said, "I didn't think it was in you to say a thing like that. Those flowers were a sacred thing. You wouldn't understand that, would you? I'd have starved to send them. I may have sunk pretty low, but I have some decency left, and that's more than some people can say even if they belong to posh clubs and look down on fellows who earn a decent living. Good-bye, Plant. We shall not meet again. D'you mind if I don't shake hands."

That was how he left me, but it was not the last of him. That evening I was called to the telephone to speak to a Mr. Long. Familiar tones, jaunty once more, greeted me. "That you, Plant? Atwater here. Excuse the alias, won't you. I say, I hope you didn't take offence at the way I went off to-day. I've been thinking, and I see you were perfectly right. May I come round for another yarn?"

"No."

"To-morrow, then?"

"No."

"Well, when shall I come?"

"I'm afraid I can't see you."

"No, I quite understand, old man. I'd feel the same myself. It's only this. In the circumstances I'd like to accept your very sporting offer to pay for those flowers. I'll call round for the money if you like or will you send it?"

"I'll send it."

"Care of the Holborn Post Office finds me. Fifteen bob, they cost."

"You said ten this afternoon."

"Did I? I meant fifteen."

"I will send you ten shillings. Good-bye."

"Good scout," said Atwater.

So I put a note in an envelope and sent it to the man who killed my father.

VI

Time dragged[; April, May, the beginning of June. I left my club and visited my Uncle Andrew for an uneasy week; then back to the club. I took the manuscript of *Murder at Mountrichard Castle* to the seaside, to an hotel where I once spent three months in great contentment writing *The Frightened Footman*: they gave me the best suite, at this time of year, for five guineas a week. The forlorn, out-of-season atmosphere was just as I knew it – the shuttered ballroom, the gusts of rain on the roof of the "sun lounge", the black esplanade, the crocodiles of private-school boys on their way to football, the fanatical bathers hissing like ostlers as they limped over the shingle into the breakers; the visitors' high church, the visitors' low church, and the church of the residents – all empty. Everything was as it had been three years before, but in a week I was back in London with nothing written. It was no good until I got things settled, I told myself; but "getting things settled" merely meant waiting until the house was sold and the lawyers had finished with the will. I took furnished rooms in Ebury Street and waited there, my thoughts more and more turning towards the country and the need of a house there, a permanent home of my own possession. I began to study the house-agents' advertisements on the back page of *The Times*. Finally I notified two or three firms of my needs, and was soon amply supplied with specifications and orders-to-view.

During this time I received a call from young Mr. Godley of Goodchild and Godley. There was nothing at all artistic about young Mr. Godley. He looked and spoke like a motor salesman; his galleries were his "shop" and their contents "stuff" and "things". He would have seemed at ease, if we had met casually, but the long preamble of small talk – references to mutual acquaintances, holiday resorts abroad, sport, politics, a "first-class man for job lots of wine" – suggested uncertainty; he was trying to decide how to take me. Finally he came to the point.

"Your father used to do a certain amount of work for us, you know."

"I know."

"Restorations mostly. Occasionally he used to make a fac-simile for a client who was selling a picture to America and wanted one to take its place. That kind of work."

"Often they were his own compositions."

"Well, yes, I believe a few of them were. What we call in the trade 'pastiche', you know."

"I saw some of them," I said.

"He was wonderfully gifted."

"Wonderfully."

A pause. Mr. Godley twiddled his Old Harrovian tie. "His work with us was highly confidential."

"Of course."

"I was wondering – our firm was, whether you had been through his papers yet. I mean, did he keep any records of his work or anything of the kind?"

"I'm afraid I haven't been through his things yet. I should think it quite likely. He was very methodical in some ways."

"The papers are all in your own hands?"

"So far as I know."

"If anything of the kind was to turn up, we could rely on your discretion. I mean it would do no one any good . . . I mean you would want your father to be remembered by his exhibited work."

"You need not worry," I said.

"Splendid. I was sure you would understand. We had a spot of unpleasantness with his man."

"Jellaby?"

"Yes. They both came to see us, husband and wife, immediately after the accident. You might almost say they tried to blackmail us."

"Did you give them anything?"

"No. Goodchild saw them and I imagine he gave them a good flea in the ear. They had nothing to go on."

"Odd pair the Jellabys."

"I don't think we shall be worried by them again."

"Nor by me. Blackmail is not quite in my line."

"No, no, my dear fellow, of course, I didn't for a moment mean to suggest . . . Ha, ha, ha."

"Ha, ha, ha."

"But if anything should turn up . . ."

"I shall be discreet about it."

"Or any studies for the paintings he did for us."

"Anything incriminating," I said.

"Trade secrets," said Mr. Godley.

"Trade secrets," I repeated.

That was almost the only amusing incident in my London season].

The sale of the house in St. John's Wood proved more irksome than I had expected. Ten years before the St. John's Wood Residential Amenities Company who built the neighbouring flats had offered my father £6,000 for his freehold; he had preserved the letter, which was signed, "Alfred Hardcastle, Chairman". Their successors, the Hill Crest Court Exploitation Co., now offered me £2,500; their letter was also signed Mr. Hardcastle. I refused, and put the house into an agent's hands; after two months they reported one offer – of £2,500 from a Mr. Hardcastle, the managing director of St. John's Wood Residential Estates Ltd. "In the circumstances," they wrote, "we consider this a satisfactory price." The circumstances were that no one who liked that kind of house would tolerate its surroundings; having dominated the district, the flats could make their own price. I accepted it and went to sign the final papers at Mr. Hardcastle's office, expecting an atmosphere of opulence and bluster; instead, I found a modest pair of rooms, one of the unlet flats at the top of the building; on the door were painted the names of half a dozen real estate companies and the woodwork bore traces of other names which had stood there and been obliterated; the chairman opened the door himself and let me in. He was[, as my father had supposed, a Jew;] a large, neat, middle-aged, melancholy, likeable fellow, who before coming to business, praised my father's painting with what I believe was complete sincerity.

There was no other visible staff; just Mr. Hardcastle sitting among his folders and filing cabinets, telling me how he had felt when he lost his own father. Throughout all the vicissitudes of the flats this man had controlled them and lived for them; little companies had gone into liquidation; little, allied companies had been floated; the names of nephews and brothers-in-law had come and gone at the head of the notepaper; stocks had been written down and up, new shares had been issued, bonuses and dividends declared, mortgages transferred and foreclosed, little blocks of figures moved from one balance sheet to another, all in this single room. For the last ten years a few thousand pounds capital had been borrowed and lent backwards and forwards from one account to another and, somehow, working sixteen hours a day, doing his own typing and accountancy, Mr. Hardcastle had sustained life, kept his shoes polished and his trousers creased, had his hair cut regularly and often, bought occasional concert tickets on family anniversaries and educated, he told me, a son in the United States and a daughter in Belgium. The company to which I finally conveyed my freehold was a brand-new one, registered for the occasion and soon, no doubt, doomed to lose its identity in the kaleidoscopic changes of small finance. The cheque, signed by Mr. Hardcastle, was duly honoured, and when the sum, largely depleted by my solicitor, was paid into my account, I found that with the insurance money added and my overdraft taken away, I had a credit balance for the first time in my life, of rather more than £3,500. With this I set about planning a new life.

Mr. Hardcastle had been willing to wait a long time to make his purchase; once it was done, however, his plans developed with surprising speed. Workmen were cutting the trees and erecting a screen of hoarding while the vans were removing the furniture to store; a week later I came to visit the house; it was a ruin; it might have been mined. Presumably there is some method in the business of demolition; none was apparent to a layman, the roof was off, the front was down, and on one side the basement lay open; on the other the walls still stood their full height, and the rooms, three-sided like stage settings, exposed their Morris papers, flapping loose in the wind where the fireplaces and window-frames had been torn out. The studio had disappeared, leaving a square of rubble to mark its site; new shoots appeared here and there in the trampled mess of the garden. A dozen or more workmen were there, two or three of them delving away in a leisurely fashion, the rest leaning on their tools and talking; it seemed inconceivable that in this fashion they could have done so much in such little time. The air was full of flying grit. It was no place to linger. When next I passed that way, a great concrete wing covered the site; it was cleaner than the rest of the block and by a miscalculation of the architects, the windows were each a foot or two below the general line; but, like them, were devoid of curtains.

CHAPTER II
LUCY SIMMONDS[1]

M Y PROJECT of settling in the country was well received by my friends.

Each saw in it a likely convenience for himself. I understood their attitude well. Country houses meant something particular and important in their lives, a system of permanent bolt-holes. They had, most of them, gradually dropped out of the round of formal entertaining; country life, for them, meant not a series of invitations, but of successful, predatory raids. Their lives were liable to sharp reverses; their quarters in London were camps which could be struck at an hour's notice, as soon as the telephone was cut off. Country houses were permanent; even when the owner was abroad, the house was there, with a couple of servants or, at the worst, someone at a cottage who came in to light fires and open windows, someone who, at a pinch, could be persuaded also to make the bed and wash up. They were places where wives and children could be left for long periods, where one retired to write a book, where one could be ill, where, in the course of a love affair, one could take a girl and by being her guide and sponsor in strange surroundings, establish a degree of proprietorship impossible on the neutral ground of London. The owners of these places were, by their nature, a patient race, but repeated abuse was apt to sour them; new blood in their ranks was highly welcome. I detected this greeting in every eye [and could not resent it].

There was also another, more amiable reason for their interest. Nearly all of them – and, for that matter, myself as well – professed a specialized enthusiasm for domestic architecture. It was one of the peculiarities of my generation and there is no accounting for it. In youth we had pruned our aesthetic emotions

1 PART TWO
  A Birth

hard back so that in many cases they had reverted to briar stock; we, none of us, wrote or read poetry, or, if we did, it was of a kind which left unsatisfied those wistful, half-romantic, half-aesthetic, peculiarly British longings, which, in the past, used to find expression in so many slim lambskin volumes. When the poetic mood was on us, we turned to buildings, and gave them the place which our fathers accorded to Nature – to almost any buildings, but particularly those in the classical tradition, and, more particularly, in its decay. It was a kind of nostalgia for the style of living which we emphatically rejected in practical affairs. The notabilities of Whig society became, for us, what the Arthurian paladins were in the time of Tennyson. There was never a time when so many landless men could talk at length about landscape gardening. Even Roger compromised with his Marxist austerities so far as to keep up his collection of the works of Batty Langley and William Halfpenny. "The nucleus of my museum," he explained. "When the revolution comes, I've no ambitions to be a commissar or a secret policeman. I want to be director of the Museum of Bourgeois Art."

He was overworking the Marxist vocabulary. That was always Roger's way, to become obsessed with a new set of words and to extend them, deliberately, beyond the limits of sense; it corresponded to some sombre, interior need of his to parody whatever, for the moment, he found venerable; when he indulged it I was reminded of the ecclesiastical jokes of those on the verge of religious melancholy. Roger had been in that phase himself when I first met him.

One evening, at his house, the talk was all about the kind of house I should buy. It was clear that my friends had very much more elaborate plans for me than I had for myself. After dinner Roger produced a copper-engraving of 1767 of *A Composed Hermitage in the Chinese Taste*. It was a preposterous design. "He actually built it," Roger said, "and it's still standing a mile or two out of Bath. We went to see it the other day. It only wants putting into repair. Just the house for you."

Everyone seemed to agree.

I knew exactly what he meant. It *was* just the house one would want someone else to have. I was graduating from the exploiting to the exploited class.

But Lucy said: "I can't think why John should want to have a house like that."

When she said that I had a sudden sense of keen pleasure. She and I were on the same side.

Roger and Lucy had become my main interest during the months while I was waiting to settle up in St. John's Wood. They lived in Victoria Square where they had taken three years' lease of a furnished house. "Bourgeois furniture," Roger complained, rather more accurately than usual. They shut away the model ships and fire-bucket waste paper baskets in a store cupboard and introduced a prodigious radio-gramophone; they hung their own pictures in place of the Bartolozzi prints, but the house retained its character, and Roger and Lucy, each in a different way, looked out of place there. It was here that Roger had written his ideological play.

They had been married in November. I had spent all the previous autumn abroad on a leisurely, aimless trip before settling at Fez for the winter's work. My mail at Malta, in September, told me that Roger had taken up with a rich girl and was having difficulty with her family; at Tetuan I learned that he was married. Apparently he had been in pursuit of her all the summer, unknown to us. It was not until I reached London that I heard the full story. Basil Seal told me, rather resentfully, because for many years now he had himself been in search of an heiress and had evolved theories on the subject of how and where they might be taken. "You must go to the provinces," he used to say. "The competition in London is far too hot for chaps like us. Americans and Colonials want value for money. The trouble is that the very rich have a natural affinity for one another. You can see it happening all the time – stinking rich people getting fixed up. And what happens? They simply double their super tax and no one is the better off. But they respect brains in the provinces. They like a man to be ambitious there, with his way to make in the world, and there

WORK SUSPENDED 273

are plenty of solid, mercantile families who can settle a hundred thousand on a daughter without turning a hair, who don't care a hoot about polo, but think a Member of Parliament very fine. That's the way to get in with them. Stand for Parliament."

In accordance with this plan Basil had stood three times – or rather had three times been adopted as candidate; on two occasions he fell out with his committee before the election. At least, that was his excuse to his friends for standing; in fact he, too, thought it a fine thing to be a Member of Parliament. He never got in and he was still unmarried. A kind of truculent honesty which he could never dissemble for long, always stood in his way. It was bitter for him to be still living at home, dependent on his mother for pocket money, liable to be impelled by her into unwelcome jobs two or three times a year while Roger had established himself almost effortlessly and was sitting back in comfort to await the World Revolution.

Not that Lucy was really rich, Basil hastened to assure me, but she had been left an orphan at an early age and her originally modest fortune had doubled itself. "Fifty-eight thousand in trustee stock, old boy. I wanted Lucy to take it out and let me handle it for her. I could have fixed her up very nicely. But Roger wasn't playing. He's always groaning about things being bourgeois. I can't think of anything more bourgeois than three and a half per cent."

"Is she hideous?" I asked.

"No, that's the worst part about it. She's a grand girl. She's all right for a chap."

"What like?"

"Remember Trixie?"

"Vaguely."

"Well not at all like her."

Trixie had been Roger's last girl. Basil had passed her on to him, [then taken her back]¹ for a week or two, then passed her [on to him again]². None of us had liked Trixie. She always

1 resumed the use of her
2 back

gave the impression that she was not being treated with the respect she was used to.

"How did he come by her?"

Basil told me at length, unable to hide his admiration for Roger's duplicity in the matter. All the previous summer, during the second Trixie period, Roger had been at work, without a word to any of us. I remembered, now, that he had suddenly become rather conspicuous in his clothes, affecting dark shirts and light ties, and a generally artistic appearance which, had he not been so bald, would have gone with long, untidy hair. It had embarrassed Trixie, she said, when at a bar they saw cousins of hers who were in the Air Force. "They'll tell everyone I'm going about with a pansy." So that was the explanation. It was greatly to Roger's credit we agreed.

Improbable as it sounded, the truth was that they had met at a ball in Pont Street, given by a relative of Roger's. He had gone, under protest, to make up the table at dinner in answer to an S.O.S. half an hour before the time. Someone had fallen out. It was five or six years since he had been in a London ballroom and, he explained afterwards, the spectacle of his pimply and inept juniors had inflated him with a self-esteem which must, he said, have been infectious. He had sat next to Lucy at dinner. She was, for our world, very young but, for her own, of a hoary age; that is to say, she was twenty-four. For six years she had been sent to dances by her aunt, keeping in an unfashionable, middle-strata of life in which her contemporaries had either married or taken to other occupations. This aunt occupied a peculiar position with regard to Lucy; she had brought her up and now did what she described as "making a home" for her, which meant that she subsisted largely upon Lucy's income. She had two other nieces younger than Lucy, and it was greatly to their interest that they should move to London annually for the season. The aunt was a lady of delicate conscience where the issues of Lucy's marriage were involved. Once or twice before she had been apprehensive – without cause as it happened – that Lucy was preparing to "throw herself away". Roger, however, was a case that admitted of no doubt. Everything she learned about him was reprehensible; she fought him in the full confidence of a just cause, but she had no serviceable weapon. In six years of social life Lucy had never met anyone the least like Roger.

"And he took care she shouldn't meet us," said Basil. "What's more, she thinks him a great writer."

This was true. I did not believe Basil, but after I had seen her and Roger together I was forced to accept it. It was one of the most disconcerting features of the marriage for all of us. It is hard to explain exactly why I found it so shocking. Roger was a very good novelist – every bit as good in his own way as I in mine; when one came to think of it, it was impossible to name anyone else, alive, who could do what he did; there was no good reason why his books should not be compared with those of prominent writers of the past, nor why we should not speculate about their ultimate fame. But to do so struck us all as the worst of taste. Whatever, secretly, we thought about our own work we professed, in public, to regard it as drudgery and our triumphs as successful impostures on the world at large. To speak otherwise would be to suggest that we were concerned with anyone else's interest but our own; it would be a denial of the *sauve qui peut* principle which we had all adopted. But Lucy, I soon realized, found this attitude unintelligible. She was a serious girl. When we talked cynically about our own work she simply thought less of it and of us; if we treated Roger in the same way, she resented it as bad manners. It was greatly to Roger's credit that he had spotted this idiosyncrasy of hers at once and played his game accordingly. Hence the undergraduate costume and the talk about the Art of the Transition. Lucy had not abandoned her young cousins without grave thought. She perfectly understood that, for them, happiness of a particular kind depended on her continued support; but she also thought it a great wrong that a man of Roger's genius should waste his talents on film scenarios and advertisements. Roger convinced her that a succession of London seasons and marriage to a well-born chartered accountant were not really the highest possible good. Moreover, she was in love with Roger.

"So the poor fellow has had to become a highbrow again,"

said Basil. "Back exactly where he started in the New College Essay Society."

"She doesn't sound too keen on this play of his."

"She isn't. She's a critical girl. That's going to be Roger's headache."

This was Basil's version of the marriage and it was substantially accurate. It omits, however, as any narrative of Basil's was bound to, the consideration that Roger was, in his way, in love with Lucy. Her fortune was a secondary attraction; he lacked the Mediterranean mentality that can regard marriage as an honourable profession, perhaps because he lacked Mediterranean respect for the permanence of the arrangement. At the time when he met Lucy he was earning an ample income without undue exertion; money alone would not have been worth the pains he had taken for her; [nor were the pains unique; he habitually went to great inconvenience in pursuit of his girls; even for Trixie he took tepidly to horse-racing for a time;] the artistic clothes and the intellectual talk were measures of the respect in which he held Lucy. Her fifty-eight thousand in trustee stock was, no doubt, what made him push his suit to the extreme of marriage, but the prime motive and zest of the campaign came from Lucy herself.

To write of someone loved, of oneself loving, above all of oneself being loved – how can these things be done with propriety? How can they be done at all? I have treated of love in my published work; I have used it, – with avarice, envy, revenge – as one of the compelling motives of conduct. I have written it up as something prolonged and passionate and tragic; I have written it down as a modest but sufficient annuity with which to reward the just; I have spoken of it continually as a game of profit and loss. How does any of this avail for the simple task of describing, so that others may see her, the woman one loves? How can others see her except through one's own eyes, and how, so seeing her, can they turn the pages and close the book and live on as they have lived before, without becoming themselves the author and themselves the lover? The catalogues of excellencies of the renaissance poets, those competitive advertisements, each man outdoing the next in metaphor, that great blurb – like a [Jewish] publisher's list in the Sunday newspapers – the Song of Solomon, how do these accord with the voice of love – love that delights in weakness, seeks out and fills the empty places and completes itself in its work of completion? How can one transcribe those accents? Love, which has its own life, its hours of sleep and waking, its health and sickness, growth, death and immortality, its ignorance and knowledge, experiment and mastery – how can one relate this hooded stranger to the men and women with whom he keeps pace? It is a problem beyond the proper scope of letters.

[In the criminal code of Haiti, Basil tells me, there is a provision designed to relieve unemployment, forbidding farmers to raise the dead from their graves and work them in the fields. Some such rule should be observed against the use of live men in books. The algebra of fiction must reduce its problems to symbols if they are to be soluble at all. I am shy of a book commended to me on the grounds that the "characters are alive". There is no place in literature for a live man, solid and active. At best the author may maintain a kind of Dickensian menagerie, where his characters live behind bars, in darkness, to be liberated twice nightly for a brief gambol under the arc lamps; in they come to the whip crack, dazzled, deafened and doped, tumble through their tricks and scamper out again, to the cages behind which the real business of life, eating and mating, is carried on out of sight of the audience. "Are the lions really alive?" "Yes, lovey." "Will they eat us up?" "No, lovey, the man won't let them" – that is all the reviewers mean as a rule when they talk of "life". The alternative, classical expedient is to take the whole man and reduce him to a manageable abstraction. Set up your picture plain, fix your point of vision, make your figure twenty foot high or the size of a thumbnail, he will be life-size on your canvas; hang your picture in the darkest corner, your heaven will still be its one source of light. Beyond these limits lie only the real trouser buttons and the crepe hair with which the futurists used to adorn

their paintings. It is, anyway, in the classical way that I have
striven to write; how else can I now write of Lucy?]

I met [her]¹ first after I had been some weeks in London[;
after my return, in fact, from my week at the seaside]. I had seen
Roger several times; he always said, "You must come and meet
Lucy," but nothing came of these vague proposals until finally,
full of curiosity, I went with Basil uninvited.

I met him in the London library, late one afternoon.

"Are you going to the young Simmondses'?" he said.

"Not so far as I know."

"They've a party to-day."

"Roger never said anything to me about it."

"He told me to tell everyone. I'm just on my way there now.
Why don't you come along?"

So we took a taxi to Victoria Square, for which I paid.

As it turned out, Roger and Lucy were not expecting anyone.
He went to work now, in the afternoons, with a committee [who
were engaged in some fashion in sending supplies to the Red Army
in China]²; he had only just come in and was in his bath. Lucy was
listening to the six o'clock news on the wireless. She said, "D'you
mind if I keep it on for a minute? There may be something about
the dock strike in Madras. Roger will be down in a minute."

She did not say anything about a drink so Basil said, "May I go
and look for the whisky?"

"Yes, of course. How stupid of me. I always forget. There's
probably some in the dining-room."

He went out and I stayed with Lucy in her hired drawing-
room. She sat quite still listening to the announcer's voice. She
was five months gone with child – "Even Roger has to admit that
it's proletarian action," she said later – but as yet scarcely showed
it in body; but she was pale, paler, I guessed, than normal, and
she wore that incurious, self-regarding expression which sometimes goes with a first pregnancy. Above the sound of the wireless
I heard Basil outside, calling upstairs, "Roger. Where do you
keep the corkscrew?" When they got to the stock prices, Lucy

1 Lucy
2 for the relief of Spanish refugees

switched off. "Nothing from Madras," she said. "But perhaps you aren't interested in politics."

"Not much," I said.

"Very few of Roger's friends seem to be."

"It's rather a new thing with him," I said.

"I expect he doesn't talk about it unless he thinks people are interested."

That was outrageous, first because it amounted to the claim to know Roger better than I did and, secondly, because I was still smarting from the ruthless boredom of my last two or three meetings with him.

"You'd be doing us all a great service if you could keep him to that," I said.

It is a most painful experience to find, when one has been rude, that one has caused no surprise. That is how Lucy received my remark. She merely said, "We've got to go out almost at once. We're going to the theatre in Finsbury and it starts at seven."

"Very inconvenient."

"It suits the workers," she said. "They have to get up earlier than we do, you see."

Then Roger and Basil came in with the drinks. Roger said, "We're just going out. They're doing the Tractor Trilogy at Finsbury. Why don't you come too. We could probably get another seat, couldn't we, Lucy?"

"I doubt it," said Lucy. "They're tremendously booked up."

"I don't think I will," I said.

"Anyway join us afterwards at the Café Royal."

"I might," I said.

"What have you and Lucy been talking about?"

"We listened to the news," said Lucy. "Nothing from Madras."

"They've probably got orders to shut down on it. I.D.C. have got the B.B.C. in their pocket."

"I.D.C.?" I asked.

"Imperial Defence College. They're the new hush-hush crypto-fascist department. They're in up to the neck with I.C.I. and the oil companies."

"I.C.I.?"

"Imperial Chemicals."

"Roger," said Lucy, "we really must go if we're to get anything to eat."

"All right," he said. "See you later at the Café."

I waited for Lucy to say something encouraging. She said, "We shall be there by eleven," and began looking for her bag among the chintz cushions.

I said, "I doubt if I can manage it."

"Are we taking the car?" Roger asked.

"No, I sent it away. I've had him out all day."

"I'll order some taxis."

"We could drop Basil and John somewhere," said Lucy.

"No," I said, "get two."

"We're going by way of Appenrodts," said Lucy.

"No good for me," I said, although, in fact, they would pass the corner of St. James's where I was bound.

"I'll come and watch you eat your sandwiches," said Basil.

That was the end of our first meeting. I came away feeling badly about it, particularly the way in which she had used my Christian name and acquiesced in my joining them later. A commonplace girl who wanted to be snubbing, would have been conspicuously aloof and have said "Mr. Plant", and I should have recovered some of the lost ground. But Lucy was faultless.

I have seen so many young wives go wrong on this point. They have either tried to force an intimacy with their husbands' friends, claiming, as it were, continuity and identity with the powers of the invaded territory or they have cancelled the pass-ports of the old régime and proclaimed that fresh application must be made to the new authorities and applicants be treated strictly on their merits. Lucy seemed serenely unaware of either danger. I had come inopportunely and been rather rude, but I was one of Roger's friends; they were like his family to her, or hers to him; we had manifest defects which it was none of her business to reform; we had the right to come to her house unexpectedly, to shout upstairs for the corkscrew, to join her table at supper. The question of intrusion did not arise. It was simply that as far as she was concerned we had no separate or individual existence. It was, as I say, a faultless and highly provocative attitude. I found that in the next few days a surprising amount of my time, which, any-way, was lying heavy on me, was occupied in considering how this attitude, with regard to myself, could be altered.

My first move was to ask her and Roger to luncheon. I was confident that none of their other friends – none of those, that is to say, from whom I wished to dissociate myself – would have done such a thing. I did it formally, some days ahead, by letter to Lucy. All this, I knew, would come as a surprise to Roger. He telephoned me to ask, "What's all this Lucy tells me about your asking us to luncheon?"

"Can you come?"

"Yes, I suppose so. But what's it all about?"

"It's not 'about' anything. I just want you to lunch with me."

"Why?"

"It's quite usual, you know, when one's friends marry. Just politeness."

"You haven't got some ghastly foreigners you stayed with abroad?"

"No, nothing like that."

"Well, it all seems very odd to me. Writing a letter, I mean, and everything . . ."

I rang off.

Lucy answered with a formal acceptance. I studied her writing. [I had expected, I do not know why, a round girlish hand of the post-copper-plate era. Instead] she wrote like a man. [She used a fountain pen, I noticed; that was unusual in a girl.]

Dear John,

Roger and I shall be delighted to lunch with you at the Ritz on Thursday week at 1.30.

Yours sincerely,

Lucy Simmonds.

Should it not have been "Yours ever" after the "Dear John"? I wondered whether she had wondered what to put. Another girl might have written "Yours" with a non-committal squiggle, but her writing did not lend itself to that kind of evasion. I had ended my note, "Love to Roger".

Was she not a little over-formal in repeating the place and time? Had she written straight off, without thinking, or had she sucked the top of her pen a little?

The paper was presumably the choice of their landlord, in unobtrusive good taste. I smelled it and thought I detected a whiff of soap.

At this point I lost patience with myself; it was ludicrous to sit brooding over a note of this kind. I began, instead, to wonder whom I should ask to meet her – certainly none of the gang she had learned to look on as "Roger's friends". On the other hand it must be clear that the party was for her. Roger would be the first to impute that they were being made use of. In the end, after due thought and one or two failures, I secured a middle-aged, highly reputable woman-novelist and Andrew Desert and his wife – an eminently sociable couple. When Roger saw his fellow guests he was more puzzled than ever. I could see him all through luncheon trying to work it out, why I should have spent five pounds in this peculiar fashion.

I enjoyed my party. Lucy began by talking about my father's painting.

"Yes," I said, "it's very fashionable at the moment."

"Oh, I don't mean that," she said in frank surprise, and went on to tell me how she had stopped before a shop window in Duke Street where a battle picture of my father's was on view; there had been two private soldiers construing it together, point by point. "I think that's worth a dozen columns of praise in the weekly papers," she said.

"Just like Kipling's *Light that Failed*," said the woman-novelist.

"Is it? I didn't know." She told us she had never read any Kipling.

"That shows the ten years between us," I said, and so the conversation became a little more personal as we discussed the differences between those who were born before the Great War and those born after it; in fact, so far as it could be worked, the differences between Lucy and myself.

Roger always showed signs of persecution-mania in the Ritz. He did not like it when we knew people at other tables whom he didn't know and, when the waiter brought him the wrong dish [by mistake], he began on a set-piece which I had heard him use before in this same place. "Fashionable restaurants are the same all over the world," he said. "There are always exactly twenty per cent. more tables than the waiters can manage. It's a very good thing for the workers' cause that no one except the rich know the deficiencies of the luxury world. Think of the idea Hollywood gives of a place like this," he said, warming to his subject. "A *maître d'hôtel* like an ambassador, bowing famous beauties across acres of unencumbered carpet – and look at poor Lorenzo there, sweating under his collar, jostling a way through for dowdy Middle West Americans . . ." But it was not a success. Lucy, I could see, thought it odd of him to complain when he was a guest. I pointed out that the couple whom Roger condemned as Middle West Americans were in fact called Lord and Lady Settringham, and Andrew led the conversation, where Roger could not follow it, to the topic of which ambassadors looked like *maîtres d'hôtel*. The woman-novelist began a eulogy of the Middle West which she knew and Roger did not. So he was left with his theme undeveloped. All this was worth five pounds to me, and more.

I thought it typical of the way Lucy had been brought up that she returned my invitation in a day or two.

Roger got in first on the telephone. "I say, are you free on Wednesday evening?"

"I'm not sure. Why?"

"I wondered if you'd dine with us."

"Not at half-past six for the Finsbury Theatre?"

"No. I work late these days at the [Red China Supply][1] Committee."

[1] Relief

"What time then?"

"Oh, any time after eight. Dress or not, just as you feel like it."

"What will you and Lucy be doing?"

"Well, I suppose we shall dress. In case anyone wants to go on anywhere."

"In fact, it's a dinner party?"

"Well, yes, in a kind of way."

It was plain that poor Roger was dismayed at this social mushroom which had sprung up under his nose. As a face-saver the telephone call was misconceived, for a little note from Lucy was already in the post for me. It was not for me to mock these little notes; I had begun it. But an end had to be made to them, so I decided to answer this by telephone, choosing the early afternoon when I assumed Roger would be out. He was in, and answered me. "I wanted to speak to Lucy."

"Yes?"

"Just to accept her invitation to dinner."

"But you've already accepted."

"Yes, but I thought I'd better just tell her."

"I told her. What d'you think?"

"Ah, good, I was afraid you might have forgotten."

I had come badly out of that.

From first to last the whole episode of the dinner was calamitous. It was a party of ten, and one glance round the room showed me that this was an occasion of what Lucy had been brought up to call "duty". That is to say, we were all people whom for one reason or another she had felt obliged to ask. She was offering us all up together in a single propitiatory holocaust to the gods of the schoolroom. Even Mr. Benwell was there. He did not realize that Lucy had taken the house furnished and was congratulating her upon the decorations; "I like a London house to look like a London house," he was saying.

Roger was carrying things off rather splendidly with a kind of sardonic gusto which he could often assume in times of stress. I knew him in that mood and respected it. I knew, too, that my presence added a particular zest to his performance. Throughout the evening I caught him in constant enquiry of me; was

I attending to this parody of himself? I was his audience, not
Lucy.

The fate in store for myself was manifest as soon as I came into
the room. It was Lucy's cousin Julia, the younger of the two girls
Basil had told me of, the one whose début had been so disturbed
by Lucy's marriage. It would not, I felt, be a grave set-back. Julia
had that particular kind of succulent charm – bright, dotty, soft,
eager, acquiescent, flattering, impudent – that is specially, it
seems, produced for the delight of Anglo-Saxon manhood. She
had no need of a London season to find a happy future. "Julia is
staying with us. She is a great fan of yours," said Lucy in her Pont
Street manner; a manner which, like Roger's, but much more
subtly, had an element of dumb crambo in it. What she said
turned out to be true.

"My word, this *is* exciting," said Julia, and settled down to
enjoy me as though I were a box of chocolates open on her knees.

"What a lot of people Lucy's got here tonight."

"Yes, it's her first real dinner party, and she says it will be her
last. She says she doesn't like parties any more."

"Did she ever?" I was ready to talk about Lucy at length, but
this was not Julia's plan.

"Everyone does at first," she said briefly, and then began the
conversation as she had rehearsed it, I am sure, in her bath. "I
knew you the moment you came into the room. Guess how."

"You heard my name announced."

"Oh, no. Guess again."

An American hero would have said, "For Christ's sake," but
I said, "Really I've no idea, unless perhaps you knew everyone
else already."

"Oh, no. Shall I tell you? I saw you in the Ritz the day Lucy
lunched with you."

"Why didn't you come and talk to us?"

"Lucy wouldn't let me. She said she'd ask you to dinner
instead."

"Ah."

"You see, for years and years the one thing in the world I've
wanted most – or nearly most – was to meet you and when Lucy

calmly said she was going to lunch with you I cried with envy –
literally so I had to put a cold sponge on my eyes before going
out."

Talking to this delicious girl about Lucy, I thought, was like
sitting in the dentist's chair with one's mouth full of instruments
and the certainty that, all in good time, he would begin to hurt.

"Did she talk about it much, before she came to lunch?"

"Oh no, she just said 'I'm afraid I've got to leave you to-day as
Roger wants me to lunch with one of his old friends.' So I said,
'How rotten, who?' and she said, 'John Plant,' just like that, and I
said, '*John Plant*,' and she said, 'Oh, I forgot you were keen on
thrillers.' *Thrillers*, as though you were just anybody. And I said,
'Couldn't I possibly come,' and she said, 'Not possibly,' and then
when I was crying she said I might come with her to the lounge
and sit behind a pillar and see you come in."

"How did she describe me?"

"She just said you'd be the one who paid for the cocktails. Isn't
that just like Lucy, or don't you know her well enough to tell?"

"What did she say about the lunch afterwards?"

"She said everyone talked about Kipling."

"Was that all?"

"And she thought Roger had behaved badly because he
doesn't like smart restaurants, and she said neither did she, but
it had cost you a lot of money so it was nasty to complain. Of
course, I wanted to hear all about *you* and what *you* said, and she
couldn't remember anything. She just said you seemed very
clever."

"Oh, she said that?"

"She says that about all Roger's friends. But, anyway, it's my
turn now. I've got you to myself for the evening."

She had. We were sitting at dinner now. Lucy was still talking
to Mr. Benwell. On my other side there was some kind of relative
of Roger's. She talked to me for a bit about how Roger had settled
down since marriage. "I don't take those political opinions of his
seriously," she said, "and, anyway, it's all right to be a communist
nowadays. Everyone is."

"I'm not," I said.

"Well, I mean all the clever young people."

So I turned back to Julia. She was waiting for me. "D'you know you once wrote me a letter?"

"Good gracious. Why?"

"Dear Madam, Thank you for your letter. If you will read the passage in question more attentively you will note that the down train was four minutes late at Frasham. There was thus ample time for the disposal of the bicycle bell. Yours faithfully, John Plant," she quoted.

"Did I write that?"

"Don't you remember?"

"Vaguely. It was about *The Frightened Footman*, wasn't it?"

"Mm. Of course I knew perfectly well about the train. I just wrote in the hopes of getting an answer and it worked. I liked you for being so severe. There was another girl at school was literary too, and she had a crush on Gilbert Warwick. *He* wrote *her* three pages beginning, My Dear Anthea, all about his house and the tithe barn he's turned into his work-room and ending, Write to me again; I hope you like Silvia as much as Heather, those were two of his heroines, and she thought it showed what a better writer he was than you, but I knew just the opposite. And later Anthea did write again, and she had another long letter just like the first all about his tithe barn, and that made her very cynical. So I wrote to you again to show how different you were."

"Did I answer?"

"No. So then all the Literary Club took to admiring you instead of Gilbert Warwick."

"Because I didn't answer letters?"

"Yes. You see, it showed you were a real artist and didn't care a bit for your public, and just lived for your work."

"I see."

After dinner Roger said, "Has little Julia been boring you frightfully?"

"Yes."

"I thought she was. She's very pretty. It's a great evening for her."

Eventually we returned to the drawing-room and sat about.

Roger did not know how to manage this stage of this party. He talked vaguely of going on somewhere to dance and of playing a new parlour game that had lately arrived from New York. No one encouraged him. I did not speak to Lucy until I came to say good-bye, which was very early, as soon as the first guest moved and everyone, on the instant, rose too. When I said good-bye to her, Julia said, "Please, I must tell you. You're a thousand times grander than I ever imagined. It was half a game before – now it's serious."

I could imagine the relief in the house as the last of us left, Roger and Lucy emerging into one another's arms as though from shelter after a storm . . . "So that's over. Was it as bad as you expected?" "Worse, worse. You were splendid" . . . perhaps they – and Julia too? – were cutting a caper on the drawing-room carpet in an ecstasy of liberation.

"That," I said to myself, "is what you have bought with your five pounds."

That evening, next day and for several days, I disliked Lucy. I made a story for all who knew him, of Roger's dinner party, leaving the impression that this was the kind of life Lucy enjoyed and that she was driving Roger into it. But for all that I did not abate my resolve to force my friendship upon her. [I can give no plausible account of this inconsistency. I was certainly not, consciously, in love with her. I did not, even, at that time find her conspicuously beautiful. In seeking her friendship I did not look for affection nor, exactly, for esteem.] I sought recognition. I wanted to assert the simple fact of my separate and individual existence. I could not by any effort of will regard her as being, like Trixie, "one of Roger's girls", and I demanded reciprocation; I would not be regarded as, like Basil, "one of Roger's friends"; still less, like Mr. Benwell, as someone who had to be asked to dinner every now and then. I had little else to think about at the time, and the thing became an itch with me. I felt about her, I suppose, as old men feel who are impelled by habit to touch every third lamp-post on their walks; occasionally something happens to distract them, they see a friend or a street accident and they pass a lamp-post by; then all day they fret and fidget until, after tea, they set out shamefacedly to put the matter right. That was how I felt about Lucy; our relationship constituted a tiny disorder in my life that had to be adjusted.

That at least is how, in those earliest days, I explained my obsession to myself, but looking at it now, down the long, mirrored corridor of cumulative emotion, I see no beginning to the perspective. There is in the apprehension of woman's beauty an exquisite, early intimation of loveliness when, seeing some face, strange or familiar, one gains, suddenly, a further glimpse and foresees, out of a thousand possible futures, how it might be transfigured by love[; the vision is often momentary and transient, never to return in waking life, or else precipitately succeeded by the reality, and so forgotten]. With Lucy – her grace daily more encumbered by her pregnancy; deprived of sex, as women are, by its own fulfilment – the vision was extended and clarified until, with no perceptible transition, it became the reality. But I cannot say when it first appeared. Perhaps, that evening, when she said, about the *Composed Hermitage in the Chinese Taste*, "I can't think why John should want to have a house like that," but it came without surprise; I had sensed it on its way, as an animal, still in profound darkness and surrounded by all the sounds of night, will lift its head, sniff, and know, inwardly, that dawn is near. Meanwhile, I moved for advantage as in a parlour game.

Julia brought me success. Our meeting, so far from disillusioning her, made her cult of me keener and more direct. It was no fault of mine, I assured Roger, when he came to grumble about it; I had not been in the least agreeable to her; indeed towards the end of the evening I had been openly savage.

"The girl's a masochist," he said, adding with deeper gloom, "and Lucy says she's a virgin."

"There's plenty of time for her. The two troubles are often cured simultaneously."

"That's all very well, but she's staying another ten days. She never stops talking about you."

"Does Lucy mind?"

"Of course she minds. It's driving us both nuts. Does she write you a lot of letters?"

"Yes."

"What does she say?"

"I don't read them. I feel as though they were meant for somebody else. Besides they're in pencil."

"I expect she writes them in bed. No one's ever gone for me like that."

"Nor for me," I said. "It's not really at all disagreeable."

"I daresay not," said Roger. "I thought only actors and sex-novelists and clergymen came in for it."

"No, no, anybody may – scientists, politicians, professional cyclists – anyone whose name gets into the papers. It's just that young girls are naturally religious."

"Julia's eighteen."

"She'll get over it soon. She's been stirred up by suddenly meeting me in the flesh after two or three years' distant devotion. She's a nice child."

"That's all very well," said Roger, returning sulkily to his original point. "It isn't Julia I'm worried about, it's ourselves, Lucy and me – she's staying another ten days. Lucy says you've got to be nice about it, and come out this evening, the four of us. I'm sorry, but there it is."

So for a week I went often to Victoria Square, and there was the beginning of a half-secret joke between Lucy and me in Julia's devotion. While I was there Julia sat smug and gay; she was a child of enchanting prettiness; when I was absent, Roger told me, she moped a good deal and spent much time in her bedroom writing and destroying letters to me. She talked about herself, mostly, and her sister and family. Her father was a major and they lived at Aldershot; they would have to stay there all the year round now that Lucy no longer needed their company in London. She did not like Roger. "He's not very nice about you," she said.

"Roger and I are like that," I explained. "We're always foul about each other. It's our fun. Is Lucy nice about me?"

"Lucy's an angel," said Julia, "that's why we hate Roger so."

Finally there was the evening of Julia's last party. Eight of us went to dance at a restaurant. Julia was at first very gay, but her spirits dropped towards the end of the evening. I was living in Ebury Street; it was easy for me to walk home from Victoria Square, so I went back with them and had a last drink. "Lucy's promised to leave us alone, just for a minute, to say good-bye," Julia whispered.

When we were alone, she said, "It's been absolutely wonderful the last two weeks. I didn't know it was possible to be so happy. I wish you'd give me something as a kind of souvenir."

"Of course. I'll send you one of my books, shall I?"

"No," she said, "I'm not interested in your books any more. At least, of course, I am, terribly, but I mean it's *you* I love."

"Nonsense," I said.

"Will you kiss me, once, just to say good-bye."

["Certainly not."][1]

Then she said suddenly, "You're in love with Lucy, aren't you?"

"Good heavens, no. What on earth put that into your head?"

"I can tell. Through loving you so much, I expect. You may not know it, but you are. And it's no good. She loves that horrid Roger. Oh, dear, they're coming back. I'll come and say good-bye to you to-morrow, may I?"

"No."

"*Please.* This hasn't been how I planned it at all."

Then Roger and Lucy came into the room with a sly look as though they had been discussing what was going on and how long they should give us. So I shook hands with Julia and went home.

She came to my rooms at ten next morning. Mrs. Legge, the landlady, showed her up. She stood in the door, swinging a small parcel. "I've got five minutes," she said, "the taxi's waiting. I told Lucy I had some last-minute shopping."

"You know you oughtn't to do this sort of thing."

1 I kissed her paternally on the cheek.

"I've been here before. When I knew you were out. I pretended I was your sister and had come to fetch something for you."

"Mrs. Legge never said anything to me about it."

"No. I asked her not to. In fact I gave her ten shillings. You see she caught me at it."

"At what?"

"Well, it sounds rather silly. I was in your bedroom, kissing things – you know, pillows, pyjamas, hair brushes. I'd just got to the wash-stand and was kissing your razor when I looked up and found Mrs. Whatever-she's-called standing in the door."

"Good God, I shall never be able to look her in the face again."

"Oh, she was quite sympathetic. I suppose I must have looked funny, like a goose grazing." She gave a little, rather hysterical giggle, and added, "Oh, John, I do love you so."

"Nonsense. I shall turn you out if you talk like that."

"Well, I do. And I've got you a present." She gave me the square parcel. "Open it."

"I shan't accept it," I said unwrapping a box of cigars.

"But you must. You see, they'd be no good to me, would they? Are they good ones?"

"Yes," I said, looking at the box. "Very good ones indeed."

"The best?"

"Quite the best, but..."

"That's what the man in the shop said. Smoke one now."

"Julia dear, I couldn't. I've only just finished breakfast."

She saw the point of that. "When will you smoke the first one? After luncheon? I'd like to think of you smoking the first one."

"Julia, dear, it's perfectly sweet of you, but I can't, honestly..."

"I know what you're thinking, that I can't afford it. Well, that's all right. You see, Lucy gave me five pounds yesterday to buy a hat. I thought she would – she often does. But I had to wait and be sure. I'd got them ready, hidden yesterday evening. I meant to give you them then. But I never got a proper chance. So here they are." And then, as I hesitated, with rising voice, "Don't you see I'd much rather give you cigars than have a new hat? Don't you see I shall go back to Aldershot absolutely miserable, the whole time in London quite spoilt, if you won't take them?"

She had clearly been crying that morning and was near tears again.

"Of course I'll take them," I said. "I think it's perfectly sweet of you."

Her face cleared in sudden, infectious joy.

"There. Now we can say good-bye."

She stood waiting for me, not petitioning this time, but claiming her right. I put my hands on her shoulders and gave her a single, warm kiss on the lips. She shut her eyes and sighed. "Thank you," she said in a small voice, and hurried out to her waiting taxi, leaving the box of cigars on my table.

Sweet Julia! I thought; it was a supremely unselfish present; something quite impersonal and unsentimental – no keep-sake – something which would be gone, literally in smoke, in less than six weeks; a thing she had not even the fun of choosing for herself; she had gone to the counter and left it to the shopman – "I want a box of the best cigars you keep, please – as many as I can get for five pounds." She just wanted something which she could be sure would give pleasure.

And chiefly because she thought I had been kind to her cousin, Lucy took me into her friendship.

Roger's engraving showed a pavilion, still rigidly orthodox in plan, but, in elevation decked with ornament conceived in a wild ignorance of oriental forms; there were balconies and balustrades of geometric patterns; the cornice swerved upwards at the corners in the lines of a pagoda; the roof was crowned with an onion cupola which might have been Russian, bells hung from the capitals of barley-sugar columns; the windows were freely derived from the Alhambra; there was a minaret. To complete the atmosphere the engraver had added a little group of Turkish military performing the bastinado upon a curiously complacent malefactor, an Arabian camel and a mandarin carrying a bird in a cage.

"My word, what a gem," they said. "Is it really all there?"

"The minaret's down and it's all rather overgrown."

"What a chance. John must get it."

"It will be fun to furnish. I know just the chairs for it."

This was the first time I had been to Victoria Square since Julia left.

And Lucy said, "I can't think why John should want to have a house like that."

II

Lucy was a girl of few friends; she had, in fact, at the time I was admitted to their number, only two; a man named Peter Baverstock, in the Malay States, whom I never saw, and a Miss Muriel Meikeljohn whom I saw all too often. Peter Baverstock had wanted to marry Lucy since she was seven and proposed to her whenever he came home on leave, every eighteen months, until she married Roger, when he sent her a very elaborate wedding present, an immense thing in carved wood, ivory and gilt which caused much speculation with regard to its purpose; later he wrote and explained; I forget the explanation. I think it was the gift which, by local usage, men of high birth gave to their grand-daughters when they were delivered of male twins; it was, anyway, connected with twins and grandparents, of great rarity, and a token of high esteem in the parts he came from. Lucy wrote long letters to Baverstock every fortnight. I often watched her at work on those letters, sitting square to her table, head bowed, hand travelling evenly across the page, as, I remembered reading in some books of memoirs, Sir Walter Scott's had been seen at a lighted window, writing the Waverley novels. It was a tradition of her upbringing that letters for the East must always be written on very thin, lined paper. "I'm just telling Peter about your house," she would say.

"How can that possibly interest him?"

"Oh, he's interested in everything. He's so far away."

It seemed an odd reason.

Miss Meikeljohn was a pale, possessive girl, who had been a fellow boarder with Lucy in the house of a distressed gentle-woman in Vienna where they had both been sent to learn sing-ing. They had shared a passion for a leading tenor, and had once got into his dressing-room at the Opera House by wearing mackintoshes and pretending to be reporters sent to interview him. Lucy still kept a photograph of this tenor, in costume, on her dressing-table, but she had shed her musical aspirations with the rest of her Pont Street life. Miss Meikeljohn still sang, once a week to a tutor. It was after these lessons that she came to luncheon with Lucy, and the afternoon was hers by prescriptive right for shopping, or for a cinema, or for what she liked best, a "good talk". These Tuesdays were "Muriel's days", and no one might interfere with them.

"They are the only times she comes into London. Her parents are separated and terribly poor," Lucy said, as though in com-plete explanation.

When they went to the cinema or play together they went in the cheap seats because Miss Meikeljohn insisted on paying her share. Lucy thought this evidence of Miss Meikeljohn's integrity of character; she often came back from [their common][1] enter-tainments with a headache from having had to sit so close to the screen.

The friendship was odd in many ways, notably because Miss Meikeljohn luxuriated in heart-to-heart confidences – in what my father's generation coarsely called "taking down her back hair" – an exhibition that was abhorrent to Lucy, who in friend-ship had all the modesty of the naked savage.

I must accept the modesty of the naked savage on trust, on the authority of numerous travel books. The savages I have met on my travels have all been formidably overdressed. But if there existed nowhere else on the globe that lithe, chaste and unstudied nudity of which I have so often read, it was there, dazzlingly, in the mind of Lucy. There were no reservations in her friendship, and it was an experience for which I was little qualified, to be

1 these

admitted, as it were, through a door in the wall to wander at will over that rich estate. The idea of an occasional opening to the public in aid of the cottage hospital, of extra gardeners working a week beforehand to tidy the walks, of an upper housemaid to act as guide, of red cord looped across the arms of the chairs, of special objects of value to be noted, of "that door leads to the family's private apartments. They are never shown," of vigilance at the hot-house for fear of a nectarine being pocketed, of "now you have seen *everything*: please make way for the next party," and of the open palm – of all, in fact, which constituted Miss Meikeljohn's, and most people's, habit of intimacy, was inconceivable to Lucy.

When I began to realize the spaces and treasures of which I had been made free, I was like a slum child alternately afraid to touch or impudently curious. Or, rather, I felt too old. Years earlier when Lucy was in her cradle, I had known this kind of friendship. There was a boy at my private school with whom I enjoyed a week of unrestrained confidence; one afternoon sitting with him in a kind of nest, itself a secret, which we had devised for ourselves from a gym mat and piled benches in a corner of the place where we played on wet afternoons, I revealed my greatest secret, that my father was an artist and not, as I had given it out, an officer in the Navy; by tea-time the story was all over the school, that Plant's pater had long hair and did not wash. (Revenge came sooner than I could have hoped, for this was the summer term, 1914, and my betrayer had an aunt married to an Austrian nobleman; he had boasted at length of staying in their castle; when school reassembled in September I was at the head of the mob which hounded him in tears to the matron's room with cries of "German spy".) It was the first and, to my mind, most dramatic of the normal betrayals of adolescence. With the years I had grown cautious. There was little love and no trust at all between any of my friends. Moreover, we were bored; each knew the other so well that it was only by making our relationship into a kind of competitive parlour game that we kept it alive at all. We had all from time to time cut out divergent trails and camped in new ground, but we always, as it were, returned to the same base for supplies, and swapped yarns of our exploration.

That was what I meant by friendship at the age of [thirty-three][1],
and Lucy, finding herself without preparation [for them] among
people like myself, had been disconcerted. That was the origin of
what, at first, I took for priggishness in her. Her lack of shyness
cut her off from us. She could not cope with the attack and
defence, deception and exposure, which was our habitual
intercourse. Anything less than absolute intimacy embarrassed
her, so she fell back upon her good upbringing, that armoury of
school-room virtues and graces with which she had been
equipped, and lived, as best she could, independently, rather as,
it is said, Chinese gentlemen of the old school can pursue
interminable, courteous, traditionally prescribed conversations
with their minds abstracted in realms of distant beauty.

But it was not enough. She was lonely. In particular she was
cut off by her pregnancy from Roger. For a term of months she
was unsexed, the roots of her love for Roger wintering, out of
sight in the ground, without leaf. So she looked for a friend and,
because she thought I had been kind to Julia, and because, in a
way, I had responded to her in her schoolroom mood, she chose
me. I had not misinterpreted her change of manner. She had
made up her mind that I was to be a friend [and, as her intimation of this had been in talking of my house, that became for
many weeks a main bond between us]. I began, almost at once, to
spend the greater part of the day in her company, and as my
preoccupation at the time was in finding a house that quest
became the structure of our friendship. Together we went over
the sheaves of house-agents' notices and several times we went on
long expeditions together to look at houses in the country. [Once
on our quest she took me to stay the night with relatives of hers.]
We talked of everything except the single topic of politics. [On
that we were agreed; I, because it was old stuff to me; I had been
over it all, time and again, since the age of seventeen; she
because, I think, she felt her political opinions to be a part of
her marriage with Roger. I have known countless communists
and not one of them was moved by anything remotely resembling

1 thirty-four

compassion.] The attraction of [communism][1] for Lucy was
double. It was a part of the break she had made with Aldershot
and Pont Street, and it relieved her of the responsibility she felt
for her own private fortune. Money, her money, was of great
importance to her. If she had lived among the rich it would have
been different; she would then have thought it normal to be
assured, for life, of the possessions for which others toiled; she
would, indeed, have thought herself rather meagrely provided.
But she had been brought up among people poorer than herself
to regard herself as somebody quite singular. When the age came
of her going to dances, her aunt had impressed on her the danger
she ran of fortune-hunters and, indeed, nearly all the young men
with whom she consorted, and their mothers, regarded £58,000
as a notable prize. "Sometimes by the way that girl talks," Basil
had said, "you'd think she was the Woolworth heiress." It was
quite true. She did think herself extremely rich and responsible.
One of the advantages to her of marrying Roger was the belief
that her money was being put to good use in rescuing a literary
genius from wage-slavery. She was much more afraid of misusing
her money than of losing it. Thus when she was convinced that all
private fortunes like her own were very shortly to be abolished
and all undeserved prominence levelled, she was delighted.
Moreover, her conversion had coincided with her falling in
love. She and Roger had been to meetings together, and together
read epitomes of Marxist philosophy. Her faith, like a Christian's,
was essential to her marriage, so, knowing that I was hostile, she
sequestered it from me [by making it a joke between us. That
defence, at least, she had already picked up from watching Roger
and his friends].

It was convenient for Roger to have me in attendance. He was
not domestic by nature[, and it was inevitable that these months
should come to him as an anticlimax after the adventure of
marriage]. He did not, as some husbands do, resent his wife's
pregnancy. It was as though he had bought a hunter at the end
of the season and turned him out; discerning friends, he

1 Socialism

knew, would appreciate the fine lines under the rough coat, but he would sooner have shown something glossy in the stable. He had summer business to do, moreover; the horse must wait till the late autumn. That, at least, was one way in which he saw the situation, but the analogy was incomplete. It was rather *he* that had been acquired and put to grass, and he was conscious of that aspect too. Roger was hobbled and prevented from taking the full stride required of him, by the habit, long settled, of regarding sex relationships in terms of ownership and use. Confronted with the new fact of pregnancy, of joint ownership, his terms failed him. As a result he was restless and no longer master of the situation; the practical business of getting through the day was becoming onerous so that my adhesion was agreeable to him. Grossly, it confirmed his opinion of Lucy's value and at the same time took her off his hands. Then one morning, when I made my now habitual call at Victoria Square, Lucy, not yet up but lying in bed in a chaos of newspapers, letters and manicure tools, greeted me by saying, "Roger's writing."

Couched as she was, amid quilted bed-jacket and tumbled sheets – one arm bare to the elbow where the wide sleeve fell back and showed the tender places of wrist and forearm, the other lost in the warm depths of the bed, with her pale skin taking colour against the dead white linen, and her smile of confident, morning welcome; as I had greeted her countless times and always with a keener joy, until that morning I seemed to have come to the end of an investigation and hold as a certainty what before I had roughly surmised – her beauty rang through the room like a peal of bells; thus I have stood, stunned, in a Somerset garden, with the close turf wet and glittering underfoot in the dew, when, from beyond the walls of box, the grey church tower has suddenly scattered the heavens in tumult.

"Poor fellow," I said. "What about?"

"It's my fault," she said, "a detective story," and she went on to explain that since I had talked to her about my books, she had read them – "You were perfectly right. They *are* works of art. I had no idea" – and talked of them to Roger until he had suddenly said, "Oh, God, another Julia." Then he had told her that for many years he had kept a plot in his mind, waiting for a suitable time to put it into writing.

"He'll do it very well," I said, "Roger can write anything."

"Yes."

But while she was telling me this and I was answering, I thought only of Lucy's new beauty. I knew that beauty of that kind did not come from a suitable light or a lucky way with the hair or a sound eight hours' sleep, but from an inner secret; and I knew this morning that the secret was the fact of Roger's jealousy. So another stage was reached in my falling in love with Lucy, while each week she grew heavier and slower and less apt for love, so that I accepted the joy of her companionship without reasoning. [Later, on looking back on those unusual weeks, I saw myself and Lucy as][1] characters in the stock intrigue of renaissance comedy, where the heroine follows the hero in male attire and is wooed by him, unknowing, in the terms of rough friendship.

In these weeks Lucy and I grew adept in construing the jargon of the estate agents. [We knew that "substantially built" meant "hideous", "ripe for modernization" "ruinous", that "matured grounds" were a jungle of unkempt laurel; all that belonged to the underworld of *Punch* humour. We learned, what was far more valuable, to detect omissions; nothing could be taken for granted, and if the agent did not specify a staircase, it had in all probability disappeared. Basil explained to me how much more practical it was to purchase a mansion; really large houses, he said, were sold for the sake of the timber in the park; he had a scheme, rather hazily worked out, by which I should make myself a private company for the development of a thousand acres, a mile of fishing, a castle and two secondary residences which he knew of in Cumberland, and by a system of mortgages, sub-tenancies, directors' fees and declared trading losses, inhabit the castle, as he expressed it, "free"; somewhere, in the legal manoeuvres,

1 Lucy and I were like

Basil was to have acquired and divested himself, at a profit, of a controlling interest in the estate. Roger produced a series of derelict "follies" which he thought it my duty to save for the nation. Other friends asked why I did not settle in Portugal where, they said, Jesuit Convents in the Manuelo style could be picked up for a song. But] I had a clear idea of what I required. In the first place it must not cost, all told, when the decorators and plumbers had moved out and the lawyers been paid for the conveyance, more than £3,000; it must be in agricultural country, preferably within five miles of an antiquated market town, it must be at least a hundred years old, and it must be a *house*, no matter how dingy, rather than a cottage, however luxurious; there must be a cellar, two staircases, high ceilings, a marble chimney-piece in the drawing-room, room to turn a car at the front door, a coach-house and stable yard, a walled kitchen garden, a paddock and one or two substantial trees – these seemed to me the minimum requisites of the standard of gentility at which I aimed, something between the squire's and the retired admiral's. Lucy had a womanly love of sunlight and a Marxist faith in the superior beauties of concrete and steel. She had, moreover, a horror, born of long association, of the rural bourgeoisie with whom I was determined to enrol myself. I was able to excuse my predilection to others by describing it as Gallic; French writers, I explained, owed their great strength, as had the writers of nineteenth-century England, to their middle-class status; the best of them all owned square white houses, saved their money, dined with the mayor and had their eyes closed for them at death by faithful, repellent housekeepers; English and American writers squandered their energy in being fashionable or bohemian or, worst of all, in an unhappy alternation between the two. This theme went down well with Mr. Benwell who, in the week or two after I expounded it to him, gave deathless offence to several of his authors by exhorting them to be middle-class too, but it left Lucy unimpressed. She thought the object of my search grotesque, but followed in a cheerful and purely sporting spirit as one may hunt a fox which one has no taste to eat.

The last occasion of her leaving London before her confinement, was to look at a house with me, below the Berkshire downs.
It was too far to travel comfortably in a day, and we spent the
night with relatives of hers near Abingdon. We had by now
grown so accustomed to one another's company that there
seemed nothing odd to us in Lucy proposing me as a guest.
Our host and hostess, however, thought it most irregular, and
their manifest surprise was a further bond between us. Lucy was
by now [seven][1] months with child and at the back of her
relatives' concern was the fear that she might be delivered prematurely in their house. They treated her with a solicitude that all
too clearly was a rebuke to my own easy-going acceptance of the
situation. Try how I might to realize the dangers she ran, I could
never feel protective towards Lucy. She looked, we agreed, like
Tweedledum armed for battle, and I saw her at this time as
preternaturally solid, with an armour of new life defending her
from the world. Biologically, no doubt, this was a fallacy, but it
was the attitude we jointly accepted, so that we made an immediate bad impression by being struck with *fourire* in the first five
minutes of our visit, when our hostess whispered that she had
fitted up a bedroom for Lucy on the ground floor so that she
should not be troubled by stairs.

The house we had come to see proved, like so many others, to
be quite uninhabitable. Its owner, in fact, was living in his lodge.
"Too big for me these days," he said of the house which, when he
opened it to us, gave the impression of having been designed as a
small villa and wantonly extended, as though no one had remembered to tell the workmen when to stop and they had gone on
adding room to room like cells in a wasp-nest. "I never had the
money to spend on it," the owner said gloomily, "you could make
something of it with a little money."

We went upstairs and along a lightless passage. He had been
showing people over this house since [1920][2], he said, and with
the years he had adopted a regular patter. "Nice little room this,

1 eight
2 1902

very warm in the winter. . . . You get a good view of the downs here, if you stand in the corner. . . . It's a dry house. You can see that. I've never had any trouble with damp. . . . These used to be the nurseries. They'd make a nice suite of spare bedroom, dressing-room and bath if you didn't . . ." and at that point, remembering Lucy, he stopped abruptly and in such embarrassment that he scarcely spoke until we left him.

"I'll write to you," I said.

"Yes," he said with great gloom, knowing what I meant, "I sometimes think the place might do as a school. It's very healthy."

So we drove back to Lucy's relatives. They wanted her to dine in bed or, anyway, to go to her room and lie down until dinner. Instead she came out with me into the evening sunlight and we sat in what Lucy's relatives called their "blue garden", reconstructing a life history of the sad little man who had shown us his house. Lucy's relatives thought us and our presence there and our whole expedition extremely odd. There was something going on, they felt, which they did not understand, and Lucy and I, infected by the atmosphere, became, as it were, confederates in this house which she had known all her life, in the garden where, as a little girl, she had once, she told me, buried a dead starling, with tears.

After this expedition Lucy remained in London, spending more and more of her time indoors. When I finally found a house to suit me, I was alone.

"You might have waited," said Lucy. It seemed quite natural that she should reproach me. She had a share in my house. "Damn this baby," she added.

III

In the last week before the birth of her child, Lucy began for the first time to betray impatience; she was never, at any time, at all apprehensive – merely bored and weary and vexed, past bearing, by the nurse who had now taken up residence in the house. Roger and Miss Meikeljohn had made up their minds that she was going to die. "It's all this damned pre-natal care," said Roger. "Do you realize that maternal mortality is higher in this

country than it's ever been? D'you know there are cases of
women going completely bald after childbirth? And permanently insane? It's worse among the rich than the poor, too."

Miss Meikeljohn said: "Lucy's being so wonderful. She
doesn't *realize*."

The nurse occupied herself with extravagant shopping lists;
"Does *everyone* have to have all these things?" Lucy asked, aghast
at the multitude of medical and nursery supplies which began to
pour into the house. "Everyone who can afford them," said Sister
Kemp briskly, unconscious of irony. Roger found some comfort
in generalizing. "It's anthropologically very interesting," he said,
"all this purely ceremonial accumulation of rubbish – like turtle
doves brought to the gates of a temple. Everyone according to his
means sacrificing to the racial god of hygiene."

He showed remarkable forbearance to Sister Kemp, who
brought with her an atmosphere of impending doom and
accepted a cocktail every evening, saying, "I'm not really on
duty *yet*," or "No time for this *after the day*."

She watched confidently for The Day, her apotheosis, when
Lucy would have no need for Roger or me or Miss Meikeljohn,
only for herself.

"I shall call you Mrs. Simmonds until The Day," she said.
"After that you will be my Lucy." She sat about with us in the
drawing-room, and in Lucy's bedroom where we spent most of
the day, now; like an alien, sitting at a café; an alien anarchist,
with a bomb beside him, watching the passing life of a foreign
city, waiting for his signal from the higher powers, the password
which might come at once or in a very few days, whispered in his
ear, perhaps, by the waiter, or scrawled on the corner of his
evening newspaper – the signal that the hour of liberation had
come when he would take possession of all he beheld. "The
fathers need nearly as much care as the mothers," said Sister
Kemp. "No, not another thank you, Mr. Simmonds. I've got to
keep in readiness, you know. It would never do if baby came
knocking at the door and found Sister unable to lift the latch."

"No," said Roger. "No, I suppose it wouldn't."

Sister Kemp belonged to a particularly select and highly paid corps of nurses. A baby wheeled out by her, as it would be daily for the first month, would have access to certain paths in the Park where inferior nurses trespassed at the risk of cold looks. Lucy's perambulator would thus be socially established and the regular nurse, when she took over, would find her charge already well known and respected. Sister Kemp explained this, adding as a concession to Lucy's political opinions, "The snobbery among nurses is terrible. I've seen many a girl go home from Stanhope Gate in tears." And then, *ésprit de corps* asserting itself, "Of course, they ought to have known. There's always Kensington Gardens for *them*."

Once Sister Kemp had attended a house in Seamore Place, in nodding distance of Royalty, but the gardens there, though supremely grand, had been, she said, "dull", by which we understood that even for her there were close circles. Roger was delighted with this. "It's like something out of Thackeray," he said and pressed for further details, but Lucy was past taking relish in social survivals; she was concerned only with the single, physical fact of her own exhaustion. "I hate this baby already," she said. "I'm going to hate it all my life."

Roger worked hard at this time, in the morning at his detective story, in the afternoons at his committee for [Chinese][1] aid. Miss Meikeljohn and I tried to keep Lucy amused with increasingly little success. Miss Meikeljohn took her to concerts and cinemas where, now, she allowed Lucy to buy the seats as extreme comfort was clearly necessary for her. I took her to the Zoo, every morning at twelve o'clock. There was a sooty, devilish creature in the monkey house named Humboldt's Gibbon which we would watch morosely for half an hour at a time; he seemed to exercise some kind of hypnotic fascination over Lucy; she could not be got to other cages. "If I have a boy I'll call him Humboldt," she said. "D'you know that before I was born, so Aunt Maureen says, my mother used to sit in front of a Flaxman bas-relief so as to give me ideal beauty. Poor mother, she died when I was born." Lucy could say that without embarrassment because she felt no

1 Spanish

danger in her own future. "I don't care how disagreeable it's going to be," she said, "I only want it soon."

Because of my confidence in her, and my resentment of the proprietary qualms of Roger and Miss Meikeljohn, I accepted her attitude; and was correspondingly shocked when the actual day came.

Roger telephoned to me at breakfast time. "The baby's begun."

"Good," I said.

"What d'you mean, good?"

"Well, it is good, isn't it? When did it start?"

"Last night, about an hour after you left."

"It ought to be over soon."

"I suppose so. Shall I come round?"

He came, yawning a great deal from having been up all night. "I was with her for an hour or two. I always imagined people in bed when they were having babies. Lucy's up, going about the house. It was horrible. Now she doesn't want me."

"What happened exactly?"

He began to tell me and then I was sorry I had asked. "That nurse seems very good," he said at the end. "The doctor didn't come until half an hour ago. He went away again right away. They haven't given her any chloroform yet. They say they are keeping that until the pains get worse. I don't see how they could be. You've no conception what it was like." He stayed with me for half an hour and read my newspapers. Then he went home. "I'll telephone you when there's any news," he said.

Two hours later I rang up. "No," he said, "there's no news. I said I'd telephone you if there was."

"But what's happening?"

"I don't know. Some kind of lull."

"But she's all right, isn't she? I mean they're not anxious."

"I don't know. The doctor's coming again. I went in to see her, but she didn't say anything. She was just crying quietly."

"Nothing I can do, is there?"

"No, how could there be?"

"I mean about lunch or anything. You don't feel like coming out?"

"No, I ought to stay around here."

The thought of the lull, of Lucy not speaking, but lying there, in tears, waiting for her labour to start again, pierced me as no tale could have done of cumulative pain; but beyond my sense of compassion I was now scared. I had been smoking a pipe; my mouth had gone dry, and when I knocked out the smouldering tobacco the smell of it sickened me. I went out into Ebury Street as though to the deck of a ship, breathing hard against nausea, and from habit more than sentiment, took a cab to the Zoo.

The man at the turnstile knew me as a familiar figure. "Your lady not with you to-day, sir?"

"No, not to-day."

"I've got five myself," he said.

I did not understand him and repeated foolishly, "Five?"

"Being a married man," he added.

Humboldt's Gibbon seemed disinclined for company. He sat hunched up at the back of his cage, fixing on me a steady, and rather bilious stare. He was never, at the best of times, an animal who courted popularity. In the cage on his left lived a sycophant-ish, shrivelled, grey monkey from India who salaamed for titbits of food; on his right were a troup of patchy buffoons who swung and tumbled about their cage to attract attention. Not so Humboldt's Gibbon; visitors passed him by – often with almost superstitious aversion and some such comment as "Nasty thing"; he had no tricks, or, if he had, he performed them alone, for his own satisfaction, after dark, ritualistically, when, in that exotic enclave among the stucco terraces, the prisoners awake and commemorate the jungles where they had their birth, as exiled darkies, when their work is done, will tread out the music of Africa in a vacant lot behind the drug store.

Lucy used always to bring fruit to the ape; I had nothing, but, to deceive him, I rattled the wire and held out my empty fingers as though they held a gift. He unrolled himself, revealing an extraordinary length of black limb, and came delicately towards me on toes and finger tips; his body was slightly pigeon chested and his fur dense and short, his head was spherical, without the poodle-snout of his neighbours – merely two eyes and a line of yellow teeth set in leather, like a bare patch worn in a rug. He was less like a man than any of his kind and he lacked their human vulgarity. When, at short range, he realized that I held nothing for him he leapt suddenly at the bars and hung there, spread out to his full span, spiderish, snarling with contempt; then dropped to the floor and turning about walked delicately back to the corner from which I had lured him. So I looked at him and thought of Lucy, and the minutes passed.

Presently I was aware of someone passing behind me from the salaaming monkey to the troup of tumblers, and back again, and at either side peering not at the animals but at me. I gazed fixedly at the ape, hoping that this nuisance would pass. Finally a voice said, "I say."

I turned and found Arthur Atwater. He was dressed as I had seen him before, in his raincoat, though it was a fine, warm day, and his soft grey hat, worn at what should have been a raffish angle but which, in effect, looked merely lopsided. (He explained the raincoat in the course of our conversation, saying, "You know how it is in digs. If you leave anything behind when you go out for the day, someone's sure to take a fancy to it.") "It is Plant, isn't it?" he said.

"Yes."

"Thought so. I never forget a face. They call it the royal gift, don't they?"

"Do they?"

"Yes, that and punctuality. I'm punctual too. It's a curious thing because you see, actually, though I don't make any fuss about it in the position I'm in, I'm descended from Henry VII." There seemed no suitable answer to this piece of information so, since I was silent, he added suddenly, "I say, you do remember me, don't you?"

"Vividly."

He came closer and leant beside me on the rail which separated us from the cage. It was as though we stood on board ship and were looking out to sea, only instead of the passing waters we saw the solitary, still person of Humboldt's Gibbon. "I don't mind telling you," said Atwater, "I've had a pretty thin time of it since we last met."

"I saw you were acquitted at the trial. I thought you were very fortunate."

"Fortunate! You should have heard the things the beak said. Things he had no right to say and wouldn't have dared say to a rich man, and said in a very nasty way, too – things I shan't forget in a hurry. Mr. Justice Longworth – *Justice*, that's funny. Acquitted without a stain! – innocent! Does that give me back my job?"

"But I understood from the evidence at the trial that you were under notice to go anyway."

"Yes. And why? Because sales were dropping. Why should I sell their beastly stockings for them anyway? Money – that's all anyone cares about now. And I'm beginning to feel the same way. When do you suppose I had my last meal – my last square meal?"

"I've really no idea, I'm afraid."

"Tuesday. I'm hungry, Plant – literally hungry."

"You could have saved yourself the sixpence admission here, couldn't you?"

"I'm a Fellow," said Atwater with surprising readiness.

"Oh."

"You don't believe that, do you?"

"I have no reason not to."

"I can prove it; look here – Fellow's tickets, two of them." He produced and pressed on my attention two tickets of admission signed in a thin, feminine hand. "My dear Atwater," I said, "these don't make you a Fellow; they've merely been given you by someone who is – not that it matters."

"Not that it matters! Let me tell you this: D'you know who gave me these? – the mother of a chap I know; chap I know well. I dropped round to see him the other evening, at the address I found in the telephone book. It was his mother's house as it happened. My pal was abroad. But, anyway, I got talking to the

mother and told her about how I was placed and what pals her
son and I had been. She seemed a decent old bird. At the end she
said, 'How very sad. Do let me give you something,' and began
fumbling in her bag. I thought at least a quid was coming, and
what did she give me? These tickets for the Zoo. I ask you!"

"Well," I said, with a tone as encouraging as I could manage,
for it did seem to me that in this instance he had been unfairly
disappointed, "the Zoo is a very pleasant place."

At this suggestion Atwater showed one of those mercurial
changes of mood [which later became familiar to me but
which, at this stage of our acquaintance, I found rather disconcerting,] from resentment to simple enthusiasm. "It's wonderful," he said, "there's nothing like it. All these animals from all
over the world brought here to London. Think what they've seen
– forests and rivers, places probably where no white man's ever
been. It makes you long to get away, doesn't it? Think of pad-
dling your canoe upstream in undiscovered country, with strings
of orchids overhead and parrots in the trees and great butterflies,
and native servants, and hanging your hammock in the open at
night and starting off in the morning with no one to worry you,
living on fish and fruit – that's life," said Atwater.

Once again I felt impelled to correct his misconceptions of
colonial life. "If you are still thinking of settling in Rhodesia,"
I said, "I must warn you you will find conditions very different
from those you describe."

"Rhodesia's off," said Atwater. "I've other plans."

He told me of them at length, and because they distracted me
from thinking of Lucy, I listened gratefully. They depended,
primarily, on his finding a man of his acquaintance – a good
scout named Appleby – who had lately disappeared as so many of
Atwater's associates seemed to have done, leaving no indication
of his whereabouts. Appleby knew of a cave in Bolivia where the
Jesuits, in bygone years, had stored their treasure. When they
were driven out, they put a curse on the place, so that the superstitious natives left the hoard inviolate. Appleby had old parch-
ments which made the matter clear. More than this Appleby had
an aerial photograph of the locality, and by a special process

known to himself, was able to treat the plate so that auriferous ground came out dark; the hill where the Jesuits had left their treasure was almost solid black; the few white spots indicated chests of jewels and, possibly, bar platinum. "Appleby's idea was to collect ten stout fellows who would put up a hundred quid each for our fares and digging expenses. I'd have gone like a shot. Had it all fixed up. The only snag was that just at that time I couldn't put my hands on a hundred quid."

"Did the expedition ever start?"

"I don't think so. You see a lot of the chaps were in the same position. Besides old Appleby would never start without me. He's a good scout. If I only knew where he hung out I should be all right."

"Where used he to hang out?"

"You could always find him at the old Wimpole. He was what our barman called one of the regulars."

"Surely they would know his address there?" I kept talking. As long as I was learning about old Appleby I had only half my mind for Lucy.

"Well, you see the Wimpole's rather free and easy in some ways. As long as you're a good chap you're taken as you come and no questions asked. Subs are paid by the month; you know the kind of place. If you're shy of the ante, as we used to call it, the doorman doesn't let you in."

"And old Appleby was shy of the ante?"

"That's it. It wasn't a thing to worry about. Most of the chaps one time or another have been shown the door. I expect it's the same at your club. No disgrace attached. But old Appleby's a bit touchy and began telling off the doorman good and proper and then the secretary butted in and, to cut a long story short, there was something of a shemozzle."

"Yes," I said, "I see." And even as I spoke all interest in Appleby's shemozzle faded completely away and I thought of Lucy, lying at home in tears, waiting for her pain. "For God's sake tell me some more," I said.

"More about Appleby?"

"More about anything. Tell me about all the chaps in the

Wimpole. Tell me their names one by one and exactly what they look like. Tell me your family history. Tell me the full details of every job you have ever lost. Tell me all the funny stories you have ever heard. Tell my fortune. Don't you see, I want to be *told*?"

"I don't quite twig," said Atwater. "But if you are trying to hint that I'm boring you . . ."

"Atwater," I said earnestly, "I will [give you a pound][1] just to talk to me. Here [it is][2], look, take it. There. Does that look as though I was bored?"

"It looks to me as though you were barmy," said Atwater, pocketing the note. "Much obliged all the same. It'll come in handy just at the moment, only as a loan, mind."

"Only as a loan," I said, and we both of us lapsed into silence, he, no doubt, thinking of my barminess, I of Lucy. The black ape walked slowly round his cage raking the sawdust and nut shells with the back of his hand, looking vainly for some neglected morsel of food. Presently there was an excited scurry in the cage next to us; two women had appeared with a bunch of bananas. "Excuse me, please," they said and pushed in front of us to feed Humboldt's Gibbon; then they passed on to the grey sycophant beyond, and so down all the cages until their bag was empty. "Where shall we go now?" one of them said. "I don't see the point of animals you aren't allowed to feed."

Atwater overheard this remark; it worked in his mind so that by the time they had left the monkey house, he was in another mood. Atwater the dreamer, Atwater the good scout, and Atwater the underdog seemed to appear in more or less regular sequence. It was Atwater the good scout I liked best, but one clearly had to take him as he came. "Feeding animals while men and women starve," he said bitterly.

It was a topic; a topic dry, scentless and colourless as a pressed flower; a topic on which, in the school debating society, one had despaired of finding anything new to say – "The motion before

1 pay you
2 is a pound

the House is that too much kindness is shown to animals, proposed by Mr. John Plant, Headmaster's House" – nevertheless, it
was something to talk about.

"The animals are paid for their entertainment value," I said.
"We don't send out hampers to monkeys in their own forests." –
Or did we? There was no knowing what humane ladies in England
would not do – "We bring the monkeys here to amuse us."

"What's amusing about that black creature there?"

"Well, he's very beautiful."

"Beautiful?" Atwater stared into the hostile little face beyond
the bars. "Can't see it myself." Then rather truculently, "I suppose you'd say he was more beautiful than me."

"Well, as a matter of fact, since you raise the point . . ."

"You think that thing beautiful and feed it and shelter it, while
you leave me to starve."

This seemed unfair. I had just given Atwater a pound; moreover, it was not I who had fed the ape. I pointed this out.

"I see," said Atwater. "You're paying me for my entertainment value. You think I'm a kind of monkey."

This was uncomfortably near the truth. "You misunderstand
me," I said.

"I hope I do. A remark like that would start a rough-house at
the Wimpole."

A new and glorious idea came to me. "Atwater," I said,
cautiously for his oppressed mood was still on him. "Please do
not take offence at my suggestion but, supposing I were to pay –
as a loan, of course – would it be possible for us, do you think, to
lunch at the Wimpole?"

He took the suggestion quite well. "I'll be frank with you," he
said. "I haven't paid this month's sub yet. It's seven and
sixpence."

"We'll include that in the loan."

"Good scout. I know you'll like the place."

The taxi driver, to whom I gave the address "Wimpole Club",
was nonplussed. "Now you've got me," he said. "I thought
I knew them all. It's not what used to be called the 'Palm
Beach'?"

"No," said Atwater, and gave more exact directions.

We drove to a mews off Wimpole Street. ("It's handy for chaps in the motor business Great Portland Street way," said Atwater.) "By the way, I may as well explain, I'm known as Norton at the club."

"Why?"

"Lots of the chaps there use a different name. I expect it's the same at your club."

"I shouldn't be surprised," I said.

I paid the taxi. Atwater kicked open a green door and led me into the hall where a porter, behind the counter, was lunching off tea and sandwiches.

"I've been out of town," said Atwater. "Just dropped in to pay my subscription. Anyone about?"

"Very quiet," said the porter.

The room into which he led me was entirely empty. It was at once bar, lounge and dining-room, but mostly bar, for which a kind of film-set had been erected, built far into the room, with oak rafters, a thatched roof, a wrought iron lantern and an inn-sign painted in mock heraldry with quartered bottles and tankards. ["Please don't take this wrong," I said, "but I'm really interested to know what was the resemblance you saw between your club and the room where we talked in mine?"

"You can't compare them really, can you? I just didn't want to seem snooty. Jim!"][1]

"Sir." A head appeared above the bar. "Well, Mr. Norton, we haven't seen you for a long time. I was just having my bit of dinner."

"May I interrupt that important function and give my friend here something in the nature of a snorter." – This was a new and greatly expanded version of Atwater the good scout – "Two of your specials, please, Jim." To me, "Jim's specials are famous." To Jim, "This is one of my best pals, Mr. Plant." To me, "There's not much Jim doesn't know about me." To Jim, "Where's the gang?"

---

1 "Jim!" cried Atwater.

"They don't seem to come here like they did, Mr. Norton. There's not the money about."

"You've said it." Jim put two cocktails on the bar before us. "I presume, Jim, that since this is Mr. Plant's first time among us, in pursuance of the old Wimpole custom, these are on the house?"

Jim laughed rather anxiously. "Mr. Norton likes his joke."

"Joke? Jim, you shame me before my friends. But never fear. I have found a rich backer; if we aren't having this with you, you must have one with us."

The barman poured himself out something from a bottle which he kept for the purpose on a shelf below the bar, and said, "First to-day," as we toasted one another. Atwater said, "It's one of the mysteries of the club what Jim keeps in that bottle of his." I knew; it was what every barman kept, cold tea, but I thought it would spoil Atwater's treat if I told him.

Jim's "special" was strong and agreeable.

"Is it all right for me to order a round?" I asked.

"It's more than all right. It's perfect."

Jim shook up another cocktail and refilled his own glass.

"D'you remember the time I drank twelve of your specials before dinner with Mr. Appleby?"

"I do, sir."

"A tiny bit spifflicated that night, eh, Jim?"

"A tiny bit, sir."

We had further rounds; Jim took cash for the drinks; three shillings [a time][1]. After the first round, when Atwater broke into his pound note, I paid. Every other time he said, "Chalk it up to the national debt," or some similar reference to the fiction of our loan. Soon Jim and Atwater were deep in reminiscence of Atwater's past.

After a time I found my thoughts wandering and went to telephone to Victoria Square. Roger answered. "It seems things are coming more or less normally," he said.

"How is she?"

"I haven't been in. The doctor's here now, in a white coat like an umpire. He keeps saying I'm not to worry."

1 round

"But is she in danger?"

"Of course she is, it's a dangerous business."

"But I mean, more than most people?"

"Yes. No. I don't know. They said everything was quite normal whatever that means."

"I suppose it means she's not in more danger than most people."

"I suppose so."

"Does it bore you my ringing up to ask?"

"No, not really. Where are you?"

"At a club called the Wimpole."

"Never heard of it."

"No. I'll tell you about it later. Very interesting."

"Good. Do tell me later."

I returned to the bar. "I thought our old comrade had passed out on us," said Atwater. "Been sick?"

"Good heavens, no."

"You look a terrible colour, doesn't he, Jim? Perhaps a special is what he needs. I was sick that night old Grainger sold his Bentley, sick as a dog." . . .

When I had spent about thirty shillings Jim began to tire of his cold tea. "Why don't you gentlemen sit down at a table and let me order you a nice grill?" he asked.

"All in good time, Jim, all in good time. Mr. Plant here would like one of your specials first just to give him an appetite, and I think rather than see an old pal drink alone, I'll join him."

Later, when we were very drunk, steaks appeared which neither of us remembered ordering. We ate them at the bar with, at Jim's advice, great quantities of Worcester sauce. Our conversation, I think, was mainly about Appleby and the need of finding him. We rang up one or two people of that name, whom we found in the telephone book, but they disclaimed all knowledge of Jesuit treasure.

It must have been four o'clock in the afternoon when we left the Wimpole. Atwater was more drunk than I. Next day

I remembered most of our conversation verbatim. In the mews I asked him: "Where are you living?"

"Digs. Awful hole. But it's all right now I've got money – I can sleep on the embankment. Police won't let you sleep on the embankment unless you've got money. Vagrancy. One law for the rich, one for the poor. Iniquitous system."

"Why don't you come and live with me. I've got a house in the country, plenty of room. Stay as long as you like. Die there."

"Thanks, I will. Must go to the embankment first and pack."

And we separated, for the time, he sauntering unsteadily along Wimpole Street, past the rows of brass plates, I driving in a taxi to my rooms in Ebury Street where I undressed, folded my clothes and went quietly to bed. I awoke, in the dark, hours later, in confusion as to where I was and how I had got there.

The telephone was ringing next door in my sitting-room. It was Roger. He said that Lucy had had a son two hours ago; he had been ringing up relatives ever since; she was perfectly well; the first thing she had asked for when she came round from the chloroform was a cigarette. "I feel like going out and getting drunk," said Roger. "Don't you?"

"No," I said. "No, I'm afraid not," and returned to bed.

IV

When I got drunk I could sleep it off and wake in tolerable health; Roger could not; in the past we had often discussed this alcoholic insomnia of his and found no remedy for it except temperance; after telephoning to me he had gone out with Basil; he looked a wreck next morning.

"It's extraordinary," he said. "I've got absolutely no feeling about this baby at all. I kept telling myself all these last months that when I actually saw it, all manner of deep-rooted, atavistic emotions would come surging up. I was all set for a deep spiritual experience. They brought the thing in and showed it to me, I looked at it and waited – and nothing at all happened. It was just like the first time one takes hashish – or being 'confirmed' at school."

"I knew a man who had five children," I said. "He felt just as you do until the fifth. Then he was suddenly overcome with love; he bought a thermometer and kept taking its temperature when the nurse was out of the room. I daresay it's a habit, like hashish."

"I don't feel as if I had anything to do with it. It's as though they showed me Lucy's appendix or a tooth they'd pulled out of her."

"What's it like? I mean, it isn't a freak or anything?"

"No, I've been into that; two arms, two legs, one head, white – just a baby. Of course, you can't tell for some time if it's sane or not. I believe the first sign is that it can't take hold of things with its hands. Did you know that Lucy's grandmother was shut up?"

"I had no idea."

"Yes. Lucy never saw her, of course. It's why she's anxious about Julia."

"Is she anxious about Julia?"

"Who wouldn't be?"

"How soon can you tell if they're blind?"

"Not for weeks, I believe. I asked Sister Kemp. She said, 'The very idea,' and whisked the baby off as if I wanted to injure it, poor little brute. D'you know what Lucy calls Sister Kemp now? – Kempy."

"It's not possible."

It was true. I went in to see her for five minutes and twice during that time she said "Kempy". When we were alone for a minute I asked her why. "She asked me to," said Lucy, "and she's really very sweet."

"Sweet?"

"She was absolutely sweet to me yesterday."

I had brought some flowers, but the room was full of them. Lucy lay in bed; slack and smiling. I sat down by her and held her hand. "Everyone's been so sweet," she said. "Have you seen my baby?"

"No."

"He's in the dressing-room. Ask Kempy to show you."

"Are you pleased with him?"

"I love him. I do really. I never thought I should. He's such a *person*."

This was incomprehensible.

"You haven't gone bald," I said.

"No, but my hair's terrible. What did you do yesterday?"

"I got drunk."

"So did poor Roger. Were you with him?"

"No," I said, "it was really very amusing." I began to tell her about Atwater, but she was not listening.

Then Sister Kemp came in with more flowers – from Mr. Benwell.

"How sweet he is," said Lucy.

This was past bearing – first Sister Kemp, now Mr. Benwell. I felt stifled in this pastry-cook's atmosphere. "I've come to say good-bye," I said. "I'm going back to the country to see about my house."

"I'm so glad. It's lovely for you. I'm coming to see it as soon as I'm better."

She did not want me, I thought; Humboldt's Gibbon and I had done our part. "You'll be my first guest," I said.

"Yes. Quite soon."

Sister Kemp went with me to the landing.

"Now," she said, "come and see something very precious."

There was a cradle in Roger's dressing-room, made of white stuff and ribbons, and a baby in it.

"Isn't he a fine big man?"

"Magnificent," I said, "and very sweet ... Kempy." [1]

POST SCRIPT

[1]The date of this child's birth was 25 August, 1939, and while Lucy was still in bed the air-raid sirens sounded the first false alarm of the second World War. And so an epoch, my epoch, came to an end. Intellectually we had forseen the event, and had calmly discussed it, but our inherited habits continued to the last moment.

Beavers bred in captivity, inhabiting a concrete pool, will, if given the timber, fatuously go through all the motions of damming an ancestral stream. So I and my friends busied ourselves with our privacies and intimacies. My father's death, the abandonment of my home, my quickening love of Lucy, my literary innovations, my house in the country – all these had seemed to presage a new life. The new life came, not by my contrivance.

Neither book – the last of my old life, the first of my new – was ever finished. As for my house, I never spent a night there. It was requisitioned, filled with pregnant women, and through five years bit by bit befouled and dismembered. My friends were dispersed. Lucy and her baby moved back to her aunt's. Roger rose from department to department in the office of Political Warfare. Basil sought and found a series of irregular adventures. For myself plain regimental soldiering proved an orderly and not disagreeable way of life.

I met Atwater several times in the couse of the war – the Good-scout of the officer's club, the Under-dog in the transit-camp, the Dreamer lecturing troops about post-war conditions. He was reunited, it seemed, with all his legendary lost friends, he prospered and the Good-scout predominated. Today, I believe, he holds sway over a large area of Germany. No one of my close acquaintance was killed, but all our lives, as we had constructed them, quietly came to an end. Our story, like my novel, remained unfinished – a heap of neglected foolscap at the back of a drawer.

'The Tragical Death of Mr. Will. Huskisson, Sept. MDCCCXXX', *The Golden Hind II*, July 1924, pp. 22. [See Introduction, p. xi.]

CHARLES RYDER'S SCHOOLDAYS

T HERE WAS a scent of dust in the air; a thin vestige surviving in the twilight from the golden clouds with which before chapel the House Room fags had filled the evening sunshine. Light was failing. Beyond the trefoils and branched mullions of the windows the towering autumnal leaf was now flat and colourless. All the eastward slope of Spierpoint Down, where the College buildings stood, lay lost in shadow; above and behind, on the high lines of Chanctonbury and Spierpoint Ring, the first day of term was gently dying.

In the House Room thirty heads were bent over their books. Few form-masters had set any preparation that day. The Classical Upper Fifth, Charles Ryder's new form, were "revising last term's work" and Charles was writing his diary under cover of Hassall's *History.* He looked up from the page to the darkling texts which ran in Gothic script around the frieze. "*Qui diligit Deum diligit et fratrem suum.*"

"Get on with your work, Ryder," said Apthorpe.

Apthorpe has greased into being a house-captain this term, Charles wrote. *This is his first Evening School. He is being thoroughly officious and on his dignity.*

"Can we have the light on, please?"

"All right. Wykham-Blake, put it on." A small boy rose from the under-school table. "Wykham-Blake, I said. There's no need for everyone to move."

A rattle of the chain, a hiss of gas, a brilliant white light over half the room. The other light hung over the new boys' table.

"Put the light on, one of you, whatever your names are."

Six startled little boys looked at Apthorpe and at one another, all began to rise together, all sat down, all looked at Apthorpe in consternation.

"Oh, for heaven's sake."

Apthorpe leaned over their heads and pulled the chain; there was a hiss of gas but no light. "The bye-pass is out. Light it, you." He threw a box of matches to one of the new boys who dropped it, picked it up, climbed on the table and looked miserably at the white glass shade, the three hissing mantles and at Apthorpe. He had never seen a lamp of this kind before; at home and at his private school there was electricity. He lit a match and poked at the lamp, at first without effect; then there was a loud explosion; he stepped back, stumbled and nearly lost his footing among the books and ink-pots, blushed hotly and regained the bench. The matches remained in his hand and he stared at them, lost in an agony of indecision. How should he dispose of them? No head was raised but everyone in the House Room exulted in the drama. From the other side of the room Apthorpe held out his hand invitingly.

"When you have quite finished with my matches perhaps you'll be so kind as to give them back."

In despair the new boy threw them towards the house-captain; in despair he threw slightly wide. Apthorpe made no attempt to catch them, but watched them curiously as they fell to the floor. "How very extraordinary," he said. The new boy looked at the match-box; Apthorpe looked at the new boy. "Would it be troubling you too much if I asked you to give me my matches?" he said.

The new boy rose to his feet, walked the few steps, picked up the match-box and gave it to the house-captain, with the ghastly semblance of a smile.

"Extraordinary crew of new men we have this term," said Apthorpe. "They seem to be entirely half-witted. Has anyone been turned on to look after this man?"

"Please, I have," said Wykham-Blake.

"A grave responsibility for one so young. Try and convey to his limited intelligence that it may prove a painful practice here to throw match-boxes about in Evening School, and laugh at house officials. By the way, is that a work-book you're reading?"

"Oh, yes, Apthorpe." Wykham-Blake raised a face of cherubic innocence and presented the back of the *Golden Treasury*.

"Who's it for?"

"Mr. Graves. We're to learn any poem we like."

"And what have you chosen?"

"Milton-on-his-blindness."

"How, may one ask, did that take your fancy?"

"I learned it once before," said Wykham-Blake and Apthorpe laughed indulgently.

"Young blighter," he said.

Charles wrote: *Now he is snooping round seeing what books men are reading. It would be typical if he got someone beaten his first Evening School. The day before yesterday this time I was in my dinner-jacket just setting out for dinner at the d'Italie with Aunt Philippa before going to* The Choice *at Wyndhams.* Quantum mutatus ab illo Hectore. *We live in water-tight compartments. Now I am absorbed in the trivial round of House politics. Graves has played hell with the house. Apthorpe a house-captain and O'Malley on the Settle. The only consolation was seeing the woe on Wheatley's fat face when the locker list went up. He thought he was a cert for the Settle this term. Bad luck on Tamplin though. I never expected to get on but I ought by all rights to have been above O'Malley. What a tick Graves is. It all comes of this rotten system of switching round house-tutors. We ought to have the best of Heads instead of which they try out ticks like Graves on us before giving them a house. If only we still had Frank.*

Charles's handwriting had lately begun to develop certain ornamental features – Greek E's and flourished crossings. He wrote with conscious style. Whenever Apthorpe came past he would turn a page in the history book, hesitate and then write as though making a note from the text. The hands of the clock crept on to half past seven when the porter's handbell began to sound in the cloisters on the far side of Lower Quad. This was the signal of release. Throughout the House Room heads were raised, pages blotted, books closed, fountain-pens screwed up. "Get on with your work," said Apthorpe; "I haven't said anything about moving." The porter and his bell passed up the cloisters, grew faint under the arch by the library steps, were barely audible in the Upper Quad, grew louder on the steps of Old's House and very loud in the cloister outside Head's. At last Apthorpe tossed the *Bystander* on the table and said "All right."

The House Room rose noisily. Charles underlined the date at the head of his page – *Wednesday Sept. 24th, 1919* – blotted it and put the note-book in his locker. Then with his hands in his pockets he followed the crowd into the dusk.

To keep his hands in his pockets thus – with his coat back and the middle button alone fastened – was now his privilege, for he was in his third year. He could also wear coloured socks and was indeed at the moment wearing a pair of heliotrope silk with white clocks, purchased the day before in Jermyn Street. There were several things, formerly forbidden, which were now his right. He could link his arm in a friend's and he did so now, strolling across to Hall arm-in-arm with Tamplin.

They paused at the top of the steps and stared out in the gloaming. To their left the great bulk of the chapel loomed immensely; below them the land fell away in terraces to the playing-fields with their dark fringe of elm; headlights moved continuously up and down the coast road; the estuary was just traceable, a lighter streak across the grey lowland, before it merged into the calm and invisible sea.

"Same old view," said Tamplin.

"Give me the lights of London," said Charles. "I say, it's rotten luck for you about the Settle."

"Oh, I never had a chance. It's rotten luck on *you*."

"Oh, I never had a chance. But *O'Malley*."

"It all comes of having that tick Graves instead of Frank."

"The buxom Wheatley looked jolly bored. Anyway, I don't envy O'Malley's job as head of the dormitory."

"That's how he got on the Settle. Tell you later."

From the moment they reached the Hall steps they had to unlink their arms, take their hands out of their pockets and stop talking. When Grace had been said Tamplin took up the story.

"Graves had him in at the end of last term and said he was making him head of the dormitory. The head of Upper Dormitory never has been on the Settle before last term when they moved Easton up from Lower Anteroom after we ragged

Fletcher. O'Malley told Graves he couldn't take it unless he had an official position."

"How d'you know?"

"O'Malley told me. He thought he'd been rather fly."

"Typical of Graves to fall for a tick like that."

"It's all very well," said Wheatley, plaintively, from across the table; "I don't think they've any right to put Graves in like this. I only came to Spierpoint because my father knew Frank's brother in the Guards. I was jolly bored, I can tell you, when they moved Frank. I think he wrote to the Head about it. We pay more in Head's and get the worst of everything."

"Tea, please."

"Same old College tea."

"Same old College eggs."

"It always takes a week before one gets used to College food."

"I never get used to it."

"Did you go to many London restaurants in the holidays?"

"I was only in London a week. My brother took me to lunch at the Berkeley. Wish I was there now. I had two glasses of port."

"The Berkeley's all right in the evening," said Charles, "if you want to dance."

"It's jolly well all right for luncheon. You should see their hors d'oeuvres. I reckon there were twenty or thirty things to choose from. After that we had grouse and meringues with ices in them."

"I went to dinner at the d'Italie."

"Oh, where's that?"

"It's a little place in Soho not many people know about. My aunt speaks Italian like a native so she knows all those places. Of course, there's no marble or music. It just exists for the cooking. Literary people and artists go there. My aunt knows lots of them."

"My brother says all the men from Sandhurst go to the Berkeley. Of course, they fairly rook you."

"I always think the Berkeley's rather rowdy," said Wheatley. "We stayed at Claridges after we came back from Scotland because our flat was still being done up."

"My brother says Claridges is a deadly hole."

"Of course, it isn't everyone's taste. It's rather exclusive."

"Then how did our buxom Wheatley come to be staying there, I wonder?"

"There's no need to be cheap, Tamplin."

"I always say," suddenly said a boy named Jorkins, "that you get the best meal in London at the Holborn Grill."

Charles, Tamplin and Wheatley turned with cold curiosity on the interrupter, united at last in their disdain. "*Do* you, Jorkins? How very original of you."

"Do you *always* say that, Jorkins? Don't you sometimes get tired of *always* saying the same thing?"

"There's a four-and-sixpenny table d'hôte."

"Please, Jorkins, spare us the hideous details of your gormandizing."

"Oh, all right. I thought you were interested, that's all."

"Do you think," said Tamplin, confining himself ostentatiously to Charles and Wheatley, "that Apthorpe is keen on Wykham-Blake?"

"No, is he?"

"Well, he couldn't keep away from him in Evening School."

"I suppose the boy had to find consolation now his case Sugdon's left. He hasn't a friend among the under-schools."

"What d'you make of the man Peacock?" (Charles, Tamplin and Wheatley were all in the Classical Upper Fifth under Mr. Peacock.)

"He's started decently. No work tonight."

"Raggable?"

"I doubt it. But slack."

"I'd sooner a master were slack than raggable. I got quite exhausted last term ragging the Tea-cake."

"It was witty, though."

"I hope he's not so slack that we shan't get our Certificates next summer."

"One can always sweat the last term. At the University no one ever does any work until just before the exams. Then they sit up all night with black coffee and strychnine."

"It would be jolly witty if no one passed his Certificate."

"I wonder what they'd do."

"Give Peacock the push, I should think."

Presently Grace was said and the school streamed out into the cloisters. It was now dark. The cloisters were lit at intervals by gas-lamps. As one walked, one's shadow lengthened and grew fainter before one until, approaching the next source of light, it disappeared, fell behind, followed one's heels, shortened, deepened, disappeared and started again at one's toes. The quarter of an hour between Hall and Second Evening was mainly spent in walking the cloisters in pairs or in threes; to walk four abreast was the privilege of school prefects. On the steps of Hall, Charles was approached by O'Malley. He was an ungainly boy, an upstart who had come to Spierpoint late, in a bye-term. He was in Army Class B and his sole distinction was staying-power in cross-country running.

"Coming to the Graves?"

"No."

"D'you mind if I hitch on to you for a minute?"

"Not particularly."

They joined the conventional, perambulating couples, their shadows, lengthened before them, apart. Charles did not take O'Malley's arm. O'Malley might not take Charles's. The Settle was purely a House Dignity. In the cloisters Charles was senior by right of his two years at Spierpoint.

"I'm awfully sorry about the Settle," said O'Malley.

"I should have thought you'd be pleased."

"I'm not, honestly. It's the last thing I wanted. Graves sent me a postcard a week ago. It spoiled the end of the holidays. I'll tell you what happened. Graves had me in on the last day last term. You know the way he has. He said, 'I've some unpleasant news for you, O'Malley. I'm putting you head of the Upper Dormitory.' I said, 'It ought to be someone on the Settle. No one else could keep order.' I thought he'd keep Easton up there. He said, 'These things are a matter of personality, not of official position.' I said, 'It's been proved you have an official. You know how bolshie we were with Fletcher.' He said, 'Fletcher wasn't the man for the job. He wasn't my appointment.'"

"Typical of his lip. Fletcher was Frank's appointment."

"I wish we had Frank still."

"So does everyone. Anyway, why are you telling me all this?"

"I didn't want you to think I'd been greasing. I heard Tamplin say I had."

"Well, you are on the Settle and you are head of the dormitory, so what's the trouble?"

"Will you back me up, Ryder?"

"Have you ever known me back anyone up, as you call it?"

"No," said O'Malley miserably, "that's just it."

"Well, why d'you suppose I should start with you?"

"I just thought you might."

"Well, think again."

They had walked three sides of the square and were now at the door of Head's House. Mr. Graves was standing outside his own room talking to Mr. Peacock.

"Charles," he said, "come here a minute. Have you met this young man yet, Peacock? He's one of yours."

"Yes, I think so," said Mr. Peacock doubtfully.

"He's one of my problem children. Come in here, Charles. I want to have a chat to you."

Mr. Graves took him by the elbow and led him into his room.

There were no fires yet and the two armchairs stood before an empty grate; everything was unnaturally bare and neat after the holiday cleaning.

"Sit you down."

Mr. Graves filled his pipe and gave Charles a long, soft and quizzical stare. He was a man still under thirty, dressed in Lovat tweed with an Old Rugbeian tie. He had been at Spierpoint during Charles's first term and they had met once on the miniature range; in that bleak, untouchable epoch Charles had been warmed by his affability. Then Mr. Graves was called up for the army and now had returned, the term before, as House Tutor of Head's. Charles had grown confident in the meantime and felt no need of affable masters; only for Frank whom Mr. Graves had supplanted. The ghost of Frank filled the room. Mr. Graves had hung some Medici prints in the place of Frank's football groups. The set of *Georgian Poetry* in the bookcase was his, not Frank's. His college arms embellished the tobacco jar on the chimney-piece.

"Well, Charles Ryder," said Mr. Graves at length, "are you feeling sore with me?"

"Sir?"

Mr. Graves became suddenly snappish. "If you choose to sit there like a stone image, I can't help you."

Still Charles said nothing.

"I have a friend," said Mr. Graves, "who goes in for illumination. I thought you might like me to show him the work you sent in to the Art Competition last term."

"I'm afraid I left it at home, sir."

"Did you do any during the holidays?"

"One or two things, sir."

"You never try painting from nature?"

"Never, sir."

"It seems rather a crabbed, shut-in sort of pursuit for a boy of your age. Still, that's your own business."

"Yes, sir."

"Difficult chap to talk to, aren't you, Charles?"

"Not with everyone. Not with Frank," Charles wished to say; "I could talk to Frank by the hour." Instead he said, "I suppose I am, sir."

"Well, I want to talk to you. I dare say you feel you have been a little ill-used this term. Of course, all your year are in rather a difficult position. Normally there would have been seven or eight people leaving at the end of last term but with the war coming to an end they are staying on an extra year, trying for University scholarships and so on. Only Sugdon left, so instead of a general move there was only one vacancy at the top. That meant only one vacancy on the Settle. I dare say you think you ought to have had it."

"No, sir. There were two people ahead of me."

"But not O'Malley. I wonder if I can make you understand why I put him over you. You were the obvious man in many ways. The thing is, some people *need* authority, others don't.

You've got plenty of personality. O'Malley isn't at all sure of himself. He might easily develop into rather a second-rater. You're in no danger of that. What's more, there's the dormitory to consider. I think I can trust you to work loyally under O'Malley. I'm not so sure I could trust him to work under you. See? It's always been a difficult dormitory. I don't want a repetition of what happened with Fletcher. Do you understand?"

"I understand what you mean, sir."

"Grim young devil, aren't you?"

"Sir?"

"Oh, all right, go away. I shan't waste any more time with you."

"Thank you, sir."

Charles rose to go.

"I'm getting a small hand printing-press this term," said Mr. Graves. "I thought it might interest you."

It did interest Charles intensely. It was one of the large features of his day-dreams; in chapel, in school, in bed, in all the rare periods of abstraction, when others thought of racing motor-cars and hunters and speed-boats, Charles thought long and often of a private press. But he would not betray to Mr. Graves the intense surge of images that rose in his mind.

"I think the invention of movable type was a disaster, sir. It destroyed calligraphy."

"You're a prig, Charles," said Mr. Graves. "I'm sick of you. Go away. Tell Wheatley I want him. And try not to dislike me so much. It wastes both our time."

Second Evening had begun when Charles returned to the House Room; he reported to the house-captain in charge, despatched Wheatley to Mr. Graves and settled down over his Hassall to half an hour's day-dream, imagining the tall folios, the wide margins, the deckle-edged mould-made paper, the engraved initials, the rubrics and colophons of his private press. In Third Evening one could "read"; Charles read Hugh Walpole's *Fortitude*.

Wheatley did not return until the bell was ringing for the end of Evening School.

Tamplin greeted him with "Bad luck, Wheatley. How many did you get? Was he tight?"; Charles with "Well, you've had a long hot-air with Graves. What on earth did he talk about?"

"It was all rather confidential," said Wheatley solemnly.

"Oh, sorry."

"No, I'll tell *you* sometime if you promise to keep it to yourself." Together they ascended the turret stair to their dormitory. "I say, have you noticed something? Apthorpe is in the Upper Anteroom this term. Have you ever known the junior house-captain anywhere except in the Lower Anteroom? I wonder how he worked it."

"Why should he want to?"

"Because, my innocent, Wykham-Blake has been moved into the Upper Anteroom."

"Tactful of Graves."

"You know, I sometimes think perhaps we've rather misjudged Graves."

"You didn't think so in Hall."

"No, but I've been thinking since."

"You mean he's been greasing up to you."

"Well, all I can say is, when he wants to be decent, he *is* decent. I find we know quite a lot of the same people in the holidays. He once stayed on the moor next to ours."

"I don't see anything particularly decent in that."

"Well, it makes a sort of link. He explained why he put O'Malley on the Settle. He's a student of character, you know."

"Who? O'Malley?"

"No, Graves. He said that's the only reason he is a schoolmaster."

"I expect he's a schoolmaster because it's so jolly slack."

"Not at all. As a matter of fact, he was going into the Diplomatic, just as I am."

"I don't expect he could pass the exam. It's frightfully stiff. Graves only takes the Middle Fourth."

"The exam is only to keep out undesirable types."

"Then it would floor Graves."

"He says schoolmastering is the most *human* calling in the

world. Spierpoint is not an arena for competition. We have to stop the weakest going to the wall."

"Did Graves say that?"

"Yes."

"I must remember that if there's any unpleasantness with Peacock. What else did he say?"

"Oh, we talked about people, you know, and their characters. Would you say O'Malley had poise?"

"Good God, no."

"That's just what Graves thinks. He says some people have it naturally and they can look after themselves. Others, like O'Malley, need bringing on. He thinks authority will give O'Malley poise."

"Well, it doesn't seem to have worked yet," said Charles, as O'Malley loped past their beds to his corner.

"Welcome to the head of the dormitory," said Tamplin. "Are we all late? Are you going to report us?"

O'Malley looked at his watch. "As a matter of fact, you have exactly seven minutes."

"Not by my watch."

"We go by mine."

"Really," said Tamplin. "Has your watch been put on the Settle, too? It looks a cheap kind of instrument to me."

"When I am speaking officially I don't want any impertinence, Tamplin."

"His watch *has* been put on the Settle. It's the first time I ever heard one could be impertinent to a watch."

They undressed and washed their teeth. O'Malley looked repeatedly at his watch and at last said, "Say your dibs."

Everyone knelt at his bedside and buried his face in the bedclothes. After a minute, in quick succession, they rose and got into bed; all save Tamplin who remained kneeling. O'Malley stood in the middle of the dormitory, irresolute, his hand on the chain of the gas-lamp. Three minutes passed; it was the convention that no one spoke while anyone was still saying his prayers; several boys began to giggle. "Hurry up," said O'Malley.

Tamplin raised a face of pained rebuke. "*Please*, O'Malley. I'm saying my dibs."

"Well, you're late."

Tamplin remained with his face buried in the blanket. O'Malley pulled the chain and extinguished the light, all save the pale glow of the bye-pass under the white enamel shade. It was the custom, when doing this, to say "Goodnight"; but Tamplin was still ostensibly in prayer; in this black predicament O'Malley stalked to his bed in silence.

"Aren't you going to say 'Goodnight' to us?" asked Charles.

"Goodnight."

A dozen voices irregularly took up the cry. "Goodnight, O'Malley...I hope the official watch doesn't stop in the night...happy dreams, O'Malley."

"Really, you know," said Wheatley, "there's a man still saying his prayers."

"Stop talking."

"*Please*," said Tamplin, on his knees. He remained there for half a minute more, then rose and got into bed.

"You understand, Tamplin? You're late."

"Oh, but I don't think I can be, even by your watch. I was perfectly ready when you said 'Say your dibs.'"

"If you want to take as long as that you must start sooner."

"But I couldn't with all that noise going on, could I, O'Malley? All that wrangling about watches?"

"We'll talk about it in the morning."

"Goodnight, O'Malley."

At this moment the door opened and the house-captain in charge of the dormitory came in. "What the devil's all this talking about?" he asked.

Now, O'Malley had not the smallest intention of giving Tamplin a "late". It was a delicate legal point, of the kind that was debated endlessly at Spierpoint, whether in the circumstances he could properly do so. It had been in O'Malley's mind to appeal to Tamplin's better nature in the morning, to say that he could take a joke as well as the next man, that his official position was repugnant to him, that the last thing he wished to do was start the term by using his new authority on his former associates; he would say all this and ask Tamplin to "back him up". But now, suddenly challenged out of the darkness, he lost his head and said, "I was giving Tamplin a 'late', Anderson."

"Well, remind me in the morning and for Christ's sake don't make such a racket over it."

"Please, Anderson, I don't think I was late," said Tamplin; "it's just that I took longer than the others over my prayers. I was perfectly ready when we were told to say them."

"But he was still out of bed when I put the light out," said O'Malley.

"Well, it's usual to wait until everyone's ready, isn't it?"

"Yes, Anderson. I did wait about five minutes."

"I see. Anyhow, lates count from the time you start saying your dibs. You know that. Better wash the whole thing out."

"Thank you, Anderson," said Tamplin.

The house-captain lit the candle which stood in a biscuit-box shade on the press by his bed. He undressed slowly, washed and, without saying prayers, got into bed. Then he lay there reading. The tin hid the light from the dormitory and cast a small, yellow patch over his book and pillow; that and the faint circle of the gas-lamp were the only lights; gradually in the darkness the lancet windows became dimly visible. Charles lay on his back thinking; O'Malley had made a fiasco of his first evening; first and last he could not have done things worse; it seemed a rough and tortuous road on which Mr. Graves had set his feet, to self-confidence and poise.

Then, as he grew sleepier, Charles's thoughts, like a roulette ball when the wheel runs slow, sought their lodging and came at last firmly to rest on that day, never far distant, at the end of his second term; the raw and gusty day of the junior steeplechase when, shivering and half-changed, queasy with apprehension of the trial ahead, he had been summoned by Frank, had shuffled into his clothes, run headlong down the turret stairs and with a new and deeper alarm knocked at the door.

"Charles, I have just had a telegram from your father which you must read. I'll leave you alone with it."

He shed no tear, then or later; he did not remember what was said when two minutes later Frank returned; there was a numb, anaesthetized patch at the heart of his sorrow; he remembered, rather, the order of the day. Instead of running he had gone down in his overcoat with Frank to watch the finish of the race; word had gone round the house and no questions were asked; he had tea with the matron, spent the evening in her room and slept that night in a room in the Headmaster's private house; next morning his Aunt Philippa came and took him home. He remembered all that went on outside himself, the sight and sound and smell of the place, so that, on his return to them, they all spoke of his loss, of the sharp severance of all the bonds of childhood, and it seemed to him that it was not in the uplands of Bosnia but here at Spierpoint, on the turret stairs, in the unlighted box-room passage, in the windy cloisters, that his mother had fallen, killed not by a German shell but by the shrill voice sounding across the changing room, "Ryder here? Ryder? Frank wants him at the double."

II

Thursday, September 25th, 1919. Peacock began well by not turning up for early school so at five past we walked out and went back to our House Rooms and I read Fortitude *by Walpole; it is strong meat but rather unnecessary in places. After breakfast O'Malley came greasing up to Tamplin and apologized. Everyone is against him. I maintain he was in the right until he reported him late to Anderson. No possible defence for that – sheer windiness. Peacock deigned to turn up for Double Greek. We mocked him somewhat. He is trying to make us use the new pronunciation; when he said o'ú there was a wail of "ooh" and Tamplin pronounced subjunctive soo-byoongteeway – very witty. Peacock got bored and said he'd report him to Graves but relented. Library was open 5–6 tonight. I went meaning to put in some time on Walter Crane's* Bases of Design *but Mercer came up with that weird man in Brent's called Curtis-Dunne. I envy them having Frank as house-master. He is talking of starting a literary and artistic society for men not in the Sixth. Curtis-Dunne wants to start a political group. Pretty good lift considering this is his second term although he is sixteen and has been at*

Dartmouth. Mercer gave me a poem to read – very sloppy. Before this there was a House Game. Everyone puffing and blowing after the holidays. Anderson said I shall probably be centre-half in the Under Sixteens – the sweatiest place in the field. I must get into training quickly.

Friday 26th. Corps day but quite slack. Reorganization. I am in A Company at last. A tick in Boucher's called Spratt is platoon commander. We ragged him a bit. Wheatley is a section commander! Peacock sent Bankes out of the room in Greek Testament for saying "Who will rid me of this turbulent priest" when put on to translate. Jolly witty. He began to argue. Peacock said, "Must I throw you out by force?" Bankes began to go but muttered "Muscular Christianity." Peacock: "What did you say?"; "Nothing, sir"; "Get out before I kick you." Things got a bit duller after that. Uncle George gave Bankes three.

Saturday 27th. Things very dull in school. Luckily Peacock forgot to set any preparation. Pop. Sci. in last period. Tamplin and Mercer got some of the weights that are so precious they are kept in a glass case and picked up with tweezers, made them red hot on a bunsen burner and dropped them in cold water. A witty thing to do. House Game – Under Sixteen team against a mixed side. They have put Wykham-Blake centre-half and me in goal; a godless place. Library again. Curtis-Dunne buttonholed me again. He drawled "My father is in parliament but he is a very unenlightened conservative. I of course am a socialist. That's the reason I chucked the Navy." I said, "Or did they chuck you?" "The pangs of parting were endured by both sides with mutual stoicism". He spoke of Frank as "essentially a well-intentioned fellow". Sunday tomorrow thank God. I may be able to get on with illuminating "The Bells of Heaven".

III

Normally on Sundays there was a choice of service. Matins at a quarter to eight or Communion at quarter past. On the first Sunday of term there was Choral Communion for all at eight o'clock.

The chapel was huge, bare, and still unfinished, one of the great monuments of the Oxford Movement and the Gothic revival. Like an iceberg it revealed only a small part of its bulk above the surface of the terraced down; below lay a crypt and below that foundations of great depth. The Founder had chosen the site and stubbornly refused to change it so that the original estimates had been exceeded before the upper chapel was begun. Visiting preachers frequently drew a lesson from the disappointments, uncertainties and final achievement of the Founder's "vision". Now the whole nave rose triumphantly over the surrounding landscape, immense, clustered shafts supporting the groined roof; at the west it ended abruptly in concrete and timber and corrugated iron, while behind, in a waste land near the kitchens, where the Corps band practised their bugles in the early morning, lay a nettle-and-bramble-grown ruin, the base of a tower, twice as high as the chapel, which one day was to rise so that on stormy nights, the Founder had decreed, prayers might be sung at its summit for sailors in peril on the sea.

From outside the windows had a deep, submarine tinge, but from inside they were clear white, and the morning sun streamed in over the altar and the assembled school. The prefect in Charles's row was Symonds, editor of the Magazine, president of the Debating Society, the leading intellectual. Symonds was in Head's; he pursued a course of lonely study, seldom taking Evening School, never playing any game except, late in the evenings of the summer term, an occasional single of lawn tennis, appearing rarely even in the Sixth Form, but working in private under Mr. A. A. Carmichael for the Balliol scholarship. Symonds kept a leather-bound copy of the *Greek Anthology* in his place in chapel and read it throughout the services with a finely negligent air.

The masters sat in stalls orientated between the columns, the clergy in surplices, laymen in gowns. Some of the masters who taught the Modern Side wore hoods of the newer universities; Major Stebbing, the adjutant of the O.T.C., had no gown at all; Mr. A. A. Carmichael – awfully known at Spierpoint as "A. A.", the splendid dandy and wit, fine flower of the Oxford Union and the New College Essay Society, the reviewer of works of classical scholarship for the *New Statesman*, to whom Charles had never yet spoken; whom Charles had never yet heard speak directly, but only at third hand as his *mots*, in their idiosyncratic modulations, passed from mouth to mouth from the Sixth in sanctuary to the

catechumens in the porch; whom Charles worshipped from afar
– Mr. Carmichael, from a variety of academic costume, was this
morning robed as a baccalaureate of Salamanca. He looked, as
he stooped over his desk, like the prosecuting counsel in a cartoon
by Daumier.

Nearly opposite him across the chapel stood Frank Bates; an
unbridged gulf of boys separated these rival and contrasted
deities, that one the ineffable dweller on cloud-capped Olympus,
this the homely clay image, the intimate of hearth and household,
the patron of threshing-floor and olive-press. Frank wore only an
ermine hood, a B.A.'s gown, and loose, unremarkable clothes,
subfusc today, with the Corinthian tie which alternated with the
Carthusian, week in, week out. He was a clean, curly, spare
fellow; a little wan for he was in constant pain from an injury
on the football field which had left him lame and kept him at
Spierpoint throughout the war. This pain of his redeemed him
from heartiness. In chapel his innocent, blue eyes assumed a
puzzled, rather glum expression like those of an old-fashioned
child in a room full of grown-ups. Frank was a bishop's son.

Behind the masters, out of sight in the side aisles, was a dowdy
huddle of matrons and wives.

The service began with a procession of the choir: "Hail Festal
Day", with Wykham-Blake as the treble cantor. At the rear of the
procession came Mr. Peacock, the Chaplain and the Headmaster. A week ago Charles had gone to church in London with Aunt
Philippa. He did not as a rule go to church in the holidays, but
being in London for the last week Aunt Philippa had said,
"There's nothing much we can do today. Let's see what entertainment the Church can offer. I'm told there is a very remarkable freak named Father Wimperis." So, together, they had gone
on the top of a bus to a northern suburb where Mr. Wimperis was
at the time drawing great congregations. His preaching was not
theatrical by Neapolitan standards, Aunt Philippa said afterwards; "However, I enjoyed him hugely. He is irresistibly
common." For twenty minutes Mr. Wimperis alternately fluted
and boomed from the pulpit, wrestled with the reading-stand
and summoned the country to industrial peace. At the end he

performed a little ceremony of his own invention, advancing to the church steps in cope and biretta with what proved to be a large silver salt cellar in his hands. "My people," he said simply, scattering salt before him, "you are the salt of the earth."

"I believe he has something new like that every week," said Aunt Philippa. "It must be lovely to live in his neighbourhood."

Charles's was not a God-fearing home. Until August 1914 his father had been accustomed to read family prayers every morning; on the outbreak of war he abruptly stopped the practice, explaining, when asked, that there was now nothing left to pray for. When Charles's mother was killed there was a memorial service for her at Boughton, his home village, but Charles's father did not go with him and Aunt Philippa. "It was all her confounded patriotism," he said, not to Charles but to Aunt Philippa, who did not repeat the remark until many years later. "She had no business to go off to Serbia like that. Do you think it my duty to marry again?"

"No," said Aunt Philippa.

"Nothing would induce me to – least of all my duty."

The service followed its course. As often happened, two small boys fainted and were carried out by house-captains; a third left bleeding at the nose. Mr. Peacock sang the Gospel over-loudly. It was his first public appearance. Symonds looked up from his Greek, frowned and continued reading. Presently it was time for Communion; most of the boys who had been confirmed went up to the chancel rails, Charles with them. Symonds sat back, twisted his long legs into the aisle to allow his row to pass, and remained in his place. Charles took Communion and returned to his row. He had been confirmed the term before, incuriously, without expectation or disappointment. When, later in life, he read accounts of the emotional disturbances caused in other boys by the ceremony he found them unintelligible; to Charles it was one of the rites of adolescence, like being made, when a new boy, to stand on the table and sing. The Chaplain had "prepared" him and had confined his conferences to theology. There had been no probing of his sexual life; he had no sexual life to probe. Instead they had talked of prayer and the sacraments.

Spierpoint was a product of the Oxford Movement, founded with definite religious aims; in eighty years it had grown more and more to resemble the older Public Schools, but there was still a strong ecclesiastical flavour in the place. Some boys were genuinely devout and their peculiarity was respected; in general profanity was rare and ill-looked-on. Most of the Sixth professed themselves agnostic or atheist.

The school had been chosen for Charles because, at the age of eleven, he had had a "religious phase" and told his father that he wished to become a priest.

"Good heavens," his father said; "or do you mean a parson?"

"A priest of the Anglican Church," said Charles precisely.

"That's better. I thought you meant a Roman Catholic. Well, a parson's is not at all a bad life for a man with a little money of his own. They can't remove you except for flagrant immorality. Your uncle has been trying to get rid of his fellow at Boughton for ten years – a most offensive fellow but perfectly chaste. He won't budge. It's a great thing in life to have a place you can't be removed from – too few of them."

But the "phase" had passed and lingered now only in Charles's love of Gothic architecture and breviaries.

After Communion Charles sat back in his chair thinking about the secular, indeed slightly anti-clerical, lyric which, already inscribed, he was about to illuminate, while the masters and, after them, the women from the side aisles, went up to the rails.

The food on Sundays was always appreciably worse than on other days; breakfast invariably consisted of boiled eggs, over-boiled and lukewarm.

Wheatley said, "How many ties do you suppose A. A.'s got?"

"I began counting last term," said Tamplin, "and got to thirty."

"Including bows?"

"Yes."

"Of course, he's jolly rich."

"Why doesn't he keep a car, then?" asked Jorkins.

The hour after breakfast was normally devoted to letter-writing, but today a railway strike had been called and there were no posts. Moreover, since it was the start of term, there was no Sunday Lesson. The whole morning was therefore free and Charles had extracted permission to spend it in the Drawing School. He collected his materials and was soon happily at work.

The poem – Ralph Hodgson's " 'Twould ring the bells of Heaven The wildest peal for years, If Parson lost his senses And people came to theirs . . ." – was one of Frank's favourites. In the happy days when he had been House Tutor of Head's, Frank had read poetry aloud on Sunday evenings to any in Head's who cared to come, which was mostly the lower half of the House. He read "There swimmeth One Who swam e'er rivers were begun, And under that Almighty Fin the littlest fish may enter in" and "Abou Ben Adhem, may his tribe increase" and "Under the wide and starry sky" and "What have I done for you, England, my England . . . ?" and many others of the same comfortable kind; but always before the end of the evening someone would say "Please, sir, can we have 'The Bells of Heaven'?" Now he read only to his own house but the poems, Frank's pleasant voices, his nightingales, were awake still, warm and bright with remembered firelight.

Charles did not question whether the poem was not perfectly suited to the compressed thirteenth-century script in which he had written it. His method of writing was first to draw the letters faintly, free-hand in pencil; then with a ruler and ruling-pen to ink in the uprights firmly in Indian ink until the page consisted of lines of short and long black perpendiculars; then with a mapping-pen he joined them with hair strokes and completed their lozenge-shaped terminals. It was a method he had evolved for himself by trial and error. The initial letters of each line were left blank and these, during the last week of the holidays, he had filled with vermilion, carefully drawn, "Old English" capitals. The *T* alone remained to do and for this he had selected a model from Shaw's *Alphabets*, now open before him on the table. It was a florid fifteenth-century letter which needed considerable ingenuity of adaption, for he had decided to attach to it the decorative tail of the *J*. He worked happily, entirely absorbed, drawing in pencil, then tensely, with breath held, inking the outline with a mapping-pen; then, when it was dry – how often, in his impatience, he had ruined his work by attempting this too soon – rubbing away the pencil lines. Finally he got out his water colours and his red sable brushes. At heart he knew he was going too fast – a monk would take a week over a single letter – but he worked with intensity and in less than two hours the initial with its pendant, convoluted border was finished. Then, as he put away his brushes, the exhilaration left him. It was no good; it was botched; the ink outline varied in thickness, the curves seemed to feel their way cautiously where they should have been bold; in places the colour overran the line and everywhere in contrast to the opaque litho-graphic ink it was watery and transparent. It was no good.

Despondently Charles shut his drawing book and put his things together. Outside the Drawing School, steps led down to the Upper Quad past the doors of Brent's House – Frank's. Here he met Mercer.

"Hullo, been painting?"

"Yes, if you can call it that."

"Let me see."

"No."

"Please."

"It's absolutely beastly. I hate it, I tell you. I'd have torn it up if I wasn't going to keep it as a humiliation to look at in case I ever begin to feel I know anything about art."

"You're always dissatisfied, Ryder. It's the mark of a true artist, I suppose."

"If I was an artist I shouldn't do things I'd be dissatisfied with. Here, look at it, if you must."

Mercer gazed at the open page. "What don't you like about it?"

"The whole thing's nauseating."

"I suppose it *is* a bit ornate."

"There, my dear Mercer, with your usual unerring discern-ment you have hit upon the one quality that is at all tolerable."

"Oh, sorry. Anyway, I think the whole thing absolutely first-class."

"Do you, Mercer. I'm greatly encouraged."

"You know you're a frightfully difficult man. I don't know why I like you."

"I know why I like you. Because you are so extremely easy."

"Coming to the library?"

"I suppose so."

When the library was open a prefect sat there entering in a ledger the books which boys took out. Charles as usual made his way to the case where the Art books were kept but before he had time to settle down, as he liked to do, he was accosted by Curtis-Dunne, the old new boy of last term in Brent's. "Don't you think it scandalous," he said, "that on one of the few days of the week when we have the chance to use the library, we should have to kick our heels waiting until some semi-literate prefect chooses to turn up and take us in? I've taken the matter up with the good Frank."

"Oh, and what did he say to that?"

"We're trying to work out a scheme by which library privileges can be extended to those who seriously want them, people like you and me and I suppose the good Mercer."

"I forget for the moment what form you are in."

"Modern Upper. Please don't think from that that I am a scientist. It's simply that in the Navy we had to drop Classics. My interests are entirely literary and political. And of course hedonistic."

"Oh."

"Hedonistic above all. By the way, I've been looking through the political and economic section. It's very quaintly chosen, with glaring lacunae. I've just filled three pages in the Suggestions Book. I thought perhaps you'd care to append your signature."

"No thanks. It's not usual for people without library privileges to write in the Suggestions Book. Besides, I've no interest in economics."

"I've also written a suggestion about extending the library privileges. Frank needs something to work on, that he can put before the committee."

He brought the book to the Art bay; Charles read "That since seniority is no indication of literary taste the system of library privileges be revised to provide facilities for those genuinely desirous of using them to advantage."

"Neatly put, I think," said Curtis-Dunne.

"You'll be thought frightfully above yourself, writing this."

"It is already generally recognized that I *am* above myself, but I want other signatures."

Charles hesitated. To gain time he said, "I say, what on earth have you got on your feet? Aren't those house shoes?"

Curtis-Dunne pointed a toe shod in shabby, soft black leather; a laced shoe without a toecap, in surface like the cover of a well-worn Bible. "Ah, you have observed my labour-saving device. I wear them night and morning. They are a constant perplexity to those in authority. When questioned, as happened two or three times a week during my first term, I say they are a naval pattern which my father, on account of extreme poverty, has asked me to wear out. That embarrasses them. But I am sure you do not share these middle-class prejudices. Dear boy, your name, please, to this subversive manifesto."

Still Charles hesitated. The suggestion outraged Spierpoint taste in all particulars. Whatever intrigues, blandishments and self-advertisements were employed by the ambitious at Spierpoint were always elaborately disguised. Self-effacement and depreciation were the rule. To put oneself explicitly forward for preferment was literally not done. Moreover, the lead came from a boy who was not only in another house and immeasurably Charles's inferior, but also a notorious eccentric. A term back Charles would have rejected the proposal with horror, but today and all this term he was aware of a new voice in his inner counsels, a detached, critical Hyde who intruded his presence more and more often on the conventional, intolerant, subhuman, wholly respectable Dr. Jekyll; a voice, as it were, from a more civilized age, as from the chimney corner in mid-Victorian times there used to break sometimes the sardonic laughter of grandmama, relic of Regency, a clear, outrageous, entirely self-assured disturber among the high and muddled thoughts of her whiskered descendants.

"Frank's all for the suggestion, you know," said Curtis-Dunne. "He says the initiative must come from us. He can't go pushing reforms which he'll be told nobody really wants. He wants a concrete proposal to put before the library committee."

That silenced Jekyll. Charles signed.

"Now," said Curtis-Dunne, "there should be little difficulty with the lad Mercer. He said he'd sign if you would."

By lunch-time there were twenty-three signatories, including the prefect-in-charge.

"We have this day lit a candle," said Curtis-Dunne.

There was some comment around Charles in Hall about his conduct in the library.

"I know he's awful," said Charles, "but he happens to amuse me."

"They all think he's barmy in Brent's."

"Frank doesn't. And anyway I call that a recommendation. As a matter of fact, he's one of the most intelligent men I ever met. If he'd come at the proper time he'd probably be senior to all of us."

Support came unexpectedly from Wheatley. "I happen to know the Head took him in as a special favour to his father. He's Sir Samson Curtis-Dunne's son, the Member for this division. They've got a big place near Steyning. I wouldn't at all mind having a day's shooting there next Veniam day."

On Sunday afternoons, for two hours, the House Room was out of bounds to all except the Settle; in their black coats and with straw hats under their arms the school scattered over the country-side in groups, pairs and occasional disconsolate single figures, for "walks". All human habitations were barred; the choice lay between the open down behind Spierpoint Ring and the single country road to the isolated Norman church of St. Botolph. Tamplin and Charles usually walked together.

"How I hate Sunday afternoons," said Charles.

"We might get some blackberries."

But at the door of the house they were stopped by Mr. Graves.

"Hullo, you two," he said, "would you like to make yourselves useful? My press has arrived. I thought you might help put it together." He led them into his room, where half-opened crates filled most of the floor. "It was all in one piece when I bought it. All I've got to go on is this." He showed them a woodcut in an old book. "They didn't change much from Caxton's day until the steam presses came in. This one is about a hundred years old."

"Damned sweat," muttered Tamplin.

"And here, young Ryder, is the 'movable type' you deplore so much."

"What sort of type is it, sir?"

"We'll have to find out. I bought the whole thing in one lot from a village stationer."

They took out letters at random, set them, and took an impression by pressing them, inked, on a sheet of writing paper. Mr. Graves had an album of typefaces.

"They all look the same to me," said Tamplin.

In spite of his prejudice, Charles was interested. "I've got it, I think, sir; Baskerville."

"No. Look at the serifs. How about Caslon Old Style?"

At last it was identified. Then Charles found a box full of ornamental initials, menu headings of decanters and dessert, foxes' heads and running hounds for sporting announcements, ecclesiastical devices and monograms, crowns, Odd Fellows' arms, the wood-cut of a prize bull, decorative bands, the splendid jumble of a century of English job-printing.

"I say, sir, what fun. You could do all sorts of things with these."

"We will, Charles."

Tamplin looked at the amateurs with disgust. "I say, sir, I've just remembered something I must do. Do you mind awfully if I don't stay?"

"Run along, old Tamplin." When he had gone, Mr. Graves said, "I'm sorry Tamplin doesn't like me."

"Why can he not let things pass?" thought Charles. "Why does he always have to comment on everything?"

"You don't like me either, Charles. But you like the press."

"Yes," said Charles, "I like the press."

The type was tied up in little bags. They poured it out, each bagful into the tray provided for it in the worn oak tray.

"Now for the press. This looks like the base."

It took them two hours to rebuild. When at last it was assembled, it looked small, far too small for the number and size of the cases in which it had travelled. The main cast-iron supports terminated in brass Corinthian capitals and the summit was embellished with a brass urn bearing the engraved date 1824. The common labour, the problems and discoveries, of erection had drawn the two together; now they surveyed its completion in common pride. Tamplin was forgotten.

"It's a lovely thing, sir. Could you print a book on it?"

"It would take time. Thank you very much for your help. And now," Mr. Graves looked at his watch, "as, through some grave miscarriage of justice, you are not on the Settle, I expect you have no engagement for tea. See what you can find in the locker."

The mention of the Settle disturbed their intimacy. Mr. Graves repeated the mistake a few minutes later when they had boiled the kettle and were making toast on the gas-ring. "So at this moment Desmond O'Malley is sitting down to his first Settle tea. I hope he's enjoying it. I don't think somehow he is enjoying this term very much so far." Charles said nothing. "Do you know, he came to me two days ago and asked to resign from it? He said that if I didn't let him he would do something that would make me degrade him. He's an odd boy, Desmond. It was an odd request."

"I don't suppose he'd want me to know about it."

"Of course he wouldn't. Do you know why I'm telling you? Do you?"

"No, sir."

"I think you could make all the difference to him, whether his life is tolerable or not. I gather all you little beasts in the Upper Dormitory have been giving him hell."

"If we have, it's because he asked for it."

"I dare say, but don't you think it rather sad that in life there are so many different things different people are asking for, and the only people who get what they ask for are the Desmond O'Malleys?"

At that moment, beyond the box-room, the Settle tea had

reached its second stage; surfeited with crumpets, five or six each, they were starting on the éclairs and cream-slices. There was still a warm, soggy pile of crumpets left uneaten and according to custom O'Malley, as junior man, was deputed to hand them round the House Room.

Wheatley was supercilious. "What is that, O'Malley? Crumpets? How very kind of you, but I am afraid I never eat them. My digestion, you know."

Tamplin was comic. "My figure, you know," he said.

Jorkins was rude. "No, thanks. They look stale."

There was loud laughter among the third-year men and some of their more precocious juniors. In strict order of seniority, O'Malley travelled from boy to boy, rebuffed, crimson. All the Upper Dormitory refused. Only the fags watched, first in wonder that anyone should refuse crumpets on a cold afternoon, later with brightening expectancy as the full plate came nearer to them.

"I say, thanks awfully, O'Malley." They soon went at the under-school table and O'Malley returned to his chair before the empty grate, where he sat until chapel silently eating confectionery.

"You see," said Mr. Graves, "the beastlier you are to O'Malley, the beastlier he'll become. People are like that."

IV

Sunday, Sept. 28th. Choral. Two or three faints otherwise uneventful. Tried to do the initial and border for "The Bells of Heaven" but made a mess of it. Afterwards talked to Curtis-Dunne in the library. He intrigues me. With Frank's approval we are agitating for library privileges. I don't suppose anything will come of it except that everyone will say we are above ourselves. After luncheon Tamplin and I were going for a walk when Graves called us in and made us help put up his printing press. Tamplin escaped. Graves tried to get things out of me about ragging Dirty Desmond but without success. In the evening we had another rag. Tamplin, Wheatley, Jorkins and I hurried up to the dormitory as soon as the bell went and said our prayers before Dirty D. arrived. Then when he said, "Say your dibs" we just sat on our beds. He

*looked frightfully bored and said "Must I repeat my instructions?" As the
other men were praying we said nothing. Then he said, "I give you one more
chance to say your dibs. If you don't I'll report you." We said nothing so off
Dirty D. went in his dressing-gown to Anderson who was with the other
house-captains at hot-air with Graves. Up came Anderson. "What's all this
about your prayers?" "We've said them already." "Why?" "Because
Tamplin got a late for taking too long so we thought we'd better start
early." "I see. Well we'll talk about it tomorrow." So far nothing has been
said. Everyone thinks we shall get beaten but I don't see how we can be. We
are entirely in our rights. Geoghegan has just been round to all four of us to say
we are to stay behind after First Evening so I suppose we are going to be
beaten.*

After First Evening, when the House Room was clear of all
save the four and the bell for Hall had died away and ceased,
Geoghegan, the head of the house, came in carrying two canes,
accompanied by Anderson.

"I am going to beat you for disobeying an order from the head
of your dormitory. Have you anything to say?"

"Yes," said Wheatley. "We had already said our prayers."

"It is a matter of indifference to me how often you pray. You
have spent most of the day on your knees in chapel, praying all
the time, I hope. All I am concerned about is that you obey the
orders of the head of the dormitory. Anyone else anything to say?
Then get the room ready."

They pushed back the new men's table and laid a bench on its
side across the front of the fireplace. The routine was familiar.
They were beaten in the House Room twice a term, on the
average.

"Who's senior? You, I think, Wheatley."

Wheatley bent over the bench.

"Knees straight." Geoghegan took his hips and arranged him
to his liking, slightly oblique to the line of advance. From the
corner he had three steps to the point of delivery. He skipped
forward, struck and slowly turned back to the corner. They were
given three strokes each; none of them moved. As they walked
across the Hall, Charles felt the slight nausea turn to exhilaration.

"Was he tight?"

'Heard at the College Debating Society: "The honourable mover, sir, is standing with his eyes fixed upon the setting sun, while, if he only turns, behold! a new day is even now breaking gloriously in the East"', *The Isis*, 18 October 1922, p. 7.

SCOTT-KING'S
MODERN EUROPE

MARIAE IMMACULATAE ANTONIAE
CONIUGIS PRUDENTIORIS
AUDACI CONIUGI

SCOTT-KING'S MODERN EUROPE

I

IN 1946 Scott-King had been classical master at Granchester for twenty-one years. He was himself a Granchesterian and had returned straight from the University after failing for a fellowship. There he had remained, growing slightly bald and slightly corpulent, known to generations of boys first as "Scottie", then of late years, while barely middle-aged, as "old Scottie"; a school "institution", whose precise and slightly nasal lamentations of modern decadence were widely parodied.

Granchester is not the most illustrious of English public schools but it is, or, as Scott-King would maintain, was, entirely respectable; it plays an annual cricket match at Lord's; it numbers a dozen or so famous men among its old boys, who, in general, declare without apology: "I was at Granchester" – unlike the sons of lesser places who are apt to say: "As a matter of fact I was at a place called —. You see at the time my father…"

When Scott-King was a boy and when he first returned as a master, the school was almost equally divided into a Classical and a Modern Side, with a group of negligible and neglected specialists called "the Army Class". Now the case was altered and out of 450 boys scarcely 50 read Greek. Scott-King had watched his classical colleagues fall away one by one, some to rural rectories, some to the British Council and the B.B.C., to be replaced by physicists and economists from the provincial universities, until now, instead of inhabiting solely the rare intellectual atmosphere of the Classical Sixth, he was obliged to descend for many periods a week to cram lower boys with Xenophon and Sallust. But Scott-King did not repine. On the contrary he found a peculiar relish in contemplating the victories of barbarism and positively rejoiced in his reduced station, for he was of a type, unknown in the New World but quite common in Europe, which is fascinated by obscurity and failure.

"Dim" is the epithet for Scott-King and it was a fellow-feeling, a blood-brotherhood in dimness, which first drew him to study the works of the poet Bellorius.

No one, except perhaps Scott-King himself, could be dimmer. When, poor and in some discredit, Bellorius died in 1646 in his native town of what was then a happy kingdom of the Hapsburg Empire and is now the turbulent modern state of Neutralia,[1] he left as his life's work a single folio volume containing a poem of some 1500 lines of Latin hexameters. In his lifetime the only effect of the publication was to annoy the Court and cause his pension to be cancelled. After his death it was entirely forgotten until the middle of the last century when it was reprinted in Germany in a collection of late Renaissance texts. It was in this edition that Scott-King found it during a holiday on the Rhine, and at once his heart stirred with the recognition of kinship. The subject was irredeemably tedious – a visit to an imaginary island of the New World where in primitive simplicity, untainted by tyranny or dogma, there subsisted a virtuous, chaste and reasonable community. The lines were correct and melodious, enriched by many happy figures of speech; Scott-King read them on the deck of the river steamer as vine and turret, cliff and terrace and park, swept smoothly past. How they offended – by what intended or unintended jab of satire, blunted today; by what dangerous speculation – is not now apparent. That they should have been forgotten is readily intelligible to anyone acquainted with the history of Neutralia.

Something must be known of this history if we are to follow Scott-King with understanding. Let us eschew detail and observe that for three hundred years since Bellorius's death his country has suffered every conceivable ill the body politic is heir to. Dynastic wars, foreign invasion, disputed successions, revolting colonies, endemic syphilis, impoverished soil, masonic intrigues,

---

[1] The Republic of Neutralia is imaginary and composite and represents no existing state.

revolutions, restorations, cabals, juntas, pronunciamentos, lib-
erations, constitutions, *coups d'état*, dictatorships, assassinations,
agrarian reforms, popular elections, foreign intervention, repu-
diation of loans, inflations of currency, trades unions, massacres,
arson, atheism, secret societies – make the list full, slip in as many
personal foibles as you will, you will find all these in the last three
centuries of Neutralian history. Out of it emerged the present
republic of Neutralia, a typical modern state, governed by a
single party, acclaiming a dominant Marshal, supporting a vast
ill-paid bureaucracy whose work is tempered and humanized by
corruption. This you must know; also that the Neutralians being
a clever Latin race are little given to hero-worship and make
considerable fun of their Marshal behind his back. In one thing
only did he earn their full-hearted esteem. He kept out of the
Second World War. Neutralia sequestered herself and, from
having been the cockpit of factious sympathies, became remote,
unconsidered, *dim*; so that, as the face of Europe coarsened and
the war, as it appeared in the common-room newspapers and the
common-room wireless, cast its heroic and chivalrous disguise
and became a sweaty tug-of-war between teams of indistinguishable louts, Scott-King, who had never set foot there, became
Neutralian in his loyalty and as an act of homage resumed with
fervour the task on which he had intermittently worked, the
translation of Bellorius into Spenserian stanzas. The work was
finished at the time of the Normandy landings – translation,
introduction, notes. He sent it to the Oxford University Press.
It came back to him. He put it away in a drawer of the pitch-pine
desk in his smoky gothic study above the Granchester quadrangle. He did not repine. It was his opus, his monument to
dimness.

But still the shade of Bellorius stood at his elbow demanding
placation. There was unfinished business between these two. You
cannot keep close company with a man, even though he be dead
three centuries, without incurring obligations. Therefore at the
time of the peace celebrations Scott-King distilled his learning
and wrote a little essay, 4000 words long, entitled *The Last Latinist*,
to commemorate the coming tercentenary of Bellorius's death. It

appeared in a learned journal. Scott-King was paid twelve
guineas for this fruit of fifteen years' devoted labour; six of
them he paid in income tax; with six he purchased a large gun-
metal watch which worked irregularly for a month or two and
then finally failed. There the matter might well have ended.

These, then, in a general, distant view, are the circumstances –
Scott-King's history; Bellorius; the history of Neutralia; the year of
Grace 1946 – all quite credible, quite humdrum, which together
produced the odd events of Scott-King's summer holiday. Let us
now "truck" the camera forward and see him "close-up". You
have heard all about Scott-King but you have not yet met him.

Meet him, then, at breakfast on a bleak morning at the
beginning of the summer term. Unmarried assistant masters at
Granchester enjoyed the use of a pair of collegiate rooms in the
school buildings and took their meals in the common-room.
Scott-King came from his class-room where he had been taking
early school, with his gown flowing behind him and a sheaf of
fluttering exercise papers in his numb fingers. There had been no
remission of war-time privations at Granchester. The cold grate
was used as ashtray and waste-paper basket and was rarely
emptied. The breakfast-table was a litter of small pots, each
labelled with a master's name, containing rations of sugar, margarine and a spurious marmalade. The breakfast dish was a slop
of "dried" eggs. Scott-King turned sadly from the sideboard.
"Anyone", he said, "is welcome to my share in this triumph of
modern science."

"Letter for you, Scottie," said one of his colleagues. " 'The
Honourable Professor Scott-King Esquire.' Congratulations."

It was a large, stiff envelope, thus oddly addressed, em-
blazoned on the flap with a coat of arms. Inside were a card
and a letter. The card read: *His Magnificence the Very Reverend the
Rector of the University of Simona and the Committee of the Bellorius
Tercentenary Celebration Association request the honour of Professor Scott-
King's assistance at the public acts to be held at Simona on July 28th–August
5th, 1946. R.S.V.P. His Excellency Dr. Bogdan Antonic, International
Secretary of the Association, Simona University, Neutralia.*

The letter was signed by the Neutralian Ambassador to the

Court of St. James's. It announced that a number of distinguished scholars were assembling from all over the world to do honour to the illustrious Neutralian political thinker Bellorius and delicately intimated that the trip would be without expense on the part of the guests.

Scott-King's first thought on reading the communication was that he was the victim of a hoax. He looked round the table expecting to surprise a glance of complicity between his colleagues, but they appeared to be busy with their own concerns. Second thoughts convinced him that this sumptuous embossing and engraving was beyond their resources. The thing was authentic, then; but Scott-King was not pleased. He felt, rather, that a long-standing private intimacy between himself and Bellorius was being rudely disturbed. He put the envelope into his pocket, ate his bread and margarine, and presently made ready for morning chapel. He stopped at the secretary's office to purchase a packet of crested school writing paper on which to inscribe "*Mr. Scott-King regrets...*"

For the strange thing is that Scott-King was definitely blasé. Something of the kind has been hinted before, yet, seeing him cross the quadrangle to the chapel steps, middle-aged, shabby, unhonoured and unknown, his round and learned face puckered against the wind, you would have said: "There goes a man who has missed all the compensations of life – and knows it." But that is because you do not yet know Scott-King; no voluptuary surfeited by conquest, no colossus of the drama bruised and rent by doting adolescents, not Alexander, nor Talleyrand, was more blasé than Scott-King. He was an adult, an intellectual, a classical scholar, almost a poet; he was travel-worn in the large periphery of his own mind, jaded with accumulated experience of his imagination. He was older, it might have been written, than the rocks on which he sat; older, anyway, than his stall in chapel; he had died many times, had Scott-King, had dived deep, had trafficked for strange webs with Eastern merchants. And all this had been but the sound of lyres and flutes to him. Thus musing, he left the chapel and went to his class-room, where for the first hours he had the lowest set.

They coughed and sneezed. One, more ingenious than the rest, attempted at length to draw him out as, it was known, he might sometimes be drawn: "Please, sir, Mr. Griggs says it's a pure waste of our time learning classics," but Scott-King merely replied: "It's a waste of time coming to me and *not* learning them."

After Latin gerunds they stumbled through half a page of Thucydides. He said: "These last episodes of the siege have been described as tolling like a great bell," at which a chorus rose from the back bench – "The bell? Did you say it was the bell, sir?" and books were noisily shut. "There are another twenty minutes. I said the book tolled like a bell."

"Please, sir, I don't quite get that, sir, how can a book be like a bell, sir?"

"If you wish to talk, Ambrose, you can start construing."

"Please, sir, that's as far as I got, sir."

"Has anyone done any more?" (Scott-King still attempted to import into the lower school the adult politeness of the Classical Sixth.) "Very well, then, you can all spend the rest of the hour preparing the next twenty lines."

Silence, of a sort, reigned. There was a low muttering from the back of the room, a perpetual shuffling and snuffling, but no one spoke directly to Scott-King. He gazed through the leaded panes to the leaden sky. He could hear through the wall behind him the strident tones of Griggs, the civics master, extolling the Tolpuddle martyrs. Scott-King put his hand in his coat-pocket and felt the crisp edges of the Neutralian invitation.

He had not been abroad since 1939. He had not tasted wine for a year, and he was filled, suddenly, with deep home-sickness for the South. He had not often nor for long visited those enchanted lands; a dozen times perhaps, for a few weeks – for one year in total of his forty-three years of life – but his treasure and his heart lay buried there. Hot oil and garlic and spilled wine; luminous pinnacles above a dusky wall; fireworks at night, fountains at noonday; the impudent, inoffensive hawkers of lottery tickets moving from table to table on to the crowded pavement; the shepherd's pipe on the scented hillside – all that travel agent ever sought to put in a folder, fumed in Scott-King's mind that drab morning. He had left his coin in the waters of Trevi; he had wedded the Adriatic; he was a Mediterranean man.

In the mid-morning break, on the crested school paper, he wrote his acceptance of the Neutralian invitation. That evening, and on many subsequent evenings, the talk in the common-room was about plans for the holidays. All despaired of getting abroad; all save Griggs who was cock-a-hoop about an International Rally of Progressive Youth Leadership in Prague to which he had got himself appointed. Scott-King said nothing even when Neutralia was mentioned.

"I'd like to go somewhere I could get a decent meal," said one of his colleagues. "Ireland or Neutralia, or somewhere like that."

"They'd never let you into Neutralia," said Griggs. "Far too much to hide. They've got teams of German physicists making atomic bombs."

"Civil war raging."

"Half the population in concentration camps."

"No decent-minded man would go to Neutralia."

"Or to Ireland for that matter," said Griggs.

And Scott-King sat tight.

II

Some weeks later Scott-King sat in the aerodrome waiting-room. His overcoat lay across his knees, his hand luggage at his feet. A loudspeaker, set high out of harm's way in the dun concrete wall, discoursed dance music and official announcements. This room, like all the others to which he had been driven in the course of the morning, was sparsely furnished and indifferently clean; on its walls, sole concession to literary curiosity, hung commendations of government savings bonds and precautions against gas attack. Scott-King was hungry, weary and dispirited for he was new to the amenities of modern travel.

He had left his hotel in London at seven o'clock that morning; it was now past noon and he was still on English soil. He had not been ignored. He had been shepherded in and out of charabancs and offices like an idiot child; he had been weighed and measured like a load of merchandise; he had been searched like a criminal; he had been cross-questioned about his past and his future, the state of his health and of his finances, as though he were applying for permanent employment of a confidential nature. Scott-King had not been nurtured in luxury and privilege, but this was not how he used to travel. And he had eaten nothing except a piece of flaccid toast and margarine in his bedroom. The ultimate asylum where he now sat proclaimed itself on the door as "For the use of V.I.P.s only".

"V.I.P.?" he asked their conductress.

She was a neat, impersonal young woman, part midwife, part governess, part shop-walker, in manner. "Very Important Persons," she replied without evident embarrassment.

"But is it all right for me to be here?"

"It is essential. You are a V.I.P."

I wonder, thought Scott-King, how they treat quite ordinary, unimportant people?

There were two fellow-travellers, male and female, similarly distinguished, both bound for Bellacita, capital city of Neutralia; both, it presently transpired, guests of the Bellorius Celebration Committee.

The man was a familiar type to Scott-King; his name Whitemaid, his calling academic, a dim man like himself, much of an age with him.

"Tell me," said Whitemaid, "tell me frankly" – and he looked furtive as men do when they employ that ambiguous expression – "have you ever heard of the worthy Bellorius?"

"I know his work. I have seldom heard it discussed."

"Ah, well, of course, he's not in my subject. I'm Roman Law," said Whitemaid, with an accession of furtiveness that took all grandiosity from the claim. "They asked the Professor of Poetry, you know, but he couldn't get away. Then they tried the Professor of Latin. He's red. Then they asked for anyone to represent the University. No one else was enthusiastic so I put myself forward. I find expeditions of this kind highly diverting. You are familiar with them?"

"No."

"I went to Upsala last vacation and ate very passable caviare twice a day for a week. Neutralia is not known for delicate living, alas, but one may count on rude plenty – and, of course, wine."

"It's all a racket, anyhow," said the third Very Important Person.

This was a woman no longer very young. Her name, Scott-King and Whitemaid had learned through hearing it frequently called through the loudspeaker and seeing it chalked on blackboards, calling her to receive urgent messages at every stage of their journey, was Miss Bombaum. It was a name notorious to almost all the world except, as it happened, to Scott-King and Whitemaid. She was far from dim; once a roving, indeed a dashing, reporter who in the days before the war had popped up wherever there was unpleasantness – Danzig, the Alcazar, Shanghai, Wal-Wal; now a columnist whose weekly articles were syndicated in the popular press of four continents. Scott-King did not read such articles and he had wondered idly at frequent intervals during the morning what she could be. She did not look a lady; she did not even look quite respectable, but he could not reconcile her typewriter with the calling of actress or court-esan; nor for that matter the sharp little sexless face under the too feminine hat and the lavish style of hair-dressing. He came near the truth in suspecting her of being, what he had often heard of but never seen in the life, a female novelist.

"It's all a racket," said Miss Bombaum, "of the Neutralian Propaganda Bureau. I reckon they feel kind of left out of things now the war's over and want to make some nice new friends among the United Nations. We're only part of it. They've got a religious pilgrimage and a Congress of Physical Culture and an International Philatelists' Convention and heaven knows what else. I reckon there's a story in it – in Neutralia, I mean; not in Bellorius, of course, he's been done."

"Done?"

"Yes, I've a copy somewhere," she said, rummaging in her bag. "Thought it might come in useful for the speeches."

"You don't think," said Scott-King, "that we are in danger of being required to make speeches?"

"I can't think what else we've been asked for," said Miss Bombaum. "Can you?"

"I made three long speeches at Upsala," said Whitemaid. "They were ecstatically received."

"Oh, dear, and I have left all my papers at home."

"Borrow this any time you like," said Miss Bombaum, producing Mr. Robert Graves's *Count Belisarius*. "It's sad though. He ends up blind."

The music suddenly ceased and a voice said: "Passengers for Bellacita will now proceed to Exit D. Passengers for Bellacita will now proceed to Exit D," while, simultaneously, the conductress appeared in the door-way and said: "Follow me, please. Have your embarkation papers, medical cards, customs clearance slips, currency control vouchers, passports, tickets, identity dockets, travel orders, emigration certificates, baggage checks and security sheets ready for inspection at the barrier, please."

The Very Important Persons followed her out, mingled with the less important persons who had been waiting in a nearby room, stepped into a dusty gale behind the four spinning screws of the aeroplane, mounted the step-ladder and were soon strapped into their seats as though waiting the attention of the dentist. A steward gave them brief instructions in the case of their being forced down over the sea and announced: "We shall arrive at Bellacita at sixteen hours Neutralian time."

"An appalling thought occurs to me," said Whitemaid, "can this mean we get no luncheon?"

"They eat very late in Neutralia, I believe."

"Yes, but four o'clock!"

"I'm sure they will have arranged something for us."

"I pray they have."

Something had been arranged but not a luncheon. The Very Important Persons stepped out some hours later into the brilliant sunshine of Bellacita airport and at once found their hands shaken in swift succession by a deputation of their hosts. "I bid you welcome to the land of Bellorius," said their spokesman.

His name, he told them with a neat bow, was Arturo Fe; his rank Doctor of Bellacita University; but there was nothing academic in his appearance. Rather, Scott-King thought, he might be a slightly ageing film actor. He had thin, calligraphic moustaches, a hint of side-whisker, sparse but well-ordered hair, a gold-rimmed monocle, three gold teeth, and neat, dark clothes.

"Madam," he said, "gentlemen, your luggage will be cared for. The motor-cars await you. Come with me. Passports? Papers? Do not give them a thought. Everything is arranged. Come."

At this stage Scott-King became aware of a young woman standing stolidly among them. He had taken notice of her in London where she had towered some six inches above the heads of the crowd.

"I come," she said.

Dr. Fe bowed. "Fe," he said.

"Sveningen," she answered.

"You are one of us? Of the Bellorius Association?" asked Dr. Fe.

"I speak not English well. I come."

Dr. Fe tried her in Neutralian, French, Italian and German. She replied in her own remote Nordic tongue. Dr. Fe raised hands and eyes in a pantomime of despair.

"You speak much English. I speak little English. So we speak English, yes? I come."

"You come?" said Dr. Fe.

"I come."

"We are honoured," said Dr. Fe.

He led them between flowering oleanders and borders of camomile, past shaded café tables at which Whitemaid longingly looked, through the airport vestibule to the glass doors beyond.

Here there was a hitch. Two sentries, shabbily uniformed but armed for action, war-worn, it seemed, but tigers for duty, barred their passage. Dr. Fe tried a high hand, he tried charm, he offered them cigarettes; suddenly a new side of his character was revealed; he fell into demoniac rage, he shook his fists, he bared his chryselephantine teeth, he narrowed his eyes to Mongol slits of hate; what he said was unintelligible to Scott-King but it was plainly designed to wound. The men stood firm.

Then, as suddenly as it had arisen, the squall passed. He turned to his guests. "Excuse one moment," he said. "These stupid fellows do not understand their orders. It will be arranged by the officer." He despatched an underling.

"We box the rude mens?" suggested Miss Sveningen, moving cat-like towards the soldiers.

"No. Forgive them I beg you. They think it their duty."

"Such little men should be polite," said the giantess.

The officer came; the doors flew open; the soldiers did something with their tommy-guns which passed as a salute. Scott-King raised his hat as the little party swept out into the blaze of sunshine to the waiting cars.

"This superb young creature," said Scott-King, "would you say she was a slightly incongruous figure?"

"I find her eminently, transcendently congruous," said White-maid. "I exult in her."

Dr. Fe gallantly took the ladies under his own charge. Scott-King and Whitemaid rode with an underling. They bowled along through the suburbs of Bellacita; tram-lines, half-finished villas, a rush of hot wind, a dazzle of white concrete. At first, when they were fresh from the upper air, the heat had been agreeable; now his skin began to prick and tickle and Scott-King realized that he was unsuitably dressed.

"Exactly ten hours and a half since I had anything to eat," said Whitemaid.

The underling leaned towards them from the front seat and pointed out places of interest. "Here," he said, "the anarchists shot General Cardenas. Here syndico-radicals shot the auxiliary bishop. Here the Agrarian League buried alive ten Teaching Brothers. Here the bimetallists committed unspeakable atrocities on the wife of Senator Mendoza."

"Forgive me for interrupting you," said Whitemaid, "but could you tell us where we are going?"

"To the Ministry. They are all happy to meet you."

"And we are happy to meet them. But just at the moment my friend and I are rather hungry."

"Yes," said the underling with compassion. "We have heard of it in our papers. Your rations in England, your strikes. Here things are very expensive but there is plenty for all who pay, so our people do not strike but work hard to become rich. It is better so, no?"

"Perhaps. We must have a talk about it some time. But at the moment it is not so much the general economic question as a personal immediate need —"

"We arrive," said the underling. "Here is the Ministry."

Like much modern Neutralian building the Ministry was unfinished, but it was conceived in severe one-party style. A portico of unembellished columns, a vast, blank door-way, a bas-relief symbolizing Revolution and Youth and Technical Progress and the National Genius. Inside, a staircase. On the staircase was a less predictable feature; ranged on either side like playing-cards, like a startling hand composed entirely of Kings and Knaves, stood ascending ranks of trumpeters aged from sixty to sixteen, dressed in the tabards of medieval heralds; more than this they wore blond bobbed wigs; more than this their cheeks were palpably rouged. As Scott-King and Whitemaid set foot on the lowest step these figures of fantasy raised their trumpets to their lips and sounded a flourish, while one who might from his extreme age have been father to them all, rattled in a feeble way on a little kettle-drum. "Frankly," said Whitemaid, "I am not in good heart for this kind of thing."

They mounted between the blaring ranks, were greeted on the piano nobile by a man in plain evening-dress, and led to the reception hall which with its pews and thrones had somewhat the air of a court of law and was in fact not infrequently used for condemning aspiring politicians to exile on one or other of the inhospitable islands that lay off the coast of the country.

Here they found an assembly. Under a canopy, on the central throne, sat the Minister of Rest and Culture, a saturnine young man who had lost most of his fingers while playing with a bomb during the last revolution. Scott-King and Whitemaid were presented to him by Dr. Fe. He smiled rather horribly and extended a maimed hand. Half a dozen worthies stood round him. Dr. Fe introduced them. Honorific titles, bows, smiles, shakes of the hand; then Scott-King and Whitemaid were led to their stalls amid their fellow-guests, now about twelve in number. In each place, on the red-plush seat, lay a little pile of printed matter. "Not precisely esculent," said Whitemaid. Trumpets and drum sounded without; another and final party arrived and was presented; then the proceedings began.

The Minister of Rest and Culture had a voice, never soft perhaps, now roughened by a career of street-corner harangues. He spoke at length and was succeeded by the venerable Rector of Bellacita University. Meanwhile Scott-King studied the books and leaflets provided for him, lavish productions of the Ministry of Popular Enlightenment – selected speeches by the Marshal, a monograph on Neutralian pre-History, an illustrated guide to the ski-ing resorts of the country, the annual report of the Corporation of Viticulture. Nothing seemed to have bearing upon the immediate situation except one, a polyglot programme of the coming celebrations. "*17.00 hrs.*," he read. "*Inauguration of the Ceremonies by the Minister of Rest and Culture. 18.00 hrs. Reception of delegates at the University of Bellacita. Official dress. 19.30 hrs. Vin d'honneur offered to the delegates by the Municipality of Bellacita. 21.00 hrs. Banquet offered by the Committee of the Bellorius Tercentenary Committee. Music by Bellacita Philharmonic Youth Squadron. Evening dress. Delegates will spend the night at the Hôtel 22nd March.*"

"Look," said Whitemaid, "nothing to eat until nine o'clock and, mark my words, they will be late."

"In Neutralia," said Dr. Arturo Fe, "in Neutralia, when we are happy, we take no account of time. Today we are *very* happy."

The Hôtel 22nd March was the name, derived from some forgotten event in the Marshal's rise to power, by which the chief hotel of the place was momentarily graced. It had had as many official names in its time as the square in which it stood – the Royal, the Reform, the October Revolution, the Empire, the President Coolidge, the Duchess of Windsor – according to the humours of local history, but Neutralians invariably spoke of it quite simply as the "Ritz". It rose amid sub-tropical vegetation, fountains and statuary, a solid structure, ornamented in the rococo style of fifty years ago. Neutralians of the upper class congregated there, sauntered about its ample corridors, sat in its comfortable foyer, used the concierge as a poste restante, borrowed small sums from its barmen, telephoned sometimes, gossiped always, now and then lightly dozed. They did not spend any money there. They could not afford to. The prices were fixed, and fixed high, by law; to them were added a series of baffling taxes – 30 per cent. for service, 2 per cent. for stamp duty, 30 per cent. for luxury tax, 5 per cent. for the winter relief fund, 12 per cent. for those mutilated in the revolution, 4 per cent. municipal dues, 2 per cent. federal tax, 8 per cent. for living accommodation in excess of minimum requirements, and others of the same kind; they mounted up, they put the bedroom floors and the brilliant dining-rooms beyond the reach of all but foreigners.

There had been few in recent years; official hospitality alone flourished at the Ritz; but still the sombre circle of Neutralian male aristocracy – for, in spite of numberless revolutions and the gross dissemination of free-thought, Neutralian ladies still modestly kept the house – foregathered there; it was their club. They wore very dark suits and very stiff collars, black ties, black buttoned boots; they smoked their cigarettes in long tortoise-shell holders; their faces were brown and wizened; they spoke of money and women, dryly and distantly, for they had never enough of either.

On this afternoon of summer when the traditional Bellacita season was in its last week and they were all preparing to remove to the seaside or to their family estates, about twenty of these descendants of the crusaders sat in the cool of the Ritz lounge. They were rewarded first by the spectacle of the foreign professors' arrival from the Ministry of Rest and Culture. Already they seemed hot and weary; they had come to fetch their academic dress for the reception at the University. The last-comers – Scott-King, Whitemaid, Miss Sveningen and Miss Bombaum – had lost their luggage. Dr. Arturo Fe was like a flame at the reception desk; he pleaded, he threatened, he telephoned. Some said the luggage was impounded at the customs, others that the taxi driver had stolen it. Presently it was discovered in a service lift abandoned on the top storey.

At last Dr. Fe assembled his scholars, Scott-King in his M.A. gown and hood, Whitemaid, more flamboyantly, in the robes of his new doctorate of Upsala. Among the vestments of many seats of learning, some reminiscent of Daumier's law courts, some of Mr. Will Hay of the music-hall stage, Miss Sveningen stood conspicuous in sports dress of zephyr and white shorts. Miss Bombaum refused to go. She had a story to file, she said.

The party trailed out through the swing doors into the dusty evening heat, leaving the noblemen to compare their impressions of Miss Sveningen's legs. The subject was not exhausted when they returned; indeed, had it risen earlier in the year it would have served as staple conversation for the whole Bellacita season.

The visit to the University had been severe, an hour of speeches followed by a detailed survey of the archives. "Miss Sveningen, gentlemen," said Dr. Fe. "We are a little behind. The Municipality is already awaiting us. I shall telephone them that we are delayed. Do not put yourselves out."

The party dispersed to their rooms and reassembled in due time dressed in varying degrees of elegance. Dr. Fe was splendid, tight white waistcoat, onyx buttons, a gardenia, half a dozen miniature medals, a kind of sash. Scott-King and Whitemaid seemed definitely seedy beside him. But the little brown marquesses and counts had no eye for these things. They were waiting for Miss Sveningen. If her academic dress had exposed such uncovenanted mercies, such superb, such unpredictable expanses and lengths of flesh, what would she not show them when gowned for the evening?

She came.

Chocolate-coloured silk enveloped her from collar-bone to humerus and hung to within a foot of the ground; low-heeled black satin shoes covered feet which seemed now unusually large. She had bound a tartan fillet in her hair. She wore a broad patent-leather belt. She had a handkerchief artfully attached to her wrist by her watch-strap. For perhaps a minute the inky,

simian eyes regarded her aghast; then, one by one, with the
languor born of centuries of hereditary disillusionment, the
Knights of Malta rose from their places and sauntered with
many nods to the bowing footmen towards the swing doors,
towards the breathless square, towards the subdivided palaces
where their wives awaited them.

"Come, lady and gentlemen," said Dr. Arturo Fe. "The cars
are here. We are eagerly expected at the Hôtel de Ville."

No paunch, no jowl, no ponderous dignity of the counting-
house or of civic office, no hint indeed of pomp or affluence,
marked the Lord Mayor of Bellacita. He was young, lean and
plainly ill at ease; he was much scarred by his revolutionary
exploits, wore a patch on one eye and supported himself on a
crutch-stick. "His Excellency, alas, does not speak English," said
Dr. Fe as he presented Scott-King and Whitemaid.

They shook hands. The Lord Mayor scowled and muttered
something in Dr. Fe's ear.

"His Excellency says it is a great pleasure to welcome such
illustrious guests. In the phrase of our people he says his house is
yours."

The English stood aside and separated. Whitemaid had
sighted a buffet at the far end of the tapestried hall. Scott-King
stood diffidently alone; a footman brought him a glass of sweet
effervescent wine. Dr. Fe brought him someone to talk to.

"Allow me to present Engineer Garcia. He is an ardent lover
of England."

"Engineer Garcia," said the newcomer.

"Scott-King," said Scott-King.

"I have work seven years with the firm Green, Gorridge and
Wright Limited at Salford. You know them well, no doubt?"

"I am afraid not."

"They are a very well-known firm, I think. Do you go often to
Salford?"

"I'm afraid I've never been there."

"It is a very well-known town. What, please, is your town?"

"I suppose, Granchester."

"I am not knowing Granchester. It is a bigger town than Salford?"

"No, much smaller."

"Ah. In Salford is much industry."

"So I believe."

"How do you find our Neutralian champagne?"

"Excellent."

"It is sweet, eh? That is because of our Neutralian sun. You prefer it to the champagne of France?"

"Well, it is quite different, isn't it?"

"I see you are a connoisseur. In France is no sun. Do you know the Duke of Westminster?"

"No."

"I saw him once at Biarritz. A fine man. A man of great propriety."

"Indeed?"

"Indeed. London is his propriety. Have you a propriety?"

"No."

"My mother had a propriety but it is lost."

The clamour in the hall was tremendous. Scott-King found himself the centre of an English-speaking group. Fresh faces, new voices crowded in on him. His glass was repeatedly filled; it was over-filled and boiled and cascaded on his cuff. Dr. Fe passed and re-passed. "Ah, you have soon made friends." He brought reinforcements; he brought more wine. "This is a special bottle," he whispered. "Special for you, Professor," and refilled Scott-King's glass with the same sugary froth as before. The din swelled. The tapestried walls, the painted ceiling, the chandeliers, the gilded architrave, danced and dazzled before his eyes.

Scott-King became conscious that Engineer Garcia was seeking to draw him into a more confidential quarter.

"How do you find our country, Professor?"

"Very pleasant, I assure you."

"Not how you expected it, eh? Your papers do not say it is pleasant. How is it allowed to scandalize our country? Your papers tell many lies about us."

"They tell lies about everyone, you know."

"Please?"

"They tell lies about everyone," shouted Scott-King.

"Yes, lies. You see for yourself it is perfectly quiet."

"Perfectly quiet."

"How, please?"

"Quiet," yelled Scott-King.

"You find it too quiet? It will become more gay soon. You are a writer?"

"No, merely a poor scholar."

"How, poor? In England you are rich, no? Here we must work very hard for we are a poor country. In Neutralia for a scholar of the first class the salary is 500 ducats a month. The rent of his apartment is perhaps 450 ducats. His taxes are 100. Oil is 30 ducats a litre. Meat is 45 ducats a kilo. So you see, we work.

"Dr. Fe is a scholar. He is also a lawyer, a judge of the Lower Court. He edits the *Historical Review*. He has a high position in the Ministry of Rest and Culture, also at the Foreign Office and the Bureau of Enlightenment and Tourism. He speaks often on the radio about the international situation. He owns one-third share in the Sporting Club. In all the New Neutralia I do not think there is anyone works harder than Dr. Fe, yet he is not rich as Mr. Green, Mr. Gorridge and Mr. Wright were rich in Salford. And they scarcely worked at all. There are injustices in the world, Professor."

"I think we must be quiet. The Lord Mayor wishes to make a speech."

"He is a man of no cultivation. A politician. They say his mother..."

"Hush."

"This speech will not be interesting, I believe."

Something like silence fell on the central part of the hall. The Lord Mayor had his speech ready typed on a sheaf of papers. He squinnied at it with his single eye and began haltingly to read.

Scott-King slipped away. As though at a great distance he descried Whitemaid, alone at the buffet, and unsteadily made his way towards him.

"Are you drunk?" whispered Whitemaid.

"I don't think so – just giddy. Exhaustion and the noise."

"I am drunk."

"Yes. I can see you are."

"How drunk would you say I was?"

"Just drunk."

"My dear, my dear Scott-King, there if I may say so, you are wrong. In every degree and by every known standard I am very, very much more drunk than you give me credit for."

"Very well. But let's not make a noise while the Mayor's speaking."

"I do not profess to know very much Neutralian but it strikes me that the Mayor, as you call him, is talking the most consummate rot. What is more, I doubt very much that he is a mayor. Looks to me like a gangster."

"Merely a politician, I believe."

"That is worse."

"The essential, the immediate need is somewhere to sit down."

Though they were friends only of a day, Scott-King loved this man; they had suffered, were suffering, together; they spoke, pre-eminently, the same language; they were comrades in arms. He took Whitemaid by the arm and led him out of the hall to a cool and secluded landing where stood a little settee of gilt and plush, a thing not made for sitting on. Here they sat, the two dim men, while very faintly from behind them came the sound of oratory and applause.

"They were putting it in their pockets," said Whitemaid.

"Who? What?"

"The servants. The food. In the pockets of those long braided coats they wear. They were taking it away for their families. I got four macaroons." And then swiftly veering he remarked: "She looks terrible."

"Miss Sveningen?"

"That glorious creature. It was a terrible shock to see her when she came down changed for the party. It killed something here," he said, touching his heart.

"Don't cry."

"I can't help crying. You've seen her brown dress? And the hair ribbon? And the handkerchief?"

"Yes, yes, I saw it all. And the belt."

"The belt," said Whitemaid, "was more than flesh and blood could bear. Something snapped, here," he said, touching his forehead. "You must remember how she looked in shorts? A Valkyrie. Something from the heroic age. Like some god-like, some unimaginably strict school prefect, *a dormitory monitor*," he said in a kind of ecstasy. "Think of her striding between the beds, a pigtail, bare feet, in her hand a threatening hairbrush. Oh, Scott-King, do you think she rides a bicycle?"

"I'm sure of it."

"In shorts?"

"Certainly in shorts."

"I can imagine a whole life lived riding tandem behind her, through endless forests of conifers, and at midday sitting down among the pine needles to eat hard-boiled eggs. Think of those strong fingers peeling an egg, Scott-King, the brown of it, the white of it, the shine. Think of her *biting* it."

"Yes, it would be a splendid spectacle."

"And then think of her now, in there, in that brown dress."

"There are things not to be thought of, Whitemaid." And Scott-King, too, shed a few tears of sympathy, of common sorrow in the ineffable, the cosmic sadness of Miss Sveningen's party frock.

"What is this?" said Dr. Fe, joining them some minutes later. "Tears? You are not enjoying it?"

"It is only," said Scott-King, "Miss Sveningen's dress."

"This is tragic, yes. But in Neutralia we take such things bravely, with a laugh. I came, not to intrude, simply to ask, Professor, you have your little speech ready for this evening? We count on you at the banquet to say a few words."

For the banquet they returned to the Ritz. The foyer was empty save for Miss Bombaum who sat smoking a cigar with a man of repellent aspect. "I have had my dinner. I'm going out after a story," she explained.

It was half-past ten when they sat down at a table spread with arabesques of flower-heads, petals, moss, trailing racemes and sprays of foliage until it resembled a parterre by Le Nôtre. Scott-King counted six wineglasses of various shapes standing before him amid the vegetation. A menu of enormous length, printed in gold, lay on his plate beside a typewritten place-card "*Dr. Scotch-Kink*". Like many explorers before him, he found that prolonged absence from food destroyed the appetite. The waiters had already devoured the hors-d'oeuvre, but when at length the soup arrived, the first mouthful made him hiccup. This, too, he remembered, had befallen Captain Scott's doomed party in the Antarctic.

"Comment dit-on en français 'hiccup'?" he asked his neighbour.

"Plaît-il, mon professeur?"

Scott-King hiccuped. "Ça," he said.

"Ça c'est le hoquet."

"J'en ai affreusement."

"Évidemment, mon professeur. Il faut du cognac."

The waiters had drunk and were drinking profusely of brandy and there was a bottle at hand. Scott-King tossed off a glassful and his affliction was doubled. He hiccuped without intermission throughout the long dinner.

This neighbour, who had so ill-advised him, was, Scott-King saw from the card, Dr. Bogdan Antonic, the International Secretary of the Association, a middle-aged, gentle man whose face was lined with settled distress and weariness. They conversed, as far as the hiccups permitted, in French.

"You are not Neutralian?"

"Not yet. I hope to be. Every week I make my application to the Foreign Office and always I am told it will be next week. It is not so much for myself I am anxious – though death is a fearful thing – as for my family. I have seven children, all born in Neutralia, all without nationality. If we are sent back to my unhappy country they would hang us all without doubt."

"Jugo-Slavia?"

"I am a Croat, born under the Hapsburg Empire. That was a true League of Nations. As a young man I studied in Zagreb, Budapest, Prague, Vienna – one was free, one moved where one would; one was a citizen of Europe. Then we were liberated and put under the Serbs. Now we are liberated again and put under the Russians. And always more police, more prisons, more hanging. My poor wife is Czech. Her nervous constitution is quite deranged by our troubles. She thinks all the time she is being watched."

Scott-King essayed one of those little, inarticulate, non-committal grunts of sympathy which come easily to the embarrassed Englishman; to an Englishman, that is, who is not troubled by the hiccups. The sound which in the event issued from him might have been taken as derisive by a less sensitive man than Dr. Antonic.

"I think so, too," he said severely. "There are spies everywhere. You saw that man, as we came in, sitting with the woman with the cigar. He is one of them. I have been here ten years and know them all. I was second secretary to our Legation. It was a great thing, you must believe, for a Croat to enter our diplomatic service. All the appointments went to Serbs. Now there is no Legation. My salary has not been paid since 1940. I have a few friends at the Foreign Office. They are sometimes kind and give me employment, as at the present occasion. But at any moment they may make a trade agreement with the Russians and hand us over."

Scott-King attempted to reply.

"You must take some more brandy, Professor. It is the only thing. Often, I remember, in Ragusa I have had the hiccups from laughing. . . . Never again, I suppose."

Though the company was smaller at the banquet than at the *vin d'honneur*, the noise was more oppressive. The private dining-room of the Ritz, spacious as it was, had been built in a more trumpery style than the Hôtel de Ville. There the lofty roof had seemed to draw the discordant voices upwards into the cerulean perspective with which it was painted, and disperse them there amid the floating deities; the Flemish hunting scenes on the walls seemed to envelop and muffle them in their million stitches. But here the din banged back from gilding and mirrors; above the clatter and chatter of the dinner-table and the altercations of the waiters, a mixed choir of young people sang folk-songs, calculated to depress the most jovial village festival. It was not thus, in his class-room at Granchester, that Scott-King had imagined himself dining.

"At my little house on the point at Lapad, we used to sit on the terrace laughing so loudly, sometimes, that the passing fishermen called up to us from their decks asking to share the joke. They sailed close inshore and one could follow their lights far out towards the islands. When we were silent, *their* laughter came to us across the water when they were out of sight."

The neighbour on Scott-King's left did not speak until the dessert, except to the waiters; to them he spoke loudly and often, sometimes blustering, sometimes cajoling, and by this means got two helpings of nearly every course. His napkin was tucked into his collar. He ate intently with his head bowed over his plate so that the morsels which frequently fell from his lips were not permanently lost to him. He swigged his wine with relish, sighing after each draught and tapping the glass with his knife to call the waiter's attention to the need of refilling it. Often he jammed glasses on his nose and studied the menu, not so much, it seemed, for fear of missing anything, as to fix in his memory the fleeting delights of the moment. It is not entirely easy to achieve a Bohemian appearance in evening-dress but this man did so with his shock of grizzled hair, the broad ribbon of his pince-nez, and a three days' growth of beard and whisker.

With the arrival of the dessert, he raised his countenance, fixed on Scott-King his large and rather bloodshot eyes, belched mildly and then spoke. The words were English; the accent had been formed in many cities from Memphis (Mo.) to Smyrna. "Shakespeare, Dickens, Byron, Galsworthy," he seemed to say.

This late birth of a troublesome gestation took Scott-King by surprise; he hiccuped non-committally.

"They are all great English writers."

"Well, yes."

"Your favourite, please?"

"I suppose Shakespeare."

"He is the more dramatic, the more poetic, no?"

"Yes."

"But Galsworthy is the more modern."

"Very true."

"I am modern. You are a poet?"

"Hardly that. A few translations."

"I am an original poet. I translate my poems myself into English prose. They have been published in the United States. Do you read the *New Destiny*?"

"I am afraid not."

"It is the magazine which publishes my translations. Last year they sent me ten dollars."

"No one has ever paid me for my translations."

"You should send them to the *New Destiny*. It is not possible, I think," continued the Poet, "to render the poetry of one language into the poetry of another. Sometimes I translate English prose into Neutralian poetry. I have done a very beautiful rendering of some selected passages of your great Priestley. I hoped it would be used in the High Schools but it is not. There is jealousy and intrigue everywhere – even at the Ministry of Education."

At this moment a splendid figure at the centre of the table rose to make the first speech. "Now to work," said his neighbour, produced a note-book and pencil and began busily writing in shorthand. "In the new Neutralia we all work."

The speech was long and provoked much applause. In the course of it a note came to Scott-King by the hand of a waiter: *"I shall call on you to reply to his Excellency. Fe"*.

Scott-King wrote in answer: *"Terribly sorry. Not tonight. Indisposed. Ask Whitemaid,"* stealthily left his place and, still hiccuping, passed behind the table to the dining-room door.

Outside the foyer was almost deserted; the great glass dome which throughout the years of war had blazed aloft nightly, a candle in a naughty world, rose darkly. Two night porters shared a cigar behind one of the pillars; a huge empty carpet, strewn with empty chairs, lay before Scott-King in the subdued light to which a parsimonious management had reduced the earlier blaze. It was not much past midnight but in the New Neutralia memories persisted of the revolutionary curfew, of police round-ups, of firing squads in the public gardens; New Neutralians liked to get home early and bolt their doors.

As Scott-King stepped into this silent space, his hiccups mys-teriously ceased. He went through the swing doors and breathed the air of the piazza where under the arc-lamps workmen were washing away with hoses the dust and refuse of the day; the last of the trams, which all day long rattled round the fountains, had long since returned to its shed. He breathed deeply, testing, as it were, the limits of his miraculous recovery, and knew it to be complete. Then he turned back, took his key and, barely con-scious, ascended.

During the first tumultuous afternoon and evening in Bella-cita there had been little opportunity for more than the barest acquaintance between Scott-King and his fellow-guests of the Bellorius Association. Indeed he had scarcely distinguished them from their hosts. They had bowed and shaken hands, they had exchanged nods among the University archives, they had apol-ogized one to the other as they jostled and jogged elbows at the *vin d'honneur*; Scott-King had no share in whatever intimacies flour-ished after the banquet. He remembered an affable American and a Swiss of extreme hauteur and an Oriental whom on general principles he assumed to be Chinese. Now on the morn-ing following he came cheerfully to join them in the Ritz foyer in accordance with the printed programme. They were to leave at 10.30 for Simona. His bags were packed; the sun, not yet oppres-sive, shone brilliantly through the glass dome. He was in the best of tempers.

He had awoken in this rare mood after a night of untroubled sleep. He had breakfasted on a tray of fruit, sitting on his ver-andah above the square, showering copious blessings on the palms and fountains and trams and patriotic statuary. He approached the group in the foyer with the intention of making himself peculiarly agreeable.

Of the festive Neutralians of the day before only Dr. Fe and the Poet remained. The rest were at work elsewhere constructing the New Neutralia.

"Professor Scott-King, how are you this morning?"

There was more than politeness in Dr. Fe's greeting; there was definite solicitude.

"Extremely well, thank you. Oh, of course, I had forgotten about last night's speech. I was very sorry to fail you; the truth was . . ."

"Professor Scott-King, say no more. Your friend Whitemaid I fear is not so well."

"No?"

"No. He has sent word that he cannot join us." Dr. Fe raised exquisitely expressive eyebrows.

The Poet drew Scott-King momentarily aside. "Do not be alarmed," he said. "Reassure your friend. Not a hint of last night's occurrences shall appear. I speak with the authority of the Ministry."

"You know I'm completely in the dark."

"So are the public. So they shall remain. You sometimes laugh at us in your democratic way for our little controls, but they have their uses, you see."

"But I don't know what has happened."

"So far as the press of Neutralia is concerned, nothing happened."

The Poet had shaved that morning and shaved ruthlessly. The face he thrust near Scott-King's was tufted with cotton-wool. Now he withdrew it and edged away. Scott-King joined the group of delegates.

"Well," said Miss Bombaum, "I seem to have missed a whole packet of fun last night."

"I seem to have missed it too."

"And how's the head this morning?" asked the American scholar.

"Seems like you had fun," said Miss Bombaum.

"I went to bed early," said Scott-King coldly. "I was thoroughly over-tired."

"Well, I've heard it called plenty of things in my time. I reckon that covers it too."

Scott-King was an adult, an intellectual, a classical scholar, almost a poet; provident Nature who shields the slow tortoise and points the quills of the porcupine, has given to such tender spirits their appropriate armour. A shutter, an iron curtain, fell between Scott-King and these two jokers. He turned to the rest of the company and realized too late that jocularity was the least he had to fear. The Swiss had not been cordial the day before; this morning he was theatrical in his coldness; the Asiatic seemed to have spun himself a cocoon of silken aloofness. The assembled scholars did not positively cut Scott-King; in their several national fashions they signified that they were not unaware of Scott-King's presence amongst them. Further than this they did not go. They too had their shutters, their iron curtains. Scott-King was in disgrace. Something unmentionable had happened in which he was vicariously but inextricably implicated; a gross, black, inexpungible blot had fallen on Scott-King overnight.

He did not wish to know more. He was an adult, an intellectual; he was all that has already been predicated of him. He was no chauvinist. Throughout six embattled years he had remained resolutely impartial. But now his hackles rose; quite literally he felt the roots of his sparse hairs prick and tingle. Like the immortal private of the Buffs he stood in Elgin's place; not untaught certainly, nor rude, nor abysmally low-born, but poor and, at the moment, reckless, bewildered and alone, a heart with English instinct fraught he yet could call his own.

"I may have to keep the party waiting a few minutes," he said. "I must go and call on my colleague Mr. Whitemaid."

He found him in bed looking strange rather than ill; almost exalted. He was still rather drunk. The windows stood wide open on to the balcony and on the balcony, modestly robed in bath towels, sat Miss Sveningen eating beefsteak.

"They tell me downstairs that you are not coming with us to Simona?"

"No. I'm not quite up to it this morning. I have things to

attend to here. It is not easy for me to explain." He nodded towards the giant carnivore on the balcony.

"You spent an agreeable evening?"

"A total blank, Scott-King. I remember being with you at some kind of civic reception. I remember a fracas with the police, but that was much later. Hours must have intervened."

"The police?"

"Yes. At some kind of dancing place. Irma here was splendid – like something in a film. They went down like nine-pins. But for her I suppose I should be in a cell at this moment instead of happily consuming Bromo-Seltzer in your company."

"You made a speech."

"So I gather. You missed it? Then we shall never know what I said. Irma in her blunt way described it as long and impassioned but incomprehensible."

"Was it about Bellorius?"

"I rather suppose not. Love was uppermost in my mind, I think. To tell you the truth I have lost my interest in Bellorius. It was never strong. It wilted and died this morning when I learned that Irma was not of us. She has come for the Physical Training Congress."

"I shall miss you."

"Stay with us for the gymnastics."

For a second Scott-King hesitated. The future at Simona was obscure and rather threatening.

"There are to be five hundred female athletes. Contortionists perhaps from the Indies."

"No," said Scott-King at length firmly. "I must keep faith with Bellorius."

And he returned to the delegates who now sat impatiently in a charabanc at the doors of the Ritz.

III

The town of Simona stands within sight of the Mediterranean Sea on the foothills of the great massif which fills half the map of Neutralia. Groves of walnut and cork-oak, little orchards of almond and lemon, cover the surrounding country and grow to the foot of the walls which jut out among them in a series of sharp bastions, ingeniously contrived in the seventeenth century and never, in a long history of strife, put to the test of assault; for they enclose little of military significance. The medieval university, the baroque cathedral, twenty churches in whose delicate limestone belfries the storks build and multiply, a rococo square, two or three tiny shabby palaces, a market and a street of shops are all that can be found there and all that the heart of man can properly desire. The railway runs well clear of the town and betrays its presence only by rare puffs of white smoke among the tree-tops.

At the hour of the angelus Scott-King sat with Dr. Bogdan Antonic at a café table on the ramparts.

"I suppose Bellorius must have looked out on almost precisely the same prospect as we see today."

"Yes, the buildings at least do not change. There is still the illusion of peace while, as in Bellorius's time, the hills behind us are a nest of brigands."

"He alludes to them, I remember, in the eighth canto, but surely today? . . ."

"It is still the same. Now they call them by different names – partisans, resistance groups, unreconcilables, what you will. The effect is the same. You need police escort to travel many of the roads."

They fell silent. In the course of the circuitous journey to Simona, sympathy had sprung up between Scott-King and the International Secretary.

Bells deliciously chimed in the sunlit towers of twenty shadowy churches.

At length Scott-King said: "You know I suspect that you and I are the only members of our party who have read Bellorius."

"My own knowledge of him is slight. But Mr. Fu has written of him very feelingly, I believe, in demotic Cantonese. Tell me, Professor, do you think the celebration is a success?"

"I'm not really a professor, you know."

"No, but for the occasion all are professors. You are more professor than some who are here. I was obliged to cast my net rather wide to have all countries represented. Mr. Jungman, for example, is simply a gynaecologist from The Hague, and Miss Bombaum is I do not know what. The Argentine and the Peruvian are mere students who happened to be in the country at this time. I tell you these things because I trust you and because I think you suspect them already. You have not perceived an element of deception?"

"Well, yes."

"It is the wish of the Ministry. You see, I am their cultural adviser. They required a celebration this summer. I searched the records for an anniversary. I was in despair until by chance I hit on the name of Bellorius. They had not heard of him, of course, but then they would have been equally in the dark if he had been Dante or Goethe. I told them," said Dr. Antonic with a sad, sly, highly civilized little smile, "that he was one of the greatest figures of European letters."

"So he should be."

"You really think so? You do not find the whole thing a masquerade? You think it is a success? I hope so, for you see my position at the Ministry is far from secure. There is jealousy everywhere. Imagine it, that anyone should be jealous of *me*. But in the New Neutralia all are so eager to work. They would snap up my little post greedily. Dr. Arturo Fe would like it."

"Surely not? He seems fully employed already."

"That man collects government posts as in the old days churchmen collected benefices. He has a dozen already and he covets mine. That is why it is such a triumph to have brought him here. If the celebration is not a success, he will be implicated. Already, today, the Ministry have shown displeasure that the statue of Bellorius is not ready to be unveiled tomorrow. It is not our fault. It is the Office of Rest and Culture. It is the plot of an enemy named Engineer Garcia, who seeks to ruin Dr. Fe and to succeed him in some of his posts. But Dr. Fe will explain; he will improvise. He is of the country."

Dr. Fe improvised next day.

The party of savants were quartered in the main hotel of
Simona, which that morning had the aspect of a war-time railway station owing to the arrival some time after midnight of fifty
or sixty international philatelists for whom no accommodation
had been arranged. They had slept in the lounge and hall; were,
some of them, still sleeping when the Bellorius delegation
assembled.

This was the day set down in the programme for the unveiling
of the Bellorius statue. Hoarding and scaffolding in the town
square marked the site of the proposed monument, but it was
already well known among the delegates that the statue had not
arrived. They had lived by rumour during the past three days for
nothing in their exhilarating experiences had quite corresponded
with the printed plan. "They say the 'bus has gone back to
Bellacita for new tyres." – "Have you heard we are to dine with
the Lord Mayor?" – "I heard Dr. Fe say we should not leave till
three o'clock." "I believe we ought all to be at the Chapter
House" . . . and so on. This was the atmosphere of the tour, and
in it the social barriers which had threatened to divide them at
Bellacita had quickly broken down. Whitemaid was forgotten,
Scott-King found himself once more befriended, made part of a
fellowship of bewilderment. They were two days on the road
sleeping at places far from their original route; they were wined
and feasted at unexpected hours, disconcertingly greeted by brass
bands and deputations, disconcertingly left stranded in deserted
squares; once they crossed paths and for several frantic hours
exchanged luggage with a party of religious pilgrims; once they
had two dinners within an hour of each other; once they had
none. But here they were in the end where they should be, at
Simona. The only absentee was Bellorius.

Dr. Fe improvised.

"Miss Bombaum, gentlemen, a little addition to our programme. Today we go to pay homage to the National Memorial." Obediently they trooped out to the 'bus. Some philatelists
were sleeping there and had to be dislodged. With them were
embarked a dozen vast wreaths of laurel.

"What are these?"

"Those are our homage."

Red ribbons across the foliage bore the names of the countries thus curiously represented.

They drove out of the town into the land of cork-oak and almond. After an hour they were stopped and an escort of armoured cars formed up before and behind them.

"A little token of our esteem," said Dr. Fe.

"It is for fear of the partisans," whispered Dr. Antonic.

Dust from the military enveloped the 'bus and hid the landscape. After two hours they halted. Here on a bare hillock stood the National Memorial. Like all modern state-architecture it was a loveless, unadorned object saved from insignificance only by its bulk; a great truncated pyramid of stone. A squad of soldiers were at work seeking lethargically to expunge a message daubed across the inscribed face in red paint: "Death to the Marshal".

Dr. Fe ignored their activities and led his party to the further side which was innocent of any legend, patriotic or subversive. Here under a fierce sun they left their wreaths, Scott-King stepping forward, when called, to represent Great Britain. The poet-journalist crouched and snapped with his camera. The escort cheered. The fatigue-men came round with their mops to see what was going on. Dr. Fe said a few words in Neutralian. The ceremony was over. They had luncheon in a neighbouring town at what seemed to be a kind of barrack-canteen, a bare room decorated only by a large photograph of the Marshal; a substantial but far from sumptuous meal eaten at narrow tables on thick earthenware plates. Scott-King drank several glasses of the heavy, purplish wine. The 'bus had stood long in the sun and was scorching hot. The wine and the thick stew induced sleep, and Scott-King lolled away the hours of the return journey unconscious of the jungle-whispering which prevailed around him in that tropic air.

Whispering, however, there was, and it found full voice when at length the party returned to Simona.

Scott-King awoke to it as he entered the hotel. "We must call a meeting," the American professor was saying. "We must vote a resolution."

"We want a show-down," said Miss Bombaum. "Not here," she added, taking stock of the stamp-collectors who still squatted in the public rooms. "Upstairs."

It would be tedious in the extreme to recount all that was said in Miss Bombaum's bedroom after the expulsion of two philatelists who had taken refuge there. It was tedious to sit there, thought Scott-King, while the fountains were splashing in the square and the breeze stirring among the orange leaves on the city walls. Speeches were made, repeated, translated and mis-translated; there were calls for order and small private explosions of ill-temper. Not all the delegates were present. The Swiss Professor and the Chinese could not be found; the Peruvian and Argentine students refused to come, but there were six savants in the little bedroom besides Miss Bombaum, all of them, except Scott-King, very indignant about something.

The cause of offence emerged through many words and the haze of tobacco smoke. In brief it was this: the Bellorius Association had been made dupes of the politicians. But for Miss Bombaum's insatiable curiosity nothing need ever have been known of it. She had nosed out the grim truth like a truffle and the fact was plain. The National Monument was nothing more or less than a fetish of civil strife. It commemorated the massacre, execution, liquidation – what you will – ten years back on that sunny spot of some fifty leaders of the now dominant Neutralian party by those then dominant. The delegates of the Bellorius Association had been tricked into leaving wreaths there and, worse than this, had been photographed in the act. Miss Bombaum's picture was at that moment, she said, being rushed out to the newspapers of the world. More than this they had lunched at the party Headquarters at the very tables where the ruffians of the party were wont to refresh themselves after their orgies of terrorization. What was more, Miss Bombaum said, she had just learned from a book in her possession that Bellorius had never had any connection with Neutralia at all; he had been a Byzantine general.

Scott-King petulantly joined issue on this point. Strong words were used of him. "Fascist beast." – "Reactionary cannibal." – "Bourgeois escapist."

Scott-King withdrew from the meeting.

Dr. Fe was in the passage. He took Scott-King's arm and silently led him downstairs and out into the arcaded street.

"They are not content," said Dr. Fe. "It is a tragedy of the first magnitude."

"You shouldn't have done it, you know," said Scott-King.

"I should not have done it? My dear Professor, I wept when it was first suggested. I delayed our journey two days on the road precisely to avoid this. But would they listen? I said to the Minister of Popular Enlightenment: 'Excellency, this is an international occasion. It is in the realm of pure scholarship. These great men have not come to Neutralia for political purposes.' He replied coarsely: 'They are eating and drinking at our expense. They should show their respect for the Régime. The Physical Training delegates have all saluted the Marshal in the Sports Stadium. The philatelists have been issued with the party badge and many of them wear it. The professors, too, must help the New Neutralia.' What could I say? He is a person of no delicacy, of the lowest origins. It was he, I have no doubt, who induced the Ministry of Rest and Culture to delay sending the statue. Professor, you do not understand politics. I will be frank with you. It was all a plot."

"So Miss Bombaum says."

"A plot against me. For a long time now they have been plotting my downfall. I am not a party man. You think because I wear the badge and give the salute I am of the New Neutralia. Professor, I have six children, two of them girls of marriageable age. What can one do but seek one's fortune? And now I think I am ruined."

"Is it as bad as that?"

"I cannot express how bad it is. Professor, you must go back to that room and persuade them to be calm. You are English. You have great influence. I have remarked during our journey together how they have all respected you."

"They called me 'a fascist beast'."

"Yes," said Dr. Fe simply, "I heard it through the keyhole. They were very discontented."

After Miss Bombaum's bedroom, the streets were cool and sweet; the touch of Dr. Fe's fingers on Scott-King's sleeve was light as a moth. They walked on in silence. At a dewy flower-stall Dr. Fe chose a buttonhole, haggled fiercely over the price, presented it with Arcadian grace to Scott-King and then resumed the sorrowful promenade.

"You will not go back?"

"It would do no good, you know."

"An Englishman admits himself beaten," said Dr. Fe desperately.

"It amounts to that."

"But you yourself will stay with us to the end?"

"Oh certainly."

"Why, then, we have lost nothing of consequence. The celebrations can proceed." He said it politely, gallantly, but he sighed as they parted.

Scott-King climbed the worn steps of the ramparts and sat alone under the orange trees watching the sun set.

The hotel was tranquil that evening. The philatelists had been collected and carted off; they left dumbly and glumly for an unknown destination like Displaced Persons swept up in the machinery of "social engineering". The six dissident delegates went with them, in default of other transport. The Swiss, the Chinese, the Peruvian and the Argentine alone remained. They dined together, silently, lacking a common tongue, but in good humour. Dr. Fe, Dr. Antonic and the Poet dined at another table, also silent, but sorrowful.

Next day the errant effigy arrived by lorry and the day following was fixed for the unveiling. Scott-King passed the time happily. He studied the daily papers, all of which, true to Miss Bombaum's forecast, displayed large photographs of the ceremony at the National Monument. He pieced together the sense of a leading article on the subject, he ate, he dozed, he visited the cool and glowing churches of the town, he composed the speech which, he was told, was expected of him on the morrow. Dr. Fe, when they met, showed the reserve proper to a man of delicate feeling who had in emotion revealed too much of himself. It was a happy day for Scott-King.

Not so for his colleagues. Two disasters befell them severally, while he was pottering around. The Swiss Professor and the Chinese went for a little drive together in the hills. Their companionship was grounded on economy rather than mutual liking. An importunate guide; insensibility to the contemplative pleasures of Western architecture; a seemingly advantageous price; the promise of cool breezes, a wide panorama, a little restaurant; these undid them. When at evening they had not returned, their fate was certain.

"They should have consulted Dr. Fe," said Dr. Antonic. "He would have chosen a more suitable road and found them an escort."

"What will become of them?"

"With the partisans you cannot say. Many of them are worthy, old-fashioned fellows who will treat them hospitably and wait for a ransom. But some are occupied with politics. If our friends have fallen among those, I am afraid they will certainly be murdered."

"I did not like the Swiss."

"Nor I. A Calvinist. But the Ministry will not be pleased that he is murdered."

The fate of the South Americans was less romantic. The police took them off during luncheon.

"It seems they were not Argentine or Peruvian," said Dr. Antonic. "Not even students."

"What had they done?"

"I suppose they were informed against."

"They certainly had a villainous appearance."

"Oh yes, I suppose they were desperate fellows – spies, bimetallists, who can say? Nowadays it is not what you do that counts, but who informs against you. I think someone very high up must have informed against that pair. Otherwise Dr. Fe could have had the business postponed until after our little ceremony. Or perhaps Dr. Fe's influence is on the wane."

So in the end, as was indeed most fitting, one voice only was raised to honour Bellorius.

The statue, when at last after many ineffective tugs at the controlling cord it was undraped and stood clear, stonily, insolently unabashed under the fierce Neutralian sun, while the populace huzzaed and, according to their custom, threw firecrackers under the feet of the notables, as the pigeons fluttered above in high alarm and the full weight of the band followed the opening trumpets – the statue was appalling.

There are no contemporary portraits of Bellorius still extant. In their absence some sharp business had been done in the Ministry of Rest and Culture. The figure now so frankly brought to view had lain long years in a mason's yard. It had been commissioned in an age of free enterprise for the tomb of a commercial magnate whose estate, on his death, had proved to be illusory. It was not Bellorius; it was not the fraudulent merchant prince; it was not even unambiguously male; it was scarcely human; it represented perhaps one of the virtues.

Scott-King stood aghast at the outrage he had unwittingly committed on that gracious square. But he had already spoken and his speech had been a success. He had spoken in Latin; he had spoken from the heart. He had said that a torn and embittered world was that day united in dedicating itself to the majestic concept of Bellorius, in rebuilding itself first in Neutralia, then among all the yearning peoples of the West, on the foundations Bellorius had so securely laid. He had said that they were lighting a candle that day which by the Grace of God should never be put out.

And after the oration came a prodigious luncheon at the University. And after the luncheon he was invested with a Doctorate of International Law. And after the investiture he was put into a 'bus and driven with Dr. Fe, Dr. Antonic and the Poet, back to Bellacita.

By the direct road the journey took barely five hours. It was not yet midnight when they drove down the brilliant boulevard of the capital city. Little had been said on the road. When they drew up at the Ministry, Dr. Fe said: "So our little expedition is over. I can only hope, Professor, that you have enjoyed it a particle as much as we." He held out his hand and smiled under the arc-lamps. Dr. Antonic and the Poet collected their modest luggage. "Good night," they said. "Good night. We shall walk from here. The taxis are so expensive – the double fare operates after nine o'clock."

They walked. Dr. Fe ascended the steps of the Ministry. "Back to work," he said. "I have had an urgent summons to report to my chief. We work late in the New Neutralia."

There was nothing furtive about his ascent but it was swift. Scott-King caught him as he was about to enter a lift.

"But, I say, where am I to go?"

"Professor, our humble town is yours. Where would you like to go?"

"Well, I suppose I must go to an hotel. We were at the Ritz before."

"I am sure you will be comfortable there. Tell the porter to get you a taxi and see he does not try to overcharge you. Double fare but not more."

"But I shall see you tomorrow?"

"I hope *very* often."

Dr. Fe bowed and the doors of the lift shut upon his bow and his smile.

There was in his manner something more than the reserve proper to a man of delicate feeling who had in emotion revealed too much of himself.

IV

Officially," said Mr. Horace Smudge, "we don't even know you're here."

He gazed at Scott-King through hexagonal spectacles across the Pending Tray and twiddled a new-fangled fountain pen; a multiplicity of pencils protruding from his breast-pocket and his face seemed to suggest that he expected one of the telephones on his desk to ring at any moment with a message about something far more important than the matter under discussion; he was for all the world, Scott-King thought, like the clerk in the food office at Granchester.

Scott-King's life had been lived far from chanceries, but once, very many years ago at Stockholm, he had been asked to luncheon, by mistake for someone else, at the British Embassy. Sir Samson Courtenay had been *chargé d'affaires* at the time and Scott-King gratefully recalled the air of nonchalant benevolence with which he had received a callow undergraduate where he had expected a Cabinet Minister. Sir Samson had not gone far in his profession but for one man at least, for Scott-King, he remained the fixed type of English diplomat.

Smudge was not as Sir Samson; he was the child of sterner circumstances and a more recent theory of public service; no uncle had put in a bland word for Smudge in high places; honest toil, a clear head in the examination room, a genuine enthusiasm for Commercial Geography, had brought him to his present position as second secretary at Bellacita. "You've no conception," said Smudge, "what a time we have with Priorities. I've had to put the Ambassadress off the plane twice, at the last moment, to make room for I.C.I. men. As it is I have four electrical engineers, two British Council lecturers and a trades unionist all wanting passages. Officially we have not heard of Bellorius. The Neutralians brought you here. It's their business to get you back."

"I've been to them twice a day for three days. The man who organized everything, Dr. Fe, seems to have left the Ministry."

"You could always go by train, of course. It takes a little time but it would probably be quicker in the end. I presume you have all the necessary visas?"

"No. How long would they take to get?"

"Perhaps three weeks, perhaps longer. It's the Inter-Allied Zone Authority which holds things up."

"But I can't afford to go on living here indefinitely. I was only allowed to bring £75 and the prices are terrible."

"Yes, we had a case like that the other day. A man called Whitemaid. He'd run out of money and wanted to cash a cheque, but of course that is specifically contrary to the currency regulations. The consul took charge of him."

"Did he get home?"

"I doubt it. They used to ship them by sea, you know, as Distressed British Subjects and hand them over to the police on arrival, but all that has been discontinued since the war. He was connected with your Bellorius celebration I think. It has caused a good deal of work to us one way and another. But it's worse for the Swiss. They've had a professor murdered and that always involves a special report on counsellor-level. I'm sorry I can't do more for you. I only deal with air priorities. You are the business of the consulate really. You had better let them know in a week or two how things turn out."

The heat was scarcely endurable. In the ten days Scott-King had been in the country, the summer seemed to change temper and set its face angrily against him. The grass had turned brown in the square. Men still hosed the streets but the burning stone was dry again in an instant. The season was over; half the shops were shut and the little brown noblemen had left their chairs in the Ritz.

It was no great distance from the Embassy to the hotel, but Scott-King was stumbling with exhaustion before he reached the revolving doors. He went on foot for he was obsessed now by parsimony; he could no longer eat with pleasure, counting the price of each mouthful, calculating the charge for service, the stamp duty, the luxury taxes; groaning in that scorching summer under the weight of the Winter Relief Fund. He should leave the Ritz without delay, he resolved, and yet he hesitated; once ensconced in some modest pension, in some remote side street where no telephone ever rang and no one in passage from the outer world ever set foot, might he not be lost irretrievably, submerged, unrecognizable in his dimness, unremembered? Would he perhaps, years hence, exhibit a little discoloured card advertising lessons in English conversation, grow shabbier and greyer and plumper with the limp accretions of despair and destitution and die there at last nameless? He was an adult, an intellectual, a classical scholar, almost a poet, but he could not face that future without terror. So he clung to the Ritz, empty as it was, contemptuously as he felt himself regarded there, as the one place in Neutralia where salvation might still be found. If he left, he knew it would be for ever. He lacked the assurance of the native nobility who could sit there day by day, as though by right. Scott-King's only right lay in his travellers' cheques. He worked out his bill from hour to hour. At the moment he had nearly forty pounds in hand. When he was down to twenty, he decided, he would move. Meanwhile he looked anxiously round the dining-room before starting the daily calculation of how cheaply he could lunch.

And that day he was rewarded. His number turned up. Sitting not two tables away, alone, was Miss Bombaum. He rose to greet her. All the hard epithets with which they had parted were forgotten.

"May I sit here?"

She looked up, first without recognition, then with pleasure. Perhaps there was something in his forlorn appearance, in the diffidence of his appeal, which cleared him in Miss Bombaum's mind. This was no fascist beast that stood before her, no reactionary cannibal.

"Surely," she said. "The guy who invited me hasn't shown up."

A ghastly fear, cold in that torrid room, struck Scott-King, that he would have to pay for Miss Bombaum's luncheon. She was eating a lobster, he noted, and drinking hock.

"When you've finished," he said. "Afterwards, with coffee perhaps in the lounge."

"I've a date in twenty minutes," she said. "Sit down."

He sat and at once, in answer to her casual enquiry, poured out the details of his predicament. He laid particular stress on his financial problems and, as pointedly as he could, ordered the humblest dish on the menu. "It's a fallacy not to eat in hot weather," said Miss Bombaum. "You need to keep your resistance up."

When he had finished the recital she said, "Well, I reckon it shouldn't be hard to fix you up. Go by the Underground."

Blacker despair in Scott-King's haunted face told Miss Bombaum that she had not made herself clear.

"You've surely heard of the Underground? It's –" she quoted from one of her recent articles on the subject – "it's an alternative map of Europe, like a tracing overlying all the established frontiers and routes of communication. It's the new world taking shape below the surface of the old. It's the new ultra-national citizenship."

"Well I'm blessed."

"Look, I can't stop now. Be here this evening and I'll take you to see the key man."

That afternoon, his last, as it turned out, in Bellacita, Scott-King received his first caller. He had gone to his room to sleep through the heat of the day, when his telephone rang and a voice announced Dr. Antonic. He asked for him to be sent up.

The Croat entered and sat by his bed.

"So you have acquired the Neutralian custom of the *siesta*. I am too old. I cannot adapt myself to new customs. Everything in this country is as strange to me as when I first came here.

"I was at the Foreign Office this morning enquiring about my papers of naturalization and I heard by chance you were still here. So I came at once. I do not intrude? I thought you would have left by now. You have heard of our misfortunes? Poor Dr. Fe is disgraced. All his offices taken from him. More than this there is trouble with his accounts. He spent more, it appears, on the Bellorius celebrations than the Treasury authorized. Since he is out of office he has no access to the books and cannot adjust them. They say he will be prosecuted, perhaps sent to the islands."

"And you, Dr. Antonic?"

"I am never fortunate. I relied on Dr. Fe for my naturalization. Whom shall I turn to now? My wife thought that perhaps you could do something for us in England to make us British subjects."

"There is nothing I can do."

"No, I suppose not. Nor in America?"

"Still less there."

"So I told my wife. But she is a Czech and so more hopeful. We Croats do not hope. It would be a great honour if you would come and explain these things to her. She will not believe me when I say there is no hope. I promised I would bring you."

So Scott-King dressed and was led through the heat to a new quarter on the edge of the town, to a block of flats.

"We came here because of the elevator. My wife was so weary of Neutralian stairs. But alas the elevator no longer works."

They trudged to the top floor, to a single sitting-room full of children, heavy with the smell of coffee and cigarette smoke.

"I am ashamed to receive you in a house without an elevator," said Mme. Antonic in French; then turning to the children, she addressed them in another tongue. They bowed, curtsied, and left the room. Mme. Antonic prepared coffee and brought a plate of biscuits from the cupboard.

"I was sure you would come," she said. "My husband is too timid. You will take us with you to America."

"Dear madam, I have never been there."

"To England then. We must leave this country. We are not at our ease here."

"I am finding the utmost difficulty in getting to England myself."

"We are respectable people. My husband is a diplomat. My father had his own factory at Budweis. Do you know Mr. Mackenzie?"

"No, I don't think so."

"He was a *very* respectable Englishman. He would explain that we come of good people. He visited often to my father's factory. If you will find Mr. Mackenzie he will help us."

So the conversation wore on. "If we could only find Mr. Mackenzie," Mme. Antonic repeated, "all our troubles would be at an end." Presently the children returned.

"I will take them to the kitchen," said Mme. Antonic, "and give them some jam. Then they will not be a nuisance."

"You see," said Dr. Antonic, as the door closed, "she is always hopeful. Now I do not hope. Do you think," he asked, "that in Neutralia Western Culture might be born again? That this country has been preserved by Destiny from the horrors of war so that it can become a beacon of hope for the world?"

"No," said Scott-King.

"Do you not?" asked Dr. Antonic anxiously. "Do you not? Neither do I."

That evening Miss Bombaum and Scott-King took a cab to the suburbs and left it at a café where they met a man who had sat with Miss Bombaum in the Ritz on her first evening. No names were exchanged.

"Who's this guy, Martha?"

"An English friend of mine I want you to help."

"Going far?"

"England. Can he see the chief?"

"I go ask. He's on the level?"

"Surely."

"Well, stick around while I ask."

He went to telephone and returned saying, "The chief 'll see him. We can drop him off there, then have our talk."

They took another cab and drove further from the city into a district of tanneries and slaughterhouses, recognizable by their smell in the hot darkness. Presently they stopped at a lightless villa.

"In there. Don't ring. Just push the door."

"Hope you have a good trip," said Miss Bombaum.

Scott-King was not a reader of popular novels and so was unfamiliar with the phrase "It all happened so quickly that it was not until afterwards . . ." That, however, expressed his situation. The cab drove off as he was still stumbling up the garden path. He pushed the door, entered an empty and lightless hall, heard a voice from another room call "Come in," went in, and found himself in a shabby office confronting a Neutralian in the uniform of a major of police.

The man addressed him in English. "You are Miss

Bombaum's friend? Sit down. Do not be alarmed by my uniform. Some of our clients are *very* much alarmed. A silly boy tried to shoot me last week when he saw me like this. He suspected a trap. You want to go to England, I think. That is very difficult. Now if you had said Mexico or Brazil or Switzerland it would be easier. You have reasons which make England preferable?"

"I have reasons."

"Curious. I spent many years there and found it a place of few attractions. The women had no modesty, the food upset my stomach. I have a little party on their way to Sicily. That would not do instead?"

"I am afraid not."

"Well, we must see what can be done. You have a passport? This is lucky. English passports come very dear just now. I hope Miss Bombaum explained to you that mine is not a charitable organization. We exist to make profits and our expenses are high. I am constantly bothered by people who come to me supposing I work for the love of it. I do love my work, but love is not enough. The young man I spoke of just now, who tried to shoot me – he is buried just outside under the wall – he thought this was a political organization. We help people irrespective of class, race, party, creed or colour – for cash in advance. It is true, when I first took over, there were certain amateur associations that had sprung up during the World War – escaping prisoners, communist agents, Zionists, spies and so on. I soon put them out of business. That is where my position in the police is a help. Now I can say I have a virtual monopoly. Our work increases every day. It is extraordinary how many people without the requisite facilities seem anxious to cross frontiers today. I also have a valued connection with the Neutralian government. Troublesome fellows whom they want to dispose of pass through my hands in large numbers. How much have you got?"

"About forty pounds."

"Show me."

Scott-King handed him his book of travellers' cheques.

"But there are seventy pounds here."

"Yes, but my hotel bill . . ."

"There will be no time for that."

"I am sorry," said Scott-King firmly. "I could not possibly leave an hotel with my bill unpaid, especially in a foreign country. It may seem absurdly scrupulous to you but it is one of the things a Granchesterian simply cannot do."

The Major was not a man to argue from first principles. He took men as they came and in his humane calling he dealt with many types.

"Well, I shan't pay it," he said. "Do you know anyone else in Bellacita?"

"No one."

"Think."

"There was a man called Smudge at our Embassy."

"Smudge shall have your bill. These cheques want signing."

Despite his high training Scott-King signed and the cheques were put away in the bureau drawer.

"My luggage?"

"We do not handle luggage. You will start this evening. I have a small party leaving for the coast. We have our main clearing-house at Santa Maria. From there you will travel by steamer, perhaps not in the grand luxury, but what will you? No doubt as an Englishman you are a good sailor."

He rang a bell on his desk and spoke to the answering secretary in rapid Neutralian.

"My man here will take charge of you and fit you out. You speak Neutralian? No? Perhaps it is as well. We do not encourage talk in my business, and I must warn you, the strictest discipline has to be observed. From now on you are under orders. Those who disobey never reach their destinations. Good-bye and a good journey."

Some few hours later a large and antiquated saloon car was bumping towards the sea. In it sat in extreme discomfort seven men habited as Ursuline nuns. Scott-King was among them.

The little Mediterranean seaport of Santa Maria lay very near the heart of Europe. An Athenian colony had thrived there in the

days of Pericles and built a shrine to Poseidon; Carthaginian
slaves had built the breakwater and deepened the basin; Romans
had brought fresh water from the mountain springs; Dominican
friars had raised the great church which gave the place its present
name; the Hapsburgs had laid out the elaborate little piazza; one
of Napoleon's marshals had made it his base and left a classical
garden there. The footprints of all these gentler conquerors were
still plain to see but Scott-King saw nothing as, at dawn, he
bowled over the cobbles to the water-front.

The Underground dispersal centre was a warehouse; three
wide floors, unpartitioned, with boarded windows, joined by an
iron staircase. There was one door near which the guardian had
set her large brass bedstead. At most hours of the day she reclined
there under a coverlet littered with various kinds of food, weap-
ons, tobacco and a little bolster on which she sometimes made
lace of an ecclesiastical pattern. She had the face of a *tricoteuse* of
the Terror. "Welcome to Modern Europe," she said as the seven
Ursulines entered.

The place was crowded. In the six days which he spent there
Scott-King identified most of the groups who messed together by
languages. There were a detachment of Slovene royalists, a few
Algerian nationals, the remnants of a Syrian anarchist association, ten patient Turkish prostitutes, four French Pétainist mil-
lionaires, a few Bulgarian terrorists, a half-dozen former Gestapo
men, an Italian air-marshal and his suite, a Hungarian ballet,
some Portuguese Trotskyites. The English-speaking group consisted chiefly of armed deserters from the American and British
Armies of Liberation. They had huge sums of money distributed
about the linings of their clothes, the reward of many months'
traffic round the docks of the central sea.

Such activity as there was took place in the hour before dawn.
Then the officer in charge, husband, it seemed, of the guardian
hag, would appear with lists and a handful of passports; a roll
would be called and a party despatched. During the day the
soldiers played poker – a fifty-dollar ante and a hundred-dollar
raise. Sometimes in the hours of darkness there were newcomers.
The total number at the clearing station remained fairly constant.

At last on the sixth day there was a commotion. It began at midday with a call from the chief of police. He came with sword and epaulettes and he talked intently and crossly in Neutralian with the custodian.

One of the Americans, who had picked up more languages during his time in the Old World than most diplomats, explained: "The guy with the fancy fixings says we got to get the hell out of here. Seems there's a new officer going to raid this joint."

When the officer had gone, the custodian and his wife debated the question. "The old girl says why don't he hand us over and get rewarded. The guy says Hell, the most likely reward they'd get would be hanging. Seems there's some stiffs planted round about."

Presently a sea-captain appeared and talked Greek. All the Underground travellers sat stock-still listening, picking up a word here and there. "This guy's got a ship can take us off."

"Where?"

"Aw, some place. Seems they're kinda more interested in finance than geography."

A bargain was struck. The captain departed, and the Underground conductor explained to each language group in turn that there had been a slight dislocation of plan. "Don't worry," he said. "Just go quiet. Everything's all right. We'll look after you. You'll all get where you want to in time. Just at the moment you got to move quick and quiet, that's all."

So, unprotesting, at nightfall, the strangely assorted party was hustled on board a schooner. Noah's animals cannot have embarked with less sense of the object of their journey. The little ship was not built for such cargo. Down they went into a dark hold; hatches were battened down; the unmistakeable sound of moorings being cast off came to them in their timbered prison; an auxiliary Diesel engine started up; sails were hoisted; soon they were on the high seas in very nasty weather.

This is the story of a summer holiday; a light tale. It treats, at the worst, with solid discomfort and intellectual doubt. It would be inappropriate to speak here of those depths of the human spirit, the agony and despair, of the next few days of Scott-King's life. To even the Comic Muse, the gadabout, the adventurous one of those heavenly sisters, to whom so little that is human comes amiss, who can mix in almost any company and find a welcome at almost every door – even to her there are forbidden places. Let us leave Scott-King then on the high seas and meet him again as, sadly changed, he comes at length into harbour. The hatches are off, the August sun seems cool and breathless, Mediterranean air fresh and spring-like as at length he climbs on deck. There are soldiers; there is barbed wire; there is a waiting lorry; there is a drive through a sandy landscape, more soldiers, more wire. All the time Scott-King is in a daze. He is first fully conscious in a tent, sitting stark naked while a man in khaki drill taps his knee with a ruler.

"I say, Doc, I know this man." He looks up into a vaguely familiar face. "You *are* Mr. Scott-King, aren't you? What on earth are you doing with this bunch, sir?"

"Lockwood! Good gracious, you used to be in my Greek set! Where am I?"

"No. 64 Jewish Illicit Immigrants' Camp, Palestine."

Granchester reassembled in the third week of September. On the first evening of term, Scott-King sat in the masters' common-room and half heard Griggs telling of his trip abroad. "It gives one a new angle to things, getting out of England for a bit. What did you do, Scottie?"

"Oh, nothing much. I met Lockwood. You remember him. Sad case, he was a sitter for the Balliol scholarship. Then he had to go into the army."

"I thought he was still in it. How typical of old Scottie that all he has to tell us after eight weeks away is that he met a prize pupil! I shouldn't be surprised to hear you did some work, too, you old blackleg."

"To tell you the truth I feel a little *désoeuvré*. I must look for a new subject."

"You've come to the end of old Bellorius at last?"

"Quite to the end."

Later the headmaster sent for Scott-King.

"You know," he said, "we are starting this year with fifteen fewer classical specialists than we had last term?"

"I thought that would be about the number."

"As you know I'm an old Greats man myself. I deplore it as much as you do. But what are we to do? Parents are not interested in producing the 'complete man' any more. They want to qualify their boys for jobs in the modern world. You can hardly blame them, can you?"

"Oh yes," said Scott-King. "I can and do."

"I always say you are a much more important man here than I am. One couldn't conceive of Granchester without Scott-King. But has it ever occurred to you that a time may come when there will be no more classical boys at all?"

"Oh yes. Often."

"What I was going to suggest was – I wonder if you will consider taking some other subject as well as the classics? History, for example, preferably economic history?"

"No, headmaster."

"But, you know, there may be something of a crisis ahead."

"Yes, headmaster."

"Then what do you intend to do?"

"If you approve, headmaster, I will stay as I am here as long as any boy wants to read the classics. I think it would be very wicked indeed to do anything to fit a boy for the modern world."

"It's a short-sighted view, Scott-King."

"There, headmaster, with all respect, I differ from you profoundly. I think it the most long-sighted view it is possible to take."

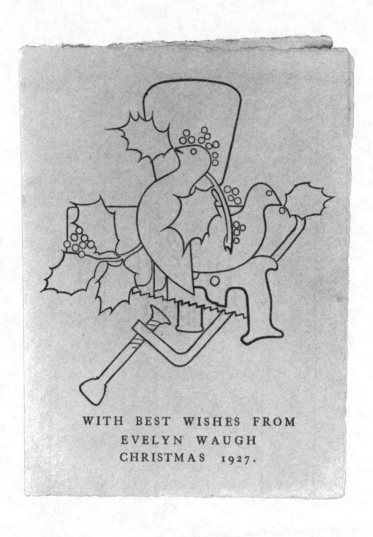

WITH BEST WISHES FROM
EVELYN WAUGH
CHRISTMAS 1927.

Christmas Card, 1927.

TACTICAL EXERCISE

JOHN VERNEY married Elizabeth in 1938, but it was not until the winter of 1945 that he came to hate her steadily and fiercely. There had been countless brief gusts of hate before this, for it was a thing which came easily to him. He was not what is normally described as a bad-tempered man, rather the reverse; a look of fatigue and abstraction was the only visible sign of the passion which possessed him, as others are possessed by laughter or desire, several times a day.

During the war he passed among those he served with as a phlegmatic fellow. He did not have his good or his bad days; they were all uniformly good and bad; good, in that he did what had to be done, expeditiously without ever "getting in a flap" or "going off the deep end"; bad, from the intermittent, invisible sheet-lightning of hate which flashed and flickered deep inside him at every obstruction or reverse. In his orderly room when, as a company commander, he faced the morning procession of defaulters and malingerers; in the mess when the subalterns disturbed his reading by playing the wireless; at the Staff College when the "syndicate" disagreed with his solution; at Brigade H.Q. when the staff-sergeant mislaid a file or the telephone orderly muddled a call; when the driver of his car missed a turning; later, in hospital, when the doctor seemed to look too cursorily at his wound and the nurses stood gossiping jauntily at the beds of more likeable patients instead of doing their duty to him – in all the annoyances of army life which others dismissed with an oath and a shrug, John Verney's eyelids drooped wearily, a tiny grenade of hate exploded and the fragments rang and ricocheted round the steel walls of his mind.

There had been less to annoy him before the war. He had some money and the hope of a career in politics. Before marriage he served his apprenticeship to the Liberal party in two hopeless by-elections. The Central Office then rewarded him with a constituency in outer London which offered a fair chance in the next General Election. In the eighteen months before the war he nursed this constituency from his flat in Belgravia and travelled frequently on the continent to study political conditions. These studies convinced him that war was inevitable; he denounced the Munich agreement pungently and secured a commission in the territorial army.

Into this peacetime life Elizabeth fitted unobtrusively. She was his cousin. In 1938 she had reached the age of twenty-six, four years his junior, without falling in love. She was a calm, handsome young woman, an only child, with some money of her own and more to come. As a girl, in her first season, an injudicious remark, let slip and overheard, got her the reputation of cleverness. Those who knew her best ruthlessly called her "deep".

Thus condemned to social failure, she languished in the ballrooms of Pont Street for another year and then settled down to a life of concert-going and shopping with her mother, until she surprised her small circle of friends by marrying John Verney. Courtship and consummation were tepid, cousinly, harmonious. They agreed, in face of the coming war, to remain childless. No one knew what Elizabeth felt or thought about anything. Her judgements were mainly negative, deep or dull as you cared to take them. She had none of the appearance of a woman likely to inflame great hate.

John Verney was discharged from the Army early in 1945 with a M.C. and one leg, for the future, two inches shorter than the other. He found Elizabeth living in Hampstead with her parents, his uncle and aunt. She had kept him informed by letter of the changes in her condition but, preoccupied, he had not clearly imagined them. Their flat had been requisitioned by a government office; their furniture and books sent to a repository and totally lost, partly burned by a bomb, partly pillaged by firemen. Elizabeth, who was a linguist, had gone to work in a clandestine branch of the Foreign Office.

Her parents' house had once been a substantial Georgian villa overlooking the Heath. John Verney arrived there early in the morning after a crowded night's journey from Liverpool. The wrought-iron railings and gates had been rudely torn away by the salvage collectors, and in the front garden, once so neat, weeds and shrubs grew in a rank jungle trampled at night by courting soldiers. The back garden was a single, small bomb-crater; heaped clay, statuary and the bricks and glass of ruined greenhouses; dry stalks of willow-herb stood breast high over the mounds. All the windows were gone from the back of the house, replaced by shutters of card and board, which put the main rooms in perpetual darkness. "Welcome to Chaos and Old Night," said his uncle genially.

There were no servants; the old had fled, the young had been conscripted for service. Elizabeth made him some tea before leaving for her office.

Here he lived, lucky, Elizabeth told him, to have a home. Furniture was unprocurable, furnished flats commanded a price beyond their income, which was now taxed to a bare wage. They might have found something in the country, but Elizabeth, being childless, could not get release from her work. Moreover, he had his constituency.

This, too, was transformed. A factory, wired round like a prisoner-of-war camp, stood in the public gardens. The streets surrounding it, once the trim houses of potential Liberals, had been bombed, patched, confiscated, and filled with an immigrant proletarian population. Every day he received a heap of complaining letters from constituents exiled in provincial boarding-houses. He had hoped that his decoration and his limp might earn him sympathy, but he found the new inhabitants indifferent to the fortunes of war. Instead they showed a sceptical curiosity about Social Security. "They're nothing but a lot of reds," said the Liberal agent.

"You mean I shan't get in?"

"Well, we'll give them a good fight. The Tories are putting up a Battle-of-Britain pilot. I'm afraid he'll get most of what's left of the middle-class vote."

In the event John Verney came bottom of the poll, badly. A rancorous Jewish schoolteacher was elected. The Central Office paid his deposit, but the election had cost him dear. And when it was over there was absolutely nothing for John Verney to do.

He remained in Hampstead, helped his aunt make the beds after Elizabeth had gone to her office, limped to the greengrocer and fishmonger and stood, full of hate, in the queues; helped Elizabeth wash up at night. They ate in the kitchen, where his aunt cooked deliciously the scanty rations. His uncle went three days a week to help pack parcels for Java.

Elizabeth, the deep one, never spoke of her work, which, in fact, was concerned with setting up hostile and oppressive governments in Eastern Europe. One evening at a restaurant, a man came and spoke to her, a tall young man whose sallow, aquiline face was full of intellect and humour. "That's the head of my department," she said. "He's so amusing."

"Looks like a Jew."

"I believe he is. He's a strong Conservative and hates the work," she added hastily, for since his defeat in the election John had become fiercely anti-Semitic.

"There is absolutely no need to work for the State now," he said. "The war's over."

"Our work is just beginning. They won't let any of us go. You must understand what conditions are in this country."

It often fell to Elizabeth to explain "conditions" to him. Strand by strand, knot by knot, through the coalless winter, she exposed the vast net of government control which had been woven in his absence. He had been reared in traditional Liberalism and the system revolted him. More than this, it had him caught, personally, tripped up, tied, tangled; wherever he wanted to go, whatever he wanted to do or have done, he found himself baffled and frustrated. And as Elizabeth explained she found herself defending. This regulation was necessary to avoid that ill; such a country was suffering, as Britain was not, for having neglected such a precaution; and so on, calmly and reasonably.

"I know it's maddening, John, but you must realize it's the same for everyone."

"That's what all you bureaucrats want," he said. "Equality through slavery. The two-class state – proletarians and officials."

Elizabeth was part and parcel of it. She worked for the State and the Jews. She was a collaborator with the new, alien, occupying power. And as the winter wore on and the gas burned feebly in the stove, and the rain blew in through the patched windows, as at length spring came and buds broke in the obscene wilderness round the house, Elizabeth in his mind became something more important. She became a symbol. For just as soldiers in far-distant camps think of their wives, with a tenderness they seldom felt at home, as the embodiment of all the good things they have left behind, wives who perhaps were scolds and drabs, but in the desert and jungle become transfigured until their trite air-letters become texts of hope, so Elizabeth grew in John Verney's despairing mind to more than human malevolence as the archpriestess and maenad of the century of the common man.

"You aren't looking well, John," said his aunt. "You and Elizabeth ought to get away for a bit. She is due for leave at Easter."

"The State is granting her a supplementary ration of her husband's company, you mean. Are we sure she has filled in all the correct forms? Or are commissars of her rank above such things?"

Uncle and aunt laughed uneasily. John made his little jokes with such an air of weariness, with such a droop of the eyelids that they sometimes struck chill in that family circle. Elizabeth regarded him gravely and silently.

John was far from well. His leg was in constant pain so that he no longer stood in queues. He slept badly; as also, for the first time in her life, did Elizabeth. They shared a room now, for the winter rains had brought down ceilings in many parts of the shaken house and the upper rooms were thought to be unsafe. They had twin beds on the ground floor in what had once been her father's library.

In the first days of his homecoming John had been amorous. Now he never approached her. They lay night after night six feet apart in the darkness. Once when John had been awake for two hours he turned on the lamp that stood on the table between them. Elizabeth was lying with her eyes wide open staring at the ceiling.

"I'm sorry. Did I wake you?"

"I haven't been asleep."

"I thought I'd read for a bit. Will it disturb you?"

"Not at all."

She turned away. John read for an hour. He did not know whether she was awake or asleep when he turned off the light.

Often after that he longed to put on the light, but was afraid to find her awake and staring. Instead he lay, as others lie in a luxurious rapture of love, hating her.

It did not occur to him to leave her; or, rather, it did occur from time to time, but he hopelessly dismissed the thought. Her life was bound tight to his; her family was his family; their finances were intertangled and their expectations lay together in the same quarters. To leave her would be to start fresh, alone and naked in a strange world; and lame and weary at the age of thirty-eight, John Verney had not the heart to move.

He loved no one else. He had nowhere to go, nothing to do. Moreover he suspected, of late, that it would not hurt her if he went. And, above all, the single steadfast desire left to him was to do her ill. "I wish she were dead," he said to himself as he lay awake at night. "I wish she were dead."

Sometimes they went out together. As the winter passed, John took to dining once or twice a week at his club. He assumed that on these occasions she stayed at home, but one morning it transpired that she too had dined out the evening before. He did not ask with whom, but his aunt did, and Elizabeth replied, "Just someone from the office."

"The Jew?" John asked.

"As a matter of fact, it was."

"I hope you enjoyed it."

"Quite. A beastly dinner, of course, but he's very amusing."

One night when he returned from his club, after a dismal little dinner and two crowded Tube journeys, he found Elizabeth in bed and deeply asleep. She did not stir when he entered. Unlike her normal habit, she was snoring. He stood for a minute, fascinated by this new and unlovely aspect of her, her head thrown back, her mouth open and slightly dribbling at the corner. Then he shook her. She muttered something, turned over and slept heavily and soundlessly.

Half an hour later, as he was striving to compose himself for sleep, she began to snore again. He turned on the light, looked at her more closely and noticed with surprise, which suddenly changed to joyous hope, that there was a tube of unfamiliar pills, half empty, beside her on the bed table.

He examined it. "*24 Comprimés narcotiques, hypnotiques*," he read, and then in large, scarlet letters, "NE PAS DEPASSER DEUX." He counted those which were left. Eleven.

With tremulous butterfly wings Hope began to flutter in his heart, became a certainty. He felt a fire kindle and spread inside him until he was deliciously suffused in every limb and organ. He lay, listening to the snores, with the pure excitement of a child on Christmas Eve. "I shall wake up tomorrow and find her dead," he told himself, as once he had felt the flaccid stocking at the foot of his bed and told himself, "Tomorrow I shall wake up and find it full." Like a child, he longed to sleep to hasten the morning and, like a child, he was wildly, ecstatically sleepless. Presently he swallowed two of the pills himself and almost at once was unconscious.

Elizabeth always rose first to make breakfast for the family. She was at the dressing-table when sharply, without drowsiness, his memory stereoscopically clear about the incidents of the night before, John awoke. "You've been snoring," she said.

Disappointment was so intense that at first he could not speak. Then he said, "You snored, too, last night."

"It must be the sleeping-tablet I took. I must say it gave me a good night."

"Only one?"

"Yes, two's the most that's safe."

"Where did you get them?"

"A friend at the office – the one you called the Jew. He has them prescribed by a doctor for when he's working too hard. I told him I wasn't sleeping, so he gave me half a bottle."

"Could he get me some?"

"I expect so. He can do most things like that."

So he and Elizabeth began to drug themselves regularly and passed long, vacuous nights. But often John delayed, letting the beatific pill lie beside his glass of water, while, knowing the vigil was terminable at will, he postponed the joy of unconsciousness, heard Elizabeth's snores, and hated her sumptuously.

One evening while the plans for the holiday were still under discussion, John and Elizabeth went to the cinema. The film was a murder story of no great ingenuity but with showy scenery. A bride murdered her husband by throwing him out of a window, down a cliff. Things were made easy for her by his taking a lonely lighthouse for their honeymoon. He was very rich and she wanted his money. All she had to do was confide in the local doctor and a few neighbours that her husband frightened her by walking in his sleep; she doped his coffee, dragged him from the bed to the balcony – a feat of some strength – where she had already broken away a yard of balustrade, and rolled him over. Then she went back to bed, gave the alarm next morning, and wept over the mangled body which was presently discovered half awash on the rocks. Retribution overtook her later, but at the time the thing was a complete success.

"I wish it were as easy as that," thought John, and in a few hours the whole tale had floated away in those lightless attics of the mind where films and dreams and funny stories lie spider-shrouded for a lifetime unless, as sometimes happens, an intruder brings them to light.

Such a thing happened a few weeks later when John and Elizabeth went for their holiday. Elizabeth found the place. It belonged to someone in her office. It was named Good Hope Fort, and stood on the Cornish coast. "It's only just been de-requisitioned," she said: "I expect we shall find it in pretty bad condition."

"We're used to that," said John. It did not occur to him that she should spend her leave anywhere but with him. She was as much part of him as his maimed and aching leg.

They arrived on a gusty April afternoon after a train journey of normal discomfort. A taxi dove them eight miles from the station, through deep Cornish lanes, past granite cottages and disused, archaic tin-workings. They reached the village which gave the house its postal address, passed through it and out along a track which suddenly emerged from its high banks into open grazing land on the cliff's edge, high, swift clouds and sea-birds wheeling overhead, the turf at their feet alive with fluttering wild flowers, salt in the air, below them the roar of the Atlantic breaking on the rocks, a middle-distance of indigo and white tumbled waters and beyond it the serene arc of the horizon. Here was the house.

"Your father," said John, "would now say, 'Your castle hath a pleasant seat.'"

"Well, it has rather, hasn't it?"

It was a small stone building on the very edge of the cliff, built a century or so ago for defensive purposes, converted to a private house in the years of peace, taken again by the Navy during the war as a signal station, now once more reverting to gentler uses. Some coils of rusty wire, a mast, the concrete foundations of a hut, gave evidence of its former masters.

They carried their things into the house and paid the taxi.

"A woman comes up every morning from the village. I said we shouldn't want her this evening. I see she's left us some oil for the lamps. She's got a fire going, too, bless her, and plenty of wood. Oh, and look what I've got as a present from father. I promised not to tell you until we arrived. A bottle of whisky. Wasn't it sweet of him. He's been hoarding his ration for three months..." Elizabeth talked brightly as she began to arrange the luggage. "There's a room for each of us. This is the only proper living-room, but there's a study in case you feel like doing any work. I believe we shall be quite comfortable..."

The living-room was built with two stout bays, each with a french window opening on a balcony which overhung the sea. John opened one and the sea-wind filled the room. He stepped out, breathed deeply, and then said suddenly: "Hullo, this is dangerous."

At one place, between the windows, the cast-iron balustrade had broken away and the stone ledge lay open over the cliff. He looked at the gap and at the foaming rocks below, momentarily puzzled. The irregular polyhedron of memory rolled uncertainly and came to rest.

He had been here before, a few weeks ago, on the gallery of the lighthouse in that swiftly forgotten film. He stood there, looking down. It was exactly thus that the waves had come swirling over the rocks, had broken and dropped back with the spray falling about them. This was the sound they had made; this was the broken ironwork and the sheer edge.

Elizabeth was still talking in the room, her voice drowned by wind and sea. John returned to the room, shut and fastened the door. In the quiet she was saying "... only got the furniture out of store last week. He left the woman from the village to arrange it. She's got some queer ideas, I must say. Just look where she put..."

"What did you say this house was called?"

"Good Hope."

"A good name."

That evening John drank a glass of his father-in-law's whisky, smoked a pipe and planned. He had been a good tactician. He made a leisurely, mental "appreciation of the situation". Object: murder.

When they rose to go to bed he asked: "You packed the tablets?"

"Yes, a new tube. But I am sure I shan't want any tonight."

"Neither shall I," said John, "the air is wonderful."

During the following days he considered the tactical problem. It was entirely simple. He had the "staff-solution" already. He considered it in the words and form he had used in the army. "... Courses open to the enemy... achievement of surprise... consolidation of success." The staff-solution was exemplary. At the beginning of the first week, he began to put it into execution.

Already, by easy stages, he had made himself known in the village. Elizabeth was a friend of the owner; he the returned hero, still a little strange in civvy street. "The first holiday my wife and I have had together for six years," he told them in the golf club and, growing more confidential at the bar, hinted that they were thinking of making up for lost time and starting a family.

On another evening he spoke of war-strain, of how in this war the civilians had had a worse time of it than the services. His wife, for instance; stuck it all through the blitz; office work all day, bombs at night. She ought to get right away, alone somewhere for a long stretch; her nerves had suffered; nothing serious, but to tell the truth he wasn't quite happy about it. As a matter of fact, he had found her walking in her sleep once or twice in London.

His companions knew of similar cases; nothing to worry about, but it wanted watching; didn't want it to develop into anything worse. Had she seen a doctor?

Not yet, John said. In fact she didn't know she had been sleep-walking. He had got her back to bed without waking her. He hoped the sea air would do her good. In fact, she seemed much better already. If she showed any more signs of the trouble when they got home, he knew a very good man to take her to.

The golf club was full of sympathy. John asked if there were a good doctor in the neighbourhood. Yes, they said, old Mackenzie in the village, a first-class man, wasted in a little place like that; not at all a stick-in-the-mud. Read the latest books; psychology and all that. They couldn't think why Old Mack had never specialized and made a name for himself.

"I think I might go and talk to Old Mack about it," said John.

"Do. You couldn't find a better fellow."

Elizabeth had a fortnight's leave. There were still three days to go when John went off to the village to consult Dr. Mackenzie. He found a grey-haired, genial bachelor in a consulting room that was more like a lawyer's office than a physician's, book-lined, dark, permeated by tobacco smoke.

Seated in the shabby leather armchair he developed in more precise language the story he had told in the golf club. Dr. Mackenzie listened without comment.

"It's the first time I've run up against anything like this," he concluded.

At length Dr. Mackenzie said: "You got pretty badly knocked about in the war, Mr. Verney?"

"My knee. It still gives me trouble."

"Bad time in hospital?"

"Three months. A beastly place outside Rome."

"There's always a good deal of nervous shock in an injury of that kind. It often persists when the wound is healed."

"Yes, but I don't quite understand..."

"My dear Mr. Verney, your wife asked me to say nothing about it, but I think I must tell you that she has already been here to consult me on this matter."

"About her sleep-walking? But she can't..." then John stopped.

"My dear fellow, I quite understand. She thought you didn't know. Twice lately you've been out of bed and she had to lead you back. She knows all about it."

John could find nothing to say.

"It's not the first time," Dr. Mackenzie continued, "that I've been consulted by patients who have told me their symptoms and said they had come on behalf of friends or relations. Usually it's girls who think they're in the family-way. It's an interesting feature of your case that you should want to ascribe the trouble to someone else, probably the decisive feature. I've given your wife the name of a man in London who I think will be able to help you. Meanwhile I can only advise plenty of exercise, light meals at night..."

John Verney limped back to Good Hope Fort in a state of consternation. Security had been compromised; the operation must be cancelled; initiative had been lost... all the phrases of the tactical school came to his mind, but he was still numb after this unexpected reverse. A vast and naked horror peeped at him and was thrust aside.

When he got back Elizabeth was laying the supper table. He stood on the balcony and stared at the gaping rails with eyes smarting with disappointment. It was dead calm that evening. The rising tide lapped and fell and mounted again silently among the rocks below. He stood gazing down, then he turned back into the room.

There was one large drink left in the whisky bottle. He poured it out and swallowed it. Elizabeth brought in the supper and they sat down. Gradually his mind grew a little calmer. They usually ate in silence. At last he said: "Elizabeth, why did you tell the doctor I had been walking in my sleep?"

She quietly put down the plate she had been holding and looked at him curiously. "Why?" she said gently. "Because I was worried, of course. I didn't think you knew about it."

"But have I been?"

"Oh yes, several times – in London and here. I didn't think it mattered at first, but the night before last I found you on the balcony, quite near that dreadful hole in the rails. I was really frightened. But it's going to be all right now. Dr. Mackenzie has given me the name..."

It was possible, thought John Verney; nothing was more likely. He had lived night and day for ten days thinking of that opening, of the sea and rock below, the ragged ironwork and the sharp edge of stone. He suddenly felt defeated, sick and stupid, as he had as he lay on the Italian hillside with his smashed knee. Then as now he had felt weariness even more than pain.

"Coffee, darling."

Suddenly he roused himself. "No," he almost shouted. "No, no, no."

"Darling, what is the matter? Don't get excited. Are you feeling ill? Lie down on the sofa near the window."

He did as he was told. He felt so weary that he could barely move from his chair.

"Do you think coffee would keep you awake, love? You look quite fit to drop already. There, lie down."

He lay down and, like the tide slowly mounting among the rocks below, sleep rose and spread in his mind. He nodded and woke with a start.

"Shall I open the window, darling, and give you some air?"

"Elizabeth," he said, "I feel as if I have been drugged." Like the rocks below the window – now awash, now emerging clear from falling water; now awash again, deeper; now barely visible, mere patches on the face of gently eddying foam – his brain was softly drowning. He roused himself, as children do in nightmare, still scared, still half asleep. "I can't be drugged," he said loudly, "I never touched the coffee."

"Drugs in the coffee?" said Elizabeth gently, like a nurse soothing a fractious child. "Drugs in the *coffee*? What an absurd idea. That's the kind of thing that only happens on the films, darling."

He did not hear her. He was fast asleep, snoring stertorously by the open window.

'Angostura and Soda', *The Isis*, 30 January 1924, p. 5.

COMPASSION

THE MILITARY organization into which Major Gordon drifted during the last stages of the war enjoyed several changes of name as its function became less secret. At first it was called "Force X"; then "Special Liaison Balkan Irregular Operations"; finally, "Joint Allied Mission to the Jugo-Slav Army of Liberation". Its work was to send observing officers and wireless operators to Tito's partisans.

Most of these appointments were dangerous and uncomfortable. The liaison parties parachuted into the forests and the mountains and lived like brigands. They were often hungry, always dirty, always on the alert, prepared to decamp at any move of the enemy's. The post to which Major Gordon was sent was one of the safest and softest. Begoy was the headquarters of a partisan corps in Northern Croatia. It lay in a large area, ten miles by twenty, of what was called "Liberated Territory", well clear of the essential lines of communication. The Germans were pulling out of Greece and Dalmatia and were concerned only with main roads and supply points. They made no attempt now to administer or patrol the hinterland. There was a field near Begoy where aircraft could land unmolested. They did so nearly every week in the summer of 1944 coming from Bari with partisan officials and modest supplies of equipment. In this area congregated a number of men and women who called themselves the Praesidium of the Federal Republic of Croatia. There was even a Minister of Fine Arts. The peasants worked their land undisturbed except by requisitions for the support of the politicians. Besides the British Military Mission, there was a villa full of invisible Russians, half a dozen R.A.F. men who managed the landing ground and an inexplicable Australian doctor who had parachuted into the country a year before with orders to instruct the partisans in field hygiene and had wandered about with them ever since rendering first aid. There were also one hundred and eight Jews.

Major Gordon met them on the third day of his residence. He had been given a small farmhouse half a mile outside the town and the services of an interpreter who had lived for some years in the United States and spoke English of a kind. This man, Bakic, was in the secret police. His duty was to keep Major Gordon under close attention and to report every evening at OZNA headquarters. Major Gordon's predecessor had warned him of this man's proclivities, but Major Gordon was sceptical for such things were beyond his experience. Three Slav widows were also attached to the household. They slept in a loft and acted as willing and tireless servants.

After breakfast on the third day Bakic announced to Major Gordon: "Dere's de Jews outside."

"What Jews?"

"Dey been dere two hour, maybe more. I said to wait."

"What do they want?"

"Dey're Jews. I reckon dey always want sometin. Dey want see de British major. I said to wait."

"Well, ask them to come in."

"Dey can't come in. Why, dere's more'n a hundred of dem."

Major Gordon went out and found the farmyard and the lane beyond thronged. There were some children in the crowd, but most seemed old, too old to be the parents, for they were unnaturally aged by their condition. Everyone in Begoy except the peasant women was in rags, but the partisans kept regimental barbers and there was a kind of dignity about their tattered uniforms. The Jews were grotesque in their remnants of bourgeois civility. They showed little trace of racial kinship. There were Semites among them, but the majority were fair, snub-nosed, high-cheek-boned, the descendants of Slav tribes judaized long after the Dispersal. Few of them, probably, now worshipped the God of Israel in the manner of their ancestors.

A low chatter broke out as Major Gordon appeared. Then three leaders came forward, a youngish woman of better appearance than the rest and two crumpled old men. The woman asked him if he spoke French, and when Major Gordon nodded introduced her companions – a grocer from Mostar, a lawyer from Zagreb – and herself – a Viennese, wife of a Hungarian engineer.

Here Bakic roughly interrupted in Serbo-Croat and the three fell humbly and hopelessly silent. He said to Major Gordon: "I tell dese peoples dey better talk Slav. I will speak for dem."

The woman said: "I only speak German and French."

Major Gordon said: "We will speak French. I can't ask you all in. You three had better come and leave the others outside."

Bakic scowled. A chatter broke out in the crowd. Then the three with timid little bows crossed the threshold, carefully wiping their dilapidated boots before treading the rough board floor of the interior.

"I shan't want you, Bakic."

The spy went out to bully the crowd, hustling them out of the farmyard into the lane.

There were only two chairs in Major Gordon's living-room. He took one and invited the woman to use the other. The men huddled behind and then began to prompt her. They spoke to one another in a mixture of German and Serbo-Croat; the lawyer knew a little French; enough to make him listen anxiously to all the woman said, and to interrupt. The grocer gazed steadily at the floor and seemed to take no interest in the proceedings. He was there because he commanded respect and trust among the waiting crowd. He had been in a big way of business with branch stores throughout all the villages of Bosnia.

With a sudden vehemence the woman, Mme. Kanyi, shook off her advisers and began her story. The people outside, she explained, were the survivors of an Italian concentration camp on the island of Rab. Most were Jugo-Slav nationals, but some, like herself, were refugees from Central Europe. She and her husband were on their way to Australia in 1939; their papers were in order; he had a job waiting for him in Brisbane. Then they had been caught by the war.

When the King fled the Ustashi began massacring Jews. The Italians rounded them up and took them to the Adriatic. When Italy surrendered, the partisans for a few weeks held the coast.

They brought the Jews to the mainland, conscripted all who seemed capable of useful work, and imprisoned the rest. Her husband had been attached to the army headquarters as electrician. Then the Germans moved in; the partisans fled, taking the Jews with them. And here they were, a hundred and eight of them, half starving in Begoy.

Major Gordon was not an imaginative man. He saw the complex historical situation in which he participated, quite simply in terms of friends and enemies and the paramount importance of the war-effort. He had nothing against Jews and nothing against communists. He wanted to defeat the Germans and go home. Here it seemed were a lot of tiresome civilians getting in the way of this object. He said cheerfully: "Well, I congratulate you."

Mme. Kanyi looked up quickly to see if he were mocking her, found that he was not, and continued to regard him now with sad, blank wonder.

"After all," he continued, "you're among friends."

"Yes," she said, too doleful for irony, "we heard that the British and Americans were friends of the partisans. It is true, then?"

"Of course it's true. Why do you suppose I am here?"

"It is not true that the British and Americans are coming to take over the country?"

"First I've heard of it."

"But it is well known that Churchill is a friend of the Jews."

"I'm sorry, madam, but I simply do not see what the Jews have got to do with it."

"But we are Jews. One hundred and eight of us."

"Well, what do you expect me to do about that?"

"We want to go to Italy. We have relations there, some of us. There is an organization at Bari. My husband and I had our papers to go to Brisbane. Only get us to Italy and we shall be no more trouble. We cannot live as we are here. When winter comes we shall all die. We hear aeroplanes almost every night. Three aeroplanes could take us all. We have no luggage left."

"My dear madam, those aeroplanes are carrying essential war

equipment, they are taking out wounded and officials. I'm very sorry you are having a hard time, but so are plenty of other people in this country. It won't last long now. We've got the Germans on the run. I hope by Christmas to be in Zagreb."

"We must say nothing against the partisans?"

"Not to me. Look here, let me give you a cup of cocoa. Then I have work to do."

He went to the window and called to Bakic for cocoa and biscuits. While it was coming the lawyer said in English: "We were better in Rab." Then suddenly all three broke into a chatter of polyglot complaint, about their house, about their property which had been stolen, about their rations. If Churchill knew he would have them sent to Italy. Major Gordon said: "If it was not for the partisans you would now be in the hands of the Nazis," but that word had no terror for them now. They shrugged hopelessly.

One of the widows brought in a tray of cups and a tin of biscuits. "Help yourselves," said Major Gordon.

"How many, please, may we take?"

"Oh, two or three."

With tense self-control each took three biscuits, watching the others to see they did not disgrace the meeting by greed. The grocer whispered to Mme. Kanyi and she explained: "He says will you excuse him if he keeps one for a friend?" The man had tears in his eyes as he snuffed his cocoa; once he had handled sacks of the stuff.

They rose to go. Mme. Kanyi made a last attempt to attract his sympathy. "Will you please come and see the place where they have put us?"

"I am sorry, madam, it simply is not my business. I am a military liaison officer, nothing more."

They thanked him humbly and profusely for the cocoa and left the house. Major Gordon saw them in the farmyard disputing. The men seemed to think Mme. Kanyi had mishandled the affair. Then Bakic hustled them out. Major Gordon saw the crowd close round them and then move off down the lane in a babel of explanation and reproach.

II

There were thermal springs at Begoy. The little town had
come into being about them. Never a fashionable spa, it had
attracted genuine invalids of modest means from all over the
Hapsburg Empire. Serbian rule changed it very little. Until 1940
it retained its Austrian style; now the place was ravaged. Partisans
and Ustashi had fought there, or, rather, each in turn had fired it
and fled. Most houses were gutted and the occupants camped
in basements or improvised shelters. Major Gordon's normal
routine did not take him into the town, for the officials and
military were in farmhouses like his own on the outskirts, but
he daily frequented the little park and public gardens. These had
been charmingly laid out sixty years before and were, surprisingly, still kept in order by two old gardeners who had stayed on
quietly weeding and pruning while the streets were in flames
and noisy with machine-gun fire. There were winding paths
and specimen trees, statuary, a bandstand, a pond with carp
and exotic ducks, and the ornamental cages of what had once
been a little zoo. The gardeners kept rabbits in one of these, fowls
in another, a red squirrel in a third. The partisans had shown a
peculiar solicitude for these gardens; they had cut a bed in the
centre of the principal lawn in the shape of the Soviet star and
had shot a man whom they caught chopping a rustic seat for
firewood. Above the gardens lay a slope wooded with chestnut
and full of paths carefully graded for the convalescent with
kiosks every kilometre, where once postcards and coffee and
medicinal water had been on sale. Here for an hour a day in
the soft autumn sunshine Major Gordon could forget the war.
More than once on his walks there he met Mme. Kanyi, saluted
her, and smiled.

Then, after a week, he received a signal from his headquarters
in Bari saying: *Unrra research team require particulars displaced persons
Jugo-Slavia stop report any your district*. He replied: *One hundred and
eight Jews*. Next day (there was wireless communication for only
two hours daily): *Expedite details Jews names nationality conditions*. So
his duty took him away from the gardens into the streets where

the lime trees still flourished between the stucco shells. He passed ragged, swaggering partisans, all young, some scarcely more than children; girls in battle dress, bandaged, bemedalled, girdled with grenades, squat, chaste, cheerful, sexless, barely human, who had grown up in mountain bivouacs, singing patriotic songs, arm-in-arm along the pavements where a few years earlier rheumatics had crept with parasols and light, romantic novels.

The Jews lived in a school near the ruined church. Bakic led him there. They found the house in half darkness for the glass had all gone from the windows and been replaced with bits of wood and tin collected from other ruins. There was no furniture. The inmates for the most part lay huddled in little nests of straw and rags. As Major Gordon and Bakic entered they roused themselves, got to their feet and retreated towards the walls and darker corners, some raising their fists in salute, others hugging bundles of small possessions. Bakic called one of them forward and questioned him roughly in Serbo-Croat.

"He says de others gone for firewood. Dese ones sick. What you want me tell em?"

"Say that the Americans in Italy want to help them. I have come to make a report on what they need."

The announcement brought them volubly to life. They crowded round, were joined by others from other parts of the house until Major Gordon stood surrounded by thirty or more all asking for things, asking frantically for whatever came first to mind – a needle, a lamp, butter, soap, a pillow; for remote dreams – a passage to Telaviv, an aeroplane to New York, news of a sister last seen in Bucharest, a bed in a hospital.

"You see dey all want somepin different, and dis is only a half of dem."

For twenty minutes or so Major Gordon remained, overpowered, half-suffocated. Then he said: "Well, I think we've seen enough. I shan't get much further in this crowd. Before we can do anything we've got to get them organized. They must make out their own list. I wish we could find that Hungarian woman who talked French. She made some sense."

Bakic inquired and reported: "She don't live here. Her

husband works on the electric light so dey got a house to dem-
selves in de park."

"Well, let's get out of here and try to find her."

They left the house and emerged into the fresh air and
sunshine and the singing companies of young warriors. Major
Gordon breathed gratefully. This was the world he understood,
arms, an army, allies, an enemy, injuries given and taken honourably. Very high above them a huge force of minute shining
bombers hummed across the sky in perfect formation on its daily
route from Foggia to somewhere east of Vienna.

"There they go again," he said. "I wouldn't care to be under-
neath when they unload."

It was one of his duties to impress the partisans with the might
of their allies, with the great destruction and slaughter on distant
fields which would one day, somehow, bring happiness here
where they seemed forgotten. He delivered a little statistical
lecture to Bakic about block-busters and pattern-bombing. But
another part of his mind was all the time slowly being set in
motion. He had seen something entirely new, which needed new
eyes to see clearly: humanity in the depths, misery of quite
another order from anything he had guessed before. He was as
yet not conscious of terror or pity. His steady Scottish mind
would take some time to assimilate the experience.

III

They found the Kanyis' house. It was a tool shed hidden by
shrubs from the public park. A single room, an earth floor, a bed,
a table, a dangling electric globe; compared with the schoolhouse, a place of delicious comfort and privacy. Major Gordon
did not see the interior that afternoon for Mme. Kanyi was
hanging washing on a line outside, and she led him away from
the hut, saying that her husband was asleep. "He was up all night
and did not come home until nearly midday. There was a breakdown at the plant."

"Yes," said Major Gordon, "I had to go to bed in the dark at
nine."

"It is always breaking. It is quite worn out. He cannot get the proper fuel. And all the cables are rotten. The General does not understand and blames him for everything. Often he is out all night."

Major Gordon dismissed Bakic and talked about U.N.R.R.A. Mme. Kanyi did not react in the same way as the wretches in the schoolhouse; she was younger and better fed and therefore more hopeless. "What can they do for us?" she asked. "How can they? Why should they? We are of no importance. You told us so yourself. You must see the Commissar," she said. "Otherwise he will think there is some plot going on. We can do nothing, accept nothing, without the Commissar's permission. You will only make more trouble for us."

"But at least you can produce the list they want in Bari."

"Yes, if the Commissar says so. Already my husband has been questioned about why I have talked to you. He was very much upset. The General was beginning to trust him. Now they think he is connected with the British, and last night the lights failed when there was an important conference. It is better that you do nothing except through the Commissar. I know these people. My husband works with them."

"You have rather a privileged position with them."

"Do you believe that for that reason I do not want to help my people?"

Some such thoughts had passed through Major Gordon's mind. Now he paused, looked at Mme. Kanyi and was ashamed. "No," he said.

"I suppose it would be natural to think so," said Mme. Kanyi gravely. "It is not always true that suffering makes people unselfish. But sometimes it is."

Major Gordon returned to his quarters in a reflective mood that was unusual to him.

IV

The partisans were nocturnal in their habits. They slept late in the mornings, idled about at midday smoking, ate in the early afternoon, and then towards sundown seemed to come alive. Most of their conferences took place after dark.

That evening Major Gordon was thinking of going to bed when he was summoned to the General. He and Bakic stumbled along cart tracks to the villa which housed the general staff. They found the General, his second-in-command, the Commissar, and the old lawyer who was called the Minister of the Interior.

Most meetings in this room were concerned with supplies. The General would submit a detailed, exorbitant list of immediate requirements – field artillery, boots, hospital equipment, wireless apparatus – and so forth. They worked on the principle of asking for everything and item by item reducing their demands to practicable size. In these tedious negotiations Major Gordon enjoyed the slight advantage of being the giver and the final judge of what was reasonable; all the partisans could do was dissipate any sense he might have of vicarious benefaction. He always left feeling a skinflint. Formal politeness was maintained and sometimes even a faint breath of cordiality.

To-night, however, the atmosphere was entirely changed. The General and the Commissar had served together in Spain, the second-in-command was a professional officer from the Royal Jugo-Slav Army, the Minister of the Interior was a nonentity introduced to give solemnity to the occasion. They sat round the table. Bakic stood in the background. His place as interpreter was taken by a young communist of undefined position whom Major Gordon had met once or twice before at headquarters. He spoke excellent English.

"The General wishes to know why you went to visit the Jews to-day."

"I was acting on orders from my headquarters."

"The General does not understand how the Jews are the concern of the Military Mission."

Major Gordon attempted an explanation of the aims and organization of U.N.R.R.A. He did not know a great deal about them and had no great respect for the members he had met, but he did his best. General and Commissar conferred.

Then: "The Commissar says if those measures will take place after the war, what are they doing now?"

Major Gordon described the need for planning. U.N.R.R.A. must know what quantities of seed corn, bridge-building materials, rolling stock and so on were needed to put ravaged countries on their feet.

"The Commissar does not understand how this concerns the Jews."

Major Gordon spoke of the millions of displaced persons all over Europe who must be returned to their homes.

"The Commissar says that is an internal matter."

"So is bridge-building."

"The Commissar says bridge-building is a good thing."

"So is helping displaced persons."

Commissar and General conferred. "The General says any questions of internal affairs should be addressed to the Minister of the Interior."

"Tell him that I am very sorry if I have acted incorrectly. I merely wished to save everyone trouble. I was sent a question by my superiors. I did my best to answer it in the simplest way. May I now request the Minister of the Interior to furnish me with a list of the Jews?"

"The General is glad that you understand that you have acted incorrectly."

"Will the Minister of the Interior be so kind as to make the list for me?"

"The General does not understand why a list is needed."

And so it began again. They talked for an hour. At length Major Gordon lost patience and said: "Very well. Am I to report that you refuse all co-operation with Unrra?"

"We will co-operate in all necessary matters."

"But with regard to the Jews?"

"It must be decided by the Central Government whether that is a necessary matter."

At length they parted. On the way home Bakic said: "Dey mighty sore with you, Major. What for you make trouble with dese Jews?"

"Orders," said Major Gordon, and before going to bed drafted a signal: "*Jews condition now gravely distressed will become desperate winter stop Local authorities unco-operative stop Only hope higher level.*"

A fortnight passed. Three aeroplanes landed, delivered their loads and took off. The R.A.F. officer said: "There won't be many more of these trips. They usually get snow by the end of October."

The partisans punctiliously checked all supplies and never failed to complain of their quantity or quality.

Major Gordon did not forget the Jews. Their plight oppressed him on his daily walks in the gardens, where the leaves were now falling fast and burning smokily in the misty air. The Jews were numbered, very specially, among his allies and the partisans lapsed from his friendship. He saw them now as a part of the thing he had set out hopefully to fight in the days when there had been a plain, unequivocal issue between right and wrong. Uppermost in his conscious mind was resentment against the General and Commissar for their reprimand. By such strange entrances does compassion sometimes slip, disguised, into the human heart.

At the end of the fortnight he was elated to receive the signal: "*Central Government approves in principle evacuation Jews stop Dispatch two repeat two next plane discuss problem with Unrra.*"

Major Gordon went with this signal to the Minister of the Interior who was lying in bed drinking weak tea. Bakic explained, "He's sick and don't know nothing. You better talk to de Commissar."

The Commissar confirmed that he had received instructions.

"I suggest we send the Kanyis."

"He say, why de Kanyis?"

"Because they make most sense."

"Pardon me?"

"Because they seem the most responsible pair."

"De Commissar says, responsible for what?"

"They are the best able to put their case sensibly."

A long discussion followed between the Commissar and Bakic. "He won't send de Kanyis."

"Why not?"

"Kanyi got plenty work with de dynamo."

So another pair was chosen and sent to Bari, the grocer and the lawyer who had first called on him. Major Gordon saw them off. They seemed stupefied and sat huddled among bundles and blankets on the airfield during the long wait. Only when the aeroplane was actually there, illumined by the long line of bon-fires lit to guide it, did they both suddenly break into tears. When Major Gordon held out his hand to them, they bent and kissed it.

Two days later Bari signalled: "*Receive special flight four Dakotas 1130 hrs tonight stop dispatch all Jews.*" In a mood of real joy Major Gordon set about making the arrangements.

V

The landing-strip was eight miles from the town. Before dusk the procession started. Some had somehow contrived to hire peasant carts. Most went on foot, bowed and laden. At ten o'clock Major Gordon drove out and found them, a dark mass, on the embankment of what had once been a railway. Most were asleep. There was mist on the ground. He said to the Squadron Leader: "Is this going to lift?"

"It's been getting thicker for the last hour."

"Will they be able to land?"

"Not a chance."

"We'd better get these people home."

"Yes, I'm just sending the cancellation signal now."

Major Gordon could not bear to wait. He drove back alone but could not rest; hours later, he went out and waited in the mist at the junction of lane and road until the weary people hobbled past into the town.

Twice in the next three weeks the grim scene was repeated. On the second occasion the fires were lit, the aeroplanes were overhead and could be heard circling, recircling and at length heading west again. That evening, Major Gordon prayed: "Please God make it all right. You've done things like that before. Just make the mist clear. Please God help these people." But the sound of the engines dwindled and died away, and the hopeless Jews stirred themselves and set off again on the way they had come.

That week came the first heavy fall of snow. There would be no more landing until the spring.

Major Gordon despaired of doing anything for the Jews, but powerful forces were at work on their behalf in Bari. He soon received a signal: "*Expect special drop shortly relief supplies for Jews stop Explain partisan HQ these supplies only repeat only for distribution Jews.*" He called on the General with this communication.

"What supplies?"

"I presume food and clothing and medicine."

"For three months I have been asking for these things for my men. The Third Corps have no boots. In the hospital they are operating without anaesthetics. Last week we had to withdraw from two forward positions because there were no rations."

"I know. I have signalled about it repeatedly."

"Why is there food and clothes for the Jews and not for my men?"

"I cannot explain. All I have come to ask is whether you can guarantee distribution."

"I will see."

Major Gordon signalled: "*Respectfully submit most injudicious discriminate in favour of Jews stop Will endeavour secure proportionate share for them of general relief supplies,*" and received in answer: "*Three aircraft will drop Jewish supplies point C 1130 hrs 21st stop These supplies from private source not military stop Distribute according previous signal.*"

On the afternoon of the 21st the Squadron Leader came to see Major Gordon.

"What's the idea?" he said. "I've just been having the hell of a schemozzle with the Air Liaison comrade about to-night's drop. He wants the stuff put in bond or something till he gets orders from higher up. He's a reasonable sort of chap usually. I've never seen him on such a high horse. Wanted everything checked in the presence of the Minister of the Interior and put under joint guard. Never heard such a lot of rot. I suppose someone at Bari has been playing at politics as usual."

That night the air was full of parachutes and of "free-drops" whistling down like bombs. The Anti-Fascist Youth retrieved them. They were loaded on carts, taken to a barn near the General's headquarters and formally impounded.

VI

The war in Jugo-Slavia took a new turn. The first stage of German withdrawal was complete; they stood now on a line across Croatia and Slovenia. Marshal Tito flew from Vis to join the Russian and Bulgarian columns in Belgrade. A process of reprisal began in the "liberated" areas. The Germans remained twenty miles to the north of Begoy, but behind nothing except snow now closed the road to Dalmatia. Major Gordon took part in many Victory Celebrations. But he did not forget the Jews; nor did their friends at Bari. In mid-December Bakic one day announced: "De Jews again", and going out into the yard Major Gordon found it full of his former visitors, but now transformed into a kind of farcical army. All of them, men and women, wore military greatcoats, Balaclava helmets, and knitted woollen gloves. Orders had been received from Belgrade, and distribution of the stores had suddenly taken place, and here were the recipients to thank him. The spokesmen were different on this occasion. The grocer and lawyer had disappeared for ever. Madame Kanyi kept away for reasons of her own; an old man made a longish speech which Bakic rendered "Dis guy say dey's all very happy."

For the next few days a deplorable kind of ostentation seemed to possess the Jews. A curse seemed to have been lifted. They appeared everywhere, trailing the skirts of their greatcoats in the snow, stamping their huge new boots, gesticulating with their gloved hands. Their faces shone with soap, they were full of Spam and dehydrated fruits. They were a living psalm. And then, as suddenly, they disappeared.

"What has happened to them?"

"I guess dey been moved some other place," said Bakic.

"Why?"

"People make trouble for them."

"Who?"

"Partisan people dat hadn't got no coats and boots. Dey make trouble wid de Commissar so de Commissar move dem on last night."

Major Gordon had business with the Commissar. The Anti-Fascist Theatre Group was organizing a Liberation Concert and had politely asked him to supply words and music of English anti-fascist songs, so that all the allies would be suitably represented. Major Gordon had to explain that his country had no anti-fascist songs and no patriotic songs that anyone cared to sing. The Commissar noted this further evidence of Western decadence with grim satisfaction. For once there was no need to elaborate. The Commissar understood. It was just as he had been told years before in Moscow. It had been the same thing in Spain. The Attlee Brigade would never sing.

When the business was over Major Gordon said: "I see the Jews have moved."

Bakic was left outside nowadays, and the intellectual young man acted as interpreter. Without consulting his chief he answered: "Their house was required for the Ministry of Rural Economy. New quarters have been found for them a few miles away."

The Commissar asked what was being said, grunted and rose. Major Gordon saluted and the interview was at an end. On the steps the young interpreter joined him.

"The question of the Jews, Major Gordon. It was necessary for them to go. Our people could not understand why they should have special treatment. We have partisan women who work all day and have no boots or overcoats. How are we to explain that these old people who are doing nothing for our cause, should have such things?"

"Perhaps by saying that they *are* old and *have* no cause. Their need is greater than a young enthusiast's."

"Besides, Major Gordon, they were trying to make business. They were bartering the things they had been given. My parents are Jewish and I understand these people. They want always to make some trade."

"Well, what's wrong with that?"

"War is not a time for trade."

"Well, anyway, I hope they have decent quarters."

"They have what is suitable."

VII

The gardens in winter seemed smaller than they had done in full leaf. You could see right through them from fence to fence; snow obliterated lawns and beds; the paths were only traceable by boot-prints. Major Gordon daily took a handful of broken biscuits to the squirrel and fed him through the bars. One day while he was thus engaged, watching the little creature go through the motions of concealment, cautiously return, grasp the food, jump away and once more perform the mime of digging and covering, he saw Mme. Kanyi approach down the path. She was carrying a load of brushwood, stooping under it, so that she did not see him until she was quite close.

Major Gordon was particularly despondent that day for he had just received a signal for recall. The force was being re-named and re-organized. He was to report as soon as feasible to Bari. Major Gordon was confident that word had come from Belgrade that he was no longer *persona grata*.

He greeted Mme. Kanyi with warm pleasure. "Let me carry that."

"No, please. It is better not."

"I insist."

Mme. Kanyi looked about her. No one was in sight. She let Major Gordon take the load and carry it towards her hut.

"You have not gone with the others?"

"No, my husband is needed."

"And you don't wear your greatcoat."

"Not out of doors. I wear it at night in the hut. The coats and boots make everyone hate us, even those who had been kind before."

"But partisan discipline is so firm. Surely there was no danger of violence?"

"No, that was not the trouble. It was the peasants. The partisans are frightened of the peasants. They will settle with them later, but at present they are dependent on them for food. Our people began to exchange things with the peasants. They would give needles and thread, razors, things no one can get, for turkeys and apples. No one wants money. The peasants preferred bartering with our people to taking the partisans' bank-notes. That was what made the trouble."

"Where have the others gone?"

She spoke a name which meant nothing to Major Gordon. "You have not heard of that place? It is twenty miles away. It is where the Germans and Ustashi made a camp. They kept the Jews and gypsies and communists and royalists there, to work on the canal. Before they left they killed what were left of the prisoners – not many. Now the partisans have found new inhabitants for it."

They had reached the hut and Major Gordon entered to place his load in a corner near the little stove. It was the first and last time he crossed the threshold. He had a brief impression of orderly poverty and then was outside in the snow. "Listen, Mme. Kanyi," he said. "Don't lose heart. I am being recalled to Bari. As soon as the road is clear I shall be leaving. When I get there I promise I'll raise Cain about this. You've plenty of friends there and I'll explain the whole situation to them. We'll get you all out, I promise."

Major Gordon had one further transaction with Mme. Kanyi before his departure. There fell from the heavens one night a huge parcel of assorted literature – the gift of one of the more preposterous organizations which abounded in Bari. This department aimed at re-educating the Balkans by distributing *Fortune, The Illustrated London News* and handbooks of popular, old-fashioned agnosticism. From time to time during Major Gordon's tour of duty bundles of this kind had arrived. He had hitherto deposited them in the empty office of the Director of Rest and Culture. On this last occasion, however, he thought of Mme. Kanyi. She had a long, lonely winter ahead of her. She might find something amusing in the pile. So he despatched it to her by one of the widows, who finding her out, left it on the step in the snow. Then within a few days the road to the coast was declared open and Major Gordon laboriously made his way to Split and so to Bari.

VIII

Bari had much besides the bones of St. Nicholas. Those who were quartered there complained but they constituted the Mont Parnasse of the Allied Armies. One met more queer old friends in its messes and clubs than anywhere else in the world at this last stage of the war, and to those on leave from the Balkans its modest amenities seemed the height of luxury. But Major Gordon, during his fortnight of "reporting to headquarters" had deeper interests than on earlier leaves. He was determined to get the Jews out of Croatia and by dint of exploring the by-ways of semi-official life, of visiting committees and units with non-committal designations in obscure offices, he was in fact able to quicken interest, supply detailed information and in the end set the official machine to work which eventually resulted in a con-voy of new Ford trucks making the journey from the coast to Begoy and back for the sole and specific purpose of rescuing the Jews.

By the time that they arrived in Italy Major Gordon was back in Jugo-Slavia for a brief appointment as liaison with a camp of escaped prisoners of war, but he got news of the move and for the first time tasted the sweet and heady cup of victory. "At least I've done something worthwhile in this bloody war," he said.

When next he passed through Bari it was on his way home to England, for the military mission was being wound up and replaced by regular diplomatic and consular officials. He had not forgotten his Jews, however, and, having with difficulty located them, drove out to a camp near Lecce, in a flat country of olive and almond and white beehive huts. Here they rested, part of a collection of four or five hundred, all old and all baffled, all in army greatcoats and Balaclava helmets.

"I can't see the point of their being here," said the

Commandant. "We feed them and doctor them and house them. That's all we can do. No one wants them. The Zionists are only interested in the young. I suppose they'll just sit here till they die."

"Are they happy?"

"They complain the hell of a lot but then they've got quite a lot to complain about. It's a lousy place to be stuck in."

"I'm particularly interested in a pair called Kanyi."

The Commandant looked down his list. "No trace of them here."

"Good. That probably means they got off to Australia all right."

"Not from here, old man. I've been here all along. No one has ever left."

"Could you make sure? Anyone in the Begoy draft would know about them."

The Commandant sent his interpreter to inquire while he took Major Gordon into the shed he called his mess, and gave him a drink. Presently the man returned. "All correct, sir. The Kanyis never left Begoy. They got into some kind of trouble there and were jugged."

"May I go with the interpreter and ask about it?"

"By all means, old man. But aren't you making rather heavy weather of it? What do two more or less matter?"

Major Gordon went into the compound with the interpreter. Some of the Jews recognized him and crowded round with complaints and petitions. All he could learn about the Kanyis was that they had been taken off the truck by the partisan police just as it was about to start.

He had one more day in Bari before his flight home. He spent it revisiting the offices where he had begun his work of liberation. But this time he received little sympathy. "We don't really want to bother the Jugs any more. They really co-operated very well about the whole business. Besides the war's over now in that part. There's no particular point in moving people out. We're busy at the moment moving people in." This man was in fact at that moment busy despatching royalist officers to certain execution.

The Jewish office showed no interest when they understood that he had not come to sell them illicit arms. "We must first set up the State," they said. "Then it will be a refuge for all. First things first."

So Major Gordon returned to England unsatisfied and he might never have heard any more of the matter, had he not a cousin in the newly reopened Ministry at Belgrade. Months later he heard from him: *"I've been to a lot of trouble and made myself quite unpopular in getting information about the couple you're interested in. The Jugs are very close but at last I got matey with the head of the police who wants us to return some refugees we've got in our zone in Austria. He dug out the file for me. Both were condemned by a Peoples' Court and executed. The man had committed sabotage on the electric light plant. The woman had been a spy for a "foreign power". Apparently she was the mistress of a foreign agent who frequented her house while the husband was busy destroying the dynamo. A lot of foreign propaganda publications were found in her house and produced as evidence. What very unsavoury friends you seem to have."*

It so happened that this letter arrived on the day when the Allies were celebrating the end of the war in Asia. Major Gordon was back with his regiment. He did not feel inclined to go out that evening and join in the rejoicing. The mess was empty save for the misanthropic second-in-command and the chaplain (although of Highland origin the regiment was full of Glasgow Irish and had a Benedictine monk attached to them).

The second-in-command spoke as he had spoken most evenings since the General Election.... "I don't know what they mean by 'Victory'. We start the bloody war for Poland. Well that's ceased to exist. We fight it in Burma and Egypt – and you can bet your boots we shall give them up in a few months to the very fellows who've been against us. We spent millions knocking Germany down and now we shall spend millions building it up again...."

"Don't you think, perhaps, people feel better than they did in 1938?" said the chaplain.

"No," said the second-in-command.

"They haven't got rid of that unhealthy sense of guilt they had?"

"No," said Major Gordon. "I never had it before. Now I have."

And he told the story of the Kanyis. "Those are the real horrors of war − not just people having their legs blown off," he concluded. "How do you explain that, padre?"

There was no immediate answer until the second-in-command said: "You did all you could. A darn sight more than most people would have done."

"That's your answer," said the chaplain. "You mustn't judge actions by their apparent success. Everything you did was good in itself."

"A fat lot of good it did the Kanyis."

"No. But don't you think it just possible that *they* did *you* good? No suffering need ever be wasted. It is just as much part of Charity to receive cheerfully as to give."

"Well, if you're going to start preaching a sermon, padre," said the second-in-command, "I'm off to bed."

"I'd like you to tell me a bit more about that," said Major Gordon.

BOOK REVIEWS

'Book Reviews' (column head cartoon), *The Cherwell*, 15 August 1923, p. 59 and thereafter.

LOVE
AMONG
THE RUINS

A. CANOVA ET E. WAUGH FEC RUNT

LOVE AMONG
THE RUINS

A ROMANCE OF
THE NEAR FUTURE

BY

Evelyn Waugh

WITH DECORATIONS BY VARIOUS
EMINENT HANDS INCLUDING
THE AUTHOR'S

MCMLXII
CHAPMAN & HALL
LONDON

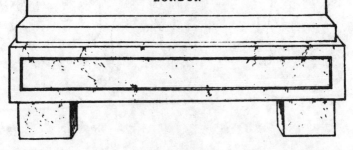

LOVE AMONG THE RUINS

A Romance of the Near Future

I

DESPITE THEIR promises at the last Election, the politicians had not yet changed the climate. The State Meteorological Institute had so far produced only an unseasonable fall of snow and two little thunderbolts no larger than apricots. The weather varied from day to day and from county to county as it had done of old, most anomalously.

This was a rich, old-fashioned Tennysonian night.

Strains of a string quartet floated out from the drawing-room windows and were lost amid the splash and murmur of the gardens. In the basin the folded lilies had left a brooding sweetness over the water. No gold fin winked in the porphyry font and any peacock which seemed to be milkily drooping in the moon-shadows was indeed a ghost, for the whole flock of them had been found mysteriously and rudely slaughtered a day or two ago in the first disturbing flush of this sudden summer.

Miles, sauntering among the sleeping flowers, was suffused with melancholy. He did not much care for music and this was his last evening at Mountjoy. Never again, perhaps, would he be free to roam these walks.

Mountjoy had been planned and planted in the years of which he knew nothing; generations of skilled and patient husbandmen had weeded and dunged and pruned; generations of dilettanti had watered it with cascades and jets; generations of collectors had lugged statuary here; all, it seemed, for his enjoyment this very night under this huge moon. Miles knew nothing of such periods and processes, but he felt an incomprehensible tidal pull towards the circumjacent splendours.

Eleven struck from the stables. The music ceased. Miles turned back and, as he reached the terrace, the shutters began to close and the great chandeliers were one by one extinguished.

By the light of the sconces which still shone on their panels of faded satin and clouded gold, he joined the company dispersing to bed through the islands of old furniture.

His room was not one of the grand succession which lay along the garden front. Those were reserved for murderers. Nor was it on the floor above, tenanted mostly by sexual offenders. His was a humbler wing. Indeed he overlooked the luggage porch and the coal bunker. Only professional men visiting Mountjoy on professional business and very poor relations had been put here in the old days. But Miles was attached to this room, which was the first he had ever called his own in all his twenty years of Progress.

His next-door neighbour, a Mr. Sweat, paused at his door to say good-night. It was only now after twenty months' proximity, when Miles's time was up, that this veteran had begun to unbend. He and a man named Soapy, survivals of another age, had kept themselves to themselves, talking wistfully of cribs they had cracked, of sparklers, of snug bar-parlours where they had met their favourite fences, of strenuous penal days at the Scrubs and on the Moor. They had small use for the younger generation; crime, calvinism and classical music were their interests. But at last Mr. Sweat had taken to nodding, to grunting, and finally, too late for friendship, to speaking to Miles.

"What price the old strings tonight, chum?" he asked.

"I wasn't there, Mr. Sweat."

"You missed a treat. Of course nothing's ever good enough for old Soapy. Made me fair sick to hear Soapy going on all the time. The viola was scratchy, Soapy says. They played the Mozart just like it was Haydn. No feeling in the Debussy pizzicato, says Soapy."

"Soapy knows too much."

"Soapy knows a lot more than some I could mention, schooling or no schooling. Next time they're going to do the Grosse Fugue as the last movement of the B flat. That's something to look forward to, that is, though Soapy says no late Beethoven comes off. We'll see. Leastways, me and Soapy will; *you* won't. You're off tomorrow. Pleased?"

"Not particularly."

"No, no more wouldn't I be. It's a funny thing but I've settled down here wonderful. Never thought I should. It all seemed a bit too posh at first. Not like the old Scrubs. But it's a real pretty place once you're used to it. Wouldn't mind settling here for a lifer if they'd let me. The trouble is there's no security in crime these days. Time was, you knew just what a job was worth, six months, three years; whatever it was, you knew where you were. Now what with prison commissioners and Preventative Custody and Corrective Treatment they can keep you in or push you out just as it suits them. It's not right.

"I'll tell you what it is, chum," continued Mr. Sweat. "There's no understanding of crime these days like what there was. I remember when I was a nipper, the first time I came up before the beak, he spoke up straight: 'My lad,' he says, 'you are embarking upon a course of life that can only lead to disaster and degradation in this world and everlasting damnation in the next.' Now that's talking. It's plain sense and it shows a personal interest. But last time I was up, when they sent me here, they called me an 'antisocial phenomenon'; said I was 'maladjusted'. That's no way to speak of a man what was doing time before they was in long trousers, now is it?"

"They said something of the same kind to me."

"Yes and now they're giving you the push, just like you hadn't no Rights. I tell you it's made a lot of the boys uncomfortable your going out all of a sudden like this. Who'll it be next time, that's what we're wondering?

"I tell you where you went wrong, chum. You didn't give enough trouble. You made it too easy for them to say you was cured. Soapy and me got wise to that. You remember them birds as got done in? That was Soapy and me. They took a lot of killing too; powerful great bastards. But we got the evidence all hid away tidy and if there's ever any talk of me and Soapy being 'rehabilitated' we'll lay it out conspicuous.

"Well, so long, chum. Tomorrow's my morning for Remedial Repose so I daresay you'll be off before I get down. Come back soon."

"I hope so," said Miles and turned alone into his own room.

He stood briefly at the window and gazed his last on the
cobbled-yard. He made a good figure of a man, for he came of
handsome parents and all his life had been carefully fed and
doctored and exercised; well clothed too. He wore the drab
serge dress that was the normal garb of the period – only certified
homosexuals wore colours – but there were differences of fit and
condition among these uniforms. Miles displayed the handiwork
of tailor and valet. He belonged to a privileged class.

The State had made him.

No clean-living, God-fearing, Victorian gentleman, he; no
complete man of the renaissance; no gentil knight nor dutiful
pagan nor, even, noble savage. All that succession of past
worthies had gone its way, content to play a prelude to Miles.
He was the Modern Man.

His history, as it appeared in multuplet in the filing cabinets of
numberless State departments, was typical of a thousand others.
Before his birth the politicians had succeeded in bringing down
his father and mother to penury; they, destitute, had thrown
themselves into the simple diversions of the very poor and thus,
between one war and the next, set in motion a chain-reaction of
divorces which scattered them and their various associates in
forlorn couples all over the Free World. The aunt on whom the
infant Miles had been quartered was conscripted for work in a
factory and shortly afterwards died of boredom at the conveyer-
belt. The child was put to safety in an Orphanage.

Huge sums were thenceforward spent upon him; sums which,
fifty years earlier, would have sent whole quiversful of boys to
Winchester and New College and established them in the learned
professions. In halls adorned with Picassos and Legers he yawned
through long periods of Constructive Play. He never lacked the
requisite cubic feet of air. His diet was balanced and on the first
Friday of every month he was psychoanalysed. Every detail of
his adolescence was recorded and microfilmed and filed, until at
the appropriate age he was transferred to the Air Force.

There were no aeroplanes at the station to which he was
posted. It was an institution to train instructors to train instructors to train instructors in Personal Recreation.

There for some weeks he tended a dish-washing machine and tended it, as his adjutant testified at his trial, in an exemplary fashion. The work in itself lacked glory, but it was the normal novitiate. Men from the Orphanages provided the hard core of the Forces, a caste apart which united the formidable qualities of Janissary and Junker. Miles had been picked early for high command. Dish-washing was only the beginning. The adjutant, an Orphan too, had himself washed both dishes and officers' underclothes, he testified, before rising to his present position.

Courts Martial had been abolished some years before this. The Forces handed their defaulters over to the civil arm for treatment. Miles came up at quarter sessions. It was plain from the start, when Arson, Wilful Damage, Manslaughter, Prejudicial Conduct and Treason were struck out of the Indictment and the whole reduced to a simple charge of Antisocial Activity, that the sympathies of the Court were with the prisoner.

The Station Psychologist gave his opinion that an element of incendiarism was inseparable from adolescence. Indeed, if checked, it might produce morbid neuroses. For his part he thought the prisoner had performed a perfectly normal act and, moreover, had shown more than normal intelligence in its execution.

At this point some widows, mothers and orphans of the incinerated airmen set up an outcry from the public gallery and were sharply reminded from the Bench that this was a Court of Welfare and not a meeting of the Housewives' Union.

The case developed into a concerted eulogy of the accused. An attempt by the prosecution to emphasize the extent of the damage was rebuked from the Bench.

"The jury," he said, "will expunge from their memories these sentimental details which have been most improperly introduced."

"May be a detail to you," said a voice from the gallery. "He was a good husband to me."

"Arrest that woman," said the Judge.

Order was restored and the panegyrics continued.

At last the Bench summed up. He reminded the jury that it was a first principle of the New Law that no man could be held responsible for the consequences of his own acts. The jury must dismiss from their minds the consideration that much valuable property and many valuable lives had been lost and the cause of Personal Recreation gravely retarded. They had merely to decide whether in fact the prisoner had arranged inflammable material at various judiciously selected points in the Institution and had ignited them. If he had done so, and the evidence plainly indicated that he had, he contravened the Standing Orders of the Institution and was thereby liable to the appropriate penalties.

Thus directed the jury brought in a verdict of guilty coupled with a recommendation of mercy towards the various bereaved persons who from time to time in the course of the hearing had been committed for contempt. The Bench reprimanded the jury for presumption and impertinence in the matter of the prisoners held in contempt, and sentenced Miles to residence during the State's pleasure at Mountjoy Castle (the ancestral seat of a maimed V.C. of the Second World War, who had been sent to a Home for the Handicapped when the place was converted into a gaol).

The State was capricious in her pleasures. For nearly two years Miles enjoyed her particular favours. Every agreeable remedial device was applied to him and applied, it was now proclaimed, successfully. Then without warning a few days back, while he lay dozing under a mulberry tree, the unexpected blow had fallen; they had come to him, the Deputy Chief-Guide and the sub-Deputy, and told him bluntly and brutally that he was rehabilitated.

Now on this last night he knew he was to wake tomorrow on a harsh world. Nevertheless he slept and was gently awoken for the last time to the familiar scent of china tea on his bed table, the thin bread and butter, the curtains drawn above the luggage porch, the sunlit kitchen-yard and the stable clock just visible behind the cut-leaf copper beech.

He breakfasted late and alone. The rest of the household were already engaged in the first community-songs of the day. Presently he was called to the Guidance Office.

Since his first day at Mountjoy, when with other entrants Miles had been addressed at length by the Chief Guide on the Aims and Achievements of the New Penology, they had seldom met. The Chief Guide was almost always away addressing penological conferences.

The Guidance Office was the former house-keeper's room stripped now of its plush and patriotic pictures; sadly tricked out instead with standard civil-service equipment, class A.

It was full of people.

"This is Miles Plastic," said the Chief Guide. "Sit down, Miles. You can see from the presence of our visitors this morning what an important occasion this is."

Miles took a chair and looked and saw seated beside the Chief Guide two elderly men whose faces were familiar from the television screen as prominent colleagues in the Coalition Government. They wore open flannel shirts, blazers with numerous pens and pencils protruding from the breast pocket, and baggy trousers. This was the dress of very high politicians.

"The Minister of Welfare and the Minister of Rest and Culture," continued the Chief Guide. "The stars to which we have hitched our waggon. Have the press got the hand-out?"

"Yes, Chief."

"And the photographers are all ready?"

"Yes, Chief."

"Then I can proceed."

He proceeded as he had done at countless congresses, at countless spas and university cities. He concluded, as he always did: "In the New Britain which we are building, there are no criminals. There are only the victims of inadequate social services."

The Minister of Welfare, who had not reached his present eminence without the help of a certain sharpness in debate, remarked: "But I understood that Plastic is from one of our own Orphanages..."

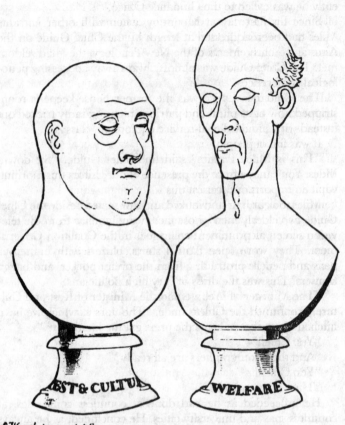

EST & CULTURE

WELFARE

E. Waugh inven et delin.

Coalition

"Plastic is recognized as a Special Case," said the Chief Guide.

The Minister of Rest and Culture, who in the old days had more than once done time himself, said: "Well, Plastic, lad, from all they do say I reckon you've been uncommon smart."

"Exactly," said the Chief Guide. "Miles is our first success, the vindication of the Method."

"Of all the new prisons established in the first glorious wave of Reform, Mountjoy alone has produced a complete case of re-habilitation," the Minister of Welfare said. "You may or may not be aware that the Method has come in for a good deal of criticism both in Parliament and outside. There are a lot of young hot-heads who take their inspiration from our Great Neighbour in the East. You can quote the authorities to them till you're black in the face but they are always pressing for the all latest gadgets of capital and corporal punishment, for chain gangs and solitary confinement, bread and water, the cat-o'-nine-tails, the rope and the block, and all manner of new-fangled nonsense. They think we're a lot of old fogeys. Thank goodness we've still got the solid sense of the people behind us, but we're on the defensive now. We have to show results. That's why we're here this morning. To show them results. *You* are our Result."

These were solemn words and Miles in some measure responded to the occasion. He gazed before him blankly with an expression that might seem to be awe.

"You'd best watch your step now, lad," said the Minister of Rest and Culture.

"Photographs," said the Minister of Welfare. "Yes, shake *my* hand. Turn towards the cameras. Try to smile."

Bulbs flashed all over the dreary little room.

"State be with you," said the Minister of Welfare.

"Give us a paw, lad," said the Minister of Rest and Culture, taking Miles's hand in his turn. "And no funny business, mind."

Then the politicians departed.

"The Deputy-Chief will attend to all the practical matters," said the Chief wearily. "Go and see him now."

Miles went.

"Well, Miles, from now on I must call you Mr. Plastic," said the Deputy-Chief. "In less than a minute you become a Citizen. This little pile of papers is *You*. When I stamp them, Miles the Problem ceases to exist and Mr. Plastic the Citizen is born. We are sending you to Satellite City, the nearest Population Centre, where you will be attached to the Ministry of Welfare as a sub-official. In view of your special training you are not being classi-fied as a Worker. The immediate material rewards, of course, are not as great. But you are definitely in the Service. We have set your foot on the bottom rung of the non-competitive ladder."

The Deputy Chief Guide picked up the rubber stamp and proceeded to his work of creation. Flip-thump, flip-thump the papers were turned and stained.

"There you are, Mr. Plastic," said the Deputy-Chief handing Miles, as it were, the baby.

At last Miles spoke: "What must I do to get back here?" he asked.

"Come, come, you're rehabilitated now, remember. It is your turn to give back to the State some of the service the State has given you. You will report this morning to the Area Progressive. Transport has been laid on. State be with you, Mr. Plastic. Be careful, that's your Certificate of Human Personality you've dropped – a *vital* document."

II

Satellite City, one of a hundred such grand conceptions, was not yet in its teens but already the Dome of Security showed signs of wear. This was the name of the great municipal edifice about which the city was planned. The eponymous dome had looked well enough in the architect's model, shallow certainly but amply making up in girth what it lacked in height, the daring exercise of some new trick of construction. But to the surprise of all, when the building arose and was seen from the ground, the dome blandly vanished. It was hidden for ever among the roofs and butting shoulders of the ancillary wings and was never seen again from the outside except by airmen and steeplejacks. Only the name remained. On the day of its dedication, among massed politicians and People's Choirs the great lump of building materials had shone fine as a factory in all its brilliance of glass and new concrete. Since then, during one of the rather frequent week-ends of international panic, it had been camouflaged and its windows blackened. Cleaners were few and usually on strike. So the Dome of Security remained blotched and dingy, the sole permanent building of Satellite City. There were no workers' flats, no officials' garden suburb, no parks, no playgrounds yet. These were all on the drawing-boards in the surveyor's office, tattered at the edges, ringed by tea cups; their designer long since cremated and his ashes scattered among the docks and nettles. Thus the Dome of Security comprised, even more than had been intended, all the aspirations and amenities of the city.

The officials subsisted in perpetual twilight. Great sheets of glass, planned to "trap" the sun, admitted few gleams from scratches in their coat of tar. At evening when the electric light came on, there was a faint glow, here and there. When, as often, the power-station was "shedding its load" the officials stopped work early and groped their way back to their darkened huts where in the useless refrigerators their tiny rations were quietly putrefying. On working days the officials, male and female,

ΠΑΝΔΑΙΜΟΝΙΑ
CLOSED
DURING
STRIKE.

Canova fec. Moses delin. Waugh perfec.

Exiles from Welfare

trudged through cigarette ends round and round, up and down
what had once been lift-shafts, in a silent, shabby, shadowy
procession.

Among these pilgrims of the dusk, in the weeks that followed
his discharge from Mountjoy, moved the exiled Miles Plastic.

He was in a key department.

Euthanasia had not been part of the original 1945 Health
Service; it was a Tory measure designed to attract votes from
the aged and the mortally sick. Under the Bevan–Eden Coalition
the service came into general use and won instant popularity.
The Union of Teachers was pressing for its application to difficult
children. Foreigners came in such numbers to take advantage of
the service that immigration authorities now turned back the
bearers of single tickets.

Miles recognized the importance of his appointment even
before he began work. On his first evening in the hostel his fellow
sub-officials gathered round to question him.

"Euthanasia? I say, you're in luck. They work you jolly hard,
of course, but it's the one department that's expanding."

"You'll get promoted before you know your way about."

"Great State! You *must* have pull. Only the very bright boys
get posted to Euthanasia."

"I've been in Contraception for five years. It's a blind alley."

"They say that in a year or two Euthanasia will have taken
over Pensions."

"You must be an Orphan."

"Yes, I am."

"That accounts for it. Orphans get all the plums. I had a Full
Family Life, State help me."

It was gratifying, of course, this respect and envy. It was well to
have fine prospects; but for the time being Miles's duties were
humble enough.

He was junior sub-official in a staff of half a dozen. The
Director was an elderly man called Dr. Beamish, a man whose
character had been formed in the nervous '30s, now much
embittered, like many of his contemporaries, by the fulfilment
of his early hopes. He had signed manifestos in his hot youth, had

raised his fist in Barcelona and had painted abstractedly for
Horizon; he had stood beside Spender at great concourses of
Youth, and written "publicity" for the Last Viceroy. Now his
reward had come to him. He held the most envied post in
Satellite City and, sardonically, he was making the worst of it.
Dr. Beamish rejoiced in every attenuation of official difficulties.

Satellite City was said to be the worst served Euthanasia
Centre in the State. Dr. Beamish's patients were kept waiting so
long that often they died natural deaths before he found it
convenient to poison them.

His small staff respected Dr. Beamish. They were all of the
official class, for it was part of the grim little game which Dr.
Beamish played with the higher authorities to economize extravagantly. His department, he maintained, could not, on its present allotment, afford workers. Even the furnace-man and the girl
who despatched unwanted false teeth to the Dental Redistribu-
tion Centre were sub-officials.

Sub-officials were cheap and plentiful. The Universities
turned them out in thousands every year. Indeed, ever since the
Incitement to Industry Act of 1955, which exempted workers
from taxation – that great and popular measure of reform
which had consolidated the now permanent Coalition Government – there had been a nefarious one-way traffic of expensively
State-educated officials "passing", as it was called, into the ranks
of the workers.

Miles's duties required no special skill. Daily at ten the service
opened its doors to welfare-weary citizens. Miles was the man
who opened them, stemmed the too eager rush and admitted the
first half-dozen; then he closed the doors on the waiting multitude until a Higher Official gave the signal for the admission of
another batch.

Once inside they came briefly under his charge; he set them in
order, saw that they did not press ahead of their turn, and
adjusted the television-set for their amusement. A Higher Official
interviewed them, checked their papers and arranged for the
confiscation of their property. Miles never passed the door
through which they were finally one by one conducted. A faint

whiff of cyanide sometimes gave a hint of the mysteries beyond. Meanwhile he swept the waiting-room, emptied the waste-paper basket and brewed tea – a worker's job, for which the refinements of Mountjoy proved a too rich apprenticeship.

In his hostel the same reproductions of Leger and Picasso as had haunted his childhood still stared down on him. At the cinema, to which he could afford, at the best, a weekly visit, the same films as he had seen free at Orphanage, Air Force station and prison, flickered and drawled before him. He was a child of Welfare, strictly schooled to a life of boredom, but he had known better than this. He had known the tranquil melancholy of the gardens at Mountjoy. He had known ecstasy when the Air Force Training School had whirled to the stars in a typhoon of flame. And as he moved sluggishly between Dome and hostel there rang in his ears the words of the old lag: "You didn't give enough trouble."

Then one day, in the least expected quarter, in his own drab department, hope appeared.

Miles later remembered every detail of that morning. It had started in the normal way; rather below normal indeed, for they were reopening after a week's enforced idleness. There had been a strike among the coal-miners and Euthanasia had been at a standstill. Now the necessary capitulations had been signed, the ovens glowed again, and the queue at the patients' entrance stretched halfway round the Dome. Dr. Beamish squinted at the waiting crowd through the periscope and said with some satisfaction: "It will take months to catch up on the waiting list now. We shall have to start making a charge for the service. It's the only way to keep down the demand."

"The Ministry will never agree to that, surely, sir?"

"Damned sentimentalists. My father and mother hanged themselves in their own back-yard with their own clothes-line. Now no one will lift a finger to help himself. There's something wrong in the system, Plastic. There are still rivers to drown in, trains – every now and then – to put your head under; gas-fires in some of the huts. The country is full of the natural resources of death, but everyone has to come to us."

It was not often he spoke so frankly before his subordinates. He had overspent during the week's holiday, drunk too much at his hostel with other unemployed colleagues. Always after a strike the senior officials returned to work in low spirits.

"Shall I let the first batch in, sir?"

"Not for the moment," said Dr. Beamish. "There's a priority case to see first, sent over with a pink chit from Drama. She's in the private waiting-room now. Fetch her in."

Miles went to the room reserved for patients of importance. All one wall was of glass. Pressed to it a girl was standing, turned away from him, looking out at the glum queue below. Miles stood, the light in his eyes, conscious only of a shadow which stirred at the sound of the latch and turned, still a shadow merely but of exquisite grace, to meet him. He stood at the door, momentarily struck silent at this blind glance of beauty. Then he said: "We're quite ready for you now, miss."

The girl came nearer. Miles's eyes adjusted themselves to the light. The shadow took form. The full vision was all that the first glance had hinted; more than all, for every slight movement revealed perfection. One feature only broke the canon of pure beauty; a long, silken, corn-gold beard.

She said, with a deep, sweet tone, all unlike the flat conventional accent of the age: "Let it be quite understood that I don't want anything done to me. I consented to come here. The Director of Drama and the Director of Health were so pathetic about it all that I thought it was the least I could do. I said I was quite willing to hear about your service, but I do *not* want anything *done*."

"Better tell him inside," said Miles.

He led her to Dr. Beamish's room.

"Great State!" said Dr. Beamish, with eyes for the beard alone.

"Yes," she said. "It is a shock, isn't it? I've got used to it by now but I can understand how people feel seeing it for the first time."

"Is it real?"

"Pull."

"It *is* strong. Can't they do anything about it?"

"Oh they've tried everything."

Dr. Beamish was so deeply interested that he forgot Miles's presence. "Klugmann's Operation, I suppose?"

"Yes."

"It does go wrong like that every now and then. They had two or three cases at Cambridge."

"I never wanted it done. I never want anything done. It was the Head of the Ballet. He insists on all the girls being sterilized. Apparently you can never dance really well again after you've had a baby. And I did want to dance really well. Now this is what's happened."

"Yes," said Dr. Beamish. "Yes. They're far too slap-dash. They had to put down those girls at Cambridge, too. There was no cure. Well, we'll attend to you, young lady. Have you any arrangements to make or shall I take you straight away?"

"But I don't want to be put down. I told your assistant here, I've simply consented to come at all, because the Director of Drama cried so, and he's rather a darling. I've not the smallest intention of letting you kill me."

While she spoke, Dr. Beamish's geniality froze. He looked at her with hatred, not speaking. Then he picked up the pink form. "Then this no longer applies?"

"No."

"Then for State's sake," said Dr. Beamish, very angry, "what are you wasting my time for? I've got more than a hundred urgent cases waiting outside and you come in here to tell me that the Director of Drama is a darling. I know the Director of Drama. We live side by side in the same ghastly hostel. He's a pest. And I'm going to write a report to the Ministry about this tomfoolery which will make him and the lunatic who thinks he can perform a Klugmann, come round to me begging for extermination. And then I'll put them at the bottom of the queue. Get her out of here, Plastic, and let some sane people in."

Miles led her into the public waiting-room. "What an old beast," she said. "What a perfect beast. I've never been spoken to like that before even in the ballet-school. He seemed so nice at first."

"It's his professional feeling," said Miles. "He was naturally put out at losing such an attractive patient."

She smiled. Her beard was not so thick as quite to obscure her delicate ovoid of cheek and chin. She might have been peeping at him over ripe heads of barley.

Her smile started in her wide grey eyes. Her lips under her golden moustachios were unpainted, tactile. A line of pale down sprang below them and ran through the centre of the chin, spreading and thickening and growing richer in colour till it met the full flow of the whiskers, but leaving on either side, clear and tender, two symmetrical zones, naked and provocative. So might have smiled some carefree deacon in the colonnaded schools of fifth-century Alexandria and struck dumb the heresiarchs.

"I think your beard is beautiful."

"Do you really? I can't help liking it too. I can't help liking anything about myself, can you?"

"Yes. Oh, yes."

"That's not natural."

Clamour at the outer door interrupted the talk. Like gulls round a lighthouse the impatient victims kept up an irregular flap and slap on the panels.

"We're all ready, Plastic," said a senior official. "What's going on this morning?"

What was going on? Miles could not answer. Turbulent sea birds seemed to be dashing themselves against the light in his own heart.

"Don't go," he said to the girl. "Please, I shan't be a minute."

"Oh, I've nothing to take me away. My department all think I'm half dead by now."

Miles opened the door and admitted an indignant half-dozen. He directed them to their chairs, to the registry. Then he went back to the girl who had turned away slightly from the crowd and drawn a scarf peasantwise round her head, hiding her beard.

"I still don't quite like people staring," she said.

"Our patients are far too busy with their own affairs to notice anyone else," said Miles. "Besides you'd have been stared at all right if you'd stayed on in ballet."

Miles adjusted the television but few eyes in the waiting-room glanced towards it; all were fixed on the registrar's table and the doors beyond.

"Think of them all coming here," said the bearded girl.

"We give them the best service we can," said Miles.

"Yes, of course, I know you do. Please don't think I was finding fault. I only meant, fancy wanting to die."

"One or two have good reasons."

"I suppose you would say that I had. Everyone has been trying to persuade me, since my operation. The medical officials were the worst. They're afraid they may get into trouble for doing it wrong. And then the ballet people were almost as bad. They are so keen on Art that they say: 'You were the best of your class. You can never dance again. How can life be worth living?' What I try to explain is that it's just because I could dance that I *know* life is worth living. That's what Art means to me. Does that sound very silly?"

"It sounds unorthodox."

"Ah, but you're not an artist."

"Oh, I've danced all right. Twice a week all through my time at the Orphanage."

"Therapeutic dancing?"

"That's what they called it."

"But, you see, that's quite different from Art."

"Why?"

"Oh," she said with a sudden full intimacy, with fondness. "Oh what a lot you don't know."

The dancer's name was Clara.

III

Courtship was free and easy in this epoch but Miles was Clara's first lover. The strenuous exercises of her training, the austere standards of the corps-de-ballet and her devotion to her art had kept her body and soul unencumbered.

For Miles, child of the State, Sex had been part of the curriculum at every stage of his education; first in diagrams, then in demonstrations, then in application, he had mastered all the antics of procreation. Love was a word seldom used except by politicians and by them only in moments of pure fatuity. Nothing that he had been taught prepared him for Clara.

Once in drama, always in drama. Clara now spent her days mending ballet shoes and helping neophytes on the wall bars. She had a cubicle in a Nissen hut and it was there that she and Miles spent most of their evenings. It was unlike anyone else's quarters in Satellite City.

Two little paintings hung on the walls, unlike any paintings Miles had seen before, unlike anything approved by the Ministry of Art. One represented a goddess of antiquity, naked and rosy, fondling a peacock on a bank of flowers; the other a vast, tree-fringed lake and a party in spreading silken clothes embarking in a pleasure boat under a broken arch. The gilt frames were much chipped but what remained of them was elaborately foliated.

"They're French," said Clara. "More than two hundred years old. My mother left them to me."

All her possessions had come from her mother, nearly enough of them to furnish the little room – a looking glass framed in porcelain flowers, a gilt, irregular clock. She and Miles drank their sad, officially compounded coffee out of brilliant, riveted cups.

"It reminds me of prison," said Miles when he was first admitted there.

It was the highest praise he knew.

On the first evening among this delicate bric-a-brac his lips found the bare twin spaces of her chin.

"I knew it would be a mistake to let the beastly doctor poison me," said Clara complacently.

Full summer came. Another moon waxed over these rare lovers. Once they sought coolness and secrecy among the high cow-parsley and willow-herb of the waste building sites. Clara's beard was all silvered like a patriarch's in the midnight radiance.

"On such a night as this," said Miles, supine, gazing into the face of the moon, "on such a night as this I burned an Air Force Station and half its occupants."

Clara sat up and began lazily smoothing her whiskers, then more vigorously tugged the comb through the thicker, tangled growth of her head, dragging it from her forehead; re-ordered the clothing which their embraces had loosed. She was full of womanly content and ready to go home. But Miles, all male, *post coitum tristis*, was struck by a chill sense of loss. No demonstration or exercise had prepared him for this strange new experience of the sudden loneliness that follows requited love.

Walking home they talked casually and rather crossly.

"You never go to the ballet now."

"No."

"Won't they give you seats?"

"I suppose they would."

"Then why don't you go?"

"I don't think I should like it. I see them often rehearsing. I don't like it."

"But you lived for it."

"Other interests now."

"Me?"

"Of course."

"You love me more than the ballet?"

"I am very happy."

"Happier than if you were dancing?"

"I can't tell, can I? You're all I've got now."

"But if you could change?"

"I can't."

"If?"

"There's no 'if'."

"Damn."

"Don't fret, darling. It's only the moon."

And they parted in silence.

November came, a season of strikes; leisure for Miles, unsought and unvalued; lonely periods when the ballet school worked on and the death house stood cold and empty.

Clara began to complain of ill health. She was growing stout.

"Just contentment," she said at first, but the change worried her. "Can it be that beastly operation?" she asked. "I heard the reason they put down one of the Cambridge girls was that she kept growing fatter and fatter."

"She weighed nineteen stone," said Miles. "I know because Dr. Beamish mentioned it. He has strong professional objections to the Klugmann operation."

"I'm going to see the Director of Medicine. There's a new one now."

When she returned from her appointment, Miles, still left idle by the strikers, was waiting for her among her pictures and china. She sat beside him on the bed.

"Let's have a drink," she said.

They had taken to drinking wine together, very rarely because of the expense. The State chose and named the vintage. This month the issue was "Progress Port". Clara kept it in a crimson, white-cut, Bohemian flagon. The glasses were modern, unbreakable and unsightly.

"What did the doctor say?"

"He's very sweet."

"Well?"

"Much cleverer than the one before."

"Did he say it was anything to do with your operation?"

"Oh, yes. Everything to do with it."

"Can he put you right?"

"Yes, he thinks so."

"Good."

They drank their wine.

"That first doctor did make a mess of the operation, didn't he?"

"Such a mess. The new doctor says I'm a unique case. You see, I'm pregnant."

"*Clara.*"

"Yes, it is a surprise, isn't it?"

"This needs thinking about," said Miles.

He thought.

He refilled their glasses.

He said: "It's hard luck on the poor little beast not being an Orphan. Not much opportunity for it. If he's a boy we must try and get him registered as a worker. Of course it might be a girl. Then," brightly, "we could make her a dancer."

"Oh, don't mention dancing," cried Clara, and suddenly began weeping. "Don't speak to me of dancing."

Her tears fell fast. No tantrum this, but deep uncontrolled inconsolable sorrow.

And next day she disappeared.

IV

Santa-Claus-tide was near. Shops were full of shoddy little dolls. Children in the schools sang old ditties about peace and goodwill. Strikers went back to work in order to qualify for their seasonal bonus. Electric bulbs were hung in the conifers and the furnaces in the Dome of Security roared again. Miles had been promoted. He now sat beside the assistant registrar and helped stamp and file the documents of the dead. It was harder work than he was used to and Miles was hungry for Clara's company. The lights were going out in the Dome and on the Goodwill Tree in the car park. He walked the half-mile of hutments to Clara's quarters. Other girls were waiting for their consorts or setting out to find them in the Recreatorium, but Clara's door was locked. A note, pinned to it, read: *Miles, Going away for a bit. C.* Angry and puzzled he returned to his hostel.

Clara, unlike himself, had uncles and cousins scattered about the country. Since her operation she had been shy of visiting them. Now, Miles supposed, she was taking cover among them. It was the manner of her flight, so unlike her gentle ways, that tortured him. For a busy week he thought of nothing else. His reproaches sang in his head as the undertone to all the activities of the day and at night he lay sleepless, repeating in his mind every word spoken between them and every act of intimacy.

After a week the thought of her became spasmodic and regular. The subject bored him unendurably. He strove to keep it out of his mind as a man might strive to control an attack of hiccups, and as impotently. Spasmodically, mechanically, the thought of Clara returned. He timed it and found that it came every $7\frac{1}{2}$ minutes. He went to sleep thinking of her, he woke up thinking of her. But between times he slept. He consulted the departmental psychiatrist who told him that he was burdened by the responsibility of parentage. But it was not Clara the mother who haunted him, but Clara the betrayer.

Tidings of Comfort and Joy

Next week he thought of her every twenty minutes. The week after that he thought of her irregularly, though often; only when something outside himself reminded him of her. He began to look at other girls and considered himself cured.

He looked hard at other girls as he passed them in the dim corridors of the Dome and they looked boldly back at him. Then one of them stopped him and said: "I've seen you before with Clara" and at the mention of her name all interest in the other girl ceased in pain. "I went to visit her yesterday."

"Where?"

"In hospital, of course. Didn't you know?"

"What's the matter with her?"

"She won't say. Nor will anyone else at the hospital. She's top secret. If you ask me she's been in an accident and there's some politician involved. I can't think of any other reason for all the fuss. She's covered in bandages and gay as a lark."

Next day, December 25th, was Santa Claus Day; no holiday in the department of Euthanasia, which was an essential service. At dusk Miles walked to the hospital, one of the unfinished edifices, all concrete and steel and glass in front and a jumble of huts behind. The hall porter was engrossed in the television, which was performing an old obscure folk play which past generations had performed on Santa Claus Day, and was now revived and revised as a matter of historical interest.

It was of professional interest to the porter for it dealt with maternity services before the days of Welfare. He gave the number of Clara's room without glancing up from the strange spectacle of an ox and an ass, an old man with a lantern, and a young mother. "People here are always complaining," he said. "They ought to realize what things were like before Progress."

The corridors were loud with relayed music. Miles found the hut he sought. It was marked "Experimental Surgery. Health Officers Only". He found the cubicle. He found Clara sleeping, the sheet pulled up to her eyes, her hair loose on the pillow. She had brought some of her property with her. An old shawl lay across the bed-table. A painted fan stood against the television-set. She awoke, her eyes full of frank welcome, and pulled the sheet higher, speaking through it.

"Darling, you shouldn't have come. I was keeping it for a surprise."

Miles sat by the bed and thought of nothing to say except: "How are you?"

"Wonderful. They've taken the bandages off today. They won't let me have a looking glass yet but they say everything has been a tremendous success. I'm something very special, Miles – a new chapter in surgical progress."

"But what has happened to you? Is it something to do with the baby?"

"Oh no. At least, it was. That was the first operation. But that's all over now."

"You mean our child?"

"Yes, that had to go. I should never have been able to dance afterwards. I told you all about it. That was why I had the Klugmann operation, don't you remember?"

"But you gave up dancing."

"That's where they've been so clever. Didn't I tell you about the sweet, clever new medical director? He's cured all that."

"Your dear beard."

"Quite gone. An operation the new director invented himself. It's going to be named after him or even perhaps after me. He's so unselfish he wants to call it the Clara operation. He's taken off all the skin and put on a wonderful new substance, a sort of synthetic rubber that takes grease-paint perfectly. He says the colour isn't perfect but that it will never show on the stage. Look, feel it."

She sat up in bed, joyful and proud.

Her eyes and brow were all that was left of the loved face. Below it something quite inhuman, a tight, slippery mask, salmon pink.

Miles stared. In the television screen by the bed further characters had appeared – Food Production Workers. They seemed to declare a sudden strike, left their sheep and ran off at the bidding of some kind of shop-steward in fantastic dress. The machine by the bedside broke into song, an old, forgotten ditty:

Experimental Surgery

"O tidings of comfort and joy, comfort and joy, O tidings of comfort and joy."

Miles retched unobtrusively. The ghastly face regarded him with fondness and pride. At length the right words came to him; the trite, the traditional sentence uttered by countless lips of generations of baffled and impassioned Englishmen: "I think I shall go for a short walk."

But first he walked only as far as his hostel. There he lay down until the moon moved to his window and fell across his sleepless face. Then he set out, walking far into the fields, out of sight of the Dome of Security, for two hours until the moon was near setting.

He had travelled at random but now the white rays fell on a signpost and he read: "*Mountjoy* $\frac{3}{4}$". He strode on with only the stars to light his way till he came to the Castle gates.

They stood open as always, gracious symbol of the new penology. He followed the drive. The whole lightless face of the old house stared at him silently, without rebuke. He knew now what was needed. He carried in his pocket a cigarette lighter which often worked. It worked for him now.

No need for oil here. The dry old silk of the drawing-room curtains lit like paper. Paint and panelling, plaster and tapestry and gilding bowed to the embrace of the leaping flames. He stepped outside. Soon it was too hot on the terrace and he retreated further, to the marble temple at the end of the long walk. The murderers were leaping from the first-storey windows but the sexual offenders, trapped above, set up a wail of terror. He heard the chandeliers fall and saw the boiling lead cascading from the roof. This was something altogether finer than the strangulation of a few peacocks. He watched exultant as minute by minute the scene disclosed fresh wonders. Great timbers crashed within; outside the lily-pond hissed with falling brands; a vast ceiling of smoke shut out the stars and under it tongues of flame floated away into the tree-tops.

Two hours later when the first engine arrived, the force of the fiery storm was already spent. Miles rose from his marble throne and began the long walk home. But he was no longer at all fatigued. He strode out cheerfully with his shadow, cast by the dying blaze, stretching before him along the lane.

On the main road a motorist stopped him and asked: "What's that over there? A house on fire?"

"It was," said Miles. "It's almost out now."

"Looks like a big place. Only Government property, I suppose?"

"That's all," said Miles.

"Well hop in if you want a lift."

"Thanks," said Miles, "I'm walking for pleasure."

V

Miles rose after two hours in bed. The hostel was alive with all the normal activity of morning. The wireless was playing; the sub-officials were coughing over their wash-basins; the reek of State sausages frying in State grease filled the asbestos cubicle. He was slightly stiff after his long walk and slightly footsore, but his mind was as calm and empty as the sleep from which he had awoken. The scorched-earth policy had succeeded. He had made a desert in his imagination which he might call peace. Once before he had burned his childhood. Now his brief adult life lay in ashes; the enchantments that surrounded Clara were one with the splendours of Mountjoy; her great golden beard, one with the tongues of flame that had leaped and expired among the stars; her fans and pictures and scraps of old embroidery, one with the gilded cornices and silk hangings, black, cold and sodden. He ate his sausage with keen appetite and went to work.

All was quiet too at the Department of Euthanasia.

The first announcement of the Mountjoy disaster had been on the early news. Its proximity to Satellite City gave it a special poignancy there.

"It is a significant phenomenon," said Dr. Beamish, "that any bad news has an immediate effect on our service. You see it whenever there is an international crisis. Sometimes I think people only come to us when they have nothing to talk about. Have you looked at our queue today?"

Miles turned to the periscope. Only one man waited outside, old Parsnip, a poet of the '30s who came daily but was usually jostled to the back of the crowd. He was a comic character in the department, this veteran poet. Twice in Miles's short term he had succeeded in gaining admission but on both occasions had suddenly taken fright and bolted.

"It's a lucky day for Parsnip," said Miles.

"Yes. He deserves some luck. I knew him well once, him and his friend Pimpernell. *New Writing*, the Left Book Club, they were

all the rage. Pimpernell was one of my first patients. Hand
Parsnip in and we'll finish him off."

So old Parsnip was summoned and that day his nerve stood
firm. He passed fairly calmly through the gas chamber on his way
to rejoin Pimpernell.

"We might as well knock off for the day," said Dr. Beamish. "We shall be busy again soon when the excitement dies
down."

But the politicians seemed determined to keep the excitement
up. All the normal features of television were interrupted and
curtailed to give place to Mountjoy. Survivors appeared on the
screen, among them Soapy, who described how long practice as a
cat burglar had enabled him to escape. Mr. Sweat, he remarked
with respect, had got clear away. The ruins were surveyed by the
apparatus. A sexual maniac with broken legs gave audience from
his hospital bed. The Minister of Welfare, it was announced,
would make a special appearance that evening to comment on
the disaster.

Miles dozed intermittently beside the hostel set and at dusk
rose, still calm and free; so purged of emotion that he made his
way once more to the hospital and called on Clara.

She had spent the afternoon with looking glass and make-up
box. The new substance of her face fulfilled all the surgeon's
promises. It took paint to perfection. Clara had given herself a full
mask as though for the lights of the stage; an even creamy white
with sudden high spots of crimson on the cheek bones, huge hard
crimson lips, eyebrows extended and turned up catwise, the eyes
shaded all round with ultramarine and dotted at the corners with
crimson.

"You're the first to see me," she said. "I was half-afraid you
wouldn't come. You seemed cross yesterday."

"I wanted to see the television," said Miles. "It's so crowded at
the hostel."

"So dull today. Nothing except this prison that has been
burned down."

"I was there myself. Don't you remember? I often talked
of it."

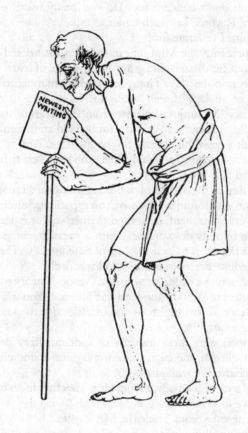

Parsnip ad Portas

"Did you, Miles? Perhaps so. I've such a bad memory for things that don't concern me. Do you really want to hear the Minister? It would be much cosier to talk."

"It's him I've come for."

And presently the Minister appeared, open-necked as always but without his usual smile; grave to the verge of tears. He spoke for twenty minutes. " . . . The great experiment must go on . . . the martyrs of maladjustment shall not have died in vain . . . A greater, new Mountjoy shall rise from the ashes of the old . . ." Eventually tears came – real tears for he held an invisible onion – and trickled down his cheeks. So the speech ended.

"That's all I came for," said Miles, and left Clara to her cocoa-butter and face-towel.

Next day all the organs of public information were still piping the theme of Mountjoy. Two or three patients, already bored with the entertainment, presented themselves for extermination and were happily despatched. Then a message came from the Regional Director, official-in-chief of Satellite City. He required the immediate presence of Miles in his office.

"I have a move order for you, Mr. Plastic. You are to report to the Ministers of Welfare and Rest and Culture. You will be issued with a Grade A hat, umbrella and briefcase for the journey. My congratulations."

Equipped with these insignia of sudden, dizzy promotion, Miles travelled to the capital leaving behind a domeful of sub-officials chattering with envy.

At the terminus an official met him. Together in an official car they drove to Whitehall.

"Let me carry your briefcase, Mr. Plastic."

"There's nothing in it."

Miles's escort laughed obsequiously at this risqué joke.

At the Ministry the lifts were in working order. It was a new and alarming experience to enter the little cage and rise to the top of the great building.

"Do they always work here?"

"Not *always*, but very very often."

Miles realized that he was indeed at the heart of things.

"Wait here. I will call you when the Ministers are ready."

Miles looked from the waiting-room window at the slow streams of traffic. Just below him stood a strange, purposeless obstruction of stone. A very old man, walking by, removed his hat to it as though saluting an acquaintance. Why? Miles wondered. Then he was summoned to the politicians.

They were alone in their office save for a gruesome young woman. The Minister of Rest and Culture said: "Ease your feet, lad" and indicated a large leatherette armchair.

"Not such a happy occasion, alas, as our last meeting," said the Minister of Welfare.

"Oh, I don't know," said Miles. He was enjoying the outing.

"The tragedy at Mountjoy Castle was a grievous loss to the cause of penology."

"But the great work of Rehabilitation will continue," said the gruesome young woman.

"A greater Mountjoy will arise from the ashes," said the Minister.

"Those noble criminal lives have not been lost in vain."

"Their memory will inspire us."

"Yes," said Miles. "I heard the broadcast."

"Exactly," said the Minister. "Precisely. Then you appreciate, perhaps, what a change the occurrence makes in your own position. From being, as we hoped, the first of a continuous series of successes, you are our only one. It would not be too much to say that the whole future of penology is in your hands. The destruction of Mountjoy Castle by itself was merely a set-back. A sad one, of course, but something which might be described as the growing pains of a great movement. But there is a darker side. I told you, I think, that our great experiment had been made only against considerable opposition. Now – I speak confidentially – that opposition has become vocal and unscrupulous. There is, in fact, a whispering campaign that the fire was no accident but the act of one of the very men whom we were seeking to serve. That campaign must be scotched."

"They can't do us down as easy as they think," said the Minister of Rest and Culture. "Us old dogs know a trick or two."

"Exactly. Counter-propaganda. You are our Exhibit A. The irrefutable evidence of the triumph of our system. We are going to send you up and down the country to lecture. My colleagues have already written your speech. You will be accompanied by Miss Flower here, who will show and explain the model of the new Mountjoy. Perhaps you will care to see it yourself. Miss Flower, the model please."

All the time they were speaking Miles had been aware of a bulky, sheeted object on a table in the window. Miss Flower now unveiled it. Miles gazed in awe.

The object displayed was a familiar, standard packing-case, set on end.

"A rush job," said the Minister of Welfare. "You will be provided with something more elaborate for your tour."

Miles gazed at the box.

It fitted. It fell into place precisely in the void of his mind, satisfying all the needs for which his education had prepared him. The conditioned personality recognized its proper pre-ordained environment. All else was insubstantial; the gardens of Mountjoy, Clara's cracked Crown Derby and her enveloping beard were trophies of a fading dream.

The Modern Man was home.

"There is one further point," continued the Minister of Welfare. "A domestic one but not as irrelevant as it may seem. Have you by any chance formed an attachment in Satellite City? Your dossier suggests that you have."

"Any woman trouble?" explained the Minister of Rest and Culture.

"Oh, yes," said Miles. "Great trouble. But that is over."

"You see, perfect rehabilitation, complete citizenship should include marriage."

"It has not," said Miles.

"That should be rectified."

"Folks like a bloke to be spliced," said the Minister of Rest and Culture. "With a couple of kids."

"There is hardly time for *them*," said the Minister of Welfare. "But we think that psychologically you will have more appeal if

you have a wife by your side. Miss Flower here has every quali-
fication."

"Looks are only skin deep, lad," said the Minister of Rest and
Culture.

"So if you have no preferable alternative to offer ...?"

"None," said Miles.

"Spoken like an Orphan. I see a splendid career ahead of the
pair of you."

"When can we get divorced?"

"Come, come, Plastic. You mustn't look too far ahead. First
things first. You have already obtained the necessary leave from
your Director, Miss Flower?"

"Yes, Minister."

"Then off you both go. And State be with you."

In perfect peace of heart Miles followed Miss Flower to the
Registrar's office.

Then the mood veered.

Miles felt ill at ease during the ceremony and fidgeted with
something small and hard which he found in his pocket. It proved
to be his cigarette-lighter, a most uncertain apparatus. He
pressed the catch and instantly, surprisingly, there burst out a
tiny flame – gemlike, hymeneal, auspicious.

BASIL SEAL RIDES AGAIN

OR

THE RAKE'S REGRESS

TO MRS. IAN FLEMING

Dear Ann

In this senile attempt to recapture the manner of my youth I have resurrected characters from earlier stories which, if you ever read them, you will have forgotten.

Basil Seal was the hero of *Black Mischief* (1932) and *Put Out More Flags* (1942). Through my ineptitude the colour of his eyes changed during the intervening decade. At the end of the latter book he considered marriage with the newly widowed, very rich Angela Lyne who had long been his mistress. Ambrose Silk, an aesthete, also appeared in that book. Peter, Lord Pastmaster, first appeared as Peter Beste-Chetwynde in *Decline and Fall* (1928). His mother, later Lady Metroland, appeared there and in *Vile Bodies* (1930). Alastair Digby-Vane-Trumpington was Lady Metroland's lover in 1928 and Sonia's husband in 1942.

Albright is new: an attempt to extract something from the rum modern world of which you afford me occasional glimpses in your hospitable house.

I should have liked to drop the title in favour of what I have here used as subtitle, but it was suggested that this might smack of sharp practice to readers who saw the story in the *Sunday Telegraph* and *Esquire* and might be led to expect something new.

Ever your affec. coz.

Combe Florey. December 1962   E. W.

BASIL SEAL RIDES AGAIN

"Y ES."

"What d'you mean: 'Yes'?"

"I didn't hear what you said."

"I said he made off with all my shirts."

"It's not that I'm the least deaf. It's simply that I can't concentrate when a lot of fellows are making a row."

"There's a row now."

"Some sort of speech."

"And a lot of fellows saying: 'Shush'."

"Exactly. I can't concentrate. What did you say?"

"This fellow made off with all my shirts."

"Fellow making the speech?"

"No, no. Quite another fellow – called Albright."

"I don't think so. I heard he was dead."

"This one isn't. You can't say he stole them exactly. My daughter gave them to him."

"All?"

"Practically all. I had a few in London and there were a few at the wash. Couldn't believe it when my man told me. Went through all the drawers myself. Nothing there."

"Bloody thing to happen. *My* daughter wouldn't do a thing like that."

Protests from neighbouring diners rose in volume.

"They can't want to hear this speech. It's the most awful rot."

"We seem to be getting unpopular."

"Don't know who all these fellows are. Never saw anyone before except old Ambrose. Thought I ought to turn out and support him."

Peter Pastmaster and Basil Seal seldom attended public banquets. They sat at the end of a long table under chandeliers and pier-glasses, looking, for all the traditional brightness of the hotel, too bright and too private for their surroundings. Peter was a year or two the younger but he, like Basil, had scorned to order his life with a view of longevity or spurious youth. They were two stout, rubicund, richly dressed old buffers who might have passed as exact contemporaries.

The frowning faces that were turned towards them were of all ages from those of a moribund Celtic bard to the cross adolescent critic's for whose dinner Mr. Bentley, the organizer, was paying. Mr. Bentley had, as he expressed it, cast his net wide. There were politicians and publicists there, dons and cultural attachés, Fulbright scholars, representatives of the Pen Club, editors; Mr. Bentley, home-sick for the *belle époque* of the American slump, when in England the worlds of art and fashion and action harmoniously mingled, had solicited the attendance of a few of the early friends of the guest of honour and Peter and Basil, meeting casually a few weeks before, had decided to go together. They were celebrating the almost coincident events of Ambrose Silk's sixtieth birthday and his investiture with the Order of Merit.

Ambrose, white-haired, pallid, emaciated, sat between Dr. Parsnip, Professor of Dramatic Poetry at Minneapolis, and Dr. Pimpernell, Professor of Poetic Drama at St. Paul. These distinguished expatriates had flown to London for the occasion. It was not the sort of party at which decorations are worn but as Ambrose delicately inclined in deprecation of the honeyed words that dripped around him, no one could doubt his effortless distinction. It was Parsnip who was now on his feet attempting to make himself heard.

"I hear the cry of 'silence'," he said with sharp spontaneity. His voice had assumed something of the accent of his place of exile but his diction was orthodox – august even; he had quite discarded the patiently acquired proletarian colloquialisms of thirty years earlier. "It is apt, for, surely?, the object of our homage tonight is epitomized in that golden word. The voice which once clearly spoke the message of what I for one, and many of us here, will always regard as the most glorious decade of English letters, the nineteen-thirties," (growls of dissent from the youthful critic) "that voice tardily perhaps, but at long last so illustriously honoured by official recognition, has been silent for a quarter of a century. Silent in Ireland, silent in Tangier, in Telaviv and Ischia and Portugal, now silent in his native London, our guest of honour has stood for us as a stern rebuke, a recall to artistic reticence and integrity. The books roll out from the presses, none by Ambrose Silk. Not for Ambrose Silk the rostrum, the television screen; for him the enigmatic and monumental silence of genius. . . ."

"I've got to pee," said Basil.

"I always want to nowadays."

"Come on then."

Slowly and stiffly they left the hotel dining-room.

As they stood side by side in the lavatory Basil said: "I'm glad Ambrose has got a gong. D'you think the fellow making the speech was pulling his leg?"

"Must have been. Stands to reason."

"You were going to tell me something about some shirts."

"I did tell you."

"What was the name of the chap who got them?"

"Albright."

"Yes, I remember; a fellow called Clarence Albright. Rather an awful chap. Got himself killed in the war."

"No one that I knew got killed in the war except Alastair Trumpington."

"And Cedric Lyne."

"Yes, there was Cedric."

"And Freddy Sothill."

"I never really considered I knew him," said Basil.

"This Albright married someone – Molly Meadows, perhaps?"

"*I* married Molly Meadows."

"So you did. I was there. Well, someone like that. One of those girls who were going round at the time – John Flintshire's sister, Sally perhaps. I expect your Albright is her son."

"He doesn't look like anyone's son."

"People always are," said Basil, "sons or daughters of people."

This truism had a secondary, antiquated and, to Peter, an obvious meaning, which was significant of the extent by which

Basil had changed from *enfant terrible* to "old Pobble", the name by which he was known to his daughter's friends.

The change had been rapid. In 1939 Basil's mother, his sister, Barbara Sothill, and his mistress, Angela Lyne, had seen the war as the opportunity for his redemption. His embattled country, they supposed, would find honourable use for those deplorable energies which had so often brought him almost into the shadows of prison. At the worst he would fill a soldier's grave; at the best he would emerge as a second Lawrence of Arabia. His fate was otherwise.

Early in his military career, he lamed himself, blowing away the toes of one foot while demonstrating to his commando section a method of his own device for demolishing railway bridges, and was discharged from the army. From this disaster was derived at a later date the sobriquet "Pobble". Then, hobbling from his hospital bed to the registry office, he married the widowed Angela Lyne. Hers was one of those few, huge, astutely dispersed fortunes which neither international calamities nor local experiments with socialism could seriously diminish. Basil accepted wealth as he accepted the loss of his toes. He forgot he had ever walked without a stick and a limp, had ever been lean and active, had ever been put to desperate shifts for quite small sums. If he ever recalled that decade of adventure it was as something remote and unrelated to man's estate, like an end-of-term shortness of pocket money at school.

For the rest of the war and for the first drab years of peace he had appeared on the national register as "farmer"; that is to say, he lived in the country in ease and plenty. Two dead men, Freddy Sothill and Cedric Lyne, had left ample cellars. Basil drained them. He had once expressed the wish to become one of the "hard-faced men who had done well out of the war". Basil's face, once very hard, softened and rounded. His scar became almost invisible in rosy suffusion. None of his few clothes, he found, now buttoned comfortably and when, in that time of European scarcity, he and Angela went to New York, where such things could then still be procured by the well-informed, he bought suits and shirts and shoes by the dozen and a whole treasury of watches, tie-pins, cuff-links and chains so that on his return, having scrupulously declared them and paid full duty at the customs – a thing he had never in his life done before – he remarked of his elder brother, who, after a tediously successful diplomatic career spent in gold-lace or starched linen allowed himself in retirement (and reduced circumstances) some laxity in dress: "Poor Tony goes about looking like a scarecrow."

Life in the country palled when food rationing ceased. Angela made over the house they had called "Cedric's Folly" and its grottoes to her son Nigel on his twenty-first birthday, and took a large, unobtrusive house in Hill Street. She had other places to live, a panelled seventeenth-century apartment in Paris, a villa on Cap Ferrat, a beach and bungalow quite lately acquired in Bermuda, a little palace in Venice which she had once bought for Cedric Lyne but never visited in his lifetime – and among them they moved with their daughter Barbara. Basil settled into the orderly round of the rich. He became a creature of habit and of set opinions. In London finding Bratt's and Bellamy's disturbingly raffish, he joined that sombre club in Pall Mall that had been the scene of so many painful interviews with his self-appointed guardian, Sir Joseph Mannering, and there often sat in the chair which had belonged prescriptively to Sir Joseph and, as Sir Joseph had done, pronounced his verdict on the day's news to any who would listen.

Basil turned, crossed to the looking glasses and straightened his tie. He brushed up the copious grey hair. He looked at himself with the blue eyes which had seen so much and now saw only the round, rosy face in which they were set, the fine clothes of English make which had replaced the American improvisations, the starched shirt which he was almost alone in wearing, the black pearl studs, the buttonhole.

A week or two ago he had had a disconcerting experience in this very hotel. It was a place he had frequented all his life, particularly in the latter years, and he was on cordial terms with the man who took the men's hats in a den by the Piccadilly entrance. Basil was never given a numbered ticket and assumed he was known by name. Then a day came when he sat longer than usual over luncheon and found the man off duty. Lifting the counter he had penetrated to the rows of pegs and retrieved his bowler and umbrella. In the ribbon of the hat he found a label, put there for identification. It bore the single pencilled word "Florid". He had told his daughter, Barbara, who said: "I wouldn't have you any different. Don't for heaven's sake go taking one of those cures. You'd go mad."

Basil was not a vain man; neither in rags nor in riches had he cared much about the impression he made. But the epithet recurred to him now as he surveyed himself in the glass.

"Would you say Ambrose was 'florid', Peter?"

"Not a word I use."

"It simply means flowery."

"Well, I suppose he is."

"Not fat and red?"

"Not Ambrose."

"Exactly."

"I've been called 'florid'."

"You're fat and red."

"So are you."

"Yes, why not? Almost everyone is."

"Except Ambrose."

"Well, he's a pansy. I expect he takes trouble."

"We don't."

"Why the hell should we?"

"We don't."

"Exactly."

The two old friends had exhausted the subject.

Basil said: "About those shirts. How did your girl ever meet a fellow like that?"

"At Oxford. She insisted on going up to read History. She picked up some awfully rum friends."

"I suppose there were girls there in my time. We never met them."

"Nor in mine."

"Stands to reason the sort of fellow who takes up with under-graduettes has something wrong with him."

"Albright certainly has."

"What does he look like?"

"I've never set an eye. My daughter asked him to King's Thursday when I was abroad. She found he had no shirts and she gave him mine."

"Was he hard up?"

"So she said."

"Clarence Albright never had any money. Sally can't have brought him much."

"There may be no connexion."

"Must be. Two fellows without money both called Albright. Stands to reason they're the same fellow."

Peter looked at his watch.

"Half past eleven. I don't feel like going back to hear those speeches. We showed up. Ambrose must have been pleased."

"He was. But he can't expect us to listen to all that rot."

"What did he mean about Ambrose's 'silence'? Never knew a fellow who talked so much."

"All a lot of rot. Where to now?"

"Come to think of it, my mother lives upstairs. We might see if she's at home."

They rose to the floor where Margot Metroland had lived ever since the destruction of Pastmaster House. The door on the corridor was not locked. As they stood in the little vestibule loud, low-bred voices came to them.

"She seems to have a party."

Peter opened the door of the sitting-room. It was in darkness save for the ghastly light of a television set. Margot crouched over it, her old taut face livid in the reflection.

"Can we come in?"

"Who are you? What d'you want? I can't see you."

Peter turned on the light at the door.

"Don't do that. Oh, it's you Peter. And Basil."

"We've been dining downstairs."

"Well, I'm sorry; I'm busy, as you can see. Turn the light out and come and sit down if you want to, but don't disturb me."

"We'd better go."

"Yes. Come and see me when I'm not so busy."

Outside Peter said: "She's always looking at that thing nowadays. It's a great pleasure to her."

"Where to now?"

"I thought of dropping in at Bellamy's."

"I'll go home. I left Angela on her own. Barbara's at a party of Robin Trumpington's."

"Well, good night."

"I say, those places where they starve you, – you know what I mean – do they do any good?"

"Molly swears by one."

"She's not fat and red."

"No. She goes to those starving places."

"Well, good night."

Peter turned east, Basil north, into the mild, misty October night. The streets at this hour were empty. Basil stumped across Piccadilly and up through Mayfair, where Angela's house was almost the sole survivor of the private houses of his youth. How many doors had been closed against him then that were now open to all comers as shops and offices!

The lights were on. He left his hat and coat on a marble table and began the ascent to the drawing-room floor, pausing on the half-landing to recuperate.

"Oh, Pobble, you toeless wonder. You always turn up just when you're wanted."

Florid he might be, but there were compensations. It was not thus that Basil had often been greeted in limber youth. Two arms embraced his neck and drew him down, an agile figure inclined over the protuberance of his starched shirt, a cheek was pressed to his and teeth tenderly nibbled the lobe of his ear.

"Babs, I thought you were at a party. Why on earth are you dressed like that?"

His daughter wore very tight very short trousers, slippers and a thin jersey. He disengaged himself and slapped her loudly on the behind.

"Sadist. It's that sort of party. It's a 'happening'."

"You speak in riddles child."

"It's a new sort of party the Americans have invented. Nothing is arranged beforehand. Things just happen. Tonight they cut off a girl's clothes with nail scissors and then painted her green. She had a mask on so I don't know who it was. She might just be someone hired. Then what happened was Robin ran out of drink so we've all gone scouring for it. Mummy's in bed and doesn't know where old Nudge keeps the key and we can't wake him up."

"You and your mother have been into Nudge's bedroom?"

"Me and Charles. He's the chap I'm scouring with. He's downstairs now trying to pick the lock. I think Nudge must be sedated, he just rolled over snoring when we shook him."

At the foot of the staircase a door led to the servants' quarters. It opened and someone very strange appeared with an armful of bottles. Basil saw below him a slender youth, perhaps a man of twenty-one, who had a mop of dishevelled black hair and a meagre black fringe of beard and whiskers; formidable, contemptuous blue eyes above grey pouches; a proud, rather childish mouth. He wore a pleated white silk shirt, open at the neck, flannel trousers, a green cummerbund and sandals. The appearance, though grotesque, was not specifically plebeian and when he spoke his tone was pure and true without a taint of accent.

"The lock was easy," he said, "but I can't find anything except wine. Where d'you keep the whisky?"

"Heavens, I don't know," said Barbara.

"Good evening," said Basil.

"Oh, good evening. Where do you keep the whisky?"

"It is a fancy dress party?" Basil asked.

"Not particularly," said the young man.

"What have you got there?"

"Champagne of some kind. I didn't notice the label."

"He's got the Cliquot rosé," said Basil.

"How clever of him," said Barbara.

"It will probably do," said the young man. "Though most people prefer whisky."

Basil attempted to speak but found no words.

Barbara quoted:

" 'His Aunt Jobiska made him drink

Lavender water tinged with pink,

For the world in general knows

There's nothing so good for a Pobble's toes.' Come along, Charles, I think we've got all we're going to get here. I sense a grudging hospitality."

She skipped downstairs, waved from the hall and was out of the front door, while Basil still stood dumbfounded.

At length, even more laboriously than he was wont, he continued upward. Angela was in bed reading.

"You're home early."

"Peter was there. No one else I knew except old Ambrose. Some booby made a speech. So I came away."

"Very wise."

Basil stood before Angela's long looking glass. He could see her behind him. She put on her spectacles and picked up her book.

"Angela, I don't drink much nowadays, do I?"

"Not as much as you used."

"Or eat?"

"More."

"But you'd say I led a temperate life?"

"Yes, on the whole."

"It's just age," said Basil. "And dammit, I'm not sixty yet."

"What's worrying you, darling?"

"It's when I meet young men. A choking feeling – as if I was going to have an apoplectic seizure. I once saw a fellow in a seizure, must have been about the age I am now – the Lieutenant-Colonel of the Bombardiers. It was a most unpleasant spectacle. I've been feeling lately something like that might strike me any day. I believe I ought to take a cure."

"I'll come too."

"Will you really, Angela? You are a saint."

"Might as well be there as anywhere. They're supposed to be good for insomnia too. The servants would like a holiday. They've been wearing awfully overworked expressions lately."

"No sense taking Babs. We could send her to Malfrey."

"Yes."

"Angela, I saw the most awful-looking fellow tonight with a sort of beard – here, in the house, a friend of Babs. She called him 'Charles'."

"Yes, he's someone new."

"What's his name?"

"I did hear. It sounded like a pack of fox hounds I once went out with. I know – Albrighton."

"Albright," cried Basil, the invisible noose tightening. "Albright, by God."

Angela looked at him with real concern. "You know," she said, "you really do look rather rum. I think we'd better go to one of those starving places at once."

And then what had seemed a death-rattle turned into a laugh.

"It was one of Peter's shirts," he said, unintelligibly to Angela.

II

It may one day occur to a pioneer of therapeutics that most of those who are willing to pay fifty pounds a week to be deprived of food and wine, seek only suffering and that they could be cheaply accommodated in rat-ridden dungeons. At present the profits of the many thriving institutions which cater for the ascetic are depleted by the maintenance of neat lawns and shrubberies and, inside, of the furniture of a private house and apparatus resembling that of a hospital.

Basil and Angela could not immediately secure rooms at the sanatorium recommended by Molly Pastmaster. There was a waiting list of people suffering from every variety of infirmity. Finally they frankly outbid rival sufferers. A man whose obesity threatened the collapse of his ankles, and a woman raging with hallucinations were informed that their bookings were defective, and on a warm afternoon Basil and Angela drove down to take possession of their rooms.

There was a resident physician at this most accommodating house. He interviewed each patient on arrival and ostensibly considered individual needs.

He saw Angela first. Basil sat stolidly in an outer room, his hands on the head of his cane, gazing blankly before him.

When at length he was admitted, he stated his needs. The doctor did not attempt any physical investigation. It was a plain case.

"To refrain from technical language you complain of speech-lessness, a sense of heat and strangulation, dizziness and subsequent trembling?" said this man of science.

"I feel I'm going to burst," said Basil.

"Exactly. And these symptoms only occur when you meet young men?"

"Hairy young men especially."

"Ah."

"*Young puppies.*"

"And with puppies too? That is very significant. How do you react to kittens?"

"I mean the young men are puppies."

"Ah. And are you fond of puppies, Mr. Seal?"

"Reasonably."

"Ah." The man of science studied the paper on his desk. "Have you always been conscious of this preference for your own sex?"

"I'm not conscious of it now."

"You are fifty-eight years and ten months. That is often a crucial age, one of change, when repressed and unsuspected inclinations emerge and take control. I should strongly recommend your putting yourself under a psychoanalyst. We do not give treatment of that kind here."

"I just want to be cured of feeling I'm going to burst."

"I've no doubt our régime will relieve the symptoms. You will not find many young men here to disturb you. Our patients are mostly mature women. There is a markedly virile young physical training instructor. His hair is quite short but you had better keep away from the gym. Ah, I see from your paper that you are handicapped by war-wounds. I will take out all physical exercise from your timetable and substitute extra periods of manipulation by one of the female staff. Here is your diet sheet. You will notice that for the first forty-eight hours you are restricted to turnip juice. At the end of that period you embark on the carrots. At the end of the fortnight, if all goes well, we will have you on raw eggs and barley. Don't hesitate to come and see me again if you have any problem to discuss."

The sleeping quarters of male and female inmates were separated by the length of the house. Basil found Angela in the drawing-room. They compared their diet sheets.

"Rum that it should be exactly the same treatment for insomnia and apoplexy."

"That booby thought I was a pansy."

"It takes a medical man to find out a thing like that. All these years and I never knew. They're always right, you know. So that's why you're always going to that odd club."

"This is no time for humour. This is going to be a very grim fortnight."

"Not for me," said Angela. "I came well provisioned. I'm only here to keep you company. And there's a Mrs. Somebody next door to me who I used to know. She's got a private cache of all the sleeping-pills in the world. I've made great friends with her already. *I* shall be all right."

On the third day of his ordeal, the worst according to *habitués* of the establishment, there came a telephone call from Barbara.

"Pobble, I want to go back to London. I'm bored."

"Bored with Aunt Barbara?"

"Not with *her*, with *here*."

"You stay where you're put, chattel."

"No. *Please*, I want to go home."

"Your home is where I am. You can't come here."

"No. I want to go to London."

"You can't. I sent the servants away for a fortnight."

"Most of my friends live without servants."

"You've sunk into a very low world, Babs."

"Don't be such an ass. Sonia Trumpington hasn't any servants."

"Well, she won't want you."

"Pobble, you sound awfully feeble."

"Who wouldn't who's only had one carrot in the last three days."

"Oh, you are brave."

"Yes."

"How's mummy?"

"Your mother is not keeping the régime as strictly as I am."

"I bet she isn't. Anyway, please, can I go back to London?"

"No."

"You mean 'No'?"

"Yes."

"Fiend."

Basil had gone hungry before. From time to time in his varied youth, in desert, tundra, glacier and jungle, in garrets and cellars, he had briefly endured extremities of privation. Now in the periods of repose and solitude, after the steam bath and the smarting deluge of the showers, after the long thumping and twisting by the huge masseuse, when the chintz curtains were drawn in his bedroom and he lay towel-wrapped and supine gazing at the pattern of the ceiling paper, familiar, forgotten pangs spoke to him of his past achievements.

He defined his condition to Angela after the first week of the régime. "I'm not rejuvenated or invigorated. I'm etherealized."

"You look like a ghost."

"Exactly. I've lost sixteen pounds three ounces."

"You're overdoing it. No one else keeps these absurd rules. We aren't expected to. It's like the '*rien ne va plus*' at roulette. Mrs. What's-her-name has found a black market in the gym kept by the sergeant-instructor. We ate a grouse pie this morning."

They were in the well-kept grounds. A chime of bells announced that the brief recreation was over. Basil tottered back to his masseuse.

Later, light-headed and limp, he lay down and stared once more at the ceiling paper.

As a convicted felon might in long vigils search his history for the first trespass that had brought him to his present state, Basil examined his conscience. Fasting, he knew, was in all religious systems the introduction to self-knowledge. Where had he first played false to his destiny? After the conception of Barbara; after her birth. She, in some way, was at the root of it. Though he had not begun to dote on her until she was eight years old, he had from the first been aware of his own paternity. In 1947, when she was a year old, he and Angela had gone to New York and California. That enterprise, in those days, was nefarious. Elaborate laws restricted the use of foreign currencies and these they had defied, drawing freely on undisclosed assets. But on his return he had made a full declaration to the customs. It was no immediate business of theirs to inquire into the sources of his laden trunks. In a mood of arrogance he had displayed everything and paid without demur. There lay the fount and origin of the deviation into rectitude that had disfigured him in recent years. As though waking after a night's drunkenness – an experience common enough in his youth – and confusedly articulating the disjointed memories of outrage and absurdity, he ruefully contemplated the change he had wrought in himself. His voice was not the same instrument as of old. He had first assumed it as a conscious imposture; it had become habitual to him; the antiquated, wordly-wise moralities which, using that voice, he had found himself obliged to utter, had become his settled opinions. It had begun as nursery clowning for the diversion of Barbara; a parody of Sir Joseph Mannering; darling, crusty old Pobble performing the part expected of him; and now the parody had become the *persona*.

His meditation was interrupted by the telephone. "Will you take a call from Mrs. Sothill?"

"Babs."

"Basil. I just wondered how you were getting on."

"They're very pleased with me."

"Thin?"

"Skinny. And concerned with my soul."

"Chump. Listen. I'm concerned with Barbara's soul."

"What's she been up to?"

"I think she's in love."

"Rot."

"Well, she's moping."

"I expect she misses me."

"When she isn't moping she's telephoning or writing letters."

"Not to me."

"Exactly. There's someone in London."

"Robin Trumpington?"

"She doesn't confide."

"Can't you listen in on the telephone?"

"I've tried that, of course. It's certainly a man she's talking to. I can't really understand their language but it sounds very affectionate. You won't like it awfully if she runs off, will you?"

"She'd never think of such a thing. Don't put ideas into the child's head, for God's sake. Give her a dose of castor oil."

"*I* don't mind, if *you* don't. I just thought I should warn."

"Tell her I'll soon be back."

"She knows that."

"Well, keep her under lock and key until I get out."

Basil reported the conversation to Angela. "Barbara says Barbara's in love."

"Which Barbara?"

"Mine. Ours."

"Well, it's quite normal at her age. Who with?"

"Robin Trumpington, I suppose."

"He'd be quite suitable."

"For heaven's sake, Angie, she's only a child."

"I fell in love at her age."

"And a nice mess that turned out. It's someone after my money."

"*My* money."

"I've always regarded it as mine. I shan't let her have a penny. Not till I'm dead anyway."

"You look half dead now."

"I've never felt better. You simply haven't got used to my new appearance."

"You're very shaky."

" 'Disembodied' is the word. Perhaps I need a drink. In fact I know I do. This whole business of Babs has come as a shock – at a most unsuitable time. I might go and see the booby doctor."

And, later, he set off along the corridor which led to the administrative office. He set off but had hardly hobbled six short paces when his newly sharpened conscience stabbed him. Was this the etherealized, the reborn, Basil slinking off like a schoolboy to seek the permission of a booby doctor for a simple adult indulgence? He turned aside and made for the gym.

There he found two large ladies in bathing-dresses sitting astride a low horse. They swallowed hastily and brushed crumbs from their lips. A rubbery young man in vest and shorts addressed him sternly: "One moment, sir. You can't come in here without an appointment."

"My visit is unprofessional," said Basil. "I want a word with you."

The young man looked doubtful. Basil drew his note case from his pocket and tapped it on the knob of his cane.

"Well, ladies, I think that finishes the work-out for this morning. We're getting along very nicely. We mustn't expect immediate results you know. Same routine tomorrow." He replaced the lid on a small enamelled bin. The ladies looked hungrily at it but went in peace.

"Whisky," said Basil.

"Whisky? Why, I couldn't give you such a thing even if I had it. It would be as much as my job's worth."

"I should think it is precisely what your job *is* worth."

"I don't quite follow, sir."

"My wife had grouse pie this morning."

He was a cheeky young man much admired in his own milieu for his bounce. He was not abashed. A horrible smirk of complicity passed over his face. "It wasn't really grouse," he said. "Just a stale liver pâté the grocer had. They get so famished here they don't care what they're eating, the poor creatures."

"Don't talk about my wife in those terms," said Basil, adding: "I shall know what I'm drinking, at a pound a snort."

"I haven't any whisky, honest. There may be a drop of brandy in the first-aid cupboard."

"Let's look at it."

It was of a reputable brand. Basil took two snorts. He gasped. Tears came to his eyes. He felt for support on the wall-bars beside him. For a moment he feared nausea. Then a great warmth and elation were kindled inside him. This was youth indeed; childhood no less. Thus he had been exalted in his first furtive swigging in his father's pantry. He had drunk as much brandy as this twice a day, most days of his adult life, after a variety of preliminary potations, and had felt merely a slight heaviness. Now in his etherealized condition he was, as it were, raised from the earth, held aloft and then lightly deposited; a mystical experience as though on Ganges bank or a spur of the Himalayas.

There was a mat near his feet, thick, padded, bed-like. Here he subsided and lay in ecstasy; quite outside his body, high and happy, his spirit soared; he shut his eyes.

"You can't stay here, sir. I've got to lock up."

"Don't worry," said Basil. "I'm not here."

The gymnast was very strong; it was a light task to hoist Basil on one of the trollies which in various sizes were part of the equipment of the sanatorium, and thus recumbent, dazed but not totally insensible, smoothly propelled up the main corridor, he was met by the presiding doctor.

"What have you there, sergeant?"

"Couldn't say at all. Never saw the gentleman before."

"It looks like Mr. Seal. Where did you find him?"

"He just walked into the gym, sir, looking rather queer and suddenly he passed out."

"Gave you a queer look? Yes."

"He rolls through the air with the greatest of ease, that darling young man on the flying trapeze," Basil chanted with some faint semblance of tune in his voice.

"Been overdoing it a bit, sir, I wouldn't wonder."

"You might be right, sergeant. You had better leave him now. The female staff can take over. Ah, Sister Gamage, Mr. Seal needs help in getting to his room. I think the régime has proved too strenuous for him. You may administer an ounce of brandy. I will come and examine him later."

But when he repaired to Basil's room he found his patient deeply sleeping.

He stood by the bed, gazing at his patient. There was an expression of peculiar innocence on the shrunken face. But the physician knew better.

"I will see him in the morning," he said and then went to instruct his secretary to inform the previous applicants that two vacancies had unexpectedly occurred.

III

"The sack, the push, the boot. I've got to be out of the place in an hour."

"Oh Basil, that *is* like old times, isn't it?"

"Only deep psychoanalysis can help me, he says, and in my present condition I am a danger to his institution."

"Where shall we go? Hill Street's locked up. There won't be anyone there until Monday."

"The odd thing is I have no hangover."

"Still ethereal?"

"Precisely. I suppose it means an hotel."

"You might telephone to Barbara and tell her to join us. She said she was keen to leave."

But when Angela telephoned to her sister-in-law, she heard: "But isn't Barbara with you in London? She told me yesterday you'd sent for her. She went up by the afternoon train."

"D'you think she can have gone to that young man?"

"I bet she has."

"Ought I to tell Basil?"

"Keep it quiet."

"I consider it very selfish of her. Basil isn't at all in good shape. He'll have a fit if he finds out. He had a sort of fit yesterday."

"Poor Basil. He may never know."

Basil and Angela settled their enormous bill. Their car was brought round to the front. The chauffeur drove. Angela sat beside Basil who huddled beside her occasionally crooning ill-remembered snatches of "the daring young man on the flying trapeze". As they approached London they met all the outgoing Friday traffic. Their own way was clear. At the hotel Basil went straight to bed – "I don't feel I shall ever want another bath as long as I live," he said – and Angela ordered a light meal for him of oysters and stout. By dusk he had rallied enough to smoke a cigar.

Next morning he was up early and spoke of going to his club.

"That dingy one?"

"Heavens no, Bellamy's. But I don't suppose there'll be many chaps there on a Saturday morning."

There was no one. The barman shook him up an egg with port and brandy. Then, with the intention of collecting some books, he took a taxi to Hill Street. It was not yet eleven o'clock. He let himself into what should have been the empty and silent house. Music came from the room on the ground floor where small parties congregated before luncheon and dinner. It was a dark room, hung with tapestry and furnished with Bühl. There he found his daughter, dressed in pyjamas and one of her mother's fur coats, seated on the floor with her face caressing a transistor radio. Behind her in the fireplace large lumps of coal lay on the ashes of the sticks and paper which had failed to kindle them.

"Darling Pobble, never more welcome. I didn't expect you till Monday and I should have been dead by then. I can't make out how the central heating works. I thought the whole point of it was it just turned on and didn't need a man. Can't get the fire to burn.

And don't start: 'Babs, what are you doing here?' I'm freezing, that's what."

"Turn that damn thing off."

In the silence Barbara regarded her father more intently. "Darling, what have they been doing to you? You aren't yourself at all. You're tottering. Not my fine stout Pobble at all. Sit down at once. Poor Pobble, all shrunk like a mummy. Beasts!"

Basil sat and Barbara wriggled round until her chin rested on his knees. "Famine baby," she said. Star-sapphire eyes in the child-like face under black touselled hair gazed deep into star-sapphire eyes sunk in empty pouches. "Belsen atrocity," she added fondly. "Wraith. Skeleton-man. Dear dug-up corpse."

"Enough of this flattery. Explain yourself."

"I told you I was bored. You know what Malfrey's like as well as I do. Oh the hell of the National Trust. It's not so bad in the summer with the charabancs. Now it's only French art experts – half a dozen a week, and all the rooms still full of oilcloth promenades and rope barriers and Aunt Barbara in the flat over the stables and those ridiculous Sothills in the bachelors' wing and the height of excitement a pheasant shoot with lunch in the hut and then nothing to eat except pheasant and... Well, I registered a formal complaint, didn't I?, but you were too busy starving to pay any attention, and if your only, adored daughter's happiness doesn't count for more than senile vanity...." she paused, exhausted.

"There's more to it than that."

"There is *something* else."

"What?"

"Now, Pobble, you have to take this calmly. For your own good, not for mine. I'm used to violence, God knows. If you had been poor the police would have been after you for the way you've knocked me about all these years. I can take it; but you, Pobble, you are at an age when it might be dangerous. So keep quite calm and I'll tell you. I'm engaged to be married."

It was not a shock; it was not a surprise. It was what Basil had expected. "Rot," he said.

"I happen to be in love. You must know what that means. You must have been in love once – with mummy or someone."

"Rot. And dammit, Babs, don't blub. If you think you're old enough to be in love, you're old enough not to blub."

"That's a silly thing to say. It's being in love makes me blub. You don't realize. Apart from being perfect and frightfully funny he's an artistic genius and everyone's after him and I'm jolly lucky to have got him and you'll love him too once you know him if only you won't be stuck-up and we got engaged on the telephone so I came up and he was out for all I know someone else *has* got him and I almost died of cold and now you come in looking more like a vampire than a papa and start saying 'rot'."

She pressed her face on his thigh and wept.

After a time Basil said: "What makes you think Robin paints?"

"Robin? Robin Trumpington? You don't imagine I'm engaged to *Robin*, do you? He's got a girl of his own he's mad about. You don't know much about what goes on, do you, Pobble? If it's only Robin you object to, everything's all right."

"Well, who the hell do you think you are engaged to?"

"Charles of course."

"Charles à Court. Never heard of him."

"Don't pretend to be deaf. You know perfectly well who I mean. You met him here the other evening only I don't think you really took him in."

"*Albright*," said Basil. It was evidence of the beneficial effect of the sanatorium that he did not turn purple in the face, did not gobble. He merely asked quietly: "Have you been to bed with this man?"

"Not to *bed*."

"Have you slept with him?"

"Oh, no *sleep*."

"You know what I mean. Have you had sexual intercourse with him?"

"Well, perhaps; not in bed; on the floor and wide awake you *might* call it intercourse, I suppose."

"Come clean, Babs. Are you a virgin?"

"It's not a thing any girl likes having said about her, but I think I am."

"*Think?*"

"Well, I suppose so. Yes, really. But we can soon change all that. Charles is set on marriage, bless him. He says it's easier to get married to girls if they're virgins. I can't think why. I don't mean a big wedding. Charles is very unsocial and he's an orphan, no father, no mother, and his relations don't like him, so we'll just be married quietly in a day or two and then I thought if you and mummy don't want it we might go to the house in Bermuda. We shan't be any trouble to you at all, really. If you want to go to Bermuda, we'll settle for Venice, but Charles says that's a bit square and getting cold in November, so Bermuda will really be better."

"Has it occurred to either of you that you need my permission to marry?"

"Now don't get legal, Pobble. You know I love you far too much ever to do anything you wouldn't like."

"You'd better get dressed and go round to your mother at Claridges."

"Can't get dressed. No hot water."

"Have a bath there. I had better see this young man."

"He's coming here at twelve."

"I'll wait for him."

"You'll freeze."

"Get up and get out."

There followed one of those scuffles that persisted between father and daughter even in her eighteenth year which ended in her propulsion, yelping.

Basil sat and waited. The bell could not be heard in the ante-room. He sat in the window and watched the doorstep, saw a taxi draw up and Barbara enter it, still in pyjamas and fur coat, carrying a small case. Later he saw his enemy strolling confidently from Berkeley Square. Basil opened the door.

"You did not expect to see me?"

"No, but I'm very glad to. We've a lot to discuss."

They went together to the ante-room. The young man was

less bizarre in costume than on their previous meeting but his hair was as copious and his beard proclaimed his chosen, deleterious status. They surveyed one another in silence. Then Basil said: "Lord Pastmaster's shirts are too big for you."

It was a weak opening.

"It's not a thing I should have brought up if you hadn't," said Albright, "but *all* your clothes look too big for *you*."

Basil covered his defeat by lighting a cigar.

"Barbara tells me you've been to that sanatorium in Kent," continued the young man easily; "there's a new place, you know, much better, in Sussex."

Basil was conscious of quickening recognition. Some faint, odious inkling of kinship; had he not once, in years far gone by, known someone who had spoken in this way to his elders? He drew deeply on his cigar and studied Albright. The eyes, the whole face seemed remotely familiar; the reflection of a reflection seen long ago in shaving-mirrors.

"Barbara tells me you have proposed marriage to her."

"Well, *she* actually popped the question. I was glad to accept."

"You are Clarence Albright's son?"

"Yes, did you know him? I barely did. I hear he was rather awful. If you want to be genealogical, I have an uncle who is a duke. But I barely know him either."

"And you are a painter?"

"Did Barbara tell you that?"

"She said you were an artistic genius."

"She's a loyal little thing. She must mean my music."

"You compose?"

"I improvise sometimes. I play the guitar."

"Professionally?"

"Sometimes – in coffee bars, you know."

"I do not know, I'm afraid. And you make a living by it?"

"Not what *you* would call a living."

"May I ask, then, how you propose to support my daughter?"

"Oh that doesn't come into it. It's the other way round. I'm doing what you did, marrying money. Now I know what's in your mind. 'Buy him off,' you think. I assure you that won't work.

Barbara is infatuated with me and, if it's not egotistical to mention it, I am with her. I'm sure you won't want one of those 'Gretna Green Romances' and press photographers following you about. Besides, Barbara doesn't want to be a nuisance to you. She's a loyal girl, as we've already remarked. The whole thing can be settled calmly. Think of the taxes your wife will save by a good solid marriage settlement. It will make no appreciable difference to your own allowance."

And still Basil sat steady, unmoved by any tremor of that volcanic senility which a fortnight ago would have exploded in scalding, blinding showers. He was doing badly in this first encounter which he had too lightly provoked. He must take thought and plan. He was not at the height of his powers. He had been prostrate yesterday. Today he was finding his strength. Tomorrow experience would conquer. This was a worthy antagonist and he felt something of the exultation which a brave of the sixteenth century might have felt when in a brawl he suddenly recognized in the clash of blades a worthy swordsman.

"Barbara's mother has the best financial advice," he said.

"By the way, where is Barbara? She arranged to meet me here."

"She's having a bath in Claridges."

"I ought to go over and see her. I'm taking her out to lunch. You couldn't lend me a fiver, could you?"

"Yes," said Basil. "Certainly."

If Albright had known him better he would have taken alarm at this urbanity. All he thought was: "Old crusty's a much softer job than anyone told me." And Basil thought: "I hope he spends it all on luncheon. That bank-note is all he will ever get. He deserved better."

IV

Sonia Trumpington had never remarried. She shared a flat with her son Robin but saw little of him. Mostly she spent her day alone with her needlework and in correspondence connected with one or two charitable organizations with which, in age, she had become involved. She was sewing when Basil sought her out after luncheon (oysters again, two dozen this time with a pint of champagne – his strength waxed hourly) and she continued to stitch at the framed grospoint while he confided his problem to her.

"Yes, I've met Charles Albright. He's rather a friend of Robin's."

"Then perhaps you can tell me what Barbara sees in him."

"Why, *you*, of course," said Sonia. "Haven't you noticed? He's the dead spit – looks, character, manner, everything."

"Looks? Character? Manner? Sonia you're raving."

"Oh, not as you are now, not even after your cure. Don't you remember at all what you were like at his age?"

"But he's a monster."

"So were you, darling. Have you quite forgotten? It's all as clear as clear to me. You Seals are so incestuous. Why do you suppose you got keen on Barbara? Because she's just like Barbara Sothill. Why is Barbara keen on Charles? Because he's *you*."

Basil considered this proposition with his newly resharpened wits.

"That beard."

"I've seen you with a beard."

"That was after I came back from the Arctic and I never played the guitar in my life," he said.

"Does Charles play the guitar? First I've heard of it. He does all sorts of things – just as you did."

"I wish you wouldn't keep bringing me into it."

"Have you quite forgotten what you were like? Have a look at some of my old albums."

Like most of her generation Sonia had in youth filled large volumes with press-cuttings and photographs of herself and her friends. They lay now in a shabby heap in a corner of the room.

"That's Peter's twenty-firster at King's Thursday. First time I met you, I think. Certainly the first time I met Alastair. He was Margot's boy-friend then, remember? She was jolly glad to be rid of him. . . . That's my marriage. I bet you were there." She turned the pages from the posed groups of bride, bridegroom and bridesmaids to the snapshots taken at the gates of St. Margaret's. "Yes, here you are."

"No beard. Perfectly properly dressed."

"Yes, there are more incriminating ones later. Look at that ... and that."

They opened successive volumes. Basil appeared often.

"I don't think any of them very good likenesses," said Basil stiffly. "I'd just come back from the Spanish front there – of course I look a bit untidy."

"It's not clothes we're talking about. Look at your expression."

"Light in my eyes," said Basil.

"1937. That's another party at King's Thursday."

"What a ghastly thing facetious photographs are. What on earth am I doing with that girl?"

"Throwing her in the lake. I remember the incident now. I took the photograph."

"Who?"

"I've no idea. Perhaps it says on the back. Just 'Basil and Betty'. She must have been much younger than us, not our kind at all. I've got an idea she was the daughter of some duke or other. The Stayles – that's who she was."

Basil studied the picture and shuddered. "What can have induced me to behave like that?"

"Youthful high spirits."

"I was thirty-four, God help me. She's very plain."

"I'll tell you who she is – was. Charles Albright's mother. That's an odd coincidence if you like. Let's look her up and make sure."

She found a *Peerage* and read: "Here we are. Fifth daughter of the late duke. Elizabeth Ermyntrude Alexandra, for whom H.R.H. The Duke of Connaught stood sponsor. Born 1920. Married 1940 Clarence Albright, killed in action 1943. Leaving issue. Died 1956. I remember hearing about it – cancer, very young. That's Charles, that issue."

Basil gazed long at the photograph. The girl was plump and, it seemed, wriggling; annoyed rather than amused by the horse-play. "How one forgets. I suppose she was quite a friend of mine once."

"No, no. She was just someone Margot produced for Peter."

Basil's imagination, once so fertile of mischief, lately so dormant, began now, in his hour of need, to quicken and stir.

"That photograph has given me an idea."

"Basil, you've got that old villainous look. What are you up to?"

"Just an idea."

"You're not going to throw Barbara into the Serpentine."

"Something not unlike it," he said.

"Let us go and sit by the Serpentine," said Basil to his daughter that afternoon.

"Won't it be rather cold?"

"It will be quiet. Wrap up well. I have to talk to you seriously."

"Good temper?"

"Never better."

"Why not talk here?"

"Your mother may come in. What I have to say doesn't concern her."

"It's about me and Charles, I bet."

"Certainly."

"Not a scolding?"

"Far from it. Warm fatherly sympathy."

"It's worth being frozen for that."

They did not speak in the car. Basil sent it away, saying they would find their own way back. At that chilly tea-time, with the leaves dry and falling, there was no difficulty in finding an empty seat. The light was soft; it was one of the days when London seems like Dublin.

"Charles said he'd talked to you. He wasn't sure you loved him."

"I love him."

"Oh, *Pobble*."

"He did not play the guitar but I recognized his genius."

"Oh, Pobble, what are you up to?"

"Just what Sonia asked." Basil leaned his chin on the knob of his cane. "You know, Babs, that all I want is your happiness."

"This doesn't sound at all like you. You've got some sly scheme."

"Far from it. You must never tell him or your mother what I am about to say. Charles's parents are dead so they are not affected. I knew his mother very well; perhaps he doesn't know how well. People often wondered why she married Albright. It was a blitz marriage, you know, while he was on leave and there were air raids every night. It was when I was first out of hospital, before I married your mother."

"Darling Pobble, it's very cold here and I don't quite see what all this past history has to do with me and Charles."

"It began," said Basil inexorably, "when – what was her name? – Betty was younger than you are now. I threw her into the lake at King's Thursday."

"What began?"

"Betty's passion for me. Funny what excites a young girl – with you a guitar, with Betty a ducking."

"Well, I think that's rather romantic. It sort of brings you and Charles closer."

"Very close indeed. It was more than romantic. She was too young at the beginning – just a girlish crush. I thought she would get over it. Then, when I was wounded, she took to visiting me every day in hospital and the first day I came out – you won't be able to understand the sort of exhilaration a man feels at a time like that, or the appeal lameness has for some women, or the sense of general irresponsibility we all had during the blitz – I'm not trying to excuse myself. I was not the first man. She had grown up since the splash in the lake. It only lasted a week. Strictly perhaps I should have married her, but I was less strict in those days. I married your mother instead. You can't complain about that. If I hadn't, you wouldn't exist. Betty had to look elsewhere and fortunately that ass Albright turned up in the nick. Yes, Charles is your brother, so how could I help loving him?"

Soundlessly Barbara rose from the seat and sped through the twilight, stumbled on her stiletto heels across the sand of the Row, disappeared behind the statuary through Edinburgh Gate. Basil at his own pace followed. He stopped a taxi, kept it waiting at the kerb while he searched Bellamy's vainly for a friendly face, drank another egg-nog at the bar, went on towards Claridges.

"What on earth's happened to Barbara?" Angela asked. "She came in with a face of tragedy, didn't speak and now she's locked herself in your bedroom."

"I think she's had a row with that fellow she was keen on. What was his name? Albright. A good thing really, a likeable fellow but not at all suitable. I daresay Babs needs a change of scene. Angie, if it suits you, I think we might all three of us go to Bermuda tomorrow."

"Can we get tickets?"

"I have them already. I stopped at the travel office on my way from Sonia's. I don't imagine Babs will want much dinner tonight. She's best left alone at the moment. I feel I could manage a square meal. We might have it downstairs."

THE OXFORD PLAYHOUSE

'The Oxford Playhouse' (column head cartoon), *The Cherwell*,
10 November 1923, p. 56 and thereafter.

JUVENILIA

THE CURSE OF THE HORSE RACE

CHAP I   BETTING

I BET YOU 500 pounds I'll win. The speaker was Rupert a man of about 25 he had a dark bushy mistarsh and flashing eyes.

I shouldn't trust to much on your horse said Tom for ineed he had not the sum to spear.

The race was to take place at ten the following moring

CHAP II

The next moring Tom took his seat in the grant stand while Rupert mounted Sally (which was his horse) with the others to wate for the pistol shot which would anounse the start.

The race was soon over and Rupet had lost. What was he to do could he do the deed? Yes I'll *kill* him in the night, he thought.

CHAP III   THE FIRE

Rupert crept stedfustly along with out a sound but as he drew his sword it squeeked a little   this awoke Tom seasing a candle he lit it just at that moment Rupert struch and sent the candle flying

The candle lit the cuntain   Rupert trying to get away tumbled over the bed   Tom maid a dash for the dorr and cleided with a perlisman who had come to see what was the matter and a panic took place.

CHAP IIII   EXPLAIND

While Tom and the peliesman were escapeing through the door Rupert was adaping quite a diffrat methand of escape he puld the matris of the bed and hurld the it out of the window then jumped out he landed safe and sound on the matris then began to run for all he was worth now let us leave Rupert and turn to Tom and the peliesman as soon as they got out Tom told the peliesman what had hapend.

CHAP V   HOT ON THE TRAIL

"See there he is" said Tom "We must folow him and take him to prizen" said the peliesman.

There's no time to spere said Tom letts get horses said the peliesman so they bort horses and and galerpin in the direcion they had seen him go.

On they went aintil they were face to face with each other. the peliesman lept from his horse only to be stabed to the hart by Rupert then Tom jumped down and got Rupert a smart blow on the cheak.

CHAP VI   A DEADLY FIGHT

This enraged Rupert thake that he shouted and made a plung but tom was too quick for him artfully dogeing the sword he brout his sword round on Rupert's other cheak.

Just at that moment Ruper slashed killed the peliesmans horse then lept on Toms horse and galapt off.

CHAP VII   THE MYSTERIOUS MAN

Of cause then was no chance of catching him on foot so Tom walked to the nearest inn to stay the night but it was ful up he had to share with a nother man.

Thou Tom was yerry tired he could not sleep, their was something about the man he was he did not like he reminded him of some one he didnot know who. Sudnly he felt something moveing on the bed looking up he saw the man fully dressed just getting off the bed.

CHAP VIII   RUN TO ERTH

Now Tom could see that the mysteraous man was Rupert. Has he come to do a merder? Or has he only come to stay the night?

thees were the thoughts that rushed throu Toms head he lay still to what Rupert would do first he opened a cubord and took out a small letter bag from this he took some thing wich made Toms blod turn cold it was a bistol Tom lept forward and seesed Rubert by the throught and flung him to the ground then snaching a bit of robe from the ground he bound Rupert hand and foot.

CHAP IX   HUNG

Then Tom drest himself then Tom took Rupert to the puliese cort Rupert was hung for killing the pulies man. I hope this story will be aleson to you never to bet.

'The Attack – The Chief's Son Killed', *In Quest of Thomas Lee*, Part III,
p. 17. Dated 1914. [See Introduction, p. xi.]

FIDON'S CONFETION

CHAPTER I

MIDNIGHT BOOMED from the old clock tower and still the two men played on. Ralfe the eldest son of Gerald Cantonville had got in debt to a villainous money lender and in desperation had taken to gambling in a great efort to "raise the wind" all in vain on he played and still Baycraw won. Sudenly the door opened and in came a young boy of nineteen he had just left his public school carrying away nearly every cup at the sports. He was certainly not clever clever for he had never got any higher than the upper fifth   "Hullo Ralfe still playing I should turn in"   The elder brother looked up sharply "Get off to bed youngster" he growled and then returned to the game. Tom Cantonville shrugged his shoulders and went out with despair in his heart.

Baycraw tiptoed down stairs and opened the window a cold draft of air blew in. He wistled softly and a dark form was siluetted for a moment against the bleu without. Then came a soft thud and a wispered warning. Then silence. The two men Baycraw and Fidon crept up stairs and having opened the door Mr. Cantonville's room switched on the light. The old man turned over binked and started only to find himself looking down the barrel of a "colt" revolver

"Make a sound and your a dead man" wispered Braycow

"Who are you" murmered the terrified man

"You know very well! You havn't such a bad memory as all that. Come no think can't remember a certain bank robery in which a certain Cargon figurgered, do you not recall what he said when you found him out eh? something about revenge? well I am he and this – Fidon at this moment broke off as Braycaw raising a knife plunged it down ward there was a strangled and stilness.

"This" continued Fidon "Is our revenge

CHAPTER II

Halfe past eight and stil no apearance of Mr. Cantonville. They began to get nervous he was always punctual. Tom went to see what it was. In a minute he staggered back white to the lips his hand on his fore head he reeled into a chair and lay their like one dead his breath coming in short gasps   Ralfe ran to the side bord and returned with a liqure glass of brandy. Tom drunk it and sat up "He's dead" he said "they bloods all over his chest. Mrs. Cantonville rushed up to the room followed by all the other. There lay Mr. Cantonville a knife embedded in his chest. "We'd better leave it as it is for the detectives to see" advised Ralfe   Tom was already at the telephone and in ten minutes a car swung up the drive and a detective alighted. All this time Braycaw was sitting in the breakfast room puffing a segar but now he followed the detective to the scene of the crime. The detective bent out of the boddy and drew out the knife it was an Idian dagger which had belonged to Ralfe but which he had given as security to Braycaw on not being able to pay for the gambling. "Why" cried Barbarous his sister "That's Ralfe's knife"

the detective turned on Ralfe "Can you acount for this?" he demanded

"I think I can" said Braycaw stepping forward   "He was in debt and he was heir to all his father's property and money

"You cad" cried Ralfe leaping forward but was brough up by the detectives revolver leveled at him

"Mr Ralfe Cantonville" he said dryly "you can make all your excuses in court untill then consider yourselfe under arest."

Tom buried his face in his hands. He heard a click and saw Ralfe handcuffed. He turned and ran down stairs and buring his face in his hands sobbed like a child. Suddenly the door swung open and in walked Braycaw a cynical smile on his lips   Tom leapt to his feet his eyes blazing   "Rather unfortunate about your brother eh? what?" drawled Braycaw. Tom's reply was a terific swing of his fist. Braycaw who was not a big man stagered back his hands on his face and colapsed on the floor. Tom turned on his heel and left the room leaving Braycaw in a heap on the ground with a broken nose.

CHAPTER III

Now what ever falts Fidon might have he was not a cad and upon hearing of Ralfes arrest he quicly resolved to turn kings evidence and so it was that at halfe past five that evening there was a knock at the door and a clean shaven made steped into the spaceous hall of Cantonville Chase. He was ushered into the drawing room where he found Tom dedjectedly trying to read. He came quickly to the point and told everything. Tom escitedly brought paper and pen and the confetion was written. Sudenly there came a report the smashing of glass and a cry from Fidon a small figure rushed in flung some thing on the ground and the whole room was full of smoke. Tom stagered to the window and let in a cool draft of night air. As smoke cleared away he saw Fidon lying with a bullet in his head and the precious confetion was gone. Then he heard the purr of a motor car outside he rushed only to see Braycaw in a motor disapearing outside he seize his bike and in a second was following. On and on they went in a mad chase the result of which would mean a mans life Tom drew his "Browning" revolver and fire into the darkness ahead he fired again and saw a jet of flame shoot out of the car, he had fired the petrol! the car lurched and swurved; a dark form lept from it. Tom jumped from his bike and seized Braycaw by the coat. A swift turn and Braycaw was gone leaving Tom holding the coat. But Tom could see in the light of the blazing car something that made his heart leap with joy-out of the pocket petruded the confetion. Ralfe was safe!

CHAPTER IV

The light streamed in at the window and Tom sat up his first
action was to feel under the pillow and a sigh of relief broke from
his lips as he felt the paper but he must get on the trial was
tomorro and he had a long way to go. He looked at the clockit
was 10 o'clock in 24 hours the trial would take place. He dressed
and after a hasty meal hurried to the station the train was waiting
and he got in. Five minutes later the train had started and was just
getting up steam when a bearded gentleman rushed up the platform and leapt at the train. With agility that did not suite his years
he swung onto the footbord and so in to the window where Tom
was seated. Having apologies for his strange entrance he settled
down and to all apearances slept   Tom looked him up and down
and noticed he had a broken nose. He began to suspect something. He sliped his hand behind the visitor and pulled one of the
locks and he saw it was a wig. Then he lept forward and seized the
beared it came away in his hand revealing Braycaw who leapt at
him. The two struggled feercly together for some time then as
they realed against the door it gave and they fell out on the hill
down which the roled until it came to are shere drop Tom lost
contitiousness.

When Tom recovered his senses it was dark he felt in his
pocett and struck a light he was lying on a bush petruding from
the side. Braycaw had been caught in the bush also but by his
neck and he lay dead   Tom shuddered. But he had other thinks
than a murderer's fate to trouble his mind. In a few hours his
brother would be tried and he must get there with the confetion.
He looked about him and saw the only possible way to escape was
by most dangerous and wll nigh imposiple climb. But he saw that
if he was to save his brother he must act and act quicly slowly
raised himself to a stanidng possition then he felt above him and
gripped the rock above slowly he puled himselfe up and then he
found himselfe looking into a cave. He then remembered that it

was a sumuggler's cave that led to the old inn. He made his way up and opened the trap door which opened into the inn yard he pulled himselfe up and then began the race against time he rushed to the station just as the train was starting and leapt to the footboard of the engin "Would you like to earn a five pound note and save a man's life" he cried The man looked amazed "Then reach Sherborough before ten" that was all. The driver opened the throttle of the engine and she sped forward into the night

CHAPTER V

Nine o'clock struck and Ralfe paced his sell restlesly He put his hand to his hot head "could it be true? or was only a dreadful nightmare?" he flung himselfe on the hard bench "What if the trial did go against him? hung" he shuddered there was one window in his sell a small grating he could not escape.

Ralfe clung to the rail of the box as one witness after another rose and then suddenly there staggered into the room a young man his colar undone his tie twisted and blood on his face a bandage round his head. it was Tom. It is needless to desscribe the whole trial. Let it be said only that Tom's arival saved Ralfe who was aquitted "without a stain on his character. Now he has a pretty wife and two children and often on Autumn evening they sit round the fire never tiered of following with their father his adventures and those of his brother in the race against time to get Fidon's confetion.

The End

'Paris Letter' (column head cartoon), *The Isis*, 28 November 1923, p. 13 and thereafter.

MULTA PECUNIA

CHAPTER I

SIR ALFRED James, a great collector of books, one day chanced to look at an old volume which had the curious name of "Multa Pecunia", which told him that under his house there was a cave in which was untold of wealth. He did not trouble to read any more, for he had heard the yarn before, and did not believe it.

When Tom came home, being Sir Alfred's son, he was treated with great respect by the servants and therefore was allowed to go into every nook and corner of the house. He was in a little poky room one day, when he saw this carving "Multa Pecunia". He stared for some time at the carving, when suddenly he remembered seeing a book in the library with the same title. Immediately he ran to the library and took out the catalogue. There he saw these words, "Multa Pecunia, shelf 7, place 13". He was immediately at shelf 7, but place 13 was empty!

CHAPTER II

What could it mean? Why had the book gone? He was quite bewildered. "Jumping Golliwogs" cried Tom at last, "I must tell the Pater." He left the room with the intention of going to tell his father about the mysterious disappearance of the old volume; perhaps his father had it, or — Hark! what was that! the rustling of stiff paper was audible. He was now quite close to Smith, the butler's room. The door was open so he looked in. There he saw Smith leaning over the old volume deeply engrossed. Suddenly he got up and walked stealthily to the door. Then he walked off in the direction of the room with the carving. When he got there he pressed the letter "U" and immediately a little trap door opened which was about 17 by 13 inches. Into this crept Smith followed by Tom. The two crept along a passage, and stopped at the sight of a great granite door. "Smith! what does this mean?" cried Tom putting his hand on Smith's collar. Smith fairly staggered when he saw Tom; in fact he simply lost his head, and flew at Tom's throat. A tremendous fight ensued in which Tom with his knowledge of boxing gave him, gave Smith an "up shot" blow that fairly staggered him. But in the end weight won and Tom was knocked senseless to the ground: but Smith was not a fellow to leave him there, he carried him up the steps and laying him down at the door of the library, then closing the door of the secret cave, and putting back the old volume in the library as he found it, he went back to bed.

Sir Alfred came striding along the passage to the library when he suddenly stopped in utter astonishment. "Tom!" he gasped as he saw the boy's pale face.

CHAPTER III

When Tom came to consciousness he found himself in a soft feather bed with a nurse at his bedside. "Ah! that's good, he is conscious now" she whispered. "Why did Smith attack me? asked Tom feebly. "He's delirious" said the nurse turning to the doctor, "I thought he would be after that fall, poor boy"; for the library being at the foot of a flight of steps, Sir Alfred and the nurse naturally thought he had fallen down them.

A long time had past and Tom had not been allowed to see anyone as he had concussion of the brain. At last he was allowed to see someone and nurse asked him who he would choose for his first visitor. "Smith" was the reply. In came Smith very shyly. Why did you fling me down on that stone" demanded Tom.

CHAPTER IV

Now Smith was not usually a butler. He was really a prof-fesional thief and so he soon thought of what to say, so turning to the nurse he said "I think I had better go for the excitement of seeing anybody after such a long time of quiet has made him a bit mad," with that he left the room.

Tom was quite well and able to run about the house, so he thought he would see Smith. Smith was not in his room, so Tom thought that he would go into the secret cave. He went to the old carving, pressed the letter "U", immediately the same door opened. He went along the passage. Suddenly he stopped abruptly, for footsteps could be heard coming towards him. He crouched down waiting ready to spring. The footsteps came nearer and nearer. Tom could feel his heart thumping against his ribs. Suddenly appeared round the corner of the passage, Tom was on his in a minute and taken by surprise Smith was flung senseless to the ground. Tom was just getting up when he saw a piece of old parchment, he opened it and this is what he read – "I, Wilfred James have stolen these articles of great price from Queen Elizabeth. I could not keep the secret so I put my confidence in Sir Walter Raleigh who gave a hint about it to the great statesman Bacon, who told Queen Elizabeth. The troops of soldiers will be here in one hour and if they find the jewels I shall be locked in the Tower." There the paper ended, so Tom began to look for the jewels, and found them in Smith's pocket. Then putting Smith back on his bed he went to his father's study and told Sir Alfred all the paper had said, and showed him the jewels.

The next day Sir Alfred gave Smith the "sack" and the day after he was found to be the worst thief that ever puzzled Scotland Yard and was arrested and sent to Dartmoor convict prison.

The End

'Evolution and Plus Fours', *The Isis*, 1 November 1922, p. 10.

FRAGMENT OF A NOVEL

To myself,

Evelyn Arthur St. John Waugh

to whose sympathy and appreciation
alone it owes its being,
this book is dedicated.

Dedicatory letter,

My dear Evelyn,

Much has been written and spoken about the lot of the boy with literary aspirations in a philistine family; little can adequately convey his difficulties, when the surroundings, which he has known from childhood, have been entirely literary. It is a sign of victory over these difficulties that this book is chiefly, if at all, worthy of attention.

Many of your relatives and most of your father's friends are more or less directly interested in paper and print. Ever since you first left the nursery for meals with your parents downstairs, the conversation, to which you were an insatiable listener, has been of books, their writers and producers; ever since, as a sleepy but triumphantly emancipate school-boy, you were allowed to sit up with our elders in the "bookroom" after dinner, you have heard little but discussion about books. Your home has always been full of them; all new books of any merit, and most of none, seem by one way or another to find their place in the files which have long overflowed the shelves. Among books your whole life has been layed and you are now rising up in your turn to add one more to the everlasting bonfire of the ephemeral.

And all this will be brought up against you. "Another of these precocious Waughs," they will say, "one more nursery novel." So be it. There is always a certain romance, to the author at least, about a first novel which no reviewer can quite shatter. Good luck! You have still high hopes and big ambitions and have not yet been crushed in the mill of professionalism. Soon perhaps you will join the "wordsmiths" jostling one another for royalties and contracts, meanwhile you are still very young.

Yourself,
Evelyn

I

Peter Audley awoke with "second bell" ringing dismally down the cloisters and rolling over in bed looked at his watch. Re-assured that he had another five minutes before he need begin getting up, he pulled his rug up over his shoulders and lay back gazing contentedly down the dormitory, which was already stir-ring with the profoundly comforting sounds made by other people dressing. The splashing of the showers next door, the chipping of the thick crockery and the muttered oaths at back-studs accentuated the pleasure of the last minutes.

Early school was kept up practically all the year round at Selchurch, which took a certain pride in the gloom of these early mornings. Peter, however, had got his "privileges" which took away the bitterest sting of frantic punctuality and allowed him, after reporting to his form master, to sit out and work in his study.

With a heave he got out of bed and went to wash. The showers looked singularly uninviting but the water for the basins was stone cold – the furnaces were not lit until midday in March 1918 – and with rising gloom he returned shivering and half dry to the dormitory. Some fanatic had opened one of the high Gothic windows and a cold gust of wind swept down the room. There was a chorus of protestation and the window was closed. He dressed dully and leaving the dormitory at a few minutes past seven crossed the quad to "report". Several fags, laden with books, dashed past him, trying desperately to avoid recognition by the prefect "taking lates". His form master nodded to him and he turned on his heel and made for his study. The gravel was dark with fallen rain, the sky menacing with monstrous rough hewn clouds; over everything spread a fine, wet mist.

The handle of his study door was cold; he went in, kicked the door to and fell into an easy chair gazing round the tiny room. It was pleasant enough and he had spent considerable pains on it, but this morning it afforded him no pleasure.

The carpet was black – a burst of aestheticism which he had long regretted as it took a great deal of brushing and earned his study the name of the "coal cellar" – and the walls distempered a bluish grey. On them were hung four large Medici prints, the gift of his grandmother but his own choice; Botticelli's Mars & Venus – he had had some difficulty over this with his house master, to whom a nude was indecent whether it came from the National Gallery or La Vie Parisienne – Beatrice d'Este, Rembrandt's "Philosopher" and Holbein's Duchess of Milan. These he liked either because they were very beautiful or because they gave an air of distinction which his friends' Harrison Fishers and Rilette pictures lacked. The curtains, cushions on the window seat and table cloth were blue; the whole room was pleasantly redolent of the coffee of the evening before.

Peter, however, lay back staring gloomily at the grey block of class rooms opposite. It was Saturday morning and Saturday afternoon was the time chosen, as being the longest uninter-rupted time in the week, for the uniform parade. He could just remember when, his first term, summer 1914, it had been the great social time of the week when tea was brewed and quantities of eclaires eaten, and now that he had grown to an age to have a study and enjoy these things, they were all blotted out and from two to six he would have to manoeuvre a section of sullen fags over the wet downs in some futile "attack scheme".

He knew exactly what would happen. They would fall in on one of the quads and be inspected – that meant half an hours work with reeking brasso and s.a.p. cleaning his uniform and equipment. They would then march up to the downs and in a driving wind stand easy while the O.C. explained the afternoons

work. Ordnance maps would be issued to all N.C.O.s with which
to follow the explanation; these always bulged with incorrect
folding and flapped in the wind.

It was never considered sufficient for one company merely to
come and attack the other; a huge campaign of which they
formed a tiny part would have to be elaborated. A company
would be the advanced guard of part of an army, which had
landed at Littlehampton and was advancing upon Hasting,
intending to capture important bridge heads on the local river
on their way; B company, with white hat bands, would be a force
set to hold the spur of the downs above the Sanatorium cooperat-
ing with hypothetical divisions on either flank, until another
division could arrive from Arundel. Rattles would be issued to
serve as Lewis guns and this game of make-believe would go on
for three hours, with extreme discomfort to both sides, when
whistles and bugles would sound and the corps form up again for
a criticism of the afternoon's work. They would be told that,
when the parade was dismissed, all rifles were to be wiped over
with an oily rag before being returned to the armoury and that all
uniforms were to be back in the lockers before six o'clock. They
would then dismiss, hungry, bad tempered and with only twenty
minutes in which to change for Chapel.

He hated the corps and all the more now that he had to take it
seriously. He was seventeen and a half; next year, if the war was
still on, as it showed every sign of being, would see him fighting. It
brought everything terribly near. He had learnt much of what it
was like over there from his brother, but Ralf saw everything so
abstractedly with such imperturbable cynicism. Peter flattered
himself that he was far more sensitive and temperamental. He
was sure that he would not be able to stand it; Ralf had won the
D.S.O. some months ago.

He collected his thoughts with a start and looked at his
time table. He had to finish the chapter of Economics which
he had left the evening before. The book was lying where he had
tossed it and, like everything that morning, looked singularly
uninviting. It was bound in a sort of greasy, limp, oil cloth,
"owing", a label half scraped off the back proclaimed, "to

shortage of labour"; it was printed crookedly on a thin greyish paper with little brown splinters of wood in it; it was altogether a typical piece of wartime workmanship. He took it up with listless repulsion and began to read.

"From considerations of this nature," he read, "which, while not true of every person, taken individually, are yet on the average true, it may be inferred, with approximate accuracy, that by adding to the wealth of the poor, something taken, by some recognised and legal process, from the wealth of the rich, while some dissatisfaction as well as satisfaction is inevitably caused, yet, provided that the poor be greater in number than the rich, the satisfaction is greater than the dissatisfaction. Inequality of wealth, insofar as ... "

It was all ineffably tedious. He tossed the book on to the table in the corner and taking up a novel passed the next half hour in dissatisfied gloom.

II

The clock in the quad struck quarter to eight and voices and shuffling sounded across the gravel as the forms began emptying. The door of his study was burst open and Bellinger came in.

"Edifying spectacle of history specialist at work! Here have I been doing geography with the 'door mouse' for three mortal quarters of an hour, while you read low novels."

Bellinger was in the army class, a cheery soul, athletic, vacant, with an obsession for clothes. This was the only subject about which he could talk; he was always perfectly dressed himself and had earned something of a reputation by it. People would bring him patterns of cloth and consult him when they were getting suits, which was complimentary, although they never took his advice. It was said of him that he had once cut the headmaster in London because he met him wearing a brown overcoat with evening dress.

Peter turned down the corner of his page – a pernicious habit even in a wartime "Outlines of Economics" of which he could never cure himself – and got up.

"Come across to hall, you silly old ass, and tell me the latest bulletins from Sackville Street."

"Nothing doing," said Bellinger with the self righteous gloom of one whose religion has been insulted and pulled at the points of his waistcoat, "nothing doing at all. It's the curse of this infernal war. While all the best people are in uniform they don't pay any attention to civilian fashions. Thank the Lord I shall be in khaki in a couple of months."

They linked up and walked down to hall, Bellinger earnestly enlarging upon the advantages of the R.A.F. over the ordinary uniform.

When they arrived at the "pits-table", where people with studies sat, a heated discussion was going on. The head, Peter gathered, had proposed to the Games Committee the night before that none of the house cups should be competed for until after the war and that the time saved should be devoted to more parades and longer digging upon the house potatoe plots. Cook, the captain of Lane's, had apparently been the only one with the courage to hold out against him. Lane's were certain to get the open football and stood a good chance for the Five Mile.

Beaton, a small science specialist, was voluble in the head's defence.

"After all," he was saying, "what effects has the war had on us here? We've had a little less food and coal, people have been leaving a little earlier, the young masters have gone and these antiquated old fools like Boyle have taken their places, parades have become a bit longer, but is this enough? Has anything been done to make us realize that we are in the middle of the biggest war in history?"

"Everything has been done," said Peter, "to make school life excessively unpleasant – after you with the bread, please Travers – what little of the old life does remain, is what keeps it just tolerable. Good God, isn't it bad enough for you. I pity the men who've come during the last year and know only this side of Selchurch. I hate school, now, and shall be only too glad to get away; why utterly spoil it for the 'underschools'?"

"Yes," said Travers a large, sad "historian" on the other side of the table, "You seem to be one of the maniacs who believe in making themselves wretched because other people are. It's only by the misery of three quarters, that life can be even tolerable for a quarter of society. It's unjust but it's better than the whole show being miserable. It's a fundamental principle of political science" – any particularly sweeping cynicism was a "fundamental principle" with Travers.

"My pater had that craze badly in 1914," said Garth, a pleasant, spotty youth, next to Peter, "he dug up the tennis court to grow vegetables when there was plenty of waste ground behind the stable yard."

"And the mater makes me wear old clothes," said Bellinger, "because she thinks it looks bad to wear new ones in war time."

"Everyone is quite imbecile about the war" – Travers loved dismissing subjects – "they don't realize that it is a natural function of development. It's a fundamental principle that society can only remain normal if it is decimated at regular periods."

The "paper boy" came to the table. Every day it was the duty of one of the fags to fetch the house papers from the porter's lodge, as soon as he came out of early school, and bring them up to hall. They were supposed to go to the people who had bought them at the "paper auction" at the beginning of term, but in practice they went first to the high table where the prefects sat with the housemaster; when they had made their choice, he took them to the "pits-table" and distributed what were left as he liked.

"Times, please" said Peter over his shoulder.

"I'm sorry, Audley, that's gone."

"All right, Morning Post. Thanks."

He spread it out over the table and glanced down the columns. It was full of the usual war news (Peter wondered vaguely what they managed to put in the papers in peace time); there were rumours of preparations for a big German offensive, factious political questions in the house, pages of minor engagements in the East. He folded it and passed it on to Bellinger.

III

It was a gloomy morning; gloomy even for the Easter term 1918. For half an hour after breakfast he sat in his study cleaning his uniform; in chapel he could smell the cleaning stuff up his nails. After chapel he had to go in for a double period of European History. He went into school profoundly depressed.

The "historians" were now taken by one Boyle. He had been, until the outbreak of war, the headmaster of a prosperous preparitory school on the East coast and had lived a life of lucrative dignity, making himself agreeable to distinguished parents and employing a large and competent staff to do the teaching. For two years he had kept doggedly on, feeling that it would be a surrender to the barbarian enemy if he left, but the numbers steadily sank, until one night a bomb was actually dropped onto the gymnasium breaking every frame of glass in the house. Then he realized that he must give it up, "St. Pendred's" was commandeered to house a garrison staff, and Mr. Boyle set about finding other employment. The head forced to choose between Mr. Boyle and a mistress, to his eternal discredit chose Mr. Boyle and in less than a year the Senior History Specialist Set had sunk from the intellectual mekka of the school to the haven which sheltered those who considered that the work they had had to do to pass the School Certificate absolved them from any further exertions, at any rate, while they were at Selchurch. Not that he was ragged – that would have been beneath the dignity of a Sixth Form set – They merely sat through his hours in complete apathy. His predecessor had been a young man fresh from Cambridge and had made his history extremely entertaining, they had held debates, read each other papers and discussed current politics, but now there were no Varsity scholarships, the battle clouds of France shut out all but the immediate future and no one had any particular motive for, or interest in, working. Mr. Boyle certainly had not and Youth, far from being the time of burning quests and wild, gloriously vain ideals beloved of the minor poets, is essentially one of languor and repose. Every hour he dictated notes, from a large leather bound note book, which most people took; every week he set an essay which several people wrote; every month he gave out a syllabus of books for out of school study, which nobody read. He asked for little and was content with far less but the Senior History Specialist set often seemed unsatisfactory even to Mr. Boyle.

He came into the class room smiling a dignified welcome all round, laid his note book on one side of the high oak desk, his mortar board on the other, and sat down smoothing out his gown.

"Good morning, gentlemen," he began in his usual formula, "What are we doing this morning? European history, isn't it Travers? Thank you. Ah yes, well I don't think we can do better than go on with our notes for a little. Now let me see where was it we had got to. Alberoni? Yes I see I have the place marked. The last thing I gave you was 'willing to cede Sardinia to secure her nephew's succession to the Duchy of Parma' wasn't it? Well then, head this 'D. Alberoni's third coalition'." For two hours he dictated an essay on XVIIth diplomacy.

Peter had reduced the taking of notes to an entirely subconscious exercise. He could now sit schooled by long practice, with his mind completely blank or filled with other things while his pen wrote out pages of notes industriously and quite correctly. Sometimes he would be woken from his reverie by a pause over some proper name, but often on looking them through he would find names which he had no recollection of having heard before. He sat writing out,

" ... invited 'pretender' to Spain and arranged with Görz a northern alliance with Sweden and Russia to support the Stuart claims, while at the same time he entered into correspondence with Polignac and the Duchess of Main, to overthrow the Regency. The death of Charles XII, however. . . . "

Mr. Boyle's notes did not elucidate any difficult problems or sift the important facts of history from the trivial. They merely stated things in direct paraphrase of Lodge; for the whole double period Peter steadily took them down.

At last the clock chimed and Mr. Boyle stood up, shut his note book and took up his mortar board. "That will be enough for this morning, I think. Remember that I want the essays on 'The Freedom of the civilized State' by Monday evening, without fail this time please. I will ask you to read up Catherine the Great for next Tuesday, if you will – I recommend Lecky. Thank you, good morning."

Wearily they filed out for break. In the war time efficiency mania P.T. had been innovated which effectually took up all the break – ten minutes in which to change and twenty minutes drill. Peter hurried to the changing room and began undressing; he suddenly remembered that he had broken the lace of his gym shoe the day before. He succeeded in borrowing another and then realized that he had forgotten to get a new hat for parade as he had been told to last time. Everything seemed to be conspiring against him this morning.

"You never lose a stud but you lose the lot," sighed Bellinger, "Hullo, what the devil does *he* want."

Peter looked round and saw the porter's burly figure framed in the doorway.

"Telegram for Mr. Audley, sir."

"Hullo, what?" Peter tore open the orange envelope and hurriedly took out the telegram; it was getting late for P.T.

"Ralf on leave," it ran, "return home wiring head will meet 4:52 Bulfrey."

IV

One of the awfully clever things that Ralf had said was that life should be divided into water tight compartments and that no group of friends or manner of living should be allowed to encroach upon any other. Peter lay back and compared the day with the prospects early that morning.

As soon as he had got the telegram he had put on his shoes and told the porter to 'phone for a taxi. After a frantic search for his house master and an incoherent but convincing explanation to him and a hurried interview with the matron about his bag, he had managed to get away in time to catch the 11:12 to Victoria. There he had had a hasty but excellent lunch at the Grosvenor and had dashed across to Paddington and got into the train just as it was starting.

He now had a clear two hours run to Bulfrey. He lay back and took a cigarette from the box he had bought at lunch. Very contentedly he watched the telegraph wires rising falling and recrossing each other, mile after mile.

He had not had time in the rush of half packed pyjamas, moving trains and lost tickets, to think of what it all meant; now in the empty first class carriage with magazines and cigarettes he began to shake off the shadows of the prison house. He looked at his watch. At the very time that he was swaying into the country through the short wayside stations, Bellinger and Beaton and Garth and everyone else with whose lives his own had seemed so inextricably bound that morning were marching about on the downs. It was very cold at Selchurch, he reflected and the sea mist was lying in the valleys; he was warm with the close atmosphere of the carriage and the glass of port he had had after lunch and with a deep inward content.

Mile succeeded mile through the avenue of telegraph poles. Outside the weather was clearing up and a bright cool sun came out. He watched the fields reeling by and began to pass the landmarks which had grown familiar through many home comings, an imposing patent medicine factory, the neat beds of a large market garden, an Elizabethan farmhouse.

He wondered how long this unexpected holiday was going to last; he supposed about four days. This was really the first time that Ralf had made any mark in his life; he was five years older and had always kept himself very much aloof. They had had many quarrels as brothers always have. At times Ralf had been almost a prig, particularly when he was head of the house at Selchurch, and his first year at Oxford. Anyway it was through him that Peter was now sitting in comfort instead of marching his section up a wet hill in "blob" formation, and in the warmth of heart that can come only from physical comfort, Peter prepared to be very gracious towards his brother.

At last the train slowed to a stop and stood panting but unexhausted like a well trained runner. Peter suddenly realized that they had reached Bulfrey. He snatched up his hat and bag, buttoned his coat and leapt onto the platform. Ralf was striding down towards him.

Peter had seen him in uniform before but then it had been with the timid pride of a 1914 subaltern. Now after three years fighting he looked wonderfully fit and hansome. A slanting ray of sunlight lit up his fair hair; he was wearing no cap.

"Hullo, Peter," he cried, shaking hands, "we were afraid that you mightn't be able to get the train. I suppose you've had lunch?"

"Yes thanks, I managed to get some in town. Pretty fair rush though. Hold on a second while I find my ticket." He handed Ralf his bag and began exploring his pockets. Finding it, at last, between the leaves of his school "blue-book", he gave it to the collector and taking back his bag followed his brother out.

"Is that all the luggage you've got?" he asked, "That's splendid; we shall be able to bring it up with us now. I've got the dog-cart outside. Moira's looking after it. She was coming into Bulfrey to do some shopping so I asked her to come and meet you."

Moira Gage was the daughter of the vicar of Bulfrey Combe. Peter's age, she and her brother had been the constant companions of the Audley boys before they went to school. They had seen less of each other as they grew up, Chris had gone to Winchester, Ralf and Peter to Selchurch, but the Vicarage was next door to the Hall and they had seen a good deal of each other in the holidays. Their fathers were close friends.

"Good work, I was afraid she would be away doing that V.A.D. work. I only saw her once last holidays. Ah there she is."

They had come out into the small station yard. On the other side of it stood the dog-cart and in it stood Moira Gage, one hand holding the reins, the other shading her eyes. She was tall, slim and pale, not really pretty but graceful and attractive; from a distance she looked like a Shepperson drawing but when you got nearer you saw depths in her grey, scrutable eyes, which his charming mannerisms could never convey; she was dressed in a tweed coat and a skirt with a grey silk scarf over her shoulders. Peter ran forward and greeted her.

"Peter," she said, "before you do anything else, do make Ralf put his hat on. He looks simply dreadful and I'm sure he'd be court-martialled or something, if anyone saw."

"Three years of military life shatter any illusions about military discipline," Ralf replied, climbing up into the dog-cart, "the only hardened militarist nowadays is the newly conscripted civilian."

"Now he's being clever again," Moira laughed, "I really thought you lost that when you came down from Oxford. Among other things, it's very bad manners when you are in stupid company."

"Thank you," Peter expostulated, "I wish you'd speak for yourself. I'm in the sixth now and write essays on industrial history and all sorts of things."

"You seem to regard your history with most unreasonable pride," said Moira, "from all I hear it sounds only slack."

"All pride is unreasonable" said Ralf. To Peter it seemed that he had paused a moment hesitating whether "no pride is unreasonable" was the more impressive; he had long gone beyond the stage when a sweeping generalization could pass as an epigram.

"The aphorisms of a disappointed man," said Moira. "The next remark like that Ralf and I get out and walk."

Bulfrey Combe was a mile and a half out from Bulfrey and still kept most of the appearance of a country village. Bulfrey was a small town with two or three streets of cheap shops, a bank, and a small glass factory which formed the nucleus of a large area of slums which was gradually spreading its grimy tentacles along the roads into the

'Brandy', *The Isis*, 12 March 1924, p. 10.

ESSAY

"OH, YES," said Lurnstein, "I had ideals at one time all right – we all do, you know."

He was leaning back from the small table, on which the tea was set, eyeing my half finished portrait. I had had a long sitting and his beautiful china tea in his thin blue and white china came as a great relief.

He looked extremely handsome, I thought, in the golden afternoon light, in his picturesque studio overall; Jewish, of course, but with a distinguished air that made one overlook his stumpy hands and other signs of ill-breeding.

"Perhaps you'd like to hear something of my life," he said, "it has not been without interest."

He lit another cigarette, pushed the box, a beautiful piece of Moorish inlaid work, to within my easy reach, and then drawing a deep breath of smoke, began:

"I started life about as low as any new peer. My father was a Jew and we lived in the Jewish quarter off the Commercial Road. When he was sober he was very kind to me and my brothers. My mother never had any great significance for me, but I realize now that she must have been a very hard worked and hard treated woman as upon her fell the sole burden of supporting her husband and large family.

"From the time when my first memories start I have always been interested in drawing, and I used to use every scrap of paper and every stump of pencil I could find, but lines never satisfied me – I wanted colours and tones. And these I could not afford. Coloured chalks used to be my chief delight and I used to take them from the desk of the Rabbi who managed the local synagogue and to whom I used to go once a week for religious instruction. For my father, though quite indifferent himself, was always most particular that I should attend. The Rabbi used the chalks, I remember, to draw maps of the divisions of the tribes with.

"Well one day he caught me taking his chalks, but instead of beating me, as the red-haired master at the board school would have done, he asked me all about my drawing and finally persuaded me to let him take some of my work away to show to his rich friends. For he was the son of a very rich man himself and had been to the 'Varsity but had sacrificed it all to help his fellow countrymen in the slums. I tell you that there are just as fine acts of self-sacrifice done by the rabbis in the Yiddish quarter as by any of your parsons at Kennington, only they don't brag about it.

"Well, he showed my work to his friends in the West, with the result that a few days later a man with a top hat and spats came to the door and asked to see me and my work. He gave half-crowns to all my brothers but he didn't give me half a crown, and I remember, I was very offended until I heard that I was to be taken away and taught painting.

"That was the beginning of my 'career'. Those Jews ran me for the next five years, and I painted just as I was told to at the Academy school, to which I was sent. And everyone was very kind to me and I was introduced to lots of rich men, not only the moneyed Jews but men of your class who spend lots of money on being bored and are called 'in society' by lower middle class novelists. I began to acquire social polish and was being shaped into a pretty little gentleman; but all the time particularly when I could feel the grain of the canvas under my brush, I was dissatisfied.

"When I was nineteen they gave me a studio, nothing like this, of course, but a decent enough shed with a good north light – and set me up as a Society portrait painter. Well I painted and flattered the ugly old women, that came to me, for a time; but after a little I found I could stand it no longer. I was painting badly, insipidly, insincerely, and I knew I could do better. I saw that the whole Academic conception was false – yes, that sounds funny from me nowadays, doesn't it? But we all see things more clearly when we're young.

"That autumn the Italian futurists came to London and Marinetti delivered his epoch making series of broken-English lectures at the Dorée galleries. It was there, and particularly in Severini's ball-room scenes, that I found what I and half Chelsea had been looking for.

"I always acted on impulses then, and when I came back and found in my room the luggage I had been packing for a tour through Italy with the Jews, – they still ran me, though by that time I was making a fairly decent living – I was filled with revulsion. I wrote a brief, I am afraid rude, note to them, and slamming the door of my studio rushed out into the night.

"I have no clear idea of what happened that night. I went to the Café Royal and drank absinthe. And soon I joined a group at the next table and together, as the sham English Bohemians do, we drank a lot, & laughed a lot, and finally all reeled out into the cool air of Regent Street. There were girls with us too, who had their hair cut short though it was not fashionable then. The leader of the set was a beautiful youth with red-gold hair whom we all called Ronald. I never learned his sirname though I met him continually for the next year and shared his studio with him. He painted fierce warm-colored 'abstractions' in tremendous bouts of energy which left him lethargic and apathetic. He was a great friend of mine in the year I spent in our sham Quartier Latin. For after that night I left the Jews and spent my time with the young art students and futurists. We were a happy enough lot and I should always have looked back to that year as the best of my life if –

"Well, during that year I painted as I have never painted before or since. I painted as I knew I ought to without convention or restraint. I exhibited at the Mansard Gallery and in the Adelphi and reviews of my work appeared in 'Blast' and 'The Gypsy'. I was gloriously happy in my work & then it was all spoilt, and by a woman.

"I won't say much about that, if you don't mind. I was desperately in love and Ronald kept telling me not to be a fool. I wouldn't listen to him and began to break with my friends. She was a model and her vision remains to me now as the most beautiful thing I need ever fear to see. . . . Well, the crash came, as Ronald said it would, and I tore up all my drawings and stuffed the stove in the studio full of them. And I scraped the paint off my canvases with my palette knife; and I had one tremendous night with the whole set 'flung roses, roses, riotously with the throng, seeking to put thy pale lost lilies out of my mind'. We were all very noisy and drunk and we told Rabellaisian jokes till far into the morning, and then in the grey of dawn I slunk back to the respectability and the Jews."

He was speaking, up till now, very seriously and bitterly. Now he shook his great shoulders like a dog, tossed his head, & motioning me to resume my pose took up his palette.

"Oh yes, they received me with open arms. And Mayfair accepted me as its season's attraction. The old life went on. They made me an R.A. and – Happy? why yes. Why not? I've made a good thing out of life. Ask any of your club friends, they'll tell you so. But there are times when I see reviews of Ronald's work and hear my academic colleagues' sneers of him that I – Oh well; we must get on with the damned picture while the light lasts."

Cover Design, *The Oxford Broom*, April 1923.

THE HOUSE:
AN ANTI-CLIMAX

NEVER, IN its varied and not always unqualifiedly successful career, had the school been in a state of such utter disorganization and prostration, as in the Easter term, 1917. In France & Flanders, our thinly guarded, inadequately munitioned lines, were quite incapable of successfully resisting the menaced German "push", every paper brought news of further mis-management and ill-success, every post news of some friend or relation who had been killed. At school, the houses had mostly been taken over, in the absence of their younger housemasters, by well meaning but incompetent elderly assistant masters; the prefects were young, and knowing that in a few weeks, at the most a few months, they would be "called up" to go to possible death, almost certain mutilation, cared little for school or house affairs. All over the country nerves were strained to the breaking point. This must be borne in mind when reading a story which at any other period would have been utterly impossible.

Every house, of course, claims to be the best, and in all probability has hypnotized itself into believing so, but there is one House that is more exclusive, more arrogantly self-confident, more self-contained, than any other. The House has many exclusive points of etiquette that the out-houses look on with contempt or resentment. They have largely their own slang, a great many of their own customs, and above all an unshakable contempt for the corps and all its machinations. Every flight of Inspection-day oratory leaves them the same, and even when all over the country militarism was all powerful, when soldiers drilled on the Christ Church quads at Oxford, they kept up their contempt with unmitigated bitterness. And then came Ross. A prefect, an excellent all round athlete, with a high place in the Classical sixth, he had remained quite a nonentity until he returned at the beginning of the Easter term to find himself head of the House, now demoralized and bereft of all its earlier dignity.

He had to take the entire management of the House into his own hands, and very soon he made himself felt. He stopped people getting "orders" for confectionery from their temporary housemaster, he stopped people getting leaves off Clubs & Parades without consulting the matron at all, he generally raised the house to something like its former standard and on the whole people liked it, for fundamentally men rather like being kept in order if it is done in the right way.

For the first three weeks all went well – too well really. Then came the Monday afternoon parade in which the corps started organizing for the House Platoons Shield. Ross delivered a violent little speech and, as in most of his speeches, he said rather more than he meant to. "Stand easy and pay attention. The display that you have given so far has been perfectly monstrous. I've never seen such marching in my life before – might be a whole lot of boy scouts. I can tell you, that if you think that because this House has been disgustingly slack in the past, you are going to be disgustingly slack now, you are quite wrong for once in your lives. You're going to sweat for this – sweat your guts out – and I'm going to make you! Got that?" and he called the platoon up.

The House looked on him with undisguised amazement and disgust and slowly meandered through the platoon drill with their customary negligence.

Next Tuesday's uniform parade saw the House with tarnished buttons, mud caked boots, and fouled rifles as usual. Next day saw the whole platoon doing "defaulters".

And so it went on, and gradually the House began to give way to his personality and even attained a certain sullen efficiency when suddenly a few days after the House Trials, an occurrence happened which altered the whole complexion of affairs.

One afternoon Ross was sitting in the house captain's room reading, when Stewart burst in, in running change, rather dirty, obviously just returned from a run.

Stewart was captain of Running and certain, people said, to be, at any rate, in the first three in the Five Mile – very possibly a winner.

He sat down on the window seat and began idly fingering the congealing mud on his knees. Then he looked up. "Ross," he said in the drawl always affected by prefects & house captains in the House, "I suppose you know that you are playing hell with the House, with your corps-mania?" Ross said nothing but pushed his book onto the table after carefully marking the place. After a pause Stewart went on.

"The House hasn't got either the time or inclination to do your beastly corps, and clubs properly. We've no chance for the Footer, I know, but we've got a damned good chance for the Five Mile Jerry; and we aren't going to throw it away to play soldiers."

Still Ross said nothing; only the corners of his mouth moved.

"Well to give you an example. I told young Merrivale that I wanted him for a training run today and he said that he had to clean his bayonet to show to you before hall, because it was rusty yesterday. I said I would make it all right with you, of course, but I can't train a team decently if your beastly bayonets are going to get in the way every minute."

Then Ross spoke. "I'm sorry to disappoint you, but Merrivale's bayonet has got to be clean before he goes for any run."

Stewart was genuinely astounded. "D'you mean to say you put your ruddy platoon shield before the Five Mile Jerry?" he demanded.

"You put it rather crudely" drawled Ross, "but that is what, I suppose, it comes to eventually."

Then Stewart lost his temper. "There's one thing you're forgetting" he said, "and that's that I'm not going to try and train a team with you getting in my light all the time. I'm a house-captain and needn't run if I don't want to. If you don't chuck your corps-mania I shan't run in the five-mile."

Stewart of course meant this as a threat that could not be argued against, the idea that he would be taken at his word was unthinkable, as indeed in a cooler moment it would have been to Ross. But now he was out to score. "Then I suppose Caven will have to run after all – he's first spare man isn't he?"

They had both made a decision which they knew quite well would be disastrous but now neither could withdraw. Stewart, who had a great sense for the dramatic, went straight to the house board and crossed himself off the head of the list in a breathless silence.

The news spread round the House and then round the school with Oriental speed. The out-houses were openly exultant, the House sullen. Why, they asked, should they lose a cup, just because the bloods quarrelled. They split up into factions and argued incessantly. Ross had missed the House trials in the last two years & no one knew his capabilities as a runner, but he immediately began to train rigorously, and people soon saw that he meant to win the house the cup without Stewart, who watching with the appreciation of the connoisseur, saw that he was a very fine runner. The house settled down to watch the five mile as the settling of the feud.

Stewart, very repentant, came down in a great coat to watch the finish. The House did not win.

Personality and will can do as much as the Pelmen advertisements say, but they cannot force the pace up the Cow-Top and then lead a quarter mile sprint to Combs. A huddled heap after the Valley dyke was all that was left of Ross's training.

A week later came the house Platoons competition and muffled up and very white Ross came down from the San to watch. He was bitterly conscious of his failure and wondering how he would be able to endure another term of the cold superiority of Stewart and the glowering animosity of the whole House.

But suddenly he saw that the House Platoon were drilling as they had never drilled before or – thank God! – have since. Public opinion is the most unaccountable thing in the world and with his failure had suddenly come a popularity that he would never have enjoyed before had he been triumphant. The

House, in their own great way were showing him their change of opinion. Their equipment was clean, and under Stewart as platoon commander they were drilling with an enthusiasm which went far to counteract the effect of the lethargy of their previous efforts.

It would make a splendid ending if the House could be allowed to win the Shield, but this is a story of school life and anyone who knows the House will know that that is out of the question. Suffice it to say, however, that they were third, and that as Ross went down the grass slope to Chapel that evening, arm in arm with Stewart it seemed almost as if he had forgiven the House rather than that they had forgiven him. And after all that is greatness.

Dust jacket for *The Old Expedient*, by Pansy Pakenham (Chapman & Hall, London, 1928).

OXFORD

PORTRAIT OF YOUNG MAN
WITH CAREER

JEREMY came into my room at half-past six, just as I was assembling my sponge and towels and dressing gown and things for a bath. I saw him as I came out of my bedroom, looking for something to write a message on. He was making straight for my portfolio of drawing paper. I called and made myself known to him.

Jeremy was in my house at school; he has what would be known in North Oxford as a "personality". That is to say he is rather stupid, thoroughly well satisfied with himself, and acutely ambitious. Jeremy purposes to be President of the Union.

I said to him, "Hullo, Jeremy, I am afraid you find me on the point of going to have a bath. I never miss a bath before dinner; I shall to-night if I do not go at once. The bathroom is shut at seven. But do stay and drink some sherry won't you?"

"Thanks," said Jeremy, and sat down.

I reached for the decanter and found it empty. There must have been nearly a bottle there that morning.

"Jeremy, that damned man of mine has finished the sherry. I am sorry."

"Never mind. I'll just smoke a cigarette and go."

My cigarettes are particularly large and take at least a quarter of an hour to smoke. I banished all my dreams of white tiles and steam and took a cigarette myself.

"I haven't anything particular to say," said Jeremy, "I was just passing your College and thought I might as well drop in for a little. It is hard to know what to do before hall, isn't it?"

"I generally have a bath."

"Ah, our baths are not open at this hour."

He propped his feet on the side of the fireplace. He was wearing that detestable sort of dark brown suede shoes that always looks wet.

"Oh, I know one thing I wanted to ask you. I want to meet Richard Pares. I feel he is a man to know."

"An amiable rogue."

"Well, will you introduce me to him."

"You know, I hardly know him."

It was quite true and, besides, I dislike introducing Jeremy to people; as a rule he begins by calling them by their Christian names.

"Nonsense, I'm always seeing you about together. I am not doing anything 'fore lunch on Tuesday. How about then? Or Friday I could manage, but I should prefer Tuesday."

So it was arranged.

There was a pause; I looked at my watch; Jeremy took no notice; I looked again.

"What is the time," he said, "Twenty-three to. Oh, good! – hours yet."

"Before a fool's opinion of himself the gods are silent – aye and envious too," I thought.

"I'm speaking 'on the paper' on Thursday."

"Good."

"About the Near East. Macedonia. Oil, you know."

"Ah."

"I think it ought to be rather a good speech."

"Yes."

"Evelyn, you aren't listening; now seriously, what do you really think is wrong with my speaking. What I feel about the Union myself is. . . ."

A blind fury, a mist of fire. We struggled together on the carpet. He was surprisingly weak for his size. The first blow with the poker he dodged and took on his shoulder; the second and third caved his forehead in. I stood up, quivering, filled with a beastly curiosity to find what *was* inside his broken skull. Instead I restrained myself and put his handkerchief over his face.

Outside the door I met my scout. I forgot the sherry.

"Hunt" – I almost clung to him. "There is a gentleman in the room lying on the carpet."

"Yes sir. Drunk, sir?"

I remembered the sherry. "No, as a matter of fact he's dead."

"Dead, sir?"

"Yes, I killed him."

"You don't say so, sir!"

"But Hunt, what are we to do about it?"

"Well, sir, if he's dead, there doesn't seem to be much we can do, does there? Now I remember a gentleman on this staircase once, who killed himself. Poison. It must have been '93 I should think, or '94. A nice quiet gentleman, too, when he was sober. I remember he said to me...."

The voice droned on, "...I liked your speech, but I thought it was 'a little heavy'. What do you think Bagnall meant by that?"

It was the voice of Jeremy. My head cleared. We were still there on opposite sides of the fire. He was still talking.

"...Scaife said...."

At seven o'clock Jeremy rose. "Well, I mustn't keep you from your bath. Don't forget about asking Richard to lunch on Tuesday, will you? Oh, and Evelyn, if you know the man who reports the Union for the *Isis*, you might ask him to give me a decent notice this time."

I try to think that one day I shall be proud of having known Jeremy. Till then....

Scaramel.

Cover Design, *The Oxford Broom*, June 1923.

ANTONY, WHO SOUGHT
THINGS THAT WERE LOST

REVOLUTION came late to St. Romeiro and suddenly. Cazarin, the journalist who had been educated in Paris, was said to have proclaimed it. Messengers came to him with the news that students at Vienna had driven out Prince Metternich and perhaps had murdered him; that all Lombardy was in revolt, that the Pope had fled and all his cardinals. And from the coast the fishermen brought other tales, of how the foreigners were torturing men and women at Venice and of things that were done in Naples; how when the Pope left Rome the pillars of St. Peter's were shaken and many of the peasants affirmed that it was the Emperor Napoleon who had done these things, not knowing that he was dead.

Thus and thus revolution came to St. Romeiro and Cazarin and the people came out in the heat of the day and cried before the Duke's palace; Cazarin crying for liberty and the people for the removal of the duty on olives. Then the news came that the Duke had fled and with him all his family. So the people broke down the iron gates which the Duke's grandfather had brought from Milan and burst into the Palace. And they found only a very few, very young soldiers, and since these seemed ill inclined to resist, they killed them; and then feeling much enraged at their own valour, they sought what further they might do. And they cried, "To the Castle!" for there were the prisoners kept and each had some near relative who for some crime or foolishness was imprisoned.

And Cazarin remembered the Count Antony who had been shut up with his lady in the Castle ten years ago. But when the prison was broken open, they found many debtors and thieves and a poor mad woman who had thought herself to be the Queen of Heaven, but of the Count Antony they found nothing, nor of his lady.

Now this is the story of Antony, called by his friends, "Antony, who sought things that were lost". Cazarin, who had been educated at Paris, learned it, in part from what he himself knew and in part from what the turnkey told him.

He was a tall man, this Count Antony, and very beautiful and he was born of a proud family. His fathers had been great men in Italy and had fought with the Spaniards against the French and had their origin, it was said, from no less a person than a Pope himself. And Count Antony had the estates of his fathers and their beauty, but there was that in the heart of Antony which none of his fathers had known. And for this cause Antony's friends called him, "Antony, who sought things that were lost", because he seemed always to be seeking in the future for what had gone before.

And Antony was betrothed to the Lady Elizabeth who was fair and gentle, and with his sad, wondering eyes he would watch her, for she moved graciously; and in the eyes of both of them was love greater than the fathers of Antony had known.

But there were whisperings at St. Romeiro at this time; behind high shutters men would sit long over their wine and talk of "Freedom" and "Unity" and many foolish words; and they would swear oaths together round the table and sign papers, being very young and somewhat kindled with wine. And these things seemed noble to the Count Antony.

But the whisperings were too loud and echoed in the Palace; and thus it was that one day, as he returned from visiting the Lady Elizabeth, he found men of the ducal guard waiting before his house; and they took him to the Castle. Then the Lady Elizabeth, full of love for him, cried to the Duke and prayed for Antony. And when her prayers for his liberty were of no avail she prayed that she might be locked up with him, for, she said, there would be no captivity where Antony was and no freedom where he was not; for she was still a maid and very full of love. And the Duke who, albeit a great lover in his time, was now sunken into a life of gluttony, was afraid of the love in the Lady Elizabeth's eyes and so granted her wish; thus she was borne to the Castle, rejoicing.

These things Cazarin had seen with his own eyes before he went to Paris; what followed after to Antony and Elizabeth he learned from the turnkey, a lame and ugly man, before he was killed by the people of St. Romeiro.

They shut Antony and Elizabeth in a cell cut deeply in the grey stone; it was a dark place and water dripped monotonously from the damp roof to the damp floor and foul things crept about the damp walls. At the side of the cell furthest from the door was a broad step raised from the floor and covered with straw. And here the Lady Elizabeth sat and when the turnkey brought them their food, Antony knelt by her and served her. And after they had eaten thus, they wrapped their hands in each other's and talked; and as they talked, they kissed. And they made a bed of straw on the step and thus among the foul and creeping things was their marriage made; and the turnkey envied them that were so happy in so foul a place.

So a week wore itself out and another; and the cheeks of the Lady Elizabeth became pale and her hair became dull and coarse and the brows of the Count Antony that had been white, were dirty and his beard was long; but ever in his smouldering eyes there was love and a seeking for things that were lost. But the turnkey, who had so envied them, saw that now there was in the eyes of the lady Elizabeth no love but only a great weariness.

Now when the turnkey brought them their food, Antony knelt to serve his lover as he had done before. And some of the bread which the turnkey brought was rotten and the Lady Elizabeth would tear out what was good with her dirty hands and eat it, and then sullenly roll herself over on the straw and stare at the wall; and Antony would eat what the Lady Elizabeth left. And after a short time these two, who had so loved each other, slept together in the straw no longer, but Antony slept on the wet stone; and by day they talked little to each other and never kissed; and the turnkey saw that in the eyes of Antony there was a wild and bewildered sorrow and a seeking for what was no more; but in the eyes of his lover there grew hate.

So the autumn grew into winter and a new year began. And the turnkey was lame and his face was scarred with pox and his mouth was drawn with laughing at the sorrow about him; and daily he came to the cell and no other man did the Lady Elizabeth see, except Antony who had been her lover. And as winter grew into spring and the hate increased in the eyes of Elizabeth, so there grew also desire for the love of that man that was lost to her. And Antony who slept on the wet stones and ate the rotten bread was agued and sick and too weak to move from his corner; only his eyes followed Elizabeth as she moved in the cell.

One day when the food had been set before her, the Lady Elizabeth said, "Turnkey, am I still beautiful?"

And the turnkey answered:

"Not with the beauty in which I first saw you, Lady Elizabeth; for your cheeks are grown pale and your hair dull and coarse, and all your fair skin is blotched and dirty. Yet are you still very beautiful."

"I have not seen my image for many months. Let me look in your eyes and see if I am still beautiful."

So the turnkey thrust his face which was pock-marked and drawn with derision near to the face of the Lady Elizabeth; and there was desire in their eyes. And she put her hands in his hair and she leaned her breast against his and so the Lady Elizabeth, who had known the white arms of Antony, loved this turnkey who was ugly and low born. And Antony made no sound but lay in his corner burdened with his ague and the great chain which he could barely move; but in his eyes there was pain as is seldom seen in men.

And the turnkey said, "I will go and bring wine and we will make a feast for this new love which we have found." And they spoke of this new thing which had come to them, and how they would entertain it; and the turnkey promised that she should leave the cell and live with him in his lodgings, where there should be water for her to wash herself and clean food for her to eat and a small courtyard to walk in, whence could be seen the tops of trees. And she cried, "O my love, return to me soon."

Thus was she left with Antony.

And Antony was weak and burdened with his chain but there was pain in him which raised him from his corner; and he spoke no word but crept to Elizabeth, who had been his lover, silently, as the foul things on the walls. And she rose in alarm and made to escape him, but he caught at her ankle and drew her to the floor. And between his hands was the heavy chain and he stretched it across her throat and knelt on the two ends between his wrists so that the great links pressed into her neck. And Elizabeth, who had been his lover, struggled with him, but the pain lent him strength and he prevailed; and the struggling of her hands ceased and thus the Lady Elizabeth died.

And so the turnkey found them when he returned; and he uttered a cry and the flask of wine slipped from his fingers and scattered itself on the wet floor. And he ran to where the Lady Elizabeth lay and laid his hand on her breast and knew that she was dead. And spoke no word but left her with Antony and shut the great door and locked it and threw the key into the Castle moat. And he never returned to the cell to tend the body of Elizabeth, for he had known love there.

These things he told Cazarin, who had been educated at Paris, before the people of St. Romeiro killed him.

'Woodcut', *The Golden Hind II*, January 1924, p. 26.

EDWARD OF UNIQUE ACHIEVEMENT

A Tale of Blood and Alcohol in an Oxford College

I HAVE for a long time hesitated to tell this story of Edward.
For six weeks past, since Edward late one evening interrupted
my essay to grow expansive over my whiskey, I have done the
manly thing and told no one – at least practically no one. But
lately this wasting of "copy" – as all good journalists are wont to
describe the misfortunes of their friends – has been for me a
matter of increasing and intolerable regret; and now that I have
learned from Anne "in a manner which it is not convenient to
record", much of which Edward and Poxe are ignorant, I find it
wholly impossible to remain silent. I have obscured the identities
of the chief actors so far as it has been in my power to do so.
Edward at any rate I feel should be safe from detection.

The more I consider the nature of Edward the more incredible it all seems. He is to all outward showing the most wholly and
overmasteringly ordinary undergraduate. Every afternoon,
nearly, he may be heard ordering his tea down the Carlton
Club telephone, "China tea, dry toast and butter and white
cake, for one, please." He is clothed in tweeds or flannels and
usually wears an old Wykamist tie. No proctor would hesitate to
recognize him as a member of the University.

Yet in this is Edward alone among all the other young men in
Old Wykamist ties and the Carlton Club. Some few weeks ago he
murdered his tutor, a Mr. Curtis. So very few people out of
College were aware of Mr. Curtis's existence that his sudden
death was received without consternation. He was just no more
seen, as undistinguished dons do disappear in large Colleges.
After all it was to everyone's interest to keep things quiet – Mr.
Curtis's sole relative, a brother with a large practice at Pang-
bourne, quite realized this when the Warden explained things to
him. The police, I think, never heard of it; if they did it was

quite soon forgotten. It was said by Poxe – though with how much
truth I would not venture to judge – that pressure was brought on
Cockburn to keep the affair out of the *Isis* (there was some doubt
about his degree – the Dean of Edward's College was examining
it – but, as I say, I will not make myself responsible for anything
Poxe says).

I do not know why Edward hated Mr. Curtis so much. I never
had the privilege of meeting him but as I used to watch him
moving about the quad, usually alone or with Anne, who is
married to the Warden, I thought that he seemed, considering
that he was a history tutor, a pleasant young man enough. But,
however that may be, Edward hated him with an absorbing and
unmeasurable hatred, so that at last he became convinced that
Mr. Curtis's existence was not compatible with his own. This was
a state of mind into which any undergraduate might have
slipped; where Edward showed himself essentially different
from the other young men in Old Wykamist ties in the Carlton
Club, was in his immediate perception that the more convenient
solution was not suicide but murder. Most undergraduates would
kill themselves sooner or later if they stayed up long enough, very
few would kill anyone else.

Once decided upon, the murder was accomplished with the
straightforward efficiency which one would expect from a student of the cinematograph and one who, until his second failure in
History previous (through his inability to draw maps) had been a
senior History scholar.

Mr. Curtis's room was on the first floor just above the side
gate. The side gate was closed at nine and the key kept in the
porter's lodge. The other key was kept in the Bursary. Edward
knew that this was the key which he would have to take. He went
into the Bursary at lunch time and found the Bursar there. The
keys were hung on a nail by his desk. The Bursar sat at the desk.
Edward began a story of a burned carpet; the Bursar became
angry but did not move. He included the sofa; the Bursar stood
up but remained at his desk. Edward threw a chair into the
conflagration and then described how the three minimax extinguishers which he had promised were all empty, "perhaps

during the Bump Supper; you know, sir". It was enough; the Bursar strode up and down thoroughly moved; Edward secured the key and hurrying to his room burned the carpet and the sofa and the chair and emptied the extinguishers in case the Bursar should come to investigate. His scout thought him drunk.

Edward then hurried to Mr. Curtis and secured an interview for ten that evening; he sent a note to the President of the Union desiring to speak that evening, it was on Thursday that these things occurred – and then feeling that he had accomplished a good work, lunched very quietly at the Carlton Club.

After lunch Edward set out on his bicycle and rode through much dust to Abingdon. There not at the first antique shop but at the smaller one on the other side of the square, he bought a dagger; at Radley he bought a stone and sitting under a hedge, he sharpened it. Returning with this in his pocket, he lay for a long time in a very hot bath. It was with considerable contentment that he sat down to eat dinner alone at the George – there were still several details to be thought out.

The Union that evening was fuller than usual; some politician from London of enormous distinction was speaking. Edward, in private business, asked questions of force and ingenuity about the despatch boxes, the clock, the gas burners in the roof and the busts of the Prime Ministers: he was observed by all. At five-to-ten he slipped out saying to the Teller as he went that he was coming back; others were about him who were making for the coffee room while drinks could still be obtained. Edward's bicycle was among the others at the St. Michael Street gate, clustering about the notice which forbade their presence. In eight minutes he was back again in his place, reviewing with complete satisfaction his evening's achievement; almost immediately he was called upon to speak. His speech was, perhaps, more successful as an alibi than as a piece of oratory, but few were there to hear it. As he walked home that evening there was singing in his heart. It had been an admirable murder. Everything had happened perfectly. He had gone in at the side gate, unobserved, and reached Mr. Curtis's room. His tutor had that habit, more fitting for a house master than a don, of continuing to read or write some few words after his visitors entered, in order to emphasize his superiority. It was while he was finishing his sentence that Edward killed him and the sentence was merged into a pool of blood. On his way back, Edward had gone down George Street as far as the canal and there had sunk the dagger. It had been a good evening, Edward thought.

Hastings, the night porter at Edward's College, always liked to delay people and talk to them in the porch. It was a habit which many resented, but Edward to-night was so overflowing with good nature that he actually started the conversation.

"A dull debate at the Union to-night, Hastings."

"Indeed, sir; and did you speak?"

"I tried to."

"Ah, well, sir; if you wanted excitement you should have stayed in College to-night. Most unusual happenings, sir. I don't think I ever remember anything quite like it happening before, not since I've been at the College."

"Why, what's happened, Hastings?"

"You may well ask, sir. I knew his Lordship would come to a bad end."

"Do tell me what has happened, Hastings."

"Well, sir, you knows what Lord Poxe is when he gets drunk, sir. There's no stopping him. Well, he come in to-night, sir, oh, very drunk. He never see me when I opened the door – just ran straight in and fell down on the grass. Then he gets up and starts swearing something wicked – said the dons hadn't no right to put grass there for a gentleman to fall over. Said he was going to go and murder the lot of them."

"Well, Hastings?"

"Well, he's done it, sir."

"What! all of them, Hastings?"

"No, sir, not all; but Mr. Curtis sir. The Dean went to find him to tell him to go to bed and found him asleep on the floor of Mr. Curtis's room and Mr. Curtis," with great glee, "dripping blood, sir. Quite slowly, pit-a-pat, as you might say."

"Well, I'm damned!"

"Yes, indeed, sir. So was the Dean. He is with the Warden now, sir."

The sky filled with chimes; it was twelve o'clock.

"Well, I must go to bed, Hastings. It's a funny business."

"Yes, sir, and good night, sir."

"Good night, Hastings."

So Edward went to bed with a grave disquiet. It was a pity that Poxe should have done this; it was really a very great pity. But as he grew sleepier the conviction grew that perhaps this was the best that could have happened. He thought of Poxe – a sad figure. His father had been forced to resign from the Diplomatic Corps after that disgraceful business with the Montenegrin minister's younger daughter, and had then married his first cousin, begotten an heir and drunken himself to death at the age of forty-two. It was thought that Poxe would never beget an heir, and it was certain that he would not live to be forty-two. He was nearly always half-sober. And so Edward's thoughts drifted to the decay of great families, to renaissance Italy, and then far away beyond St. Mary's tower where it was just striking half-past-twelve. A good evening and sleep. . . .

Everyone in College had heard the story next morning. It reached me through my scout who called me with: "Half-past-seven sir, and Lord Poxe has murdered Mr. Curtis." I met Poxe in the bathroom, very white and dejected. I asked him about the murder.

"Well, I suppose I've rather rotted things up this time. I can't remember a thing about it except that I was furious about some grass, and that two people put me to bed. It's a melancholy business. They can't hang me, can they?"

I suggested inebriates' asylum and had my bath. I was sincerely sorry about poor Poxe, but felt he would probably be better shut up. After all it was not safe to have a man who did that sort of thing about the College; it was not as though he was seldom drunk. I went to breakfast at the Old Oak tea rooms and found Edward there. He was in great form, and for this I disliked him that he should be in good form at breakfast; however, he was really rather amusing about the Poxe murder as it was already called.

Edward asked if he might work in my rooms – he knew I never used them – as he had had a fire in his. I said that I wanted them this morning and advised the Union. Then I went back.

At about eleven, I saw from my window the Warden's side door open and Poxe come out, radiantly cheerful. I called him into my room, and he told me of what had happened. It must certainly have been a cheering interview for Poxe.

He had gone to see the Warden with all the trepidation that should befit a young nobleman suddenly confronted with the prospect of being hanged. The old man had been seated on one side of the table with the Dean next to him. Poxe had been asked to sit down. The Warden had begun:

"I have asked you to come and see me, Lord Poxe, in what for both of us, I think, and certainly for me, is a very bitter occasion. Last night, when in a state of intoxication, as you will perhaps have been informed, you entered the room of your tutor, Mr. Curtis, and stabbed him to death. I suppose that you do not deny this?"

Poxe was silent.

"It was a foolish act, Lord Poxe, an act of wanton foolishness, but I do not wish to be hard on you," the Warden's voice broke with emotion, "my poor boy, you are the fifteenth Lord Poxe and, as I have at different occasions reminded you, not unconnected with my own family. Lady Emily Crane, your great aunt, you will remember, married a Mr. Arthur Thorn, my grandfather. I feel that the College owes it to your position to treat this matter as discreetly as possible."

Poxe nodded enthusiastically. Among tradesmen and dons he had always found his title of vast value.

"The Dean and I have discussed the matter at some length and have come to the conclusion that there is no reason why this matter should be referred to the ordinary State authorities at all; it has, as, of course, you are aware, always been a principle of University government so far as is possible to impede and nullify the workings of the ordinary courts of law. In this case it seems particularly advisable, as it is only too likely that the criminal courts would be unwilling to treat this matter with the clemency which we think desirable.

"Nor, indeed, is a precedent far to seek. In the fifteenth century a commoner of this College struck off the head of the Bursar – true, that was in open fight and not before the young man had received severe injuries; but things, of course, were far rougher then. On that occasion the distinguished scholar, who held the position it is my privilege unworthily to occupy, inflicted upon the delinquent the fine of twopence to be paid to the Bursar's relatives."

Poxe brightened.

"Of course, the value of the penny has, since that time, markedly decreased, but calculating it as nearly as one can in days of rather haphazard accountancy, the Dean and I decided that the fine must have valued about thirteen shillings.

"I need hardly say, Lord Poxe, that this whole matter has been acutely distressing to the Dean and myself. We hope and trust that it will not occur again. It is probable that in the event of a second offence, the College would find itself unable to treat the matter with the same generosity. Thank you, Lord Poxe."

And thus the interview closed and Poxe went out, elated, to celebrate his escape in the manner which most immediately suggested itself to him; and Edward, in his fire-blackened room, felt that everything was turning out well.

Without difficulty, an aged and dissolute doctor was unearthed in St. Ebbs, where he lodged in squalor with one of the College servants, and earned an irregular livelihood by performing operations in North Oxford; this sorry man was persuaded to write a certificate of death from natural causes. The funeral was brief and ill-attended. The Warden toiled for three days in the composition of a Greek epitaph and on the third evening persuaded the Dean to write one in Latin. And so for Poxe and Edward the matter ended.

One thing I feel should be added. It is merely an incident that may be of no significance but which may explain much that seems improbable. I was told it in an intimate moment by Anne, who is married to the Warden, and of whom many stories are told. This is what she said, that on the night when Mr. Curtis died, she ran in a high state of emotion to her husband, the

Warden, and cried, "Oh why, why did you kill him? I never really loved him."

She stopped, seeing the Dean there also. He, a gentleman, rose to go, but the Warden detained him. And then Anne, falling on her knees, pounded out a tale of the most monstrous and unsuspected transactions between herself and Mr. Curtis.

"Supposing there were a trial," asked the Warden, "could this be kept a secret?"

The Dean doubted gravely whether this would be possible.

And then came to the Warden the full realization of the imperishable obligations of precedent, the memory of the head of the Bursar, the appreciation of the greatness of families not unconnected with his own.

"At least, I think it must have been then," Anne said as she turned up the light.

SCARAMEL.

'The New Cherwell' (cartoon title to editorial), *The Cherwell*, 1 August 1923 and thereafter. [See Introduction, p. xvi.]

FRAGMENTS:
THEY DINE WITH THE PAST

Almost the first thing which Toby said to me when we met was, "Imogen is in London again."

Even to Toby to whom this could never mean as much as to the rest of us, it seemed the only thing of immediate importance; to me, more than as pleasure or pain, though, of course, it was both of these, it came as a breaking away of near memories.

For some moment of time the bar where we stood was frozen in space; the handles, the slopped wood, the pallid man beyond them lost perspective; "If you like our beer tell your friends; if you don't tell us" stood as cut in stone, the ordainment of priest kings, immeasurably long ago; the three years or a little more that stood between now and that grim evening in April fell, unhonoured, into the remote past and there was no sound from the street.

Then, instantly almost, the machine fell to its work again and I said as though nothing had intervened between his voice and mine:

"Was she with *him*?"

For even now, after three years or more, I could not easily say his name; I spoke of him, as slatternly servants will speak of their master, impersonally. And indeed it was thus I thought of him; the name was an insignificant thing labelling an event. Toby understood something of this as anyone who had known Imogen, must have understood, even he; for he was associated with much that was wholly alien to him; he had been in Adelphi Terrace in that strange evening in April when Hauban had gazed out across the river for two, three hours, and scarely a word spoken.

To my question, down such valleys of thought, his answer made a way; she had been with him; they in a taxi; Toby had seen it from the top of a 'bus in Regent Street.

And so, quite naturally, I went to find Hauban, whom I had not thought to seek when I had landed that morning – or was it three and a half years ago? Thus suddenly had I returned to the past. And when I found Hauban, he said:

"So you, also, are returned to England."

Thus I knew that he too had seen Imogen and with his next words he invited me to dinner where I should meet many old friends, whom he would assemble to greet my return. But he and I and his guests knew that not for my welcome were we assembled, though no word was spoken of Imogen all the evening through.

And the thought of her was about and between us all; with such shy courtesy did we treat her, who had been Queen, for all who had loved her were gathered there and none dared speak even her name.

SCARAMEL.

'Drawing', *The Golden Hind II*, April 1924, p. 12.

CONSPIRACY TO MURDER

DURING the first week of term, Guy first mentioned his neighbour to me. We were sitting on my window seat looking over the quad, when I noticed slinking out of the J.C.R. a strange shambling man of middle age. He was ill-dressed and rather dirty, and he peered forward as he walked.

"That strange man," said Guy, "has got the room opposite me."

We decided that this would be dull for Guy, for we had often seen these strange old men before and knew that they had no interest to offer, except the dull curiosity of asking why they had come to Oxford. And they were nearly always ready to tell their story of miserly saving and the thirst for knowledge. Therefore when, a fortnight later, Guy began to talk of him again, I was considerably surprised.

"You know, he leads an incredible life; my scout told me that he has never been out to a meal or had a single man in to see him. He doesn't know one of the other freshers and can't find his way about Oxford. He's never heard of half the Colleges. I think I shall go in and talk to him one evening. Come up with me."

So one evening at about half-past ten, Guy and I went across to this strange man's room. We knocked, and getting no answer, opened the door. The room was in darkness, and we were about to go, when Guy said: "Let's have a look at his room."

I turned on his light and then gave a gasp of astonishment. The little man was sitting in his arm chair with his hands in his lap looking straight at us. We began to apologize, but he interrupted us.

"What do you want? I do not wish to be disturbed."

"Our names are Guy Legge and Barnes," I said, "we just came in to see you, but if you're busy –" I was strangely discomforted by this man and had not yet recovered from the shock of finding him sitting there in the dark.

"It was unnecessary to come and see me. I don't want to know you Barnes, or you Legge, or anyone else."

And outside the door I said, "Well I'm damned. Of all the abominable men –"

But Guy took me by the arm and said, "Dick, that man scared me."

So it began.

A few nights later I was engrossed in an essay when I heard someone beating on my oak.

"Go away, I'm busy."

"It's I, Guy. May I come in?"

"Oh, it's you. Well do you mind awfully if I work to-night? I've got to get this essay done by eleven to-morrow."

"Let me in, Dick. I won't disturb you. I only wanted to know if I could come in and read in here."

So I opened the oak and when he came into the light I saw that he was looking pale and worried.

"Thanks awfully, Dick. I hope you don't mind my coming in. I couldn't work in my room."

So I returned to my essay and in two hours it was finished. I turned round and saw that Guy was not working. He was just sitting gazing into my fire.

"Well," I said, "I've finished this thing and I'm going to bed."

He roused himself, "Well, I suppose I must get back," and then at the door, "You know, Dick, that man next door haunts me. I've never met a man who hated me as he does. When we meet on the stairs, he shrinks away and snarls like a beast."

And I, sleepily, laughed at him and went to bed.

And for the next week or so, Guy came to my room every evening until one Sunday night he said, "Dick, I don't want to go back, I'm not sleepy. May I read in front of your fire all night?"

I told him not to be a fool; he was looking thoroughly tired. And then he said, "Dick, don't you understand, I'm afraid of that man next door. He wants to kill me."

"Guy," I said, "go to bed and don't be an ass. You have been working too hard."

But a quarter of an hour later, I felt that I could not go to bed and leave Guy like this, so I went up to his room. As I passed the strange man's door, I could not help a little qualm of fear. I knocked at Guy's bedroom door and inside I heard a little cry of terror and the sound of bare feet. I turned the handle, but the door was locked and I could hear Guy's breathing through the door; he must have been pressed against it on the other side.

"D'you always lock your bedder door?" I asked, and at the sound of my voice I heard him sigh with relief.

"Hullo, Dick. You quite startled me. What do you want?"

So I went in and talked to him; he always slept with his door locked now, and his light on; he was very much scared but after a few minutes he became calmer and soon I went away, but behind me I heard him lock his door.

Next day he avoided me until evening; then he came in again and asked if he might work. I said:

"Look here, Guy, tell me what is the matter with you." And almost immediately I wished that I had not asked him, because he poured out his answers so eagerly.

"Dick, you can't think what I've been through in the last ten days. I'm living up there alone with only a door between me and a madman. He hates me, Dick, I know it. It is not imagination. Every night he comes and tries at my door and then shuffles off again. I can't stand it. One night I shall forget and then God knows what that man will do to me."

So it went on and one day I went up to Guy's room in the morning. He was not there, but his scout was, and I found him in the act of taking the key from Guy's bedroom door. I knew I had no right to ask him, but I said:

"Hullo, Ramsey, what are you doing with Mr. Legge's key?"

Ramsey showed, as only a scout can show, that I had been guilty of a gross breach of good manners and answered me:

"The gentleman next door wanted it, sir. He has lost his and wanted to see if it would fit."

"Did Mr. Legge say that you could take it?"

"No, sir. I did not think it necessary to ask him."

"Then put it back at once and don't touch things in his room whatever the gentleman next door says."

I had no right to say this to Guy's scout, but I was definitely frightened. A sudden realization had come to me that Guy might have some reason for his fear. That evening I went up to see him and we decided to work in his room. He did not mind if I were with him.

"But shut the oak, Dick," he said.

We worked until eleven o'clock and then we both sat up listening; someone was fumbling against the oak; then he knocked quietly.

Guy had started up white and panting.

"You see, I haven't been lying. He's coming at me. Keep him off, Dick, for God's sake."

The knocking was repeated.

"Guy," I said, "I'm going to open that oak. Brace up, man, we two can look after ourselves against anyone. Don't you see? We've got to open that oak."

"Dick, for God's sake don't. I can't stand it," but I went towards the door. I opened it and there was only the oak between us and the man beyond. Suddenly Guy's face became twisted with hatred and his voice harsh. "So you're in it, too. You're going to betray me to that fiend. He's bought you as he has bought Ramsey. There's not a man in the College he hasn't bought or bullied into it and I can't fight the lot," his voice suddenly fell to a tone of blind despair and he rushed into his bedroom, slamming the door. I hesitated between the two doors and then, picking up a heavy candlestick, opened the oak.

On the threshold, blinking in the light, was the strange man.

"So you're here, too, Barnes," he said slowly; "but that is excellent. What I wish to say is for you as well as Legge. I want to apologize for being so rude that evening when you two came up to see me. I was very nervous. But where is Legge?"

And from the bedroom came a sound of hysterical sobbing, the wild, hideous sobbing of a mad man.

'Beer', *The Isis*, 7 May 1924, p. 4.

UNACADEMIC EXERCISE:
A NATURE STORY

AFTER half-an-hour I said what I had been pondering ever since we started.

"Billy, this is a crazy business. I'm willing to call the bet off if you are."

But he answered gravely.

"I'm sorry, my friend, but I'm not going to lose the opportunity of making a fiver."

Then there was silence again until Anderson looked back from the wheel and said:

"Look here, Billy, let's stop at this pub and then go home. I can lend you a fiver or more if you want it. You needn't pay me until you want to."

But Billy was resolute:

"No, Dick, I owe enough already. I should like to earn an honest meal for once."

So Anderson drove on and soon we came into sight of the grim place which Craine had chosen for our experiment. I saw that Billy was beginning to lose his nerve for he was shivering in his big overcoat and his feet were very still, pressed down with all his might.

"Billy," I said, "I don't think we need go any further; we should only be wasting time. You've obviously won the bet."

And I think he would have yielded – for he was rather a child – when Craine's voice answered for him.

"What damned nonsense. The thing isn't begun yet. Donne's bet that he has the nerve to go through the whole werewolf ceremony. Just getting to the place is nothing. He doesn't yet know what he has to do. I've got as far as this twice before – once in Nigeria with a man of forty, but he hadn't the nerve to go through with it, and once in Wales with the bravest thing in the world, a devoted woman; but she couldn't do it. Donne may, because he's young and hasn't seen enough to make him easily frightened."

But Billy was frightened, badly, and so were Anderson and I and for this reason we let ourselves be overborne by Craine because he knew that we were; and he smiled triumphant as a stage Satan in the moonlight.

It was strange being beaten like this by Craine who in College was always regarded as a rather unsavoury joke. But then this whole expedition was strange and Craine was an old man – thirty-three – an age incalculable to the inexperience of twenty-one; and Billy was only just nineteen.

We had started off merrily enough down St. Aldate's; Billy had said:

"I wonder what human flesh tastes like; what d'you suppose one should drink with it?" and when I had answered with utter futility, "Spirits, of course," they had all laughed; which shows that we were in high good humour.

But once in Anderson's car and under that vast moon, a deep unquiet had settled upon us and when Craine said in his sinister way:

"By the way, Donne, you ought to know in case you lose us; if you want to regain your manhood all you have to do is to draw some of your own blood and take off the girdle."

Anderson and I shuddered. He said it with a slight sneer on "manhood" and we resented it that he should speak to Billy in this way, but more than this we were shocked at the way in which the joke was suddenly plunged into reality. This was the first time that evening on which I had felt fear and all through the drive it had grown more and more insistent, until on the heath, bleak and brilliantly moon-lit, I was sickeningly afraid and said:

"Billy, for God's sake let's get back."

But Craine said quietly:

"Are you ready, Donne? The first thing you have to do is to take off your clothes; yes, all of them."

And Billy without looking at us, began with slightly trembling hands to undress. When he stood, white beside his heap of clothes under the moon, he shivered and said: "I hope I get a wolf skin soon; it's damned cold." But the pathetic little joke faltered and failed and left us all shivering; all except Craine who was pouring something out into the cup of his flask.

"You have to drink this – all right it isn't poisonous. I brewed it myself out of roots and things."

So the rites began. Billy was told to draw a circle about himself in the ground and he obeyed silently. Another potion was given to him.

"Put this on your hands, eyelids, navel and feet. Just a drop or two. That's right."

I was trembling unrestrainedly and I dared not look at Anderson because I knew that he was too. Craine went on evenly:

"And now comes a less pleasant part. I am afraid that you have to taste human blood," and then to us, like a conjuror borrowing a watch, "will either of you two volunteer to lend some?"

Anderson and I started, thoroughly alarmed.

"Look here, Craine, this is beastly."

"You can't go on, Craine."

But Craine said:

"Well, Donne, what are we going to do?" and Billy answered evenly, "Go on with it, Craine."

It was the first time he had spoken since he drew the circle and he stood now quite calm and looking incredibly defenceless.

"Well, if neither of you two friends of his are willing, I suppose I must offer my blood."

But by a sudden intuition, we both of us knew that this thing must be averted at all costs; I was conscious of the most immediate and overpowering danger and dreamlike stood unmoving; Anderson had started forward.

"If Billy wants to go on with this, he had better have mine."

And Craine answered easily:

"As you like, my friend. Do not step inside the circle and cut deeply because he will need a good deal. That is all I ask you," but he and Anderson and I knew that he had been in some strange way checked.

So Anderson rolled up his sleeve and cut his arm and Billy without hesitation put his lips to the wound. After a few moments, Craine said, "That should be enough"; so Anderson bound up his arm roughly with a handkerchief and Billy straightened himself; there was a small trickle of blood running down his chin. He was made to repeat some jumbled sentences in a foreign tongue and then Craine produced a strip of fur.

"The girdle," he said, "put it on Donne."

"And now you have to kneel down and say a paternoster backwards. You had better repeat it after me."

And then there occurred something of which, I think, I shall never lose the memory. Billy did not kneel down; he crouched back on his haunches like an animal and threw his head right back; his fair hair stirred in the moonlight, but on his face there came a look of awakening and of savagery, his lips drawn back and show-ing his teeth. I stood there in wild horror and saw this happen.

"Amen, Saeculorum Saecula in gloria."

And the Thing in the circle drew in its breath. I dare not now think what that sound might have been. I refuse resolutely to let myself consider the possibility that it might not have been Billy's voice; that the Thing in the circle was not Billy, his face contorted by some trick of the moonlight. Even then, in that moment of terror, I would not let myself consider this but I knew by an animal apprehension of the Unknown that that sound must be stopped if we were to keep our sanity; that from the moment we heard it our lives must be wholly altered. Anderson knew this, too; and, always quicker to act than I, he was in the circle while I stood numb with horror. He was a strong man and he flung Billy across the scratched circumference, tearing the girdle from him; he fell in a heap and his elbow struck on a stone; a drop of blood oozed through the earth. Then he raised himself, and, holding his elbow said, "Dick, are you mad? Why on earth did you do that? You've hurt me damnably." And then suddenly turning on to his face he burst into a fit of hysterical crying and lay there shaking from head to foot and we three watching him. Craine, of course, spoke first.[1]

1 The rest omitted owing to blind stupidity of editor and printer.

'Woodcut', *The Golden Hind II*, January 1924, p. 39.

THE NATIONAL GAME

MY BROTHER said to me at breakfast:
"When you last played cricket, how many runs did you make?" And I answered him, truthfully, "Fifty."

I remembered the occasion well for this was what happened. At school, oh! many years ago now, I had had my sixth form privileges taken away for some unpunctuality or other trifling delinquency and the captain of cricket in my house, a youth with whom I had scarcely ever found myself in sympathy, took advantage of my degradation to put me in charge of a game, called quite appropriately a "Remnants' game". I had resented this distinction grimly, but as a matter of fact the afternoon had been less oppressive than I had expected. Only twenty-one boys arrived so, there being none to oppose me, I elected to play for both while they were batting. I thus ensured my rest and for an hour or so read contentedly having gone in first and failed to survive the first over. When eventually by various means the whole of one side had been dismissed – the umpire was always the next batsman, and, eager for his innings, was usually ready to prove himself sympathetic with the most extravagant appeal – I buckled on the pair of pads which a new boy had brought, although they were hotly claimed by the wicket keeper, and went out to bat. This other side bowled less well and after missing the ball once or twice, I suddenly and to my intense surprise hit it with great force. Delighted by this I did it again and again. The fielding was half-hearted and runs accumulated. I asked the scorer how many I had made and was told: "Thirty-six." Now and then I changed the bowlers, being still captain of the fielding side and denounced those who were ostentatiously slack in the field. Soon I saw a restiveness about both sides and much looking at watches. "This game shall not end," I ordained, "until I have made fifty." Almost immediately the cry came "Fifty" and with much clapping I allowed the stumps to be drawn.

Such is the history of my only athletic achievement. On hearing of it my brother said, "Well, you'd better play to-day. Anderson has just fallen through. I'm taking a side down to a village in Hertfordshire – I've forgotten the name."

And I thought of how much I had heard of the glories of village cricket and of that life into which I had never entered and so most adventurously, I accepted.

"Our train leaves King's Cross at 9:20. The taxi will be here in five minutes. You'd better get your things."

At quarter past nine we were at the station and some time before eleven the last of our team arrived. We learned that the village we were to play was called Torbridge. At half-past twelve, we were assembled with many bags on the Torbridge platform. Outside two Fords were for hire and I and the man who had turned up latest succeeded in discovering the drivers in the "Horse and Cart"; they were very largely sober; it seemed that now everything would be going well. My brother said,

"Drive us to the cricket ground."

"There isn't no cricket ground," brutishly, "is there, Bill?"

"I have heard that they do play cricket on Beesley's paddock."

"Noa, that's football they plays there."

"Ah;" very craftily, "but that's in the winter. Mebbe they plays cricket there in the summer."

"I have heard that he's got that field for hay this year."

"Why, so 'e 'ave."

"No, there ain't no cricket ground, mister." And then I noticed a sign post. On one limb was written "Lower Torbridge, Great Torbridge, Torbridge St. Swithin", and on the other "Torbridge Heath, South Torbridge, Torbridge Village", and on the third just "Torbridge Station", this pointing towards me.

We tossed up and, contrary to the lot, decided to try Torbridge Village. We stopped at the public house and made enquiries. No, he had not heard of no match here. They did say there was some sort of festification at Torbridge St. Swithin, but maybe that was the flower show. We continued the pilgrimage and at each public house we each had half-a-pint. At last after three-quarters of an hour, we found at the "Pig and Hammer" Torbridge Heath, eleven disconsolate men. They were expecting a team to play them – "the Reverend Mr. Bundles". Would they play against us instead? Another pint all round and the thing was arranged. It was past one; we decided to lunch at once. At quarter to three, very sleepily the opposing side straddled out into the field. At quarter past four, when we paused for tea, the score was thirty-one for seven, of these my brother had made twenty in two overs and had then been caught; I had made one and that ingloriously. I had hit the ball with great force on to my toe from which it had bounced into the middle of the pitch. "Yes, one," cried the tall man at the other end; he wanted the bowling; with great difficulty I limped across; I was glad that the next ball bowled him. One man did all the work for the other side – a short man with very brown forearms and a bristling moustache.

At quarter to five we went out to field and at seven, when very wearily we went back to the pavilion, only one wicket had fallen for 120. The brown-armed man was still in. Even on the occasion of my triumph I had not fielded; this afternoon, still with a crushed toe, I did not do myself credit. After a time it became the habit of the bowler whenever a ball was hit near me, immediately to move me away and put someone else there; and for this I was grateful.

In the shed at the end of the field there was no way of washing. We all had to change in one little room each with his heap of clothes; we all lost socks, studs and even waistcoats; it was all very like school. And finally when we were changed and feeling thoroughly sticky and weary, we learned from the cheery captain with the brown arms that there were no taxis in Torbridge Heath and no telephone to summon one with. It was three miles to Torbridge Station and the last train left at half-past eight. There would be no time for any dinner; we had heavy bags to carry.

One last sorrow came upon us when it would have seemed that all was finished, and just as we were coming into King's Cross I found that somewhere in that turmoil of changing I had lost my return ticket. My poor brother had to pay, I having no money. When he had paid he discovered that he would have no money left for a taxi. We must go back by tube and walk. To

Book-plate for Alexander Raban Waugh, Esquire [Evelyn's brother Alec, a keen cricketer and author].

DETAILS OF FIRST
PUBLICATION

———

'The Balance: A Yarn of the Good Old Days of Broad Trousers and High Necked Jumpers', *Georgian Stories 1926*, ed. Alec Waugh, Chapman & Hall, London, 1926.

'A House of Gentlefolks', introduced as 'The Tutor's Tale' in *The New Decameron: The Fifth Day*, ed. Hugh Chesterman, Basil Blackwell, Oxford, 1927.

'The Manager of "The Kremlin" ', for a series of 'Real Life Stories – by Famous Authors', *John Bull*, 15 February 1930.

'Love in the Slump' first appearing as 'The Patriotic Honeymoon', *Harper's Bazaar*, London, January 1932.

'Too Much Tolerance', no. 7 in a series of 'The Seven Deadly Sins of To-Day', *John Bull*, 21 May 1932.

'Excursion in Reality' first appearing as 'An Entirely New Angle', *Harper's Bazaar*, New York, July 1932, and as 'This Quota Stuff: Positive Proof that the British can make Good Films', *Harper's Bazaar*, London, August 1932.

'Incident in Azania', *Windsor Magazine*, December 1933.

'Bella Fleace Gave a Party', *Harper's Bazaar*, London, December 1932 and *Harper's Bazaar*, New York, March 1933.

'Cruise', *Harper's Bazaar*, London, February 1933.

'The Man Who Liked Dickens', *Hearst's International* combined with *Cosmopolitan*, September 1933, and *Nash's Pall Mall Magazine*, November 1933.

'Out of Depth', subtitled 'An Experiment begun in Shaftesbury Avenue and Ended in Time', *Harper's Bazaar*, London, December 1933.

'By Special Request' first appearing, subtitled 'Chapter Five. The Next Winter', as fifth and last episode in *A Flat in London* (serial version of *A Handful of Dust*), *Harper's Bazaar*, New York, October 1934 and *Harper's Bazaar*, London, October 1934.

'Period Piece', *Mr. Loveday's Little Outing and Other Sad Stories*, Chapman & Hall, London, 1936.

'On Guard', *Harper's Bazaar*, London, December 1934.

'Mr. Loveday's Little Outing' first appearing as 'Mr. Crutwell's Little Outing', *Harper's Bazaar*, New York, March 1935, and 'Mr. Crutwell's Outing', *Nash's Pall Mall Magazine*, May 1935.

'Winner Takes All', *Strand*, March 1936.

'An Englishman's Home', *Good Housekeeping*, London, August 1939.

'The Sympathetic Passenger', for the 'Tight Corner' series in *The Daily Mail*, 4 May 1939.

'Work Suspended: Two Chapters of an Unfinished Novel', Chapman & Hall, London, 1942.

'Charles Ryder's Schooldays', *The Times Literary Supplement*, 5 March 1982, with an introduction by Michael Sissons.

'Scott-King's Modern Europe' (abridged version), *Cornhill*, Summer 1947, and as 'A Sojourn in Neutralia', *Hearst's International* combined with *Cosmopolitan*, November 1947.

'Tactical Exercise', *Strand*, March 1947, and as 'The Wish', *Good Housekeeping*, New York, March 1947.

'Compassion', The Month, August 1949. First appearing as 'The Major Intervenes', *The Atlantic*, July 1949. ('Compassion' is an expansion of this text.)

'Love Among the Ruins: A Romance of the Near Future', Chapman & Hall, London, 1953.

'Basil Seal Rides Again or The Rake's Regress', Chapman & Hall, London, 1963.

DETAILS OF FIRST PUBLICATION

JUVENILIA

'The Curse of the Horse Race', *Little Innocents: Childhood Reminiscences*, by Dame Ethyl Smith and Others, Cobden-Sanderson, London, 1932.

'Fidon's Confetion', 'Fragment of a Novel', 'Essay', 'The House: An Anti-Climax', *Evelyn Waugh, Apprentice: The Early Writings, 1910–27*, edited and with an introduction by R. M. Davis, Pilgrim Books, Norman, Oklahoma, 1985.

'Multa Pecunia', *The Pistol Troop Magazine*, 1912.

OXFORD

'Portrait of Young Man With Career', *The Isis*, 30 May 1923.

'Antony, Who Sought Things That Were Lost', *The Oxford Broom*, June 1923.

'Edward of Unique Achievement', *The Cherwell*, 1 August 1923.

'Fragments: They Dine With the Past', *The Cherwell*, 15 August 1923.

'Conspiracy to Murder', *The Cherwell*, 5 September 1923.

'Unacademic Exercise: A Nature Story', *The Cherwell*, 19 September 1923.

'The National Game', *The Cherwell*, 26 September 1923.